ALSO BY JAVIER MARÍAS

Voyage Along the Horizon (1973)

The Man of Feeling (1986)

All Souls (1989)

While the Women Are Sleeping (1990)

A Heart So White (1992)

Written Lives (1992)

Tomorrow in the Battle Think on Me (1994)

When I Was Mortal (1996)

Bad Nature, or With Elvis in Mexico (1996)

Dark Back of Time (1998)

THE YOUR FACE TOMORROW TRILOGY

Fever and Spear (2002)

Dance and Dream (2004)

Poison, Shadow and Farewell (2007)

The Infatuations (2011)

Thus Bad Begins (2014)

Between Eternities (2017)

Berta Isla (2019)

TOMÁS NEVINSON

TOMÁS NEVINSON

Javier Marías

TRANSLATED WITH AN AFTERWORD BY
MARGARET JULL COSTA

ALFRED A. KNOPF
New York
2023

THIS IS A BORZOI BOOK
PUBLISHED BY ALFRED A. KNOPF

www.aaknopf.com

Library of Congress Cataloging-in-Publication Data
Names: Marías, Javier, author. | Costa, Margaret Jull, translator.
Title: Tomás Nevinson / Javier Marías ; translated with an afterword by
Margaret Jull Costa
Other titles: Tomás Nevinson. English
Description: First United States edition. | New York : Alfred A. Knopf, 2023. |
Identifiers: LCCN 2022049991 (print) | LCCN 2022049992 (ebook) |
ISBN 9780593534588 (hardcover) | ISBN 9780593467855 (trade paperback) |
ISBN 9780593534595 (ebook)
Subjects: LCGFT: Thrillers (Fiction) | Spy fiction. | Novels.
Classification: LCC PQ6663.A7218 T6613 2023 (print) |
LCC PQ6663.A7218 (ebook) | DDC 863/.64—dc23/eng/20221117
LC record available at https://lccn.loc.gov/2022049991
LC ebook record available at https://lccn.loc.gov/2022049992

Jacket design by Perry De La Vega

Manufactured in the United States of America
First American Edition

For Carme Mercader,
who, near or far, in lockdown or not,
cheerful or less so—she always more cheerful than me—
has happily kept me company in this book
from beginning to end

I

I was brought up the old-fashioned way, and could never have dreamed that I would one day be ordered to kill a woman. You don't touch women, you don't beat them, you don't do them any physical harm and you avoid all verbal violence, although in that regard they themselves don't always hold back. More than that, you protect and respect them and give way to them, shield them and help them if they're pregnant or with a child in their arms or in a pushchair, you offer them your seat on the bus or in the metro, you even safeguard them when walking down the street, keeping them away from the traffic or from the effluvia that, in the olden days, used to be tossed over balconies, and if a ship founders and seems likely to go under, the lifeboats are for them and their little ones (who belong more to them than to us men), at least the first spaces. When a group of people are about to be shot en masse, the women are sometimes spared and allowed to leave; they are then left without husbands, without fathers, without brothers and even without adolescent let alone grown-up sons, but they are allowed to go on living, mad with grief like tormented ghosts, for whom, nevertheless, the years pass and thus they grow old, chained to the memory of the world they have lost. They are obliged to become the depositories of memory, the only ones left when it seems no one is left, and the only ones who can tell what happened.

Anyway, this is what I was taught as a child, but that was then, and it wasn't always followed to the letter. Yes, that was then and was applied in theory but not in practice. After all, in 1793, a queen of France was guillotined, and before that, countless women accused of witchcraft were burned to death, as was the soldier Joan of Arc, to give just a couple of well-known examples.

Yes, of course, women have always been killed, but it's something that goes against the grain and causes great unease, it isn't clear whether Anne Boleyn was given the privilege of being put to the sword rather than beheaded with a crude, bungling axe, or indeed burned at the stake, because she was a woman or because she was the Queen, or because she was young and beautiful, beautiful according to the tastes of the time and according to reports, although reports are never to be trusted, not even those of eyewitnesses, who see and hear only vaguely, and who are often wrong or else lie. In engravings of her execution she is shown on her knees as if she were praying, her body erect and her head held high; if they had used an axe, she would have had to rest her chin or cheek on the block and adopt a more humiliating, more uncomfortable posture, to have grovelled if you like, and this would also have offered a clearer view of her backside to those who could see it from where they were standing. It's odd that she should be so concerned about comfort or composure in her final moments in this world, and even about elegance and decorum; of what possible importance could this be to someone who was about to become a corpse and disappear beneath the earth, and in two separate pieces. These depictions also include the swordsman of Calais, as he is called in various accounts, so as to distinguish him from any ordinary executioner – brought over *ex profeso* because of his great skill and, possibly, at the request of the Queen herself – and he is always shown standing behind her and out of sight, never in front of her, as if it had been agreed and decided that she would be spared having to see the coming blow, the trajectory of the heavy weapon which, nevertheless, advances swiftly and unstoppably, like a whistle once it has left the lips or like a sudden strong gust of wind (in a couple of the

4

images she has her eyes blindfolded, but not in most of them); so that she would not know the precise moment when her head would be cut off with a single clean two-handed blow and fall onto the dais face up or face down or on one side, on the neck or the top of the head – who knows, she certainly would never know; so that the movement would catch her by surprise, if there can be any surprise when the person knows why she has come and why she is kneeling there, without a cloak about her, at eight o'clock in the morning on a still-cold English day in May. She is, of course, kneeling to facilitate the executioner's task and not call into question his skill: he had been so good as to cross the Channel and offer his help, and he probably wasn't particularly tall. It seems Anne Boleyn had insisted that one blow with the sword would be enough because she only had a little neck. She must often have put her hands about it as proof.

She was, at any rate, treated more considerately than Marie Antoinette two and a half centuries later, for it is said that she was treated far worse in her October than her husband Louis XVI in his January, for he had preceded her to the guillotine by about nine months. The fact that she was a woman was of no interest to the revolutionaries, or perhaps they considered treating women differently to be in itself anti-revolutionary. A lieutenant called de Busne, who had treated her respectfully during her time in prison, was arrested and replaced by another, surlier guard. When it came to the King, they had simply tied his hands behind his back when he reached the foot of the scaffold; he had been transported there in a closed carriage, which belonged, I believe, to the mayor of Paris; and he was allowed to choose the priest who attended him (a nonjuring priest, that is, one who had not sworn loyalty to the Constitution and to the new order, which changed on a daily basis and which had condemned the King to die). His Austrian widow, however, had her hands bound before the journey, which she had to make in an open cart, thus leaving her far more vulnerable and exposed to the unbridled loathing on the faces of the rabble and to their insults; also they only offered her the services of a constitutional priest, which she politely declined. The chronicles say that although, during her reign, she had been said to be lacking in manners, these returned to her in her final moments: she went up the steps to the scaffold so quickly that she stumbled and trod on the executioner's foot, for which she immediately apologized, as if this were her usual response ('*Excusez-moi, Monsieur,*' she said).

The guillotine had its inevitably undignified preliminaries: the condemned man not only had his hands tied behind his back, he would also have his arms tightly bound to his sides, like a foreshadowing of the shroud; once rendered rigid and ungainly, almost immobilized, two assistants would have to pick him up like a parcel (or as they used to do with dwarfs in circuses before firing them from a cannon) and manoeuvre him into position, face down, prone, completely horizontal, so that his neck fitted in the designated space. In that, Marie Antoinette and husband were equals: they both found themselves objectified at the end, treated like sacks or bales of cotton or torpedoes in some archaic submarine, like bundles with a protruding head that would suddenly tumble off in no particular direction, until someone stopped it by grabbing the hair in full view of the crowd. Not one of them did what St Denis did, according to an astonished French cardinal, who described how, after St Denis' martyrdom and decapitation during Emperor Valerian's persecution of Christians, the saint-to-be picked up his head and walked with it under his arm from Montmartre to the place of his burial (thus considerately lightening the porters' load), where the abbey or church that bears his name was later built: a distance of five and a half miles. This marvel left the cardinal speechless, he said, although actually it so fired him up that a witty lady listening to his account interrupted him, cutting the incident down to size with a single sentence: 'But, sir!' she said. 'The distance is nothing, it's only the first step that is difficult.'

Only the first step is difficult. Perhaps the same could be said of any-thing, or of most things that require some effort or that one does with displeasure or repugnance or with reservations, for one does very few things without some reservations, there's almost always some-thing that prompts us not to act and not to take that step, not to leave the house and not to move, not to speak to anyone and to avoid others speaking to us, or looking at us, or telling us something. I sometimes think that our entire lives – including the lives of ambi-tious, restless, impatient, voracious souls, eager to intercede in the world and even to govern it – are merely the prolonged, postponed desire to go back to being as undetectable as before we were born, invisible, inaudible, giving off no heat; to being silent and still, to retrace our steps and undo what we have done and what can never be undone, in short, to forget, if we're lucky and no one tells on us; to erase all evidence of our past existence which is, alas, at least for a time, still present and future. And yet we are incapable of fulfilling that desire which we fail even to recognize, or only certain very brave, strong, almost inhuman creatures are capable of doing so: those who commit suicide, those who withdraw and wait, those who disappear without saying goodbye, those who truly hide themselves away, that is, those who really do their utmost never to be found: anchorites and hermits in remote places, the impersonators who shake off their identity ('I am not my former self') and take on another which they unhesitatingly embrace ('Don't imagine, fool, that you know me'). Deserters, exiles, usurpers and the forgetful, those who really do not remember who they were and convince themselves that they are not what they were when they were children or even when they were young men or young women, still less when they were born. Those who do not return.

Killing another person is the hardest thing anyone can do, a platitude largely endorsed by people who have never killed anyone. They say this because they can't imagine themselves with a pistol or a knife in their hand, or a rope to strangle with or a machete, most crimes take time and require physical effort if they involve hand-to-hand combat, they also imply a degree of danger (the other person might seize our weapon in the struggle and then we would be the ones to give up the ghost). However, people have long been accustomed to seeing characters in films using rifles with telescopic sights, then you only have to pull the trigger to hit your target and job done, a clean, aseptic task with little risk, and nowadays someone can operate a drone thousands of miles away from the target and end one life or several as if it were all a fiction, an imaginary act, like in a video game (you watch the result on a screen) or, for the more archaically minded, like on a pinball machine where you're in deadly combat with a fat steel ball. Then there is absolutely no chance of ending up spattered with blood.

It's difficult too, people think, because of the irreversible nature of the act, its finality: to kill means that the dead person will never do anything ever again, nothing more will spring from him, he won't argue or have ideas, he can't rectify or amend or right any wrong nor be persuaded; he will cease for ever to speak or act, no one will expect him to reappear, he won't even breathe or look; he will become utterly inoffensive, or worse, useless, like a domestic appliance that has gone wrong and become a mere nuisance, a piece of junk that gets in the way and has to be removed. Most people see killing as too drastic, excessive, they tend to think that anyone can be saved, they basically believe that we can all change and be forgiven, or that some human plague will cease without us having to eradicate it. Besides, in the abstract, other people fill us with pity, so how could I possibly end another person's life? Pity, though, can slacken when confronted by reality, and can even vanish, sometimes instantly. If, that is, we ourselves don't brutally suppress it

I remember an old Fritz Lang film, made in 1941, right in the middle of the war, when the United States had not yet joined in and when it seemed impossible that England could resist alone against Germany, with the rest of Europe having either submitted or willingly fallen into line. And it began like this: a man, played by Walter Pidgeon, dressed as a hunter, in hat, breeches and gaiters, and armed with a precision rifle, arrives at an outcrop or embankment or precipice in a leafy part of Bavaria. It is 29 July 1939, just thirty-six days since the beginning of the war, and the place turns out to be Berchtesgaden, where Hitler owned a villa to which he frequently retreated, even in mid-conflict, and while he was there it was the most closely guarded place in Germany. Spotting something on the other side of the embankment or precipice – or perhaps it was more like a moat surrounding a castle – the hunter lies face down in the scrub and peers through his binoculars. He looks surprised and excited by what he sees, and then he removes from his jacket pocket a telescopic sight, which he attaches to his rifle and adjusts to a distance of five hundred and fifty yards. He is staring at the Führer himself, who is strolling up and down a terrace, talking to a subordinate, a high-ranking Gestapo officer. I still remember his strange half-English name, Quive-Smith, played by George Sanders wearing a monocle, a white jacket and dark trousers, a uniform very similar to that worn in the 1970s by Franco's Falangist henchmen, who never could resist Nazi fashions.

At first, Quive-Smith blocks our view of Hitler, and the hunter, unable now to see Hitler through his front sight, nervously wipes the sweat from his brow. Shortly afterwards, though, the officer leaves and the greater criminal is left alone. Now he is within reach, the bullseye. The hunter places his finger on the trigger and, after a moment's hesitation, he fires. All we hear is a click but no explosion, the weapon is not loaded. Walter Pidgeon laughs and touches the brim of his hat in a gesture of farewell. The viewer is aware that there is an armed soldier nearby, patrolling the area, but he has not yet seen the hidden hunter.

I don't know what explanation is given in the novel on which the film is based, but what the film shows us is that Pidgeon, after that first pretend shot, suddenly realizes that he *can* kill Hitler, and that he has just done so in jest. He then hurriedly slides a bullet into the chamber and again takes aim. The Führer has not changed position, he is directly opposite him, he has not yet gone inside and his chest is still within range. When the hunter is subsequently caught and interrogated, he assures Quive-Smith or Sanders that he had never considered actually firing, that the challenge lay solely in discovering that he *could* do it, that he had succeeded in reaching Hitler's lair without being detected or intercepted. It is what he calls 'a sporting stalk'. Bringing down the prey is a mere mathematical certainty once you have it within range and in your sights. There's no merit then in squeezing the trigger, indeed he has long since given up shooting anything, even a rabbit or a partridge. However, if you're playing the game seriously and not just pretending, the rifle must be loaded. 'Your judgement of distance is uncanny,' Quive-Smith tells him, for he, too, is a keen hunter: he has checked and, given how the sight was adjusted, Pidgeon was only ten feet short of the exact range. 'Such a man cannot be allowed to live,' Sanders adds. And yet Sanders' remark remains ambiguous to the viewer. Pidgeon plays Captain Alan Thorndike, an internationally famous hunter, indeed, his interrogator knows and admires him, has read about his exploits in Africa. It's possible that the tiny error of ten feet was deliberate and that Pidgeon is telling the truth, and he really didn't intend putting a bullet through Hitler's heart.

The way in which the film develops is equally laden with ambiguity: we cannot be sure whether Thorndike happened upon the Führer by chance or if he went looking for him, however unlikely the former may seem. He gives the impression, in any case, that it only actually occurs to him to kill Hitler when he sees him in the flesh, when he realizes who he has in his sights. No, he acts much more slowly than that. After pretending to shoot, after that dull click with his weapon unloaded, after first touching the brim of his hat in a farewell gesture and after giving a cheerfully self-satisfied smile, he makes as if to leave, he sits back like someone who has fulfilled his mission and has nothing more to do there, on that outcrop overlooking the famous villa in Berchtesgaden. And it is then that the expression on his face changes, becomes grave and impatient, as if he were running out of time, more determined too (not overly determined, but more so). That is the moment when it occurs to him that what has been a rehearsal, a pantomime, an amusement – a sporting stalk – could become a reality and change the course of history. That it is in his hands, in his finger, to do his country and half the world an enormous favour, and on 29 July 1939 no one could as yet imagine just how enormous that favour would prove to be. It doesn't matter what happens to him, it would be very hard for him to escape, what matters is the excitement. And so he slides a bullet into the chamber, just one, certain that he will easily hit his target, and that he will not need to fire a second shot. He again strokes the trigger and is on the point of squeezing it, this time with consequences, both personal and historical. An instant later, the Führer will be lying there dead and bloodied, erased from the face of the earth that he is about to dominate and destroy, sprawled on the terrace, a useless piece of junk, an obstacle staining the ground he lies on, mere detritus. He would have to be removed like a squashed cat, what a brief distance there is between everything and nothing, between vigorous life and death, between panic and pity.

As I said, I haven't read the novel the film is based on, but the film never makes clear what Thorndike's intentions really were, because nothing is done until it is done completely and cannot be undone, until there is no turning back. A leaf falls from a tree and covers his rifle sight. Pidgeon rather bad-temperedly brushes it away and, for a moment, loses his line of sight and has to recover his position. He must take aim at Hitler again, he must again have him clearly in his sights or the mathematics will not agree with his infallible calculations and the cat will remain alive and on the loose, will plot and scratch and tear. It's too late now, a falling leaf is enough to end time: the patrolling soldier has found him and hurls himself upon him, and in the ensuing struggle between the two men that one bullet is fired into the air.

Who would not have done the same in his situation, who would not have hesitated and stroked the trigger and felt the temptation to fire a shot in cold blood – 'Yes, a murder, nothing more' to quote a character in a classic novel when playing down the importance of such an act – if, in 1939, he had had Hitler's chest within easy range, whether by chance or after pursuing and stalking his prey? And even long before that date, and not in a fiction. Because this other case is not fictional, unlike Fritz Lang's film: Friedrich Reck-Malleczewen was in no way a left-winger nor was he a Jew or a gipsy or a homosexual, he had six daughters and a son from his two marriages. He was born in 1884, and so was five years older than the Führer. His father was a Prussian politician and landowner. He studied Medicine in Innsbruck and served as an officer in the Prussian army, but had to abandon his military career when diagnosed with diabetes. He worked briefly as a doctor on a ship in American waters. He then moved to Stuttgart where he worked as a journalist and theatre critic, and later moved to Pasing near Munich. He wrote adventure stories for children, and one of them, *Bomben auf Monte Carlo*, proved so popular that it was made into a film four times. These facts would lead one to think him a harmless enough fellow, little given to stirring things up or to subversion. However, he was an educated man and clear-thinking enough to despise and detest the Nazis and Hitler as soon as they appeared on the horizon. And so in May 1936 he began a secret, indeed clandestine diary, which he continued to write until

October 1944, even though, from 1937 on, he took care to hide it away in a wood and to change its hiding place frequently, just in case the authorities were spying on him and keeping watch, because its discovery would have meant certain death. The diary was only published posthumously, in 1947, under the title *Tagebuch eines Verzweifelten*, and at the time it attracted little attention in Germany, perhaps because it was still too soon to remember what had only just ended. Almost twenty years later, in 1966, it was reprinted as a paperback, and that led to it being translated into English in 1970 as *Diary of a Man in Despair*, which is the version I read.

Reck-Malleczewen considered the Nazis to be 'a horde of vicious apes' by whom he felt imprisoned, and, despite having converted to Catholicism in 1933, he confessed to being filled with loathing. 'My life in this pit will soon enter its fifth year. For more than forty-two months, I have thought hate, have lain down with hate in my heart, have dreamed hate and awakened with hate,' he wrote. He saw Hitler in the flesh on four occasions. On one of these, 'behind the fence of his mamelukes' he seemed to him not to be human, but 'the Prince of Darkness himself . . . a figure out of a ghost story'. On another occasion, when he saw him at an inn, 'his oily hair falling into his face as he ranted', a sight that prevented him from eating his own sausage and veal chop in peace, he said that Hitler 'had the look of a man trying to seduce the cook' and gave an impression of 'basic stupidity'. When Hitler left and nodded a goodbye, he reminded him of 'a head-waiter closing his hand around the tip'. Of his 'melancholy jet-black eyes', he said that they were 'like raisins' set in 'a jelly-like, slag-grey face, a moonface'. On the first occasion, as early as 1920, after hearing Hitler deliver an inflammatory diatribe in a private house to which he had more or less invited himself, he and his friends, once they were free of that self-styled orator (the servants had become alarmed, thinking he was attacking his hosts, and rushed in to defend them), felt an immediate need to open a window so that the fresh air could dispel 'the feeling of oppression'. And Reck points out that 'It was not that an unclean body had been in the room, but something else: the unclean essence of a monstrosity.' Despite Hitler's meteoric rise, in the twenty years that passed between that first occasion and the last, 'there is absolutely nothing that has happened . . . since I first saw him to make me change my first view of him. The fact remains that he was, and is, without the slightest self-awareness and pleasure in himself, that he basically hates himself . . .'

The most relevant comment also dates, like the others, from 11 August 1936 (that day's entry is a long one), and in it Reck-Malleczewen describes a day in 1932 (he doesn't give the exact date) when he visited a Munich restaurant, the Osteria Bavaria, and happened to coincide with Hitler, who, strangely, arrived alone, without his usual escort of heavies and bodyguards (for, by then, he was already a celebrity), walked across the room and sat down at the table next to the one occupied by Reck-Malleczewen and his friend Mücke. Feeling himself observed and critically examined, 'he became uncomfortable. His face took on the sullen expression of a minor bureaucrat who has ventured into a place which he would not generally enter, but now that he is there demands for his good money "that he be served and treated every bit as well as the fine gentlemen over there . . ." ' Reck adds that because the streets were already quite unsafe at the time, September 1932, he always carried a loaded revolver with him whenever he went into town. And that devout Catholic, that peace-loving father of seven, that author of books for children and young adults, that educated, bourgeois man from northern Europe, writes the following words without his pen trembling or hesitating: 'In the almost deserted restaurant, I could easily have shot him. If I had had an inkling of the role this piece of filth was to play, and of the years of suffering he was to make us endure, I would have done it without a second thought. But I took him for a character out of a comic strip, and did not shoot.'

On 11 August 1936, he had still seen very little suffering and horror in comparison with what came later, and, nevertheless, Reck-Malleczewen thinks that he would not have hesitated to kill in cold blood a ridiculous man sitting down to eat lunch alone in 1932, had he known then what he knew four years later and eight and a bit years before he died, at the age of sixty, in Dachau concentration camp. On that date in his diary, when Hitler is now completely beyond his grasp and beyond that of almost every other mortal, he consoles himself for that missed opportunity in the Osteria Bavaria with an attack of fatalism which proves prescient: 'It would have done no good in any case: in the councils of the Highest, our martyr-dom had already been decided. If Hitler at that point had been taken and tied to railroad tracks, the train would have been derailed before it got to him . . . There are many rumours of attempts to assassinate him. The attempts fail, and they will continue to fail. For years (and especially in this land of successful demons) it has seemed that God is asleep.' A conservative Christian must have been very desperate indeed to feel able to scold God for not crowning with success man's attempts on the life of one of His creatures, rather than waiting for the Final Judgement. That he had not permitted, no, what am I say-ing, had not facilitated a premeditated murder.

Reck-Malleczewen, who came from a long line of military men, or so he said, was finally arrested on 13 October 1944, accused of 'undermining the morale of the armed forces' (a crime punishable by guillotining) for claiming to be suffering from angina when he was called up to the ranks of the pathetic civil militias being improvised by Goebbels out of a motley crew of adolescents and old men before the Russian advance in the east and for answering 'Blessed be God' rather than the mandatory 'Heil Hitler!' (even whores were obliged to shout this out twice per session, during the preamble and with each fake orgasm) and for some other very grave triviality. After spending a few days in prison, fearing the worst, and after attending a simul-acrum of a court hearing, he was freed thanks to the inexplicable intervention of an SS general who gently reprimanded this man ten years his senior (Reck was already sixty by then), and to whom the diarist refers in his final entries as 'General Dtl.'. This is why he could return to his home and have time to set down this experience in his diary's very secret pages. Had those pages been discovered, he would have gone straight to the gallows or the guillotine without delay or remission.

However, he was rearrested on 31 December, and this he was unable to describe in his diary, for the even more grotesque crime of 'insulting the German currency', apparently because of a letter to his publisher in which he had complained that the inflation rate was eroding the value of his royalties. This time no mysterious 'General Dtl.' appeared and he was not released, and on 9 January 1945 he was transported to Dachau, an extremely insalubrious place, where he soon fell ill. A Dutch prisoner who was there at the same time left a statement in which he described him as a sad, confused old man, weakened by hunger and trembling with nerves, who had learned nothing from his experiences. From that brief portrait one trivial detail has lodged in my memory, just the kind of detail one always remembers best: he was wearing grey linen trousers that were far too short for him and a green Italian military tunic with one sleeve missing.

A death certificate declares that Friedrich Reck died of typhus on 16 February, but another source states that, on that date, he was shot in the back of the neck, perhaps the shot he had failed to use on the piece of filth, the low-ranking bureaucrat, in September 1932. The shot from which a hungry Hitler escaped because his lazy, scornful executioner thought he was like a character out of a comic strip.

We must not be lazy or indifferent, we must not fail to take advantage of an opportunity because it will probably never come again, and we might end up paying with our own life for that scruple, that hesitation, that moment of pity, or that fear of marking ourselves indelibly – 'I killed someone once' – the ideal would be to know beforehand what each individual is going to do and what he is going to become. But if we do not know for certain what happened in the past, how can we possibly be guided by what is to come? If Reck-Malleczewen found it impossible to shoot the Führer in that restaurant, how much more impossible would it have been for him to run over an Austrian boy called Adolf as he was leaving his school in Linz or Steyr, or to throw him into a river in a sack securely tied and weighted down with rocks – yes, as if he were an unwanted cat – when he wasn't even a schoolboy, or to suffocate him with a pillow in his cradle or his carrycot, in the village of Braunau where he was born, had we had the chance and been old enough. He would not have considered the possibility however many 'inklings' he'd had, not even 'the councils of the Highest' would have provided him with a full view of what that child would bring and disseminate. To kill a child or a baby from a tiny, obscure place in Austria, on the frontier with Germany, which he would, besides, have found it difficult to leave; to suggest that, if he lived, he would exterminate millions and subjugate and bloody the world as no one had ever done before: everyone would have taken him for a madman and a maniac, an aberrant assassin, as would he himself, despite having surveyed the scene and known the horror that the defenceless creature harboured in his veins and intended to unleash from Munich, Nuremberg and Berlin.

As you see, killing is not so extreme or so difficult or unjust if you know who you are killing, what crimes he has committed or announced he is going to commit, how many evils you would save people from, how many innocent lives would be spared in exchange for a single shot, a strangling or a few knife thrusts, it lasts only a matter of seconds and then it's done, it's over, it's finished and you carry on – you do almost always carry on, lives are sometimes very long and nothing ever stops entirely – there are cases when humanity breathes easier and even applauds, and feels that a great weight has been lifted from its shoulders, when it feels grateful and lighter and safer, cheered and set free by an assassination, briefly happy.

And yet that first step is still difficult: neither Thorndike in fiction nor Reck in reality squeezed the trigger when they had the chance, even though both knew perfectly well that they would be eliminating something wicked and malign, a pestilence, a putrefaction with his 'slag-grey moonface', his body oozing consternation and oppression, 'the unclean essence of a monstrosity'. Yes, they knew, but the unimaginable worst had not yet happened. We never learn, and the abominable must be beyond abominable before we decide to act, the horror has to be actually happening and already unstoppable before we make a decision, we have to see the axe raised or already slicing through a neck before we skewer those wielding the axe, we must establish that those who appear to be the executioners really are the executioners, and that they are, moreover, executing us. What has not yet happened lacks prestige and force, the already foreseen and the imminent are not enough, clear-sighted words always go unheard, everything has to be corroborated by the terrible facts and deeds, when it's too late and nothing can be done or undone.

And what happens then, paradoxically, is punishment and revenge, which complicate matters still further and are a very different thing; because it's no longer a matter of avoiding an imminent calamity or possibly even more abominations, which really helps when justifying a murder, the act of killing (the idea of averting a new offence, of preventing a repetition and any further misfortunes). No, someone who has committed a crime, or has betrayed or denounced someone, may well have no intention of harming anyone ever again and will therefore not be a permanent danger, his punishable behaviour the product of fear or weakness or some psychological disturbance, an exception. As for revenge, what leads someone to destroy another individual is rancour or the need for redress, enduring hatred or overwhelming grief; as for punishment, it's more a chilling warning to others, the desire to set an example, to teach others a lesson, to make it perfectly clear that such acts have consequences and will not be permitted. This is how mafias work, incapable of forgiving the slightest error or the smallest debt so that there can be no dangerous precedent, so that everyone understands that no one can get away with failing to show them due respect, that no one can steal from, lie to or betray them, that they are to be feared. This, after all, is also how the State and its justice system work, with ceremony and solemnity, or without either if necessary and when everything has to be done in secret: they discourage others from doing the same, they dissuade them by condemning the bold person who preceded them. The proud or optimistic person, or perhaps the innocent who tried his luck and got in first.

My mission was of the punishment or revenge variety, not the avoidance of an individual crime or a killing (not at least immediately), and so it would be harder for me to carry out. And if it was an act of revenge, it wasn't mine. It had been delegated to me, I had been ordered to put it into practice, and, in hierarchical organizations, you get used to obeying orders without question – indeed you go along with it from the start: you sign up for it – even if you have your doubts or you find those orders repugnant (you're perfectly at liberty to feel both, but not to show those feelings or give in to them). Nowadays, we happily condemn the lowliest soldier in the story and those who do the condemning either know nothing about or else blithely ignore what would have happened to those soldiers had they refused to carry out orders. They would have suffered the same grim fate as their victims, especially in time of war, and would have been instantly replaced: another pawn would have taken their place and carried out the task, and the result would have been the same, there are deaths that are 'decided' in heaven or in hell, as Reck-Malleczewen said of the martyrdom of the Germans. Viewed calmly, from a time of peace or a period of truce, from the point of view of the present which always views the past with utter scorn, from the now that believes itself superior to any before, it is very easy to proclaim proudly 'I would have refused, I would have rebelled,' and thus feel noble and pure. It's easy to vilify and condemn the person who strangled or pulled the trigger or stabbed, and no one stops to think just who he eliminated or how many lives he saved by his actions, or how many lives the victim of the assassination would have ended or caused by his instigations and provocations, by his sermons and his moral pestilence, it comes to the same thing or worse (the person who only talks and eggs others on does not stain himself with blood, he leaves the dirty work to his followers, he instils them with venom and that's enough to set them going and for them wildly to outdo themselves), although that isn't how everyone sees it.

I had been retired for some time or 'burned out' as people say of someone who was once useful and no longer is, who has exposed himself to danger over many years and exhausted himself in the process, or of someone who has had no alternative but to remain in dry dock and who has thus lost all his abilities, reflexes and skills, or else they have rusted up. They had let me go and I had agreed. This had coincided with my discovery of the original deception (the one that got me into this life and this work, when I was too young to question it) practised on me by the person who was my recruiter and my most visible boss, Bertram Tupra, later Bertie, also called Reresby and Ure, Dundas and Nutcombe and Oxenham and other names unknown to me, just as I adopted several names during the long years when I was active, I was Fahey and MacGowran, and Avellaneda and Hörbiger and Riccardo Breda, Ley and Rowland and, very briefly, Cromer-Fytton, and a few other names that have been erased from my memory, I could recall them if I tried, because everything bad comes back and my wanderings were full of bad things which, later, once they were over, I missed as one misses everything that no longer is and once was, happiness and sadness, enthusiasm, suffering, everything that forces us to move on, that abandons us.

I had returned to Madrid, to my remote origins and to my wife and my children, whose childhood I had missed and in whose early youth I was very tentatively involving myself, as if asking their permission. She, miraculously, had not entirely rejected me after a continuous absence of about twelve years, not just a continuous absence but a continuous silence too: while I was in hiding, I could not risk being detected if I re-established contact with her, it was best if everyone thought I was dead and therefore out of the game and unreachable, and that is what Berta came to believe with some degree of earnestness but no certainty, that is, intermittently. Even more miraculous, and despite having considered herself to be a potential or de facto widow and later officially a widow and so even freer if you like, was the fact that she had not remarried or established a lasting relationship with someone else, and so she had not buried me in the depths nor had she really replaced me, although the word 'replace' was no longer appropriate. Not because of a lack of will or purpose, for she would doubtless have made a few attempts, but for one reason or another none of those relationships survived, not that I ever asked her about them, I didn't feel I had the right to feel curious and, besides, it was none of my business, just as it was none of her business what relationships I had formed during my adventures. I had even had a daughter whom I'd left behind in England. I have never seen her again nor told anyone of her existence, although her name and her face, which for me remains unchanged and will always be that of a little girl, often appears to me in my daydreams or dreams, Valerie or Val is her name, Valerie Rowland, I suppose, unless her mother has changed it as a posthumous punishment for my abandoning them, then again, James Rowland was a temporary, transient ghost, the sort who does not linger and only turns up in false documents.

Berta and I do not live together now – it's hard after such a long separation and such a long apparent death, one grows accustomed to not having witnesses to one's awakenings or one's habits – but very close, she in our old apartment in Calle de Pavía, and me on the other side of the Teatro Real, in Calle de Lepanto, I don't even need to cross the road to go from one place to the other. And she allowed me over to her place sometimes as a trusted visitor, and even invited me to stay and have supper with the children or without, and she and I

24

even went to bed together from time to time, as ex-lovers sometimes do, more out of familiarity or lingering affection than a revival of old passions, and because there's no need to toil away at courtships or engage in arduous seductions with no guaranteed result. I still didn't discount her throwing me out and replacing me with another man, any day, tomorrow even, for she led a life in which I played no part and she would feel no less free because I had returned. As for myself, the truth is that I hadn't even considered the possibility of starting anything of that sort anew. It was as if my long years of utilitarian relationships with women had left me with no real interest in them (too much time spent seeing them as purely instrumental), oblivious to anything apart from the physiological and mechanical, a mere release. Emotionally numb and desiccated. I regarded those illusions — I could see them in my children, more in Elisa than in Guillermo — as something that existed, but only in other people, a race to whom I had once belonged in some remote, innocent time, in a life so different that it seemed to me imaginary and that I found hard to recognize as mine. I was not yet forty-three when I returned to Madrid in 1994, at least I think it was 1994, I have an ever looser grip on dates, but it was as if I were a hundred years old in that regard, or more as if I were the kind of dead person who refuses to disappear or turn his back on life. I'm referring solely to emotions and expectations, not to the sexual or instinctive. Or perhaps it was simply that I was so pleased to have regained some kind of relationship with Berta (a poor imitation, a parody, a painting, a shadow, or whatever) that it did not occur to me to expect anything more or to look further than her eyes and her person. At the time, I did not dare to express myself in such clear terms, but that is probably what I felt.

Yes, I had been let go and I had agreed to that, the decision had been entirely reciprocal. I had become thoroughly fed up and disillusioned and had announced my defection or my desertion or whatever they call it in MI6 and MI5 or in the secret service of any republic or realm, and they felt they had recouped their investment and that I had performed well for them: 'We won't miss you as much as we would have years ago, you've been out of the loop for a long time now, and there's never been anything to stop you leaving,' had been the response of Bertram Tupra, who was, all in all, a pleasant, easy-going fellow, and because of that, I think, quite detached. He did whatever he liked and considered nothing to be of any great import-ance, the sort of man who wears his coat draped over his shoulders and walks along letting it float or flap about him like a cloak, not caring if its loose, unchecked skirts strike some passer-by. He left a trail of accidental victims and never gave them so much as a back-ward glance. He assumed this was the way of the world, or at least the part of the world in which he carried out his work.

I wasn't expecting to see him again, or hear his voice, when I said goodbye to him in London, preferring not to shake the hand he blithely offered me as if there were no problem at all (the party doing the deceiving or the offending tends not to see any problem; more than that, they often act as if it were all of no account, because one downplays one's own grievances while storing up and magnifying those of others). Tupra elegantly removed his hand and lit a cigarette, as if he had never held his hand out to me in the first place; he wasn't in the least offended by my scornful attitude, my snub. I had been under orders to him for two long decades, and now that this would no longer be the case, I would be cancelled out, erased, I would become instead a dull civilian, or, rather, a stranger whose behaviour didn't even merit his notice, still less his scrutiny. With a retired agent, it's only a question of keeping an eye on him to make sure he doesn't talk too much or say things he shouldn't and can't say. Knowledge of this prohibition is nearly always enough to dissuade retirees, but some do let themselves go and set off along a path of self-destruction: they take to drink or drugs, they fall into depression, they repent and seek expiation or punishment, they start gambling and run up massive debts, they take refuge in traditional religions or in new gimcrack versions, all of them absurd; or else they start to brag, they need others to know they did something worthwhile in life, they cannot bear the fact that their deeds have gone unrecorded, and in the end, their secretive existence begins to weigh on them. They feel that secrets only make sense if, one day, they cease to be secrets, and that they should be revealed at least once before they die. And often, when someone is close to death (and many are convinced they are before their actual time comes), he doesn't care about the consequences of his final words or deeds, nowadays we put little trust in funeral eulogies or in how we will be remembered. We know that, in reality, no one is remembered beyond the first sad hours, during which there is more shock and panic than recapitulation and remembrance.

And so I was hugely surprised when I received a phone call in my office at the embassy in Madrid, where I had easily slipped back into post after many years away. A more distinguished post in fact, a reward for my past sacrifices. I still have a good memory, but it isn't what it was while I was on active service and had to dovetail lies and false identities and sustain them without contradictions or mistakes. And so I had completely forgotten something I had heard Professor

27

Peter Wheeler say when I was very young and studying at Oxford and used to return to Madrid in the vacation to be with my family and my girlfriend, Berta. Wheeler was the first to see that I could be useful and to sound me out about working for the Secret Service, the first to predict the potential in my ability to learn and speak languages and to imitate different accents and ways of speaking – everyone thought it a gift, but that's rather a grand word for a gift you've had since childhood. He was also the one to put me in touch with Tupra, at which point he immediately stood aside and placed me in Tupra's hands, like a gundog bringing a rabbit or a bird to its master. On the day when he first sounded me out, and when I mentioned the rumours I'd heard about his former activities as a spy during the Second World War, and how he still helped out when asked – perhaps in the recruitment of talent, of students who stood out for some particular reason – he had said the following: 'Once you've been involved with the Secret Service, they're the ones who keep in touch with you. Rarely or frequently, as they choose. You don't abandon them, that would be an act of betrayal. We always stand and wait.' When I recalled those last words, they came to me in English, the language in which he and I usually talked: despite being a brilliant Hispanist and Lusitanist, he felt more comfortable in English and could be more precise. 'We always stand and wait.' At the time, this had sounded to me like a quotation or a reference to something else, and I am now well read enough to realize, on remembering it, that it was an allusion to the famous line in the poem by John Milton, although the two verbs have a very different meaning in the poem to the one given them by Wheeler in that context, on that afternoon in his house, adding: 'They barely ever contact me now, but, yes, there are occasional exchanges. You never completely retire if you can still be of use to them. It's a way of serving your country and not becoming an outcast. It's within your grasp not to become a complete, lifelong outcast.' I had sensed in Wheeler's voice a mixture of sadness, pride and relief.

I did feel that I had retired completely and definitively. I believed myself to be free, useless, rejected, banished and even something of a pariah on my return to my first country, Spain, not realizing that, each morning, when I went to work and to my office, I was in fact moving back into British territory, after all, I received my orders and my salary from the Foreign Office, and had for many years given priority to my second country: I had fought in its ranks with passion and without scruples, and had become a patriot, something I had never been in my first country, which had long been contaminated by Francoism. And had I not forgotten those antediluvian words of Wheeler's, Tupra's voice would not have caught me off guard, more than that, it would not have surprised me in the least. Because that is what his phone call was, a reminder that no one is ever a complete pariah nor is anyone ever let go completely if he can still be of service to the country, to the cause, to contribute to what Tupra called 'the defence of the Realm', something so wide-ranging and diffuse that it could include anything, even something that apparently had nothing to do with his country or his wide but shrinking Realm. 'You don't abandon them, they're the ones who keep in touch with you. Rarely or frequently, as they choose.' What Wheeler had said was that the Secret Service dispensed with its active agents whenever it suited them or when they were burned out or became a burden, but not the other way round. If they were needed again, they would re-recruit them so to speak; they summoned and dismissed them with a click of the fingers, or at least tried to.

Thinking it over that night, and having reluctantly arranged to meet Tupra in the next few days, I thought how closely our organizations resemble mafias, which you enter and from which you can be expelled – normally that expulsion is final and tends to come hand in hand with your expulsion from the world and from life – but which you cannot leave voluntarily; and if you do go by mutual agreement, as had been my case, you end up discovering that you were only on leave or an extended leave of absence, however long one or the other lasted. Those you have served have unlimited information about your past, they know what you did on their instructions, and therefore have the capacity to distort those deeds and present them in an ugly, incriminating light. You only have to introduce a little truth into a lie for the lie to seem not just credible, but irrefutable. We are in the hands of people who know us of old, those who can most harm us are precisely those who knew us when we were young and who shaped and moulded us, not to mention those who have employed and paid us or have been kind to us and done us favours. No one escapes this, what others know we experienced or did, the insults received, the unconquered fears and the acts of vengeance we've committed in the presence of witnesses or with their actual help. That is why many people loathe and cannot bear their former benefactors, and view those who got them out of trouble or rescued them from poverty, or even saved them from death, as their greatest danger and their greatest enemy: they are the last person they would want to meet. Tupra was definitely my greatest enemy, the person who had done most for me and against me, and the person who knew most about what I had done in the world, infinitely more than Berta, than my dead parents, than my living children, who knew absolutely nothing. And Bertram Tupra was, moreover, a past master of calumny.

I found it odd that he should be so willing to fly to Madrid, that he didn't even try to persuade or order me to travel to London, to go and see him in that building with no name where he had suggested we meet when we said goodbye and where I assumed he was working, and where I had my suspicions about what he was doing or plotting: he had taken me there once, he had put me to the test by making me watch videos, a test that, in his view, I had failed, he had spoken to me about gifts that I, of course, lacked and which very few people possessed, 'interpreters of lives' he called them, or 'interpreters of people', individuals capable of predicting someone's behaviour just from a glance, or by chatting to them or even observing them on videos, taking for granted that he himself was one of those geniuses. He wanted to gather together a group of such people and resuscitate a division dating from the war years, I think, and to rebuild it as he wanted it; perhaps he had put in an official request for such a division and been given permission in the years when we didn't see each other, my years in dry dock or enforced exile in a provincial English town, the years during which almost everyone thought me dead. And there would be many who still thought I was dead, and we tend not to hear much news about the departed.

The day we met again before my return to Madrid and when I reproached him for his by then ancient deception, I didn't ask him and he didn't tell me what he was up to, why would he? Tupra was very good at getting information out of other people, but rarely gave anything away, he wanted to be given all the information without providing any himself, or only the bare minimum so that his various schemes and machinations would meet with success. Besides, at the time, I really didn't care what he was doing or what happened to him; indeed, just in case, I had gone to that meeting with, in my overcoat pocket, my Charter Arms Undercover, the small revolver they had allowed me to keep while in exile and which had accompanied me at all times, in that town with a river. At that moment – and only at that moment, and after each moment come hours and days and sometimes very long years – nothing would have pleased me more than to have put a bullet in him. But that would have condemned me for the rest of my life, and what I most wanted was to leave that world behind and return to the one place left to me, Madrid. Madrid meant my wife, forgotten and remembered, and my children who were now strangers to me. Somehow or other, I had found them where I left them, and they had reluctantly allowed me in, well, at least they hadn't rejected me outright. In those passable circumstances, I really didn't want Tupra to reappear; nothing easy or simple would ever come from him, only murky dealings and complications, entanglements and knots. And I thought I had left all that behind me for ever, and that he would have left me even further behind, and more than for ever.

Of one thing I was certain, though, some other matter was bringing him to my city apart from the desire to talk to me, to think otherwise would have been pure vanity and believing myself to be more important than I was, and no one was of much importance to Reresby or Dundas or Ure. On the phone he had sounded polite and almost ingratiating, without, however, being obsequious, something he would never be: 'I know we didn't part on the best of terms, Tomás Nevinson, but I need you to do me a huge favour, for old times' sake.' That is how he addressed me, not as 'Tom' or by my surname, as he used to, but by my full name and in Spanish too, Tomás Nevinson was the only name that had, in a way, remained intact and uncontaminated, the name I had never used during any of my obscure exploits, or his assignments. Perhaps he did this as if to acknowledge that I had now gone back to being that person and no other, the original person, brought up in Madrid, the son of an English father and a Spanish mother, and, above all, a boy from the Chamberí district. 'So now he's come asking me for a favour,' I thought, and I couldn't help feeling a little thrill of satisfaction. 'Now he's depending on me and giving me the opportunity to pay him back, to refuse and tell him to go to hell and slam the door in his face.' But Tupra knew how to turn the tables, and immediately transformed his request for a favour into a favour he would be doing for me: 'Well,' he said, 'you won't just be doing me a favour, but a Spanish friend of mine as well, and in the country where one lives it's always useful to have people who owe you a favour, especially important people or people who are just about to become important. Now that you're living in Madrid, it would suit you down to the ground. Let's just look at the matter coolly and with an open mind. Let me explain the assignment, and then you can decide whether to take it on or not. I wouldn't ask you if I wasn't sure you were the ideal agent; more than that, you're the only one who could possibly succeed. We made a good team, you and me. You hardly ever let me down, and I couldn't tell you how often your colleagues did, the few who lasted that long, after all, you and I worked together for more than twenty years, didn't we? Or was it less? I don't know. But almost no agent ever lasts that long. They get burned out horribly fast or else make mistakes. You didn't, you lasted a long time. A very long time.'

The fact that he still referred to me as an agent seemed to me the highest possible praise, I had been retired for nearly two years and was sure that my retirement was permanent and irreversible, that what had been such a large part of my life was over and would never come back, leaving my memory in a semi-vegetative or somnambular state, simultaneously forgetting and remembering: during the day I would try to forget everything I had done and that had been

33

done to me and that I had been obliged to do, and especially what I had done off my own bat and on my own initiative (often there is no way you can receive orders and then you have to make your own decisions); while I slept, though, my head would fill up with the past, or perhaps that was a way of driving out the past when day dawned, and I woke up.

I had ended up feeling disillusioned and thoroughly sick of it, and Tupra no longer considered me to be useful, or felt he had squeezed every last drop of juice out of me. I wanted to leave, and they let me leave with no regrets. I had discovered that I'd initially been recruited thanks to a deception. But who remembers the beginning of anything, after so much time has passed? In a long love relationship, what does it matter who took the first step or made the first approach, who worked hard to build the relationship or who first noticed who, let alone who gave the other person the come-on, thus inoculating the other with the idea of love or sex, causing the other to see him or her in an entirely new light? Time suppresses time, or whatever comes next erases what moves over to make room for it and is gone; the present does not join forces with the past, but supplants it or shoos it away, and in that almost memoryless sphere continuity disperses whatever went before and whatever came after, and everything becomes an indistinguishable magma, and you can no longer conceive of the existence that was once possible but did not happen, was rejected or sidelined, to which no one paid any attention or that failed in the attempt. Whatever does not happen lacks brio and even distinction, becomes lost in the vast mist of what isn't and will not be, and no one is even remotely interested in what did not happen, even we don't care about what didn't happen to us. Thus preambles don't count. Once things have happened, these wipe out how that happening happened, just as no one wonders why they were born once they're striding smartly down the path. Or indeed, once they first start walking.

Tupra hadn't changed at all, and, besides, not that much time had passed, although to me it had seemed endless: when you think a matter has been resolved, when you cut a thread that has stretched out over decades – a love affair, a friendship, a belief, a city or a job – everything that was holding that thread in place suddenly moves off with astonishing speed and completely muddles up our idea of time. For me, Tupra was one of those men who accept the toll of the years quite early on, then keep age at bay for many more years, as if that initial acceptance of the passing years served to postpone indefinitely all the subsequent ones, as if he were in total charge of any changes in his appearance, and as if these depended on his will or agreement, his consent. As if one morning he had said to the mirror: 'The time has come to look more respectable or more authoritative or more experienced. So be it.' And as if later, on another day, he said: 'All right, enough is enough. Hold things right there, until further orders.' I had the impression that he controlled not only everything to do with his machinations and obligations, but also the way he aged or matured physically. Perhaps he shared it out among his many names, of which I could recall just six. The effect was disconcerting and disquieting, as if you had before you someone whom time obeyed, at least as regards his face. I had first seen him twenty or so years ago in Oxford, I couldn't be bothered to make an exact calculation, and he certainly didn't look weighed down by a quarter of a century, at most, by a decade, and not the cruellest of decades either.

It is also true that he dyed the grey hair around his temples, something I had noticed when I was in England.

I had left it to him to choose a meeting place even though he was the one asking to see me, it's hard to abandon hierarchies even when the subordinate has lost all respect for the subordinator and thoroughly despises him, feels resentful and insulted, and would once willingly have put a bullet in him. I found it odd that he should choose a park in winter (it was 6 January 1997, Epiphany, but he had no time for Spanish feast days, he didn't know about them and they were, besides, no excuse for not meeting) much closer to my apartment or attic in Calle de Lepanto than to wherever he would be spending his brief stay, doubtless somewhere near the British embassy. He told me only what I needed to know, and hadn't given me a phone number or the name of his hotel, or perhaps he was staying in one of the rooms in the embassy reserved for influential guests, or else had invaded the apartment of some British Council employee or one of the teachers at the Instituto Británico, where I had studied until I was fourteen, before moving on to the Colegio Estudio, where Berta had spent all her school years, and where we met as adolescents.

Tupra was definitely influential, and not only in his particular sphere or in his own country, where he was above almost all visible authorities, certainly the police, as I had found out early on in Oxford with Sergeant Morse or whoever he was, and possibly above uniformed soldiers too, I never knew his rank or ranks as he rose (he would have risen on merit), he was always in mufti. As for those invisible authorities, those who rarely leave their carpeted rooms, it's possible that he often dodged them or decided not to consult them when he could foresee raised eyebrows and long silences equivalent to a tacit no. What's more, it often suits those same authorities if some underling does take the initiative or disobeys orders or doesn't ask permission, so that if things go wrong or cause a scandal, they

36

can honestly say they knew nothing about it. Tupra was also influential in most of Europe and the Commonwealth, possibly in the United States and in allied Asian nations. It was typical of him to prefer not to be locatable, that is, not to be found out or taken by surprise, so that he could thus impose his own conditions and times, to be always the one to make contact and to appear, the one deciding on what the next steps should be and always taking the initiative. He hated anyone asking him a favour or bringing him problems, and yet he never stopped asking favours of others and putting them in tight spots, demanding they perform semi-heroic deeds and giving them instructions.

I arrived first and sat on one of the stone benches in the little park where he had arranged to meet me, a small, secluded spot next to Plaza de la Paja, a tiny scrap of greenery right in the middle of old Madrid or the Madrid of the Habsburgs. It couldn't have been the Príncipe de Anglona garden, because that wasn't opened to the public until a few years later, but in my already faltering recollections it's as if it were (my memory keeps playing terrible tricks on me: there are names, events and dates that I can reproduce with photographic exactitude, while others from the same period are lost in a mist). It was a cold day, so I had put on my peaked cap, more Dutch or French than Spanish or British, and which, according to Berta, gave me a certain sailorish air. At forty-five, I wasn't yet bald, although my hair was definitely thinner, but my receding hairline still qualified as 'interesting' and, fortunately, had stopped receding. I kept my cap on for the moment, after all, I was out in the open, for I haven't yet lost the polite custom of taking off my hat when indoors, unless I'm pretending to be someone of coarser habits. Given the date and the temperature, I wasn't surprised to find no one else there, in fact, I was surprised to find the place open at all, and I doubted Tupra would have checked beforehand. Families were strolling about in the nearby square, children were trying out or showing off their new toys, and some grown-ups were eating cakes that we traditionally eat at that time of year. A couple of the cafés had put out chairs and tables, although it wasn't really the right time of year for that, but the old *madrileño* delight in being out and about led many to sit down and, well wrapped up, enjoy a late breakfast or an aperitif. Epiphany in Spain is a quiet, late-rising day. Madrid cannot bear being stuck indoors.

After a couple of minutes, a woman dressed for winter came into the garden, she was wearing a woollen hat and, at first glance, I reckoned she was about thirty. She looked briefly across at my bench and, seeming slightly annoyed to see me there – as if I were invading her territory – went over to another one, a short distance away. I noticed she had blue eyes and I watched as she took a book out of her bag, a Pléiade edition, instantly recognizable to anyone who has ever handled one. Out of curiosity, I tried to identify the book, and before she settled down to read I saw what I took to be a picture of the author, which was undoubtedly a portrait of Chateaubriand as a young man with wild, romantic hair, which meant that the book was probably *Mémoires d'outre-tombe*. I couldn't but suspect that Tupra had sent her, perhaps as a chaperone or a distant witness; he was cultivated and pedantic despite his brisk, often abrupt and even violent manner: it was not in vain that he, like me, had studied at Oxford (History Ancient and Modern, he had told me once with great precision and a touch of pride that he could not entirely repress: getting to that university would have been quite something in his youth, given where he came from; and he had added, so as not to take credit where no credit was due: 'It helped me to know men better, because, in ordinary life, and in normal, civilized times, men now are different from men back then, but at certain key moments they're no different and can turn savage in a matter of seconds, and we witness such moments far more often than most people. However, I never took up history professionally, I wasn't good enough') and he had studied under Professor Wheeler, not in the strictly educational sense, but in the broader, deeper sense of education, the actual shaping of a person. A woman on her own reading Chateaubriand in French near the Plaza de la Paja in January (she had taken off her right woollen glove, for no one can turn the Bible-paper pages of a Pléiade edition with their gloves on) smacked of scene-setting, of some carefully prepared *tableau vivant*, or perhaps it was an obscure, convoluted warning, intended to turn my thoughts to beyond the grave before Tupra arrived, a state in which I had existed for years and years, at least as regards those closest to me and those I had offended against, those who would have liked to eliminate me out of revenge or a sense of justice (in the eyes of the condemned man these are barely distinguishable), those pursuing me. If it was some improbably abstruse warning, I had nonetheless understood it, because the concept of *outre-tombe* had already lodged in my mind. The young woman settled down to read and did not look at me again while I continued to wait.

Tupra appeared seven or eight minutes late, as was also typical, keeping others waiting, never to the point of abuse or exaggeration, but always a little bit late. He wasn't wearing his dark overcoat draped over his shoulders as he used to, but had put it on and buttoned it up, for Madrid is usually colder than London. With his mid-calf-length coat, as was the fashion in the 1980s and 1990s, a light-coloured scarf around his neck and black leather gloves, he and I were dressed very similarly. He still had the same simultaneously resolute and indolent walk, as if he never hurried and as if the world had to wait until he had absorbed all the facts that concerned him directly. And why would he have lost that energetic gait? He was, after all, only a few years older than me, although, when I first met him, I had the distinct feeling that he had lived several more lives than I had. Perhaps I had now caught him up somewhat, because, since that far-distant time, I had accumulated lives of my own, and even lost one or two, I had been declared dead *in absentia* and Berta had officially become a widow, and been duly compensated. When he entered the garden, he glanced at the young woman on the other bench. The fact that she did not look up to inspect this new intruder on her territory confirmed my suspicion that Tupra had invited her. Although who knows why. Perhaps he didn't trust me, I might have changed. He sat down beside me, undid the bottom buttons of his coat so that he could cross his legs, took out a cigarette, lit it without a word of greeting (he gave only a slight lift of his chin), as if at most a week had passed since our last meeting. That is, as if he were as used to seeing me as he was the people he continued to work with on a daily basis. I had ceased to do that in 1994, for good.

'I do like to observe the tropes,' he said. 'Have you noticed that in every spy movie, there's always a scene in which two men sit down on a bench as if by chance, as if they had just happened to coincide? Even though there are five empty benches nearby. It's quite ridiculous. Here at least, that is not the case.'

II

'What passing-bells for these who die as cattle?', that line from a popular 1917 poem suddenly came into my mind, popular, that is, in England, and written by one of those young men who cease to exist when they're only twenty or so and who die in droves. Tupra's presence almost always heralded death or suggested or recalled it, a death from before or after, past or future, to be suffered or inflicted, sometimes, but rarely, by one's own hand, more often indirectly thanks to a few murmured words. His dead did not die like cattle, in our world that occurs only sporadically in times of peace and we were living in a time of apparent peace, although for him the world was in a permanent state of war, something most people were unaware of. And in order for people to remain unaware of that or almost anything else, in order that, day after day and night after night, they could continue with their minuscule cravings, their daily tasks and tribulations, they need individuals like him or like me in my former life, sentinels or watchmen who never sleep and are constantly on the alert. He did not hold with that line from the Psalms: 'Unless the Lord watches over the city, the watchman stays awake in vain.' He knew that there was no Lord and that he doesn't watch over anything, and that even if there was a Lord, he would be drowsy or distracted, for this reason, the essential watchman never dozes and never even rests, because he is the only one defending the Realm, he and his fellow watchmen.

No, the dead that Tupra carried with him were individuals, they all had faces but not, of course, names, or not the name they had received at birth; they came marked long ago by an arrow or a bull-seye, sentenced to death in an office or an inn, and because they died alone, they deserved passing-bells to be rung for them, and bells did toll for them, for each man in his own land, in his own house, wherever he was loved despite any crimes he had committed or precisely because he had committed them, as perhaps they tolled for Hitler in his native village of Braunau, or in Steyr or in Linz where he went to school, someone would remember him as a child in those places and would mourn him in secret. And so they were the dead who were not forgotten and were not to be confused with those one had known in life and whom one had even befriended and not always on false pretences, with whom one had exchanged jokes and the occasional true or false memory. 'The pallor of girls' brows shall be their pall' was another line in that same poem, and it ended with this, the other line I remembered: 'And each slow dusk a drawing-down of blinds.'

What blinds did Tupra – or Ure or Reresby, it made no difference – want to draw down in Madrid, which window or balcony was he aiming at? I was inevitably wondering what brows would he order to grow pale on that cold January morning? Would he still be the same inside as outside, for the sentinel cannot allow change, if he does, the city will fall and be conquered, he would not have aged in mind or character either, or not yet, the day he ceased to be alert, he would know how to step aside. The fact that he wanted to see me and had arranged to meet me where no one could overhear us suggested that he must have some kind of mission in mind, that he wanted me to cease being an absentee, as they called agents who had retired, but who still benefited, financially I mean, from the institution that had expelled them or that they had abandoned, and so were not entirely set adrift, and over whom, hypothetically at least, the institution still exercised a distant degree of control: those who received pensions if they were of retirement age or burned out, or were assigned to less stressful jobs, well paid enough for them to get by, if they were, objectively speaking, young but had become too unbalanced or demotivated and were no longer right for the job. (The British Secret Service prided itself on never leaving anyone behind, not even traitors entirely, if they had fulfilled the loyal part of their duties efficiently, or before they became traitors.) Because, subjectively speaking, no one was young after a decade or two in active service and working at full capacity: there were people who had trodden every inch of the territory and were so worn down that they had been relegated to an office, and at the age of thirty-five or forty would suddenly burst into tears at their desk, in front of their colleagues, for no obvious reason and without anyone having said anything, as some older people often do, some of whom become tearful over the slightest thing, a film or a piece of music, some hidden emotion indecipherable to others, or a secret memory or the mere presence of a child, when they must think: 'Enjoy not knowing anything and not having had time to do anything, to harm anyone, even though others could easily harm you, that comes with being born and only the first step is difficult. You don't know that the time will come when you'll be old like me, you don't even understand what "old" means or else think it won't happen to you if, that is, you've already started to get some idea of its meaning by seeing me or your grandparents or others with ash on their sleeve and sitting in parks. And the last thing you can imagine is that the passing-bells will ever toll for you or that there'll be a drawing-down of blinds, if such ancient customs are still being observed then, which is unlikely, for even now they are probably only observed in small places, with so few inhabitants that each and every one is important and is missed when they cease to be. Make the most of the fact that you're fresh and ignorant and that few people can make use of you, that any orders you're given are very simple and needn't trouble your conscience. Make the most of not knowing who you are, nor what kind of man or woman you're going to

become, make the most of not having a conscience or only a rudimentary one, still under construction, and which, alas, will grow
unstoppably. However, a conscience is forged very slowly, and so
enjoy, albeit unwittingly, this long period of time during which you
are not accountable to anyone and when you cannot as yet hear any
cries and laments.'

'I assume they do it so that they can't be overheard,' I said. 'There are no concealed microphones in the open air, unless one of them is wearing one, but we wouldn't lay traps for each other, would we, not when we're working together towards the same objective. It's different when one of the two isn't working, when he's reluctant.' I wasted no time in alluding to that first deception, but he did not react, he kept silent, for him it was a matter of no importance; however hard he tried, he could never give it the same value I did, for him it was just one episode among many. 'There could be devices in any interior space. In a bar or in a café, that is, if you know beforehand where you'll be meeting. I presume that's why you chose this very central, virtually unknown place. It's very near where I live and yet I didn't even know it existed, I've never been here before.' I indicated the young reader with a nod of my head. 'She's the only danger here, but she's some way away and, besides, she appears to be absorbed in reading Chateaubriand, at least I think so. She only looked over at me because she would rather we weren't here, so that she could sit on our bench. Although her bench does get the sun, which is no small thing in January. She's either a woman who likes to have her own way or a slave to habit.'

I wasn't sure if I had used the word 'we' on purpose, to make it clear to him that I would brook no deceptions, no half-truths, or whether it had just slipped out involuntarily. It's difficult to avoid sliding back into old habits when you've spent your whole life following them, a life in which I had always felt we were 'we', wherever I happened to be and even if I was alone. That 'we' instils courage, breeds patience, provides imaginary company and banishes scruples, or at least shares out responsibilities. Tupra had been part of that 'we' from the first day to the last. The truth is, I had spoken the word as if I'd never left and was not a total 'absentee', as if I hadn't spent two years being a miserable 'I', exhausted and bewildered and nostalgic too.

'You managed to make out what she's reading? With no binoculars either? That's a good sign, it means you haven't entirely lost all your skills. That's what I like to hear.'

'No flattery, Tupra. Anyone could do that. Who is she anyway? You must know her.'

'Me. Don't be absurd, Tom, that's a sure sign you're out of practice.' It didn't take him long to put me in my place, and it served me right. 'I haven't the faintest idea. She's clearly a highly cultivated local, there must be plenty of those around.'

I looked at him and I looked at the woman. Then back at him and again at her, the briefest of glances. Of course they knew each other. Besides, she had the kind of physique Tupra found attractive. True, he was attracted to many different female physiques – although not all, he could be scornful too, woundingly indifferent – his very unEnglish blue or grey eyes, immodestly pale, communicated his verdicts all too clearly. He had always seemed to me more southern than northern, with his all-embracing gaze, his full, soft lips, his thick eyelashes, his eyebrows like black smudges, his lustrous, beer-coloured skin and thick hair, curly at the temples like that of a flamenco singer. He had never explained to me the origin of his strange surname, assuming it was his real name.

'Tell me what you want. What is this favour you're asking? Who is this Spanish friend, the father of our reader over there? Her husband, her boss, her lover? Look, I really have nothing more to say to you. Probably not even that. In fact, I really don't know why I came.'

I found it hard not to like him, it was a struggle. What he had done to me in my now distant youth was unforgivable, especially so for the youngster I was then, the student, into whose skin I could no longer put myself. It was a very long time since I had stopped being him, the main – irreversible – thing was that I had become a different person, someone dedicated to my task, diligent, highly skilled, almost a fanatical member of that 'we'. An English patriot I told myself, despite being or having been more Spanish than anything. I wasn't sure how or when or why that change, that conversion, had taken place, it was probably the natural result of my activities, it happened with no previous thought on my part. You begin to serve a cause reluctantly, and then, after a time, you feel valued and useful and never again question the cause, you embrace it unthinkingly just as you greet each dawn, because that is what gives meaning to your life or to your daily existence. Everyone has some sense of loyalty to some thing or place: even those who have renounced it for reasons of duty or principle still reserve a small space for it, normally such a very secret space that even they might not know of its existence and will discover it unexpectedly and belatedly only when it's revealed to them. It could be loyalty to a single person, to a habit, to a place, to a town; to a business or an institution; to a body whose memory lingers and refuses to leave; to the past, so as to preserve continuity, or to the present, so as not to lose sight of it; to your comrades-in-arms, to those who trust you; to your superiors, to those who feel proud of you although they never tell you so and never will. Berta had long embodied my particular scrap of loyalty, in terms of affection and perhaps sexually too. Tupra had embodied it professionally, he was for me the ultimate representative of England, just as the ship's captain is for a sailor. Now that I had him there before me again and could feel his presence, I could confirm that he was a very

49

pleasant man except when he became cutting or disdainful or violent or lecturing. Although even when he adopted that latter stance, it was still always interesting to listen to him, he never spouted nonsense or trivia and I rarely heard him utter a platitude, which is all that one hears these days, and reads too, which is even worse. He could be cordial when he wanted, he often laughed heartily, and his mere presence was enough to lift the spirits, and mine had been very low since returning to Madrid, or perhaps since long before that, ever since my years of hibernation in that English town where I had left a daughter. Tupra made one feel that the real party, the life and soul of it, was to be found wherever he happened to be, or that what really mattered was whatever he was pointing at, or focusing on through his rifle sight, wherever he was fixing his gaze or his attention.

He stubbed out his cigarette with his foot and immediately lit another, probably as a way to fend off the cold, which was starting to make itself felt. He still smoked those Rameses II cigarettes that come in a small, elaborate cardboard packet with colourful Egyptian motifs, one could apparently still buy them in London, in Smith & Sons or in Davidoff's perhaps, or in James J. Fox. Even in those pretentious or eccentric shops it was impossible now to find the Marcovitch cigarettes in their small metal box, the ones I had smoked in my distant youth and which had contributed indirectly to my fate. They are no longer made, but then everything stops being made before we die, without the slightest consideration for our habits, tastes and loyalties.

He indicated the reader with the tip of his cigarette, without actually looking at her.

'She's reading Chateaubriand you say. *Memoirs from Beyond the Grave*, I suppose,' he gave the title in English. 'I don't think anyone reads *The Genius of Christianity* any more.' And then he responded to my last comment. 'You came because you're bored and there are days when you don't know what to do with yourself. You came out of curiosity, defiance and vanity. You came in order to find out if you're still useful, because none of us is essential. You came because, even though you think you don't give a damn about anything, it's unbearable to be outside once you've been inside. You didn't leave entirely of your own will. We opened the door for you and we let you go, at the time you weren't much use to us, now, on the other hand, you are. You came because, having once been on the inside, you find it intolerable being on the outside not knowing what's going on, what plots are being hatched. Admittedly what you knew was only partial, the part you needed to know at any one time. And it's hard not to intervene, not to have some impact in the world. Not being able to stop any more misfortunes or at least try to. Once you've engaged in that life, it's very hard not to want to carry on being engaged.'

This was one of his favourite mottoes, at least with me, perhaps he offered different ones to different people. The first time we met, in Oxford, he had explained the nature of his work thus: 'We both act and don't act, Nevinson, or, rather, we don't carry out the actions we carry out, or the things we do are done by nobody. They simply happen.' In my youth, that had sounded to me like something out of a Beckett play.

'After having been Someone,' he added, 'it's very difficult to go back to being no one. Even if that Someone was invisible and almost no one would recognize him. That's why you've come, Nevinson, that's why you're here and not at home with your wife and children opening presents.' So he did know that in Spain we exchanged presents on 6 January rather than on Christmas Day. This time he addressed me as he used to do, by my surname. He usually either called me that or 'Tom'. 'To find out if you would become Someone again. Bear in mind, though, that, as usual, only you and I will know it; as well as some possible go-between should that prove necessary.'

'What, like that Molyneux fellow with his stupid Napoleonic

forelock?' I asked so as not to respond at once to his assertions, which he had strung together with such confidence. 'What an impertinent fool you sent me that last time. In the end, I had to put him firmly in his place.'

Tupra laughed. He laughed like someone confessing to a prank the thought of which still amused him.

'Ah, yes, young Molyneux. Well, believe it or not, he's making a good career for himself. Of course, we don't make great demands on people nowadays. For the first time in our history, we're having difficulty recruiting agents, and many veterans are drifting away or working part-time, combining their work for us with working for someone who pays them better, big British companies, multinationals with headquarters in the territory and who knows what else. They ask permission and we give it to them, because remaining inactive is the worst possible thing for an agent: they're better off helping to expand our economy, that at least is our bosses' patriotic-pragmatic reasoning. If it's for the benefit of the Realm, they don't frown upon a little light industrial espionage. The problem is that there are more and more agents with two masters, and that always affects discipline and, of course, concentration. But that, I fear, is a sign of the times, and will continue. It won't be long before I myself will have to think about what to do, I've had plenty of offers. The truth is that it's just impossible to find talents like yours these days. Strangely, the fall of the Iron Curtain has made us less attractive.' He had gone back to flattering me, openly this time. Then he immediately returned to Molyneux. 'That's right, I packed you off to that town where you were hidden away for a while, where was it now? Ipswich, York, Lincoln, Bristol, Bath? I don't remember. I know it was somewhere with a river. The Avon, the Orwell, the Witham, the Ouse?'

Tupra couldn't resist being irritating, or undermining your morale when he was supposed to be raising it, or playing down any sacrifices you had made. He was as likely to encourage you as to offend you, and both were ways of spurring you on. He knew perfectly well in which town and next to which river I had remained buried for several long years, not as he put it 'for a while'. That isn't how it had felt to me, but perhaps it had for him. For me, it had been a long, languishing eternity, I had even formed a small, short-lived family in order to survive it, the nurse Meg and the little girl Val. What, I wondered, would have become of them, I hoped they were all right, and that Meg had even found another husband and another father for Val. I sent them money every month from Madrid, and although Meg never acknowledged receipt and certainly never thanked me, the cheques were always cashed, one of my English accounts, the one in the name of James Rowland, which was how they had known me in that town. Dignity and scorn have their limits, those imposed by necessity. Tupra was playing with fire if he really did want a favour from me. I was tempted to get up and leave him there in that garden, and go and open some useless present or other in Calle de Pavía, which had long been my home and was now my wife's.

Yes, I was tempted, but I didn't leave. I took it on the chin, doused that flash of bad temper, and after a few seconds found myself feeling almost amused by Tupra's malice, his desire to stick his finger in your eye, only a little, not too deep, just enough to irritate. Except, that is, when things got serious, then he wouldn't use his finger, but something far worse. I hate to say it, but he knew me well, or perhaps he knew us all well, those from the past and those still to come. Perhaps we weren't so very remarkable once we had chosen to follow a path that was remarkable only as regards the world's apathetic masses, those who had no idea what was going on and didn't want to, those who simply wanted everything to work and to be in its proper place, every morning and every evening. He had hit the nail on the head, he had put it very well: 'It's unbearable to be outside once you've been inside.' I recognized myself in those words. And in his other words too, but I didn't need them. However weary of it all I had felt in the end, however retrospectively disillusioned, however resentful and even sickened, I missed the excitement . . . no, that's a stupid thing to say: I missed the *sense* of activity, of having orders, missions and operations to carry out, the sense of waiting, of being involved in the one-eyed or blind defence of the Realm (because I was always left slightly in the dark, never seeing the complete picture, perhaps even Tupra didn't either, although he would have had a wider view). What had at first been a trial and a curse, one that even used to keep me awake at night, like a knee pressing into my chest, with the passing of time and those years of activity it had become not my sustenance, but my one way of being in the world in a balanced, rational way. Without it I wandered around in a gloomy, somnambular state, lost among a lot of vague memories, and eaten away by all too precise regrets. I had only one method of dealing with the latter, and that was by adding more reasons for future regrets.

Perhaps that is precisely what leads some individuals to kill again and again, because only by being engaged in committing a new crime can they momentarily erase all the others, by focusing all one's mind and one's five senses on the planning and the execution. I've often thought this when trying to explain to myself what leads those women and men – far more men of course – to reoffend unnecessarily. I believe that the accumulation of crimes has an anaesthetizing or perhaps a narcotic effect: for those who still have some glimmer of conscience, it's easier to deal with a whole pile of deaths than just one or two, because there comes a moment when their conscience can no longer keep up with the vast numbers, its capacity not being limitless, and it eventually loses track, becomes overwhelmed, washes its hands of the whole business. Anyone responsible for having other people die like cattle has no time to notice individuals or to draw down the blinds one by one, and so those people become a mere blur, tinged with unreality, a number, a piece of flesh, and the higher the number and the heavier the flesh, the more their sense of guilt becomes benumbed, submerged, and disappears altogether when it can't cope any more. Piling death upon death is probably the only way out for mass murderers, be they dictators, terrorists, ministers who declare unnecessary wars or the generals who advise them or urge them on. That is why they must be eliminated, because they keep on adding more and more deaths and will never stop. Yes, it was very hard to be outside and unable to contribute to the restoration of life without misfortunes . . . Without misfortunes for us, you understand; after all, who cares about our enemies: their misfortunes are our good fortune, until the fighting stops and they surrender.

'You know perfectly well where you buried me, Tupra, or where I buried myself for five years, and you know perfectly well which river it was. Stop all this nonsense and tell me what you want, the cold is beginning to get to me.'

'You, like everyone else, can't bear to be sidelined. You used to be made of sterner stuff. Look at that woman, reading away, quite oblivious to us. You, and others like you, immediately grow accustomed to the untroubled life, and the slightest contretemps upsets you.'

From this response (that offensive plural, that 'like everyone else') I saw that he had been wounded by the word 'nonsense'. By my having taken the liberty of applying it to him. He needed in some way to pay me back, to re-establish the hierarchy, abolished two years earlier.

'Look, Nevinson, I'm not going to lie to you, or ask you to do something impossible or even particularly difficult. The Secret Service isn't what it used to be. It may well go back to being so if we ever come under serious attack again. But at the moment, there isn't that much to do. The fall of the Berlin Wall hasn't just made us look less attractive, it has also left us somewhat disconcerted, without that constant sense of threat or imminent combat, with no real adversary. I wouldn't say it's left us in a void, because in our profession there is no void, for those of us who remain active, I mean.' Another tiny dart aimed at me. 'There's still Ulster, of course, that interminable, tedious nightmare; but things are going better there now too, it might even be on the right path: Major has done quite a lot undercover' – John Major had been Prime Minister in Britain since 1990, and was in the last few months of his mandate – 'and if Blair is the next Prime Minister, it's likely that, in a couple of years' time, he'll impose some false remedy; and that remedy, however false, will last for a few more years, because we are all utterly exhausted and bored, even those who seem inexhaustible.' He repeated that last word, and it's true that the world does eventually get bored with everything. 'There are other things, though, there always are, just as there are always those who wish us ill. And then there are our allies, like your country, Spain, where the problem with ETA is still dragging on.' So suddenly I was Spanish. 'For the moment, though, we must act with a degree of modesty.' He paused as if tempted to light a third cigarette. He glanced at my hands and stopped. 'Have you given up smoking?' He wanted me to keep him company in his vice.

'No, I still smoke.' I took out my cigarette case. 'I just couldn't be bothered to take off my gloves.'

'You mean you don't know how to smoke with your gloves on? It's very easy. Look at that young woman over there.'

I shot a sideways glance at the reader, who was indeed smoking with one glove on, and was clearly deemed worthy of Tupra's admiration. He had kept his gloves on all the time.

'Of course I do.' I rather clumsily took a cigarette out of the case and carefully lit it. Fortunately, there was no wind, it was just very cold.

'What are you smoking? I can't see what brand it is.'

'They're German cigarettes, pretty weak stuff. I've got used to them though.'

'German?' he said, scandalized, as if I had uttered a heresy. I couldn't tell whether he had a grudge against German tobacco or against the entire nation. He had spent more time than me in East Germany, when times were harsh.

'As you said, there is no East and West there now: you've run out of adversaries.'

'Well, time will tell, who knows how the more bureaucratic part of society will evolve, authoritarianism is always the thing people miss most,' he said sceptically, then, without a pause, picked up the thread again. 'Punishment is a modest thing, Tom, but not to be scorned. Not just as a way of settling accounts or delivering justice, call it what you will, but also as a way of instilling fear and dissuading others, because there are always people ready to emulate the very worst actions and reactivate the very worst ideas.' He took off one glove and ran his fingers over his lips, as if to dry them. He had such soft lips that they always looked moist. Before putting his glove back on, he took the opportunity to light his cigarette. 'Villainy is very seductive and easily passed on. The villainy of the father proves irresistible to his children or, if not to them, then to his grandchildren. Exterminating whole families is a vile thing to do in any conflict, but you have only to look at Yugoslavia, and the reasoning behind that has to be seen from a historical-paranoiac perspective, in wartime it's best not to know your history, those with that knowledge will be aware of what those inoffensive children might well do when they grow up.'

Those Yugoslavian wars made me feel positively ill, I could barely stand to watch the TV news or read the press. I just hoped they wouldn't ask me to get involved with anything to do with that conflict.

'Besides, you and I both know that nothing ever goes away entirely, and what does appear to have gone away always returns sooner or later, although that sometimes takes thirty or even fifty years. Anyway, when it returns, it does so with renewed rancour, artificially plumped up, because there's nothing like the imagination for feeding rancour. By recalling what some of our forefathers suffered, usually remote relatives we never even knew. By transforming them into victims when they, almost every one of them, were also executioners, but the imagination chooses to ignore that part, leaves out that part of the story and lingers over what most pleases it. So you have to assume that everything bad comes back, and if *we* don't make that assumption then who will? People tend to think that once something's over or overcome, it stays quietly in the past, and that reassures them. Armies are made up of people. We, on the other hand, know that whatever has been continues to be, and that it's merely waiting in abeyance. Everyone grows tired of fighting and feels relieved when it ends; they're afraid of dying on the last day of a war, just before surrender or an armistice, and they go back home as soon as there's no longer any imminent danger. They thus allow the enemy to recover and regroup, as happened with Germany after the First World War, and look what followed only twenty years later. A country destroyed, in ruins, rose up again like a monster.'

'Yes. In Spanish we say "*A enemigo que huye, puente de plata*" – literally, "If your enemy flees, build him a silver bridge". That's considered to be good advice, a sensible attitude to take: you help your enemy to flee, and give a sigh of relief. You don't pursue or humiliate him, you don't beat him to a pulp. You choose not to destroy him.'

Tupra had now unbuttoned his overcoat, from bottom to top. Perhaps he was warming up as we talked, although that isn't usually what happened. Or else he was finding it hard to turn and face me on the bench with his coat buttoned up, the bench was fairly narrow. He rounded on me:

'It may well be a popular saying, but that's an unforgivable mistake to make. It's the saying of a suicidal country, as your history has shown. No one can guarantee that, once the enemy has crossed the bridge, he won't dismantle it and make off with the silver. Without a bridge he'll be unreachable should you change your mind, plus you'll have given him the means to gather strength again. With your silver he'll recruit mercenaries and will return to the charge with renewed energy.'

'Don't be so literal, Bertie.' That was the name I suddenly came out with, the name I'd used during all the years we were working together and before I knew of his initial deception. Perhaps because his response seemed so foreign to me and so ingenuous. He was a real Englishman, and I was not. 'It's a metaphor.'

He gave a patronizing laugh and it was my turn to feel ingenuous. He was so very quick at turning the tables on you.

'I know, Tom. And I, of course, was speaking metaphorically. Just how would you improvise a silver bridge?' Again that mocking laugh. 'Where would you get the silver from in mid-battle? And how would you have time to build a bridge? Come on now, it's not going to appear as if by magic. No matter. We say precisely the opposite, but ours isn't a saying, it comes from Shakespeare: "We have scotch'd the snake, not killed it," Macbeth says to his wife. And he adds: "She'll close and be herself, whilst our poor malice remains in danger of her former tooth." Mind, he says this just after he's killed King Duncan, realizing that even once they've eliminated him, they're still not safe, even his murder is not enough.'

I had never entirely accustomed myself to the idea that so many men and women engaged in such urgent work, men and women of action if you like, so many agents, were also highly cultivated, even though I considered myself to be. But many of them were machinators, which requires a deep knowledge of history and literature. It was not for nothing that, during training, we were given short courses on the most varied of subjects. It was not for nothing that they often recruited us from the best universities (perhaps that belonged to another era, though, and the most gifted no longer took the bait, since everyone was now obsessed with earning huge amounts of money, and you don't earn that kind of money in the service of your country, or not if that's your only source of income). After all, Tupra and I both had our Oxford past, so as well as studying our respective specialisms, we had learned a little of everything too, enough at least to be able to show it off. And to put it to use if we were lucky and if the opportunity arose.

'Ah,' I said. 'So elimination isn't enough. What do you have to do then to be completely safe?'

'Lady Macbeth answers your question in the very same scene, you really should be ashamed, Nevinson, not to have those lines fresh in your mind.' Now he sounded like a schoolmaster telling off a pupil. 'Nought's had, all's spent, where our desire is got without content: 'Tis safer to be that which we destroy than by destruction dwell in doubtful joy.'

'Sorry, I don't quite understand, Tupra.' We had gone back to being Tupra and Nevinson. 'It must be the cold.'

'Well, Macbeth, remember, is full of this stuff.' I did not remember, although I thought Berta would be sure to, she knew her English classics off pat, she taught them to university students. ' "Better be with the dead . . . than on the torture of the mind to lie in restless ecstasy." He even goes so far as to envy King Duncan whom he has, in the most cowardly fashion, dispatched to the next world, stabbing him while he was asleep and defenceless: "Duncan is in his grave; after life's fitful fever he sleeps well; treason has done his worst: nor steel, nor poison, malice domestic, foreign levy, nothing, can touch him further." '

Tupra fell silent for a few seconds, and so did I, thinking, remembering. I didn't need to say anything, because he took it upon himself to put into words my thoughts and my memories.

'You know that, and you know that it's true. You know that the only sure thing is to be dead. That's why you were dead for such a long time, so that no one would come looking for you with steel or poison, or could touch you further.'

If he had been speaking in Spanish, he would have said '*ulterior*' not 'further', because this time (as I checked later on at home), Tupra used the precise word that Shakespeare had used, he was extraordinarily accurate when quoting anyone, apart, that is, from the occasional deliberate omission or liberty taken, his memory still excellent: 'So that no one could touch you further.' He had been toying with me, for he knew perfectly well where I'd been and why I had gone into hiding, the reasons why I had been declared, first, disappeared and, later, dead, as he himself had told Berta, for he had given her the news in person on another trip to Madrid, introducing himself as Reresby, they had met, although he hadn't yet asked after her. In fact, he hadn't asked me anything, he didn't care what had become of me or how I was feeling. Or, rather, he thought he knew already, on the assumption that we were all alike.

So why had he come now to take me back to those dark and languishing days, to a time when I had not existed or only as far as a few provincials were concerned, under the name of James Rowland; when I had been completely removed from everything, waiting interminably to be rescued, improvising a deliberately anodyne, opaque passage or drift through life, the more undetectable the better, becoming more blurred and more fragmented with each unremarked day, and therefore safer too. Not that I had forgotten that period when I'd played dead and renounced life's fitful fever, as the uncontentable Macbeth says: that is hardly something one can forget; but it had been two years since I returned to life, and it was assumed that no one would come looking for me now, that I was out of danger, or almost. There might still be the odd straggler, some obstinately suspicious person in England or in Northern Ireland (it would be best if I never set foot in that latter country again, just in case, nor in Argentina, if I wanted to be extra prudent), but not in Spain. And it was unlikely that anyone would travel here to follow my trail and settle some very ancient account.

Contrary to what happens in so many novels and films, not even the betrayed can maintain the permanent tension created by hatred and the desire for revenge that remains unfulfilled. Even someone determined never to forget will eventually end up half forgetting, because to do otherwise would be the equivalent of being consumed by flames every day for years and years, and not even the most hard-hearted of men can stand that. So if a victim is told that his particular traitor has died, he will, for a time, remain unconvinced and try to ascertain if this is true, but in reality he does tend to believe that news simply so that he can finally move on and, now and then, drop off to sleep. People grow older and grow tired, and are basically grateful not to have to keep dousing their inner fires, and not think about the thing burning them up. If they do manage to accept that their enemy is safely underground, they won't, in the end, care very much that they played no part in that death, and did not themselves dig their enemy's grave. More than that, the less they had to do with it, the more quickly their grievances will dissolve and the more easily they will be able to look back with one eye or with eyes half closed. 'At least he won't be playing any more dirty tricks,' people think ingenuously, and happily resign themselves. 'Not on me or on anyone. The world is free of him and his wicked ways. He no longer sees or hears, he neither breathes nor thinks nor speaks. He carries neither poison nor steel about his person.'

'Let's go, you look half frozen. You've become very slack, Nevinson, it certainly doesn't take long for the rust to set in with you lot. Let's go to one of those taverns,' that's what he called the bars in the Plaza de la Paja, 'after all, it's highly unlikely anyone will be able to over-hear us there. Still, best keep your voice down, even if that might make it rather hard to hear each other. Everyone in this country of yours shouts so much. Why do you think that is?'

I didn't answer him because he clearly wasn't expecting an answer, he simply wanted to criticize my Spanish side, albeit mildly. He sprang to his feet without first buttoning up his coat, thus giving me to understand that the cold hadn't affected him in the least. Before leaving the garden, he made a gesture of respect or farewell to the lady reader, pretending to doff a non-existent hat, or at least touch the brim. She noticed and responded with the very slightest of nods, her hat still on, we hadn't seen her hair at all. It seemed to me now that they really didn't know each other, and that she was simply being polite. As for him, I had seen him successfully come on to many women in the past, he had even done so when we first met in Blackwell's in Oxford, some twenty-five years ago, on that occasion to a particularly luscious lecturer from Somerville College (voluptu-ous in a way not commonly found among women in her profession or indeed out of it). However, he did not approach this young woman, whereas before he would certainly not have let her escape: he would have struck up a conversation on some pretext or other

(Chateaubriand in this case) and perhaps have persuaded her to meet him that evening or night. I'd learned from him in that area too, one watches and imitates, with a greater or lesser degree of luck; and part of my job, sometimes an indispensable part, had been knowing how to charm certain women. Tupra had barely changed and was still very attractive, almost, at times, irresistible (and this wasn't so much to do with his physical appearance, for I found a couple of his features positively repellent), but perhaps an awareness of his age had made him more cautious or had cooled his ardour. Or who knows, he might well be in a serious relationship or even married, I'd never heard him say a word about his personal or sentimental or family life, as if he didn't have one, nor about his origins (he'd made only very oblique allusions to the low level of society from which he came, and it must have been very low indeed). Or perhaps he *had* invited the reader to be there and had already arranged to meet her later.

'Have you got married, Bertie, since we last saw each other?' I asked point-blank while we were still slowly making our way towards the exit.

He stopped and looked at me in surprise.

'Why do you ask? How on earth could you tell? Whatever made you think that?'

'Ah, so I was right,' I said, not giving him time to deny it, although there's always time to deny anything, even the blindingly obvious. 'And what's the lucky lady's name? Apart from Mrs Tupra of course,' I added with a faint smile. 'And Mrs Reresby and Mrs Nutcombe. Or does she not know that, on occasions, those can also be her names? I assume not, and she wouldn't be the only one. You know how much Berta, my wife, didn't know and still doesn't know. I neglected to mention that I'd be seeing you today. And I may or may not tell her later on. Congratulations, Bertie. I'll have to raise a glass to Mrs Dundas' health and to yours.'

He ignored my jokes, but I could see that he felt uneasy. It doubtless bothered him that he had somehow revealed his new marital status, and had no idea how: it's not, after all, something you would normally notice, just as one cannot usually tell if someone (unless they're a real novice) has just had a bit of rumpy-pumpy shortly before coming to meet us. It's easy enough to hide almost anything. People think it isn't, but that idea simply doesn't hold water, we are, by nature, impenetrable and opaque, and lies are invisible.

'That's very acute of you. I'm glad to see you haven't entirely rusted up. That's what we want,' he said. 'But I still don't know how you could tell.' He was clearly disconcerted, he would find it unforgivable that I had sensed something about him that was, in principle at least, undetectable; it had been a hunch on my part, a stroke of luck. 'I'm not even wearing a ring.' And he stared down, perplexed, at the back of his open hands (like someone admiring the work of a manicurist), even though he was wearing gloves. 'Hmm, perhaps someone told you, although very few people know. But I doubt very much you're going to reveal your source. Anyway, her name is Beryl.'

I found it odd that he didn't deny it, for he easily could have. I tried to conceal my look of triumph and pretended I hadn't heard his words of praise. He very rarely praised anyone. But then, of course, he was about to ask me a favour.

'Why?'

'What do you mean "why"? Why is her name Beryl?' His tone was suspicious, defensive, as if he feared I might object to that name or make fun of it.

'No, I mean, why get married now?'

He wasn't much older than me, pushing fifty, his exact age had always been the subject of conjecture. It was old for a first marriage (if it was his first), but quite a lot of men get hitched in their fifties – complete with ceremony, paperwork and all the rest – when singledom and independence are starting to look more like impotence and resignation and weakness rather than an advantage or an asset. Yes, it's an awareness of age, more than age itself, that determines our actions. Perhaps he could allow himself that bond now without too much disruption or servitude, one that I had embraced very early in life: I had imagined him ever more immersed in his work, busy creating that group where I had no place.

He remained silent for a few seconds. Then he gave me a gentle nudge, as if urging me to start walking; but that isn't what happened, or not immediately, he didn't move from the spot where we were standing by the gate, presumably still considering his response. I interpreted that nudge as mental rather than physical, as if he wanted to assure himself, through that minimal contact, that I would understand what he was about to say.

'Well, I suppose one falls in love.' I couldn't tell at first if he was saying this as a joke or was being serious. 'One knows that this will last a few years, yes, another few years, and then will probably end. But while it lasts one has to do something so as not to spend those years with an additional sadness.'

I found those last words strange. I'd never heard him mention sadnesses before, although he must have known a few, as had I, as had Mulryan and Louise Marsden, as had De Mauny and Blakeston in his absurd General Montgomery get-up, all of whom I had met: just as we had also averted a few misfortunes. One took sadnesses for granted and so never mentioned them, we each kept ours to ourselves and didn't burden others with them. No, I had never heard him refer to any sadnesses either regular or fixed, if, that is, falling in love was going to be an 'additional sadness'.

'An additional sadness?' I said, repeating his words.

'Yes, I mean avoidable, the sort that can be remedied, dodged or mitigated. There are others, as you know, that are obligatory. You've experienced those yourself, and there will be days when they weigh on you. And they may not be over yet, if, that is, you grant me the great favour I'm asking of you. If, in order to spare oneself a sadness, it's necessary to marry, then marry one must and the matter is closed, at least temporarily, as long as being-in-love lasts, for no one is entirely immune. Later, well, we'll see what happens. Anyway, that's how one gets through these years without regrets, without, as I said, an additional sadness. And without an additional distraction, one that would make it hard for us to concentrate. Thinking about a person who is absent or lost or whom we allowed to get away takes up too much time. Especially someone you allowed to get away and whom you wanted to keep by your side. It's an unnecessary waste of energy . . . Yes, best to be avoided.'

'So you're in love with Mrs Ure?' This time I called Beryl by another of Tupra's many false names. I still couldn't quite believe that he wasn't joking. His tone, though, was far from humorous. Nor was it solemn, no, it wasn't that either. It was natural, almost descriptive.

'I don't know why you find that so surprising. You've been in love with your Berta for decades. And she certainly deserves it, I don't question that. Or are you no longer in love? Is it over? Has disenchantment set in? It often happens when one goes back home, reality rarely matches up to our imagination, nor does the present match up to the future. Not that it matters: you *were* in love, and it certainly lasted a lot longer than the norm. What's wrong? Do you think I'm not allowed to fall in love? If you see it as incompatible with my habits or with my character, don't be so silly: one can be in love and remain promiscuous, although I admit the temptation does dwindle, the focus of attention is very strong. I mean that of a wife. But don't get me wrong. This doesn't mean I've become domesticated or tamed. Not when it comes to work. If you agree to my proposition, I will, as usual, expect you to see the job through to the end. Just like in the old days.'

Now it was my turn to grow thoughtful, but not because of what he had just said, that would all be explained sooner or later, although he was taking his time, and I could contain my curiosity. I immediately realized that thinking was pointless. I didn't know if I was still in love with Berta, if I was, it wasn't something I even asked myself. It just didn't interest me, let alone concern me. Life's fitful fever was taking a while to make an appearance, if and when it did. Our time together was much as it had been before, our situation was acceptable, even satisfactory for someone who expects nothing or merely hopes, which comes to the same thing, that, at least, was how it was for me, although probably not for her. For the moment, though, she hadn't distanced herself entirely nor closed the file on me, and I certainly didn't foresee myself doing that to her. If one day she became totally absorbed in some other man or determinedly, gladly picked him out and then dismissed me and vanished from my life, I would perhaps find her absence unbearable, but that could simply be a question of habituation, and we do not cope well with changes that are imposed on us. The very term 'in love' struck me as vague, juvenile – as I think I've said before – even, in a way, artificial and increasingly incomprehensible, it wasn't a concept for which one waited *nel mezzo del cammin*, and, being older than my years, I had long since passed that point. Unless it was something novel, something he was experiencing for the first time, as must have been the case with Tupra, I thought, otherwise he wouldn't have used those words so readily and so wholeheartedly, without any ironic quotation marks or hesitation.

'I'm quite sure you haven't been domesticated, Tupra.' I reverted to using his surname, we both did the same, alternating the two, depending on the degree of closeness or distance with which we approached each sentence. 'No one could tame you, that's something I've known pretty much since we first met. Just as no one could make you compassionate either.'

He did not respond. He merely nudged me again, just hard enough to indicate that we should finally leave the garden. As soon as we did, however, he noticed a yellow plaque on the wall to the right, on the Costanilla de San Andrés, and went over to read what it said like a curious tourist with plenty of time on his hands. He was in the mood to linger, to take our meeting slowly, or else he wanted to keep me out in the cold as if this were a test or part of a plan to break me, and I resigned myself to the thought that we would probably not see the inside of a building that morning. The plaque was one of those rhomboid-shaped affairs put up by the city council. He read it attentively.

'What does it say there about Tamburlaine the Great?' he asked and invited me to translate it. He said the name in English, as in the title of the play by Marlowe, Shakespeare's unfortunate contemporary, who, to his present and posthumous misfortune, lived twenty-three years less than Shakespeare.

I translated what it said: 'In this place stood the houses of Madrid resident Ruy González de Clavijo, Henry III's ambassador to the Great Tamorlán from 1403 to 1406.' That's how it was spelled, 'Tamorlán' not 'Tamerlán', presumably a more antiquated spelling.

The name Marlowe had immediately come into his head, as it had into mine, and he couldn't resist playing the pedant, a role that, given the chance, he was always happy to embrace, doubtless a legacy from his Oxford past or from Wheeler's teaching.

'So you had dealings with Transoxiana in the fifteenth century.'

I had no idea where Transoxiana was, although I assumed that it was, technically, the Kingdom of Tamburlaine the Great. By using that 'you' he was treating me again as fully Spanish, for I was only English when it suited him.

'Perhaps that explains why Marlowe wrote his play. Did you know it was based on a Spanish work, *Vida de Timur*, by a fellow called Mexía? And for some strange reason, it had been translated into English.' That scornful 'for some strange reason' just slipped out. 'Timur was his real name, by the way, Timur Lenk or Timur the Lame.' 'Lame', of course, can also mean 'cripple'. Then, pointing at the plaque, he added: 'How odd though: Tamburlaine died in 1405 when he was just about to invade China. I don't know how the ambassador who lived in this house managed to stay on in Samarkand after Tamburlaine's death rather than leave there as fast as he could. Of course, it would take some time to pack and organize his return journey. Imagine travelling a distance like that in those days. Samarkand is in modern-day Uzbekistan, which you probably wouldn't even be able to locate on a map.' He was clearly recalling his Medieval History, few people would have known the year of the death of the Great Cripple without looking it up. 'And which king of yours was this Henry III?' he asked, without pausing. 'Did he do anything important? I don't know, it vaguely rings a bell, but there are so many King Henrys: ours, the Germans', and a few French ones too . . . It's so confusing, having the same name cropping up all over the place.'

After his boastful display of recondite facts, I didn't want to look foolish. People are often surprised to learn that some intelligence officers or secret agents – or spies, as they are far less frequently known, a noble word come down in the world – are often highly cultivated. However, I could only remember two things about Enrique III:

'He died young and was nicknamed Enrique el Doliente, Enrique the Mourner.'

Amused, he muttered: 'Poor Ruy Clavijo, being Henry the Mourner's ambassador to the Great Cripple,' and he horribly mangled that name 'Clavijo'. 'The world is always in the hands of defective, tormented individuals. What is this fascination the masses have with the anomalous, be it mental or physical? Deformity and resentment and cruelty and madness, all tend to captivate and be acclaimed for a while, until the acclaimers have second thoughts and repent in private while denying in public that they ever acclaimed anyone. I imagine a lot of people find the idea comforting: if this imbecile can govern the country, so could I; all mixed up with another idea: we're in the grip of a monster, so whatever happens, it's not our fault. That's how it is and how it's always been, with very few exceptions. No, to be fair, not so very few. And what else did he do, if he had time to do anything? How old was he when he died? Very young?'

I had always respected Tupra up until the point when I stopped respecting him, but respect never completely disappears if you started out respecting someone and did so for a long time too; it even co-exists, in a strange and unresolved equilibrium, with the subsequent feeling of disdain. Not that I gave a toss for his opinion then, but in the face of his show of erudition I hated to seem to be an ignoramus. I, of course, had not studied Medieval History, my field was languages and diction and accents. Nevertheless, and as often occurs in moments of imminent humiliation, something I had read aeons ago came to my rescue, the mind is very quick to make connections and to recover what you thought had been forgotten. Or, rather, a single sentence came to my aid, one that had remained engraved on my memory at the time because I found it extremely funny, and it dated back to the fifteenth century. In Oxford, and at the insistence of Professor Wheeler, who was the author of a book on Henry the Navigator of whom he was a devotee, I had read *Generaciones y semblanzas* by Fernán Pérez de Guzmán, an almost exact contemporary of that celebrated Portuguese Prince and discoverer: a short work containing brief, superficial portraits of notable figures he had known, kings, noblemen, prelates and the occasional writer. It would doubtless have contained a sketch of Enrique III, but I could not remember a single fact about him, not a single word. I did, though, remember the portrait of his wife because of one unforgettable phrase.

'He certainly didn't reach thirty,' I ventured, more than anything to save face and to say something, as students do when cornered in an oral exam. 'He was married to Catherine of Lancaster.'

'Ah, now that name does ring a bell. And what kind of queen was she?' At the mention of someone from the English nobility, Tupra immediately perked up; for despite his very unEnglish name, he was a true patriot, when, that is, there was nothing to prevent him from being so.

'Well, she was named regent and so ruled over Castile,' I said, concealing my lack of any actual knowledge of her precise role. 'But a chronicler of the time described her as being very tall and fat, pink and white in complexion and fair. He added a less favourable remark and one, I think, that any husband would have found rather off-putting. Perhaps that's why Enrique ended up being called Enrique the Mourner.'

My comment had piqued his curiosity:

'Oh really? What did he say? I hope he didn't reflect badly on all Englishwomen. He would be a bold chronicler, though, to speak unfavourably of a queen.'

'He almost certainly described her after her death,' I said, 'when she would no longer be tall or fair or white or pink. He concluded his portrait of Catherine with this damning stroke or, rather, blot: "As regards figure and gait, she could as easily have been a man as a woman." Not very promising, eh? Not even back then, because tastes in beauty would not have been so very different.' I translated the sentence as choicely as I could.

Tupra roared with laughter, as he often did when he was in a good mood and feeling sociable; and when things went to plan. As I said earlier, he was a pleasant man, or could be, and that quality is not entirely at odds with being utterly ruthless. I found myself joining in his laughter, and on that Epiphany morning, opposite the Plaza de la Paja, surrounded by happy families with their children and their new toys, we both stood there laughing together. As if nothing had marred our friendship, as if I had not discovered the original trap he had set for me and as if he had not ruined my life in the now distant past. As if he had not plotted behind my back, without my knowledge or consent.

'I'm surprised Enrique didn't run off to Samarkand with Clavijo,' he said, when his fit of laughter had subsided a little. 'I would have. Begone vile figure, vile gait! "She could as easily have been a man as a woman," ' he repeated, savouring the words. 'How unfortunate. If he had said "she *looked* more like a man than a woman", that would have been more bearable, but figure *and* gait . . . He was very acute that chronicler, plain-speaking and mischievous too. What was his name? He's probably been translated into English by the looks of it, and I always enjoy going back to medieval texts. Not that I have the time of course.' When he finally stopped laughing, he became slightly pensive, although there was still a smile on those fleshy lips as he observed the families sitting on the café terraces or strolling about the square. Then he added: 'I hope you won't have the same experience with any of the women you'll be dealing with, if, that is, you grant me the favour I'm proposing. I don't know them myself.'

He was no longer asking for a favour, he was proposing it. That was the first warning of what awaited me.

'What women?' I said.

I felt as if I had been transported back in time, to the Eagle and Child, that Oxford pub on St Giles', to one of whose tables where Tupra and his subordinate Blakeston, disguised as Viscount Montgomery with his obligatory ornamental beret, his moustache and duffel coat, had laid out the photos of eight men to see if I recognized any of them as the possible murderer of my occasional lover Janet Jefferys, and thus save myself from becoming the principal suspect. That, more or less, marked the beginning of what would become my life, about a quarter of a century ago, when I was nearly twenty-one. As I feared, Tupra had insisted we sit down at one of the café terraces, all of which, as it turned out, were very busy.

'I know it's a bit chilly, but regard this glorious sun of York.'

I realized at once that he was referring to the opening lines of *Richard III*, a play he always reverted to even if only to indulge in a little wordplay.

'Allow me to make the most of it, I don't have many opportunities in London.'

And when a waitress brought us two beers and some olives, and I explained that it was the custom to provide a few olives along with any drink, he exclaimed:

'What? You mean they're free? What extraordinary generosity!'

He then took an envelope out of his inside overcoat pocket, removed three photographs of women and laid them out before me.

'Be careful not to stain them or get them wet. You'll need them if you agree to take on this job. Although there are, of course, copies.'

'Not this again,' I said angrily. 'You did the very same thing the first time we met, and that was in order to lay a trap for me, a trap whose consequences I still carry around with me. And will do until I die. I don't know how you dare.'

'I did *what* to you? I don't remember that.'

And he probably didn't remember, the incident had been of no importance to him, for, when necessary, he frequently ruined other people's lives. We forget the harm we cause infinitely more easily than the harm inflicted on us, we forget what we say and do and write, but rarely what we hear and read and suffer. I reminded him of the incident, I even reminded him of the name of the man I'd identified, Hugh Saumarez-Hill, Janet's permanent lover, an MP at the time, when, in fact, there was no one to identify and when there hadn't even been a murder. I'd taken far too long to discover this, by which time it was impossible to alter all that I had been through. A mature man or indeed woman cannot change their youth.

'Hugh Saumarez-Hill, doesn't that ring a bell?'

'Hmm, yes, vaguely. He didn't come to much. But this job has nothing to do with that, Tom. I'm not laying any kind of trap. It's not a matter of you being able to identify anyone, it's so that you'll be able to recognize them later on. Go on, take a look.'

I didn't want to, I couldn't believe that the same scene was being repeated, with Tupra placing a few faces before me with exactly the same sangfroid, like a card player revealing his hand at poker.

'I'm not going to look at anything, Tupra.'

I refused to look at the table, to lower my gaze, a childish act of rebellion I realized. I was looking at him, at those grey eyes with their halo of excessively thick lashes; in the wintry sun of Madrid they gleamed more brightly than they did in England and they also looked paler, as if they had taken on the consistency of sea ice. His eyes always filled one with confidence and, at the same time, sent shivers down the spine, one felt ennobled by them, appreciated, indispensable; and also on the brink of something cruel or something dirty that would do battle with something even crueller and even dirtier. No one ever emerged from those missions unsullied.

'I'm saying no to this favour, whatever it is, so don't waste your time explaining it to me. I'm not interested in starting all over again, it's too much. I'm not prepared to relive my sad history. You made it an obligatory sadness, to use your words, of the kind for which there is no remedy. And, to make matters worse, a secret sadness. I can't tell anyone about it, not even Berta. Although I doubt she would even ask about it now, or feel the slightest curiosity. Besides, I'm condemned to silence on that score. So put those photos away. Remove them from my sight. They just add insult to injury.'

But Tupra did not put them away. He distractedly drummed his fingers on them, tempting me to look at them. Distractedly, but deliberately.

'You can talk to me about it, because I already know your history,' he said, and I wasn't sure whether this comment was impertinent or ingenuous, a quality entirely untypical of him. Then again, it was hardly typical of him to have fallen in love, and to own up to it, and to have got married when he was nearly fifty. What button had Beryl pressed to make him change so radically? Although to me he didn't seem to have changed at all. He was probably one of those people who are fully formed by the age of ten, the paint already dry, their character set in stone, then all that's added is experience and, sometimes, degradation. 'You can open your heart to me if you like. I might be the only person in the world with whom you can, for whom your history is not a secret.'

'Don't be so presumptuous, Tupra. There are some areas that remain secret to you too,' I was quick to point out. 'I spent a lot of time alone, doing my own thing, without hearing your voice or receiving instructions. Making my own decisions and doing whatever I wanted.'

He ignored that remark and continued his thought.

'So you see, we do in some way share a bond. Meeting when one is still young always brings people together. Knowing what the other person did in the past and where he comes from.'

'Yes,' I said sarcastically, 'rather like two individuals who've committed a crime together. They each know what the other is capable of and have lost all respect for each other. They've seen each other without masks or make-up. It's the kind of unpleasant bond that doesn't invite one either to reminisce or to pour out one's heart. The other person is more like a mirror you avoid looking into. And if you do happen to see yourself reflected back, you quickly avert your gaze with a feeling of distaste. And I don't know where *you* come from. I can only guess.'

Tupra laughed, not the merry laugh provoked a few minutes earlier by Pérez de Guzmán's description of Catherine of Lancaster's medieval gait. He laughed with a slightly superior air, or perhaps because he really did know who I was and what I was like, and that I usually ended up doing as he asked.

'At least listen. One of those three women played a part in two very bloody attacks in your country, here in Spain. She may also have been involved in another attack as well, but definitely in those two. She played an important part, although one assumes it was from a distance.'

Oh, he knew how to arouse my curiosity, but still I resisted, and continued to look him in the eye.

'And since when have we been involved in anything that happens in Spain?'

That 'we' came out quite involuntarily, as if I were still in MI6 or MI5, because some agents do go back and forth between the two, and perhaps it was true that no one ever retires from either even when they've been thrown out. Not that I had been.

78

'I told you over the phone. This is a favour you'd be doing for me and for a Spanish friend of mine, an important man or one who will be important one day.'

'What friend? I can't imagine you have very many.'

'Tom, how can you ask me for names and facts?' was his reproachful response. Now I was Tom and he was Tupra, as long he was trying to persuade me and I was trying to dodge him it could not be otherwise. 'All right, if you prefer, let's call him a colleague . . . And for convenience's sake, let's call him Jorge. Or, rather, George, if you don't mind: I can't pronounce that name in your language, a person could choke on all those guttural sounds.'

After what he'd said, the faces in the photos called to me more loudly from the table, and I felt impelled at least to glance at them. I resisted, though, and still did not look down, I'd already noticed that all three were women when he had, without warning, placed them on the table, we can spot someone of the opposite sex at lightning speed, as if we had antennae. The waitress came over to ask if we needed anything else, and she could not help seeing the photos while she noted down our order. And so a complete stranger had seen them before I had, for our eyes are irresistibly drawn to any portrait, to the reproduction of a motionless face, which means that my obstinacy was not without merit.

'Give us five or ten minutes and then bring us another two beers, please. And, if you wouldn't mind, some *patatas bravas* too.'

I didn't know if Tupra would like those spicy potatoes, but I really didn't care, I fancied some and didn't bother to ask what he might like. He didn't appear to feel the cold, while I was still freezing, although the sun, it's true, was doing its best to warm us. The terrace was filling with people well wrapped up but determined to sit outside, a large group of nine or ten people sat right next to us, men and women talking loudly, especially, as I couldn't help but notice, one of the men.

'The two attacks took place some time ago, in 1987, one in June of

79

that year, the other in December. In both cases, these were bombings, car bombs. In the first, twenty-one people died and forty-five were hurt, some of whom suffered life-changing injuries. People don't talk much about the survivors, they tend to be forgotten. Five of the dead were children, the youngest, if I remember rightly, was only nine. In the second attack, there were eleven dead and eighty-eight injured. Another five children were among the dead, all of them little girls, the youngest of whom were only three years old.'

He was talking about two ETA killings. Like everyone else, I remembered three particularly vile attacks: one on the Hipercor shopping mall in Barcelona; one on the Civil Guard barracks in (I thought) Vic; the third on another police station in (I seemed to recall) Zaragoza. I wasn't very sure in what year these took place (I certainly wouldn't have been able to say had I been asked a minute before), and in the 1980s and the early 1990s ETA committed so many murders it was impossible to pinpoint any of them or even tell them apart, with the occasional much publicized exception (the murder of young Miguel Ángel Blanco, kidnapped by ETA, would not take place until July 1997, and that killing made a huge impression because ETA set a deadline for their demands to be met, and the clock was ticking while that modest town councillor waited either to be set free or to be killed in cold blood; their many crimes continued throughout the decade). That's one of the malign effects of sheer quantity: the more aberrant and vile the crimes, the less aberrant and vile they appear to be and the harder it is to distinguish them. Quantity achieves that very worst of perversions, making the gravest of acts less grave, that's why we stop counting the losses in wars, at least while the wars are going on and the fallen continue to fall. And sometimes those responsible prolong their wars unnecessarily for precisely that reason: to avoid anyone beginning to count the dead that they will later carry on their shoulders. And both my countries have done the same, I have no illusions about that.

III

I took out a cigarette, and Tupra immediately followed suit, for, since leaving the garden, he had, very briefly, reined himself in. He smoked more than me and more than Berta, which was quite something in 1997, when the world was not yet in the grip of hysteria and hadn't gone into full prohibitionist mode. The guy talking nineteen to the dozen on the next table soon began to annoy me and I was finding it hard to concentrate: he had a stentorian voice – like a machine gun, with every sentence a bullet that left a wound – and for some incomprehensible reason, he was dominating his group's conversation as if he were a schoolmaster. Even worse, he was holding forth on types of food I find utterly repugnant (my stomach has always been very if not entirely unSpanish): brains, tripe, liver and onions, sweetbreads and black puddings. I could only see him from behind, his shaven head and bullish neck, the very image of an oaf. He should have been called Bottomley, Puddington, Bellenden, Buttcombe or something along those lines, not that anyone is ever to blame for their actual surname.

'I assume you're referring to what happened in Zaragoza or Vic or Barcelona.'

'Barcelona and Zaragoza. The first was on 19 June 1987, the Hipercor bombing.' He pronounced the name English-fashion, 'Highpercore' or something like that. 'The second was on 11 December. That made for a very sad Christmas.'

I immediately recalled an image that had appeared in the press at the time, possibly after the Zaragoza bombing, although it really doesn't matter which, it was just one of those images you never forget; against a backdrop of desolation and destruction, the ground strewn with rubble and, hanging over it all, a malignant cloud of smoke, a policeman, his tie visible beneath his uniform, and his face all bloodied, is running towards the camera carrying in his arms a little seven- or eight-year-old girl, one of whose feet appears to have been half blown off, and whose face is a picture of pain, pure pain. In the background – it was one of those black-and-white photographs you can't take your eyes off – you could see a couple, the husband with his arms about his wife, and the wife with one hand on a buggy in which her baby is still sitting, the child is, at most, a year old, and given his or her age, would forget everything it was now hearing and seeing. Elsewhere, you can see a father (I assume he's the father) putting his arms out to another child of four or five, and beside him a taller girl, who appears to be staunchly coping on her own. What I remember most clearly, though, is the expression on the face of the young policeman, or was he perhaps a fireman, carrying the little girl. Although much of his face was covered in blood, so that you couldn't really make out his features (the blood could have been his own or someone else's, like the blood on the girl's arm), his expression was a mixture of determination and profound pity, perhaps there was also an element of postponed rage and another of sheer incredulity at what he was witnessing. Determination to save the injured child he wasn't even looking at, instead staring straight ahead, his gaze perhaps fixed on the hospital that he needs to reach as soon as possible. And profound pity for many possible reasons: not having been able to prevent the massacre, the sight of such unnecessary evil, the terror of the children who would have no idea what was going on and who lived there with their parents, or pity for his colleagues who had just been blown to pieces. I seemed to remember that, afterwards, ETA, through their journalistic and political mouthpieces, had laid the blame on the children's parents (for they would carry out these attacks and then try to wash their hands of them): if they hadn't put their families in the living quarters provided for the Civil Guard, there would have been no children among the victims, the guards themselves were using them as shields, putting them in danger and sacrificing their lives out of sheer egotism. The gang realized that killing children did not look good. It did them no harm, however, among their followers, who applauded their actions whatever they were and asked for more, you can always come up with reasons later on. Only the first step is difficult, and that had been taken centuries before, the rest was a natural consequence of that first step, that is, putting one foot in front of the other and then keeping on going.

All the while I was recalling that old press photo, I continued to avoid looking at the photos Tupra had placed before me on the table, although with every passing minute I found it harder and harder to control my gaze, which tends to be drawn to the forbidden, the tempting. Tupra was sitting closer than I was to Bottomley, almost back to back. I noticed that he, too, was becoming irritated with that harsh voice and that avalanche of words, even though fortunately he didn't understand a word. The man was now pontificating about lamb chitterlings, and even I didn't know what they were, but it sounded like something disgusting, and about fried blood, 'not as in black pudding', he was saying, 'but just as it comes'. It was astonishing that eight or nine perfectly ordinary-looking people could listen to such an enthralling lecture without butting in, without punching the orator in the face for being such a bore. It's what we call dominating the conversation, which any imbecile can do: something we've known since the 1930s.

Tupra turned his head slightly now and then, as if curious to see Buttcombe's face.

'What's the fellow saying?' he asked. 'He sounds as if he were haranguing the troops. Why does he have to talk so loudly? They're all sitting cheek by jowl as it is.'

'It's just a lot of nonsense about food. Take no notice.'

'Why does everyone nowadays have to play the gourmet? I don't understand it. What could be more tedious than talking about food and cooking? He's starting to give me a splitting headache. Can you tell him to pipe down? There's no need for the whole square to know his views. It's outrageous.'

'And what did that woman do?' I asked in order to distract him and bring him back to the business in hand. An irascible Tupra was always a danger, the last thing I needed was for him to tell me to confront the oaf, because he still had a tendency to give me orders. 'Whichever woman it was.'

'I don't know exactly, and it doesn't really matter. Obviously, she didn't drive one of the cars carrying the bombs to Barcelona or Zaragoza. She wasn't there on the spot. But she played a major role, she collaborated, she was a party to it, although, as I said, almost certainly from a distance. She organized, prepared, advised, persuaded, planned or financed, made arrangements or gave the go-ahead, I don't know. What's certain is that she was crucial to the success of those attacks. My friend George will doubtless know more, but I haven't asked him for details. It would be discourteous, and it's not what we usually do. I trust what he tells me and he trusts what I tell him. He asks me for a favour and I grant it if I can, without asking too many questions. Sometimes it's the other way round. That's how we work, I scratch his back and he scratches mine. We help them with ETA and they help us with the IRA, just as those two organizations give each other moral and financial support. We can't afford to lag behind them, can we? Anyway, if you agree, you don't need to know all the details. I only ever used to give you the essential facts, and you never asked to know more, which is as it should be. You never pestered me to fill you in on the background and never questioned my motives, that's what made you a good agent. As well as your other abilities, of course.'

Another bit of flattery.

'If I agree to what?'

'To finding her, what else? Tracking her down. Once you deign to look at the photos, we can talk about it.' He was watching my eyes, and knew I had not yet looked down.

' "That's how we work", you say. I assume, then, that your friend Jorge works for the Spanish Secret Service. For CESID, I suppose.'

Tupra shook his head.

'No, not at all, not exactly.' It never bothered him to give contradictory answers. 'Although it wouldn't surprise me if he did, one day, end up in charge. For the moment, he's an outsider, doing his own thing. Everything has to be done from a safe distance, there've been a series of blunders made already. And I won't lie to you – I'm not going to lie to you about anything – as far as this particular matter is concerned, I'm pretty much doing my own thing too.'

'You mean it's a personal favour, you haven't received any orders from above? You're doing this off your own bat and the powers-that-be don't even know about it? McColl won't know a thing, of course,' I said, referring to the last Chief of the Secret Intelligence Service under whom I had, indirectly, served.

Tupra gave a dry little laugh. Then the waitress arrived with two more beers and a dish of *patatas bravas*. Tupra carefully moved the photos to one side so as to make room for the dish and so that the photos wouldn't get stained. He asked if the potatoes were also free, given the size of the serving. I told him, no, that this time I had ordered them, and hoped he would like them. He immediately speared one with the miniature fork provided, dipped it in the red sauce and raised it hungrily to his mouth. He obviously liked it.

'Um, a touch spicy, but very nice,' he said, clearly delighted. 'Is it Mexican?' Then he answered my question. 'It's not McColl now, it's Spedding. He's been in post since 1994. You really have retired, haven't you? I can't believe you didn't know. After all, you are still working for the Foreign Office.'

'I just do my job. None of that other stuff exists for me now.'

He ignored this categorical statement. He knew that everything always exists for everyone, that nothing is ever completely left behind. The past is an intruder impossible to keep at bay.

'Orders are labyrinthine things, Tom. Now and then, someone gets lost along the way, or gets overlooked. The chain is often a long one, neither very solid nor, therefore, very taut; a link often breaks or disappears, or gets twisted and turned around and ends up facing the wrong way. As for knowing anything, that's something most would prefer to avoid, you just have to rely on your own experience. Very few high-ups want to know everything, that way they can act surprised and get angry when things backfire or can justify going too far with whatever measures or actions or, indeed, reprisals they take. But anyone can lose their head. You yourself know how difficult it is to keep your head at all times. Sometimes your head has a will of its own, which is what happened to you a while back, remember.'

I found that last statement unkind and very hurtful, a low blow. Perhaps it was simply a stratagem to get me on his side even before he'd explained what he was going to ask me to do, what was to come: he was opening the door and allowing the intruder into my mind, facilitating his entrance, his attack, as traitors and infiltrators (my peers) and the merely careless have always done in those walled cities, fortresses and castles that finally succumbed to the siege. I was, of course, constantly under siege from the past, but each morning, I made a mental – almost automatic – effort to drive it away and block it out, and I succeeded too. You become accustomed to rejecting thoughts, images, facts, even deeds that you yourself committed, and, in the end, this becomes as much a part of your routine (all right, maybe I'm exaggerating) as getting out of bed, brushing your teeth, showering, shaving, so that you can step out into the street with your body clean and your mind free of mortifying memories. It's different, more difficult, if someone sets those memories down in front of you. Tupra knew better than anyone what they were and he'd had the bad taste to mention them. I don't think he did so with intent to wound, but so as to get his own way, for he would rule out nothing as a possible means to an end.

Yes, during twenty or more years in action, in service, I had twice lost my head, and that, I assumed, was what he was referring to, I'd reported back to him orally at the time, but put nothing down in writing: I had killed two men, justifiably and out of necessity, on one occasion, to save myself and, on another, to prevent a misfortune that would probably have caused many deaths (I know, nothing is certain until it happens), like those deaths in Barcelona and Zaragoza. In the latter case, the idea – more of a flicker really – of revenge or punishment had also crossed my mind, and it's sometimes hard to differentiate between the two. I told myself this amounted to just one individual killed every ten or eleven years, and I had colleagues or predecessors who had lost their head far more often than that, the finger squeezing a trigger, the hand clasping a knife.

However hard you try to convince yourself, though, this is no consolation. 'It was a lesser evil, there was no alternative,' is a useful argument. 'It can't be undone, there's no way back, they're no longer here, whereas I am; I need to worry about myself and not about the ever-more-distant dead; I couldn't undo the deed, even if I wanted to.' And then of course, there's this: 'They were aware of the risks, aware that you don't always emerge unscathed, just as I and so many others were aware when engaged in open and in secret warfare.'

I had doubtless caused more deaths indirectly, with my investigations and my dissemblings, my warnings and my betrayals, my pretences and my wheedlings; but we're only ever fully aware of those deaths we ourselves have caused, that is, when we actually saw the other person die and their death depended on some action on our part, just as Anne Boleyn's death depended on the whistle or the strong gust of wind made or provoked by the swordsman of Calais with his swift blade, when he so kindly crossed the Channel to be there on that still-cold English day in May.

What intervenes then is will, determination, intention: even if that will is strained or vacillating, too opaque or filled with dread, a divided will, with one part belonging to us and the other to rage or fear. We defend ourselves or lash out in the heat of the moment or decide coolly to avoid a tragedy, or perhaps to punish or get payback for the harm inflicted on 'our own people', people whom we didn't actually know and who may well have been scum, there's no way of knowing once they've become victims (there's scum on all sides and, of course, on ours as well). Then there is the eye, being a witness to what we have done. 'I took that person's life with my own hands. He tried his damnedest to resist and finish me off, but failed, because I was more skilled or stronger or quicker, more underhand or had the advantage. I got rid of a truly nasty piece of work and probably saved my world from calamities, and, in a way, bearing in mind what he had already done, I dealt out justice.'

But that thought cannot erase the memory of seeing a person's life escaping through the wound you caused, the blood pouring forth, of having been a witness to his panic and his final impotence, or to his initial surprise at finding he was wounded, and imagining (because one only ever imagines it, as if it had not yet arrived) that this was the day he would die. You catch in his gaze a glimmer of incredulity or desperate denial, you believe you can see in the dying man's mind something along these lines: 'No, this can't be happening, it's just not possible that I will no longer see or hear anything or utter another word, that this still-functioning mind will stop and be snuffed out, this mind still so full of tormenting thoughts; that I will never again stand up or move so much as a finger and will be thrown in a ditch or a river or a ravine or a lake, or be burned like a lump of firewood albeit without giving off the same pleasant woody smell, that my body will send up a pestilential cloud of smoke, and I will stink of scorched flesh if, at that point, I am still me. I will be me in the eyes of the person who killed me and those who see me and pick me up and manhandle me away from the scene of the crime, who will continue to recognize my features as if I were alive, but I won't be me in my eyes or in my consciousness, because, it seems, I will have no consciousness . . .'

And you can't help retrospectively pondering the thought that there were no passing-bells for those you killed, no slow drawing-down of blinds, for they fell as single individuals, alone and with no friends near at hand.

I know this very well, or rather I can imagine it, because on several occasions — yes, there were a few — when I thought I would die in the same way, with a bullet in the back of the neck or in the head or after being stabbed in the side, or perhaps poisoned and enduring incomprehensible pain and difficulty breathing.

I remember that one of 'my' two men — once, all incredulity gone, he finally understood that he was dying — did manage to look at me without rancour, at most slightly reproachfully, a reproach directed less at me than at the order of the universe, which had brought him to that point without his consent, had kept him wrapped up and entangled for as long as it had given him shelter, and was now dispatching him without a word of warning, summarily expelling and eliminating him. And at the very final moment, he began restlessly — or as he imagined swiftly — shuffling his feet, as if he could still run away and escape, as if his feet contained what little remained of his fast-dwindling strength. He was lying on the ground, and the soles of his feet weren't touching it, but they were running in mid-air in an illusory, posthumous attempt to save himself, when, in reality, those steps, at once light and exhausted, were leading him into non-existence.

We, too, have recourse to that, to the order of the universe, so that we can begin each day without the baggage that accumulates during sleep, when the mind is defenceless and allows such distillations. We tell ourselves that everyone has to die of something, and that, as was the case with me and Tupra and indeed anyone else who decides to shape the world, even if only by one tiny insignificant detail that no one will even register or notice, ultimately, those men chose the possible form of their cancellation, which was not through illness or accident, a natural fading away or a slow decline, but at the hands of the enemy they were also trying to destroy. And we tell ourselves that, in such circumstances, we are not exactly us: I was no longer Tomás Nevinson but a mere nameless enemy who happened to have luck on his side, just as, throughout history, luck has been on the side of the survivors of wars, the ones who are never counted and who are later passed over and ignored.

There were privates in Napoleon's army who returned safe and sound after travelling thousands of miles on foot and having fought innumerable battles that often dragged on into the evening and only stopped because the light was failing and everyone was too exhausted to fight on, after suffering hunger and cold while marching through Europe, Russia and North Africa in ruined boots and carrying burdensome equipment. Some men in medieval times returned from a Crusade and lived for many years in the warmth of the homes, which, while they were either enduring or inflicting carnage in the heat of some far-off land or on board ship, they thought they would never see again. Some die in the first skirmish or during the first volleys, and some emerge from ten or fifteen years of endless campaigns without so much as a scratch (or only a couple of minor scars).

Most men do not get involved in that life voluntarily, but are called up and are obliged to go, or they enlist when they're still too young to know what they are embarking upon, and what horrors await them. We agents, on the other hand, do sign up for that life, and should therefore know or do know where a wrong move or a misstep or a moment of rash impatience might lead. While I did not sign up initially and was, moreover, easily scared and deceived – a rookie – I did not withdraw when it was still not too late and when withdrawal was perhaps still an option, that is, when I had already forgotten how I had started doing what I was doing, and which I believed I was doing out of a sense of usefulness and duty and a certain more or less unconfessed pleasure and pride: which becomes loyalty and patriotism, or the famous defence of the Realm.

Tupra had finished off the *patatas bravas* in no time, leaving me only a few guilty remnants, he was clearly hungry and had really enjoyed them. However, he quickly apologized for wolfing them down like that, and asked me to order another portion for myself. I waved to the waitress, showed her the almost empty dish, then circled my index finger to indicate that we wanted the same again. She nodded to me from the table she was currently serving, for the place had filled up as if it were spring, and I was no longer feeling so cold.

'Did she understand what you meant?'

He seemed anxious, presumably because he wanted more potatoes, and he was still grasping his fork, like a child demanding more food.

'Yes, we use gestures more than you do in England, and to more

94

effect.' And then I responded to his low blow. 'I did not ever "lose my head", Tupra. I told you what had happened at the time: on the first occasion, I had no alternative, and on the second, it was a matter of choosing the lesser of two evils. I did what you taught me to do, I averted a misfortune. Or was that misfortune inevitable? Assuming, of course, that you can remember.'

'Whatever you say, Tom. If not inevitable, it was highly likely. And that's just as well, I mean, that you always knew precisely what you were doing and acted deliberately. I hope that's still the case when you meet this woman you're refusing to look at.'

He had become diverted from that particular path in the conversation. Bellenden was driving him crazy with his tireless, strident speechifying, and was now talking about how they slaughter pigs in whatever part of the country he came from, and in gruesome detail too. Madrid under occupation by incomers.

'Will you say something to this fellow or shall I? He's been deafening us with his talk for quite long enough. Is he still ranting on about food?'

'More or less, but it's just taken a more macabre turn. Anyway, what the devil are you going to say to him? You don't speak Spanish. Look, let's just move to another café, I don't want you getting me into trouble. The last thing I need is to start a fight with that lot. They easily outnumber us. Besides, today's a public holiday.'

'We can't change cafés now. They're just about to bring us more of those potatoes,' he said eloquently and as if this were an irrefutable argument.

Bottomley was immediately behind him, and so Tupra was even more afflicted by his logorrhoea than I was, although, to a greater or lesser extent, the whole square was suffering too. Before I had time to stop or dissuade him, Tupra had half turned around and shifted his chair so that it was even nearer to Bellenden's, as if he were in the row immediately behind him in a theatre, then he leaned closer in and whispered in Buttcombe's ear. The strange thing is that Puddington did not move, he remained absolutely still with his back to Tupra. If someone were to startle you by whispering something in your ear in an unfamiliar language, the normal response would be to spin round and look him in the eye. The rest of the group immediately noticed this intrusion, and there was a brief, expectant silence while they waited for Tupra to finish and for Puddington to report back. Tupra must have given him a thorough telling-off, and in English to boot: this did not take long, but time for more than just a couple of surly sentences. Then he turned away, and before resuming his position opposite me, I saw him make a repeated gesture with his hand. A gesture that the chitterling-loving yob and, indeed, anyone else would have understood, namely that he should keep his voice down from now on.

'Who is that guy? Do you know him? What did he say?' I heard the women in the group ask, with a mixture of curiosity and alarm.

I knew my former boss was perfectly capable of instilling fear in someone, from one moment to the next; that he could move seamlessly from being all smiles and friendly words to issuing what sounded like a very serious threat. I had never learned how to do that, and no amount of watching could teach me.

Porkington replied:

'Oh, just some crazy foreign guy.' He said this in a reedy voice, and then plunged into a silence so profound that it took a few seconds for any of his companions to summon up the nerve to break it, and the conversation immediately died a death. It was as if they had all lost the slightest desire to listen to more stupid prattle about nutritional piggery or any other slightly more savoury imbecility; they couldn't come up with a single interesting thought. It was as if they had sensed danger hovering close by and could not rest easy while they remained on the table next to ours.

Tupra was pleasant and sociable when he wanted to be, but he had the ability, without warning, to cast an icy chill over any jovial gathering, with his all-embracing eyes that could suddenly turn arctic, with his serene voice that sometimes sounded like footsteps in the frost or like ice breaking. When it suited or when he wanted to, he could spread a malignant mist around him. I had tried to imitate him in this too, but again without success.

'What did you say to him?' I asked. 'He can't have understood a word you said, because the only English that bully's likely to know is "thank you".'

'He understood perfectly well that I was sticking a knife in his ribs and that he could feel the point. That all I had to do was press a little harder to push it in up to the hilt. And he had no idea how long the blade was. If you can't see it, you can't know.'

'You've got a knife on you? Are you mad? And you threatened him with it? You've clearly lost all sense of proportion. He wasn't as bad as that. Besides, I didn't see you take out a knife. Where is it?'

He was hiding his hands under the table, like a little boy caught doing something naughty. He held up one hand in which he was clutching the small fork he had used to spear the potatoes and made a brisk upward stabbing motion.

'What I've lost is my infinite patience, which does tend to wane over the years. And I see that you've forgotten your earliest lessons. They do tend to get left behind, but they are absolutely fundamental and should be engraved on your mind. Don't you remember: anything can be a knife or a weapon, what matters is how you hold it and how you use it. If you hold a ballpoint pen in the right way, or a pencil or some tweezers or a comb, or even some nail scissors or a nail file or a toothbrush, any of those things can feel like a knife to the person on the receiving end. This one has three metal prongs, but to the flesh you're prodding they become one prong.'

He threw his fork down on the dish with a smug look on his face (if he had been Spanish, he would have accompanied this gesture with a triumphant *¡ea!* – so there!) and looked round for the waitress. She was just coming over with our second portion of *patatas bravas*. Bottomley's subjects seized this opportunity to ask for the bill, having decided to leave, although without quite knowing why. He himself was still dumbstruck, unable to utter a word.

'You know what happened at Hipercor, don't you?' Tupra went on to say, having first devoured four or five more of the potatoes he had ordered as compensation to me for his earlier rapacity; other more discreet customers had hurriedly occupied the neighbouring table, it was astonishing that café terraces should be so busy on 6 January, even if it was a day when families normally like to stroll about with their children and their new toys and do some people-watching. He again pronounced the name as 'Highpercor' and I was about to correct him, but what would be the point, most English people are impervious to other languages and their pronunciation, like us Spaniards or even worse.

'You've just told me: 19 June 1987, a car bomb in a shopping mall. Twenty-one dead and forty-five injured. Five of the dead were children. The youngest only nine.' I hadn't lost my ability to retain facts.

'I don't mean that,' he said. 'Those are just the cold, superficial numbers, the final count we all end up with, from judges to encyclopaedias. I mean, do you know how it happened, what those who died actually died from, what happened to them? People who left their homes to go shopping, probably not even for anything urgent.'

'I wasn't living in Spain at the time, Bertie. I can't remember details that I probably never read or heard. I was officially dead, wasn't I? A death decreed by you. Besides, I'm not even sure I want to know, why add more horrors to my imagination, I have quite enough of my own. Anyway, I can imagine what the consequences were. I've seen what those bombs can do.' I paused to think for a moment. 'Yes, even though it happened in Spain; there were so many such attacks at the time that each new attack somehow detracted from the seriousness of the others. They still happen of course, but because they're less frequent they stand out more. It was the same in Ulster. If you were to give me those details now, they would seem far more shocking than they did then. The passage of time creates more surprise and more panic, and more clarity too. We're more easily shocked and wonder how such a thing could ever have occurred.'

Tupra couldn't care less about my thoughts on the matter. He just wanted me to look at the photos that had been sitting on the table for some time now and which I still hadn't given so much as a sideways glance. And he wanted me to say yes to that mission, to identify the one woman out of those three. The truth is, I was beginning to feel intrigued and was finding it hard not to lower my gaze, not to take a good look at those photos, those portraits, those faces. Or maybe they were full-length shots of the women walking down the street.

'The three members of ETA's Comando Barcelona placed 440 pounds of explosive in the boot of a stolen car, along with a timer. Ammonal, petrol, glue and soap flakes. Intent on causing as much damage as possible. They left the car in the shopping-mall car park. There were a few tardy, confusing phone calls that didn't leave enough time for a search to be carried out. No one could possibly find a concealed package in just ten or fifteen minutes and in such a large area. And funnily enough, the warnings failed to mention the main fact, that the bomb had been placed inside a car. So the bomb exploded at ten minutes past four on a Friday. The first floor of the car park was blown to pieces, leaving a hole five yards wide, through which a huge fireball penetrated, burning whoever was unfortunate enough to be in its path. Apparently, that particular combination of explosive materials had similar effects to napalm, that is, it stuck to the skin of the victim, raising the temperature to three thousand degrees centigrade. The thick black smoke produced by the explosion meant that there was zero visibility, and the women (because most of the victims were women shoppers) couldn't escape' – 'They, too, died as cattle,' the thought came to me in a flash, 'along with their five children and a few men' – 'The incendiary material sticking to their bodies was impossible to remove or to extinguish. Some were reduced to ashes. And then, of course, there were the toxic gases that caused others unaffected by the flames to die of asphyxia. It was just monstrous: the place, the day, the time, the manner of death, the type of victim, the completely gratuitous nature of the attack.'

'Another occasion when it would be "Better to be with the dead",' I said, returning, slightly inexactly, to the line from *Macbeth* he had quoted earlier.

'They achieved nothing, absolutely nothing. They knew this, but they did it just the same,' Tupra went on, as if he hadn't heard me or found my comment inopportune. But he had heard me, because he added, while munching his way through another potato: 'George, who knows ETA well, would tell you that those who planned the attack and carried it out would have felt ecstatic, and certainly wouldn't have felt tormented by what they'd done, not at all, according to him.'

'Well, they certainly managed to terrorize, which is what such attacks are all about.'

'Yes, they spread terror, but so what? That doesn't advance your cause one iota. You're all still here and they're still there, and ten years on nothing has changed. Nothing of any substance anyway, nothing worth setting down in the annals. The people who died on that day are still dead and the murderers are rotting in jail. The ones they caught of course. During the trial, they showed no remorse. I understand that every time their co-religionists carry out some new attack, ETA prisoners toast them with a glass of cider or champagne in their cells.'

'Were the ones who bombed Hipercor brought to trial? I don't remember that. When?'

'In 1989.'

'Oh, I was still dead then and far away. And what happened?'

'They sentenced the actual perpetrators and the man who planned the attack, as well as the then leader of ETA, Santi Potros I think his name was. They were each sentenced to almost eight hundred years, but you know as well as I do that they won't be in prison for anything like that time. I have the other names here.' He took out a folded piece of paper from his overcoat pocket and held it out to me. 'You read it, I can't cope with those Basque names.'

There were three neatly typed names, typed perhaps by Jorge: Rafael Caride, Domingo Troitiño and Josefa Ernaga. I couldn't help feeling slightly surprised, even though it wasn't that unusual to find women among the terrorists, sometimes in very responsible positions, and this was true in Spain, on both sides in Northern Ireland and indeed anywhere else (I'd had some contact with the famous Dolours Price, once she was out of prison). It was the same in Germany and Italy and, needless to say, in the Soviet Union, in Latin America and in countries in the Middle East, including, of course, Israel, there are vengeful women everywhere. We had some in our ranks too, although we weren't terrorists but, rather, their scourge, their containing wall, although the terrorists almost always took the initiative.

'A woman took part in the attack? She's the only one with a Basque surname. Troitiño is Galician and so is Caride, I think. A woman was involved in *that* attack?'

Given the sheer brutality of the bombing, I still found this hard to believe. As I said, I was brought up the old-fashioned way, and your upbringing always leaves its mark for good or ill. I had known women take part in such atrocities, but usually as collaborators in their preparation or organization. And I had seen them experience doubts more often than their male colleagues did, or reservations, or qualms, or anticipated remorse, what used to be called 'mixed feelings'. Some finished the job more out of an intense sense of loyalty to their colleagues or to the cause they had embraced, or out of defiance, rather than out of real conviction.

'She was one of the people who placed the bomb in the shopping mall, one of the actual perpetrators. I don't know why you should find that so odd when you've had dealings with such women on more than one occasion, you even went to bed with one, or was it two?' Tupra had a very good memory, he was almost like a walking archive. 'People feel safer in the presence of women, but you and I know that their compassion is purely mythical or can be. In general I mean. As well as the idea that they're less cruel. Many may not be cruel by nature, but it's not that difficult to inculcate them with cruelty, they don't put up much resistance and then there's no going back, armies should be composed entirely of such highly trained women; they're determined and persistent, and some are quite unflinching once they've resolved to act. Just think of the women who've been in positions of power. Remember our poor dear Maggie. Remember Ana Pauker, another woman nicknamed "the Iron Lady" in her day and in her country.'

'I don't know who Ana Pauker is.'

'Well, do a bit more reading instead of languishing away here, wasting your time, you'll end up a vegetable. In our work, we need to know everything, as much as possible. Especially history, because history contains all the teachings and instructions and norms of behaviour for any occasion. What we find are merely variants on what has happened before.'

He said this as if he were reprimanding me, as if I were still in training and under orders from him. He immediately moderated and modified his tone, because, although I was irritating him with my puerile refusal to look at the photos, he was still dependent on my decision, and knew he would get nothing out of me if he, in turn, irritated me. He lit another cigarette while his mouth was still busy with another *patata brava*, which he would spear every now and then with his diminutive trident.

'Cruelty is contagious. Hatred is contagious. Faith is contagious . . . It can turn into fanaticism at the speed of light . . .' Now his tone was part assertive, part recollective. 'That's why those attitudes are so dangerous, because they're hard to stop. Before you know it, they've spread like wildfire. That was one of the very first things we were taught, that you need to spot the initial symptoms and nip them in the bud. But there were two other things on Redwood's list, there were five in all, hang on . . .'

Redwood was a legendary instructor in MI5 and MI6, a philosophy teacher who had initiated past classes of agents in theory, he would doubtless have retired or died by then. Now it was Tupra who had forgotten his lessons.

'Madness is contagious. Stupidity is contagious,' he said, completing the list.

I remembered that list very well, I had all too often found out how very accurate it was. People adopt a faith and grow, first, very serious, then very solemn. They start to believe everything their faith embraces and involves, and then they become stupid. If contradicted, they fly into a rage, they won't accept you calling them stupid or challenging what has suddenly become their all-in-all and their raison d'être. From that point on, they develop a purely defensive, irrational hatred of anyone who doesn't share their fanaticism. And they treat anyone who openly opposes it with great cruelty. Once they discover cruelty, they embrace it and pass it on to others, and it takes a long time for them to grow weary of putting their cruelty into practice. According to Redwood, there was only one antidote, which is almost impossible to apply in the midst of all the madness.

'And then there was the one antidote, do you remember?' I said.

'Ah, yes, vain consolation. Laughter is contagious,' he said. 'It's just a shame that it gets swept aside when any of the other five attitudes dominate, and often all five go together, one calls to the other, and when the whole package comes complete, there's nothing to be done. You just have to declare war on it and crush it. That's right, isn't it?'

'Yes, that's what we were taught,' I replied, adding: 'Careful, Bertie, you said "our work". You're forgetting that it's no longer mine.'

He ignored my reminder or emendation.

'Don't you see that this is precisely what we're doing, and continue to do, slowly crushing fanaticism? It's a very long job and every step counts. Help us, Tom. It will do you good to return to active service, and it will only be this once.'

I sat staring at his eyes, which were now more blue than grey beneath the wintry Madrid sun that had finally succeeded in seeing off the feeling I'd had of penetrating cold. I smiled, possibly unable to conceal a slightly triumphant look, although obviously I couldn't see myself. He had asked me for help, albeit disguising his request with a plural when, here in Madrid, there was no truly legitimate plural. From what I could gather, the request came not from Spedding or from any of his subalterns, indeed, they probably knew nothing about what Tupra was up to. He was acting on his own with the support of his friend Jorge and perhaps with that of MI6 as well, although without their knowledge. Since the fall of the Berlin Wall and the break-up of the Soviet Union everything had become vaguer, more lax. Middle-management people, like him, had far more freedom of movement, they could make use of the resources of the State for matters that were not always in the interests of the Crown or that the Crown might even have categorically vetoed. They gave invented orders, that is, orders they had not received from anyone in authority or which came, at most, from private individuals, from businesses and multinationals or, sometimes, from who knows who (they might even come from some extremely rich person with particularly stubborn competitors or with unfinished business to resolve, and who employed honourable and trusted members of Her Majesty's secret services).

For ten or twelve years, let's say between 1989 and 2001, the inevitable nebulousness that hovers over that secretive world grew still denser, until, that is, the attack on the Twin Towers put an end to such indolence and dissipation. Most agents never asked themselves who would benefit from whatever operation they happened to be engaged on. We always assumed the State would benefit and obeyed our immediate superiors as a matter of course, shrugging off any rumours that, during that long period of uncertainty, confusion and relative passivity, we were working for various alternating masters.

Bearing all this in mind, why was a female ETA collaborator so important to Tupra? The problems of my second or first country did not usually affect my first or second country, and for Tupra there was only one country, as there was for all his many names. One idea immediately occurred to me of course: Spain was still being rocked by the GAL scandal, when it was revealed that a collection of anti-terrorist groups – Grupos Antiterroristas de Liberación – had been illegally set up by Spanish government officials to fight ETA; these clandestine squads had murdered and kidnapped members and sympathizers of ETA in the 1980s under the socialist governments of Felipe González; this meant that the Spanish State now had its hands tied when it came to taking any short cuts in its fight against terrorism. If someone from the British secret services were to accept an assignment, outside of official channels, no one would point the finger at the present government under Prime Minister Aznar, who, for political and propagandistic reasons, had pitilessly criticized GAL's dirty war, when, deep down, he probably thought it rather a good thing.

The newspapers were still full of the prison sentences handed down to people in high positions in the Ministry of the Interior, policemen, civil guards, military personnel and members of CESID – Centro Superior de Información de la Defensa, the Spanish intelligence agency at the time – not to mention socialist leaders accused of having set up and financed with State money the so-called *fondos de reptiles*, literally 'reptile funds' or slush funds.

'And what did that woman do after 1987?' I asked. 'We're talking about events that happened ten years ago? Has she remained active all that time? Is she still a constant threat? I don't know, I'm not very well informed, but my impression is that members of ETA are being picked off far more frequently than any such organization could possibly want. You yourself said that those responsible for the Hipercor bombing were brought to trial very quickly. Surprisingly quickly after such a bloody attack. Normally, they would have disappeared across the border into France. Or gone off to Latin America never to return.'

'It claimed more victims than any of their previous attacks: twenty-one dead and forty-five wounded, some horribly mutilated,' Tupra repeated, wanting to underline the infamous nature of that incident in his usual unmelodramatic way. 'I'm no expert on the group either, but it seems they're never satisfied even when their terrorist cells pull off a huge coup like that. They continue to exploit them relentlessly, to the point of sacrificing them or working them into the ground. A strange way of going about things. They give them one assignment after another, and don't allow them to rest or to disappear. If, after the Hipercor attack, they remained in Barcelona, as I believe they did, and they were ordered to machine-gun an army colonel or place a car bomb under a Civil Guard van, it certainly wouldn't have been long before they were captured. Do you want to know the details of what happened in the barracks in Zaragoza just six months later?'

'No, that's not necessary. I saw some pictures at the time, in whatever country I happened to be living in then, I can't remember where now. There's one particular image that stuck in my mind, it must have been all over the press. A civil guard or a fireman carrying a badly injured little girl, her foot half blown off.'

Tupra made an eloquent gesture with one hand, as if to say 'There you have it' or 'What more do you need to know.'

'And isn't someone who took part in all that,' he said, 'isn't that person a constant, albeit shadowy threat? And even if that person isn't a threat, doesn't she deserve to be punished and made to pay for the role she played? Especially since that woman doesn't belong to ETA, not in the usual, conventional way, and so hasn't been caught and shows no sign of being caught through some blunder of her own or because she's being overexploited or overworked. Unless, that is, someone makes that happen, you, for example.'

'Me, but why me, when I'm outside of all that?'

'No one is ever completely outside. And anyone who believes they are only has to take one small step to be back inside again. There's no one better placed, no one better qualified, because that woman has a lot in common with you. She doesn't wholly belong to any one country, being half Northern Irish and half Spanish. She also speaks both languages perfectly, she's bilingual, although whether she's as gifted as you are when it comes to other languages is another matter. She took part in those two attacks and probably in another earlier attack as well. Since 1987, though, at least as far as we know, she hasn't taken part in any others, either for ETA or for the IRA, not even at a distance, in the role of conspirator or ideologue or supervisor. In fact, by the time anyone knew of her involvement in the Hipercor attack, she had vanished without trace, more or less as you did when you became James Rowland, and Tom Nevinson was presumed dead. You spent years in hiding and with another identity, which is precisely what she must have done for the past nine years. So while she may appear to have retired, it's the same in those organizations as it is in ours: anyone who leaves can return again just by taking one small step, whether voluntary or under duress, and regardless of how much time has passed. With them, though, it's much worse, because very few are allowed to leave, they have to show unswerving loyalty. In the case of this woman, who knows? Perhaps they thought she'd done enough and gone beyond the call of duty given that she was an "outsider"; or else they felt she wasn't fanatical enough or had doubts and would be of little future use; or perhaps she was the one who distanced herself from them after seeing the scale of what happened in Barcelona and Zaragoza. Perhaps she thought about it and regretted having acted as collaborator, adviser or facilitator or whatever in those massacres. Too many deaths in one year, wholesale, random destruction, as if it were a lottery, and all those children dead. It could be any of those things, we never know how we're going to react, apart from those few bloodthirsty exceptions who never hesitate, like that Josefa woman in the so-called Comando Barcelona.'

He pronounced her name English-fashion with a J.

'What we know for sure is that she did do something, something for which she hasn't been arrested or punished. In fact, no one has ever tracked her down. So she may be one of those bloodthirsty exceptions and is simply inactive or, as the press always like to call such people, a sleeper, waiting to commit some new atrocity whenever it suits her. Anyway, she's one of these three women.' Tupra again pointed very deliberately at each of the photos: one two three. 'But which one? That's the problem, we haven't been able to identify her, and we're not going to resort to mafia-style methods. They would kidnap all three for a few hours, interrogate them and end up finding the culprit, unless the bloodthirsty exception in question has been trained to withstand such torture, which I very much doubt. Anyway, we don't do that kind of thing, not even when we're acting on our own: we're still part of the Realm even then. Two of those women are totally innocent, and we're not going to kidnap some poor mother or some poor teacher or an honest restaurateur. After all, we're not engaged in open warfare, when you can sacrifice whoever you need to sacrifice just so as not to put everything else at risk or leave any loose ends untied. On the other hand, they, in their madness, believe they are at war, and feel perfectly justified in doing what they do. That's what differentiates us from them and puts us at a disadvantage. They're also ahead of us when it comes to hatred. Hatred isn't our style, as you know. That's unknown territory for us.'

Tupra made these statements in such a neutral tone that one could not help but suspect that he meant the exact opposite. After all, why did they, Tupra and his Spanish friend Jorge, feel so impelled to track down a minor figure who happened to have been involved in some particularly horrible crimes, but crimes that had been committed almost ten years ago, and ten years is a long time in terrorism, because terrorists work on a cumulative basis, creating mayhem almost without pause, thus reducing all the previous attacks to an indistinguishable blur and simultaneously creating a sense of helplessness, a feeling that we've been through an awful lot already and haven't seen the last of it, their aim being to create utter confusion, utter exhaustion.

The actual perpetrators – the main culprits if you like – were given long prison sentences. So was the person who issued the definitive order, Santi Potros, the then leader of the group. Some served time in Spain, others in France. If, for every crime committed, you were to seek out those who had participated or helped in some way, either intentionally or not, either knowingly or not; or who had provided or inadvertently divulged some vital piece of information; or who had given shelter one night to a relative or neighbour unaware of what they had come to do or what they would do the following morning in their town or village; or who had lent money to a friend in difficulties, or donated their savings to an NGO or to a parish, believing they were helping someone out of a predicament or saving a few starving children or some poor wretched refugees; or who had

lent someone a screwdriver or some glue or petrol or soap or nails –
even a small fork – never imagining why these were needed or how
they were going to be used; then probably half of humanity could be
seen as a co-participant or accomplice.

Those who inflict the greatest damage, and murderers in general,
often resort to that argument, trying to make out that the victims
themselves brought about the crimes committed, were the cause of
their own deaths or amputations. There wouldn't have been any
deaths in the barracks in Zaragoza and in Vic if the civil guards hadn't
chosen to live there with their families, thus putting them at risk; and
at Hipercor, if the authorities had acted with greater diligence and
evacuated the centre after our confusing warnings (the fact that the
bomb was hidden in the boot of a car is a minor detail, they could still
easily have stopped the explosion); no policeman or soldier or journalist or judge or shopkeeper would have been executed in our
country, which has never been invaded – not even by the Romans – if
it had not, mysteriously, been occupied by others; nor would any
businessman have died if they had all promptly, patriotically, paid up
what we demanded from them for the cause; there wouldn't have
been a single death in Ulster if the English had not stolen part of our
island from us, having stolen the whole island from us centuries
before; or if the Catholics hadn't persecuted us and tried to expel us
from our land, which is as British as London or Canterbury, as much
ours as theirs or even more so, theirs is in the south, let them go and
hear mass down there and not bother us.

Responsibility always lies elsewhere, and it's so easy to spread it
around . . . I've heard all kinds of arguments throughout my life, and
the most frequent has always been this: yes, I killed him, but it was
his fault. I suppose that, to some extent, it's an argument that I've
used as well.

Why waste time, money and energy looking for that woman after
all these years? There are so many criminals who go unpunished,

there are so many cases impossible to prove or where we never even find out if such and such a person was involved, directly or indirectly; there are so many abuses we don't even hear about, that are written off as accidents or put down to a sudden illness or a reversal of fortune, to blunders, bad luck, suicides, recklessness, imprudence or some miscalculation; or that are attributed to others, scapegoats who are then condemned and punished.

That threat had hovered over me when I was young and inexperienced, and Professor Wheeler had issued this warning in words I still often recall: 'It would be far worse to be arrested on a charge of homicide, wouldn't it?' – he had said after commending me to Tupra, which is how we came to meet – 'You never know how a trial might end, however innocent you are or however well things seem to be going. The truth doesn't count, because that has to be decided upon, established by someone who can never know what the truth is, namely a judge. It's not a matter to be placed in the hands of someone who is simply flailing about in the dark or tossing a coin and who can only guess or intuit the truth. When you think about it, it's absurd that anyone should be judged.'

Perhaps that's why we defenders of the Realm sometimes tried to avoid or bypass judges. Sometimes we knew precisely what happened, we saw or heard it and didn't need a formal trial that might contradict or refute our evidence, might consider it insufficient, one person's word against another, or that it wasn't evidence at all but mere hearsay, rumour and gossip, supposition.

Having been a defender of the Realm during the war – and in time of war everything is clearer and there are fewer delays and hesitations – Wheeler had added: 'I wouldn't recognize the authority of any court. If I could avoid it, I would never submit myself to a trial of any kind. Anything but that. Something to bear in mind, Tomás. Think about it. You can be sent to prison on a mere whim. Simply because they don't like you.'

We all knew that the contrary was also possible, that a guilty party could also be let off on a mere whim, simply because he or she found favour with someone who hadn't been a witness to anything and knew only the opposing versions put forward by either side. This (I imagined) was the case here, that Tupra was endorsing Wheeler's lesson; after all, not for nothing had Wheeler been his teacher and mentor.

'If hatred is an emotion unknown to us, Bertie, why are you pursuing this woman now? Ten years is a long time, and we've let worse things go, when it suited us or our superiors. If that woman has committed no further crimes in all that time, she probably no longer represents a danger. I find it hard to believe that this is about seeing justice done. Justice is or isn't important depending on the times and on one's perspective.'

Tupra had been steadily eating his way through the second portion of *patatas bravas*, more calmly this time, one by one. He looked around him and gestured to the waitress, wanting to pay the bill, that glorious sun of York may have been taking the chill off the air, but not entirely, and it was very early in the year to spend such a long time out of doors. He had lost all patience, although he managed to control his feelings, for he was still dependent on me. With the swift aplomb of a gambler, he scooped up the three photos and returned them to their envelope, which he then held out to me.

'Fine, I can see you're not going to look at them today, you're not going to give me that pleasure. You want to play hard to get and keep me dangling, and I can understand that, why shouldn't you? It doesn't matter. Take them home with you and study them at your leisure, when the mood takes you. I'll call you tomorrow or the day after, I should still be in Madrid. I will just tell you this, though: you would have to spend a few months, or a few weeks if you're quick, in the town where they live, somewhere up in north-west Spain. You would have to be in contact with all three for as long as it took you to identify the woman in question and rule out the other two, poor things, the ones who will have done nothing wrong. I'll give you full details when you say yes. Or you could deal directly with George and he'll provide you with the details.'

'*If* I say yes,' I said.

When the waitress came with the bill, he put his hands in his overcoat pockets, giving me to understand that although he had invited me to meet him, the law of hospitality obliged me to pay. I picked up the envelope and put it away, and we both stood up; the truth is that I'd found it hard to resist looking at those photographs, for our eyes tend to be drawn to what they've decided not to see, and I was pleased to have the opportunity to look at them later at home, without Tupra there. I could always lie and say I hadn't even bothered, that I wanted nothing to do with his schemings.

As I set off, I saw the reader of Chateaubriand sitting outside another café, still with her woollen hat on, she, oddly enough, had also put up with her share of the cold, and for as long as we had. She was still holding her fat book, but she did raise her blue eyes for a moment, looking not so much at me as at Tupra. The fact that he did not, this time, return her glance convinced me that they did know each other; it was unlike him not to look, however in love and married he might be, what, I wondered, was so special about Beryl? Perhaps he had become one of those department heads who never go anywhere without their support staff, not even to the Plaza de la Paja to see a former subordinate.

'Of course you'll say yes,' he murmured.

'What?' I said, having forgotten my earlier words.

'You'll say yes and move to that town in the north-west.'

I wasn't offended by this show of confidence, because the decision lay in my hands, not his. I was no longer under his orders. I didn't respond to that remark, but said:

'You clearly do know that woman, the reader of *Outre-tombe*.

She's still on guard over there. I presume you have your reasons for bringing her with you, but she's going to catch her death out here.'

'Oh, was she still there?' he said, without looking back. 'Pure chance. Remember that other old lesson: paranoia is just as bad as being ill-prepared. Where are you going now?'

'Home. I don't live far away.'

'I'll come with you to stretch my legs. Then I'll take a taxi.'

'As you wish.'

We walked in silence towards Plaza de la Villa, up a few short flights of steps, from where I would continue on to Calle de Lepanto or drop in to see Berta and the children in Calle de Pavía. Not that we were going to celebrate Epiphany like a real family, but they would be pleased if I looked in or so I liked to think, I sometimes had the feeling that for them I was a kind of second-rank relative who is always welcome whenever he turns up – like an uncle from the Americas with lots of stories to tell and with plenty of money – but if he doesn't, no matter; there's no way to make up for all those years of absence. In Calle del Cordón, as we reached the square, Tupra stopped – as if he'd been pondering not the matter in hand, but whether it would be worthwhile giving me a brief lecture to enlighten me – and said:

'People, individuals, do grow weary of hating. Time passes, the reason for their hatred begins to fade and they find it hard to continue hating with that same initial intensity. They're alone with their hatred, and you have to be very disciplined indeed to get yourself all riled up every single day. Sooner or later, people forget or grow lazy, passive. It's not the same with organizations. They never forgive or forget because there are always members who keep the flame alive while others rest and retreat and grow old, and who pass it on before the flame burns out. It's the same with certain families and their off-spring, with the hatred being passed on indefinitely from generation to generation. That's what those organizations were created to do, that's why they're so difficult to combat and why, to the despair of the rest of the world, they sometimes last for centuries. The more depersonalized a group is, the less reflective it is, the more deaf and blind, the more adamantine and fanatical. They all have something religious about them, they inherit enemies and objects of veneration that no one ever questions, because reason has no effect on them.' He paused in Plaza de la Villa, took out another cigarette and lit it while looking up at the statue there, Don Álvaro de Bazán wielding his staff of command; he then took two puffs and indicated the statue with his cigarette. 'Who's the fellow in the tights?'

'Don Álvaro de Bazán, Marqués de Santa Cruz, the Admiral in command of the Spanish fleet at the Battle of Lepanto.'

'That's where you live, isn't it, Calle de Lepanto – 1571, right? Didn't Cervantes lose his hand in that battle?'

'Well, he lost the use of one hand when he was just twenty-four. He used to refer to himself as *el manco sano*, the sound cripple.'

'And what does it say there?'

He went over to read the inscription on the pedestal. 'Translate it for me, will you?'

'I'm not sure you're going to like it,' I said after reading what was written there.

'Why? What does it say? No censorship, please.'

I translated it as best I could:

'The Turks at Lepanto, the French in the Third Carlist War, the English from sea to sea, all eyed me with alarm.'

' "From sea to sea", eh?' he said. 'I'll need to check that. What else?'

'All right, but bear in mind that his name Santa Cruz means Holy Cross. "The King I served and the land I fought for can tell you who I was far better than I: given the Cross of my name and the many swords that crossed mine." '

'Not bad. A touch old-fashioned, but not bad.' Then he resumed his lecture. 'We never forget either, Tom, because in order to do battle with such people we must imitate them a little, must mimic them, if we didn't, we would be lost and left at an enormous disadvantage. We, too, are an organization. An institution, an ancient body, with archives that demand justice and that are, if you prefer, our commemorative cards, even objects of veneration. But we're not motivated by hatred or vengeance, or a sense of eternal grievance that can never be assuaged, as happens with terrorist groups and mafias, and even among certain people with a tendency to feel offended and oppressed, who need to feel that in order to survive and to feed those feelings, and to inoculate new followers in the simplest way possible and recruit them in their hundreds; and so that traitors and enemies will always feel they have a sword hanging over them and are never safe, however many decades they spend avoiding the sentence meted out to them. Those threatened or condemned get up each morning filled with fear, thinking: "It didn't happen yesterday, or the day before, or in the last five or ten years, which have passed so slowly night after night and day after day. But who can assure me it won't happen today, when I step nonchalantly out into the street; or that someone won't poison my food; or that a friend won't knock at my door and be the one to put a bullet in me?" Anyone who is vehemently hated, anyone who feels and knows himself to be hated, lives each day as if it were the first day of his sentence, because he must always be alert and prepared, always on guard and prepared to fight.'

Tupra continued looking at the statue as he spoke, with a mixture of understanding and antipathy, admiration and defiance. For a moment the former prevailed, because he suddenly said:

'I like that line "the King I served and the land I fought for", because that's how it is, isn't it? People weren't plagued by doubt in those days.' Then the latter feeling prevailed, because he made a ridiculous remark, directed at the bronze Don Álvaro: 'So "the

English from sea to sea eyed me with alarm", eh? Quite the braggart, aren't we?' Then he carried on as if this had been an aside to the audience, unheard by the other characters. 'Anyone who doesn't feel that hatred is more vulnerable and more trusting, he loses the desire to kill, or even, dare I say it, to defend himself. He believes that the State or the Crown or the Republic will forget, that the State has too much else to think about and little time to look back, driven on as it is by the present; that it will let old crimes go because sometimes that's politically convenient and they will benefit from burying them. He believes that, caught in the middle of so many fronts, he is insignificant, and that belief works to our advantage. But that's where he's wrong. Hatred may be an emotion unknown to us, and to which we must not succumb, but while we don't do passion, time doesn't pass and we never forget anything. For us, what happened ten years ago is yesterday or even today, and is happening right now.'

IV

I didn't speak about it to Berta for a whole week. Nor did I feel obliged to, given how little of our lives we shared, how little and how lukewarm, just occasional encounters, always entirely on her terms, visits to the home that had belonged to us both aeons ago, phone calls on practical matters such as money or about the children who were now young adults and autonomous, if not yet independent; the odd flurry of sexual activity, ever more infrequent, and the word 'flurry' is hardly the right euphemism. When such 'flurries' occurred, I always assumed they were prompted by some setback she had suffered, some momentary disappointment or cooling off, because I was sure she was in a relationship with one man if not two consecutively, she never told me and I never asked, as I said, I had no right, it would have been an invasion of privacy, an impertinence, it was quite enough that she had not completely turned her back on me, that she had not forbidden me from ever seeing her again. I had the feeling she put up with me out of obstinacy or out of a kind of superstitious loyalty to the past, as if she did not want to betray the person she had been when she was young and not so young; perhaps too because I was of some use to her on days when she felt more alone, more discontented, or when she felt she was growing older, diminished (for no reason that I could see, I still found her as attractive as ever; but we each fabricate our own reasons): we make do with what we have and what survives – yes, with what remains – and as we watch a future of infinite possibilities slowly vanish, no longer endless and abstract, a sheaf of blank sheets, becoming something ever more concrete and constrained, or more delineated, or more set in stone, that is, becoming increasingly past and present with each day that passes.

That, up to a point, was what had made me accept: the temptation to write another chapter, the idea that I had not yet finished my own little book, when I had already assumed I had reached the end. Above all, and as I have said before: even if you're weary and decide to abandon everything, even if you miss the tranquil life you've never had (and that in itself is a fantasy: you can't miss it if you've led a very different life full of tension, deception and danger), it becomes unbearable to be outside once you've been inside, where you've felt that you could, occasionally, disturb the universe, just a whisker. We cannot resist exerting some degree of influence, however minimal, to alter the course of some diminutive existence. In this case, to have someone who was living a perfectly happy life after having participated in certain repugnant crimes, a woman who had perhaps justified her actions at the time and wiped them from her memory, to have that person in some way pay for those crimes when she considered herself to be an entirely different person and therefore safe.

And so I had studied the three photos at home very carefully; I had awaited Tupra's impatient call, genuinely impatient, for it came the very next morning, Tuesday 7 January; we had agreed to meet that same day for a light lunch with his friend or colleague Jorge (well, they must already have arranged to meet), who had given me details and other material as well as my false documentation, it was astonishing that he had all this ready prepared, and indicated how transparent my final response to Tupra had been, I found it discouraging that he should know me so well, I thought I would have changed more than that since my departure from the institution, from the old firm; have become more unfathomable and erratic. On the other hand, Jorge or George did seem perfectly willing to give me another identity, another profession and another name if I didn't think those he'd chosen for me were suitable.

He was a man in his fifties with the look of a career diplomat, rather than that of an official or officious controller, not that we ever have one individual appointed to us and they're always changing. But he was too well dressed and as if he had never been anything other than well dressed, wearing an expensive double-breasted jacket and an ample camel-hair overcoat, both of which bothered me as being far too reminiscent of the numerous toffs who'd had the run of the place during the dictatorship, acting as if they were the lords and masters of the nation, which they were, and whom I had roundly despised. He even wore mother-of-pearl cufflinks and a tie pin, almost unknown in the 1990s, bearing someone's cameo portrait. Fortunately, he wasn't using brilliantine (if he had been, you wouldn't have seen me for dust), his hair combed straight back with a parting on the right, nice silvery hair like the silver glitter on the cardboard covers of certain children's books. He had very regular features, although his nose was slightly too large and his lips were thinner than he would perhaps have liked, you could tell he was something of a flirt. He had lively, very narrow brown eyes, sometimes so narrow they could be hard to find, as if they were never looking straight ahead, but had to share themselves out over too broad a horizontal plane. The only thing that didn't fit with his ambassadorial, consular, chamberlainish air was his moustache, which was darker than his hair, and neither thin nor thick, and so while verging on the out of place (out of place on that almost senatorial or patrician face), it nevertheless managed to remain discreet.

As befitted a man of a certain lineage, whether genuine or fake, he introduced himself giving only his first name and first surname, Jorge Machimbarrena, although that surname sounded invented or borrowed to me, I was sure it wasn't his real name. I looked at the names he had assigned me on the identity card and passport which as yet lacked photographs and which he handed to me with a smug expression, as if to show how efficient he had been.

'Miguel Centurión Aguilera? Centurión? Isn't that rather too odd?' I asked. 'I've never known anyone called Centurión.'

I reminded Tupra, in case he had forgotten, that in Spain it's the first of someone's two surnames that counts and by which people are usually known, the second one is the mother's surname and, in principle, is used only for official matters. At least, that's how it was until very recently.

'If it means the same as it does in English,' he said, meaning the word *centurión*, 'no one would ever have a bizarre name like that.'

We were speaking in Tupra's language out of deference to him or because we felt obliged to. Machimbarrena's English was fluent, although he did sometimes make mistakes and he had a hopelessly strong accent, of the kind that will never improve. He could, though, be understood.

'It's not that common here either, but it does exist, there are six or seven Centuriόns in Madrid,' responded the counterfeit Machimbarrena. 'And it needs to be memorable. Bland names are no use at all, in fact, they're likely to arouse more suspicion, even when there's no reason. Odd names are more credible, I even met someone called, can you believe it, Gómez-Antigüedad, the manager of a big hotel, no one would ever have invented a name like that, would they? And look at all the writers who got rid of their Martínez, Fernández and Pérez to call themselves Azorín or Clarín or Fígaro or even Savater and Guelbenzu.'

I didn't like to point out to him that Clarín and Fígaro were mere pseudonyms used respectively by Alas and Larra, neither of which were particularly common surnames. I sensed that, like a lot of diplomats, he was a literary ignoramus with a good memory for names.

'People soon get used to unusual names and feel more comfortable with them. Centurión sticks in the mind and arouses curiosity, encourages people to ask about the name and for you then to come out with your usual spiel; it makes it easy to strike up conversations, and then you don't always have to be the buttinski, constantly having to invent opening gambits. Don't forget, it's women you're out to win over, they're the ones whose trust you want to gain.' He fixed me for a second with his wandering eyes. 'But if you don't like it, we can change it. Would you prefer to be García García?'

There was a touch of sarcasm in his voice. He really was a toff and had been since Franco's day. I don't think I'd heard the word 'buttinski' since the 1960s. I wondered who he was working for, probably CESID, either from inside or from outside, he would be answerable to the Ministry of Defence where there were a lot of pro-Francoists, who, despite that, weren't anti-democratic but had all quite naturally converted to the new norm and with no twinges of conscience. It would be a very different story if those who still yearned for the old regime were to organize some kind of rogue mission either independently or in cahoots with the kind of hardline left- or right-wing high-ups who were everywhere.

I realized that, having said yes, none of this mattered to me, nor did I feel it was any of my business. The mission came from Tupra, like all the others in my past life, and I had assumed that I would deal with him or with someone he appointed, probably some new Molyneux. On this occasion, he wasn't following orders from his superiors, but then how could I be sure that he always had before? And the objective didn't present any problems, whoever was in charge. It was, after all, a question of unmasking a murderer and, if possible, bringing her to justice. Or so I believed then.

'No, no, don't worry. If you think Centurión has its advantages as a name, then let's discuss it no further. I will be Centurión until further notice. No, I really like it.'

'You see?' said Machimbarrena smugly. 'You've immediately got used to it and seen its advantages as a name.'

'And what about photos? There aren't any here, but Bertie's sure to have a few. From three or four years ago, but I imagine they'll do. I don't think I've aged that much.'

Machimbarrena and Tupra both suddenly turned towards me in perfect unison, studying me as intently as if I were an insect. The former could not venture an opinion as to the speed of my ageing; the latter could, and I hoped he wouldn't compare me with the young thing he had met in Blackwell's about two hundred years ago, and to whom, I was sure, I bore no resemblance. He had changed infinitely less than me since that morning in another life, perhaps because he had always been the same ever since he was a child, or so I imagined. He was also vainer than I was, and took great care over his appearance.

'Once you've decided what Miguel Centurión looks like and have more or less become him, we'll take some photos and put them in. There was no sense in doing it before,' said Machimbarrena. 'You choose how you want to look. Blond or dark or going grey, with a moustache or a beard or clean-shaven, long hair or short, with or without a parting. A parting looks neater, more elegant.' And he immodestly indicated his own. 'Then again, there's no time to grow a beard, because you need to start work as soon as possible. If you like, you can leave any final decision until you arrive. After all, your physical appearance is up to you, since you're the one who's going to have to live with it and, besides, according to Bertram, you've plenty of experience of such missions. The more attractive you look the better, though, just in case. Sometimes the only way to gain a woman's trust is to win her heart. I mean her love, call it what you will. Get her into bed, I mean.' He then immediately went straight into Spanish, as if he needed his own language in order to speak crudely. 'Have your wicked way with her, shag her once or even twenty times. Stick it in her up to the hilt, drive your sword in as far as you can . . .'

I stopped him before he went any further or waxed still more toreador-like. Beneath his suave manner he was a foulmouthed toff, as so many of them are.

'All right, I get your point. I don't intend to take that route, at least in principle. It only complicates matters, confuses things, muddies the water. There are other ways. And remember, Bertram doesn't understand Spanish.'

'That's true, forgive me, Bertram. When you speak the same language as someone, you always end up slipping into it without realizing,' he said in English. 'I was saying to Nevinson that he might have to screw one of the women.'

'He knows that,' responded Tupra. 'He wasn't bad at that in his day. When he was active.'

'You say there are other ways that you prefer. What others, Nevinson? I see only one.'

I didn't answer. If he couldn't think of any, there was no point in explaining.

'All right, I'll try and make myself handsome,' I said, so as to bring the discussion to a close. 'Although at my age that's not so easy. It's not like it was before, Bertie.'

They both once again scrutinized me in a way I found embarrassing. They were gauging how seductive I might prove to be to those three women, as if I wasn't there and they were watching me on a screen. I allowed myself to be observed, but felt very awkward.

'You look pretty good to me,' said Machimbarrena, 'nice regular features. You're younger than I am, but I certainly can't complain, I do brilliantly in that department. If I were to tell you what I got up to with an actress the other day . . .' No one encouraged him to go further, and, fortunately, he got the message. 'Although you could do with a bit of sprucing up. I could send you to Sigfrido.'

'Sigfrido?' I said, alarmed by that name.

'My personal hairdresser, and he knows about male make-up too.

Don't worry, he's from Pozoblanco in the province of Córdoba, he's not German or Wagnerian or anything.'

'I don't know,' murmured Tupra, examining me. 'You would have to dye your hair at the temples and on the sides higher up. That's where you're greyest and it does make you look older. I don't mean dye all your hair, just here and there. You're not grey at all on top. And the slightly receding hairline makes you look interesting and trustworthy, and you're certainly not yet bald. Best not grow a beard, though, it would probably come out almost white and you don't want to look older than your years. Just in case, as George says.'

'Dye my hair? Like you dyeing your curls since heaven knows when? You mean start imitating your little vanities at this stage in my life?'

Tupra was not in the least amused by this remark, even though my tone had been jokey and inoffensive; perhaps he thought his thick curly hair really did look like the real thing. He shot me a stern glance, then waved one hand dismissively as if to say: 'What nonsense, pure envy.' I added:

'Besides, I don't think I need change my appearance that much. I've never worked in Spain, so there's no risk of anyone recognizing me.'

Tupra reprimanded me, wagging his finger at me. 'That's where you're wrong. Don't even go there,' that finger was saying, or even: 'You really are dangerously out of practice, Tom.'

'Don't forget what I told you. The woman we're looking for is half Northern Irish, even though she's spent all if not most of her life here, but she's lived in Northern Ireland too. Things are gradually quietening down over there; there is some hope, which can't be said for the situation in the Basque Country. But we'll see, nothing is certain and it's all still very fragile. With the exception of the ghastly evangelical, presbyterian members of the DUP and those idiots belonging to the PUP, most people want it to stop, although nothing has yet been resolved.'

He was referring to the two unionist parties, the Democratic Unionist Party and the Progressive Unionist Party, the former were the cretinous extreme right and the latter the cretinous extreme left. 'Three thousand four hundred deaths is too much for such a small place. How many deaths has ETA caused?'

'Oh, far fewer, a quarter of that,' said Machimbarrena. 'Bear in mind, though, that here only one side has done the killing while the other has meekly offered up its neck, no eye for an eye, no demand for vengeance, which is pretty remarkable when you think about it. Both sides there have done the killing, with the help of the British army. That doesn't just double the number of deaths, it multiplies them.'

'When you say only one side, there have been a few exceptions,' I said, meaning the activities of GAL in the 1980s.

'But very few, very few in comparison,' said Jorge, perhaps, who knows, because he himself had participated in the events of that decade.

Not that he was altogether wrong. The crimes committed by ETA bore no comparison with those in Ulster, and they had been going on for thirty years, more or less as long as the reciprocal slaughterings in Ulster. ETA's members had been amnestied when democracy was established, regardless of whether they had committed violent crimes; ETA had shown their gratitude by turning on the new democracy with even more venom, apparently loathing the democratic government more than they had the dictatorship and continuing to murder in cold blood.

'That's probably why,' Tupra went on, 'no one's going to torpedo the negotiations or conversations by bumping off one of ours, and you are one of ours, Tom. Not just because you're returning to active service, but because we continue to subsidize your family. Or should I say families, although it's up to you what you do with your salary.'

It was my turn not to be amused. I had already said yes to his proposal, and it was completely out of order for him to threaten me with leaving me financially vulnerable. He must have been worried that I might pull out, that I might back down before I had begun or even once I had started. The last time we had met in London to say goodbye, he had warned me: 'We never abandon those who have worked to defend the Realm, you can be sure of that. However, we will abandon anyone who lets the Realm down or allows his tongue to run away with him or reveals things he shouldn't and cannot reveal. Bear that in mind if you don't want us to withdraw your maintenance payments and all financial help. We could even prosecute you.'

I hadn't allowed my tongue to run away with me, not even with Berta, I knew perfectly well that I was still bound by the Official Secrets Act and would be for the rest of my life, by the 1911 Act and by the revised 1989 Act.

I wondered if that had not just been mere talk and that more would be demanded of me, if I would be obliged to serve whenever they asked me, at the risk of suffering reprisals or being left out in the cold at an age when I was too old to serve. If you really couldn't leave, as happens in mafias, where they pretend to give you permission to leave and immediately bump you off when you do. The only way to make yourself useless was to become surplus to requirements. I thought I had achieved that, but now they were enlisting me again, albeit through rather murky channels. And I was pleased not to be deemed useless.

'But in Ulster,' Tupra went on, 'there might be certain individuals who have your photo pinned to the bullseye on their dartboard, and such photos can spread and are easily distributed. In the past, that is, probably not now, when almost no one will remember you, and any- one who does will assume you're dead. It's unlikely, almost impossible, that this woman would be familiar with your face, but it's best to take every precaution, because none of us can ever know who might have photographed us. Someone with a good hand or a good memory could even have made a drawing of us. And yet we have no reliable description of her, no photos, she has always proved elusive and has remained in the shadows. Or rather, we do have a photo now, the one I gave you yesterday along with two others, but we have no earlier photos, which is why we don't know which of the three is the woman we're after. This doesn't mean there isn't some image out there somewhere, just as there will be of you and of everyone. Our problem is that we haven't found that older image which might give her away just a little and provide us with a clue. Besides, she'll have changed her appearance countless times. That's where you come in, but it's not an easy task. She'll be entirely without scruples. If she suspects anything, she might run away or she might kill you.'

He finished the caramel dessert he was eating and lit his post- prandial cigarette, at the time, some restaurants still had smoking areas, the civilized twentieth century, well, relatively speaking.

'I'm not saying you should don some ridiculous wig or disguise yourself as a local, but don't look like your usual self in that town in the north-west. And certainly not like the you you were before you died, that will be the image best remembered by those who still bear a grudge and are eager to have their revenge. So don't make yourself look too young.'

He suddenly seemed amused by my earlier joke, because he added with a pleasant smile:

'Imitate my little vanities, as you so kindly put it, learn from me. I may prove to be a good teacher. Purely unintentionally, of course.'

What I had told Machimbarrena was true: in principle at least, I did not intend to win anyone's heart if I could avoid it, the heart of one of those three women, still less screw them, assuming any of them were interested. Besides, that wasn't an easy route to take, certainly not any longer, I mean winning them round or, to use the vocabulary of wealthy toff Jorge, having my wicked way with them. It wasn't only that, since my retirement, I was very out of practice in that area, the mere idea of it filled me with sloth. Arranging to meet, making yourself more or less attractive, getting all dressed up, going out and having long conversations, subtly – ambiguously – chatting the woman up, taking an interest in the life and opinions of that complete stranger, paying close attention and listening patiently, memorizing everything you're told – a form of adulation – as if you were drinking in the teachings of a master; being gallant without going to ridiculous extremes, making a pass without appearing salacious or needy or unctuous or aggressive, gauging their reaction to any apparently casual or naturally occurring touching, an affectionate hand on the shoulder, a protective hand on the waist when crossing the street, the closeness of my thigh to hers in a cinema or at a concert or in a taxi . . . it made me tired just to think of it. Not to mention the prospect of kissing and fondling and feeling her up (assuming she was wearing an encouraging, facilitative skirt), unzipping zips and unbuttoning buttons and panting and looking passionate and getting undressed, even if only half undressed, and pressing yourself to another person's flesh in a flattering manner, possibly putting on a fervour straight out of some wilfully fervid novel or a desperation and an urgency copied from the most idiotic and mendacious of films. And don't even mention the possibility of spending the night in someone else's bedroom or accommodating someone in my own bed, getting up in the morning with that someone and having breakfast in their rather crumpled company; in the clear light of day the previous night's excitement tends to be seen as a mistake, sheer recklessness, folly, at least after a certain age.

My needs in that regard had diminished since my return to Madrid, as if ceasing active service had laid me low in too many ways, some of them unexpected. My sporadic encounters with Berta were enough for me, and during the periods when those encounters were more or less non-existent, doubtless because she had her own dreams and discoveries to make, I would visit the apartment of an English colleague at the embassy, one of my subordinates as it happens (she had begun working there shortly before my return), and, right from the start, she had regarded me favourably and with a great deal of curiosity and a certain strange paternalism, the latter despite me being almost twice her age. I suspected that her curiosity was aroused by what she had learned about my career, or else she'd heard rumours and thought it would be exciting to add a notch to her sexual or amatory CV in the form of a real-life spy. She was also one of those young women who get satisfaction from helping the helpless, guiding the bewildered and consoling the tormented, and I must have appeared to her to fit all three categories during the time it took me to grow accustomed to the void.

Her name was Patricia Pérez Nuix, and she, too, was the child of Spanish and English parents, or so I seem to recall, the granddaughter of an obscure exile from our Civil War who had coincided in England with other more famous exiles, Arturo Barea and Manuel Chaves Nogales and possibly Luis Cernuda; she was bilingual like

135

me, but had been brought up in London and was therefore more originally British, she had only spent the summers in Spain, like a flipside version of my life. She had quick, lively, brown eyes and a ready, generous laugh that would momentarily cheer whoever happened to be near, because hers was not a profound or lasting happiness. She knew exactly what she wanted despite her extreme youth (she had recently graduated and had been taken on almost at once because of her evident abilities), she was the one who undertook the bold task of reconnaissance and approach and the subsequent task of maintenance. Well, that's not quite true, because she came and went with a whole multitude of her contemporaries and, absurd as it may sound, she saw me only as an occasional and eccentric trophy (monthly or bimonthly, it wasn't very often) from what she considered to have been heroic times, those of the Cold War.

The fact that she considered these to be almost mythical times made me feel prematurely like a dinosaur, after all, the Cold War hadn't ended that long ago and it had been such a large part of my life: looking through her eyes, I watched my life being converted into history, antiquity, the past, and when that happens, we cannot help but question ourselves bitterly as to the usefulness of what we did, and it doesn't take us long to conclude that everything would be exactly the same if we hadn't so much as lifted a finger, if we hadn't existed and hadn't tarnished our honour.

She always received me in her apartment in Calle Ponzano with a mixture of pleasure and condescension (the smugness of the young as regards their elders) and with an insatiable curiosity to hear about my legendary life, a curiosity I was prohibited from satisfying, and so she had no option but to resort to her imaginings based on her readings and to fantasize about my exploits, just as poor Berta had done for decades, except in Berta there had been no trace of frivolity or play, no sense of tales of derring-do told or rather untold. Pat, as everyone called her, belonged to an excitable, pragmatic generation free of any moral dilemmas, who did whatever they wanted to in their personal lives meanwhile fulfilling their obligations without questioning the ways of the world. Her naturally kind heart did not prevent her from being a strict, stern civil servant – which is, after all, what she and I both were, as was Tupra, and the Prime Minister – and implacable towards anyone harming or threatening the Realm in the eyes of her superiors, one of whom was Tupra himself, albeit at a distance, as I soon discovered with some surprise. So her physical relationship with me did not present her with any problems or doubts, nor would it linger in her memory. With her, in that respect, I didn't have to make any special effort.

I still didn't have all the facts – I was waiting for the full reports, which would be given to me just before my departure – but Machimbarrena and Tupra had revealed to me that two of the three women were married; the other appeared to be single, but she might be divorced or widowed – a very private person, of whom little was known in the town because she barely told her acquaintances anything about herself – but at any rate she lived alone.

If I found myself forced to follow the muddy path of sentiment and sex or just plain sex with either of the married women, I would first have to overcome the initial resistance put up by any married woman (a resistance more mental than physical, the physical is purely mechanical and the post-coital shower washes away all traces) about deceiving her husband and making a space in her daily life for a new individual, a tedious, supplementary chore. Unless they were already in the habit of cheating on them and considered it of no importance, or unless cracks had long been appearing in their marriage and they were just waiting for an opportunity to plant a small bomb to bring it crashing to the ground.

I was hoping that none of them would take me seriously or see me as a substitute. Of course if that did happen, I had considerable experience of brutal deceptions and of disappearing with no explanation, and of placing those lovers in the hands of the law or of the comrades they had betrayed, the latter usually being the worst of the two options as far as the women were concerned. I had occasionally felt pity for them, but not a paralysing pity: what happened to them next was neither my business nor my fault. They had chosen to help the people they were helping or hide the people they were hiding, or serve the cause they were serving and to dedicate themselves to whatever they were dedicated to, although they had sometimes been duped or hypnotized into doing so, as had many inexperienced men. The woman I was charged with uncovering and identifying in that town in the north-west, whichever one of the three she turned out to be, had been responsible for massacres and should pay for that. Or if not 'should', it would be appropriate that she did. Or if not 'appropriate', since she no longer presented any danger and had turned around her unhappy life, it would be best to interrupt that life just in case, and because we were by our nature avengers. If we weren't, who would be, in this forgetful world?

Tupra was right: hatred was an emotion unknown to us, but we were the archive, the record, the ones who never forgot what everyone else forgets out of weariness or so as not to wallow in bitterness. I don't know if he realized it, but the words he had spoken made us – with all our human, mortal limitations – rather like the God of all those past centuries of belief, or should that be credulity: the God who retained and stored away everything in his motley, moveless time, in which nothing was new or old, remote or recent. 'For us, what happened ten years ago is yesterday or even today, and is happening right now.' This is how that God – now outmoded, but very much a force to be reckoned with for most of recorded history – must have regarded everything. That's why he forgave nothing, for that really wasn't in his remit, for in his eyes no crime has an expiry date or grows less heinous, they are all simultaneous, and all persist.

There was, though, another motive behind my decision to return to active service, to accept this mission: the only way not to question the usefulness of what you have done in the past is to keep doing the same thing; the only justification for a murky, muddy existence is to continue to muddy it; the only justification for a long-suffering life is to perpetuate that suffering, to tend it and nourish it and complain about it, just as a life of crime is only sustainable if you persevere as a criminal, if villains persist in their villainy and do harm right left and centre, first to some and then to others until no one is left untouched.

Terrorist organizations cannot give in voluntarily, because if they do, an abyss opens up before them, they see themselves retrospectively and are horrified by their annulment, and therefore their ruin. The serial killer keeps adding to his series of murders because that's the only way he can avoid looking back to the days when he was still innocent and without stain, the only way he can have meaning. To do otherwise would be to reach Lady Macbeth's horrified realization, something almost no one is willing to do, for it requires great integrity, a quality that has vanished from the world: 'Nought's had, all's spent.' In other words: 'We have done infamous deeds and gained nothing.'

That, in our own way, was a feeling we shared with all of them, for me, it had been unbearable to go back to work in the embassy as I had before, even though I concealed this and pretended to be quite happy or grateful and contented; as if nothing had happened in between and I had never moved from there, and my years of absence and isolation and apparent death had never existed either, the years dedicated to stopping misfortunes of which no one knew, given that I averted many of them and they never happened, and what never happens is lost like a ship in a fog from which it never emerges.

On the other hand, I did know what I'd done to avert those misfortunes, so that they would not be inflicted on the very citizens who want nothing to do with us and who disapprove of us without even knowing who we are. They assume we exist and that we have a duty to shield them from dangers and save them from the atrocities committed by those stalking the Realm, eager to destroy it at whatever cost. And yet they refuse to find out more about how we work, because they sense they would feel obliged to condemn our methods and be shocked by them, people demand security but are unwilling to sully themselves, not even with the knowledge of what we do. If we fail, we're guilty of ineptitude or negligence; if we succeed, we're guilty of brutality or murder, when, by chance or by mistake, it becomes known that we succeeded, something that is always best kept under wraps. Then those same citizens complain to high heaven and reproach us for not having been more humane and gentle to the individuals who, if they'd had their way, would have lined them all up and chopped off their heads one by one, or had the whole lot of them blown to pieces.

I had done things that were very unpleasant, indeed repugnant in the eyes of my victims; I had behaved hypocritically, I had wormed and wheedled and provoked, I had won someone's trust only to betray that trust, I had endangered those who had given me their affection and even a kind of hasty, reckless love; I had sent them to prison to serve long sentences or perhaps sent them to their deaths, and I had killed two men with my own hands. That's a brief summary. In war there's no room for regrets.

And yet, when I stop to think, I recall faces and conversations, glasses clinking, people singing, ingenuous smiles and looks and friendly words, slaps on the back and caresses I did not deserve. And the occasional naked body which, believing it was embracing one of its own – a hero in the making – was actually embracing the person who would bring about its future perdition. And little by little, you start to ask if it was all necessary, every action, every promise, every half-truth and every deceit, and the torment begins to eat away at you and overwhelm you. You wake in the middle of the night in a cold, guilt-ridden sweat, assailed by terrible feelings of remorse, caught in the spider's web of what you have done and for which there is no remedy. The only escape is to go back to your old self and do what you used to do, to reoffend and continue fighting real but insignificant enemies, who are the incarnation of the abstract enemy, who will destroy you if you don't get in first and punish him. And at that moment, you understand that, once you've started, once you've taken the first twisted step, you have no alternative but to continue along that twisted path and take another twisted turning.

In fact it was Pérez Nuix or Pat or Nuix (I would call her by one of those three names depending on mood, place or time) who was initially assigned to me as my link, the Molyneux of my new period of exile, in that town in the north-west whose name I had better not mention. Another town with a river, like the English town where I'd taken refuge for several years without ever feeling I'd actually retired because every day I waited to be given permission to return, and where I'd created a temporary family, I hoped the same didn't happen in this Spanish town, though it was unlikely, I couldn't go leaving abandoned children throughout half of Europe. Tupra had reckoned the mission would take me a few months at most, but I knew from experience that everything takes longer and grows more complicated and entangled, and proves to be far more difficult than you were told; besides, our human plans never run smoothly, they always encounter bumps in the road.

I realized that Pérez Nuix was higher in the ranks or enjoyed greater respect than her youth would lead one to expect, although it still wasn't entirely clear to me if she was working for Tupra or for Machimbarrena. I assumed it was probably the former, although the latter would be dealing with the logistics *in situ*. It was, at any rate, a matter of covering up either for CESID, which, at the time, had its hands tied, or for whoever it was who had asked the favour; removing any hint of involvement by the Spanish authorities, who were still so tarnished by the GAL scandal and the subsequent trials, it was a matter of secondary importance that GAL had operated under a different government in the 1980s, the socialist government of Felipe González, who was himself under suspicion, since it was hard to believe that he had been kept completely in the dark. It was a question of shifting the focus away from any Spaniard, be they policeman, secret agent, soldier or civilian, or whoever. If there was dirty work to be done, they could blame the English, that was the idea. Or a lone Englishman acting on his own initiative, a vengeful, vindictive Englishman with scores to settle in Northern Ireland, that is, with the IRA: I was that Englishman. And I was soon to find out that I might also have to do the dirtiest deed of all, so I can't say I was lured into going to that town in the north-west on false pretences.

'If you don't find evidence of her participation in the 1987 attacks,' Pérez Nuix said to me one afternoon. 'If you don't find *enough* evidence for her to be arrested and put on trial with a guarantee of a guilty verdict . . .' She didn't finish the sentence, at least not at first.

'Finding such evidence is well-nigh impossible,' I said at once. 'She won't have kept anything incriminating, not after all these years. No one's that stupid. I'll be doing very well if, out of the three women, I manage to discover and identify with absolute certainty the one woman we're looking for. Then what happens? But what were you about to say? Finish your sentence.'

Nuix was still hesitating. We were in a café in Calle Miguel Ángel, since it was best to discuss the matter away from the embassy, near but not too near, the embassy then had its headquarters on the corner of Calle de Fernando el Santo and Calle Monte Esquinza, in the strange building designed by architects Bryant and Blanco-Soler, one of whom was a brutalist and the other a rationalist.

It was ridiculous that Pat should feel she was superior to me in any respect; her oddly paternalistic attitude towards me during our sporadic sexual encounters was one thing, but it was quite another for her to extend that paternalism into areas in which I was a veteran and she was a novice, in which she was still at the crawling stage, whereas I'd been around the world and back again, or rather had died on the journey and been buried on my return. It was ridiculous that, out of delicacy, she should be reluctant to give me the bad news, if you like. That she should see me as terribly sensitive and fragile. That's what happens when you've been discharged from the service, people imagine you can no longer take the strain and have become a wimp.

'In that case, you would have to be the one to ensure that she no longer represented a risk, that she wasn't still in circulation. That she could no longer harm anyone.' She said all this very slowly and carefully, as if not wanting to frighten me. I understood exactly what she meant though.

'And just how would I achieve that? Apart from the usual method one applies to anyone on this earth. And I don't think that's what you mean.' I wanted to force her to spell it out clearly.

'You know there's only one sure method – the usual one. According to Tupra, you're perfectly well aware of this possibility.'

I sat looking into her lively brown eyes, caught between amusement at the way she was tiptoeing around me and genuine shock at this unexpected turn of events. It hadn't occurred to me that they would go that far once the search was over. As I explained at the beginning, I was brought up the old-fashioned way.

'What, just like that? You're telling me that if there's no chance of bringing her to court, I should bump her off? A woman who may well have distanced herself from all terrorist activities, who may have small children and, for years, have been leading a quiet, peaceful life? Who may have almost half forgotten what she did, and who, if she does remember, may feel intense regret? Isn't killing her going too far? Isn't that a bit over the top?'

Nuix immediately stopped pussyfooting around and revealed her harsh, indignant side, it's so easy to be harsh and indignant when you're young, because you never see what the consequences might be. That's why fanatics court adolescents and recruit them. Tupra was certainly no fanatic, but he knew their methods and was perfectly capable of using them himself.

'If you want over-the-top, the attacks she collaborated on were certainly that. I'm sure the survivors have not "half forgotten" as you put it. I'm sure the person who lost a leg or an arm or was left permanently wheelchair-bound remembers it every day when he or she wakes up and every night on going to bed, at every hour of every day. And do *they* not have reasons for regret – either because they did leave the house or because they didn't? No, they have no reason to regret anything because someone else decided for them, decided quite randomly to eliminate them, like someone playing the lottery or throwing dice. And then there are those who died and can no longer half forget anything or indeed remember anything. Thirty-two people died, if you add up the number of dead from the two attacks. For them there is no "perhaps", all "perhapses" ended ten years ago, and some of the children killed didn't even get to live that long. What are you talking about? A woman who is now a reformed character, contrite, possibly an exemplary wife and mother who adores her children and keeps her poor husband in total ignorance? Because he'll have no idea who he's married to. Someone who has left her crimes behind her and is living a peaceful, private life? That makes it even worse. How can she possibly lead a peaceful life when she's responsible for killing thirty-two people and mutilating many more? That woman has no right to such a life.'

'Probably not,' I said, 'but she does have the right to a trial. And if she can't be tried because there isn't enough evidence, then what? We try her ourselves, sentence her and then execute her? *That's* over the top, Patricia. That's what we call State terrorism, and it puts us on the same level as the terrorists.'

Pérez Nuix's face reflected a mixture of incredulity and disappointment. No, the young find it very easy to be fierce and draconian.

She must have assumed I was battle-hardened and unscrupulous, unaware that scruples increase with experience and age.

'I can't believe you're saying that,' she said. 'Even I know that sometimes, if there's no alternative, you have to put yourself on their level in order to defeat them and so that they don't go on killing. As infrequently as possible, of course, yes, but sometimes. You've been through all that, Tom. If you deny it, I won't believe you. Besides, there is no State involved here.'

I wasn't sure that I had been through all that, not exactly, but I wasn't about to give her a review of my exploits. Nor was I authorized to give her an answer, to tell her about my past vicissitudes. I've kept the worst of them to myself and will have to do so until I die and beyond that too, for the rest of my life and during the uncountable years and centuries when I will be just another dead man, another one who will reveal nothing, and remain eternally impenetrable . . . Perhaps Tupra was right and he really was the one person in the world who knew me best and the only one with whom I could speak openly, because he did know a great deal about what I had done. And now he was once again giving me orders, but this time through Pérez Nuix. He was avoiding having to reveal to me the more unpleasant actions I would be expected to take and that might have prompted me to turn down his proposal and continue my vegetative life commuting between Calle de Lepanto and Calle de Fernando el Santo, with frequent stops in Calle de Pavía.

The café was packed, it was the time of day when people wearily leave their offices and institutes, but don't yet feel like going home. We were surrounded on all sides, and I was worried we might be overheard, although given the unmistakably Spanish clamour, it was unlikely anyone would be able to hear anything from one table to the next.

'I would just remind you that there is such a thing as a statute of limitations or prescriptive period for crimes,' I said to Nuix. 'Yes, I know, not these particular crimes. But I don't understand why we feel that a ten-year prescriptive period is somehow not enough, but that twenty years – or whatever it is in Spain – is; it must depend on the seriousness of the crime, I suppose, as it does almost everywhere in the world. However, with very few exceptions, such periods do sooner or later lapse. What does it matter if it's only ten years when the person who committed the crimes is no longer the person they were, if they no longer represent any danger? That can happen, and does. What sense does it make that after nineteen years and eleven months have elapsed a crime can still merit the severest of sentences, but not thirty days later? It's idiotic setting time limits like that. One day I'm serving a thousand-year jail term and the next I walk free because that's simply not feasible any more? Suddenly there's no guilt and no murder and everything is erased by turning over one leaf on the calendar? Does time convert something that existed into something that didn't? Justice is absurd, a fantasy, impossible. We act as if justice existed and we happily dish it out when there can be no justice. Accepting its meaningless rules is another matter, we have to do something to keep up appearances. But I'm not sure. If that woman has spent the last ten years having completely withdrawn from that world, and doubtless hidden away from her fellow terrorists too . . . She probably won't want to see hide nor hair of them, while they're probably as keen to find her as you are, to have their revenge on her because she's turned her back on them, because she's a deserter, or simply too half-hearted, who knows. But if she's no longer the person she was, if she's now the person she is in that provincial town, are we simply going to bump her off, just like that? What does it matter if the legal time limit for her crimes to be punished has not yet lapsed? If there is a statute of limitations on crimes of terrorism, then . . .'

'There shouldn't be such limitations on any crime,' said Pérez Nuix coolly. We had never discussed this kind of thing, and I was shocked by her coldness; or her absolutism. She clearly belonged to the school of Tupra, and he was in the process of moulding her; later on, he would have to tone down that absolutism though. 'You're right to say that it's absurd. Those laws are wrong and we shouldn't pay them the slightest heed. Just because something happened a long time ago, does that make it any less serious? No. It's just as you say: the passage of time doesn't annul anything, nor should it. It doesn't even mitigate. Neither should repentance, that would be far too easy: "Oh dear, I killed some children, but I'm really sorry." Enough of all this nonsense of pardoning people. That's why we're here, because justice is too lenient.'

I couldn't help looking at her with some surprise, in a new light, and not a favourable one, not at least in my eyes. We had always had an amiable, easy-going relationship, and I had never thought of her as ruthless, although, as I said, she could be uncompromising in her job, assiduous. Not that I'd had occasion to find this out. Not even

Tupra would have been so categorical in his utter contempt for pardoning criminals, he showed a degree of flexibility – often born of cynicism – that she seemed to lack. Perhaps his method was as follows: first create a fanatic who is up for anything, then gradually dial down that fanaticism, as and when you see fit. Pat had not yet reached the dialling-down stage and was still in the crudely fanatical phase.

'I don't know if time can annul or mitigate anything,' I said, 'but it does breed indifference. I don't think anyone really cares about crimes committed two hundred years ago, or even a hundred years ago, the crimes of 1897 say. If those who committed them were still alive, I very much doubt that anyone would waste their energy pursuing them, not even you. We take it for granted that there have always been crimes, that they're part and parcel of the world, that every era had their own crimes and it was up to the people then to punish them. If they failed to do so, that has nothing to do with those who come after, we have our own crimes to deal with. The sheer quantity is so vast we wouldn't be able to cope. That's why, in the days when people believed, they left it all to the Final Judgement. They were confident that God would sort everyone out and know which acts deserved to be condemned and which were justifiable; as well as whose repentance had been sincere enough to save them. It was a more comforting world, in which we expected God's justice would reach the parts that human justice did not.'

'What are you saying, Tom? You're harking back to the Stone Age there. Nowadays we know that the only justice that counts is ours, so we'd better get a move on. Even people who are still believers accept that, and they're always quick to call in any debts if they can, here and now and as soon as possible.'

She spoke in a very scornful tone, as if she considered that I too belonged in the Stone Age, simply because I'd mentioned the divine justice on which people had relied for centuries. She was the type of person of whom there appear to be more and more: they pretend that

149

anything that doesn't exist now never existed; they're determined to close down the past as quickly as possible, with no going back, as if the past were an obstacle. I didn't even bother to respond to her remarks.

'You, for example, don't give a toss about what happened in Madrid in, say, 1766. Or in 1808, when there was certainly no shortage of barbaric acts. At most, you feel a kind of abstract sadness, as fleeting as the sadness provoked by fictions, like when you read a novel or see a film. In 1808, there was a French invasion and a popular uprising, of which all that remain are Goya's images, but you go and see them in the Prado and they already feel like fictions invented by the artist. A guerrilla war that lasted several years. It happened and that's that, today no one gets all steamed up about it, and not just because both victims and executioners are dead. And distance does, of course, mitigate and annul. At some point, the woman we're looking for will also be dead. Then she will definitely be a long way away and no one will remember her or the attacks she took part in and that still make our blood run cold; but less so than when they happened ten years ago, not as much. It may be that she's horrified by what she did or helped others to do. She may no longer be a danger to anyone. On the contrary, she may want only to save lives, to make amends. Or to return to the vocabulary of the Stone Age: to redeem herself.'

'What happened here in 1766?' She had retained the date that she didn't know, because it bothered her not to know something, because she was, as I say, assiduous and punctilious.

'The Esquilache Riots.'

'Who or what was Esquilache? And what riots?'

'The Marqués de Esquilache, a Sicilian in the service of King Charles III, who was, by the way, the best king we've had. Look him up in a history book. Anyway, Esquilache decided to ban long capes and broad-brimmed hats as a way of preventing the populace from carrying concealed weapons. This annoyed the people, who were already extremely annoyed about the shortage of bread, soap and oil, but that's by the by. The fact is that the Guardia Valona, the Walloon Guard, armed with sabres and on horseback, charged the rioters, slicing open the heads of men, women and children, even babies it's said; and they fired on the crowd gathered in Plaza Mayor. You didn't even know that such a massacre ever took place, and why should you? It lasted three or four days, and hundreds died. You see how everything is annulled and forgotten. Or would you like to do something about it now? Every country and every city has witnessed similarly bloody episodes about which the living neither know nor care. It's nothing to do with them, even if the events took place in the very streets they're blithely strolling along now.'

'All right, perhaps things that happened in the remote past do have a kind of expiry date, but only because we're powerless to do anything about them, they've slipped from our grasp and there's no way of punishing them now. *A la fuerza ahorcan* we say. Needs must when the devil drives.' Like my former tutor, Mr Southworth, she knew lots of idioms, but didn't always use them appropriately, she was, after all, more English than Spanish, unlike me, I suppose, despite my career as a defender of the Realm. 'But the attacks on Hipercor and in Zaragoza, they're still warm and could be repeated at any moment. ETA are still killing like there's no tomorrow. The IRA less so, but they haven't yet disbanded and there's no signed agreement with them, assuming their signature is worth anything. Their leaders are very close to signing, some of them, before they get amnestied, which will happen sooner or later; countries give way, we don't. You yourself said as much: we should deal with the crimes of our own times, not wait until they've gone cold and are beyond reach, beyond our reach and that of those who come after us. Besides, everything is relative. If those Walloon Guards were to be brought back to life (a mad hypothesis, I know), probably no one would bother to make them or that guy Esquilache pay for slicing open the heads of women and children. But if it turned out Hitler were still alive and was found hiding away somewhere, an ancient old man . . . well, he'd be over a hundred . . . even you would put a bullet in him if you could. You would have done so ten or fifteen years ago, when he was over ninety. And you wouldn't bother with a trial, because that would create all kinds of problems: clever defence lawyers eager for their moment in the spotlight, all kinds of murderers and other idiots trooping off to prison to visit him, humanitarian protests . . . You would have got rid of him without a second thought. A bullet through the head and that would be that, isn't that right?'

Pérez Nuix amused me with her exaggerated, outlandish ideas, with her passion and her certainty, fanaticism always has an element of enthusiasm, which is why it's so dangerous and so contagious, it makes everything look very simple, which is precisely what appeals to the multitudes. Temperance and moderation don't grab the imagination, or else it takes a long time, years not days. I thought then of Walter Pidgeon or the hunter Alan Thorndike. He had hesitated at a time when people still didn't know that much about Hitler, before he opened the gates of hell. In Patricia's example, though, I would already have had all the facts, I would have known the magnitude of his crimes and the whole story, and I wouldn't have been confronted with a man in his fifties, in his toxic prime, but with an old man incapable of doing any further harm. Although who knows: as long as someone's alive, he or she can still inflict harm, even a decrepit old man. And I would have been influenced by the facts, by his identity, by his name: assuming that he was Hitler, without the shadow of a doubt, very few people would take pity on him, would feel any compassion, however defenceless he was; nor any magnanimity, however old and frail and doddery he seemed, however helpless and inoffensive.

Nuix was right: I would have put a bullet through his head without a second thought, for all the killing and the discord, for the incomprehensible carnage he had caused, a carnage that remains incomprehensible to this day and probably will until the end of time. Yes, she was right: I wouldn't have brought him to trial, I wouldn't have run the risk of today's soft-centred men letting him live out his life in a nice, civilized prison with a television in his cell (the Führer loved watching films and would have lapped up TV serials), or even set him free.

You can never be sure what might happen if you allow the murderer to speak, to deny, to explain himself, and Hitler had extraordinary oratorical gifts. True, only imbecilic, vacuous, belligerent ideas issued from his mouth, but he could convince his audience of those same vacuous, belligerent, imbecilic ideas, and the people of this new century are even more manipulable and easily impressed than those of the 1930s. However, I wasn't going to give in to Patricia's arguments so easily.

'I'm not sure,' I said. 'Possibly. But that isn't going to happen, so your imaginary scenario is pointless.'

'Not entirely pointless,' she replied, unwilling to let go. 'Transfer that hypothesis to reality, to our current situation. What that woman did may be less in quantity, but no less evil in essence. And she won't have repented or reformed. Anyone who plants bombs intending to kill a random number of people carries that capacity in her veins, and our veins don't change. I mean, you're no innocent yourself. What's more, anyone who does such a thing has no time to feel remorse, they're too busy surviving and avoiding punishment, too busy saving themselves and justifying themselves, and convincing themselves that they performed an important service for the country or the cause, a service demanded of them by country or cause. Terrorists aren't patriots or revolutionaries or believers or militants. First off, they're murderers, and they seek out a sphere or an ambit in which murder will be rewarded and applauded. When someone kills another person, their first, second or even third thought isn't for the victim, but for themselves: "Now what am I going to do?" Even if they killed someone involuntarily or unintentionally. Even if they accidentally ran over a child, most people wouldn't clutch their head in despair because of what has happened to the victim, because of the irreparable harm they've done, but because their normal life will be cut short, because of what might happen to them next. They're concerned above all with escaping the consequences of their actions. With getting rid of the corpse and inventing an alibi if necessary, with, as you well know, eliminating all evidence and covering their tracks. And then exonerating themselves. Grief for the victim comes much later, if it ever does. I'm not saying there aren't exceptions, but that's the norm. We depend on our subjectivity, our perspective and our survival instinct, which overrides everything . . . By the way, what was the Walloon Guard doing in Madrid in 1766? They're Belgians aren't they, Walloons? I mean Flemish and Walloon.'

'Efficient mercenaries, I imagine. After all, why is there a Swiss Guard in the Vatican? Why did Emperor Charles V take lansquenets with him when he sacked Rome? According to you, they were, I suppose, the murderers of their day, looking for a place where they'd have a licence to kill, with money and booty thrown in.'

'I don't know, there must have been all kinds of reasons. But, generally speaking, mercenaries were a different thing entirely. They had no better way of earning a living, they were fighting for a wage, engaging in hand-to-hand combat. They weren't fighting for their beliefs or ideals, and so they weren't vicious or brutal and didn't kill more than they needed to; nor did they operate in secret like terrorists, who don't really put themselves in danger and nearly always attack people who are unarmed,' she said confidently, as if this were a matter to which she had given much thought; or perhaps she was just very quick at improvising arguments. 'By the way, I've no idea who the lansquenets were. And I didn't know about the sack of Rome either. When was that? And why?' Pérez Nuix wasn't really up to speed on history, having studied other things.

'You don't need to know that right now, but it happened in 1527. It's all in the history books. You should try reading them some time.' How long it takes young people of all ages to learn about the past. This knowledge should be transmitted to us while we're in the womb, that way we wouldn't have to learn the same thing over and over, generation after generation, each individual on his or her own account. Me too, when I was young.

Nuix ignored my minimally malevolent comment. She read plenty of books, but they were all about the twentieth century in which she lived and never left (although she would doubtless dive eagerly into the twenty-first century), as if nothing that happened before could be of any use to her or even concern her.

'Be that as it may, the woman must pay for what she did. We have her almost in our sights, surrounded. And we must, at all costs, prevent her from one day returning to her old ways. I said if you don't find evidence. If you find irrefutable evidence, she'll be arrested and put on trial, just like the people who planted the bomb in the shopping mall. There was another woman involved I seem to remember. Or was that in Zaragoza?'

'No, that was in Barcelona. Josefa, a woman called Josefa. Apparently, she hasn't altered her ideas one iota and shows no sign of repentance. She's in prison, of course, and prison does initially, and for a number of years, succeed in blinding and enraging people still more. Then it can assuage, but only sometimes. Our Northern Irish lady, on the other hand, is leading a normal life. I may succeed in identifying her, but, as I said, there's no way I'm going to find any evidence.'

Pat looked around her again, this time as if she didn't want to be seen. No one was taking any notice of us. Then she opened her handbag, rummaged around in it a little, and placed a pocket tape recorder on the table. It was switched on.

'Draw her out. Get a confession from her and record it. I've been recording our conversation for the last couple of minutes. See how easy it is?'

I eyed her curiously, and, I fear, rather patronizingly, but not, I hope, sympathetically. She really was far too optimistic, she had never done any work in the field.

'Really? But then I didn't have a confession to make and, besides, I didn't care if you were recording me. I wasn't on my guard. Rewind a bit and see how we sound.'

She did as I asked. The hubbub, the sheer noise in the café was so deafening that our voices sounded muffled, half smothered, and you could barely make out what we were saying.

'See how easy it is,' I said, repeating her words. 'Do you really think she's going to confess to anyone that she took part in such crimes? Especially not to a stranger, a new boy in town. A lot of ETA members are stupid, but not that stupid. And the woman may have been trained by the IRA, not that they're very much brighter, but still. They're brighter than their enemies, the gun-toting unionists, and that's something.'

'Your job is to stop being a stranger and to gain her trust.'

'The trust of three women at once? Don't talk nonsense. It's not a very big town, and they may well know each other, and if they do, they're bound to talk about me, the new boy. They might confide in each other about the relationship each of them has with me. Women talk.'

'So do men.'

'No one's denying that, but women do talk. We're the same in that respect. However much some people may insist on the differences between men and women, we're really not that different.'

Pérez Nuix said nothing for a moment, biting her lower lip. I assumed that she could see the difficulty and accepted that I was right: no one is going to tell anyone that they collaborated in the slaughter of thirty-two people, including some three-year-old girls, and in the space of six months or less. (Nineteen-eighty-seven must have been unbearable in Spain, but I was far away then.) Unless you're Josefa Ernaga, Caride, Troitiño or their leader Potros, I suppose, and you boast about your exploits in prison before your fellow terrorists who have less blood on their hands and who will see those exploits as heroic deeds. But that isn't quite what she was thinking. Nuix hadn't given up, and it was as if she'd read my thoughts.

'I can't give you full details yet,' she said. 'I'll pass you the reports in a few days' time. I imagine you'll have to memorize and then destroy them before you leave. Anyway, you know what to do. But, as I understand it, you'll be able to see and hear, or only hear, I'm not sure, what's going on in the homes of two of those women; we're working on that now. There'll almost certainly be microphones, and possibly a hidden camera in one of the rooms, probably the living room, because bedrooms spend too much time empty and in silence. Apparently this isn't feasible in the home of the third woman. But you'll be living almost directly opposite her house, admittedly at a distance, on the other side of the river, but with a pair of powerful binoculars and as long as she doesn't close her curtains . . . You won't hear anything, but at least you might be able to see something. That will be of some help, and means you don't have to depend solely on getting close to all three of them. Whichever woman it is, she might make that confession to someone else and then you can hear it and record it. Or she may not even need to make a confession, but might talk about the attacks with someone who's already in the know, with a former colleague who's there on a visit, I don't know, anything's possible.'

So that was why she had fallen silent, because she wasn't supposed to give me that information, not yet. She really was an optimist.

'Don't be so sure, Patricia, don't be so naïve. Even then I probably still won't get my hands on any evidence. Or only enough to satisfy *us* perhaps, but not enough to go to court.'

'The former would be enough as far as we're concerned. Then we'd move to the second option, as planned.'

'Oh really? But what does that have to do with me? If I do succeed in identifying her, they could send in someone else afterwards, some-one more experienced. Tupra didn't say anything to me about any second option, he just asked me to find and identify her. That's all I agreed to, not to finishing anyone off.'

'That's what he asked you initially, but we need to have all eventualities covered. Plan B, C and D. Don't worry, you won't get as far as D.'

'If you could actually guarantee that, we wouldn't even be talking about it. Besides, as I said, that would be putting us on their level, it would be State terrorism.'

'But as I said, there is no State involved here. So our hands are freer, and as a Spanish general, whose name I can't recall, put it very clearly in an interview he gave some time ago: "In the struggle against terrorism, there are some things that should not be done. If they are done, then they should not be spoken about. If they are spoken about, they must be denied." He thus calmly summarized what all States, without exception, know. In this case, we're working outside the State. Or if necessary underneath it or above. But only if there's no alternative. Quite apart from that, it would be unwise to involve more people. The fewer the better, as always. The less you know the better too. You'll only know what you need to know at each stage, nothing more. As before, as usual.'

This very young young woman said 'as before' and 'as usual' as if she'd been privy to my entire career and to all my activities, and yet I'd started out before she'd even been born or was still in the cradle. She was clearly very close to Tupra, which is why she considered me a legend, and him, I imagined, a myth. She was speaking for him. All that she had said were instructions coming from him, I saw this now; I was once again under his orders, something I found both mortifying and revivifying.

'Anyway, since you'll be there on the spot, we're not going to send in anyone else. Unless it became imperative, but I don't think so. You'll know the terrain and the woman's habits. And according to Tupra, you *are* very experienced, especially when it comes to thinking on your feet.'

I wondered if that was all he'd told her, in so many words ('Tom's very good at coming up with radical solutions,' for example) or if he'd told her about the two men I'd killed. Or if he would have added a few more to my tally, who knows. That's the trouble with people who've known us since we were young, and who appear to speak with authority and on whose lips everything sounds like the truth. Both when they're telling the truth and when they're lying.

Yes, I waited a week before telling Berta of my departure, I decided to do so only when I was just about to leave so that there would be no time for her to try and dissuade me. I didn't honestly think she would bother, but you can never be sure how someone will react. One thing I could be sure of was that she would frown disapprovingly; that it would seem wrong to her, a dangerous mistake, a backward step, a relapse, a sign that my old malady was incurable. Paradoxically, she knew less about my adventures than the newbie Nuix would now know, but she had, on principle, always been opposed to my activities. She felt they were, by their very nature, grubby and immoral, that they were based on premeditated, wilful treachery and deceit, and consisted in never attacking head-on but always from behind. She was intelligent enough though (she was very intelligent in fact) to realize that they were also necessary for the world to continue functioning and for our apparent, fragile peace, and to keep shocks and tremors to a minimum.

She didn't condemn them outright, she wasn't one of those dim-witted citizens who demand transparency and fair play even when we're pitted against the most cunning, destructive and underhand of enemies, simply so that they can feel honest and decent; she wasn't the sort who demand the abolition of the secret services, of 'reptile funds', 'sleaze' and 'payola' – as the hypocritical press refer to them – to show how virtuous they are. But she hated me being part of that murky, clandestine world: others could do that work, but not her husband, with whom she still occasionally shared a pillow, although less and less frequently. Yes, other remote figures unknown to her, of whom we would never know anything, whose actions we would never find out about and whose faces we would never see. Berta was, then, not very different from most people, who basically avoid thinking about us. They rely totally on our phantasmagorical protection, like that of guardian angels who are there but never reveal themselves, except that we are very nasty angels and no one ever imagines us hovering and fluttering above them, they want us under lock and key in the catacombs. They feel ashamed of their dependence on such grim, unscrupulous individuals while, at the same time, hoping that, when it comes to defending them and saving them, we will show a total lack of scruples.

'I'm leaving the day after tomorrow,' I told Berta on 12 January, when I went to see her as I sometimes did on a Sunday; I waited until the children had disappeared off with their friends before making my announcement. 'I'll be away for a few months, I don't know how long exactly. Would you mind telling Guillermo and Elisa, it would be harder for me not to give them a proper explanation. You just have to tell them that you don't know, that it's something to do with work; after all, you and I don't always tell each other everything, and they know that.'

Berta shot me a quick, knowing look; I saw in her eyes a mixture of disappointment, pity and indifference. I had long since lost her esteem, a huge loss to which I had resigned myself; I still merited a kind of toned-down version of her affection and her tolerance, the kind you might feel for a former lover or for a brother who has had a rough ride in life and tends to be pretty much of a disaster, in life, that is, although not necessarily professionally. People who go off the rails early on and can't get back on track, or who, as you discover one day, don't want to get back on track and who, contrary to appearances, are happy with their rollercoaster existence. I still found

Berta's eyes captivating; they had lost their youthful gleam, but were full of good cheer and a feeling of confidence in the future, a vague, possibly hollow future, that went no further than the brief burst of optimism one feels on waking each morning. For some people this is enough, they're content to be and to wait, or just to be. They're nearly always women, who are fortunate enough to see simply being alive as an achievement, a triumph.

'Actually, you've never told me anything, not since we got married or even before that. Not about the really important stuff.' She said this without rancour, which, at that stage in our lives, would have been out of place; it was more a statement of fact. 'So you're not going to say goodbye to them?'

'No, there's no need. I won't be very far away and I'll be able to visit now and then. So why make a big thing out of an absence they'll barely notice. It's not as if they see me every day.'

'You don't see me every day either, so why are you telling me?'

She had realized at once that I was going back to active service, returning to the thing that had spoiled her entire life and of which she disapproved. I didn't imagine she was going to throw this in my face – it was no longer her task in life, and besides it mattered little to her now what I did or didn't do – nevertheless, I felt ashamed to have to make this confession. It was like acknowledging I was a hopeless case, a sick man, an addict, a weak character.

'It's best if you know, just in case there should be some emergency. Plus I think I owe it to you. To tell you the little I can tell you. It's never been any big deal, and I've always been grateful to you for not questioning me, for not boxing me into a corner.'

She was standing in the middle of the living room, ironing the kids' clothes. She didn't look up from the shirt on the ironing board.

'So you're going back to your old job. I thought that was all over. That you didn't want to do it any more. That you were tired.' Her tone was neutral and, I thought, without a hint of reproach.

'And there's a part of me that really doesn't want to go back, a part that's very tired,' I said, feeling awkward despite her forbearance. 'But I realize I can't go on like this, feeling useless and passive. Feeling that I'm nothing but a past. The only way not to think about, how can I describe it, an abundant past is to replace it with a busy, fully engaged present, not one of pure routine. Do you understand what I mean? You don't approve, do you?'

She was still busy ironing the shirt, but she did look up for a moment, and now I seemed to see in her eyes a sterner glint, automatic, involuntary, or perhaps retrospective.

'You know what I think about that job, about the whole business, and always have; you've obliged me only to imagine it and one always imagines the worst. But what does it matter what I think? It didn't even matter years ago, when it should have mattered. I only hope that your rejoining doesn't bring the rest of us any problems.'

No, she'd never liked it, not just because it was such a hazardous existence and because of the dangers to me as well as to her and the kids (that's what she meant by that last remark), but because she felt it was, by its nature, intellectually and morally corrupt. On one occasion, though, she had seen our activities in a more positive light, and hadn't entirely condemned the possible murder (or so she suspected) of a couple in Madrid who, during one of my absences, had befriended her and won her trust, only to end up threatening Guillermo when he was still only a baby, a terrifying incident she told me about later when I finally reappeared.

The couple gave their name as Ruiz Kindelán and claimed to be working for the Irish embassy, where, it turned out, no one had ever heard of them. I never saw them. By the time I came home, they'd already left the scene, having supposedly been transferred to Rome. The man spoke perfect Spanish with no trace of an accent; the woman, Mary Kate O'Riada or O'Reidy, her maiden name, had a very strong accent and made lots of grammatical errors. I assumed they – or at least she – were from Northern Ireland or Ireland, working for the IRA, and later on, I assured Berta that she needn't worry, that it wouldn't happen again, that there was no chance the same diabolical couple would ever reappear in her life.

I reported the incident to Blakeston, Tupra's very efficient assistant at the time; I'd left the matter in his expert hands and forgotten all about it, called away by other more urgent matters. The truth is that I hadn't kept a close eye on the sequence of events, and if I made that promise to Berta, I did so only because Blakeston had said to me: 'Don't worry, we'll look into it. It doesn't appear to be a major incident and, as I understand it, nothing actually happened, and your family is fine. You just forget about it and I'll take care of it.' Rather than because I had any reason to believe that he had identified, located and neutralized the fake Kindeláns. I trusted Blakeston and asked no more about it. To reassure my wife, though, I did say: 'I can promise you that they'll have completely forgotten about us' and 'Nothing like that will ever happen again'; and I said this in such a sombre, emphatic tone that she assumed that we – either myself or another member of that 'we' – had eliminated them.

And I saw that she didn't find this possibility particularly shocking. That it even offered her some relief, not just for herself, but the relief that comes from the sense of justice done. She had reacted as would most people who think of themselves as pure and noble: theory is one thing and practice quite another, principles and convictions are one thing and someone threatening me and mine, my children, quite another.

That fellow Ruiz Kindelán had played around with a lighter over Guillermo's cradle, after 'accidentally' sprinkling the sheets with lighter fuel. Berta had been filled with panic at the thought of her child in flames, and by Mary Kate's complete indifference. That's why the couple deserved death, or to have their legs or their back broken, they deserved never to be able to walk again or to unleash more crimes upon the earth. People are full of fine feelings when they're not directly involved or not caught up in something themselves, but become totally ruthless once they are, when they see danger hovering over them and their children.

If that had been Berta's reaction *a posteriori*, when she'd cooled off slightly, what would it have been like in the heat of the moment: the same as everyone else's. I've seen a civilized, magnanimous individual become a pitiless beast, or more than that, a creature in the grip of quite unnecessary cruelty, the product of his fear. I've seen a kind, charitable young woman in a situation of imminent threat, begging her possible saviour, 'Kill him, kill him, do whatever you need to. Pluck out his eyes, burn him, crush him,' as if she were talking about a cockroach or a sticky bat entangled in her hair. I've seen a peace-loving old man resigned to death leap to his feet with uncanny agility and beat a man on the back with his walking stick, and continue beating him on the head again and again even once the man was lying unconscious on the ground, as if he could not hit him often enough to ensure that he himself was safe. I saw him clinging on to life when he had already bidden it farewell, and he did, in fact, die of his illness a few days after beating out the brains of his attacker. What did it matter to him if he kicked the bucket a few days sooner or later, either in a swift act of violence or in a long-drawn-out agony, as subsequently proved to be the case?

Perhaps what we cannot tolerate is that we should be killed by someone else, that others should decide the time and manner of our death, and faced by that, we rebel like savages: 'I'm going to kill you or at least try to.' The only ones who don't rebel are those who have been sentenced and know the time and manner of their death beforehand, those who have already been condemned, even if it was only yesterday: Marie Antoinette, her husband, or Anne Boleyn and so many hundreds and thousands more. And even then, with their head on the block, are they not all hoping, right up until the very last moment, to be reprieved, are they not all still hoping, even when the sword has already begun its falling arc or the guillotine its descent? Perhaps they continue to hope for a couple of seconds – perhaps – when their head has already been separated from their body. 'And any action is a step to the block, to the fire, down the sea's throat or to an illegible stone . . .' I recalled those lines by Eliot that had accompanied me since the very first day I met Tupra and Blakeston.

'There's no way it'll cause you any problems,' I said. 'I've spent years away from it all, and there won't be any weirdos out there who know of your existence.'

She again raised her head, she was ironing a skirt of hers now, one that I'd seen her wearing, and that I had perhaps once pulled down or up.

'You got tired of being inside and now you're tired of being outside. I can understand that, it's a known process, a very youthful phenomenon. Your children are currently immersed in it. And who can guarantee that you won't get tired of it again? Is that how you see the rest of your life, is that your plan? Always wanting to be where you're not, always coming and going? Well, if that's what you want, fine,' she murmured with a coldness that sounded more like scorn. The tone of someone who, finding another person utterly impossible, washes her hands of him and lets him go his own sweet way, without even bothering to warn him that there's a tree directly in his path and that he's heading straight for it. 'Apart from wanting to escape the daily grind and feeling dissatisfied with your life, is there some other reason? If you don't mind my asking. If you do, then don't worry. I'm not exactly dying of curiosity.'

I could tell her something or I could say nothing. I chose the former, I think with the puerile intention of leaving her at least minimally intrigued, or very slightly shaking her out of her indifference. I accepted what she said, that I had no right to complain about our situation, since I was, after all, the main or probably the only culprit; what I couldn't bear, though, was to think that she cared nothing about my life. She had spent years not knowing if I was dead and hoping I was still alive, and her hopes had been rewarded. Now, on the other hand, or so it seemed to me, she didn't care whether I remained on earth or made a quick dash for the exit. It was on my return to life that I had ceased to exist for her. You don't dispense with a ghost, because a ghost has no expiry date; but you can disregard an unnecessary, defeated, self-absorbed, gloomy husband.

'Tupra was here. He came to Madrid to ask me a favour, something that only I can do, well, that almost no one else could do.'

Berta now set the iron down and turned it off. As if she feared she might get distracted and burn the skirt. She rested one hand on her hip, semi-akimbo, and regarded me with a mixture of irony and disillusionment, or perhaps mockery, although I didn't quite know why. She looked very attractive in that pose, but I didn't for a moment consider telling her this, still less doing anything about it.

'Ah, that explains everything. He made you feel useful and active. The persuasive Mr Tupra, capable of persuading anyone to do anything. Even something that would never even occur to you, that you would never dream of doing.' For a moment, she remained thoughtful or reflective; she pressed the back of her other hand to her cheek, as if she were tentatively taking her temperature. 'So he was here, was he?'

There was a hint of annoyance in her voice. Perhaps she thought it really was the absolute limit that my former boss should come and retrieve me and drag me off. She didn't know about the thousand and one adventures he and I had shared, stretching back into our personal antiquity, but she did know that we'd parted on bad terms, or I had.

'Why do you say that? Anyone would think he'd persuaded you to do something extraordinary too.'

'He convinced me you were dead, Tomás,' she snapped back.

'Isn't that extraordinary enough? For years, I thought he must be right, for years, I believed him.'

'But that', I thought, 'was an idea that must have occurred to Berta anyway, a thousand times, in dreams and when wide awake. She must be referring to something else, because that irritated tone borders on resentment.' For the first time, a very remote but troubling idea came into my head. Or perhaps it was the second time. However, this was not the moment to insist, to probe, to question. Our time had expired, or mine had. Yes, it was my time that had expired once again.

V

The most striking thing about the apartment they had rented in Miguel Centurión's name in that town in the north-west was the large window from which he could contemplate a stretch of the river, at the point where it narrowed, as rivers usually do when passing through expanding settlements, and to the right, as if on a stage set, he could see one of the bridges that crossed the river, the one most used by the inhabitants, and which, from his perspective, was almost perpendicular to his building. He could see the whole bridge from the left-hand side of his living room, and that was where he placed a small desk so that he could watch the parade of passers-by each time he looked up from his reading or his marking. During the first days and nights of his sojourn, when he had still only made a few contacts, and the cold weather made staying in more enticing, he tended to look up more often and for longer, intrigued or possibly absorbed by the sight of all those people, fascinated by their simultaneous variety and homogeneity. Early in the morning, before he set off for the school where, as he had requested, they had found him a post as a teacher of English and of a couple of other subjects if they came up – I was very experienced as a teacher after my years of exile in that other provincial town where I'd lived with a wife and a daughter, whose faces were gradually fading from memory – he would observe, with curiosity and a touch of envy, the toings and froings of the locals on their way to work.

Most walked with a brisk or even a hurried early-morning pace, all knew where they were going and why they were going where they were going, they'd probably spent years following the same route to carry out the same tasks, which, as tends to be the case in ordinary towns, did not actually require any great haste or getting up with the lark. However, some smaller towns do aspire to feeling big and bustling, and, basing themselves on a purely intuitive ignorance, they imitate the manners they imagine to prevail in the metropolises; this is particularly evident in the mornings, when, newly awoken and under the stimulus of the icy temperatures, often camouflaged by skies of a deceptively heraldic blue, the inhabitants feel an urgent need to be up and about, even though no one is actually summoning them to work. At that hour, the bridge was as busy with pedestrians as any bridge in London.

And this was what immediately provoked Centurión's envy, the sense that he was not part of a community where everyone had their place, that he had not been born there and so didn't naturally blend in. He saw how people greeted each other, some without stopping, with a smile or a nod or the wave of a gloved hand, while others paused to exchange a few quick words, but all were filled with an air of strange, everyday euphoria, just to be there all together with barely a single absentee – a significant proportion of the community – as had happened nearly every morning for many years; the euphoria of belonging perhaps, symbolized by that simultaneous crossing of the bridge uniting the two shores, by the mere sight of those heading over in the opposite direction, by the feeling that they were all walking on solid, common ground, just above the waters. What he almost envied were those existences which, he imagined had, from the very start, been carefully planned and mapped out, and had known none of the shocks or dramatic digressions I had experienced, and no adventures either and certainly no crimes, nor the kind of responsibilities I had shouldered for more than half my life: no one chooses a town like that – or only the extremely vindictive or evil – in order to threaten it, still less destroy it.

On those first few days, shut away in his apartment after school, in the early winter dark, he would again sit down at the window and watch the bridge, occupied now by citizens who, walking at a slower, more leisurely pace, would be heading for the older, more central part of the town, where most of the restaurants and cheap eating places were to be found, the bars and clubs, the discotheques, the cinemas, a concert hall, the occasional visiting theatre group, or else returning from work, their thoughts subdued or, rather, dejected, having discovered, yet again, after another day, that their town continued to be merely average, with room for only modest surprises, variations on the simple theme of a gentle, sleepy melody. As the day progressed, the rhythm of the place slowed, grew more languid, and those January evenings resembled 'Sundays exiled from the infinite' as a poet or a novelist once said, I can't quite remember which. When night fell, though, even on working days, there would be a sudden, restrained quickening of the pulse, and he would see lively groups of ordinary married couples crossing the bridge, along with bewildered, eager tourists whose main priority now was to party until they dropped – the Cathedral and the Monastery were a permanent draw even in the coldest months – along with disparate hordes of young people – it was a university town, with a number of different faculties – determined to have fun. Regardless of whether it was snowing or raining or if the sky was clear, cold and starry.

Miguel Centurión spied on them all from his desk, mainly in order to familiarize himself with the customs and rhythms of that northwestern town, so that he could learn to imitate them as quickly as possible. He needed to immerse himself in the town, to become just another element in the landscape. After a week, or two weeks at most, he must have been seen by most of the population, and a smaller number would have known his name and found out that he was the new English teacher in that long-established school, someone who wasn't just passing through but who had come to stay, at least for what remained of the term and possibly further terms; or who knows, gradually, from one year to the next, he would end up staying for ever and inadvertently become part of the whole.

He knew this was not the case, that his time there had an end date and that the sooner he reached it the better. His task was to get to know three women, two of whom were of no account, a waste of effort; to befriend them, talk to them, observe and draw them out, and, if feasible, coax from the one who did matter the thing she would never confess to anyone unless she needed the simulacrum of expiation involved in opening up and unburdening her conscience, although this he thought highly unlikely. To charm them or make himself attractive to them, to seduce them in the most vulgar sense or in the broader sense, that is, to flatter them, because there is nothing one treasures more nor to which one can become more easily accustomed than praise and attention – to the fond, attentive eye, adulatory and admiring – and once one has experienced it, nothing is harder to give up. Even if the flattering remark comes from a mosquito.

Many years before, nine, nine and eight respectively, those three women were in the same situation as Centurión. None of them had been born in that town in the north-west and all had once been new arrivals, intruders, incomers; they'd settled there when they were fairly young, but not so young as to have no previous career, some people are very impatient to climb aboard the wheel of the world, and anyone can commit crimes and atrocities – so much easier than becoming a benefactor or achieving great things – you don't need to study or train or have plenty of money, you just have to allow yourself to be convinced and manipulated by visionaries and have the necessary combination of nerve and anger, and quite a high percentage of adolescents do have bloodthirsty imaginations, almost as high a percentage as those who are, by nature, compassionate. Most of the former, fortunately, content themselves with just daydreaming about destruction, bombings and machine-gunnings, and very few actually take steps to carry these out. Adolescents are dangerous, as dangerous as they are endangered.

This is really why those three women were deemed suspicious: because they had arrived there after 1987 – the year of the attacks in Barcelona and Zaragoza – with hardly any verifiable references or past history. (Each of them had told a little of their story to those who had become their close or intimate friends, including two husbands; but those stories could have been invented, and we all have dark periods in our lives about which we never speak or feel no need to

177

mention; and of course no one asks about what they don't know and cannot even surmise.)

Perhaps they took fright when they saw that two of the terrorists, Domingo Troitiño and Josefa Ernaga, who had planted the bomb at Hipercor, were arrested in September of that year, having been at large for less than three months after the killings. Then they were tried and found guilty, while the ETA leader Santi Potros and the third man, Caride, who had initially fled, were detained in France in October 1989, just twenty-eight months after an act that a number of Basques considered a cruel but heroic deed. They were each sentenced to eight hundred years. Needless to say, they have all been at liberty for a long time now, but in 1997, they were still in prison, and when your colleagues are in prison, it's best to disappear and hide, because the years spent in prison can bring about a lot of changes, and someone who at first refused to give away any names might suddenly do so, out of resentment or boredom or to gain some reward in his or her cell. Or perhaps fear wasn't an element at all: perhaps those women had been horrified by their own participation in those crimes and decided to seek refuge and safety in a new place, somewhere neither too isolated nor too conspicuous, a place people rarely think about and that hardly ever appears in the news.

Of course 1988 or 1989 was still too soon for repentance. If they had repented, it would have happened later, when they were already different people, the people they had become in the neat, spotless town in the north-west that assigned a place to each of its inhabitants, as if it didn't permit any loose ends or even a hint of untidiness. The process of repentance is very slow in fanatics, so much so that they often don't even begin to repent and, at most, pretend, both to others and to themselves. It's easier to regret actions committed in a fit of rage or for personal reasons – those dictated by dislike, greed and revenge – than those committed for a faith or a cause. The perpetrator feels justified and supported by the latter, which encourage him to believe that he was merely the instrument of something more important than him or his victims, those who died, the unlucky ones, or those who had to be eliminated because of the harm they might inflict on that faith or that cause.

In fact, fanatics, and even terrorists, might say what Tupra had said to me on the day of our first encounter, an eternity ago: 'We are simultaneously someone and no one. We both exist and don't exist. We both act and don't act, Nevinson; or rather, we don't carry out the actions we carry out, or the things we do are done by no one. They simply happen.' That was all very well, even rather appealing. And yet it was also selfish and mendacious: it could be said of us and it could be said of anyone who assumed they had the right to end a life, of individual killers who murdered for purely personal reasons, those in civil society, if I can call it that, those who have no political, nationalist or religious motives, no faith or cause; those who commit mundane crimes simply to rid themselves of a rival or a competitor or in order to inherit sooner, to punish someone who had harmed them or to erase from the world someone who just won't leave them in peace, or so they believe. They all choose to change the course of history, to intervene in it. They are the ones who disturb the universe furtively from a corner, the ones who prevent things from following their usual course and reaching their natural end. They cannot be questioned because no one knows their plans. But this wasn't quite true either, and the proof of this was that now Machimbarrena, or whoever, had tracked down those three women, and one of them, the unlucky one, would, if I struck lucky, have to die.

I always thought of them in the plural, I realized, despite knowing that two had done nothing worthy of punishment, that they were probably decent, normal, possibly excellent folk. That is one of the curses of what was once more – and, as I imagined, only temporarily – becoming my profession: you live sunk in a world of conjecture, suspicion becomes your default position and you see evil everywhere, in every face and every body, even the most charming and innocent. That's it in essence, the space occupied by evil spreads and grows unstoppably and finally embraces the whole world. At least here that space was limited. There was only room for three, until I discovered and entrapped the guilty party, or until she turned on me. Centurión repeated to himself that anyone capable of blowing someone else's children to pieces, willy-nilly, would not hesitate to kill him, a grown man who inspired no pity, were he to make a mistake and arouse her suspicions, let alone give himself away. The huntsman sometimes forgets that he is not the only danger. The animal he wants to kill is dangerous too.

He did have one possible advantage, though, time and the thing that time usually brings with it, confidence. Eight or nine years had passed with no major upsets for his chosen prey, no one had come looking for her or pursued or startled her. Her heightened state of alert must inevitably have diminished. I myself, after four or five years in that provincial English town – I wasn't even sure how many years it was – where I was living under the name of James Rowland, had begun to relax beneath the sheer monotony of life. I knew the treacherous process from which no one escapes: one day passes and another, then another and they begin to meld into one so that you lose count. Nothing happens on those days, nothing abnormal or alarming, and each new night you go to bed feeling less worried and anxious, feeling less apprehensive about the following day, which you have no reason to think will be any different. Yes, you know it might well be different, that it might signal the arrival of someone carrying your sentence in his hand and with orders to carry it out. You know that, but you no longer feel it; it takes a real effort to remain always at the ready, on tenterhooks, unforgetting, and so you begin to grow comfortable, your insomnia ebbs away. Days become months and years, and no one, not even the most paranoid, can maintain that tension and remain on guard for such a long time.

That woman, whichever one she was, would have thought what I had sometimes thought in that English town: 'The truth is, they don't know who I am nor what I did. They don't know that Tom Nevinson isn't dead, nor that he's snuggled down here in his boring, placid life as a provincial gentleman. Or else they've forgotten about me because there's no longer any point in hating me, they consider me useless and inoffensive, they're not going to waste money or put one of their own people at risk just to punish someone who once did them harm but who is now long gone. If they do know I'm alive, for them I might as well be a corpse, someone who hurt them once, but who is now out of the game. They don't care if I'm still at liberty and unpunished, breathing the air of this earth. We must concentrate on today and tomorrow and not the dark yesterdays, which are already growing dim and blurred: even the most appalling of crimes fade in the fickle memories of men, and of women too, who have more of a tendency to harbour grudges. Just as even the most luminous of yesterdays gradually, inevitably, fade away. For those who have known such luminous days. I can hardly recall a single one of mine.'

As Patricia Pérez Nuix had already revealed, the spectacle of the bridge and the river was not the only thing Miguel Centurión could see from the window of his apartment in that town in the north-west, which I will perhaps call Ruán, just for convenience's sake, so as to give it a name, albeit a non-existent one, a false name, and to be able to give its inhabitants a name too, *ruaneses*.

On the other side of the river, on the opposite bank, on precisely the same level as him – on the third floor – was the apartment of Inés Marzán, the only one of the three women who was single or divorced or widowed, that is without a husband or permanent partner at this stage in her life (prior to that, who knows). The other two women were called Celia Bayo and María Viana, at least those were the names they had been known by since their move to Ruán some years before. Centurión could partially and intermittently listen to and watch these last two from his apartment, thanks to the installation of hidden cameras and microphones in their respective homes, in the living room in both cases. The cameras doggedly or blindly recorded everything – they weren't activated by movement, didn't pick up only bodies or voices, Spanish technology wasn't that sophisticated – and so Centurión would have to fast-forward through all the empty, useless sequences on his recording machine. The tapes lasted twelve hours, after which, on his return home, he would have to sift through the accumulated images and erase the irrelevant ones before starting again. This system was new at the time, certainly in Spain, like the

mobile phone Pérez Nuix had given him so that he could make immediate contact with her, or if she didn't answer and some emergency
cropped up, with Machimbarrena and even with Tupra in London.

On the other hand, he couldn't *hear* Inés Marzán at all – there had
been no way of introducing a similar device into her apartment, not
even a microphone – and so he could only view her from a distance,
from the other side of the waters, admittedly much more clearly with
binoculars than without them, although they did reduce his field of
vision, a small living room and a bedroom, the only two rooms that
gave onto the river below, a river I will perhaps call Lesmes. Sometimes the net curtains were drawn or the blinds down, but never
during the day or during the five evenings a week when she was
working at the restaurant she owned and where Centurión, therefore,
soon became a regular customer.

Inés Marzán was a strikingly tall woman, so much so that she
seemed rather embarrassed by her height, as if she felt that being a
whole head taller than most people – certainly most women, of
course, but also quite a number of men – was an irritating anomaly
for everyone else, obliged as they were to crane their necks when
speaking to her. (Doubtless certain vulgar individuals referred to her
as 'the giraffe' or 'mummy-long-legs'.) This had not, however, made
her renounce high heels, not very high, but not that low either, and
always stilettos. Perhaps she had come to the conclusion that wearing
flat shoes wouldn't really help and might betray her feelings of insecurity: better to dress as if she were a normal height and not
emphasize her size by doing something as ineffective as it was unnatural. She must also have considered, probably and quite rightly, that
her extremely long legs were, after all, one of her few attractive
features, and high heels – a magnificent invention – do, as we know,
slim and enhance the calf muscles, well, that at least was a widely
accepted truth in 1997, a lost century that some of us still miss, accustomed as we were to the way the world was then.

Her face wasn't ugly exactly, but everything about it was large: her eyes were huge, her mouth enormous, her nose less so, but generously proportioned (at least it was straight and not crooked, or perhaps she'd had plastic surgery), her chin was on the long side too, but stopped short of being prognathous, her forehead was broad, and her thick, lush, dark hair sprang from a very marked widow's peak, everything about her was excessive and possibly intimidating to some men, who steer well clear of any women who are taller than them.

In the restaurant, where Centurión immediately got to know her (being new in town, he felt it would do no harm to introduce himself and congratulate her on her restaurant), she was all smiles, sweetness and light, as she moved among the tables with extraordinary grace, almost as if her feet weren't even touching the ground, but hovering above it. She glided from one point to another, the only sound being the soft tack-tack of her heels, she must have been practising that gliding motion ad nauseam, ever since she was an adolescent. You could also hear the faint rustle of her clothes, often made of silk or satin and always deliberately timeless, as if she had decided that the look that most favoured her was that of a woman who belonged to no particular era. Her eyes were a lovely greenish colour, but this did not quite make up for their size, indeed, they still drew one's attention simply because the pupil, iris and the white of the eye were so large and took up such a lot of space in a face which, in turn, took up a lot of space in that interminable body, which it was impossible to ignore, or to resist stopping and staring at with a mixture of fascination and unease, terrified distaste and subjugation, or was it simply amazement. Because she was so tall, she appeared very slender, but if you looked closely, you could see that she was actually quite curvaceous, and her discreetly figure-hugging clothes emphasized her firm, and by no means small, breasts (her clothes were usually tastefully low cut) and her pert buttocks.

Anyone brave enough to lie with her would doubtless enjoy the experience and want to repeat it, the problem was that, in order to take that first step, you would really need to pluck up your courage, or so thought Centurión as he watched her bustling solicitously about among her customers, like a benevolent giantess seeking forgiveness for her almost freakish dimensions.

Centurión would also watch her whenever she happened to be at home in her apartment. He kept the lace curtains on his window almost closed so that she wouldn't spot him there, and would peer through the gap, sometimes with his binoculars, sometimes without; I couldn't help but feel that I was imitating James Stewart in *Rear Window* (as I always felt whenever I had to watch anyone), and having a scene laid out before one and being able to spy on it with impunity brightens up anyone's daily life. There are, of course, scenes where nothing or very little is happening, and then it's very tedious.

Since she lived alone, Inés Marzán spent most of her time alone, and when alone she was a changed woman: her movements were no longer those of some winged entity, but of a clumsy creature unaware of her real size; as she walked through her apartment, it was not uncommon for her to brush against a piece of furniture, knocking it over or sending other objects tumbling to the floor as she passed, a book, a pen, a snuffbox, a cup, a figurine or a whole chessboard, proof that her lightfootedness in the restaurant was a performance, something learned and conscious, much like an actor who has to become his character for just as long as the play lasts and not a minute longer. It must have been really exhausting, unless those transitions had by now become completely automatic. In her apartment, she often walked around barefoot, wearing a blouse or a T-shirt or a sweater and jeans, or with neither trousers nor skirt, her limitless legs free and bare; I never saw her wearing slippers, as if she scorned such a homely image, at most, she would put on a pair of moccasins that she could easily have worn in the street (in 1997, there was still a minimum of decorum in the streets). She had very long, narrow feet;

finding shoes her size must have involved travelling far afield, a veritable expedition, unless some skilled shoemaker made them to measure and sent them to her from wherever he lived. Or perhaps there was such a man in Ruán.

She found it hard to be still. If she was watching TV or a video, she would often get up and disappear into another room, the bathroom or the kitchen, I couldn't tell, or one of the other rooms that were also out of sight. If she sat reading on her large bed or on the sofa, she wouldn't last many pages before she became distracted and started moving about, not leaving the room this time, but picking up the phone and ringing someone, her conversations tended to be fairly long and usually highly expressive, and so gesticulatory that she could almost have passed for a southerner. Or she would interrupt her reading – leaving the book lying face down somewhere, anywhere, including on the floor – to turn on the radio or put on a CD and then jig about for a while in the living room. Despite her height, she wasn't a bad dancer, indeed Centurión thought she moved with a certain grace and rhythm, although who doesn't look slightly ridiculous, if not grotesque, when the person watching them dance cannot hear the music, only an awkward silence, or in this case the murmur of the River Lesmes, a constant background noise that soothed the mind, and, at night, almost lulled one to sleep; when the water wasn't about to freeze of course. Inés Marzán was a physically restless woman and couldn't keep still even when in repose or at ease, and yet she didn't seem to mind her solitude. Perhaps what she couldn't tolerate was immobility.

Given her singular appearance, it wasn't easy to guess her age. She was thirty-eight according to the report. This was the age on her identity card, but if that card was just a front for the Northern Irishwoman, if I can call her that, it was probably fake. With her hair tied back in a ponytail, with no trousers on or no skirt, she seemed younger, when she was dressed and wearing high heels slightly older.

On the two nights of the week when she wasn't working (Sundays and Mondays, on Sundays the restaurant was closed all day), she would go out or have visitors. Once I saw her spend an evening in with some girlfriends, they ordered takeaway pizzas while half watching some TV game show, laughing, but paying it scant attention, an excuse to get together more than anything, or so their observer inferred. He didn't know where she went when she left her apartment, possibly to the cinema, to have supper at some rival restaurant, to a party, or a discotheque since she enjoyed dancing, or bar-hopping in the Barrio Tinto, or visiting someone else's home. It was still early days for him to start following her: however accustomed Centurión was to doing this and however skilled at remaining undetected, it would be unwise to risk causing her any alarm or arousing the slightest suspicion that someone was on her trail and had tracked her down. It was also too early to let her know that he was a neighbour, that he lived immediately opposite, albeit separated by the width of the river; he always tried to enter or leave his building when he thought she would not yet be up (she was never up when he set off to school, because after working so late at the restaurant, she was, understandably, a late riser) or would already be at work. It didn't matter if they met in the street or in the shops in the area, because all the locals, the *ruaneses*, visited the area, and almost all of them crossed the bridge at least once a day, if not twice.

One evening, he saw a man meet her at her door, a smartly dressed individual of the old school, middle-aged and with rather bland features; through his binoculars Centurión managed to make out a colourful tie and a pair of black cufflinks – possibly onyx – and he imagined that, under his overcoat, the man would be sporting an elegant suit in a fine fabric, doubtless made to measure, for there were still tailors in Ruán who were always busy and in high demand, that's one of the advantages of small towns, which preserve the luxuries of the old days for far longer than the big cities. The man was wearing a dark hat – more broad-brimmed than narrow – which matched his heavy, dark overcoat. He doffed his hat respectfully when Inés Marzán appeared, and offered her his right arm as they walked along by the riverside, an offer she discreetly ignored. It didn't make much sense to be holding the arm of someone who was nearly four inches shorter than her, that would have been very awkward, and he certainly wasn't going to take *her* arm as if he were her nephew. That must have been one of Inés Marzán's more minor problems. In any case, they headed for the bridge, and the man, despite his smaller stature, seemed rather proud to be walking along with such a tall woman. He was probably a banker, a businessman, a property developer, one of Ruán's landed gentry, a provincial dandy. It could have been a business meeting, or a date, although, if the latter, there was little likelihood of him getting very far very fast and certainly no chance of consummation, at least according to the spy at the window's predictions.

He soon learned that a cleaning lady came to the apartment two mornings a week, before Inés Marzán set off for her long day at the restaurant, and that a man came on a different day, almost always a Thursday. (At a time when Centurión had returned from his morning classes.) He couldn't see what she got up to with that man, nor the entire sequence of events, because after the man had arrived and she had greeted him with a warm kiss and embrace, poured him a beer and chatted briefly with him, Inés Marzán would always half close the shutters, those of the bedroom and of the living room. (She didn't take pains to close them completely or hermetically, and so, if he was lucky, Centurión thought optimistically, he might glimpse something through a crack, and to this end he would take up his binoculars and search for that privileged angle.) The fact that she closed the bedroom shutters seemed to indicate that the two of them must go in there sooner or later, but the man didn't look like a lover, although we can never know who feels erotically drawn to whom or why, and everything is possible on this earth and in our imagination. (Sometimes not even the person attracted can explain why he or she feels attracted, even the object of desire cannot always understand what the other person sees in him or her, although this is usually something neither of them bothers to ask and they simply concentrate on having a good time together.)

Not that the visitor was unattractive. He had pale, almond-shaped eyes, probably blue, and a large nose slightly curved at the tip, from which, though, a perennial dewdrop seemed about to fall, as if he were suffering the remnants of a cold or some winter allergy. He had fairly long, straight, straw-coloured hair which he wore combed back, and curly sideburns that seemed more 1960s than 1990s, like a young Stephen Stills to whom he did bear a certain resemblance. However, what made him seem most unlikely as a permanent or regular lover was his height: not only was he short in comparison with Inés Marzán – a fate shared by nearly all the men in Ruán or anywhere else – he looked positively diminutive beside her, and far too frail somehow to deal with her various prominences, which, although one did not notice these initially, subsequently became unmissable, a very definite presence. He was well formed and even handsome, but one couldn't help pondering the difficulties the couple would have in the act of copulation, with, in the most traditional position, his head only level with her breasts. Centurión was sure they weren't lovers. Whatever the truth of the matter, during most of the man's visits, the bedroom remained sealed off from the out-side world.

Miguel Centurión didn't care two hoots about Inés Marzán's sex life, nor about those of Celia Bayo and María Viana, or only insofar as it could be an indication of how he might approach them: if one of them was indifferent to sex or to men, that would close one possible door into their lives, one that should never be dismissed in his profession.

The Thursday visitor was the polar opposite of the respectable local worthy who had come to pick her up one night: this man dressed in a casual and supposedly modern way, and when he removed his coat he revealed a waistcoat, leather trousers and pointy black boots like those worn by a gunman in a Western, all he lacked was a pair of tinkling spurs. He could have been a singer or a rock concert pro-moter working in that part of the country, the owner of a gaming house, an actor in Indie films (bohemians were already old hat) or a TV star, but there was no film industry in Ruán and the regional TV station was a ramshackle affair. It occurred to Centurión (who had his eyes fixed on one goal only and was blind to everything else) that he could be someone she knew from before, someone from the old days and who saw those days as older than they were and felt quite safe, and had perhaps infected Inés Marzán with his confidence: it was not impossible that he was a former member of ETA or moved in the same circles or even belonged to the IRA (perhaps they spoke to each other in English, not Spanish).

People who leave such organizations or go into the reserves, so to speak, rarely get it right when honing their 'civilian' character, which should be as ordinary as possible. In 1997, on the other hand, the monkish Basque hairstyle, often with accompanying earring (the same for men and women), was already proliferating, and while it had not yet become obligatory, this meant that it was very easy to identify sympathizers and even the more obtuse of ETA activists, and absurdly enough, they found this style very hard to give up, as if they felt it was a betrayal to pretend to be what they were not and to ward off suspicions, although to do that is, of course, the first commandment of the clandestine life. In some respects, the group were stupid out of sheer stubbornness.

After the gunman's second visit, Centurión decided to go down into the street when he saw the man leaving Inés Marzán's apartment (the shutters were still closed, so she wouldn't see) and follow him. He had to wait until he had crossed the bridge over to his side, the south side, and then he followed him, always keeping about fifty paces behind, to the Barrio Tinto, so called, according to some, although no one knows for sure, because of the red wine, the *vino tinto*, that once used to flow down its streets or because of the reddish tones of many of the façades of the buildings, which are only ever three storeys at most. They came in various bright, intense shades, including watermelon green, yellow and blue, but most were magenta, mauve, cherry, burnt sienna, crimson and purple; this barrio of tapas and stubby wine glasses, and of brothels in laxer times (although there were still a few, half camouflaged), had a certain cardinalic air.

He saw him enter one of those hundreds of bars that line the narrow, twisting, labyrinthine streets, parallel and perpendicular and oblique, the whole area had a maritime feel about it, and the River Lesmes was still semi-navigable and had, for one and a half centuries or two, been Ruán's main supply route. Despite the cold, Centurión sat down on one of the stools outside, ordered a beer and some tapas and from there kept watch on the bar, where the diminutive gunman Stills was standing, not ordering anything to drink or eat, but merely gesturing to the barman and waiting, one foot resting on that other bar, the brass one a few inches from the floor. Thirty seconds later, a huge, thickset guy with a bull neck and a shaven head emerged from the back room, a real brute, who was, nevertheless, wearing an incongruously high-quality, possibly Italian suit, shirt and tie. Not for nothing was this bar one of the three best-known and most lucrative in Ruán; at cocktail hour and at lunchtime, and from mid-afternoon onwards, it was impossible to get a table there. Perhaps the only way the owner – I presumed he was the owner – could mitigate his brutish exterior was to spend a fortune on clothes so that he would always be dressed to the nines. Even at nine in the morning.

He greeted Stephen Stills with a look that combined impatience and relief, and the two of them disappeared into the back room, where they remained for, at most, four or five minutes. This gave me just about time to drink my beer, gobble down my tapas and pay, because the gunman then came out of the bar and immediately set off again. Even though he wasn't wearing spurs, his boots did tinkle cheekily as he walked, clink-clink-clink, presumably because he had metal tips on the toes and heels. He turned to the right, to the left, to the right and to the left again, before stopping at another bar; here he knocked on a small side entrance, not accessible to the public. The door opened, he went in, and the door closed behind him. This time, I moved away a little and wandered around, always keeping one eye on that door. He reappeared after about three minutes – these were all very brief visits – and this time headed off to the bridge, whistling; he crossed over to the north side and I followed, always keeping fifty paces behind. He plunged into the high-class area near the Cathedral, where it was all tree-lined boulevards and streets and lushly planted squares, where the renovated, refurbished and beautifully kept buildings dated back to the nineteenth century and perhaps the 1920s and 1930s. Ruán had fallen to Franco's troops in 1936 and, having thus escaped bombing during the Civil War, had remained intact and as if preserved in honey.

Stills' next stop was a high, rather grand street door – formerly a carriage entrance – with, on the wall, various name plates – in brass or bakelite or slate – announcing offices or businesses or medical or legal practices. He rang a bell, and I made a note to myself that it was the second one down on the left-hand side. He must have murmured his name into the entryphone, for the door opened at once. He entered like someone totally familiar with the terrain, and I then went over to inspect. He had rung no. 4A, which, according to one of the plates, belonged to 'Gaspar Gómez-Notario, Notary', whose surname, I thought, was a clear case of predestination.

I retreated and waited, leafing through the magazines at a nearby kiosk (I bought one magazine and a newspaper), and Stills reappeared soon afterwards, six or seven minutes later, and I wondered what on earth he could be doing at a notary's office, with his long hair and leather trousers and his pointy, metal-tipped boots (perhaps they ushered him straight in, avoiding the waiting room, so that no client would catch so much as a fleeting glimpse of him). He walked a few more blocks in that same bourgeois district, his cheerful, intermittent whistling audible from a distance, he was clearly a confident, nonchalant man, pleased to be doing his rounds so seamlessly and presumably so profitably too. When he arrived at another elegant street door, he repeated the operation. He rang a bell, the door opened, and when I again went over to inspect, I found that this time he was visiting 'Dr Ruibérriz de Torres and Dr Vidal Secanell, Consulting Rooms'. 'All respectable, well-to-do people,' thought Centurión, 'Inés Marzán and the owners of affluent bars.' Then he understood what the gunman was up to in Ruán. He probably didn't even live in Ruán.

Centurión had a couple of hours before he had to resume his teaching; having just two periods in the morning and two in the afternoon, plus the fact that his school was so close to where he lived (a four-minute walk), meant that he could spend a lot of time in his apartment observing Inés Marzán, as well as watching the recordings of Celia Bayo and María Viana in their homes, or making inquiries around the town. And of course, he had the evenings entirely to himself. So for a while longer he continued to follow Stephen Stills, who was now heading to the train station, where he strode in as if he already had his ticket, and went straight to the platform. He sat on a bench, glanced up at the clock, took a small diary from his coat pocket and started making brief notes with a stubby pencil, perhaps recording the various stops he had made on his itinerary around Ruán, and perhaps the quantities sold. He continued to whistle, more quietly now, and Centurión recognized the theme tune from *High Noon*, well, it would have to be something from a Western.

Centurión looked up at the departures board and saw that the next train due to arrive on that platform wouldn't leave for another twenty minutes and only went about four or five stops down the line before terminating in Catilina, which, although smaller than Ruán, was a fierce rival, including on the football pitch: when the two teams played, it wasn't unusual for the fans or a few violent supporters to end up fighting. It was about sixty miles away and, although less historical and less stately than Ruán, and therefore boasting fewer tourists and fewer hotels, it considered itself to be more modern and dynamic and lively and with a more vibrant night life, just as Vigo does with respect to La Coruña and Pontevedra in Galicia, although Vigo actually has more inhabitants than either of those two provincial capitals. This wasn't the case here: while Ruán had about two hundred thousand inhabitants and falling, Catilina had passed the one hundred thousand mark and was on the rise.

Centurión bought a ticket to the next stop on the line just so that he could gain access to the platform, and, having asked with a gesture if the gunman minded him sharing his bench, and having sat down beside him once the gunman had shifted up a little to make room, he opened the newspaper he had bought earlier. Stills continued to make notes in his diary or notebook, but stopped whistling.

'I've been told you're a reliable supplier,' Centurión said suddenly in a friendly tone of voice.

The diminutive gunman jumped, quickly closed his notebook and turned to look coldly at Centurión, first touching the damp tip of his nose.

'I don't know what you're talking about,' he said. 'Look, I haven't got time for this. Leave me alone.' And he made as if to stand up, but Centurión held him back simply by placing one hand on the other man's forearm. He knew that, when he wanted, his hand had the weight and feel of a raw steak. This was another thing they were taught, at least in England. That dead weight was enough to keep the gunman from standing up and moving off, not that he could have gone very far on the short platform.

'You have fifteen minutes before your train leaves,' said Centurión, looking up at the clock. 'Don't worry, I'm not a policeman, although, of course, that's precisely what a policeman would say before he whips out his badge and slaps on the handcuffs. You're right to be careful though. My name's Miguel Centurión, I can show you my ID if you like.' He removed his hand – it was best not to overdo things – and held it out to Stills, who, however, declined to shake it. 'I haven't been living in Ruán for long, and I've heard good things about you at La Demanda.' That was the name of Inés Marzán's restaurant. 'And in the consulting rooms of Drs Ruibérriz and Vidal. And from a few other people.'

'Oh, yeah, like who? You're saying Dr Vidal mentioned me to you? Come off it!'

'Now, now, one shouldn't divulge the names of people whose tongues have run away with them, should one? Besides, I didn't say the doctor told me. But there are always other patients waiting and nurses and receptionists, just as, at La Demanda, there are customers and waiters and kitchen staff. And in El Búho Bizco, well, practically the whole town goes there. People like to appear to be in the know. I heard you mentioned there too.' That was the name of the first bar Stills had visited, one of the most popular in Ruán. 'I happen to know that the huge guy with the bull neck holds you in high esteem. You know, the elegantly dressed fellow, I don't know his name. He's the owner, isn't he?'

'Berua? Berua mentioned me to you? I don't think so.'

Centurión could have been mistaken, but, having taken stock of the situation, he had concluded that the fellow was clearly a provincial drug dealer, a distributor and a seller. He probably ran some after-hours business in Catilina, doubtless set up and maintained, and possibly bolstered, by the profits he made from this other activity. He had found a few steady buyers in Ruán, people who don't want to take risks or meet with any unpleasant surprises or be sold adulterated substances, and who are pleased and gratified to have such substances brought to their door, always by the same supplier, and thus avoid any dealings with shady or sinister characters. And if he lived sixty miles away and there was little chance of meeting him in their own town, all the better. He, in turn, acquired a series of civilized, influential customers who paid promptly, never caused him any problems, never asked for favours and never threatened him. The larger quantities – never huge, an ounce at most – went to the bars, which also provided him with opportunities to acquire a few more trusted patrons. Centurión was sure that if a policeman were to search Stills there and then, on the platform, he would probably find a package or two, although he would have disposed of most of what he had stuffed in his pockets that morning in readiness for his trip to Ruán. As well as a bundle of recently earned notes, of course. He would always be paid in cash, discreet transactions, clean and quick. A man like that would be keen to widen his net with a new client like Centurión. How many clients would he have, Centurión wondered: Inés Marzán's house would definitely not have been his first stop that morning.

'I didn't say he was the one who told me. As you see, I didn't even know his name. But everyone talks, people talk, and you know what El Búho Bizco is like . . . The clientele there don't just consume tapas, do they? Some pass on the word, and if you do your rounds nearly every week, well, people begin to notice and put two and two together when they realize that, after your visits, certain substances, shall we say, suddenly become available. Plus, your appearance and your clothes are not exactly run-of-the-mill, they're very . . . individual.' Stills seemed to find this last remark flattering, and gave a reluctant half-smile – the vast and universal vanity that afflicts even the most insignificant. 'And here everyone knows everyone, even the *catilinos* who are regular visitors to the town.'

'*Catilinenses*,' he said, correcting me. 'They call us *catilinos* here just to annoy us.'

'Sorry, I didn't know that, *catilinos* is what I've heard people say in Ruán. *Catilinenses* then. All I want is for you to add me to your distribution list, to become my supplier. I won't cause you any problems, I promise, and you'll do very nicely out of it. In the time we've spent sitting here you could already have made a bit of extra cash. If you like, we still have time for a first transaction.' It was now eleven or twelve minutes until his train arrived.

'And who's going to act as *your* referee? If you won't give me any names, how am I going to check you out? Anyway, I almost never go to La Demanda. Or only very occasionally for supper.'

Centurión responded quickly:

'I didn't say I was a regular customer, just that someone there mentioned you. You can ask the owner, Inés Marzán, about me. She doesn't know me well – like I said, I haven't been in town long. But we've been introduced and she knows who I am.'

'You know Inés?'

'And I hope to know her better too. She's very attractive, a fantastic woman, really amazing.'

He looked me over rather doubtfully. Sigfrido the hairdresser had done a good job on me in Madrid; he had disguised my receding hairline and dyed some of the hair on my temples, leaving only a sprinkling of grey. I was also cultivating a light brown moustache, Robert Redford-style, when, that is, he wore a moustache; it was growing fast and it suited me. Stills – who probably wasn't even thirty yet – must have decided that I wasn't bad-looking for my age, perhaps a tad antiquated, someone from the previous decade. But antiquity doesn't tend to be an obstacle, on the contrary. The antiquated have their attractions, since they have usually lost an inclination for experimentation or silliness. They even inspire confidence because they are a reminder of a cosily non-threatening past. An illusory confidence, but all the same.

Inés Marzán was very far from being a beauty, she was too insecure. Even so, that Stephen Stills impersonator was sure to raise some objection.

'Frankly, I don't think you're up to it,' he said impertinently and with the vaguely proprietorial tone of someone with a prior claim. 'In any sense.'

'When it comes to Inés, no one is. I mean, you're certainly not.' And Centurión got slowly to his feet and looked the gunman up and down. Even when seated, it had been clear that he was a few, possibly four inches, taller. Inés Marzán would be nearly eight inches taller. 'Besides, I know you've been pals for some years and that it doesn't go beyond that. Anyway, leave it to me and I'll see what I can do. So, my friend, are you putting me on your list or not?' I suddenly addressed him more familiarly, calling him *tú*, as a way of wrongfooting him or transitioning into the next phase of our relationship.

'I'll have to make some inquiries. Miguel Centurión, eh? That's some name you've got there. A bit of a joke really.' He was either playing hard to get or playing it safe. 'You never know, I might be lucky and catch Inés at home now.' And he stuck his hand in his coat pocket and produced a mobile phone, a more rudimentary, less modern one than the one I'd been given (although both were antiques compared with the phones of today), intending to call her unexpectedly.

I again placed one leaden hand on his forearm and stopped him in his tracks; certain such weights impose and frighten and seem impossible to resist.

'Look, you imbecile,' I said, again using the *tú* form, well, you need to if you want to insult someone, even when it's a fairly mild, schoolboyish insult. 'On second thoughts, I think I'd prefer her not to know what you're going to tell her about me. There's no reason why she should be introduced so early on to my most private passions. Like I said, you imbecile, I'm not a policeman,' I repeated the same insult, so that he wouldn't think he'd misheard the first time, 'but I'd have no problem reporting you to that fellow over there' – there was a policeman in the station, whether as a passenger or on duty I wasn't sure, they were always discreetly on the alert in the provinces, on the premise that ETA could strike anywhere – 'and, as the good citizen that I am, suggest to him that he search you right now. You've probably got a few druggie bags on you and a suspiciously large bundle of cash. He'd soon put two and two together. Or perhaps he'd find something else. You look like the kind of guy who carries a blade. You may never use it, but he's not to know that, and the combination of drugs and a weapon won't go down well at all. That could be enough for him to make you miss your train and perhaps have you spend the night in the police station, and after that . . . Come on, give me a couple of wraps and deal done, then everyone's happy. Give me your number so I can get in touch again, and tell me what name you want me to use when I call you. I imagine you only use your real name with Gómez-Notario the Notary? So good they named him twice, eh?'

I was bluffing of course, because I had no idea what his name was nor what nicknames he might use. In fact, I didn't know anything, it was all conjecture and guesswork on my part. I had effortlessly and speedily slipped back into my old ways.

He shot me a sidelong glance that was a mixture of bewilderment, haste, annoyance and fear. That's the trouble with some young people: they often believe the world is theirs for the taking, but are easily demoralized by the first setback, especially if that setback comes in the form of a more confident, older man. He thought he had the whip hand, but suddenly, somehow, he was afraid I might be the one to thrash him. He looked at the policeman, he looked at the clock, the train would be arriving in four minutes now, its snout already visible in the distance, approaching slowly.

'Write it down,' he said.

'Just tell me, I have a good memory.'

He gave me the number in segments, pausing in between so that I could memorize it, then added:

'I'll probably answer, but if not, ask for Comendador.'

He did not address me as *tú*, even though there was nothing to stop him, and this, I felt, was a promising sign. Often the hierarchy between people is established on that very first meeting, and then there's no changing it. The same had happened to me with Tupra all those years ago, and he was still capable of drawing me in; after all, I was there on that platform because of him, thanks to him.

'Comendador, eh? The Knight Commander. You're not short on ambition either, I see, which is a good thing,' murmured Centurión. Comendador could as easily be his real name as a nickname. He had given in very easily to reason or to a little verbal intimidation. I hadn't even had to stick him in the ribs with my old Charter Arms Under-cover, which I always had with me as naturally as I did cigarettes. Pérez Nuix had supplied me with a more modern weapon, with no serial number and completely clean, that is, one that had never been registered or used before, so that I could do what I had to do *if* I had to. I wasn't particularly adept at handling it, or any gun for that matter, and so I'd left it in a drawer in Madrid. That 1964 revolver, on the other hand, had kept me company over many years, so light, so portable, almost like a small torch or a bulky cigarette lighter.

I removed my hand from Comendador's forearm, freeing him from its weight. Then he reached into an inside pocket and placed something on the bench, covering it with his hand. I moved my hand a little closer and, when he removed his, the two little bags had gone without anyone seeing a thing. I stood up and opened wide my arms as if to give him a farewell hug.

'So we're agreed, then, Comendador, not a word to Inés Marzán. And you and I have never met, not until I get in touch with you. With her, I'm simply marking time until I decide when and what to tell her.' And I added in a whisper: 'Bon voyage, Comendador, you imbecile.' There was no harm, with a view to future encounters, in further undermining his morale and, if you like, cheapening his name. This would also make it even clearer just who was working for whom. He didn't react this third time either. He neither returned the insult nor bristled with annoyance, he simply didn't respond.

I gave him a few manly slaps on the back while I pretended to give him a hug, slipping into his coat pocket what I knew to be the going rate in Madrid. He would certainly have no reason to complain, on the contrary: everything, including cocaine probably, was cheaper in Ruán, and in Catilina it would be cheaper still. He briefly ran the back of his hand over his hip, his way of checking the amount without having to pat his pocket. It would be clear from the start that I was no sponger, nor was I a heavy or a highwayman. In the provinces – well, everywhere – every penny counts, and it was important that he should get some benefit from me.

The train was slowing as it approached the platform. Comendador didn't wait until it came to a complete halt. He moved off swiftly – his metallic footsteps clink-clink-clinking down the platform – as if he were being pursued, as if he needed to escape. He was either looking for a particular carriage or else was simply anxious to get away from me, to leave me high and dry – for the moment.

Centurión decided that he should begin his advance on Inés Marzán that same night. She was the only one of the three women who was either single, divorced or a widow, the only one who lived alone, the only one with whom he could risk taking the shortest route to gaining her confidence and trust, that is, with no conjugal obstacles. Although conjugal ties can sometimes turn out to be a gateway for the intruder, for whom languishing, vengeful wives, angry or bored, have sometimes been waiting both physically and in their imaginations, and there are quite a few of them out there, always far more wives than husbands, who are often simply lazy, superficial and optimistic. Initially, though, you have to view those ties as insurmountable obstacles, to pretend that a married woman is forbidden fruit and leave her to take the initiative. It's a way of showing respect, and women are always grateful for that, whether they expect it or not, whether they deserve it or not, and even when they don't want it at all and end up feeling irritated by such an excess of passivity and thoughtfulness. In any case, approaching them takes far longer, either because you have genuine scruples or because you are pretending in order to make that approach.

Centurión went to La Demanda that very evening; on a freezing February Thursday, it wasn't exactly crowded, and so the owner had time to spend a few minutes chatting to her customers, offering them a little company, especially those who were dining alone, unless they made it clear it was unwanted.

'How are things? How are your students? Are you getting to know the town a bit? You must find it very boring coming, as you do, from Madrid,' she said amiably while taking down his order.

She was, as usual, all smiles. She had a warm, pleasant smile, but it constituted a slight problem if you weren't simply looking at her, but were considering exploring more deeply, so to speak. Inés Marzán not only had an enormous mouth and very full lips, her teeth were far too large, like those of the Big Bad Wolf, only not as sharp. The idea of venturing in there with his tongue filled him with doubts or even fear, as if he were about to expose it to a saw or a grinder. Her friendly, even sweet expression mitigated that feeling of threat, but not enough: those teeth looked very powerful. Centurión couldn't help thinking cynically: 'Perhaps she's one of those women who's not so keen on kissing, because not all women are, and instead gives priority to other areas and other excesses. Let's hope so.'

'I don't have much time to get bored,' he said. 'Settling in and getting used to new routines is harder work than you might think. Although I'm sure it would all be much easier and more enjoyable if I had someone like you to be my guide. Just now and then, I mean, no pressure. Could I perhaps invite you out to dinner one evening? Not here, of course, but at a venue of your choice.'

As soon as he'd said this, he felt he had been too direct, had moved too fast, and he regretted having spoken at all. But Inés Marzán probably didn't have that many practical or resolute suitors. Perhaps she was used to the occasional crudely lascivious or speculative glance, aimed solely at her curvaceous figure and her discreet décolletages; glances that would, however, go no further than that, but remain no more than an ephemeral daydream, instantly cancelled out by the thought of actually being confronted by her imposing height, her anomalously large body, which could prove unmanageable, requiring the man to be directed or dominated by her, and ordinary men hate that. Ruán was full of ordinary men, as is Madrid.

This invitation took Inés Marzán completely by surprise. She paused for a moment, pen and notebook in hand, almost as if she were thinking deeply, as if she wasn't quite sure she had heard correctly. Although she knew she had. Perhaps she couldn't understand why a reasonably good-looking stranger, about three inches shorter than her – even shorter when she was wearing heels – should feel attracted to her at first or perhaps second sight and should be in such a hurry to let her know.

She wasn't of an age to blush, but Centurión noticed that she was slightly flustered and not at all displeased by his invitation. She smiled with a mixture of suspicion ('What's he really after? Is this just a passing fancy, wanting to add another notch to his bedpost, the way some people collect countries or provinces or rare specimens?') and a touch of flirtatiousness ('So the schoolteacher fancies me, does he?'). 'It's odd how insecure women are in general,' thought Centurión. 'Even women who are totally gorgeous see only their defects and are easily and absurdly driven to despair when they see their reflection in the mirror. If you inquire more closely, you discover that most do genuinely feel that they're pathetic wee things, or think they are; I wonder where that insecurity comes from? And since this woman isn't even pretty in parts, she must consider herself to be a monster when she's alone or feeling low and has, for the moment, ceased her lightfooted bustling and rustling about the restaurant; she will, at best, think of herself as a one-off. Perhaps she turns to cocaine to cheer herself up when she's down.'

Centurión could see that she wanted to gain a little time before saying yes or no. However, when the time she gained clearly wasn't much help, she said neither yes nor no:

'Thanks very much, but dinner dates are rather difficult for me. I'm here on duty most nights. You know, the eye of the owner . . .'

This sounded to Centurión like the beginning of some proverb or country saying: 'The eye of the cowherd helps the grass to grow' or

'The eye of the farmer helps to fatten the pig' or something of the sort, and then he wasn't sure if it was an English saying or a Spanish one or both; he thought it was probably English, but then everything today gets copied and translated literally, that is to say, badly.

According to the report he'd been given, the Northern Irish woman had been born in the countryside, to a father from the Rioja region or the Basque Country and a mother from Ballymena or Ballymoney, from Armagh or Fermanagh, who had spent a summer as an au pair in San Sebastián in her youth and then ended up getting married and settling down near Lequeitio, Deva or somewhere like that. Little else was known of her parents, for those were the days when the authorities didn't keep tabs on people as much as they do now, people were free to get on with their lives without interference and to come and go as they pleased without having to tell anyone. Still less was known of their daughter, as if she had proved elusive since adolescence. Her full name was María Magdalena Orúe O'Dea, in Spanish fashion, with the father's surname first and the mother's second. In the village or hamlet or house she would have been called Magdalena or Magda or even Mag. She was the ETA or IRA collaborator he had to pinpoint.

It was more likely that someone with northern blood would have ended up as tall as Inés Marzán (more likely than someone who was a full-blooded Spaniard, although that wasn't impossible, after all, we've always had female basketball players here). And she also spoke English, Centurión had heard her one night chatting to some foreigners in the restaurant. The fact that she could get by in English was hardly surprising: Ruán was becoming more and more of a tourist magnet, and she ran a restaurant that had a good reputation, but without any offputting pretensions to fancy cuisine. He had heard her say a few words from across the room, and she seemed to be pretty fluent, although with quite a strong Spanish accent. That could be put on, of course. However, for a native speaker or for someone bilingual – as I well knew – it's very hard not to slip into your natural way of speaking the language you've spoken ever since you were a child, to speak to my father in my case and, in the case of Magdalena Orúe O'Dea, to speak to her mother. It's so difficult that it would be easier to pretend you didn't speak the language at all, so as not to run the risk of speaking it suspiciously well, a fatal mistake.

Centurión had to be alert to every clue, he couldn't allow himself not to see Inés Marzán as the guilty party, and the same went for Celia Bayo and María Viana. He wasn't in the least bit interested in them as people initially, but it's impossible not to feel a degree of interest in someone you have dealings with or who you're engaged in observing and spying on, even if it's only as a spectacle or a distraction. This had happened to me in the past, during my years of wandering when I barely thought or questioned myself, and I had even become quite fond of a cold-blooded, ruthless murderer or murderess, the sort who allows others to die as cattle – like the inhabitant of Berchtesgaden whom anyone would gladly have taken a shot at – and thus deprive them of another slow dusk. The sort who accelerate time and so don't allow time to be its naturally merciful self; those who rush and shake and jostle time in a supermarket or a train station or a barracks, with no thought for who might be there.

But almost no one is cold-blooded all the time and at every moment. A murderer is sometimes affectionate and cheerful, he laughs and sings and plays musical instruments, he smiles, slaps people on the back, hugs them and often wins them over, consoles them and raises their spirits, provides them with hope and a distant goal with which to fill their existence, and so give it meaning and motivation. 'It is one of the great troubles of life that we cannot have any unmixed emotions. There is always something in our enemy that we like, and something in our sweetheart that we dislike. It is this entanglement of moods which makes us old, and puckers our brows and deepens the furrows about our eyes,' wrote an Irishman more than a century ago, the poet Yeats. And he added something along the lines of: 'We never know untrammelled hate or unmixed love, and are always wearying ourselves with a "yes" or a "no", and finding our feet entangled in the sorry net of "maybe" and "perhaps".' Knowing all this, Centurión saw evil everywhere. And he saw it in himself too, during his time in Ruán.

'I suggested dinner, but it could be lunch or breakfast, or we could go for a walk or see a film, or have an aperitif or a glass of wine or a coffee, whichever suits you best. And don't you think we should call each other *tú*? It feels so stilted now being formal in our language.' I said 'our' on purpose, when it was possible that, in her heart of hearts, she didn't consider it to be her language.

'Yes, of course. Whatever you like. It's Miguel, isn't it? My name's Inés.'

'That much I know, Inés.'

VI

Centurión found it easy enough to fix a date with her, then another and another, the look he had chosen for his time in Ruán clearly favoured him, a look achieved with the aid of that ageing toff Machimbarrena's Rossinian hairdresser and with a little additional help from elsewhere. Besides, he was still half young, and even though he felt a lot older, at the end of the twentieth century youth lasted indefinitely. On the other hand, a lot of women are less concerned with appearance and more with perception, by which I mean how they are perceived by the person standing before them or beside them or opposite them or even behind them while they sleep.

Centurión saw that Inés Marzán was flattered, although not exactly hopeful, because she was doubtless cautious and sceptical, having, since early on, known more than one disappointment in her life, inquisitive men who wanted only to experience the sensation described in Baudelaire's poem written over one hundred and sixty years ago, even if they had never read it or known of its existence; they would have wanted to experience it, once and once only, even though they had no name for it: 'I should like to have lived alongside a young giantess, like a voluptuous cat at the feet of a queen. I should like to have seen her body blossom with her soul and flourish freely during her terrifying games . . . To explore at leisure her magnificent contours; to crawl up the slope of her enormous knees and thighs, and sometimes in summer, that season of insalubrious suns . . . to fall nonchalantly asleep in the shade of her breasts . . .' That, more or less, is what the poem says, although in Baudelaire's sublime French of course.

She was neither very young nor a giantess, she was simply large and tall, but I felt an imaginary breath of wind waft towards me from those lines the first time I entered her apartment and she deliberately closed the shutters in her bedroom, with me inside and not opposite, not on the other side of the river searching with my binoculars for a chink in the shutters, trying to see what was going on. I had a front-row seat now, I was part of the action. I could see everything when it least mattered to me and, besides, I knew the play by heart, a banal act allowing for few variations, almost all of which blur into one in the memory.

Inés Marzán did not get her hopes up solely because of past experiences, hope apparently had no place in the person she was at thirty-eight, if that *was* her real age: she didn't need a man by her side, and had long since rejected the idea, if, indeed, she had ever cherished such a desire. Or, rather, having a man there was of interest to her purely pragmatically, instrumentally, so as to enjoy his company and his conversation as preamble and epilogue, and, above all, so that he could give her pleasure, or was it merely a question of physical release or sexual hygiene, or a brief and always beneficial suspension of consciousness, a chance, however fleeting, to forget what awaits us in a time we can neither comprehend nor imagine.

She was as demonstrative during sex as she was cold and mechanical when it was over. She could instantly create an aseptic, bureaucratic atmosphere as if she had no memory of what had just happened, as if what had just happened hadn't happened at all.

It was, of course, also possible that this was a defensive tactic, an act of self-preservation, that of someone wary and disillusioned, who is not only devoid of hope, but smothers the tiniest flicker; someone who, if she felt hope creeping up the ramparts would immediately pour boiling oil over it to scorch and send it plummeting back to earth, meanwhile brusquely scolding herself: 'What are you doing, you idiot, I thought you had learned not to believe in anyone, not to expect anything from anyone, to take it for granted that everything is transient and fickle and that people lie deliberately or despite themselves, even when they're convinced they're telling an immutable truth. What is certain today will be uncertain tomorrow, smoke that rises up and is lost. What is enthusiasm today will be tepid emotion tomorrow. What are heartfelt promises today will be melted snow and lamentations tomorrow. What is joy today will, tomorrow, be insalubrious suns and empty apologies for having caused you pain. Then you'll trot out the usual words of complaint: "I spent everything I had and received nothing. I should have known this before I started throwing my money around." Or, which comes to the same thing, before taking that first difficult step.'

Inés Marzán showed little interest in knowing more about Centurión, and since she didn't ask him for his life story, this meant she could keep quiet about her own, although he did, at first, try to sound her out, before pretty much giving up. As he had been warned, she was very reserved, even evasive, when asked the kind of questions that two strangers would normally ask each other, two strangers who had, nevertheless, wasted no time in sharing the kind of intimacy that many, mistakenly, consider to be the greatest possible intimacy.

To quote Baudelaire, Centurión saw her body blossom, but not her soul, either in evocation or in recollection. Her body was very quick to respond, with a moderate or perhaps elegant voracity, with no coyness or timidity, no sense of subjugation or tyranny, an active and, at the same time, cautious body, that paused when it might be inflicting pain and stopped to ask: 'Am I hurting you? Are you uncomfortable like that? Am I squeezing you too hard with my thighs? Do tell me, won't you?' The expression 'terrifying games' did not apply to her, for to her this was pure play. Her soul, though, its evocation and its recollection, withdrew, retreated, did not appear, as if it did not exist or as if, at some remote point in her life, she had abandoned and lost sight of it.

This did make me suspicious. Perhaps she was someone condemned never to dwell on the before, never to remember, because among her visions and memories there were one or two that were simply inadmissible, the kind that can only be kept at bay if you decide to erase all memories, the good, the consoling, the bad and the frightening. If you can get up each morning as if it were the first morning of your existence, which is how babies must wake up in the weeks following their birth, not knowing what's going on or what they're doing here, where they fit in, nor who this soft, loving being is, a being in whom they see or smell only food; nor, of course, what they themselves are, *who* they are, an instinctive animal state that they soon, to their great regret, leave behind, even if it takes them years to recognize that sorrow and they sometimes reach the grave still not knowing its name. Perhaps she simply dealt with each day's tasks and nothing more, with whatever urgent matters arose, with the now that existed with no day-before-yesterday. Anyone who allows herself the luxury or the torment of never looking back always arouses suspicion.

And so, after three or four encounters with her 'magnificent curves' (hers were not exactly magnificent, but substantial and satisfactory, far more so than her problematic face with its enormous features, although familiarity does breed acceptance), Centurión still hadn't manage to find out if she was single or divorced or widowed, a fact equally unknown to her fellow citizens, among whom she had been living for several years. If one of them did know, they too were a mystery and an exception. When he asked her, in the neutral, uninvasive tone of someone who feels it would be discourteous not to take an interest or to inquire, she would say something like this, although in far simpler terms that I cannot now reproduce: 'It really doesn't matter, and besides it's none of your business. Why should you care about my past life? You can't sneak in there or intervene, you can't *be* there. You're here and now, which, by definition, means very little. Not even a whole accumulation of nows would mean a great deal, each now would be just that, a now. And the rest, the what-comes-next, a sheer waste of time, one big yawn. And, yes, sometimes a feeling of grief. Almost no one can talk about their past without feeling a little grief.'

Inés Marzán did tell him that she had lived in various places, in Oviedo, in Salamanca, in Madrid, where she, like me, had been born, in her case by chance; that she had spent a year in London in her youth, and had landed in Ruán by pure chance; that she enjoyed her restaurant and, despite the sometimes icy temperatures, was very happy in the town, and wanted nothing more. She gave the impression that she aspired only to keeping that life on an even keel, that is, repeating the same routine over and over. Someone who has no vision of, no ambitions for, the future is usually someone resigned to the circumstances of their birth or someone with such a heavy, burdensome past that it takes all their energy and imagination to occupy themselves exclusively with that past, with no room for anything else. They are usually someone who feels they have filled their quota of experiences or revenges or evils before their time, and that it now behoves them simply to stay very still and not cause more misfortunes or more harm by their movements or actions, their meanderings.

I know this because that is also my situation, I mean that of Tomás Nevinson, who has spent decades just waiting, and yet who, as you see, still counts for something. That was my situation in 1997, but it didn't stop me listening to Tupra again and to Machimbarrena and to Pérez Nuix and thus emerge from my state of waiting and move to a town in the north-west in order to establish contact with three women, and with bad intentions too, or perhaps they were good. It's always easy to persuade yourself that your intentions are good when they are still only that, intentions. Only when they have ceased to be 'only that', when they become reality, can you truly judge, and then, sometimes, feelings of remorse surface. I took it for granted that the woman I was looking for must have felt remorse if she had spent all that time in hiding and living a different life and without reoffending. I was aware that I could be wrong, but I accepted my supposition as true. I fought against it and told myself: 'If I do identify and eliminate her, there will be only one way of being sure. Of knowing she will never do it again.'

Whatever the truth, Inés Marzán did not tell him about her parents or her family or her origins, she was very miserly with memories, very stingy with information. And so, just in case she was Magdalena Orúe O'Dea, and so as not to alarm her by being overly inquisitive, Centurión did not insist. (In Northern Ireland, she would probably have become Maggie or Maddie or Molly O'Dea.) He decided to wait, knowing that people always talk in the end, that they cannot bear to remain silent for ever and not tell other people's stories or their own, cannot resist boasting a little or intriguing their listeners or provoking their compassion, horror or admiration, inspiring pity or terror, be it future or retrospective. Yes, people talk too much and without meaning to, even when they have resolved not to talk.

Centurión also waited until that fourth date to offer her a line of coke. He had kept some of the cocaine he'd been buying from Comendador, whom he met briefly each week at the station and tried gently to pump for information, although without applying too much pressure so that he wouldn't go telling tales to Inés Marzán; and since he didn't take the stuff when he was alone, or only rarely, he had more than he needed. He flushed most of it down the toilet as soon as he received it – a justifiable expense, since, sooner or later, Comendador was sure to tell him something of interest – so as not to stockpile it and get into trouble with the school or the local police, either by accident or as the result of some random search. Anyway, he still had some left. Inés Marzán accepted his offer gladly, but didn't ask for more, and certainly didn't seem desperate; after all, she had her own supply and wasn't exactly deprived.

A mist often descends over Ruán, or perhaps rises up from the river, I don't know, but it does hover on the surface of the waters, mingling with them or wrapping about them or almost replacing them, and then you can hardly make out the people crossing the bridge and it becomes hard to tell whether they're heading north or south, if they're facing you or turning away, if they're moving off or coming closer, if their face is the back of their head or the back of their head is their face. They're all different and yet they seem always to be the same, which is what happens when the shape that defines and distinguishes us one from the other grows blurred. It's as if they were walking in slow motion, because they seem to walk at a grave, spectral pace even when they walk more quickly, but also as if they were in fast-forward mode, because they appear for just a few seconds then disappear into the mist, which, at times, mysteriously, as if there were a pact between them, coincides with the wild clanging of the bells of numerous churches – San Bernabé, Santa Catarina, El Cantuariense and Santa Decapitación; Santa Águeda, San Edmundo, San Juan Puerta Latina, San Bartolomé and La Trinidad, as well as the Monastery and the Cathedral – calling people to mass or whatever.

One morning of early mist it became clear that they were definitely calling people to mass, because Inés Marzán unexpectedly answered their call. I had spent the night in her apartment, taking advantage of the fact that the following day was a holiday, which meant that her cleaner would not be coming; I had no classes, nor was it one of Comendador's Thursdays, for he never failed. The idea was to get up late and laze around until she had to go off to her restaurantly tasks. But she got up earlier than planned, at around ten, put on her best clothes – I could see her through half-closed eyes from where I lay on the bed – and just before the bells started their usual clamour, she said:

'Do you mind if I leave you alone for a while? I thought I'd go to mass.'

'To mass? I didn't know you went to mass.'

'Only from time to time, it's true, but everyone will be there today, and I like that, taking part in what everybody else is doing and being one of them. You don't mind, do you?'

'How long does the thing last?' I asked, feigning total ignorance. 'I haven't been since I was a child.' This was a lie, because I'd been obliged to attend a few Northern Irish masses as a grown-up, albeit some years ago.

'Oh, about forty-five minutes. It depends how long the priest's homily goes on for and how many people are taking communion. We'll still have a bit of time together before I head off to the restaurant though.'

'Are you going to take communion?' I asked slightly mockingly. 'You'd have to confess first, wouldn't you? And then come back determined to mend your ways, and we wouldn't want that now, would we? Or are the sins of the flesh now deemed to be only venial sins and so there's no need to confess to them? The Church is prone to making these capricious, arbitrary changes . . .'

She looked at me with a serious, almost scornful expression, the way women look at men who don't know when they've gone too far with their so-called jokes. She didn't respond and left just as the bells were beginning their madness; it took a few minutes for them to get going and reach their climax, which then deafened the whole of Ruán. I'd meant to ask her which church she was going to, but had missed my chance. I imagined she would choose Santa Águeda or Puerta Latina, as it was known there, which were both ancient, dignified, beautiful churches and fairly near at hand.

I was left alone in the apartment, and then I realized that I must act quickly. I got dressed without even bothering to shower, eager to start sniffing around. It didn't enter my head to do a thorough search, there was no time for that, only for a quick snoop; but once you begin, there's no stopping, just as when you start tidying your own bookshelves, and I would have to keep an eye out for her return. I looked in the drawers of a dresser and a wardrobe, clothes, more clothes, bedclothes, a few small boxes containing some fairly ordinary jewellery: earrings, bracelets, necklaces, pins and brooches, two plain rings and one rather elaborate one, as well as a lady's watch; now I know nothing about such things, but, to my inexperienced eyes, none of this seemed to be of any great value, although neither were they mere bling. In another two boxes, I found an old pocket watch on a chain, which would have been worth something (the maker was Breguet I noticed), and a pair of cufflinks, which made me think that there had once been a man in her life, important enough for her to have kept them as a souvenir. Or perhaps they had been a present from her that he had rejected, and which she hadn't then wanted to send back or change so that she could relive his scorn more intensely. Or, if she was a widow, to feel still sadder. Objects are very silent when you know nothing about their owner.

I went into the living room, where I searched the few shelves for any photo albums, which always tell you so much, but there didn't appear to be any. I looked at the one framed photo on display, which, when she was there, I had never wanted to look at closely for fear of appearing inquisitive. People always ask about any photos on show, but I tend not to. Now, though, I studied it carefully: a man in his thirties, smiling, holding a little girl – she looked about two – who was staring uncomprehendingly at the camera. That must have been her and her father, I thought at first. The little girl had dark hair, whereas the man was fairer, it would have been more interesting to find one of her mother, the one who, before she married, would have been called O'Dea, if, that is, Inés Marzán was Orúe O'Dea. It was a colour photo in which the background was too blurred to be of any use. It was so hard to put a date on it (I took the picture out of its frame and turned it over, but the back of the photo was blank) that it suddenly occurred to me that it could be the man of the cufflinks and the daughter she'd had with him. Perhaps Inés Marzán had had a daughter and, given her circumstances – her choices – had been obliged to leave her behind with the father, as I had done in England with little Val, who would still be growing up at her mother's side, I continued to send them money, but preferred to know nothing about them. I had done the same, to a lesser degree, with Guillermo and Elisa, my Madrid children by Berta, my first children, whom I had now superficially reclaimed, although there was never really room for them in my life . . .

Perhaps both had died, both Inés Marzán's husband and daughter, and she was just one of the living dead left merely waiting. Or perhaps those cufflinks were older and had belonged to her father, that was another possibility. When someone tells you nothing about their past, everything is possible in that past, which seems as smooth and featureless as the future, not ridged and furrowed as all pasts are, but full of incisions and creases and inscriptions that cannot be erased.

In the case of that woman, the husband could be a father and the father could be a husband, everything was like the mist that had descended on Ruán that morning, summoned by the bells or vice versa. I looked out of the window and saw how hard it was to make out the passers-by. If Inés had gone to Santa Águeda or Puerta Latina, she would have to cross the bridge when she returned, and I would find it difficult to recognize her then. All those individuals seemed completely interchangeable, like ghosts who are visible for an instant, then scamper off to make us doubt our eyes.

Inés Marzán had an office at the restaurant, where she kept all her business papers, I could find no files or folders or account books in her apartment, not even any notebooks. For lack of anything else to examine, I took a few books off the shelves at random, and leafed through the pages, hoping there might be letters or photos inside, something that might provide me with some information. I had no luck with the books I chose, and so I tried a few more. As I said: once you start, you think: 'Come on, one more, and another, or even a whole shelf full,' and so time passes without you even noticing. In four or five of the books, I found money, several thousand pesetas in each one, and I wondered if she would remember where she had hidden them; now this could indicate that she was expecting to have to leave in a hurry one day, or it could indicate nothing at all. I ended up looking through most of her books, she had only a modest collection, an eclectic selection as far as I could tell from the titles I bothered to read.

It would seem that Inés Marzán kept nothing. This in itself was very strange, because we all tend to accumulate things. Yes, it was suspicious. It was typical of someone who, at best, feels no attachment to her past, and, at worst, has tried to leave behind her no trail, no footprints, not a trace. It was understandable that, if she was Magdalena Orúe, she would carefully have covered the tracks of the person she had ceased to be and whom she now perhaps denied ever being. What was not at all understandable, though, was that there should also be no trace of Inés Marzán, the person she had been for many years, the person who had saved her and allowed her to live an untroubled existence, the only person she had been in Ruán.

Then I remembered how it was for me, how you so thoroughly internalize the total erasure of your identity that, sometimes, without realizing, you also erase your newly acquired identity, your false identity, the one that protects you: like an Indian on the run, you become accustomed to immediately erasing every footprint, to walking on tiptoe so as not to make noise, to ensuring that the dust from your fleeing feet cannot even be seen in the distance. Even if they advance confidently and unhurriedly, the feet of people like us are always fleeing from reality. Even the last step we take, the one that will finally remove us from the world and bid us farewell, even then we will be running away.

Feeling somewhat perplexed, I looked out of the window, then at my watch. Thirty-five minutes had passed since Inés Marzán's unexpected and possibly impromptu departure, it would never have occurred to me that she would go to mass. The Basques and the Irish do tend to be very Catholic, not that this means very much: most Spaniards are as well, which explains why we've allowed ourselves to be manipulated by the clergy since time immemorial. I didn't know much about the history of ETA, I'd never felt very interested, not that I did now, nor was I going to read up about it for the sake of what was a purely temporary posting, I couldn't be less interested in such utter imbecility, but I had the impression that the organization had begun in seminaries, inspired by antiquated, Carlist priests who fancied themselves as Moses liberating an entirely invented chosen people. There were doubtless some who gave the murders and kidnappings their blessing, and simply by the mere fact that they did not condemn those acts in mellifluous, charitable words, they were encouraging the faithful to go and commit more; in this respect, they were no different from the most patriotic of Irish people. It's rare to find a terrorist group that does not give off a stench of religion, whether faint or full on. Even anarchists and anticapitalists have dogmas, obediences, and positively ooze worship and devotion.

Inés would still not be back for a while, she had left before mass began, and it would not yet have finished; it was a five-minute walk from Santa Águeda and about eight from Puerta Latina, assuming she had gone to either of those, longer if she had opted for the Cathe-dral or Santa Decapitación. And longer still if she had hung around at the end, chatting to people, the whole population distributed among its various churches as if it were a holiday, that's what she had said . . . I suddenly found myself reciting: 'As if it were a holiday, the countryman sallies forth in the morning to view the fields after the hot night of endless, cooling lightning, the thunder still rumbling in the distance, and the river once again returning to its banks, and the earth so fresh and green, and the vines dripping with the gladdening rain from heaven, and the trees in the wood gleaming in the tranquil sunlight . . .' Lines I had known from when I was very young. As if it were a holiday.

The bedside table, I had forgotten to look there. It had three drawers. In the first, there were the usual pills, some for high blood pressure, well, she probably suffered from hypertension like most of the population, and a small box of condoms, although I hadn't given her the chance to offer me one, since I usually carried my own. In the second, there were some more odd bits of stray jewel-lery, and a forgotten novel or one that she was perhaps reading a little at a time before falling asleep: a contemporary Spanish novel, that is, from the 1990s, with a long title and by an author on whom a lot of frivolous praise had been heaped, as happens with almost everything when it's just published, just appeared, just born; so Inés Marzán was not immune to fashion, at least not to literary fashions, I should try talking to her about literature. Finally, in the bottom drawer, I saw a neat pile of diaries, about fifteen I reckoned. I looked at the one on the top, which belonged to that year, or rather, to 1996–1997, as it said in gold print on the top right-hand corner. I recognized them at once, despite all the time that had passed, for they were the same diaries I had used while I was study-ing at Oxford, the ones bought each year by teachers and students and many other Oxfordians who did not belong to what is called, with somewhat ecclesiastical pomp, 'the Congregation'; the ones that my tutor, Mr Eric Southworth, always used, as did Professor Peter Wheeler, the person who, with a single phone call, had propelled me into a life that both wasn't and irreversibly was mine.

The diaries had hard navy-blue covers and were all the same size. On the inside front cover was a simple map of the city indicating the location of all the colleges; and, at the back, a map of the London Underground, which is always useful, with its different coloured lines. 'So she keeps in touch with England,' I thought, 'someone must send her a diary every year, and from Oxford too, I don't think they're sold anywhere else, certainly not in Belfast.' Precisely because they were exclusive to Oxford, they gave the dates not of a normal year, but of the academic year and a little beyond, which is why the most recent began in September 1996 and ended on 20 December 1997. They were all identical and bore the university's coat of arms in the bottom right-hand corner, in fact the name on the front was *Oxford University Pocket Diary*. Each week was spread over two pages, on the left were what appeared to be appointments, things to do, phone calls to make, the usual list of reminders. On the right (on the recto, so to speak) things were more confusing or more enigmatic, brief notes and a lot of initials, as well as the occasional full name. Each day was crossed through, although this did not stop me reading what she had written. But it was odd that she should strike out each day when it was over, which is normally what people do when they're waiting for something that may never happen. Perhaps, if she *was* Magdalena Orúe O'Dea, it was her way of saying: 'No one came for me today, no one unmasked me, I survived another day, I'm free, and I'm still here. The night when I don't put a cross through the day will mean either that I've been arrested or have died.'

I picked up the diary at the very bottom of the pile, and which corresponded to 1983–1984. Inés Marzán had been using the same diary ever since, and she kept them too, but why, since most people throw their diary away at the end of the year, nor do they usually put a cross through each day as if it were accursed or simply another day they had survived unscathed? It immediately occurred to me that the 1987 diary must be there too, and that it would be worth checking 19 June and 11 December, when the carnage of the Hipercor and the barracks bombings had taken place. And on 29 May 1991, there had been another bombing in Vic, forty-two deaths and one hundred and seventy-seven wounded in those three attacks, it's extraordinary that, thirty years later, young people know nothing about them. The perpetrators are out there somewhere. Not many of them by now, but the collaborator Orúe O'Dea definitely was.

However, I didn't have time to do this, because it would have taken hours to decipher what her notes meant. The initials presumably belonged to the people she would have seen on the day, I thought. But for example, what did 'Cn AG T' and 'Cp TDY' mean?

I again picked up the most recent diary, and turned to the date when she and I had first met up. Along with some other scribbles, I saw this, which I did understand, but probably no one else would: 'L MC': 'Lunch with Miguel Centurión'. I looked further back, to the night when I had seen her go out with that dapper middle-aged man four inches shorter than her, the sleek politician or vain property developer, and I found 'S R de T', 'S' doubtless being an abbreviation for 'supper'. After that, in brackets, was '(f)'. It was impossible to know what that '(f)' meant, but then it suddenly dawned on me, dimly and improbably. I looked up the first day that Inés Marzán and I had gone to bed together, and there it was, the note said 'Dr MC (f). 'Dr' could be drinks, because we had had a few drinks beforehand. I checked the other dates when we'd had 'carnal union', which didn't take me long because 'carnal union' had not as yet happened very often, and there it was every time: 'Vt MC (f)'. So perhaps '(f)' meant something as prosaic and vulgar as 'fuck', however strange that word seemed to me in the mind of someone like Inés Marzán, the owner of La Demanda, who would, of course, quite naturally use a word like 'lunch'. But the language in which people express themselves and language in which they think are very different, especially regarding anything to do with sex, and we had already reached the age when women could be as foulmouthed as men, at least when speaking to themselves.

If '(f)' was 'fuck', this meant two things: one, that she noted down her sexual encounters in this succinct rather dismissive fashion – but at least she did record them – and two, that she had gone to bed with that antiquated, anodyne fellow of the onyx cufflinks and the bright kipper tie. So Centurión had been wrong in his emphatic judgement: when he saw them walking along by the river, so unequal in stature and style, he had predicted that, if this was a romantic date, then there was zero chance of consummation. So, either Inés Marzán already had a sporadic and often repeated relationship with that man R de T, or she was in great need of human warmth (Centurión had not yet entered the scene at that point), or she was just very open to such amorous effusions, to which she gave not the slightest importance, which was exactly how it was before and after her wild effusions with him. One of these possibilities was the only way to explain her screwing that pretentious hick, he thought, feeling not exactly jealous but slightly put out to find himself being compared with him in a field which, however bereft of sentiment, is always very personal: when you discover who the person you're sleeping with has slept with most often or is still sleeping with (it's the same with men and women, in that respect there's very little difference), the person in question sometimes becomes devalued in our eyes and we're filled with a sudden, quite unjustifiable disdain; it's very rare for their value to increase.

As for 'Vt', it could simply mean 'Visit', on the occasions when he had gone to her apartment, which was the only setting for her bouts of tempestuousness and for her coldness before and after.

What if I took one of those old diaries with me to study at leisure in my apartment, for example the 1986–1987 or the 1987–1988 diaries? In one or the other I would find the date of the Hipercor or the Zaragoza bombings, probably in the first. She surely wouldn't notice, she wouldn't miss it as she would the current diary, assuming she was in the habit of noting down her trivial daily activities in Ruán and, now and again, I noticed, making some brief comment, for example: 'What a godawful day', 'Now what do I do?' or 'Dreadful'. Yes, it would be interesting to see if she had written something similar on 19 June 1987 or 11 December of the same year or 29 May 1991, or if, on the contrary, she would have celebrated those massacres with a 'Fantastic' or a 'Great'. It seemed that ETA never killed soberly or sorrowfully; they didn't do so thinking 'It's sad, but there's no alternative', or 'A shame, but necessary for our cause'. No, the normal response was what we found out happened less than a year later, in January 1998 I believe: following the murder in cold blood (a bullet in the back of the neck if I remember rightly) in a street in Seville of a town councillor for the Partido Popular and his wife, who was walking home with him and had nothing to do with anything, several ETA prisoners celebrated this in their cells with bottles of wine or champagne and possibly, who knows, a few tapas. They must have had money even though they were in prison, or else their relatives brought them food on such celebratory days as if it was the obvious thing to do.

So there was the distinct possibility of a 'Splendid' if Inés Marzán had been far more thoughtless and reckless than she was now; she certainly would have been if she really was Magdalena Orúe O'Dea; more than that, she would be a criminal who would have deserved to die. What was still unclear was whether she deserved to die now too, under the name of Inés Marzán, in her now long life as Inés Marzán. Not that having met her and having fucked her a few times presented an insuperable obstacle to me. But I did have my doubts about killing a lonely woman who was focused solely on running her restaurant and who might well have forsworn her previously implacable nature, her blind rage. You can never know when a person stops being that person, when they eradicate the person they were. Perhaps that simply isn't even feasible, it would require them to wipe their memory clean, absolutely clean.

Taking one of the diaries could be risky, but then Centurión was in the risk business. Once he had examined it, he could easily return it to the drawer on a future visit or 'Vt', when she was in the bathroom or had left the bedroom to get a drink of water, after her brief flurry of passion.

Time was slipping by, as it always does when you make discoveries that require hasty analysis, you tend to lose track or not keep track at all. Still hesitating with the 1986–1987 diary in his hand, he again went over to the window. The mist hadn't lifted and had grown so dense that he couldn't make out the figures coming and going, they were a uniform, shapeless mass, as if wrapped in a static column of smoke or a feeble, stagnant cloud of steam. What he *could* see was a stream of people crossing the bridge in both directions (their feet were more easily visible), which indicated that some of the church services must already have finished and the parishioners were heading off for an aperitif in one or other part of the city, most of them to the Barrio Tinto. At no point had the bells stopped or diminished their pealing or ringing, as if the services were staggered on purpose or as if the fact that the service had started was no reason to cease summoning the faithful to mass.

During all the time Centurión was left alone in the apartment, the noise remained constant and unbearable – Ruán's churches all fired up – making it hard for him to concentrate or to think clearly. Because of the clamour he failed to hear Inés Marzán's returning footsteps or her key in the door. If she had returned alone, she would have caught him mid-snoop, fortunately, though, he was saved by the sound of voices, for he realized at once that she had returned with a male companion, with whom she was laughing and talking.

Purely instinctively, before he had made a final decision whether or not to make off with the diary, Centurión stuffed it down the back of his shirt, where it slithered along his spine as far as his belt, leaving a bulge that Inés might notice if, at any point, he had to turn away from her. At least he was still in the bedroom, so he closed the drawer and lay on his back on the bed, as if he hadn't even moved since she left. Although he was, of course, now dressed, albeit unshowered.

'Are you presentable, Miguel?' Inés asked, opening the door, from where she could see that he was. 'I want to introduce you to an old friend I bumped into and who just happens to be passing through Ruán.'

'I'll be right there.'

Centurión sat up, discreetly tucked the diary more firmly under his belt and went into the living room, where he saw a fat man wearing a gabardine-coloured gabardine, not really warm enough for visiting Ruán at that time of year. He was fifty-something, perhaps a little more, perhaps a little less, fat people look older when they're young and younger when they're old, they can often be very deceptive. He had thick, curly, greying hair which he wore fairly long, rather like a helmet. His glasses were too large for his beady eyes, and his other features were equally diminutive or perhaps it was just that his excess flesh made them look smaller than they were. His nose was brief and his lips thin, and he was smiling broadly, in friendly fashion, revealing almost square teeth, which resembled the pearly chewing-gum pastilles of my childhood, Chiew I think they were called; all in all, he appeared to be an affable man, who inspired confidence. He was, I sensed, one of those rather nimble fatsos.

For a moment, I had the impression that he knew me or recognized me, but I must have been mistaken, and he was merely looking at me sympathetically, for I was sure I'd never seen him in my life, anywhere. Then again, I'd seen too many people and frequented too many places, some so long ago that I barely remembered them.

Inés Marzán introduced him to me as Gonzalo de la Rica, and she didn't specify what kind of old friend he was, how they knew each other nor when they had met, dismissing the matter with an 'Oh, we've known each other for ever, we're almost family.' They chatted lightly about shared memories and people, and the only certain fact I gleaned was that they had coincided in two places, Madrid and Oviedo. De la Rica was a pleasant, talkative fellow, he made jokes that mostly went over my head because I didn't know the references, but which clearly amused Inés Marzán. After a while, he decided to show a little interest in me, or to appear to:

'Inés tells me you're a teacher, a schoolteacher.' And without waiting for me to respond, he came out with a stream of vagaries about the current state of education. 'I really don't know how you teachers cope these days, when everything seems entirely geared up to creating a load of ignoramuses. Of course, no one would dare say as much, on the contrary, but it does feel as if the government was longing to return to the nineteenth century, if not still further back, when the majority of the population were illiterate, knew nothing and so never protested or questioned anything. People then didn't have the means to do so, they could barely put their thoughts into words. Certainly not in writing, needless to say, and not even when speaking. Are your students capable of stringing together a few coherent sentences? How old are they?'

He had immediately addressed me as *tú*: well, if I was Inés' friend or lover (I wondered what she would have told him about me), then I was to be trusted. He asked questions without waiting for a reply.

'In a way, it's only logical that they should want to go back to that, to create more donkeys on the sly so to speak, it's an excellent idea, because as soon as people think they know a little, they think they know everything and that their every opinion about absolutely any-thing should be taken into account, should actually take precedence over the views of experts and scholars, and that's a recipe for paralysis: if you have to find a consensus for every tiny thing, then everything, absurdly, becomes an obstacle and nothing ever gets done. We've lived through a couple of decades now in which everyone objects and takes exception to things, and if someone doesn't put a stop to it, things will get completely out of hand. Why should people have a say in matters they know nothing about and aren't even interested in? Are people interested in astrophysics, neurosurgery, technological innovations, the arms race or space exploration? Of course they're not. Ninety per cent of people have never even taken the trouble to find out how a gun works. Or their own body for that matter, who cares about anatomy these days? Apart from a few curious folk and a few pedants who like to show off to friends at dinner parties, all they want are results, benefits, advantages. Profits. In fact, no one cares how things are organized, and so it's best if we leave it to those with real vision, real plans and real knowledge to deal with those matters, and such individuals have always been few in number everywhere, as they are now.'

I sat staring at this talkative fatso with a certain degree of curiosity, almost bewilderment. His lecture seemed, initially, to be a criticism of society's wilful and growing ignorance, but then he had gone on to praise that very thing or at least to consider it a good idea. I wondered suddenly if Inés Marzán would agree with his views, for the truth is she and I rarely talked about anything, I mean about serious subjects like that. I knew nothing about her ideas on politics or society, if she had any, because some people simply get on with their lives and let everything else wash over them. If, however, she was Magdalena Orúe, she would probably have no problem in subscribing to what her friend was saying: ETA passed themselves off as a left-wing organization, an organization 'of the people', but the fact is, they were old-school, selective, elitist, conservative, and as allergic to progress as the priests, and utterly dictatorial in spirit and in its intentions. Just like the two extremes in Northern Ireland, the IRA and the unionist paramilitaries, it was very hard to decide which of them was worse or did more damage. They all concurred in their disdain for people, in being prepared to kill arbitrarily and ruin the lives of the youngsters they attracted and trained; in their desire to dominate ordinary citizens and force them to accept what they ('the few') decided and wanted. In one sense, they weren't very different from the secret services who had attracted and trained me, except that we averted misfortunes, rather than caused them. We were reactive and preventive, we didn't initiate massacres.

Why had Inés brought de la Rica to meet me, why had she wanted to introduce him to me, or me to him, yes, perhaps it was the latter? If he really was an old friend she hadn't seen for ages, she could have gone off and had a drink with him without involving me; she could have phoned and made her excuses, and I would have understood: 'Listen, we just met by chance on our way out of church, let's see each other tomorrow or another day.'

Besides, what was she doing going to mass? I wanted to ask her about that, it wasn't very common among people her age in 1997.

'Do you know how a gun works?' the nimble fat man asked, taking advantage of my silence. I bet he was a good mover on the dance floor.

'No, I've never even held one in my hand,' I responded without batting an eyelid, since it would be unlikely that a teacher would have any experience of guns, at least in Europe. 'And I've never really wanted to. I suppose we pick up a bit about guns from watching films though.'

'You see? There you are, someone charged with educating and passing on knowledge, and you don't even know something as simple as that. As simple and as commonplace, there are millions of guns in the world in the hands of mindless idiots, any delinquent would know how to use one. Yet ordinary people don't care, they see that things exist, but have no interest in knowing any more than that. And yet at the same time, they want to have a say in everything and to intervene in everything. Don't get me wrong, democracy's a great thing, I'm a firm believer, but no one has ever really grasped either its real reach or its limitations. On the contrary, it continues to extend into areas

234

where it has no place. What sense is there in the ignorant making decisions about how to manage the economy or what our defence policy should be or even which laws are just or unjust? The process will be a slow one, it will take at least a couple of generations, but once people go back to accepting that they actually don't know, then they'll stop poking their noses in where they're not wanted, into matters that are no concern of theirs.'

I didn't know if Inés Marzán was expecting me to agree with Gonzalo de la Rica and his vast generalizations (he didn't seem to like democracy at all, or the idea that people should be educated) or to oppose him. She had never asked me about my beliefs either. I didn't want to alarm her by coming out with some stupid, off-the-cuff response, I didn't want to disappoint her, to alienate her; I needed to stay close to her until I had either identified her as Maddie O'Dea or ruled her out. It occurred to me that she was putting me to some kind of test by introducing me to this curly-haired fatty.

'Well,' I began very prudently, 'I think, ultimately, everything is their concern, whether directly or indirectly. People vote for politicians who inspire the most confidence – based on their gut feeling of course – or those who are least frightening, and in reality they put everything in the hands of those who govern them. Electing politicians is the least they can do, because they know that, afterwards, the politicians will do as they like. We can protest and criticize and go on strike, but always in the sure knowledge that it will make no difference. The people in government make the rules, even if they won by just a single vote. What do you think, Inés?' She had said nothing since de la Rica began his harangue, perhaps she was simply bored.

'I don't know,' she said, 'the world seems to me an impossible place. I just get on with my own life, because if I start thinking beyond that, I immediately feel overwhelmed.'

'What do you mean?'

'It sometimes amazes me that everything does actually function reasonably well, that it's fairly organized, that everyone has their duties to perform and pretty much do as they're told. There are too many people in the world, thousands of millions of heads, each filled with its own ambitions, passions, grievances and frustrations. I don't know how anyone can manage or even bear that. How can so many views, so many contrary interests be reconciled? When I think about it, I'm just astonished that the world isn't in a permanent state of war and hasn't long since destroyed itself or simply blown itself to pieces. That would be the only way to silence us all. There are always too many voices, and each voice moans on about all the other voices and blames them for its discontents. Even here, in Ruán, which rarely makes the headlines, there are conflicts and squabbles. I've had dealings with local politicians and the powers-that-be, and most of them hate each other's guts, are at daggers drawn. Imagine what it must be like in bigger, more densely populated towns.'

I meanwhile hadn't moved an inch, afraid that the diary held in place by my belt might fall out.

Centurión was familiar with one of those local politicians, because he was the husband of Celia Bayo, a fellow teacher at the school where he worked, and, thanks to the hidden cameras installed in their home, he was witness to a good part of their daily life, when he wanted to be, that is, and when he had time to review the hours of recordings. Not that there was much to look at, because husband and wife were rarely at home, and when they were, they usually didn't get in until late afternoon or evening. Their children were mainly looked after by a live-in nanny, and when the couple went out to supper or whatever, a young babysitter was brought in to provide extra support. Centurión assumed that the husband must earn a good salary or else had inherited or accumulated a small fortune that meant he could pay for what was pretty much full-time childcare and a comfortable, semi-luxurious life.

Nor did he rule out the possibility that the politician, like most politicians in 1997, then and even now, earned extraordinary amounts of money from commissions undertaken, favours done, contacts shared and various other underhand dealings. This was and is as easy in the autonomous regions of Spain as it is in Madrid, where, of course, it's commonplace. But perhaps the smaller the town, the more prone it is to bribery and corruption or to being corrupted, which becomes a natural part of life in the community with only a few rare exceptions who go unappreciated and despised and end up being shut out of the circle. If the whole population participates, then impunity and silence are guaranteed: no one is going to take the lid off a scandal that will send the dominoes tumbling one after the other; once reprisals begin, there's no stopping them, so it's best not to set them in motion, even the local schoolkids know that. It's best to make sure everyone is more or less a part of it. The Sicilians have their population well trained.

Celia Bayo was a jovial soul in her early forties and very slightly on the plump side. Not that she was overweight, but everything about her was rounded. Her face was round and dimpled; her bust was round, slightly too much so given her moderate stature; her hips were also round – perhaps having given birth to two children was to blame for that, rather than any kind of neglect on her part – as were her powerful thighs and calves, and the high wedge heels she wore gave her a brisk, resolute gait, rather as if she were wearing horseshoes. She was perennially cheerful and ready to help her students (she taught Geography and History to those still at the innocent age), as well as any colleagues who felt overworked or were otherwise struggling. From the very first day, she had greeted Centurión with a motherly, affable smile, as if aware that new arrivals are always particularly glad to receive a cordial welcome. She herself had been new some years before, when she had settled in Ruán, where she met and married the aforementioned politician (who was, at the time, only an aspiring politician).

It was initially difficult to imagine that she could actually be Magdalena Orúe O'Dea, apart from her red hair, her very pale eyes and her freckled skin. Of course, none of these features are exclusive to the Irish or the half Irish, there are plenty of women like that in Galicia, in Castilla y León and even quite a few in the more western parts of Andalusia. She might also dye her hair, although, for decades now, it's been impossible to know what anyone's original hair colour might have been. She seemed totally straightforward and transparent. Her far from stupid brain was what one would usually describe as a simple mechanism, naïve, perhaps too naïve to be genuine: she laughed when she should laugh and was moved when she should be moved, she cried when she watched a film intended as a tear-jerker, or would, without a hint of embarrassment, admit to having been reduced to tears, as if to say, how could one possibly react otherwise? If you told her a joke or made a joke at her expense, she would burst out laughing even if the former was not particularly funny and she hadn't instantly caught on to the latter, as if, at first, she had taken it completely literally; if someone suffered a serious setback, let alone a real misfortune, she would immediately sympathize and console and encourage them; if she spotted some injustice, she would speak out, but without making a fuss, because she was discreet even in her spontaneity.

She was really the ideal viewer or reader, because she responded obediently to the demands of the artists, even if those artists lacked expertise and their resources were fairly rough and ready. She was, if you like, 'a docile, grateful audience', one of those people who made Centurión think that the world would be an infinitely more bearable and less wretched place if there were more people like her. 'They are few, very few, a person without a drop of malice or resentment is a rare thing.'

From what he had seen of her at school, Centurión thought it was inconceivable that she could be the woman he was looking for, that she could have been involved, either closely or at a distance, with atrocities such as those perpetrated in Barcelona and Zaragoza only ten years earlier, and maybe, who knows, with others too. The adverb 'only' is justifiable here: it was too short a time for Celia Bayo to have become someone so guileless and so honest, so naturally given to feelings of delight and pity, so helpful and obliging. She could not have been further removed from Inés Marzán's chiaroscuro moods, her careful avoidance of the past, her hermetic, taciturn nature.

And yet her name appeared on that list of three, so there must be some reason; and her photo was among those Tupra had shown me when we were sitting outside that café in Plaza de la Paja and which I had studied closely when I got home, and I had recognized her at once, for she had barely changed since the photo was taken: the same bluish eyes caught unawares, the same sweet dimples in cheeks and chin, the freckles so tiny that, from a distance, they were invisible, the fine complexion that would soon be home to lines and wrinkles (she was perhaps on the outer limit before they made their first appearance and rapidly proliferated), her absent-minded gaze, her almost moon-shaped face.

Centurión forced himself to think that he must remain suspicious precisely because it seemed so unlikely. Perhaps her tendency to be obliging and helpful had led her, all unsuspecting, to be equally obliging and helpful to some very bad people. Perhaps it was all a front, or she had managed to forget what she had been, which is, of course, a fairly common phenomenon: you only have to look at politicians.

Inés Marzán had a past that she wanted to keep to herself. And Celia Bayo didn't talk much about hers either, as if she didn't have one, or not one worth mentioning, as would befit *un coeur simple* (but simple hearts have always known some sorrow). She clearly lived strictly in the present, or more than that, in the day-to-day, busy with her work, her husband, her children, her colleagues and her students, her citizenly duties and her endless social engagements. By temperament, and because she was a kind of conjugal 'power-that-be', she was also occupied with things both necessary and superfluous. She wouldn't have a moment for reflection, rumination, contemplation, to look to the future, still less look back at the past, and there are people for whom yesterday is merely an obstacle, a nuisance, the very embodiment of the useless, a burden that prevents them from getting on with today, yes, always driven on by the all-absorbing today. One night – it's usually at night – time stops for whatever reason, and then they discover that they can't remember what they have done with what they have already lived and consumed.

The fact is that in Ruán no one had a bad word to say about her, not even an averagely bad word. This might have been because everyone was vaguely afraid of her rather shady politician husband, or because she had the ability to win people over and have them forgive her virtues and her advantageous social position. At least she wasn't elegant or pretty or impertinently intelligent, qualities that are much harder to forgive.

Her husband was another matter, the influential councillor with a finger in every pie, regardless of whether or not it was his pie, and with a name that was as bizarre as his appearance. His original name was Liudwino López López, and everyone knew the story behind that: he had been born on 29 September, which is the day of San Miguel, San Rafael, and San Gabriel and All Angels. In Ruán, as in many provincial towns, it was the custom to christen babies according to the saint's day on which they were born, but being called Miguel or Gabriel López López was tantamount to being called nothing at all, and so his parents consulted the calendar of saints' days and saw that the 29th was also the day of San Liudwino, a name that seemed to them striking, distinguished and almost unique, and so they hurried to bestow that name on their new son, without even bothering to find out who the saint was, nor what his merits were nor what presumably good deeds he had performed. I don't know much about him either, but I think he was a bishop, possibly from Central Europe, who didn't actually do very much, and who, in my second or first language, would be Ledwin. I can't help associating him with a few other very strange saints who, for some reason, appeared on the Oxford calendar: from my student years the ones I recall, because they're so unforgettable, are Swithun, Dunstan, Blasius (who may have been San Blas), Cuthbert, Frideswide, Evurtius, Etheldreda, Prisca, Machutus and Britius.

However, so mortified was Liudwino of Ruán by his two redundant surnames that, when already a grown man, he managed to have the second one officially changed to another very secondary name from his mother's side of the family, and became Liudwino López Xirau. Alas, this artificially imposed surname was so peculiar (the only other person I could remember with that name was a footballer from my childhood collection of cigarette cards, a forward who played for Oviedo) and people found it so difficult to pronounce the initial x that, fortunately, everyone ended up calling him 'Ludvino', which was shortened to 'Ludi' by those closest to him, and by his affectionate wife to 'Vino' or, worse still, 'Vinito' when they had sex. Liudwino was quite unfazed by any of these corruptions.

Ruán was what used to be called 'a most noble and most loyal city', which means that it was, insofar as such a thing is possible in Spain, a serious city, verging on the austere and grave, proud of its remote past, when it had been rather important and the scene of some extraordinarily heroic episodes; it was, to be frank, arrogant. The inhabitants despised most other regions, which they considered to be mere upstarts, or else market traders and shopkeepers, or else egotistical whingers or else tricksters or else neurotic and conceited individuals, qualities that tend to go together. All the defects that Ruán saw in other cities were just as likely to be found there, for there was no shortage of trickery or whingeing or conceit or commerce, not to mention a large dose of wounded amour propre. But places try hard to appear to be what they believe they are and to live up to their reputation, and Ruán dealt with this position with sobriety and discretion.

Liudwino López Xirau's popularity probably came about because he was the very opposite of sober and discreet; he was extrovert, foulmouthed, boastful, histrionic and brazen, and, contrary to what one might expect, his brazenness fascinated many of his fellow citizens, who laughed at his jokes, thought him cheeky, astute and pragmatic, and were left flabbergasted and openmouthed by his risqué comments and tactless remarks, and even by the casual threats he issued to anyone who put obstacles in his path or refused to humour him. (Those cheerful threats would be followed by effusive embraces, pats on the cheek and a whole string of compliments, for example: 'God, you've more balls than any man I know,' or 'I love you to bits, just like Abelard and Héloïse only without the castration; oh, all right, if you want something a tad purer, like St Teresa and Christ,' or 'I'm going to place you on a solid gold pedestal, because you deserve it, the gold and the pedestal, you bastard.' Regardless of who he was speaking to, he addressed them all familiarly as *tú*.)

It's not so very strange that a place should allow itself to be charmed by what it most disdains and detests; that it should grow weary of itself and its decorum, its prudence and its culture, its supposed virtues, and quite simply adore someone who represents the polar opposite of all those things. While there is, of course, no comparison, the same thing happened with the inhabitant of Berchtesgaden.

For Liudwino López Xirau or López López, being a councillor was enough, and he had no need to aspire to anything higher or to carry a big stick. He had the ear of the mayor and of nearly all of Ruán's rich and powerful – businessmen, landowners, property developers, bankers, stock breeders, hoteliers, trades unionists and bishops – and could somehow, despite any initial misgivings on their part, bring them around to his views. He was enterprising, hyperactive, indefatigably cheerful, and it was rumoured that, from his position on the council, he had established an armour-plated network of corruption that benefited everyone, at least to begin with.

Centurión only had to see him once to know that he was the very last person you should make a deal with. You could tell from his face that he was an intriguer and a deceiver, what used to be called a chiseller and a cozener, a smooth operator with the gift of the gab and an infinite capacity for soft-soaping people. This, Centurión assumed, was the secret of his success: he was so transparent, so nonchalant and so brazenly sycophantic, that no one could imagine he actually was what he appeared to be, no one could believe he really was such a shyster. Or perhaps his particular style was so unfamiliar to the inhabitants of Ruán that they did not grasp what Centurión grasped at once, and saw him simply as a sassy, jolly, colourful, affectionate fellow with bags of initiative. He dressed loudly and eccentrically, he was somewhat lewd in his language, but they put this down to his energy, his vitality and his boldness. He seemed to them exotic and picturesque even though he had been born in the rival town of Catilina. Even his accent and diction were alien, vague and unpindownable, as if he came from somewhere further south, perhaps with some of the chutzpah of ill-mannered Madrid. Whatever the truth, both accent and diction had clearly been tried and tested and were a conscious choice.

Centurión found the man's whole appearance deplorable. As a way of compensating for his lack of height, he wore his hair in a quiff, doubtless lacquered in place, in the style of Elvis Presley, Johnny Burnette, Little Richard and other singers from his youth. His upper lip was adorned with a thin moustache with the ends curled up like a Napoleonic hussar's. Beneath his lower lip was a musketeer-ish goatee, although his muttonchop sideburns were at least fairly neat and modest, so that he didn't look too much like a highwayman straight out of the nineteenth century. Nothing he wore went with anything else, and the result was a kind of gaudy mishmash. He dressed stridently, the most discreet item of clothing he owned was a double-breasted jacket whose three silver buttons (or rather six) he always wore scrupulously buttoned up. Usually, he went for three-piece suits in strange colours, with a predilection for different shades of green (Nile green, chrysolite green, android green) or brown and magenta, none of which suited him, but he wore them with boyish pleasure. A waistcoat – which again didn't always match – was, he felt, indispensable, and he would take off his jacket and stride about the offices in the town hall, wearing either a floral waistcoat or an iridescent one better suited to a cardsharp, and with his shirtsleeves rolled up to his biceps to give an impression of dynamism and being all hands to the pump. In the street, you could spot him a mile off, not just because of his capillary ornaments, but because, even in winter, he wore light tan winklepickers, and didn't give a toss whether they did or didn't go with the rest of his attire. He must have spent a fortune at the tailor's, although not at any of Ruán's tailors, who didn't stock such garish or original fabrics.

At home, things were sometimes even worse. Centurión only had access to what was recorded by the hidden camera in the living room, and when Liudwino and Celia returned, presumably exhausted from their endless working days, they would somehow dredge up the necessary energy to perform their salacious acts right there on the carpet rather than in the bedroom (the children and the nanny having already gone to bed). They would indulge in absurd role-plays, and I mean absurd, because I once saw Liudwino López enter the room dressed as a gaucho, complete with baggy trousers and boots, a scarf knotted around his neck and a cotton shirt open to the waist. With his trousers flapping and skilfully whirling his *boleadoras* around his head, he swaggered over to his wife. He then did a terrible imitation of an Argentine accent and pretended to be a native of the pampas who just happened to have turned up at her ranch.

Celia Bayo laughingly joined in with this pantomime, and, being a simple soul, according to whom, it seemed, everything was always absolutely splendid, she happily embraced whatever he threw at her, or perhaps she was just trying to show willing. Whatever the reason, she threw herself wholeheartedly, even enthusiastically – as she did with everything – into the libidinous acts that followed these performances or fantasies.

Centurión felt embarrassed to witness what followed this display of fake gauchoism and to hear what he heard, but he couldn't stop watching or listening. He could have speeded up the tape and half seen it in fast-forward mode or stopped the tape and erased it, but he felt like one of those viewers incapable of changing channels or turning off the TV when they're presented with something that horrifies or repels them or with someone who angers or infuriates them. They remain captive to stupefaction, incredulity and the immeasurable pleasure of disgust.

Anyway, it was very clear to him that the couple did genuinely love each other and enjoy each other sexually, and it would therefore be an impossible task to develop any kind of intimate relationship with Celia Bayo, something that always facilitates investigations, like the relationship he had so easily established with Inés Marzán. He rather regretted this because he found Celia Bayo's roundness, once revealed and in action, rather tempting, at least in theory.

She and Liudwino did not confine themselves solely to these lewd excesses, which usually began as fictions (albeit not very subtle ones) and ended in purely animal fashion. When they were together in the living room, they would also exchange a few words, or, rather, the husband would update her briefly on the day's successes. Without going into detail, he would boast of his achievements in the same coarse, vulgar language he often used, even with the more distinguished *ruaneses* who had no choice but to accept it.

'Today, I finally got Gausi to kiss arse,' he said (Gausi was a very well-known property developer with operations in Castilla y León, Asturias and Cantabria), 'and as for Valderas, I've got him on such a tight lead, I can take him anywhere I want, it's amazing how quickly I broke him in.' Valderas was his boss, the mayor: 'Pee here, Mr Mayor, now stop here, and here is where I relax the lead for a second so that you can imagine you're free, but now we've got to get a move on, Mr Mayor, and if you need a shit, tough titty. The only one I'm kind of worried about at the moment is Peporro, I haven't yet got him eating out of my hand, and he's still up to his old tricks, but I keep passing him expensive little presents and when he does finally pocket them, he'll be sure to drop his trousers and offer me his cock to tickle with a feather or beat with a whip as the mood takes me. That's what I tell myself anyway. What pisses me off, though, is that recently, for his birthday, I gave him a really fancy-ass minute-repeater, which cost me a bomb. And then he was all "oh you shouldn't have" and all that crap, before strapping it on his wrist. But is he on his knees to me? No. It's as if the watch had appeared by magic and he'd forgotten where it came from. God, the guy's got a nerve! But, don't worry, I'll soon be sending him my bill.'

Centurión had no idea who Peporro was, but he was clearly someone with influence, despite his silly, childish name.

Liudwino's shady dealings were not Centurión's business, he wasn't in Ruán to right wrongs or to prevent or denounce abuses. The only thing that interested him about López Xirau was his wife. She clearly knew all about the bribery and the corruption and the scheming, although doubtless in a very broad-brush way, and didn't seem to mind in the least, well, why would she, when, thanks to all that, she could live so comfortably? Such an easy-going attitude, however, didn't chime with that of a former member of the IRA or an ETA collaborator or whatever; for while they will murder whoever they have in their sights without a twinge of remorse and place a bomb in a public place without a thought for those who'll be blown to pieces, yet, at the same time, they consider themselves so puritanical and upright that they frown at a thief benefiting from his thieving or someone selling drugs on the cheap (the extortions and robberies they commit are different of course, undertaken for the good of the country and the cause; and if a little of the money ends up in their pockets, why that's just support for the soldiers).

My immediate response was to cross her off the list and not bother about her. However, I resisted that temptation out of a sense of duty or discipline, and also because the more improbable Magdalena Orúe's new personality was, the cleverer she must be. True, unlike Inés Marzán – as one would have expected of someone whose mother was from Northern Ireland – Celia Bayo didn't speak a word of English (she spoke Italian, which she'd studied at school); then again, in 1997, almost everyone in Spain thought they could speak English and would happily attempt a few garbled, incomprehensible words. Anyone in hiding, though, if she's smart, must appear to be the opposite of – or as far removed from – what she was and possibly still is. I know from personal experience how difficult this is, and I have, on occasion, allowed my real or my old me to resurface, or have sometimes aroused suspicions by not totally rejecting the old me: one's natural tendency is to discourage or avert misfortunes when what you should be doing is fomenting and even precipitating them.

Even the loutish Liudwino could speak a kind of mangled English in his *sans-façon* way, well, everything he did was *sans-façon*. Celia Bayo introduced him to me one day when he came to pick her up after school, and on learning that I taught English he immediately let fly at me the following absurdly ungrammatical statement spoken in the most hideous accent: '*You don't steal me, pal, not steal wife's heart, not steal body, too many hours together, eh?*' And he tapped his index fingers together in a very graphic manner. When I looked at him, blank-faced or astonished and speechless, he grasped me by the elbow and drew me aside a little, then lowered his voice so that Celia wouldn't hear and so that he could explain in Spanish what he had said, summoning me to his side with a loud 'Psst' (he often addressed people with that particularly contemptuous sound, the way someone, in the old days, might have summoned a waiter or a street urchin). 'You're a bit of a looker, you are, and still young enough to keep your end up, if you know what I mean. Anyway, stay away from my wife, because she's very innocent and very sensitive, and you do, after all, spend hours together all day with bugger all else to do. You don't know me, but I'm the sort who comes to the boil very quickly and I'd make a fritter of your cock in no time at all.' I didn't fully grasp what he said, with his mixed metaphors of boiling and frying, but he could always somehow make himself understood, that was one of his virtues, clarity emerging from a tangled skein, clear messages wrapped in verbal mists. I merely smiled from my great height, patted him on the shoulder and said reassuringly: 'Don't worry.'

I later learned that, for all his bluster and his midget-hitman appearance, his wife was his weak point: when it came to her, he felt under threat and was extremely jealous. Even though she was neither pretty nor elegant, nor did she have the irresistible attraction of great intelligence, to him she must have seemed so alluring that he imagined any man must inevitably aspire to carry her off, even if it was only for a morning or an afternoon. And because she was so kind and friendly with everyone, and, therefore, in his mind, rather ingenuous, he was afraid that her attitude might give rise to misunderstandings and that, purely out of charity, amiability, pity or mistaken solidarity – in short, out of a desire not to disappoint – she would find herself being unwittingly lured away into well-intentioned carnal encounters. Indeed, the only thing that distracted him from his bungled schemes and complicated plotting was his preoccupation with Celia Bayo.

It was said that, in the middle of an important meeting with some Catalan politicians from Reus, who had come to Ruán *ex profeso* in order to talk to him and, hopefully, get a cut of his financial shenanigans, he had upped and left the meeting for a whole twenty minutes because he had suddenly had a vision of his wife, at that very moment, lying in the back room with the hairdresser she went to every week. This made no sense at all because the place was usually packed with impatient, complaining women, and the aforementioned back room wasn't a back room at all, but a tiny toilet usually with a queue outside. Nevertheless, the vision took such a firm hold on him that he rushed over to the salon – ruining his quiff and scuffing his winklepickers in the process – only to find Celia safely seated in a swivel chair and swathed in a very ample gown, while the suspect hairdresser carefully tended to her hair. After that morbid premonition, though, he made his wife go elsewhere to have her split ends repaired and her hair dye touched up, so that she was always a redhead.

He thus lost that opportunity to do business with the Catalans, who felt humiliated and cursed his behaviour as typical Spanish contempt. ('You see, there's no point even coming to this country,' one of them said. 'They don't respect us, they don't take us seriously and are sure to screw us over.')

After those initial words of warning, I got on well with Liudwino López. The poor fellow came to consider me Celia's protector, little knowing that, depending on how things turned out, I might carry her off for ever, either by handing her over to the law or – if that proved impossible – giving her a clean, merciful death. I found it hard even to consider the latter option, a woman is a woman, my upbringing kept repeating. And I would have hated to deceive him. He was such an optimist, so boastful and so over the top, that I found him very amusing. He convinced other people, which was a mystery, because basically he seemed to me to be a disaster waiting to happen, with his head stuffed full of delusions of grandeur and preposterous plans which, incredibly, often worked out well, at least initially. On the other hand, I was sure that one day he would get nicked and end up in prison. I felt rather sad about that, because he really enjoyed life. Then again, I knew he wouldn't stay in prison for long and would emerge unbowed. He'd find a way to wheedle his way to the top, one rung below the prison governor.

VII

The winter months passed as did one or two spring months, and there was still no sign of the cold easing or of the occasional mists dispersing, the mists that accentuated the ghostly aspect of that town in the north-west, indeed, some people told me it had even been known to snow in May. It's true that in the provinces time does pass more slowly, as if its inhabitants enjoyed double the usual lifespan, as if the hours made themselves felt one by one, stretching out, and weighing more heavily. It's a pleasant weight, though, like a friendly hand on your shoulder. It allows you to time to look up for a moment from whatever you're doing and find out what the storks are doing in their gigantic nests, or to listen to and count the chimes of the town-hall clock or those of a particularly insistent church, or the beckoning whistle of the knife grinders who still occasionally visit, or even the postmen whose whistles can be heard outside those houses that have no lift, summoning the tenants downstairs to collect their post: one whistle means there's something for the people on the first floor, two for the second floor, three for the third and so on, a system dating back to the 1950s and that still survives and persists in the Cathedral area, in El Cantuariense and Santa Águeda, in the areas that have remained almost unchanged for centuries. There are parts of Ruán that appear to have been frozen in that decade, and living there isn't in the least unpleasant, in fact, it's very pleasing and slow and nice. I realized that I was getting used to that rhythm, as I had during my long period of exile in that English town, which also had a river and a welcoming hotel, the Jerrold, the town where I had left Meg and Valerie – who was born there – never to see them again, that at least would be the advisable thing to do, more so for me than for them. For however much you watch over other people's interests, you keep a still closer watch on your own.

Tupra and Machimbarrena's calculations had been overly optimistic, or perhaps the former had more faith in me than I deserved, or perhaps I had grown rusty after so long out of action, or, rather, after having permanently retired, which is what I had wanted, but what we want, our will if you like, is a very feeble, fickle thing, and can do nothing on its own. Patricia Pérez Nuix phoned me now and again to find out how my investigations were progressing and to ask if I needed any help, and I began to feel rather embarrassed when I told her that I was making little or no progress.

Inés Marzán's diary, which I had taken (and which I had no problem returning to its drawer on my next visit) had proved fruitless. On the date of the Hipercor attack, all she had noted on the odd-numbered page was that she had dined with four people, giving only their initials. I passed these on to Pérez Nuix in case they coincided with those of some known terrorist, either on the files or in prison, but her response was negative. Obviously, such individuals usually have one-word aliases, and the initials in the diary appeared to include first names and surnames as they did with the men with whom I presumed she had slept. I also took her diary for 1987–1988, to see what she had written six months later, on 11 December, when the barracks had been blown up along with five little girls (I again returned it to its drawer without any difficulty and without Inés having noticed its brief disappearance, or so I assumed, since she clearly hadn't missed it and so hadn't asked me about it or said anything). The most striking thing was that, on the night of 11 December, she had again dined with two of the four individuals she had met up with on 19 June, they had the same initials. This was odd, but didn't prove anything.

There were so few notes that they didn't even allow me to work out which city she was living in during those years, or, rather, between November 1986 and October 1988, which was when the two *Oxford Pocket Diaries* I was able to consult at leisure began and ended. Wherever it was, she might well have had friends there with whom she went out to supper on a regular basis, although the same initials only appeared on those two dates. And so, as is only natural (suspicion and paranoia *are* natural feelings when you're on the hunt, like Pidgeon or Thorndike in that Fritz Lang film), it occurred to me that both those suppers could have been festive occasions, with glasses raised to the havoc that had been caused that same day. It was known, it is known (as I've said), that it was a custom among *etarras*, whether at liberty or in prison, to openly celebrate the success of an attack.

If that '(f)' I had noticed before did mean 'fuck', she must have recorded all or most of them, because it appeared with some frequency – every two or three weeks – always after someone's initials, not always the same ones (so she was rather promiscuous, and certainly not monogamous), but 'AG' turned up fairly often during that same time period. She also recorded the films she had seen, always on an even-numbered page and always, strangely enough, with the original English title, and so I learned, for example, that on 6 December 1987, she had seen Nicholas Meyer's *Time After Time*; on 15 January 1988, Kubrick's *Full Metal Jacket*; on 5 February, Alan Rudolph's *Choose Me* (she usually wrote the name of the director in brackets after the title, as if she were a film buff), and on the 7th, Powell and Pressburger's *Black Narcissus*, probably not at the cinema but on video at home. Either she had lost her love of cinema or she had simply never shared it with me, for she had never once talked to me about films.

What I gleaned from the second diary was that, shortly before the December carnage, she had made a long journey: on 29 November 1987, on the even-numbered page (the things-to-do page), she had written: 'Md → New York IB951, 13.35' and immediately underneath

'Phew, I nearly didn't make it.' She had obviously flown with Iberia that day and had either nearly missed the flight or had a very bumpy ride or else met with problems at immigration or customs when she arrived in New York, as frequently happens, but otherwise, who knows why she so very nearly hadn't made it? On 2 December she had written this: 'NY → Boston. Amtrak'. Amtrak is or was the national American railroad company, I'd made that same journey in the past, and, if I remember rightly, it took about four hours. On 4 December came this: 'Boston → NY. Amtrak', so she had returned two days later, having spent two nights in Massachusetts. And finally, on 7 December, just four days before the attack: 'New York → Md IB 952, 18.30', her return to Spain. The fact that the flights departed from and arrived at Barajas airport didn't tell me anything, not even that she was living in Madrid at the time: to get to New York you had to fly either from Madrid or from Barcelona.

She had spent a week in America, with a brief visit to Boston. My suspicions told me at once that both cities (but especially Boston) were not just full of Irish Americans, with remote or more recent family connections, but full of overt IRA sympathizers; some wealthy businessmen sent generous amounts of money to the IRA on a regular basis, many people on more modest incomes contributed what they could, and they could all count on the unspoken blessing of the American Catholic hierarchy, at least in New England; they didn't see the IRA as a terrorist organization, but as brave, patriotic soldiers fighting for the reunification and freedom of the 'old country', which had been subjugated by the Protestant English since time immemorial.

They were right in theory (my country, if it *was* still mine, had done its fair share of subjugation), but they blithely ignored the fact that Ulster was divided, that it was home to two equally murderous factions (unlike in the Basque Country, which had never been subjugated by anyone and had only one murderous faction) and that the IRA was responsible for the murder of many innocent people.

I made a careful study of the notes written during her American trip, but they were equally incomprehensible. On 2 December, she had dined in Boston with 'RR and NR', who could have been a married couple or two siblings, and on 3 December, she had met up with 'MS, JL, WL and AKK', whoever they were. During her time in New York, the most explicit bit of information was that on 5 December she had dined at the Waldorf Hotel (a legendary place and very expensive, which is perhaps why she could not resist noting it down) in company with 'BS, BE, RS, RHK, MRK, MW and SM', a large gathering; it occurred to me that, if she ever did go through her diaries, she herself would have found it hard to remember whose initials those were, especially as some would be English names, unless they belonged not to passing acquaintances, but to familiar figures. I could make nothing of it.

And so as regards my suspicions about Inés Marzán, I continued to nourish them, but could find no solid trail, let alone an irrefutable one. I asked Pérez Nuix to follow up on Inés Marzán's friend Gonzalo de la Rica, but she drew a blank. The name meant nothing to either the Spanish or the British secret services, which made me conclude, with no need for further proof, that it was false. Possibly even invented on that day of bells and mist, before they came into the apartment, on the landing, or as they were walking back from mass at Puerta Latina.

I wasted no time in questioning her about that. When we next met, I said:

'I didn't know you were religious, or even a Catholic. But since you never talk about yourself . . .'

We were sitting on a bench in Ruán's lovely main park, a beautiful place which I still miss. Like all couples (not that we were a couple, nor could we ever be; more than that, our mutual physical attraction soon waned, too primitive, I suppose, or too elemental, and we began to meet less frequently), we tended always to sit on the same bench after our brief stroll, as if what had been pleasant once should always be pleasant, or as if mere repetition protected one from the unpleasant and from things ending, from the final ending.

One of the problems with Inés Marzán, or one of her charms, was that she was a serious person. The friendliness and cordiality, the smiles she bestowed on her customers at La Demanda, barely appeared in her private domain, not even during intimate moments shared in bed or on the floor: what she revealed then was more a desire to forget than to accumulate memories for the future, I never had the feeling she wanted to treasure our moments of passion, she consumed them then coolly let them vanish, perhaps it helped her to feel momentarily carried away or took her out of herself for a few minutes, I'm more than familiar with the ephemeral benefits of that kind of impersonal sex. She only very rarely laughed, and when she did, her laughter was always forced. Not out of antipathy or bitterness, it was more that life, to her, was a serious business that didn't allow for many jokes, or even mere indifference. As if she thought it was a space through which we had no alternative but to travel, a vast space plagued with sorrows, some unsought and others foolishly brought upon ourselves, a space we crossed very slowly, ticking off each day, distinguishing each day from the last however identical, as tended to be the case in Ruán. Perhaps in the years she had spent there, she had become infected or impregnated with the town's slow pace. As I've said before, she gave one the impression that she was carrying some very heavy memories, so many that she could not speak of them; that she had suffered as a child or perhaps later on, in her early adulthood, which tends to be one's youth; that she had made her way in the world with enormous difficulty and effort, possibly having to humiliate or even prostitute herself, not necessarily in the literal sense of the word, or perhaps that too. Perhaps she'd had to pay for the favours of fickle men who had simply wanted to try their luck with a giantess, for novelty's sake, but never out of real sentiment, still less tenderness. For no other reason at all.

While this made it hard to have an easy relationship with her, it was also her charm. In a world of light, frivolous people, of ambitious or solemn or fanatical people, it's well-nigh impossible to find anyone serious and responsible, someone who isn't trying to make her way greedily through the world, nor to change it from top to bottom, nor to prosper and grow endlessly rich, someone who puts up with the world without making a great fuss, but, at the same time, pays proper attention, trying to understand how the world functions, in the certain knowledge that it's impossible to escape the world's mutable but eternal functions. All we can do is observe it, step aside and pass by unnoticed, so that it doesn't swallow us down like the sea's dark throat, so that we don't go the same way as those who die only at the very moment of their death. Because, believe me, such people resist with all their strength until that strength abandons them, and only then do they desist.

'Who told you I was?' she said.

'Well, a few days ago, you went racing off to mass. As if you'd forgotten your duty and had to rush to church in order not to break a commandment or whatever. I was surprised at such urgency. I was surprised that you'd leave me alone like that, with no warning.'

'Oh, it doesn't mean anything. As I said, sometimes I like to do what everyone else is doing, to feel part of the community.'

'So you're not a believer, and you just go to mass because everyone else does, for the company?'

It was with something akin to resignation that she looked at me with her very large eyes, large pupils, large sclera, large iris. The winter sun accentuated their greenish colour, it was like being looked at by the eye of a cyclops, and sometimes made me feel very ill at ease. I think I looked away whenever I had sex with her, and perhaps imagined I was with someone else, someone vaguely like Berta.

'No, I'm not. I haven't been a believer for a long time.' Her tone was also one of resignation and of slight forbearance, as if she were summoning up all her patience and what she really meant was: 'You've learned not to ask me questions, but you still ask far too many. I'll answer this one, though, because it's not that difficult and won't embarrass me.' 'But it's impossible to rid yourself completely of what you were taught as a child, that takes a permanent effort of will, and I'm not in favour of making permanent efforts about anything. It's exhausting always to be going against the grain, and it's far easier not to resist and just go with the flow. Even if you don't believe, you can still pray or murmur a few words, it doesn't matter. Pray to whom? Not to God or a saint or the Virgin, but to no one in particular, you don't have to pray to anyone. You just whisper to yourself: "Please, please". Or "Not yet, not yet". Or even "Forgive me, forgive me". Churches are usually silent places, or, if you're lucky, you'll hear some beautiful hymns or, if you're luckier still, an organ playing. You can be alone there, with no noise, no interruptions. Sometimes you just feel like going in and lighting a candle, knowing full well that, though this is an entirely empty gesture, it's still comforting, because it's the same gesture made by many people full of hope and devotion, and somehow you become like them, like the people who lived in an age when the world was more innocent and apparently more orderly. It's nice being in the church when the whole town is there too, rather than with four superstitious old ladies for company. That seems so sad, so anachronistic. It wasn't like that the other day. Even if everyone was only there because it was traditional, the churches were all packed . . .'

'Why "Please, please"?' I asked, making the most of the fact that she had given me an answer, a generous one too. ' "Not yet" what? And who do you want to forgive you? You must have someone in mind.'

She looked away, and I felt relieved. She looked instead at the Olmo de las Melodías, a huge, ancient elm tree, the top half of which was surrounded by a wooden platform with green wrought-iron railings, and which could be accessed via a small spiral staircase also made of green wrought iron. On public holidays and when the weather was fine, the municipal band would play up there among the leaves, the musicians dressed in old-fashioned uniforms long past their sell-by date. Another tradition that would not survive much longer.

'What I pray or wish for is that nothing bad happens to my daughter. It's like saying "I wish, I wish". You don't expect anyone to listen to you, of course. It's just an expression, because sometimes you need to imagine there's someone listening intently to your thoughts, that's all. There are statues in the church. They're only effigies, and most are pretty ugly, but they're more deceiving than that elm tree, for example. Churches have been receiving people's heartfelt prayers and pleas for centuries, and some remnant, some trace of that must be there hanging in the air.'

'You have a daughter?' So the little girl in the photo wasn't her, but her daughter. 'Why doesn't she live with you? Where is she?'

She looked at me again, impatiently this time or almost sternly. But she wasn't going to tell me off for my lack of tact, which was to be expected, at least in a man.

'You've seen the photo in my apartment. Why would she necessarily live with me? People always assume that any children will stay with the mothers, but it's not always so.'

'Yes, I'm sorry, I know that, but it is what usually happens, and still tends to be the case. Would you prefer her to be with you? What happened? Wouldn't they let you keep her?'

She hesitated for a few seconds as if pondering whether she should make any more concessions or if she had already told me enough. She again fixed her gaze on the top of the bare elm tree, it would be months before it was once more filled with simple music and restored to its former glory. I think she realized that my questions were inevitable, that not to ask them would have been inconsiderate on my part, however reserved I knew her to be. You can't respond with indifference to a revelation, to a secret sadness, the term Berta once used when I had been standing for a long time on the balcony at her apartment, staring into space, shortly after I had returned to Madrid after being lost for years, after being dead for years. 'I know we all have our secret sadnesses, I have mine too,' she said. 'I won't burden you with them, though, and I don't want you to tell me yours, not at this stage in our lives. We can keep our accumulated sadnesses to ourselves. Just tell me if that is what you're thinking about right now, and then I'll leave you alone.'

Finally, Inés decided to say something more:

'I don't usually know where she is. At most, I know where she's been, afterwards, I mean. Her father occasionally phones me up to give me a brief report. He lets me know that she's well, that she's not ill, that there's nothing seriously wrong, that everything is carrying on as usual somewhere far away, but not much more than that. I don't even know where he's phoning from. He doesn't want to run the risk of me suddenly, out of the blue, turning up on their doorstep, wherever that is, because sometimes they go travelling, and he only tells me when they get back. He should know by now that I would never do that, that I've accepted the situation and am resigned to it. Not happy, but resigned. I have no choice. He has paternal authority, custody, everything, she's his. We agreed that I would keep away, that I wouldn't try to get in touch or interfere. And I've kept my word. I don't know what he tells her about me, if he tells her anything. She may not even know I exist, or that I'm even alive. She's ten years old now, well, she soon will be. She's sure to ask him about me, and must have been asking about me for some years. I don't know what he'll have told her, what he'll have invented, what explanations he'll have given her. What story she'll have been given about me, because she must have been given a story. He has the privilege of deciding what that story is, from before she was born until now. Sometimes I think it would be worse if he told her the truth, and it would be better to make up some fairy tale. It may be that she knows nothing, that she thinks I'm dead, that would be the easiest thing, the most convenient and the kindest; people ask fewer questions about the dead. Or you're always given the same answers, because there's nothing more to add, never any news, they're paintings that have long been finished and can't even be retouched. The truth is, I haven't the slightest idea what she might think of me. Or even if she does think of me. Perhaps she's used to me not existing. I don't exist, I didn't exist, and that's all there is to say.'

I remained silent at first. Very silent. I found it hard to make any kind of comment, and I didn't want to arouse her suspicions by turning her confession into an opportunity for me to interrogate her. The prudent thing was to wait, but I had the impression that she wasn't going to say any more, that she'd told me the most important part. Nor could I remain silent indefinitely or change the subject just like that.

'When did you stop seeing her? Or did you never have her with you?' This struck me as unintrusive, as showing genuine interest or politeness.

'When she was one year old or less. I never saw her again. It was best that I should disappear. That was what I wanted at the time, I needed to disappear and I did. You never know what you might want afterwards, after a year or five or ten. You can't even imagine an afterwards. We live so much in the moment that there is no afterwards. We live so fast, with such immediacy, that we forget there always is an afterwards. Even when we think we're dying and it's all over, even then, there's an afterwards.'

She was becoming increasingly lost in thought, and I wasn't sure how to continue. I went back to concrete facts:

'And is there no way of changing things? Couldn't you come to another agreement now? A lot of time has passed, and you would obviously like to see her, to meet her.'

'No, her father would never allow that.'

'Why not? Everything can be revisited, revised.'

She said nothing and looked away. She stared intensely down at the ground, or so it seemed to me, but perhaps I was imagining it. As if she wanted to pierce the grass and penetrate the park's usually moist soil with those enormous eyes set in that vast face in that over-sized body.

'No, there are some things that can never be revised or changed. Isn't it absurd? I gave birth to that child and saw her every day for several months, and yet if I passed her in the street now, I wouldn't recognize her, I would have no idea it was her. When I see girls her age, I sometimes think: what if she happened to be visiting Ruán?

What if she's on a school trip and she's part of that group visiting the Cathedral? School groups come from all over, so who knows. I've no idea where she lives, but she must have a routine and go to school, she must.'

She was still staring down at the ground. I fancied that she was trying to imagine the indecipherable face of that intimate stranger beneath the grass, beneath the earth. She paused, then added very softly, as if she were no longer speaking to me:

'I behaved badly.' Her soft voice trembled, and, when she realized this, she immediately fell silent to avoid that tremor, which, however, reappeared shortly afterwards, when she said again: 'I behaved badly.'

I couldn't now see her vast eyes, but I could have sworn they were filling with tears. This clearly embarrassed her, and so I tried to help her out.

'Badly? What did you do?'

She looked up from the grass and once more gazed across at the top of the tree (perhaps this was her way of driving away her tears, of fending them off), then got to her feet, smoothing her skirt. I stood up too, and she again towered over me, in that sense, she was always my superior. She obviously felt our stroll had reached a natural conclusion, as had our conversation. Thus ended the brief story of her secret sadness, so strangely similar to the story I could have told her about my daughter Val. I wouldn't recognize Val either, although much less time had passed since I last saw her, only three or so years, I didn't want to keep track, I didn't want to have to imagine her at various different ages.

I can't deny that I was tempted to tell Inés: 'I know exactly how you feel, I've been through the same thing. I brought a little girl into the world, then parted from her, left her behind. She isn't mine either, she belongs to her mother, it happened in another country. For me, though, there is no afterwards, I stopped having an afterwards decades ago, when I believed a young woman I'd just been to bed with had died. But that was in another country, and she wasn't as young as I was at the time.'

I did not, of course, give in to that temptation, although hearing a confidence always invites you to share one of your own, it almost never fails, as if a confidence shared were a gift, a present, and not infrequently a poison, a burden, an attack, a curse. And if someone curses us, we usually curse them back, we need to correspond in kind, to restore the balance. But she would then have asked me to explain, and I could not and must not on any account give her an explanation. Besides, I felt that my revelation wouldn't have the same weight. I was more battle-hardened than she was, or more inured, a battle-hardened wretch. What I'd been through was a secret, but it didn't make me sad and my voice would not have trembled as I told it. It was something that had happened as all things happened, nothing more. Most things do just happen, with or without our intervention.

'That's none of your business, Miguel.' This was one of her favourite sayings, she had clearly recovered from her emotional state. 'I've told you before: you weren't there in my past life and you can't intervene in it. What's the point of you knowing about it if it's not in your power to put it right even if you did know? I don't have that power either of course. Nor does that God in whom I don't believe, even though I do occasionally visit his chosen places and light a candle and murmur "I wish, I wish" as if I did believe. No one has that power . . .'

She gave a timid smile, as if she were ashamed of having told me anything, a lot in fact, and without intending to. Before that moment vanished completely, I tried to press her a little further, to cautiously find out more:

'According to you, that isn't what you murmur, but "Please, please" and "Not yet, not yet" and "Forgive me, forgive me". Some day you'll have to tell me why you're asking forgiveness like that and what it is you're so afraid of that makes you say "Not yet, not yet". That's not referring back to your past life, but to the future.'

She smiled again, but not timidly this time.

'To be honest, I really don't think you're going to be part of my future life.'

In this, Inés Marzán was absolutely right, she had guessed correctly. In theory, I was going to be in Ruán for what remained of that term and perhaps a term or two longer, and, in theory, if the school renewed my contract and I signed up for it, I could settle down in that town in the north-west just as those three women, those three incomers, had done ten years earlier, although when they arrived they had never imagined they would stay. You move to a place not knowing you'll be trapped there, that you'll establish a business or your entire life, that you'll marry and have children and embrace the local customs, and that what was provisional will become perpetual. That it will become harder and harder to leave, firstly out of inertia and later out of fear, as if life beyond those walls posed real dangers, like setting off across the ocean in an antiquated sailing ship you've forgotten how to steer.

Miguel Centurión could become one of those people who watch the weeks and months and years go by and suddenly discover that the only sensible thing to do is to continue watching them go by, to continue watching the stream of individuals who, every day, cross the long bridge over the Lesmes river, the precursors of those who will cross it the day after tomorrow and the heirs of those who crossed it the day before yesterday, all of them oblivious to each other's existence, not even sensing their presence or recalling them, all of them different and all of them identical, equalized by the mist of the days that pass as slyly and monotonously as the waters of the river, equally imperceptible to young and old, to the newborn and those about to depart this life. Miguel Centurión could have carried on indefinitely watching their slow or hurrying steps, without ever really mixing with them, merely contemplating the passing of those who coincided with him during his time there, merely recognizing them day after day until he no longer noticed any change of personnel.

But I was Tomás Nevinson and there was nothing to keep me there once I'd fulfilled the task assigned to me, although who knows why I'd agreed to it on that January day. So Inés Marzán was quite right, I wasn't going to be part of her future life, indeed, in the worst-case scenario, I might even be the one to end her life: if I was convinced she was Magdalena Orúe O'Dea; if I couldn't find enough evidence to take her to court, but was still absolutely sure, then I would simply have to eliminate her, because of what she had done and to prevent her doing it again.

'Extrajudicial killings', people say in outraged tones; it happens more often than those honest citizens might think, citizens who pay only lip service to honesty and do so from the safety of their living rooms and when they themselves aren't under direct threat. Nowadays, no one minds if someone preparing or carrying out an indiscriminate attack is eliminated on the spot, and if those virtuous, upright folk were armed, even they would gladly shoot a man they saw randomly stabbing people in the street or about to squeeze the trigger of a semi-automatic rifle and fire into a crowd; more than that, they would beg and demand that the person be killed instantly, without a word and without a thought for legality, just so that he could no longer do any further harm, so that he won't knife me or shoot my poor child, whose fragile body wouldn't survive a bullet, let alone five or six. Finish him off, crush him, kill him and tear him to pieces here and now, don't wait for him to be arrested or put on trial, don't bother with any of that nonsense, after all, what has he done to deserve such guarantees, can't you see he might kill us, blow us to pieces, slash us and make us bleed? Exterminate him, annihilate him, tear him limb from limb once and for all.

However, I was still very far from achieving such certainty and, to be honest, I wasn't making any progress and was still very far from reaching any conclusion. Inés Marzán's story about her lost daughter was a touch too melodramatic, it could be pure invention intended to gain my sympathy and doubtless my pity too, if, that is, she had her suspicions about me, because one must never discount that as a possibility. Or it could be true, and if her daughter really was about to turn ten, then Inés Marzán would have given birth in early 1987, only months before that year's attacks, just a few months before the Hipercor attack. We tend to think that no mother, holding a new baby in her arms, would ever be prepared to allow others to die on her account or with her collaboration, but that is to misunderstand the nature of murderers by vocation.

'All those guerrillas idolized by people, all those terrorists, those supposedly idealistic liberators, are, first and foremost, clever, cunning killers,' the Anglo-Cuban writer Cabrera Infante had said to me once when I visited him in London, where he had been living in exile with his wife Miriam since the mid-1960s, despite having initially supported the Castro revolution and represented it as a diplomat. I had gone to visit him in his house in Gloucester Road, passing myself off as a Spanish novelist. This wasn't so very different from what Pérez Nuix had told me, perhaps she had visited Cabrera too, he was a very hospitable man. 'All those people, young and old, who adorn their walls with that Che Guevara poster, as if he were Elvis or the Immaculate Conception, have chosen not to find out what he was like in real life. And they cover their ears if you tell them, and look at you as if you were a worm. After all, that's what the Castro regime and their international acolytes call us, isn't it? *Gusanos*. Well, I knew him personally, I knew him before he became a celebrity, and I can assure you, Señor Manera, that, right from the start, he was a murderer by vocation. He was a cruel, ruthless man with a real taste for killing. Many people are killers by instinct, by impulse, out of necessity, because they carry it in their veins, out of necessity. The more astute among them come up with excuses, alibis, and these work so well for them that, far from receiving recriminations for their murders, they are applauded and become heroes. A brilliant move. "You see, I kill the oppressors in order to save the oppressed," people just lap that up, and then, not only do they forgive them, they venerate them and ask for more and more and more. I've seen a few of them in action, I've seen them put on that aura of heroic abnegation, I've seen them pass themselves off as martyrs. In fact, they were all executioners. Policemen, judges, executioners, all in one. They would arrest or kidnap someone, then sentence and execute them that same day. Summary trials, a term I'm sure you know. There were loads of such trials in Spain in 1939.'

If Cabrera Infante was right and was telling the truth (he certainly didn't strike me as a deceitful man), such individuals are capable of killing children even while holding their own child with infinite tenderness, cradling its head with their free hand. I've known a few of them, Irishmen who would plant a bomb and Englishmen who would shoot someone in cold blood, only to go back home at night to tuck their children up in bed. For them 'the others' don't exist, they are tyrants or the offspring of tyrants destined to reproduce more tyrants and perpetuate them, they are tarnished from birth and should not exist, for the good of the pure, of the truly clean, of the empire, the captive homeland, liberation, or whatever. I sometimes wondered if Tupra perhaps belonged to that same class of person, he had the look of someone who had left a few corpses behind him before serving the Crown, of someone who had not set out to avert misfortunes, to defend the Realm and certainly not out of a sense of duty.

And so if Inés was Magdalena . . . Even if her story wasn't invented and she *had* just given birth, that wouldn't have prevented her from cooperating with those murderers in Barcelona and Zaragoza, nor, prior to that, with other murderers in Ulster. However, nothing was clear or definite. Everything could be seen in that light, just as you can see anything in whatever light most favours or justifies or suits you. 'I behaved badly,' could mean 'I took part in vile, entirely gratuitous crimes.' 'I wanted, needed to disappear' was perhaps a way of saying that if she had stayed where she was, suckling and caring for her daughter, she would have been found and arrested. Even her abstract prayers in Ruán's silent churches allowed for that interpretation: 'Please, please': don't let anyone ever find me out or put an end to the tolerable, tranquil, fake life I've built for myself as Inés Marzán, so much so that at times I can almost forget stern, radical Magdalena O'Rue, who, in Belfast or in Derry, where they couldn't pronounce her Basque name, would become Maddie O'Rue, where even during her childhood visits, the other kids would poke fun at her, singing: 'Rueful, rueful Maddie O'Rue', who would have thought those childish words would prove so prophetic. 'Not yet, not yet': they haven't found me yet, the day when everything will come crashing down hasn't yet come, no one knows who I am or who I was, please don't let that happen yet, not yet, give me a few more months, at least one more night when no one will come pounding on my door and drag me off in my nightclothes. 'Forgive me, forgive me': forgiveness for the irreparable harm done, forgiveness for having helped kill people who had cheerfully got out of bed one morning, never imagining that what awaited them that afternoon or later that same morning was their violent death, people who would never return to life.

But it could all mean a thousand other things, forgiveness for mistakes she'd made or sometimes for her own intransigence or her fits of rage, her blunders, sudden acts of desertion, foolish decisions, unimportant infidelities that had unforeseen and unstoppable consequences, matters that seem unimportant to anyone listening, just the usual baggage carried around by anyone set down in this world and obliged to traverse it, no one stays forever safe and warm in the cradle.

I sometimes put pressure on Comendador, openly now (he had even given me a key to his apartment in Catilina, in case I needed to stock up when he was away): 'Tell me what you know about Inés, when was the first time you saw her, why did she move here, who did she come with, who brought her here, who visits her, who does she go and see, you've been visiting her every Thursday for years now, she must have told you something or let something slip, think, man, think, or do you want me to turn up one day with the police and search your apartment?'

The spurless gunman had felt afraid of me right from the very first day, and that fear had gradually grown. His nocturnal instincts were telling him that I wasn't just an English teacher, but he couldn't work out what else I was. This meant that he didn't resist, he volunteered information, tried to please me, to collaborate. All he told me, though, were trivial details, the odd bit of gossip, that Inés, for example, had been briefly involved, years ago, with some man or other. None of this shone any light on her, none of it interested me, and poor Stephen Stills was trying so hard, struggling to remember something more. It was clear that Inés Marzán had revealed nothing to him either about her life before her move to Ruán, keeping her past safely under lock and key.

Shortly after that walk in the park with her, after what she had confided beneath the Olmo de las Melodías, I asked Comendador:

'Did you know she had a daughter?'

The look of surprise on his face was completely genuine.

'What!' he said. 'How come we've never seen her? Where is she?'

'How should I know? And if you know nothing about her, I can't even be sure it's true. Do you have no idea who the father might be? Has she never spoken to you about some significant other in her life? Or insignificant for that matter?'

275

'No, she's never mentioned anyone. She's very reserved, very professional. We've known each other for years, but she is just a customer, nothing more.'

I eyed him scornfully as we sat together on the bench at the station.

'The truth is, Comendador, you're no use to me at all. I'm not going to buy from you any more. Or only very occasionally. Meanwhile, I'll consider what I should do with you, whether to leave you to your shady dealings or give you the punishment you deserve for being useless and disappointing. I've wasted too much time with you, as well as money that isn't mine.'

'What do you mean, Centurión? How have I let you down?'

They should never have given me that name. There we were, the two of us, Centurión and Comendador, like some old-fashioned comic duo.

'As a creature of the night, you must see dozens of people from every social class, and some of them must owe you money. And yet you can't bring me the tiniest bit of useful information about Inés Marzán. You can't tell me who she was or what she did before coming here.'

'What do you expect me to do? No one knew her before, no one in Catilina or Ruán has tried to investigate or draw her out. And if she clams up and won't say a dickybird, what are we supposed to do, torture her?'

I was bewildered by my lack of progress, I was irritable and bad-tempered, and I needed to put the blame on someone. And that wimpish gunman was the ideal candidate.

'It doesn't matter, there are lots of different ways. She must have told someone something during the last nine years, and you know almost everyone. You're a complete waste of space, Comendador. I don't want to see you again. I might call you one day, though, and see if you've finally pulled your finger out.'

I could see that he was taking a while to get the message. He was puzzled and disappointed too. Finally, he said in a rather weary, plaintive voice:

'So I'm just incidental, then. All you're interested in is Inés. But why?'

I wasn't afraid that he would go telling tales to her, that didn't worry me in the least. When you instil fear in someone at your very first meeting, that fear lasts a long time, or else it takes a superhuman effort to shake off that initial sense of intimidation, and Comendador wasn't going to make that effort. However much he respected Inés, she was, as he had said, just a customer. And if he did warn her about my overzealous interest in her, I could always say that I was falling in love with her and lovers are so foolish that they need to know everything about their beloved, even what they shouldn't know or what might be prejudicial for them to know.

I fixed him with that same cold gaze, he was just another provincial dope peddler, one of many. His Stephen Stills sideburns were totally over the top, not like Liudwino López's, who at least made up for his generally over-the-top appearance with a few more moderate details. Comendador wasn't ugly, but nor was he pleasant to look at, with that nose which always looked as if it were about to drip but never did, with that narrow body encased in leather, with that mixture of straight and curly hair. With the clink of his metal-tipped boots that announced his arrival ahead of time and made his departure seem to last for ever, continuing to clink for a long while after he had disappeared from view, clink-clink-clink.

'Yeah, right, like I would tell you.'

March and April passed, May arrived, followed by June, the last month of the school year, after which it really wasn't clear what Centurión should do, whether he should stay in that town in the north-west or leave until September. Tupra, or was it Machimbarrena, had been ridiculously optimistic, this whole business was going to take much longer.

He found it embarrassing talking to Pérez Nuix whenever they spoke on the phone. She couldn't understand why he was being so slow, why he was making such minimal progress, everyone wants quick results even if they turn out to be wrong and are of no help at all, and she made no attempt to conceal her disappointment at the fact that he hadn't even managed to make contact with the third woman, María Viana.

What neither she nor Machimbarrena had foreseen (still less Tupra, who had assigned him this mission, but who, once back in London, seemed to be taking absolutely no interest) was that she was beyond the reach of a modest schoolteacher. There was no reason why he should ever meet her, coincide with her or get to know her, their worlds were too far apart. María Viana was married to Gausi, a wealthy property developer, and one of the many who, according to Liudwino López, had kissed his arse, as he had boasted to his wife Celia Bayo during one of the domestic recordings at Centurión's disposal.

From what he knew and could see from a distance, Centurión

found it hard to believe that Folcuino Gausi (Ruán abounded in eccentric names even in families of so-called noble descent, a desire perhaps to stand out from the rest of upstart humanity) would kiss anyone's arse, still less that of Liudwino, the local thug and wheeler-dealer, who, the more I saw of him, seemed more and more like a poor, pathetic wretch. A clever, conniving trickster, yes, but still a poor, pathetic wretch. Gausi belonged to Ruán's high society, which – as is usually the case in small and medium-sized and, so to speak, uncontaminated towns – did its best not to mix with the other classes any more than was necessary. In such towns, the old customs prevail, everyone knows who is seriously rich, who is less rich, who doesn't pay their rent and who works their socks off just to keep their head above water, if that; and the former make no effort to be forgiven or tolerated for their good fortune, whereas in big cities, people mix a little more, and the social classes are becoming ever more blurred, something that works to the advantage of the powerful. It wasn't like that in Ruán, where the social compartments remained well sealed.

With a view to being introduced to the Gausis, Centurión had asked Comendador if, by any chance, he'd had anything to do with them, that is, if he provided them with any of his products, either husband and wife as a unit or separately. The answer had been a resounding, almost scandalized *no*: 'Good grief. It's one thing dealing with a doctor, a judge or a notary, but quite another dealing with a little prince like him. He would never risk being involved in anything murky or grubby. If he was into coke, for example, which can happen to even the most aristocratic of folk, he'd use sources we wouldn't even get a whiff of, that leave no trace. It would be brought to him from Madrid in a leather briefcase full of documents and plans, or even from Amsterdam. The briefcase would remain locked throughout the journey and it would never ever be handed to him personally. A little prince couldn't trust someone like me, someone who goes here, there and everywhere and has dealings with far too many people, well, I could easily spill the beans. To him, I'm trash mixed with shit, real shit, I mean, the kind that sticks. They only mix with people like them. All the others are just servants, lackeys, some more important than others, but lackeys nonetheless. It's acceptable to have brief contact with some, but with others none at all. They even see Inés as a kind of servant who has done well in life, but when it comes down to it, she's just serving them food. Gómez-Notario they see as a kind of personal accountant who they consult now and then, and as for Dr Ruibérriz de Torres, he's a mere pharmacist they phone up when there's no alternative. And they treat Judge Monreal, for example, as they would a bureaucrat with enormous power, a power that only affects others, because they themselves will never have to appear before him, that would be unimaginable. Needless to say, they see poor Berua as what he is, a bartender, however fashionable his bar might be and however much dosh he rakes in every day. As for Mayor Valderas, well, they know he's only temporary, and it's always easier to persuade and buy off those who are merely passing through, because they're all too aware that they must make the most of their moment in the limelight. The Gausis and their fellows (not many, mind, if there were they wouldn't have so much power) consider that everyone should be grateful to them for visiting their establishments and using their services. I'm completely out of their orbit, I'm not even *semi*-respectable, worse still, I'm from Catilina. So I've no idea what kind of life they lead, apart from seeing them out shopping or at the theatre or the cinema or at the airport about to fly off somewhere. They travel a lot, especially him. They travel together too, and I have occasionally seen her on her own. Gausi likes to go hunting when the season starts. He gets together before dawn with his mates and the occasional invited lackey, then they all set off in their little feathered hats and their green hunting gear. A right band of dickheads. Not that I've ever seen them, of course, because at that time in the morning I'm barely alive. But the town's early birds laugh themselves silly over their get-up.'

'Like Walter Pidgeon,' I thought, 'except he was no dickhead. Then again, he was in Germany in 1939.'

Ruán had for some time had a small airport from which planes, rarely even half full, set off to Madrid, Barcelona, Bilbao and Seville. It was said that it existed thanks to Gausi's personal efforts, that he'd persuaded the necessary authorities and had himself financed the remodelling or conversion of that old airfield built in the 1950s and mainly used by amateur pilots.

Despite being a recent arrival in town, Centurión knew more than Comendador about the life the Gausis led, thanks to the camera and microphone installed in their living room by CESID, or Machimbarrena's fake parallel CESID or whoever, as they had in the home of Celia Bayo and Liudwino. So he knew more, but not much more.

The Gausis lived in a two-storey, detached quasi-mansion in the most residential part of the town, and they probably didn't lack for living rooms. They spent very little time in the one he could see and hear, in fact, they didn't seem to spend much time at home at all, at least Folcuino didn't; María Viana spent rather longer, perhaps because she had to take care of the children, not that she did much of that: they had a maid, a cook, a kind of governess and a kind of secretary to lighten her load, as if theirs were an affluent, nineteenth-century household. None of the staff ever sat in the above-mentioned living room, they merely walked through it on their way to other rooms.

Machimbarrena or Pérez Nuix really hadn't done a very good job; they had chosen the room at random and left him to spy on one that seemed more like an ornament for visitors to admire than one where people might actually live. In that living-room-cum-museum, there were original paintings, rugs, a library of beautifully bound books and a large collection of fencing foils, sabres and swords (their points embedded in spongy bases) inside a huge glass cabinet. In a moment of profound boredom, I had counted twenty-six. Folcuino was clearly an enthusiastic collector of bladed weapons, all of which were doubtless authentic, historic, and, in their day, had possibly been stained with blood.

Nevertheless, even though most of the footage was of an empty room, Centurión did see something from time to time. He at least had a clear view of the Gausis. Folcuino was about sixty, fairly well preserved apart from his shiny bald pate, although he looked as if he had gone bald early on, when he was still young, and doubtless because of that, and given his upbringing and character, this didn't bother him at all. Although he was only of medium height, he strode through the town as though he were six foot two, with his head very erect and looking down his nose at everyone, as if his physical height were purely accidental and secondary in comparison with that of his mind, or perhaps it was the height bestowed by money or by his imagined noble ancestry. His facial features, so very regular that he was almost a handsome baldy (he bore a certain resemblance to the Russian pianist Sviatoslav Richter), had a certain power, or perhaps this was the effect of his habitually stern expression. Those features were neither very fine nor very coarse, and had he not been, or believed himself to be, a little prince, to use the trashy, piece-of-shit gunman's term, from a distance he would have passed for a perfectly ordinary fellow. However, since he would have been imbued with a sense of his own importance ever since he lay crying in his cradle only to be immediately picked up and comforted, his presence instilled fear and respect in everyone he had dealings with (although this may perhaps only have been the case in Ruán, where it was taken for granted).

This is what comes of being accustomed to giving orders from infancy, although, when you think about it, it's a trait easily and quickly acquired, consider only the pestilential inhabitant of Berchtesgaden and so many, many other despots, by whom we live permanently surrounded, and always have.

Folcuino had a square jaw which helped when he was in authoritarian mode, and to judge by the way he sometimes spoke to María Viana, this was not infrequent. His eyes seemed to have a naturally choleric glow, which he could conceal or at least temper at will, as if he were saying: 'Now I'm softening my gaze, now I'm releasing it and I know it's growing harder, now I have it completely under control and am making it more mellow, now it's a lightning bolt.' He even appeared to be able to change the colour of his eyes, from soft grey to severe brown, from dark blue to opaque green. He smiled little, but when he did he was clearly conscious of his very regular and sometimes captivating teeth.

Not at all in keeping with his otherwise sturdy physique, in which one could glimpse his rural ancestors as soon as some wrinkles began to appear (deep peasant wrinkles), were his anomalously broad hips, which, when he walked, slightly diminished his carefully cultivated masculinity. Instead of the firm, heavy step one would expect, he had a light, almost bouncy gait, as if his shoes had thick soles made not of rubber but of foam, which they certainly did not. Centurión imagined that those hips and that walk would, much to Gausi's chagrin, have caused him some grief as a boy at school, where fortune and ancestry still count for little, and where both girls and boys learn the infinite ways of being cruel. Some give these up when they reach adulthood, while others magnify, perfect and amplify them. Indeed, they become so addicted to them that, on occasions, they end up killing people against whom they have no grievance, as was the case with one of those three women, Inés Marzán, Celia Bayo and María Viana.

Yes, it was hard to imagine Folcuino licking anyone's arse in that town in the north-west, and certainly not smug Liudwino's arse, goodness, what names they had, the two husbands of my married suspects. Although, of course, Centurión had seen little of Folcuino and mostly only at home, where no one behaves quite as they do when they go out in the street and put on a front. Still less in a deserted room. During those months, from the end of January to the end of June, he saw him eight or nine times alone in that room, always late at night, perhaps so as to avoid being seen. It was as though he were suffering from insomnia, and crept downstairs to kill time or to calm down or wait for sleep to come.

He would appear in that living-room-cum-museum wearing light-coloured pyjamas and a dark dressing gown, either black or navy blue. No longer subject to a belt and trousers, his hips looked even wider than usual. He gazed smugly at his paintings – Centurión could have sworn that among these was quite a large Van Dyck portrait of a gentleman or wealthy merchant, a small Napoleonic Meissonier (possibly a study for a larger painting) and a Vallotton, all of them authentic; the camera showed him nothing more, the others being out of sight – and then his precious cabinet full of slender swords. He lingered over these like someone studying a work of art that is very nearly finished, but still requires a few final touches – there was always room for a new sabre or a new fencing foil; indeed, as with all collections, it was an unending task. Then he would unlock the cabinet and choose the blade with which he would, for a few minutes, make various thrusts and parries. He looked less like a fencer practising his moves and more like an imaginative boy emulating what he had seen in films or read about in novels, challenging and vanquishing his enemies. He lacked skill and grace, unlike Liudwino who must at least have taken a few lessons in how to use his gaucho *boleadoras*. Folcuino parried and thrust completely at random, and any real opponent would have skewered him like a chicken.

Centurión watched him with a mixture of curiosity, restrained hilarity and a feeling of slight concern whenever Folcuino chose a medieval broadsword, so heavy and unmanageable that he had to grasp it with both hands to lift it up and angrily strike at nothing at all. He was afraid the man might hurt himself, for although he was quite strong, he was neither young nor agile, and all those weapons looked dangerously sharp.

Folcuino soon tired of his fighting and then he would slump into an armchair to catch his breath, with, between his legs, whichever sabre, foil or sword he had used – the point resting on the floor – as if he were a warrior in repose or a sentinel on night duty, such a late night duty that he was already in his pyjamas and silk dressing gown. In those weary moments, his eyes took on a fierce, furious light, as if he really had fought in a battle and had not yet shaken off his anger and loathing. Then, little by little, his gaze softened or perhaps glazed over with just a hint of annoyance, then, placing hands and chin on the pommel or guard or hilt, he would eventually nod off, only to start awake shortly afterwards, as if the feel of metal on skin would not allow him to abandon himself to sleep. He would then struggle awkwardly to his feet, return the weapon to its appointed place – very carefully so as not to provoke a domino effect – lock the cabinet door, take one last look around the room with a kind of premature nostalgia, and, his pallid fantasies doubtless appeased, he would then turn out the lights and leave, ready to return to his bed or to the one he shared with María Viana – it was impossible to know whether they slept together, all the bedrooms were on the first floor, and those of the servants in the low-ceilinged attic rooms – where, all energy spent, he would perhaps placidly drift off into sleep.

He appeared to be such a profoundly irascible man that, every now and then, he needed to give vent to his rage by lungeing and stabbing. Given his position in society, he would have to suppress his anger for hours and days and weeks. When he launched into one of those solitary duels, his nostrils would flare – and they were already quite large enough when he was at rest – although perhaps that 'at rest' was only ever apparent. Those flared nostrils gave his face a slightly equine look, except that horses tend not to express fury, only fear.

On one such occasion, in March, when he was wielding a Katzbalger sword from the sixteenth or seventeenth century, one with a fairly short, double-edged blade – perhaps deployed against the Ottomans in the siege of Vienna, or against clerics in the sack of Rome – he was interrupted by the arrival of his wife in the living-room-cum-museum. She too was wearing a dressing gown, beneath which her bare calves were visible, suggesting that she probably slept in a short nightdress. She wasn't wearing slippers, but some delicate, flat, Roman sandals, which, in warmer weather, she could have worn out in the street. She stood frozen to the spot, possibly from fear, at the sight of her husband brutally slashing the air with a sword, which made me think that she was probably unaware of her insomniac husband's bellicose activities.

'What the fuck are you doing here? What the fuck do you want?' yelled Gausi, his eyes aflame. The belt of his dressing gown had come undone, so that it now flapped open to reveal beneath his pyjama trousers a rather unseemly suggestion of an erection, unseemly because it had been provoked not by María Viana's sudden appearance in the room, but by the imaginary clamour of battle.

I thought – a very fleeting thought – that one should never trust anyone who gets aroused for reasons other than sex; one should, rather, avoid them as being rudimentary, nasty individuals. Gausi was extremely foulmouthed, at home that is, with his wife.

María Viana pressed her hands to her cheeks in a gesture worthy of a silent-film actress, as if she wanted to cover her blushes (whether because of the erection or the sword, I don't know), then she stammered out a response:

'Sorry, sorry, I didn't know you were in here. I woke up and came downstairs for a glass of milk, saw the light on and heard noises and panting. I thought someone might have broken in. What are you doing in here in the middle of the night and holding that sword? Aren't they dangerous?'

'Can't I use my own swords when I feel like it? I don't have to ask your permission first, do I?'

María Viana was a submissive woman, or else she lived in dread of the potentially violent Folcuino, for he clearly could be violent: those flared, almost inflamed nostrils, that powerful jaw which, whatever the circumstances, always made him look either defiant or offended, that smooth, imperious bald pate like a blunt mountain peak, rectangular or truncated, those ever-changing eyes. María literally shrank back, like a daughter being scolded by an unyielding father, and apologized for no reason:

'No, no, of course not, I'll go away and leave you in peace, I'm sorry. I didn't mean to intrude, you know I never intrude on your business. It's just that when I looked in just now, I felt afraid for you. You could cut yourself. You're not as young as you were. Are you going to be much longer in here thrusting away?' In those last words and in the words 'leave you in peace' ('peace' being the least appropriate term to describe Folcuino when he was in battle mode), I thought I heard a hint of irony, as if, for a second, she was the mother and he the stubborn, sullen adolescent.

'What kind of imbecile are you? Do you really think that, having spent half my life buying these weapons, I don't know how to handle them? Do you really think I have them just because they look nice? And besides, what's it to do with you how long I stay in here? Given how rarely we see each other at night . . . And don't you dare so much as mention my age, you're a fine one to talk. So just shut up.'

I deduced from this that they must sleep in separate rooms. Then it occurred to me that they might still share a bed, in which, for a long time now, night after night, they had neither spoken nor touched each other with hand or foot or look, a situation dictated by one or the other or by a long-defunct love.

'Go back to bed, will you, and stop getting on my tits. You've made me lose my fucking concentration.'

He was speaking figuratively, of course, but it struck me that the reference to tits and fucking wasn't the happiest choice of words at that moment: his erection had vanished along with his harsh words, and no amount of getting on anyone's tits would have revived it. Perhaps only a little elementary fencing, a fight to the death with a few phantom Turks, the slaughter of cardinals and bishops.

In an innocent, genuinely interested tone María Viana nevertheless ventured to ask:

'Oh, no, have you lost your concentration? That could be very dangerous. May I help you find it again? Please, tell me, what can I do to get it back? I wouldn't want you to cut yourself on one of your swords because I distracted you.' There was no mistaking the irony even if it was disguised beneath that silly, childish tone of voice.

Folcuino wrapped his dressing gown around him like someone slamming a door shut and energetically knotted his belt, which he then had to loosen slightly because it was too tight around his belly.

'Oh fuck off, you stupid cow!'

No, no hypothetical caresses or kisses, no getting up close and personal, would have helped. And María Viana was a real beauty, although 'beauty' isn't really the right word. If she was a beauty (and I insist she wasn't), hers was a somehow inexplicable beauty: languid and apathetic while at home with Gausi, where it lay diminished, undermined, hidden; in the street, in the shops, at the theatre, she was like a magnet for men's eyes (a relative or rather haughty magnet, for it kept at bay any overfamiliar familiarity or probing looks, which remained at a respectful distance and never lingered on her in a brazen, obscene or insistent way).

She must have been well into her forties (she was the oldest of my three candidates), which did not prevent her face and body giving off a strong current – or was it a mist? – of involuntary, probably unintentional sensuality, and she certainly did nothing to promote or broadcast it. Objectively, there was nothing striking about her, because she was neither tall nor well built nor shapely like Inés Marzán, nor, of course, was she buxom or even plump and firm like Celia Bayo, who was demure despite her outgoing nature. She dressed neither very provocatively nor very elegantly. There was nothing remarkable about her at all, which is why, in private, she sometimes belittled herself, put on a childish voice, even played the poor wee thing and almost provoked one's pity. The result, I suppose, of Folcuino's continual rudeness and intimidation.

And yet when she went out and about in the town, alone or with her children or with her husband, people would slow down in order to catch an instinctively furtive glimpse, as if a mere glimpse were reward enough. Other women, amazed by her natural air of distinction and silently envying her undeniable allure, which they could neither define nor pin down, simply muttered to themselves about her, but felt no resentment. It was the same with men too, because they couldn't help feeling a kind of abstract carnal desire, if that isn't a complete contradiction in terms.

I can only speak from my own experience, and since I consider myself to be a fairly average man, I imagine my experience would be the same as everyone else's: seeing her, I felt a desire that was as unreal as it was irresistible. Unreal because it never even occurred to me that it could come to anything, that it would be possible to touch or caress her, still less penetrate her, as if María Viana were a painting, an effigy or a celluloid image, or as if she didn't belong to the same time as me, but to the past or the future or to a non-existent time, that we didn't even inhabit the same dimension, neither that of the living nor of the dead.

Although we probably did share the same dimension as the living dead who nevertheless continue to exist, to move and think and act, and who can still avert or inflict harm, and experience pity or inclemency. I was one of the living dead, and had been for many years, and she might be too if she was hiding Magdalena Orúe O'Dea in some forgotten corner of her being. That is, if she had buried her in order to be only María Viana, Gausi's wife in that town in the north-west, as discreet, esteemed and respected as she was troubling. I was sometimes assailed by the idea that, if I did make some fateful discovery, I might be the one to remove her from that world and send her to the land of the dead, and that, I felt, would be unacceptable and unbearable: someone like her deserved to linger and to last in the world, a world she improved simply by walking through it. Perhaps not by her deeds, but certainly visually. She added a new brilliance to the world, which she enhanced and ennobled.

Whenever she walked past the other inhabitants of Ruán, they would eye her surreptitiously, not because it was forbidden (she was warm and friendly with everyone), but because to look at her openly – let alone salaciously – felt inconsiderate, disrespectful. If I can put it like this, she inspired in the viewer a modesty they might never otherwise have felt. Even Liudwino López Xirau, bold and brazen in all aspects of life (including with the opposite sex, despite his weakness for Celia Bayo), would open his eyes wide in her presence, then half close them as if he needed swiftly to attenuate that vision, as though he could not withstand such an utterly disarming image, one that demanded that he suddenly develop scruples, something that ran contrary to his boastful nature and his wheedling ways. And as if he could think only one brief, simple thought, which, to be fair to him, was perhaps the only thought any of us could have: 'Wow, what a woman! She isn't pretty exactly, but there's something about her. If only she could be mine. Not that I'd know how to tackle her, how to approach her or what to do with her. If she offered herself to me naked, I wouldn't believe it, and wouldn't even dare to touch her, I would freeze. So it's best just to look at her. And best, too, if she doesn't belong to me or to anyone.'

No, were one to describe María Viana impartially, ignoring whatever pure or murky or lascivious sensations she provoked, she wasn't pretty exactly. However, subjectively speaking, she was, and, oddly, this was the view of most people regardless of age, social class or, almost, gender, a view arrived at independently by each individual, with no need to consult with others or reach a consensus. Centurión told himself that no one as captivating as her could possibly be Magdalena Orúe. Anyone endowed with such an unconscious ability to seduce would have had many doors open to her and could have followed whatever career path she chose, and she certainly wouldn't have chosen to collaborate with terrorists and lead a grim, clandestine life, perennially at risk, both pursuing and pursued, killing or helping to kill and in permanent danger of being killed herself or of spending long years in prison.

Needless to say, he immediately thought again and realized his mistake: this was an ingenuous, conventional, even idiotic response, an echo of the ancient association made between goodness and beauty, so often refuted by experience and discarded by history, and yet one that persists in our superficial human eyes.

One militant ETA member was, at least to judge from photos, an equally disquieting figure (in 1997 she was still free and, if I remember rightly, still active, and she was both clever and elusive; I think she is free now, and has been for some time, having completed a rather mild sentence for the crimes attributed to her). I can't remember her real name, and I can't bear to go online in search of something that really doesn't matter: her name may have been Idoia, followed by a very unBasque and unequivocally Castilian surname; and I do remember her famous nickname 'The Tigress', given to her because of her dazzlingly cold and possibly green eyes in the black-and-white photos that appeared in the press. She was tried and sentenced for multiple murders, she was famed for her heartlessness and for using her physical appearance to attract and entrap some of her victims and to get information and facts that would not have been available to an uglier woman; or, rather, an ugly woman would have found it infinitely more difficult. Ugliness is a limitation and a problem, both of which can be overcome. Beauty is also a limitation and a problem, but sometimes neither can be overcome.

Centurión also told himself that María Viana seemed so terribly fragile and vulnerable when confronted by Gausi, and that this hardly fitted with such an implacable image: Magdalena Orúe wouldn't have thought twice about putting a few bullets in Folcuino, especially when he was in scornful, commanding mode, even if he was the father of her children. The half-Northern Irish Maddie O'Dea wouldn't for one moment have stood for his insolence, let alone his insults. According to the incomplete reports I'd been given – which were, in fact, fragmentary, forming a kind of nebulous whole – she wasn't noted for her patience, and years ago in Belfast and in Derry had been known for her angry outbursts; and yet María Viana was perhaps too patient, and no one in Ruán would ever have described her as irascible.

When there's no alternative, anyone can pretend to be what they are not. More than that, those of us whose job it is to protect ourselves and divert misfortunes must do so whether we need to or not, and must deceive others as much as possible without wavering and without betraying ourselves, as if we were experienced actors and actresses or had forgotten our true identities. In 1997, I was like that, well, not exactly, or rather I'd gone back to being like that provisionally, in a kind of sceptical, faithless, temporary fashion. I didn't belong to any organization or body, nor was I officially under orders to anyone. I had left all that behind me, or so I thought, always in the certain knowledge that every one of my past actions was and always would be subject to secrecy, and that's an infallible way of never breaking free completely, and of never forgetting anything ever.

This, more or less, was what Tupra had told me in Plaza de la Paja, or what I myself had said or thought: those who share secrets that are condemned to remain secret for the rest of their lives or beyond are bound together indefinitely. They know everything about each other, what they are capable of and possibly what they would not be capable of, because the latter is always open to change, pending more trials, more requests and demands, more unforeseen or desperate situations. But they don't respect each other, because they know too much, they know, for example, that they are dishonest, have frequently abandoned all scruples and have neither recovered them nor particularly missed them; that they have often gone too far when they should have held back, that they have killed or ordered others to be killed and yet appear to be able to live with that knowledge. And that, despite all this, they can nevertheless fall in love and get married, as was the case with Tupra and Nutcombe and Reresby and all the other Berties. Something must have changed for him to have fallen in love and thus find a quick fix for that weakness, that passing unhappiness, without waiting for it to pass.

'No one is ever completely outside,' those, more or less, had been his words as we sat on the cold café terrace. 'One small step and you're back inside again. The distance is tiny, although it can appear huge. It's as simple as that.' In that respect, we definitely resembled members of the IRA and ETA, some of whose members, when they stepped outside of the circle, were murdered by their colleagues, the immovable ones, those whose minds are set in stone, who never think or stop. Contrary to what I had imagined when I returned to Madrid to take up a quiet job at the embassy, I hadn't actually left at all. I had been a victim of myself, of my stupor, my emptiness, my lost habits, my wounding memories, my unwelcome nostalgia, which was, nevertheless, poisoning and overpowering me. And when I recognized myself in those words, 'It's unbearable to be outside once you've been inside,' I had simply stepped back inside again.

But now, in Ruán, where I had grown accustomed to the bells and the mists, to the monotonous flow of the river and the throng of people calmly or unhurriedly crossing the bridge, to the town's peaceful rhythm in which the only conceivable acts of violence were a scorned husband killing his runaway wife – a rare occurrence – or an occasional mugging in one of the rougher parts of town or a Saturday-night bust-up, or a beating in a dark alleyway to intimidate a competitor or a businessman who then preferred to say nothing, the allowable, acceptable crimes committed by Comendador and his fellows, and so on, now I often asked myself how I had succumbed, how I had agreed to take on that unpleasant task only to find myself once again sunk in my old world of assumptions and permanent suspicion, distrust and callousness, of pretence and deliberate betrayals. No, I was no longer the man I had been after the long years that followed my enforced or voluntary recruitment. I had grown rusty, my faculties and my resolve had waned, perhaps I had grown lazy. I no longer believed in the defence of the Realm, in the purity of democracies or of the Crown, nor in the aseptic nature of the State or indeed in anything. Or perhaps only in the need to avert misfortunes, those that befall the innocent, the unprepared populace busy with their daily tasks. I wasn't even sure I wanted to punish crimes already committed. What was the point, what did it solve, since they could not be undone?

But above all I had become fragile, that is, hesitant. While I was on active service, I had followed orders, which I didn't usually question unless they placed me in an absurd amount of danger, and I never ever hesitated, or only when plans and circumstances took a bad turn. I never lost sight of my objective, not even when I had to improvise or change tack or rethink. I realized now that I didn't really want to find Magdalena Orúe O'Dea. Or, rather, I didn't want any of my three candidates to be that pitiless woman, a mixture of Northern Irish and *riojana*; well, they weren't my candidates, of course, they belonged to Tupra and Pérez Nuix and Machimbarrena or whoever was behind them, CESID and MI6 or MI5. I realized that getting to know people or watching them, something that had never affected me before, still less stopped me (or only momentarily, the time it took for the bomb to go off), was now determining my instincts and inclinations.

Tupra had handed me three photographs, three names and three incomplete reports, full of lacunae, just as he could have handed me three completely different ones, on which I would then have focused. He could have sent me to a town in the south-west or a village right up in the north, and I would have gone there. As is usual in our line of work, he had chosen to tell me as little as possible: the less known by the person carrying out decisions and conclusions reached at the very top of the chain of command, the more successful the operation is likely to be. Each link in the chain should do only what he or she is asked to do, it's too dangerous for them to know the whole plan; more than that, knowing too much prompts doubts and perplexities and questions, which bring in their train objections, arguments and suggestions, and then you're only one step away from rebellions or a reluctance to follow instructions, from indiscipline and disobedience. In order for this not to happen and for instructions to be followed to the letter, the agents, the foot soldiers, the lower ranks must have a blind trust in the invisible leaders who make the decisions and in their immediate superiors, and I no longer felt that trust. I no longer trusted the unknowable State or Bertram Tupra, who had diverted and directed my life for far too long, and had even diverted me into a transitory premature death, something that had marked me for the rest of my days.

I had nothing against those three women, against the women they were in that provincial town in 1997, leading normal, happier or possibly unhappier lives, the women I had dealings with in the bedroom or else spied on from my window overlooking the river. I found it impossible not to like Inés Marzán, Celia Bayo and María Viana, each for different reasons. I couldn't help wishing them well in the lives they had built or forged, yielded to or taken refuge in or hidden behind, it didn't matter, we all do at least one of those things with our lives.

Two of those women were not Magdalena Orúe, that much was certain, and therefore did not deserve anything bad to happen to them, not even the monitoring or surveillance to which I was subjecting them. They didn't know that someone, Miguel Centurión, the new English teacher at the school, was seeking their possible ruin, their collapse, and was silently threatening them like a bird of ill omen watching and hovering and observing them from a great height, so high up that, for them, it was an undetectable dot in the sky. No, they had no idea, unless . . . Ah, there was always that 'unless', like a stabbing pain. Unless one of them was Magdalena Orúe, and had participated from a distance in those cruellest of attacks. No, that woman would be constantly on the alert and would spend each night on tenterhooks, afraid that someone would unmask her and say: 'You're not Inés Marzán, you're not Celia Bayo, you're not María Viana, they're just invented names like the ones a novelist arbitrarily gives his characters, on a whim or out of boredom. Those people were born long after their actual birth and don't actually exist, but were created by a wretch with a heart of stone in order to avoid justice and go unpunished and to continue breathing the air her victims can no longer breathe. Or by someone who, in 1987, still was that hard-hearted wretch, and remained so for who knows how much longer and who may, who knows, still be a wretch today. But the past always leaves a trace and can never be entirely erased as long as some of us can remember it, and there always comes a moment when the false Inés Marzán or the false Celia Bayo or the false María Viana – that is you, Magdalena Orúe – finds herself obliged to admit: 'Nought's had, all's spent. 'Tis safer to be that which we destroy than by destruction dwell in doubtful joy. It's time to surrender. Or time to die.'

VIII

Ah, yes, I had grown soft. I felt constrained and troubled by the very idea that, because of me, one of those women was destined either to spend many long years in prison, or – if I failed to find sufficient proof and there was no way I could hand her over to Machimbarrena or to the police with guarantees that she would face trial – to die by my hand, when I had never closed my hands around a woman's throat or wielded a knife or an axe or a sword or any kind of weapon against someone of the opposite sex. More than that, I loathed men who used violence, those who, without redress, abused their power to give vent to their anger, their troubles or their wounded pride.

For me to reach that point, for me to eradicate one of those three ordinary and apparently inoffensive lives, I would need to be absolutely certain, or to have heard or received some confession that would not stand up in court, but that would either totally convince or totally enrage me, something that would place the memory of the poor victims of the Zaragoza and the Barcelona bombings – who were, for me, distant and unknown – above any personal feelings of affection or pity. And I could not see that happening. Indeed, with the term coming to an end, at which point I should be awaiting new instructions, it seemed to me quite impossible. Then again, given that Ruán was fairly cool in summer, most of its inhabitants stayed put, or moved to their residences or houses on the outskirts – the wealthy and the semi-well-to-do that is – into the mountains or the hills or the valley, all of which were very green.

As I mentioned, María Viana had proved inaccessible to me, and I hadn't dared to contrive some encounter or conversation with her, so as not to arouse suspicions or risk being seen as some busybody interloper. I only knew her image from seeing her out in the street with Folcuino or with her twins, or occasionally in society – I had twice coincided with her at La Demanda, and had thus been able to see and compare two of my suspects in the same setting, one serving and the other being served; I had also seen her at the cinema and at a couple of concerts, and had been able to study her more closely in the very few video recordings I had of her. In her life outside the house, she seemed like a woman of importance, while in her domestic life she inspired only pity, possibly undeserved.

The property developer Gausi could be brutal sometimes. His civilized bald pate – his attractive cranium, protected and framed by his neatly trimmed side hair – was in marked contrast to his brutish or drunken reactions when something annoyed him or put him in a bad mood. One quiet evening, when he was lounging in an armchair reading *The Day of the Jackal* by Frederick Forsyth, two small, excitable mutts of some kind – I know nothing about breeds of dog – belonging either to the family or to the twins, burst into that living-room-cum-museum, a place they were probably forbidden to enter, I certainly hadn't seen them before in any of the video recordings. Behind them came María Viana, from whom they had evidently escaped. One of the pups ran straight over to Folcuino, put its front paws on his knees and started sniffing the very place where the Katzbalger broadsword had once, in the small hours, provoked a modest protuberance. Gausi eyed the hound with disgust and disapproval – his easily roused anger did not immediately erupt; this was, after all, a defenceless enemy – and, with one foot, he catapulted or flicked the dog's small body upwards and away from him.

The mutt was lucky not to be hurled against the brick and stone fireplace or the ceiling for that matter, but instead struck one of the bookshelves, and books are not quite so hard, even leather-bound ones. The creature collided with Gausi's Agatha Christie collection and dropped to the floor like a stone. It immediately staggered to its feet, shook itself as if to make sure everything was still in place, then tottered drunkenly over to María Viana, who snatched it up and felt it all over, stroking its head and snout to quiet its childish whimperings. It appeared not to be hurt, having suffered only a passing shock, and it soon trotted smartly out of the room followed by its less lascivious companion, both of them doubtless filled with terror of this violent ogre. María Viana could not hold back:

'Are you mad? How could you? Poor little thing, you might have killed him.'

'It's your fault, you should keep them out of here. The last thing I want when I'm concentrating is for some poovy dog to come sniffing my privates. You saw him. You ought to have them castrated, I'm up to my balls with the little shits. God, they're more like Sumatran rats than dogs.'

'The children adore them, you know that. And don't talk such nonsense. The poor little things are very well trained and never cause any trouble. Anyway, what's Sumatra got to do with it? Why Sumatra?' This reference had confused her, but Gausi was in no mood to offer unnecessary explanations.

'Well trained, eh? So what were they doing in here, then? And what were you doing with them? They're not your responsibility. And you know they're forbidden to come in here. What if they'd chewed one of the paintings or knocked over my sword collection?'

'They only escaped for a moment, they must have smelled you in here and since they're really fond of you and almost never see you . . . Besides, there are other ways of getting rid of them rather than kicking them, Folqui.' So that was her affectionate diminutive for him, hardly appropriate in the circumstances. And 'Folcuino' with its diphthong was a hard name to pronounce.

The tone in which she said this seemed to require her to add something along the lines of: 'You can be such a brute sometimes.' But María Viana clearly didn't dare insult him, not even with some milder, more colloquial expression. She was serene and patient, possibly even sweet, although it's dangerous to say that about anyone, because we all have a temper, which might burst forth one day. She was afraid of him, that much was clear and that, I told myself again, did not square with her being Magdalena Orúe. Unless – always that 'unless', because this was all conjecture and supposition, as it had been so often in my past life – she could be cruel at a distance but spineless in person, it's not unusual for heartless people to appear gentle and humble. Everything is possible for someone advancing through a mist, and to begin with, there is only mist.

'If something or someone gets in my way, I get rid of them, right. That can hardly be news to you, so don't pretend to be all shocked and upset. Besides, the poovy little bugger's fine, you saw him, didn't you, trotting off as if nothing had happened. I do gauge my blows, you know. I wasn't going to kill the thing just for being horny.'

When I heard him say this, and having seen proof that he wasn't lying, I thought that, as usual, Liudwino had been over-optimistic in his predictions. There was no way Folcuino was going to lick anything, let alone Liudwino's arse. These were mere illusions on his part.

In another recording, a couple of weeks later, I heard a sort of conversation, if you could call it that, between Folcuino and María. He was reading, this time *The Pillars of the Earth* by Ken Follett; he read a lot, and was clearly unconcerned about being up to date or lagging behind. The door was open, but his wife knocked anyway, as if asking permission to come in and interrupt him. Folcuino looked up and, with his nostrils already threatening to flare, asked:

'What's wrong? Be brief, please.'

'I can't be that brief, Folqui. We need to talk about us. If this isn't a good time for you, then let's leave it for another occasion.'

'About us? For fuck's sake, haven't we talked enough?' Neverthe-less, he calmly closed his book and prepared to listen, leaving behind him the Middle Ages, which he may not have found that alluring. 'What's got into your little head now?'

María Viana came into the room and sat down in an armchair next to his. There was a small table between them, and they looked almost like passengers on a train, gazing off in the same direction, at the sword cabinet, and each observing the other out of the corner of one eye.

'Yes, we have talked about it, but talking doesn't get us anywhere. I'm not unhappy with you, all things considered, but neither am I happy, and you, at best, probably tolerate me. Now I know you don't feel the same as I do, but I'm finding it harder and harder to come up with a reason to get out of bed in the morning. It's a real struggle. If it wasn't for the kids . . . Well, they're the ones who give me the will to live and to start the day, but as they get older, they're going to have their own lives to lead, and will end up relegating me to the sidelines, apart from when they need something, money, help or being looked after when they're ill. It seems that's always the way. You have your thousands of deals to keep you busy. I don't have that many incen-tives, or only the shop, which is hardly what you'd call a reason to live . . .' She was referring to a bijou little interior design shop that belonged to Gausi, along with a few others in the town, and which she, in theory, ran. In practice it was run by a colleague and friend, a *ruanesa* through and through, whose family had lived in Ruán since the Middle Ages or thereabouts, and who had slowly but emphat-ically taken it out of her hands.

'I know that, so what is it you want, then? Do you want us to sepa-rate? That's another thing we've talked about until the cows come home. Do you want to go and live on your own, in your own house? Because I'm not shifting from this one, as you well know. Go to another town and start a new life? Please do, we give each other complete freedom as it is. You can always leave, but until you do, you've got a role to play here. Have you thought where you would go, what you would do there, how you would live? Because you're not getting anything from me. Would you give up the kids? They would stay with me, and you'd see them now and then, that's what we agreed before they were even born, from the very first day. What do you want? What are we going to talk about that we haven't talked about already? Oh, just leave me alone, will you?' He made as if to reopen his book, but stopped so as not to appear too brusque. His immaculate bald pate, like that Russian pianist's, was even shinier than usual, as if it were the summation of all the smug satisfaction of being right and having always had the last word.

At the time, prenuptial agreements were not that common, but I assumed from these comments that they had signed such an agreement when they married or before. If the twins – a boy and a girl – were about seven, then the couple would have been pioneers in that field, at least in Spain. That exchange of complaints and cutting remarks indicated that theirs was a kind of arranged marriage, a marriage of convenience. It was odd that an excellent match like Gausi, who had apparently been widowed before he was forty and had remained single into his fifties or slightly later, should have opted to get married again and to a woman from out of town whom he didn't care about and possibly never had, when he could have had his pick of women, if, for example, he wanted to have an heir. It was equally odd that a highly sensual person like María Viana, who perhaps, for that very reason, did not easily arouse passions, because no one dared attempt a serious relationship with her, because her excessive 'beauty' frightened men off, but who would doubtless still never have lacked for reckless, dazzled or suicidal suitors . . . yes, it was odd that, when she was no longer in the first flush of youth, she should have chosen such a surly, arrogant man, the only man, it seemed, who remained immune to her irresistible charms.

Perhaps he was also the only man who could cope with being married to her without suffering panic attacks or palpitations. There are women whose beauty is so inexplicable and so all-enveloping that they cause trouble and torment to anyone brave enough to be with them. The man in question cannot believe what he has done, he pinches himself when he wakes each morning, filled with amazement; he lives in a permanent state of alarm and fear even though she gives him no reason to be afraid. He feels like someone who has found a treasure. He admires her, watches over her, guards her, hides her, buries her if he can (but you can only bury a woman after you've killed her and no one destroys his treasure: despite everything, he prefers to wait for someone to snatch her from him, or to lose her through his own ill luck or stupidity). He fears the envy of other men, he fears in others what he himself feels, attributing to them his own greed and delirium, the feelings that obscured his will and judgement and entirely mastered him before he won her.

Most men would run a mile from such a singular woman; they would feel they didn't deserve her, they would overcome their elemental longing and escape while there was still time, before the vertigo took hold. Women who have this disturbing effect find it very difficult to lead a balanced existence, if that's what they want. Without intending to, they command respect, I mean, people naturally respect them, too much so for their own taste; they see man after man disappear. I myself, an observant, devoted victim of María Viana's sensuality, realized that I would never take a step in her direction, not even in the most propitious circumstances. Not because I was like those men who are cautious out of an instinct for self-preservation and an aversion to avoidable suffering (I was just passing through and would sooner or later disappear just as I had disappeared from so many places and so many people, I was in no danger of getting involved), but because I respected her from afar.

María Viana said nothing for a few seconds, still not looking at Gausi, but staring resignedly ahead of her, her gaze fixed on the swords, fencing foils and sabres, as if she were observing them curiously for the first time and wondering what those weapons, the real ones, had done in the past, what bodies they had pierced and what heads they had sliced off, and how they had managed to survive there long after the lives they had cut short had been forgotten. The swordsman of Calais' weapon would certainly not be there, the one used by the man who came to England to sever the head of a queen with a single blow, in a strange show of sympathy for the prisoner's fate. If it still existed, it would be safe in some museum, for museums never spurn macabre objects as long as they are 'historical' and flatter the vanity of tourists with a pleasant, remote shudder. Folcuino was waiting impatiently, drumming his fingers on the cover of *The Pillars of the Earth*.

'You're quite right, we have talked about it all already,' she murmured at last. 'We should still keep thinking about it, though. Even the things we think we know still need to be thought about; you can't dismiss them just like that, if they're the cause of unhappiness or, without wishing to exaggerate, chronic melancholy. However, since it doesn't affect you and only affects me, I suppose it's up to me to continue worrying away at it until I find a solution, even if there isn't one. The problem won't go away simply because there's no solution, and believe me, I would love to forget about it. You've always put your cards on the table, I can't deny that and have no complaints in that regard. And yes, I knew what to expect right from the start, but being told what to expect is not the same as experiencing it day after unchanging day. We think we're capable of so much before we begin a journey. Then we find our endurance has its limits, that we're weaker and more vulnerable than we thought, and hadn't taken into account the sheer upheaval it would cause. And the years eat away at us too, simply by accumulating year on year. And then it turns out that nothing ends, even when it seems to have ended already.'

I thought: 'So María Viana is like me and like Berta, or as we both were for a long time and possibly are again now: those who merely exist and wait.'

'Fine, whatever, only don't go on and on about something I don't give a toss about,' her husband said. 'What am I supposed to do? It is what it is, and will be until I die. You'll probably outlive me anyway. And you've always been free to make your own decisions, while always keeping a careful eye on the consequences, of course, the discomforts, the risks and the costs. You certainly don't lack for comfort here, ninety per cent of humanity would change places with you in an instant. Ninety per cent? No, what am I saying? Ninety-nine per cent.' He took out an impatient cigarette, lit it and only afterwards offered her one, which she took and put between her lips with an unexpectedly coarse expression on her face, like a billiards player with both hands occupied. 'As far as I know, you haven't taken any lovers during the years we've been together. Not as far as I know . . . Wouldn't that help with your melancholy? It works for a lot of women and for a few men too. Except that, of course, no one, absolutely no one must know about it, and that, I realize, is an impossibility, a paradox or whatever, because the lover in question would have to be aware of our situation, and lovers do tend to blab. That's the worst of things you can't do on your own, of which there are still a few.'

María got up and went over to the door, her eyes still fixed on the collection of swords. From there, having vented her feelings in that brief, pointless conversation, she said:

'Just forget it. I'm sorry to have bothered you with my problems, but, precisely for the reason you've just given, I have no one else to talk to about them. I can talk to myself for a while, but that soon grows tiresome and leads to despair. Anyway, I'm sorry: here I am coming to you with my problems when you're already doing your bit and can't really do much more.'

Gausi resumed his reading, and I fast-forwarded over the rest of the recording which clearly wasn't going to tell me anything of interest.

Nevertheless, it was the most instructive recording I'd seen after months of watching that unfrequented living-room-cum-museum. It occurred to me that Magdalena Orúe O'Dea might well have accepted any agreement that would provide her with cover and would allow her to go unnoticed, to hide away: it wasn't a bad idea to become the irreproachable wife of a wealthy, significant individual, albeit significant only in his local area, for no one would suspect her of having a sinister past, as stained with blood as those old swords in the glass cabinet, the blood now erased and invisible. This would have been a good solution for that half-Northern Irishwoman: you'll do anything when you're cornered and have no idea what the future might hold, unaware that time will continue to accumulate and that none of us can know what the future will hold. If she *was* Magdalena and had collaborated on or planned those attacks, perhaps she had grown more confident after ten years of impunity and thought she could now aspire to another more satisfying life, whatever that might be.

Perhaps she had come to feel that she was more María Viana than the person María Viana had replaced, just as I had felt myself to be more James Rowland than Tomás Nevinson and as I was now beginning to feel, although still only sporadically, that I was more the obscure English teacher Miguel Centurión than I was Tom Nevinson with all his baggage. It had happened to me before, you end up fusing the two because you can't be two people at once, and one of the two always ends up being excluded or placed in parenthesis. Until he returns.

Folcuino had used the word 'risks'. This was a very general term and could mean anything, but it didn't rule out the certain and very concrete risks that Magdalena Orúe O'Dea would run if she threw off her disguise and emerged from her hiding place. I wondered if Gausi knew about her background, but had felt no qualms about marrying someone sought by the police of two countries, a woman who had, according to my information, belonged to the IRA, and had, in fact, been on loan from them to ETA. He appeared to be a man of few principles, interested only in himself, but in that case he would be putting himself in danger (although she might have told him only half the story, have trivialized and played down her crimes).

The advantage of such a situation was that he had her caught, trapped, until those offences had expired: if she didn't obey him in everything, he would turn her in, he could always say she had deceived him and that he had known nothing about her past. That would be equivalent to having a slave happy to be a slave because any freedom, however tempting, would not last and her subsequent life would be incomparably worse than the one she led in Ruán by his side, where she was a pampered slave at home and admired by those in the world outside. And if she did end up in prison, she would certainly only see the twins now and again, always assuming Gausi were prepared to subject them to sordid and incomprehensible prison visits. And I don't know about Magdalena Orúe, but María Viana clearly loved them madly, as mothers usually do, with almost all their heart, which is very easily broken.

So it was not that difficult to understand why Maddie O'Dea would enter a sham marriage (the same applied to María Viana if she had always been María Viana). What was harder to understand was why Folcuino Gausi would choose to spend his years with a woman whom everyone else found attractive, but whom he, bizarrely, did not. If he did know her true identity that might provoke in him overwhelming feelings of repulsion: he might place her in the shop window, so to speak, as an adornment, and take advantage of her to have children, but not to share her bed. If he didn't know, that was even more difficult to explain. Why had that respectable, long-time widower remarried? The usual simplistic conjectures immediately occurred to me: he was a closet homosexual and had to keep up appearances in that proud, ancient town, where no woman would have been able to seduce him; the twins could be the product of artificial insemination or something else, given that the mother was not exactly young when she gave birth, past forty according to my calculations. Folcuino had, of course, scornfully called the poor mutt a poofter. Then again, many homosexuals, precisely because they are homosexual, feel they have the right to use terms that would cause outrage if spoken by a heterosexual. Or he might be impotent and therefore not interested in sex (age does tame us in some respects), but I had noticed that chance erection provoked by the ardour of his imaginary battle against a horde of Turks. It could be that he had once desired her so intensely ('an additional sadness') that he had agreed to marry, and afterwards had lost all interest in her or, still worse, that she had, for some reason, become repulsive to him.

After all, this can happen: according to the chroniclers and to legend, Henry VIII had been quite sick with lust for Anne Boleyn, so much so that he rejected his worthy Spanish Queen and caused a schism with the Church. In 1533, he had, with great pomp, crowned his mistress in Westminster Hall on Pentecost Sunday. By 1536, though, all trace of passion and sweet offerings had vanished, and at eight o'clock in the morning on a still-cold English day in May, she was taken to the block to have her head cut off. (The truth is, he saved her the humiliation of kneeling down and placing her head on the block, perhaps out of consideration for his former lust, which one never completely forgets: although he did swiftly erase her from his memory, for only eleven days later he married Jane Seymour.)

'And any action is a step to the block, to the fire with its smell and its smoke, down the sea's throat that always draws us down to the depths . . .' Those old lines of Eliot's were always resurfacing in my mind and always changing too through sheer repetition, lines I had first read in Blackwell's in Oxford when I still didn't understand what they meant and when I was still plain, untainted Tomás Nevinson. If the King's febrile passion had burned out in only three years or less, in impatient Folcuino's case it could have vanished entirely in eight or even seven, like the snow that falls and doesn't settle, or like the rain that once drenched us and has since dried. Everything is possible in long lives, especially the lives of the powerful which are, by definition, the most subject to change.

I found that couple truly disconcerting, far more so than Celia Bayo and Liudwino López, who, in comparison, seemed simple, contented souls who threw themselves with blithe obscenity into their role-playing and their childish games and never questioned anything, not even the husband happily deceiving every other living creature in Ruán. Celia Bayo must have thought this absolutely normal. And to me, she seemed so elementary, so nonchalant and pleasant and so well disposed towards everyone, that, despite her red hair, I discounted her as being Magdalena Orúe more confidently than I did the other two. Not entirely, of course: you have to see evil everywhere, when the finger wavers and repents and takes a while to point it out without a tremor.

Needless to say, I made my own inquiries, and needless to say, Centurión found out what he could in Ruán, from other sources than poor, dim Comendador, whose lank hair, curly sideburns and weird attire frightened off any notables, who would only meet him in secret for, at most, a couple of minutes, which is how long a transaction would normally take, a transaction that was, for them, deeply embarrassing.

The best-informed person in Ruán was the society columnist for *El Esperado de Ruán* – the *Ruán Herald* – the local newspaper as archaic as its name, yet which a lot of people continued to buy and read because they had no interest in what was going on beyond the city walls, in the land of savages. It was said that the columnist actually wrote the entire newspaper under different names; that he did so out of sheer enthusiasm and by dint of being everywhere at once, and could as easily be announcing a wedding as writing an over-the-top account of a party or indirectly denouncing – always carefully weighing his words – the underhand dealings of the local politicians. He had a reputation for being very much in the know, but he only showed his real face in the society and gossip columns – although this is just a manner of speaking, for while he opted, out of tradition and choice, to use a nom de plume, this was not in order to conceal his identity, which was known to everyone. More than that, since the creation of the TV channel TeleRuán a couple of years before, he had succumbed to the lure of being seen and heard, and had become a frequent participant on chat shows, occasionally doing 'frank' and slightly 'daring' interviews, well, daring compared with what had always been the norm in that discreet, respectful town in the northwest. His name was José Corripio, and he had the misfortune to be known by the nickname Peporro – a kind of augmentative diminutive – to all those who had watched him grow up and therefore had known him for years. For someone like him, being known as Peporro Corripio was more than a misfortune, it was an affront, and so for years he had chosen to adopt the pseudonym 'Florentín' for his more frivolous writings. For his more serious, incisive, political articles he had a whole array of constantly changing names, which went from the presumptuous and Frenchified 'Champfleury', 'Lorédan Larchey' and 'Louvet de Couvray' to the sternly Spanish 'Federico Gomez Gutiérrez' and 'Fernanda Mesnadero', and dozens more. When Centurión learned this, he recalled something Liudwino had said in one of the video recordings – Centurión couldn't quite remember if it was the one that ended with Liudwino in full gaucho mode and wielding those dangerous *boleadoras*, or the one that culminated in him wearing only a white apron and a chef's hat (his bare buttocks all too visible) and Celia Bayo almost naked apart from an eighteenth-century beret and a torn skirt. He'd said something like 'The only one who's still putting up any resistance is Peporro, I haven't quite got him eating out of my hand, and he's still up to his old tricks,' adding that he had given him a really flash watch, for which Peporro hadn't even thanked him properly, even though it now adorned his wrist as if it were an heirloom from his grandfather and he'd had it since he was an adolescent. He was sure he'd also said something about Peporro having the cheek of the devil, and predicted that Corripio would eventually offer up his 'cock' for him to do with as he pleased.

When Centurión met Florentín, this immediately confirmed him in his belief that Liudwino's refusal to take No for an answer would eventually be his downfall. Florentín or Peporro seemed to be slippery and disloyal, and a very hard nut to crack. His intention may have been to play the dandy – of which there are a surprising number in the provinces – but the end result was rather more eccentric than that. He always wore a very long, ankle-length overcoat or raincoat, like Fagin's, presumably so that he would cut a striking figure on his strolls along by the river, hands behind his back as if he were in a tremendous hurry, and so that from a distance he would be easily recognized, unmistakable. He also had a strange beard like that worn by an old-fashioned Quaker or Captain Ahab or Abraham Lincoln, except that it was pointed like Fagin's beard – indeed he may well have been modelling himself on Fagin. Otherwise, he was always immaculately dressed, in good-quality new clothes, which were very tasteful apart from the predominance of different shades of red, as if he wanted to blend in with the façades of the bars in the Barrio Tinto, to which he was a frequent visitor. He was a drinker, but never drunk, as if alcohol had no effect on him, or none that might discredit or shame him. He was about forty-five, nimble in conversation, extremely cultivated and definitely no fool despite a certain feigned frivolity. He smoked slender cigarettes which he kept in a silver cigarette case, and it was thus, in his red or burgundy clothes, cotton scarves and blood-red ties, that he appeared on the local television. Since then, he had managed to impose himself as 'Florentín' – the public enjoyed his witty comments, which were amusing and never too sharp – and those other troublesome names, Peporro and Corripio, more or less fell into disuse, apart from among people who disliked him or had it in for him, and who were fewer than they might have been, because they were also rather afraid of him and, far from provoking, were hoping to win him over. He allowed himself to be flattered, but would commit himself to nothing. People recognized him in the street now, especially in the villages, and this pleased him enormously. Perhaps to counteract the over-familiarity with which viewers treat those they see on the screen, he made a point of addressing even children formally as *usted*. When he smoked, he did not inhale.

Centurión could not conceal from him who he was or what he did – Florentín always made a point of finding out a little about any new arrivals, purely out of journalistic habit – but he did come up with a pretext, saying he was planning to write a novel set in Ruán, for which he requested Florentín's help, promising to mention him in the acknowledgements and even, if he liked, to introduce him as a character.

'It will be my first novel, but I'm sure it will be a success,' he told him with an aplomb he felt should serve as a letter of introduction, for Florentín would have immediately lost interest in anyone too timid. 'It's been decades since anyone paid any attention to these small towns. Readers know nothing about them and it will open up a whole new world to them, Señor Corripio.'

'Please, call me Florentín.'

'Forgive me, Señor Florentín. I wasn't sure how you preferred to be addressed.'

'No, no, just plain Florentín. I mean, can you imagine anyone addressing Clarín as "Señor Clarín"? That would sound ridiculous. It would be like calling Larra "Señor Fígaro" or Dickens "Mr Boz".' Centurión was only half surprised that Peporro should know that Dickensian pen name: you could tell from his programmes and articles that he was very well read. 'Where are you from originally?'

'From Madrid.' This reply instilled a minimum of respect. Madrid still had a certain prestige in 1997. Not much, but more than other places.

'And how come you speak English so well? I've heard that you speak it like a native. A native of England, of course.'

'I spent a few years studying at Oxford, and before that, as a boy, at the British Institute in Calle Martínez Campos, if you know Madrid.'

'Yes, yes, of course. Believe it or not, I've travelled quite a bit. I'm not like my fellow citizens, who despise everything that is not Ruán and barely go anywhere. Oxford eh? And the British Institute too? An excellent school I've heard. And, I believe, co-educational, even when that was forbidden under Franco.' This was another fact he found pleasing. It doubtless led him to think that Centurión might have some useful contacts. 'And do you have a publisher for this novel? And will it be translated into English?'

'It's rather early to say at the moment. But Alfaguara, Seix Barral, Tusquets or Anagrama will be sure to snap it up. They're all posh publishing houses, and this novel, because it's so unusual, will be a must-read for any neo-toffs who want to keep up to date. Ruán will become fashionable, you'll see, although I'll give it another name to feel freer when I'm writing about it. If you stick to facts that can be checked, the imagination suffers, you clip its wings.'

'So you won't use any real names, then?' This seemed both to relieve and disappoint him. 'But people in Ruán will, I suppose, know.'

'No, no real names. Depending on what I describe or invent, that might cause me legal problems. I could be accused of libel, as the English are always so quick to do at the slightest insinuation or hint of a slur. The libel laws are very strict there, and one can easily get caught in that trap. Here you're free to say terrible things about anyone, with no consequences at all. But if we did want to have it translated one day . . .' With that plural, I was already including him in that phantom project.

Florentín was both an anglophile and a francophile, and he was clearly excited by the idea of crossing borders, even if only as a character unrecognizable to the hypothetical French or English readers of a novel that did not yet exist.

He ran the back of his hand over his beard. If he had been Italian, which he wasn't, that gesture would have meant 'I don't give a damn.'

That day, he was wearing a beautifully cut suit in a ghastly colour, that of dried blood, along with a lemon-yellow tie and a pink shirt. As a whole, he managed to be a stain that wounded your eyes until your eyes got used to it. This was his distinguishing mark, his brand, to both dazzle and wound with his presence.

'Well, if you do use me as a character, you can keep the name "Florentín" if you like. Definitely not Corripio though. Absolutely not. After all, "Florentín" is a nom de plume, and only people in Ruán would put two and two together, and I really don't care if they do. There have already been all kinds of rumours and stories about me. Whatever you said would fall far short, I assure you, the imagination of the many is always madder and more villainous that that of a single individual, however professional he may be. And you, of course, are not yet a professional. Your first novel, you say. Or have you written others that haven't been published? Were they rejected? Or did you consider them immature?'

Centurión ignored those last few questions.

'And it's a really magnificent nom de plume. I congratulate you.'

'Oh, do you like it? I'm so used to it, I can't tell any more . . .'

'Yes, it sticks in the mind. In fact, they all do, I was told that you use several, depending on what you're writing about. Would you prefer to be "Lorédan Larchey"? That would suit my "creature of the air" as Savater called characters in that excellent book of his, which I'm sure you've read. So I have your permission then? I'm free to include you in the plot?'

'Absolutely. In principle that is. And what would my role be? After all, we have only just met.'

'You've already described your role. There are a thousand stories about Florentín, so many that I wouldn't have to invent any . . . But it's likely that the protagonist would, at some point, come to you and ask you for information, as I'm doing now. To ask the man whom nothing escapes, the town's watchman, who lets no crime go unnoticed apart from any crime that might unleash other crimes, and about which he keeps silent. Who is always aware of what should be revealed and what should be kept secret. An alert but prudent mind, neither obsessive nor self-righteous.'

This very brief, improvised biographical sketch pleased Florentín and, above all, intrigued him, as if he were curious to see himself in a portrait that was not as he would have portrayed himself. He took out one of his skinny cigarettes, which were far too thin, so much so that when he tapped it lightly on his cigarette case, it broke in two. He angrily, discreetly, threw it on the floor, even though there was an ashtray in front of him, and then with his slender, nimble fingers took out another. They were sitting at a table in El Búho Bizco, where he had arranged to meet Centurión, the rather drab teacher. He was clearly flattered by the prospect of existing in a fiction, regardless of who wrote it, even an unpublished, no longer young author, an idiot far too full of himself, and Centurión played on this by flattering him, taking care not to overegg the pudding so as to avoid arousing suspicions. Florentín's face lit up with rather ingenuous excitement as he flicked on his cheap Bic lighter, which really didn't tally with his long silver cigarette case, almost certainly an antique (perhaps this was another gift from Liudwino for which Florentín had felt neither beholden nor grateful). Florentín clearly wasn't always immaculate in every detail, or perhaps he had run out of fuel for the elegant matching lighter and had had to resort to a plastic one.

Into my mind like a flash came the old story a terrified Berta had once told me, and which had obliged me to make a partial confession to her about my activities: a threat to our son when he was still a baby and I was away, involving a Zippo lighter and that Irish couple (well, the woman was Irish) who had courted and flattered her and then threatened her. The details were slightly vague to me, because I'd only heard about it, not experienced it, and I had never seen the couple. Anyway, it had ultimately come to nothing, just a brief terrifying moment. Something still niggled at me, however (although this feeling was as fleeting as that initial flash), as if, twenty years later, that episode were still not quite over. And yet it was, nothing had occurred in the time that had elapsed since then. Of course it's hard to remember clearly something that happened twenty years ago, imagine how twenty years in a prison cell must feel. That more or less is what I would be condemning one of my three women to, if I could come up with the evidence. And it would be better if I could; if I didn't, Tupra could well order me to unceremoniously dispatch the most likely candidate, just in case and so as not to disappoint his friend George. To drive her up into the hills, tell her to get out of the car for some reason, then run her down at high speed, driving over her body a few times just to be sure. Or push her off a cliff, a cleaner option, after all, people can go foolishly close to the edge and fall. It would have to be a stolen car, of course, like the ones ETA and IRA terrorists would load with bombs, then leave parked outside whatever their target might be, a vehicle owned by a soldier or a judge or a businessman, or a supermarket. Tupra was perfectly capable of issuing such an order. Fortunately, I hadn't yet received an impatient phone call from him, but I feared it would not be long in coming, his impatience that is. It was hard to stop when it came.

Florentín repeated my words, 'The town's watchman, the man whom nothing escapes,' then went on: 'An ambiguous fellow, sometimes tormented by all that he knows, someone who has to weigh carefully what to reveal and what not to reveal. Yes, an attractive character for a novel. But obviously that's not what I'm really like. Thoughtful and measured. And I don't tell the stories I choose not to tell as a way of avoiding further collateral damage, just as I remain silent about certain corrupt practices so as not to provoke still worse evils. I keep some things to myself either because it suits me or simply because I can't reveal them. There are some powerful people around, and I'm certainly not untouchable. True, people do respect and fear me, and try to keep me on their side, but I'm not untouchable, I wish I were.' He paused, then in a different tone of voice said, 'Now here's an intriguing, fascinating thought: could we, unbeknown to ourselves, be playing or rehearsing a scene from the novel right now?' And he asked this with a mixture of almost childlike innocence and barely disguised excitement, as if he had suddenly, unwittingly, grown in stature. All that was lacking then was for him to take out his comb and smooth his hair a little, in fact, he did almost do just that, but stopped himself in time.

'Oh, yes, one hundred per cent, Florentín. This scene will definitely be in the book, slightly embellished and tweaked, of course. So we'd better watch what we say and how we look,' said Centurión with a broad smile to indicate that he was joking. Or that while he was joking, he was also telling the truth.

He realized that, from then on, when in his presence, the man-who-was-*El Esperado* would always behave as if he were in front of an audience, a more mysterious, more demanding audience, less tame and less homogeneous than the television audience he was used to; like a great actor conscious of being the focus of many expectant eyes. As if the mere suggestion that, from this moment on, whatever he did or said, his every gesture and word would be used to create a character in a novel and possibly, later on, in a film.

Literature allows us to see people as they truly are, even though those people do not exist, but will, with luck, always exist, which is why literature will never entirely lose its prestige. Besides, Florentín was very keen on literature, his articles were stuffed with quotations and learned references, as were his lightweight appearances on TeleRuán, even though he knew full well that they would go straight over the heads of most viewers. Not that he cared, indeed he would sometimes even say as much on air, brazenly, but not smugly: 'Now I'm aware that most of you won't know who Cardinal de Retz or Erckmann-Chatrian or Shaftesbury were. It doesn't matter though, because I know, and I know, too, that they're highly relevant to this rather frivolous situation. If you did know who they were, you'd have got far more juice out of what I said, but however little time you have, there's always time to read and study, that's what the town's library is there for.' And then he would resume his usual stream of mischievous nonsense. People liked him so much that, in the days that followed, the library would be visited by artisans and curious ladies asking if they had anything by 'Cardinal Derrez' or 'German Chatrian' or 'Shakesberry', often without success. Centurión knew that he had, in one fell swoop, won over Louvet de Couvray and Lorédan Larchey and even Champfleury and Fernanda Mesnadero, because he was about to add a new dimension to Florentín's life, give him an importance he could never have dreamed of.

'So what do you want me to tell you, my battle-hardened

Centurión?' Florentín liked to tease. 'Ask away, and I'll see if I can answer your questions and contribute a few ideas to our novel. It will be packed with characters, won't it? Any portrait of a town has to be.'

Not wanting to betray his real interests or come straight to the point, Centurión asked him first about Berua, the owner of El Búho Bizco, the doctors Vidal Secanell and Ruibérriz de Torres and the notary Gaspar Gómez-Notario, about whom he already knew a little; he wanted to test out just how indiscreet Florentín was prepared to be. To some degree, Florentín threw discretion to the winds, confirming that Berua facilitated and arranged the occasional bit of prostitution for posh girls who did it to amuse themselves or to earn some quick cash, and that he sold cocaine on the premises, and that all three of the other men bought it; however, he then warned him that he could not, for the moment, tell him absolutely everything:

'The most interesting of the four is Vidal Secanell. Behind that amiable façade lies a very dark, truly horrifying tale. In any other country, he'd be behind bars. Here, they don't investigate anything, they just let matters ride so as not to ruffle any feathers, which is how a lot of things get swept under the carpet. Anyway, it's still early days for me to tell you all the gory details. Best take it slowly. One must be sparing with information, even when it's in the noble name of fiction.'

Centurión couldn't care less what crimes that very competent cardiologist Vidal Secanell might have committed; he had seen him around town and he really did give off an air of sympathy and bonhomie. But these questions were really just a distraction technique, he actually found Florentín's anecdotes deeply boring – fortunately he was not too prolix – and while he pretended to be listening intently and reluctantly taking a few notes, he more or less switched off. He wasn't there to find out about Ruán's scandals. Then he asked about Inés Marzán, and a few expressions flickered across Florentín's face:

'I imagine you know rather more about her than I do, my brave Centurión. It hasn't escaped my notice that you have been seen out and about together a few times, not that you've been trying to hide this. Although you have been seeing slightly less of each other lately, am I right?' And he accompanied these words with a rather coarse gesture, interlacing his fingers, then moving them back and forth in a movement intended to evoke the culminating point of sexual intercourse. Then he drew them apart and held them up, as if they were paralysed, in keeping with his last remark. Florentín may have been clever, well read and always scrupulously polite, but he wasn't so very refined, and at that moment he was more Peporro than Florentín. That ugly Abraham Lincoln-cum-Fagin beard was a sign, another of Peporro Corripio's ideas.

'That isn't what I was asking. Where did she come from? What's her story? As you know, she never talks about the past, she avoids it like the plague, as if it filled her with disgust or fear. How did she end up in Ruán?'

'Oh, she's certainly very reserved. No one knows much about her previous adventures, not even her women friends, and she doesn't have many of those. She claims she came from Salamanca or Logroño or Gijón. She gives different people different versions or maybe she did once live in all those places. Although, to be honest, she doesn't interest me much as a character. She's had a couple of affairs with people here, but then who hasn't? She's far too discreet for my taste, she runs her restaurant very efficiently and apparently has no ambitions to rise in society. She has her minor vices, but keeps quiet about them, and you'll doubtless know about those anyway. Or possibly even share them. Noisy, histrionic, ambitious people are more my type. Needless to say, in circumspect Ruán there aren't too many of those. If I were ever invited to work in Madrid, though, well, that's where the truly shameless and the pompous hang out, that's where you can really shine . . .'

Centurión kept his eyes fixed on him, saying nothing, hoping to be told something of more substance. Noticing this, Florentín shook off his little metropolitan daydream and looked slightly guilty, as if he were afraid to disappoint and cut a poor figure in the novel. He half apologized:

'Look, I know a lot about what goes on in Ruán, but not everything. If you're interested, I can tell you the names of little Inés' lovers, but they're all men who've had brief flings with a number of women, and you know how it works: one woman tells another woman and that woman feels left out or simply curious, a desire to say "What about me?" Local, inconsequential trivia; well, originality is positively frowned on here. Now, as for what happened elsewhere . . . That's not my job, it's out of my jurisdiction. The most I can offer you are rumours, and I don't know if there's any truth in them or if they're mere inventions. You know how it is in these ordinary little towns: when someone doesn't talk much about themselves, people feel a need to invent something, and that something immediately becomes engraved in stone. And then your guess is as good as mine. Most of us can't bear to be in the dark about anyone, that's why my particular profession prospers and is so lucrative. People like me fill in the gaps and provide a soothing sense of cause-and-effect, of order. It's not so very different from what you novelists do; your worlds, your selective realities, seem more orderly and comprehensible and easier to grasp than reality. Those of us who make accusations and spread rumours are helping to soothe minds, as well as providing distraction and topics of conversation. I really don't know why we're so despised. We contribute to tightening the bonds in our community, bringing harmony and direction . . .'

Florentín was becoming lost in his own thoughts, he probably didn't often have a chance to share his musings with someone he considered his equal. He expressed himself rather well, but Centurión wasn't interested in the names of Inés Marzán's lovers or in Champfleury's ruminations on life. He found it odd, though, that he should have said 'little Inés' when referring to that very tall, very large woman, perhaps an indication that he felt a certain fondness, had a soft spot, for her. Such a diminutive was hardly appropriate for that near-giantess, who grew still larger during sex, as he well knew.

'What rumours have you heard, then?'

Florentín leaned back in his armchair and stuck one thumb in the breast pocket of that jacket the colour of dried blood, as if he suddenly felt rather pleased with himself or were about to give a professorial lecture.

'Oh, I don't give them much credence. A vulgar, melodramatic story, adored as much by ladies as it is by their cooks and hairdressers, who are all one and the same really, and who would happily spend their lives together if they weren't so concerned about appearances. They say her husband kicked her out and that he got custody of their daughter, who she's not even allowed to see. That she had cuckolded him so outrageously that she had no choice but to leave Salamanca or Logroño or Gijón, and pretty sharpish too. Nowadays, this sounds most unlikely and all rather nineteenth-century. Or that it was something more than just a case of adultery with aggravation, that she embezzled money, was involved in some kind of fraud or thievery, or even violent crime. Only violent, I imagine, I doubt she would have actually killed anyone. She probably just stuck a kitchen knife in her husband in a fit of rage, or in her lover, I really can't see her doing anything worse. They say the only reason her husband didn't report her to the police was because she promised to disappear for ever and never go near their daughter again. Others say she did kill someone, shortly before she moved to Ruán, but people quickly absorb and forget everything, and for a long time now, she's just been Inés Marzán, the owner of La Demanda, and it wouldn't occur to anyone not to have supper there. As in all moderate societies, the locals, at least initially, are drawn to shocking, gruesome stories. That's certainly the case in England, as you will know better than me: the English like to think that someone's quiet, peaceful life must inevitably be a front for horrific murders and unimaginable sexual perversions. It's their way of making up for so much quietude.'

Centurión realized that these rumours were not markedly different from what Inés Marzán herself had told him that day in the park, when she had spoken more openly than she ever had before. Not that this necessarily meant anything: perhaps she had decided to adopt as her own, in her own interests, the gossip that had grown up around her, that she'd heard over the years and may even have found amusing. The only thing that did catch his attention was the reference to Logroño, the capital of La Rioja, the region of Spain from which Magdalena Orúe's father came. Inés had never mentioned that town. Nor, of course, Gijón. This information was of little use to him unless Florentín actually knew what had happened in those other towns. After all, Florentín wasn't a detective, and Centurión couldn't really expect him to tell him much more.

It was time to change tack:

'And what about Liudwino López Xirau? And his wife Celia Bayo? What can you tell me about them?'

Florentín puffed out his chest like a bird, stood up and made a sweeping gesture with his hand meaning: 'Where to begin?' or 'What can I say?' But it was Liudwino he was clearly most prepared to talk about, because he immediately focused on him, and Centurión wasn't interested in Liudwino, but in Celia. Nevertheless, he had to ask about them both.

'He's a felon and a fugitive,' he said.

'A fugitive from what?'

'The guy was born in Catilina and has always been a rogue. He moved to the east coast of Spain when he was very young, because there was more money to be made there, more action, more opportunities. After a couple of years in prison in Castellón, though, he had no choice but to hotfoot it out of there. And he only got out of jail because he collaborated with the police and snitched on a few accomplices, which, apparently, made things very awkward for some poor sod in the council offices. Now, Liudwino really *was* an embezzler, a swindler, and anything else you care to name. Having made a fair few enemies in the area, he had to leave in a hurry, which means he won't be going east again any time soon. Anyway, he came home years ago, and put into practice what he had learned, except that he did it much better this time and made sure to cover his back.'

'That's all very well, Florentín, but I already knew that, and, besides, if you know it too, why don't you expose all his tricks and fiddles? I mean more openly.'

'For two reasons: first, he's got far too many people involved who would be really badly affected if the whole house of cards were to collapse now; second, because, as you'll have seen for yourself, people genuinely like him, they think he's great. And that's what makes me hold my fire, that and the possible harm one of the town's bigwigs might inflict on me. With them I make a few lighthearted, mischievous jokes, but no more than that. And you can't and shouldn't swim against the tide of popular opinion. Or only very tentatively, sowing a few doubts here and there and allowing yourself the occasional sarcastic comment. Any full-frontal attack on Liudwino would backfire on me, unless one day he falls from favour or I become even more popular than him. I'm getting there thanks to my TV appearances, but I haven't quite arrived yet. It's a real mystery how Ruán could have fallen for such a coarse, brazen fellow. Anyway, for the time being, I make the occasional wicked or mocking remark and ask a few trick rhetorical questions, just now and then, mind, and without laying it on too thick.'

Florentín paused for a moment, smoothed his jacket and his trousers, and once again seemed to be on the point of taking out his comb. He must have thought that all this speechifying would make him a better character for my book.

'People are very dangerous, the most dangerous thing there

is – simultaneously frightening and repellent. People en masse tend to be pretty nasty, they infect each other with their vile deeds and their resentments, encouraging each other to give free rein to them and furiously unleash them on anyone. You should always feel nervous of crowds and be prepared to run, even if, at least initially, they're guided by reason, because they always end up transformed into irrational beasts. If you fall out with them, you're lost, they'll crucify you. They won't hear a word against their chosen favourite, not until doubt begins to set in, as it always does, but it can be a very slow process, it can take years and destroy many people in its path. And no amount of remorse, if anyone ever feels remorse, can bring those people back; the mob judges itself very leniently, and exonerates itself of even the worst crimes. You just have to look at history, both remote and recent, it's full of once-venerated assassins. Look at what's happening today in the Basque Country, just next door if you like.'

This comment interested Centurión:

'Why, what's happening in the Basque Country?'

'What do you mean "what's happening"? Don't you read the papers? Don't you look at the election results? Every single time, about one hundred and eighty thousand votes go to the party that supports and cheers on those terrorists with all their multiple aliases. Start counting them one by one and you'll have died of boredom before you reach a thousand. Think of it, one hundred and eighty thousand people applauding and egging on a few murderers. It sends shivers down your spine, doesn't it?' Florentín had grown serious, and Centurión felt sure that if Florentín had suspected one of those three women of being in some way involved in terrorism, he would have had no qualms about saying so. It clearly wouldn't have occurred to him to connect any of them with ETA, let alone the distant IRA. Florentín looked down at his lemon-yellow tie and flicked away a few insignificant or rather imaginary specks. 'And then . . .'

'Then what?'

'One can never entirely resist those currents of opinion, it's very difficult not to succumb, however marginally, to the general mood. What I mean is that, even though I know precisely who and what Liudwino is, namely a scoundrel, I still quite like him. He's good at getting people on side, and he, of course, does his best to keep me sweet. He lionizes me and sucks up to me and tries to please me. It's difficult to pick on someone you have any kind of relationship with, and in a town this size everyone has a relationship with everyone else, whether they want to or not. With a few exceptions of course. Agreements are reached, truces called; say, for example, you pass your enemy on the bridge; what are you going to do, given that you've known him half your life? You stop and talk to him.'

'Does Liudwino give you presents?'

'Oh, he gives presents to anyone of any importance. "A little something for your children or for your wife", the usual thing. Don't worry, though, that doesn't cut any ice with me. Although I do rein myself in a little and watch my back. We journalists have to do that – better to keep pecking away at something than be dead and buried and with no beak at all.'

'Dead and buried?'

'Don't be so literal-minded, Centurión, that's just a manner of speaking. Although you only have to remember those journalists in Mexico: they would have been better off saying nothing for a while before returning to the fray, rather than going on and on about it only to end up hanging from a bridge, with their heads chopped off and some word or other scrawled on their chest. As I say, it's one thing to rein myself in and quite another to have my rifle loaded and ready for the first opportunity to fire. There's always a moment when the mob begins to doubt its hero. Look at Mussolini. Did you know that Franco kept a photo in his office of Mussolini hanging from his feet like a pig? When someone asked him why, he said: "To remind myself that the same thing is never going to happen to me." That's one thing he got right.'

'The rifle Walter Pidgeon or Alan Thorndike failed to have ready and loaded on the leafy outskirts of Berchtesgaden, even though he was a professional hunter. A mistake that made him delay giving that first playful squeeze of the trigger; and when it did occur to him that he could actually shoot, he had to put in a real bullet and start again. Then, of course, that leaf fluttered down, and just having to brush it away meant that he ran out of time and missed his chance,' I thought. 'As Florentín had said metaphorically, you should always have your rifle loaded, because you never know what you might find. "If I had had an inkling of the role this piece of filth was to play, I would have shot him without a second thought," Reck-Malleczewen wrote in his diary. That was the reality, whereas Fritz Lang's film was a fiction, based on another fiction. The problem is that we don't always get an inkling, let alone the necessary foresight and certainty, and so our finger trembles and hesitates, is about to squeeze the trigger then relaxes, then squeezes again, our eye remains fixed on the target, then blinks and looks away, then looks again. The problem is time and the moment, which nearly always arrives too late or too early: when we know the magnitude of the harm we will cause, it's no longer possible to kill, and yet it *was* possible when we sensed it as a possibility, but one doesn't shoot someone based on a supposed sixth sense. Well, some do, Tupra certainly could. I don't think I could though.'

'And what about Celia Bayo?' I asked Florentín.

'Why ask me about her? You know her, she's a colleague of yours.'

'Yes, but she's so nice she must be hiding something. Where's she from originally? How did she and Liudwino meet?'

'She's originally from Galicia, isn't she? She doesn't have an accent because she spent part of her childhood in Madrid, and she's very proud of the Italian she learned there at the Liceo. She's from La Coruña or Santiago, I can't quite remember which, but she and Liudwino met here. There's really nothing more to tell or know. With her, what you see is what you get. She's a real darling, a sweetheart, well, you've had dealings with her yourself. A genuinely kind soul. A very simple, trusting creature who sees the good in everything, even the tricks her husband gets up to, assuming she knows about them. She doesn't ask any questions, not even of him. If everything's fine with her husband and he's earning money, she's happy; she's not the sort to demand explanations, not the inquisitive type. She is what she is. I agree, though, that she wouldn't make for a very interesting character in the book.'

'Are you sure about that, Florentín? No one is ever precisely what they seem to be. My experience has been quite different: the more diaphanous someone appears to be, the more things they're hiding. Not necessarily bad things. It could be certain talents and virtues that modesty prevents them from revealing. I don't know, I've known ordinary housewives who turned out to be consummate pianists, as good as Horowitz, but without the necessary confidence or ambition. What did Celia do before she came to Ruán?'

'The same as here. She taught in Santiago or in La Coruña. She got bored there and the pay was better here. It's colder, but it rains less and there's more sun. What makes you think she's hiding something? She seems perfectly straightforward to me. If you press me, I would say that the only real mystery is why she's so in love with that lout of a husband of hers. Have you seen the way he dresses? And his vocabulary, well . . .'

I was amused to hear Florentín criticize someone else's dress sense, when he himself was a red blot on the landscape in his ankle-length overcoat. True, he was less eclectic and more coordinated colour-wise than López López. Anyway, everything he was telling me chimed with the reports I'd been given, indeed I wondered who had written those reports and what they had based them on, perhaps there was nothing more to be learned using traditional methods.

'Not that she's the epitome of refinement, with that rather equine, ponyish gait of hers, but compared with him . . . They do love each other though, and perhaps she loves him because he's so madly in love with her. He's very jealous, you know. He thinks he has a thoroughbred in the house, not a pony.'

'I know, he warned me off her the very first time we met. And I've heard a few other stories too . . .'

'Look,' and Florentín took the chance to drop the subject of Celia, of whom, like everyone else, he had the highest opinion, but whom he didn't find particularly interesting, precisely because she was so uncomplicated, 'the other thing that makes me hold off is how much Liudwino adores his wife. If, one day, I were to put him in the pillory; if I were to reveal his tangled web of bribes, blackmail and corruption; if he were tried and sent to prison, as he thoroughly deserves to . . . Well, I'd feel really sorry for her, I'd be taking away half or more than half of her happiness. His too in a way. He'd go crazy without her at his side, especially because he'd no longer be able to control her: he'd go completely mental thinking she was with some young jackass or other, because he thinks every man who sees her fancies her and is making a play for her. What binds them together is enthusiasm and optimism, frivolity and *joie de vivre*, although in his case that would be a *joie criminelle* and in hers an unconscious, easy-going *joie*. But this is all such small beer that it cries out for a certain leniency. Or not. What do you think?'

Florentín was very careful in his choice of words: 'equine' not 'horsey', 'leniency' not 'mercy' or 'pity'. He had pronounced *pony*

English-fashion, although on his lips it sounded more like 'po-oo-nee'. He had clearly done his reading so as to live up to his other pseudonyms, Louvet de Couvray, Lorédan Larchey and Champfleury. I began to wonder if he was the right man for my needs. He had told me nothing strange or grubby that wasn't already public knowledge. He didn't think badly of Inés Marzán, he thought Celia Bayo an angel, and he didn't even loathe Liudwino, even though he despised him and considered him a felon. Despite his reputation, he didn't have a viperish tongue, and was rather kind to his fellow citizens. Perhaps it was as he said: in a town the size of Ruán, it wasn't easy to cultivate a long-lasting enmity with anyone. He could play at that, making the occasional barbed comment in his newspaper or on the chat show, but a barb never really penetrates the flesh, it leaves only a superficial wound.

Perhaps in Ruán people lived willingly and calmly with whatever life threw at them, showing a kind of stoical fatalism. It wasn't as life so often is in villages (at least in Spanish and Irish villages), where the few inhabitants actually seem to need mortal, enduring enmities to feed their spirit, to combat and justify their misfortunes, from generation to generation. They have to blame someone for their own indolence, for the setbacks they bring upon themselves, for the unhappiness they're told they were born with, that they will live and die with. The fault lies in the past, with your great-grandfather or with someone else's great-great-grandfather, there are too many memories in villages, and people are constantly plunging back into them.

In Ruán, on the other hand, people accepted as a lesser evil, as something almost natural, the existence of drug dealers like Comendador, Berua and other far worse people, likeable manipulators and blackmailers like López Xirau, unscrupulous doctors disguised as lambs (or so I had been told) like Vidal Secanell, brutish exploiters like Folcuino Gausi, and it had probably always been so: a permeable, assimilative town, in which each individual played the role assigned to him by a throw of the dice, be it good or bad or only average. And if someone were erased from the picture, it would remain smudged, incomplete, imperfect; and so they allowed in whoever turned up at the gates, and quietly adopted and incorporated them. Becoming part of the landscape, whether to uglify or beautify it, was enough in itself, and when, inevitably, there was a casualty, it would be followed by a tolling of bells summoning the mist, 'and each slow dusk a drawing-down of blinds': every amputated limb, however gangrenous, demanding to be mourned.

That town in the north-west was doubtless ruled by this quotation from the Psalms: 'Unless the Lord builds the house, its builders labour in vain. Unless the Lord watches over the city, the watchmen stand guard in vain. In vain you rise early and stay up late, toiling for food to eat . . .' Why bother Ruán's watchmen when the Lord has spent centuries and centuries watching over the town, and it's still standing, just as Santa Águeda and El Cantuariense, Puerta Latina and the Cathedral still rise up almost intact, and people continue to go back and forth across the bridge, over the choppy but never turbulent waters of the Lesmes?

'I see,' I said. 'And what about María Viana? What can you tell me about her? Apart from what we all know, of course. Where is *she* from? Where did she suddenly appear from? Who was she before she married Gausi? Why did he cease being a widower to marry her? She must have had plenty of suitors over the years, which, I have to say, is hardly surprising, because while she isn't spectacularly beautiful, she does exude a kind of . . .' I deliberately avoided using the word 'sensuality'. 'Distinction, I don't know how else to put it. At least that's my feeling.'

Florentín jumped, cringed, looked nervously about him as if in search of an escape route. He nervously twizzled the glass of beer he was drinking and lit one of his ridiculous cigarettes, as if he'd been dreading that question right from the start of our conversation. The foam from his beer had left a faint white stain on his shaven upper lip, which made him look even more like that Dickensian teacher of petty thieves.

'You've caught me with my pants down there,' he said regretfully, and by using that colloquial expression he had clearly fallen into the grasp of Peporro, Corripio and possibly even Pepón, all three of them, momentarily driving out that throng of Frenchified people and even Fernanda Mesnadero, who would never have referred to such an intimate garment to express her utter ignorance; unless she was one of the ever-growing band of vigorously coarse young women. 'I know very few facts about María Viana, no one does, so there's not much to say. I mean about what she was before she came here. You'll have seen, though, that she's absolutely perfect and is as much a part of the town as if she were a real Ruán princess. Despite being extremely wealthy by marriage as well as extremely elegant, she's achieved the impossible by offending no one either intentionally or unintentionally. No one dislikes her. She's rather aloof as are all the family, but not proud. She's not what you'd call communicative, she's discreet, but cordial too. She has a smile and a friendly word for everyone, even though her smile isn't exactly warm, but that, I suppose, is just the way she is . . . Would she be a good character for the novel, do you think? Or would she seem too vacuous, a sphinx with no riddle, a screen concealing nothing? Gausi turned up with her, already married, on his return from a long journey. Some say he picked her up in Madrid, others in Santander and still others in Seville, but she certainly doesn't have a southern accent or manner. There is a very brief official version, if you like, but who knows if it's true. She was the daughter of a late friend and work colleague of Gausi's, a diplomat who never stayed in one place for very long. María isn't from nowhere exactly, but she would have spent her child-hood and adolescence moving from country to country without ever

337

settling in one place. That's why she speaks several languages, all of them badly, because none of them really took root. The only person who knows the truth is Gausi, but he's never been one for answering probing questions, not even from his friends. Indeed, he avoids such questions, he doesn't like anyone poking their nose into his business, still less into family matters. His attitude would be: "She's my wife, and that's that. Nothing to see, nothing to object to, nothing to gossip or even ask about. Asking any questions about her would be an act of sheer impertinence, since I stand as her guarantor. The same goes for my children, for my staff and even for my dogs." He's the classic authoritarian male who believes he ennobles everyone around him by his mere presence, or that the fortunate few in his immediate circle clearly have a natural aptitude for nobility. You know the sort: "Everything I have is first class, from my chauffeur to my wife." What he doesn't like, though, is for even his closest collaborators to know everything he does, all the strings he pulls, all his plans and projects. Each person should know only what he needs to know.'

'Just like in our secret services,' I thought, and, as it usually did in my mind, 'our' meant British. 'It's best if every pawn in the game knows only his particular task and never the whole scheme or plan. Even right now, I'm only partially informed and, as usual, I'm working pretty much in the dark with only a rather dim torch to light my way. And why would I need more than that? The rest doesn't concern me, and that's fine.'

'Yes, but what about María?' I didn't want him to launch into a speech about Folcuino, who, to me, seemed like a peasant who had made his fortune and acquired a little light culture (I say this more because of the paintings he had collected than because of his reading matter). I wasn't in the least bit interested in him.

'Well, there's not much more to say. According to his version she's from an upper-class family originally from Madrid. A cosmopolitan family, and I take "cosmopolitan" to mean rootless, nomadic, with not much money, the kind who live comfortably enough as long as the father brings in a good salary from his government post. Once he dies, though, it's back to basics. And that could be the reason why she married a rich, arrogant provincial like him. What else could she do?'

'But María is hardly a young woman. She must have done something else when she was younger, before she came to Ruán. It's been quite a while since women had to live like the heroines in Jane Austen or even Balzac novels.'

Florentín stroked his beard, indeed, he almost scratched it (it must have been itchy sometimes) and gave a theatrical sigh.

'She must, yes, but, alas, I know nothing about that. You see what a disappointment I am to you, my valiant Centurión. I have nothing useful to tell you at all, what a disaster, what a disappointment. At this rate, I'm not even going to have a walk-on part in your blockbuster of a novel.'

There was a definite ironic edge to his words. Perhaps he wasn't entirely convinced by my story, or perhaps he didn't give a toss about appearing in that dubious *opera prima* by an unknown writer no longer in the springtime of his life. Perhaps, more than anything, he was only talking to me in order to study *me* more closely. After all, he was probably vaguely curious to find out about Inés Marzán's latest lover, a woman who kept these things to herself. I might prove useful to him as a half-page filler in *El Esperado* or to show viewers how up to speed he was on local news.

'As you see, I leave a lot to be desired as the town gossip.'

This encounter was clearly coming to an end, and it was unlikely there would be another one.

'Don't do yourself down, Florentín. You've been really useful, and just to hear you talk is a pleasure. You're a masterly storyteller, but I'm sure everyone tells you that. And if they don't, they should, because that's what they think.'

'Really? Have you heard people say so?' Vanity did occasionally get the better of him, albeit a very flimsy vanity, like that of a poet or an artist. Or of a local celebrity, which is what he was.

'Oh yes. My students' parents often mention you, although, to be honest, the mothers more than the fathers. And my female colleagues too. They obviously follow you and find you amusing. And ninety per cent of the time they agree with you. You should make the leap into the national press. I'm amazed you haven't had any offers. Or join some private TV channel. You'd be a big hit with that Fagin-esque look of yours, with your erudition and your wit and . . .' I didn't want to overdo the flattery, and so I stopped. 'May I ask you one last question?'

'Ah, so you picked up on that,' he said smugly, referring to my Fagin comment. 'But then you're a cultivated man and an anglophile. I have had a few offers, but I wouldn't feel I was on firm ground in Madrid or Barcelona. It would take me a while to acclimatize. Ninety per cent, eh?' That figure had worried him. 'Anyway, go ahead, ask away.'

However, even while encouraging me to go on, he began gathering up his coat from the next bench, thus indicating that this would indeed be my last question. And, as was only logical, he was clearly expecting me to pay the bill. I immediately took out my wallet and held it up, a gesture meaning: 'Don't even think about paying. This is on me, after all, I've been taking up your valuable time.'

'What can you tell me about Gonzalo de la Rica?'

He looked puzzled, then slightly annoyed, as if it irked him not to know a name.

'I don't think I've ever heard or seen that name before. Who is he? Not from here, I assume.'

'No, I don't think he is. I met him only briefly, when he was passing through. He's an old friend of Inés Marzán, at least that's how she introduced him. He could be from Madrid or from Oviedo.

Maybe you've seen him with her occasionally, without knowing his name, or perhaps with someone else. A fat man, in his late fifties I'd say, and although he's going grey, he still has very thick, curly hair. He's got rather beady eyes and wears glasses, and has teeth like tiny square chewing-gum pastilles. He's very chatty too, a real talker. He didn't seem to have much time for democracy and was in favour of limiting how much ordinary people knew. Or rather, limiting the kind of information they glean from the press, from the television and the radio, which, according to him, just encourages them to put their two cents in on any subject you care to name.'

'No, I don't recall seeing anyone like that. I'm so sorry. You see, I've failed you again. But what I will say, and I'm sure you'll agree, is that he isn't entirely wrong, that de la Rica fellow. Democracy does have its faults and can sometimes create unnecessary problems. Of course, the alternatives are far worse, or usually are. Tocqueville foresaw this, and Ortega y Gasset said as much in 1929: the mass-man is the one who thinks he knows everything, but in fact knows nothing. He would never have imagined how, seventy years on, the mass-man would have proliferated. But that's not the fault of democracy, not at all. Because in 1929 it didn't exist in Spain, as it almost never has.'

IX

As I had feared, Tupra did eventually grow impatient enough to phone me. It wasn't enough for him that Pérez Nuix kept in fairly regular contact, always ringing me from Madrid, sometimes on her own behalf and sometimes on behalf of Machimbarrena, who must have considered himself far too delicate to actually pick up the phone himself. I am more than familiar with such middle-aged Spanish gentlemen, and with the English variety too, not in vain did I spend part of my childhood among the former and my university years among the latter. They are all, in their different ways, extremely blasé, they delegate and outsource, then await the results without so much as lifting the index finger with which they would have dialled a number in the days before mobile phones imposed their tyranny. Age does not wither them nor does it improve them or teach them any manners. They will die as they were born, always keeping a safe distance and using that same finger to indicate what they need at each and every moment. They are not, of course, alone in this, such an attitude can be easily and quickly learned, I've seen it in people who were born in a slum or in some hamlet in the middle of nowhere.

Pérez Nuix put only moderate pressure on me, we had, after all, shared certain intimacies that tend to blunt any cutting remarks, the memory of skin on skin prompts us to be gentler. Machimbarrena applied pressure too, but only through her, although when she acted as his messenger girl I could hear his threatening tone and she would speak in a more imperative fashion until I reminded her who she was speaking to and put her firmly in her place with the calm words of a veteran, and then she would back off. From an office everything seems so simple and soluble, but on the ground nothing is easy and time passes very slowly.

Tupra, who knew very well what life was like on the ground and who was in no way a 'gentleman' either by birth or by inheritance, proved to be no different (although he had come a long way from Streatham or Bethnal Green or wherever it was his mother had deposited him on giving birth). He did, however, wait until 13 July, when a few things had happened in Ruán and, more importantly, in Spain itself. By then, though, he'd grown so impatient that he summoned me to London to discuss things face to face, a short visit, a day trip. He had doubtless washed his hands of my mission once he'd got me involved, well, he had plenty to do in his own country and this wasn't a matter that concerned him directly. The fact that he had got in touch with me himself and issued such a peremptory order (his 'suggestions' always used to be orders in the old days, and he tended to allow the old days to infiltrate the present) must mean that he was giving in to pressure from Machimbarrena, to whom he owed favours and whom he wanted to keep sweet, with a view to being able to ask *him* for a favour or two in the future.

'Tom,' he said on the phone, with no prefacing remarks, as if we had spoken just a couple of days before, 'you see how things are in your country.' That day 'my country' was obviously Spain. 'Are you on such poor form that you still haven't sorted this business out? Pat and George are getting very nervous about recent events there and have asked me to intervene. In fact, George is demanding an explanation, presumably because his bosses are demanding the same of him. He considers you to be under my orders, to be my appointee, my man. And you are. Or were, I trained you, and, at least for the moment, you are my man again. Come on, hop on a plane and come to London for a few hours. You can explain what's going on at your end and I'll let you know what I think: perhaps you need to revisit a few old lessons. You've made things very awkward for me, which doesn't please me at all, especially not now. We're getting closer and closer to an agreement or a truce here, although that will still take time, and it's best to defuse any dangers while we still have the freedom to do so.'

He was referring to a possible agreement or truce in Ulster. Once that happened, persecution would stop or would have to be greatly reduced. Tupra would prefer to clean out the ranks of the IRA as much as possible before that pact tied his hands. I assumed Maddie O'Dea could still be an active member of the IRA even though she had been living far from Northern Ireland for eight or nine years, if not longer.

'There's one old lesson I haven't forgotten, Tupra,' I said. 'You know perfectly well that these things are never simple. They sometimes take years. Perhaps you were too optimistic in your calculations. And yes, I'm probably not on top form. I've been retired for a while and we do tend to lose our reflexes, our mental agility, our ability to take the initiative. But you knew all that. And I would just remind you that you were the one who came looking for me and that, at first, I resisted. Besides, as we get older, we take longer to make decisions. We become less intuitive, more cautious.'

I heard him tut-tutting in ironic disapproval, or in the condescending manner that he sometimes either couldn't or chose not to avoid.

'Initial resistance doesn't count once you've agreed to take on a mission, Nevinson, your "Yes" erases it completely. I can't believe you need to be reminded of that. Didn't they teach you anything at Inverailort or in Abergavenny or wherever it was you did your training? No, what am I saying?' he said scornfully. 'You didn't go to either place, you're too young.'

Inverailort House was in Scotland, and it was where Wheeler had received his harsh training during the Second World War;

Abergavenny was in Wales, and from 1942 to 1945 Rudolf Hess, Hitler's Minister without Portfolio, had been held prisoner in Abergavenny's Maindiff Court Hospital, following his arrest in Scotland. These were all places from the past, and I didn't even know if they were still used. Tupra would have loved to have taken part in that war and it was often present in his imagination and on his lips. In a way, he despised all those who hadn't been involved, and therefore despised himself, because he had missed that chance. Hess had died in Spandau in 1987, having hanged himself at the age of ninety-three. Tupra regretted having had all that time and yet never managed to see him.

'No matter. Get on a plane as soon as you can. Tomorrow if possible, or the day after.'

I hesitated for a few seconds. It would be a real hassle to fly to London. In a city like Ruán, everything seems distant and difficult, even getting a train to Catilina. This is what these small towns do to you: you fall asleep in them and end up viewing the outside world just as the locals do, as wild places, full of obstacles. The effort of leaving them fills one with infinite sloth, it feels almost impossible to set off, and the idea of trains, taxis, airports and flights seems inconceivable. I didn't fancy having to confront Tupra either, to endure his reproaches and his possibly mocking remarks, or to have him go over those old lessons, all of which belonged to the life I had assumed was over. I both was and wasn't his man. I could refuse, I could remove myself from the project entirely and leave him, in the eyes of Machimbarrena, looking like a fool, or *brutta figura* as the Italians would say. I hesitated for a few seconds, but it was already too late. When you've invested time and thought and expertise in something, you become a hostage to those things until you reach the point when you're forced to recognize that you really cannot complete the task.

'There aren't any flights from here, so I'll have to travel via Madrid and spend at least one night there,' I said. 'I haven't seen

Berta or the children since I moved to Ruán. We've only spoken on the phone.'

'Well, do that then, but why tell me? I don't see why you need to tell Berta either, you can always see them later. But if you want to see them, go ahead. Besides, when I think about it, the day after tomorrow would actually suit me better. Let me know when it's all arranged and I'll find a window when we can speak on whichever day you choose, so don't worry. The Spaniards are getting tired of waiting, as you know. How have things been in Ruán?'

'Oh, the same as everywhere else.'

The term had ended before all this, before 13 July, and I had been instructed by Pérez Nuix and a disdainful (or was he just bone-idle?) Machimbarrena to stay in that town in the north-west throughout the school holidays, once I'd ascertained that none of the three women, Inés Marzán, Celia Bayo or María Viana, were considering going away for the summer, as traditionally happened in Madrid and other cities, which, overwhelmed by the heat, virtually emptied out in the hottest months. People tended not to leave Ruán in July and August, almost the reverse. The temperature was perfectly bearable, sometimes you even had to put on a sweater when going out for an evening walk, and, on some nights, you needed a light blanket in bed. Outsiders, the 'regular summer residents', came to spend the whole season there, and throngs of culturally restless tourists in search of cooler weather packed the finer churches, the Monastery and the Cathedral. The town felt livelier than it did during the endless winter and the wintry spring. Stimulated by the influx of visitors, the bell-ringers decided to interpret this as a temporary increase in religious faith and laid on positive banquets of sound. I don't know much about matins, vespers and lauds or about liturgy in general, but it seemed to me that they unloosed their bells at any old time, without rhyme or reason.

There was an increase, too, in the number of people visiting restaurants, the bars and taverns in Barrio Tinto, as well as the official stalls and kiosks in the park, and for this reason the owner of La Demanda remained on duty and was rushed off her feet (she was very hard-working and only shut her doors at the end of January or in February, just for a couple of weeks, but even then not every year).

Celia Bayo found her many social activities curtailed (the town's rhythm changed and idleness reigned), but Liudwino López López couldn't exist without his constant scheming. He was quite incapable of abandoning the territory of his many tangled plots, certainly not as long as most of his associates or cronies, both participants and patsies, remained there in a semi-active state. He was one of those self-aggrandizing men who needs to keep a watchful eye on his theatre of operations, even if it's deserted, and in Ruán it only appeared to be deserted: the Town Council may have relaxed a little when it came to handing out contracts, but it was busy organizing festivities, fun runs, rock concerts and other such nonsense, and he had to keep his hand in and get his cut of all those trifling events, which is why he felt obliged to stay in town. And being a jealous husband, he didn't want to risk his wife being alone somewhere up in the mountains, which, in summer, welcomed whole colonies of idle *madrileños* and *bilbaínos* all eager to indulge in some provincial frolic. Liudwino saw Celia as being a nice bit of stuff who would inevitably be lusted after by some unscrupulous youth or by a husband who fancied a brief summer fling he could boast about over pre-supper drinks on his return home.

Ruán's beautiful, immaculate park – which had, I think, been known as El Boscoso since it was first opened in the mid-nineteenth century and which contained a careful selection of native and exotic trees all meticulously labelled – was at its most resplendent then and always full of people at all hours, morning, noon and night, for its gates never closed and it was lit at night by the warm yellow light of its streetlamps. The uniformed municipal band took their places among the leaves of the Olmo de las Melodías and, from Thursday to Sunday, at midday on the dot, they would play for fifty minutes, everything from American or English military marches, pasodobles, Strauss waltzes and even settings of arias by Verdi and Puccini and from Bizet's *Carmen*. This made the people of Ruán feel very refined (indeed many actually were) as well as keeping visitors entertained.

As for María Viana and Folcuino Gausi in their quasi-mansion in the posh part of town, they had at their disposal a leafy garden with abundant shade and a swimming pool. They didn't need to go anywhere, and many of the world's men and women would have paid a fortune they could never possibly have earned just to spend a week there, let alone the whole summer. Given their dislike of the hurly-burly, the Gausis went into town less often than usual. Not that the summer visitors and tourists formed horrific, boozy, vandalistic hordes (Ruán had no beach, and if you wanted to swim in the Lesmes river, you had to walk about a mile or so out of town), but the crowds were enough for the Gausis to find it bothersome to mingle and mix. They didn't like having to queue outside the cinemas, or wait their turn in the shops, or hang around for a table to become free in the cafés and restaurants, and everywhere was relatively busy in comparison with the quieter seasons when the town was barely troubled by incomers and certainly not by foreigners.

As I have explained, my useless camera didn't show that garden, but I came to know it well. A week before the festival of San Juan, with the term in its dying days, the head teacher asked if I would be available during the holidays to give private English lessons to the Gausi twins, even though they weren't studying at my school (they went to a better one, but my school was nevertheless deeply grateful for the large donations made each year by Gausi . . .). Apparently, the children were pretty useless at languages in general (she didn't put it like that, but that's what I understood), and their parents wanted to bolster their knowledge of my first or second language (I've never really known which is which) as much as possible. The tone in which my head teacher asked me this was halfway between an order and a plea (in Ruán, it was best not to displease or disappoint Gausi), and I immediately agreed, although perhaps I should have played harder to get. I was suddenly being given a most unexpected opportunity to get a little closer to the third woman, who had previously proved so inaccessible. In the worst-case scenario, I might only pass her in a corridor in the house, on the other hand, who knows, we might get to share a few moments together in the garden.

All the details and arrangements (timetables and so on, and my fee, rather meagre given how wealthy the family was) were dealt with by a man called Higueras, who I immediately identified as the secretary-type figure who sometimes came and went in the deserted sword room. He phoned me – with my head teacher's permission – and urged or invited me to visit the house before lessons began, in order to introduce myself to the children – and, I suppose, to make sure they didn't hate me on sight – and to be examined or interrogated (again he didn't put it like that, but that's what I understood) either by him or by María Viana (as one would expect, he referred to her as *la señora*), who was the person in charge of anything to do with the children, education included.

I caught the bus there one day at noon, and the truth is I felt rather as applicants for the post of cook or maid must have felt in my Madrid childhood in the 1950s and early 1960s, when it was quite common, even in fairly poor, middle-class households, to employ such servants, something that now seems unimaginable. (There's a long tradition in Madrid of upper-crust idleness and keeping up appearances.) Those women, sometimes very young women, who were paid bed and board and a measly wage and only allowed an afternoon off a week, never went beyond the hallway. They sat with my mother on the tiny sofa placed there for that purpose – as if they were sitting together on a tram – and my mother would ask them for references and chat with them for a few minutes, I've no idea about what, to see if they made a good impression and seemed trustworthy. It must have been humiliating for the ones who were rejected after such a brief encounter; the poor things would doubtless wonder afterwards why they had been found wanting, if they'd dressed inappropriately or been too frank in their answers, in what way they had blundered. For the ones who were given the job there would also have been an element of humiliation, as I fear there still is for anyone seeking work and having to submit to an interview on which depend their immediate future and their income over the next few months.

But this is something no one can change: you can't oblige someone to take on a person who strikes them as disagreeable or problematic or slapdash or sullen, and so almost all of us, at some time, have been kept on tenterhooks while we were being scrutinized, awaiting the approval or not of our possible employer. This had happened to me only once, when I entered the British embassy for the first time, but that was two or three lifetimes ago and had been a mere bureaucratic pantomime. I arrived there with my cards already marked, because I'd been recruited for my real job by dint of force and deception.

I no longer asked myself if this had been humiliating or flattering, there was no point in doing so at that stage in a life that had been so radically diverted from what it might have been. Time races past and doesn't wait and fills up with whatever you fill it up with. In the end, it's gone, and you've gained very little from it.

At least Higueras didn't direct me to the servants' entrance, a teacher is not a delivery man or a mendicant nun. Besides, I had the endorsement of my head teacher, and the Gausis were, after all, asking *me* a favour.

Seen from close to, that Higueras fellow looked rather less secretarial than I'd thought from my sightings of him in my videos walking across that living-room-cum-museum. He wore thick, round glasses, his hair close-cropped apart from an incongruously elaborate lock of hair over his forehead, as if he were a footballer hoping to create an original 'look' (a kiss-curl or a moulding that reminded me of my former contact Molyneux during my exile in England, in that town not so very different from Ruán), and he dressed with excessive

354

sobriety, wearing almost funereally black ties even in summer. However, his features were very coarse, almost misshapen, more what one would expect in an ex-boxer or a thug (featherweight or, at most, welterweight, because although he wasn't tall, he was very sturdily built), with a slightly broken nose, a chin that was used to taking punches, thick or swollen lips that appeared to have been indelibly split by long-past blows, as if they would never heal, and a pair of bureaucratic eyes with no perceptible expression, either because they were cold and emotionless or because he was just chronically drowsy.

My cursory interview took place in a small room containing a pedestal table and two armchairs, another useless, almost empty room, which was probably used even less than the room containing the swords and pictures and books; he asked me a few predictable questions, among them how it was that I spoke English so well: he did not speak it well himself, but it seemed to him that my accent was that of a native of London or Liverpool, perhaps because those were the names of the only two towns he knew. We arranged to hold the lessons once a day from twelve until one, so that the *mellizos* or *gemelos* (for some reason we have two words in Spanish both of which simply mean 'twins') could have a splash in the pool before lunch. Except on Saturdays and Sundays of course.

Once we had agreed terms, he went off to fetch the children so that I could meet them or so that they could weigh me up, and a minute later, they appeared accompanied by their mother. They introduced themselves very politely, saying their names were Nicolás and Alejandra and they were eight years old, I would have thought they were a year younger, but I'm not good at guessing ages or perhaps, having been born to older parents, they were slightly puny, not that this mattered. Their names, those of the last tsar and tsarina of Russia, must have been Folcuino's megalomaniac choice, forgetting that the whole family had been murdered and that the Tsarina had succumbed to the influence of Rasputin, of whom there have been endless emulators ever since, all over the world, none of whom are ever detected by those they devour, not even when the latter have been half devoured already. I got the impression that they and María Viana liked me well enough. At the time, I looked pretty good and healthy, partly thanks to Sigfrido and to an excellent Ruán barber, who kept me looking spruce, my Robert Redford-style moustache included, and partly because I had spent my whole life striving to make a good impression on complete strangers – men, women, the elderly, even children – whom I needed to charm or win over. A few jokey remarks, without, of course, playing the fool, a few warm open smiles, my gaze the very picture of innocence and, above all, being a good listener, pretending that I found anything they wanted to confess or recount to me absolutely fascinating.

I have to say that I learned this from Tupra, although I never reached his magisterial heights. At first, people are so easily seduced, eager to have someone pay them attention and make them feel important, nothing more. What comes later is quite another story, when they grow suspicious or weary or irritable, and then you lose them.

This was the first time I had seen María Viana without the mediation or distance provided by the street, the cinema, the shops or my recordings of her, and the sensation I commented upon earlier was instantly confirmed. No, she wasn't in any way spectacular, neither her face nor her figure, although she was very attractive, subtly attractive. She didn't have a cleft chin, but just the hint of a dimple, as if the mark had struggled to appear while she was still in her mother's womb, only to withdraw when she left the womb, leaving just that trace of its struggle for existence. On that particular day, she was wearing her brown hair caught back in a ponytail, which made her look younger. She had a very slightly turned-up nose, again only a hint of what we normally mean by that, as if it were merely there in intent. She had a lovely firm, olive complexion as if the sun had merely lightly brushed it, but held back from turning olive to bronze.

Her eyes were a very dark blue, like that of a clear, northern river at nightfall, and her eyelids tended to droop very slightly, perhaps not so much for any physiological reason as for reasons of modesty or shyness, so that her gaze was not too intense (although the intensity was troubling even with her eyes half closed, the blinds half drawn down, oblique, entrenched). Her lips were striking too, distinctive: the outline perfect, the red or pink visible, and full and fleshy enough to imagine how they would bloom irresistibly in moments of high passion and shameless sexuality, moments she did not share with Folcuino or possibly with anyone else.

Despite the strong attraction I felt for her, despite the air of sensuality she gave off, both of which made it hard for me to resist simply gazing into her face all the time, I always felt she was beyond my reach, because of that strange feeling of respect she imposed on those around her, doubtless without her being aware of it and possibly to her relative regret. It never occurred to me on that first meeting, or indeed subsequently, that I, or anyone, could ever get close to her in that sense (I was probably mistaken though, for there are always certain individuals who know no restraint).

The only thing that could possibly make one think she could be of Irish stock were the tiny, barely visible freckles on her otherwise smooth, unblemished skin. But there are thousands of freckled women in every European country, so this was a very poor indication that she could have been born Maddie O'Dea.

I began my lessons on Monday 30 June, a week after the official end of term and once the children had been given a complete break from school during the festival of San Juan: for even though Ruán was not on the Mediterranean coast – a coast that, for *ruaneses*, was always an object of scorn and ridicule not untinged with envy – they used those festivities as an excuse, as did many other places, to hold a few absurd, noisy celebrations of their own. This meant that I didn't have much time before my trip to London with a brief stopover in Madrid. Not only because of Tupra's admonishing call on 13 July, but also because of the events that convulsed Spain from 10 July onwards.

This meant that I only had about eight or nine normal working days. I would arrive just a few minutes early, and Higueras would receive me with his usual imperturbable or stolid expression – this was, I felt, less a sign of his phlegmatic nature and more a remnant from blows sustained in his youth; if it was slightly cool at midday, the lesson would take place in Tsar Nicolás' room, which was tidier and more habitable than that of the Tsarina; if the heat began to grow oppressive, then we would sit in the garden at a white wrought-iron table.

The twins were very well brought up, in fact, they seemed to me meek, docile, disciplined, and not in the least unruly. With a father who could harden his gaze in a second, who could scoop up a pooch with one foot and hurl it against a bookshelf crammed with Agatha Christies, who could address his wife in the crudest of terms, I assumed that they lived in a permanent state of semi-terror; it was even possible that, now and then, when María Viana wasn't at home, he threatened them with a Napoleonic sabre or a sword that had once belonged to the Federfechter, the Prague fencing guild (always keeping a prudent distance, so that he wouldn't risk accidentally puncturing one of them). However, since children regard as normal whatever is put before them, from the moment they take their first breath or release their first howl, they would be accustomed to yielding and obeying. Needless to say, they obeyed me, and they liked me too, because I was friendly and good-humoured, and they worked hard as well, not that this did them much good, for as my head teacher had discreetly warned me, they found English terribly difficult. They belonged to that large band of Spaniards who have no ear for languages, and are incapable of distinguishing more than our five basic vowel sounds, and incapable, therefore, of reproducing any of the intermediary ones. If their mother *was* half Northern Irish, they certainly hadn't inherited her congenital facility for the English language. Although if she was, of course, she would not only avoid at all costs addressing her children in English, she would avoid revealing that she spoke it fluently.

María Viana was, in fact, present at some of our classes, although she always sat at another table in the garden, some way off so as not to interfere or distract, but close enough to hear us perfectly. She would sit there reading a magazine or a newspaper or a book, or lie in a recliner sunbathing – she never wore a swimming costume in my presence, never jumped into the pool to cool off – at most, she would undo three buttons on her cotton or linen skirt, so that the sun's rays could caress the bottom half of her legs but not her thighs. On the other hand, she never removed her sandals, as if she were aware that, for certain males, bare feet represent a supplementary bit of nudity, as do raised arms revealing shaven armpits. Needless to say, I often found my eyes wandering over to gaze at her knees and legs, but refrained from adopting any ludicrously awkward positions that would have provided me with a wider angle and a better view. She really didn't deserve such picaresque gawpings, and I needed to focus on my lesson.

What I did notice was that María Viana used to listen somewhat abstractedly to my words and to the exercises I set the children, teaching them grammar and syntax through examples, as well as pronunciation. It seemed to me there were two possibilities: either she knew the language perfectly and was supervising my lessons or else she knew very little and was hoping to benefit from them as well, either to learn or to refresh her memory. She would greet me warmly on my arrival and say goodbye even more warmly, as if this were her way of telling me that she approved of my methods or was amazed by my excellent accent. That family, and indeed all the other inhabitants of Ruán, had no idea that I was bilingual from birth, and assumed I was simply someone who had spent time in England and had a gift for languages, or for English in particular. She never interrupted the lessons, nor, apart from exchanging the usual polite chitchat and issuing instructions, did she encourage conversation: 'We'll be better off out in the garden today. I'd have to put on the air conditioning otherwise, and I don't want to catch one of those silly summer colds, because they take for ever to shake off. I wouldn't want you to catch one either,' things like that.

If she had once been Magdalena Orúe, she had certainly made the most of her time as Gausi's wife to settle into her role, to totally assimilate and internalize it, her role being that of a courteous, unpretentious lady, who treated everyone with the same easy manner, without ever making them feel uncomfortable or embarrassed or triggering a spontaneous inferiority complex. Perhaps she had chosen this role in order to mitigate the innate coarseness of her 'little prince' and his rustic origins. It was no surprise then that, despite her obvious gifts and her wealth by marriage, she did not provoke ill will. The only slightly jarring element on these occasions, the only thing I felt was less 'ladylike', to use the English term, and really far more suited to a boy, was that sometimes, while she was reading or sunbathing, she would start whistling and would carry on whistling for a while, clearly not even aware that she was. I mean she didn't just tootle away briefly and erratically, she would whistle a whole tune, as if this were a habit acquired in adolescence or childhood, which is when we are most likely to whistle.

I recognized one of those tunes: 'The Streets of Laredo', which is adapted from an Irish ballad entitled 'The Bard of Armagh', dating, I think, from the late seventeenth century or mid-nineteenth century, although very few people would know that, because the American version is far more popular and has been used in dozens of Westerns that anyone could have seen in any country. This wasn't necessarily a clue either.

I was constantly looking for clues and would cling to any I found, but they had to be real clues, not far-fetched or recherché. My limited or non-existent progress with María Viana, Celia Bayo and Inés Marzán hadn't yet driven me to such extremes of desperation.

As for Folcuino Gausi, out of whose pocket came my measly wages, he didn't deign to appear or to pay me any attention, indeed he barely acknowledged me. I was just another employee or subordinate, and not only was I temporary, I was also under the jurisdiction of his wife. He must have considered me to be somewhere between the pharmacist Ruibérriz de Torres and the servant Inés Marzán, to use Comendador's terminology: someone to whom one goes for a specific, non-essential task that someone else could just as easily perform.

On the first day of my lessons, Higueras introduced me to him in a corridor, where he must have brought him on purpose so that he could meet me without having to receive me in his office, so that he could cast his fiery eye over me for a moment. He stopped and looked me up and down even though he was a few inches shorter than me. I watched him approach, deep in conversation (at least he wasn't carrying a sabre or a fencing foil), discussing some matter with his valet or pretending to, with his broad hips and bouncy gait, which detracted from his otherwise virile appearance, from his very rectangular, groomed bald pate (there's a contradiction in terms), which was actually his most attractive feature. When he stopped, all he said was, 'Ah,' which, translated, meant 'So, what do we have here? Who's this?' He knew perfectly well who I was, but had come out to see for himself, to check that I was appropriately dressed for his household and not like a slob, a nobody, a punk or something. He doubtless trusted Higueras' judgement, but he was one of those businessmen who doesn't like to delegate. He gave me a supposedly perfunctory glance with his stern, severe eyes (in the gloom of the corridor, they appeared to be an opaque watermelon green) and presumably didn't find what he saw too execrable, although I was a million miles from the affected garb worn by his hunting buddies, the only ones who would have merited his total, fraternal approval. He was wearing an absurd canvas jacket replete with pockets, more suitable for going on safari in an old Stewart Granger film than for directing operations at home; on his bottom half he had a pair of jungle-green trousers with a stiff, too neatly ironed crease; and on his feet were a pair of suede shoes that I identified as being by Edward Green of Northampton, or a very good imitation. This was clearly his idea of smart-casual summer wear.

'Pleased to meet you,' he said with a slight, very affected nod, which was, in fact, a vain attempt to raise himself up, as if he wanted to be the same height as me, just for a second. He didn't thank me for my readiness or willingness to help (the words 'thank you' would have long ago been abandoned in some neglected corner of his vocabulary through lack of use). 'I hope my children will benefit from the effort we're all going to be making during the holiday period.'

I had a sense that that 'all' did not include me, but only his family and his staff. His words sounded less like a wish and more like a prayer or a warning, almost as if he had blurted out: 'I hope your presence over the next months will not prove to be a waste of money or a regrettable waste of energy and time or an unnecessary and avoidable intrusion into our lives.' He then left me with a brusque 'See you.' He didn't shake my hand when greeting me or when saying goodbye, indeed he kept both hands stuck in two of his many pockets and clearly had no intention of removing them: at least those two pockets could justify their existence in that over-pocketed item of clothing, which seemed designed to inhabit a lost or imaginary Africa, or to appear in an advertisement for watches or lotions suitable for adventurers.

Before my trip to Madrid and London, I only saw him again once, ranting and raving in the garden. But that was at a time when the whole country was in a state of uproar.

Those eight or nine days of lessons, prior to being summoned to London by Tupra and preparing to tear myself away from that town for the first time since I had arrived – which, strangely, was going to take a real effort – passed perfectly serenely, almost monotonously. I seem to recall that, from the third day on, María Viana began to take real pleasure in discreetly eavesdropping on our lessons. She remained a silent presence sitting a few yards away from us, but she observed everything, especially, I think, the progress (slow and only relative) that her twins were making in their pronunciation. I would teach them to say a word and they would repeat it as often as necessary, which tended to be fairly often, until they could reproduce it reasonably well, enough at least for it to be recognizable to an English ear, rather than a Spanish ear (fortunately I had both). Poor kids. After all, it wasn't their language. María Viana would sit in a deckchair or lie in a recliner with her book or newspaper. I saw two books in her hands at the time, more 'intellectual' than the ones Folcuino read in his living-room-cum-museum: *The Rings of Saturn* by W. G. Sebald, a writer unknown to me at the time, and *The Island of the Day Before* by Umberto Eco, which didn't prove as successful as *The Name of the Rose* (nothing else he wrote ever did), but benefited from its author's fame.

I watched her rather as a fugitive might, constantly turning to look behind him, except that I kept looking at her out of the corner of my eye, unable to help myself. I had the impression that she either didn't notice or simply ignored it and let it pass. She was probably accustomed to being the object of a hundred eyes all simultaneously drawn to her without their owners meaning anything by it – for eyes know nothing of restraint – and her normal response was to ignore it, not to feel bothered or alarmed, not to shrink back nor, of course, to reciprocate or challenge those looks, as if she really were a figure on a cinema screen or a statue or a painting, where such figures can be gazed at with impunity until the end of time, or until they disappear or are destroyed (the celluloid image, I mean, or whatever has replaced it, marble or canvas).

It seemed to me impossible that a woman who behaved so serenely in the company of others – in private with Folcuino much less so – could conceal a turbulent past or have committed atrocities. I had, of course, known individuals, men and women, although not that many, who, as I've said, would laugh and sing and gaily raise a glass after soiling their hands with other people's collective blood, having blown up or machine-gunned a truck holding a dozen policemen or English soldiers, their sole regret being that only six died rather than the whole lot of them. Nothing really surprised me, faith is unequalled as a justification, faith in causes that did not begin with us and that will outlive us.

There was only one occasion when, once the class was over and the twins had already run off to change and go swimming, María Viana kept me back for a moment and asked me a few questions and we chatted. Well, there were other occasions, very few, but those happened later, on my return from London with my new, more draconian instructions from Reresby or whoever Tupra had decided to be that day in order to reprimand me and issue me with a sinister ultimatum that caused me so much grief and anguish.

'I hope you don't mind my saying,' said María Viana, always so delicate and cautious, 'because I know very little English, just a few garbled phrases to get by in the shops in London, nothing more . . . but it seems to me that you have an English English accent, I mean from England not America. I also have a sense that it's a very good accent. How did you manage that? Most of us Spaniards are terrible at languages, here no one can even get rid of their local accent.'

She had sat up on the recliner so as to be at eye level with me. As usual, she was wearing a skirt that buttoned down the front and had undone the three lowest buttons so as to be more comfortable. My eyes kept drifting towards her thighs, but I forced myself more or less successfully to withdraw my gaze. When you speak to someone, you must look them in the eye, although staring into space is also allowed, as if you had put on a veil and could see only vague shapes.

'Most people find learning other languages difficult, regardless of where they're from. You should hear the way the English and the Americans speak Spanish, well, you probably have. Or the French or the Germans. The only ones who seem to have a natural ability, as far as I know, are the Slavs or people from that part of the world. Have you noticed how well and quickly Croatian and Serbian and Bulgarian footballers pick up Spanish, the ones who play for Spanish clubs, I mean? They've barely arrived and they're already speaking it fluently, and they're footballers, not highly educated people. On the other hand, I don't think I've heard Real Madrid's German goalkeeper, Illgner, say even half a sentence in Spanish. Everyone else – it's not just we Spaniards – tends to be pretty hopeless when it comes to speaking other languages.'

'I see you like football. I don't watch it myself, although Folcuino does. Which team do you follow?' She had always addressed me informally as *tú*, but never as 'Miguel', just as I didn't dare call her 'María'. In fact, we didn't call each other anything, and avoided addressing each other by name, something that supposes a degree of intimacy we certainly did not enjoy.

'Well, being from Madrid, of course, I'm a lifelong Real Madrid fan.'

'What about the other team, Atlético?'

'They started out as a Basque branch of Athletic Bilbao, so they're foreigners. Plus, they went on to become Franco's Spanish Air Force team, with perks for the players. If I tell you that, for years, its name was Athletic Aviación de Madrid, need I say more?' I said this in a jokey voice. She would know nothing about all that. Not as María Viana. Perhaps more if she was Magdalena Orúe, because of the Basque connection.

'And where did you get your accent?'

'I lived for some time in England, so it's only logical that I should have an English accent. From the south-east, I suppose, although I can't really tell, it's always difficult to hear your own voice. We don't even recognize our own voice when we hear a recording of it.'

'Yes, but you obviously have a gift for languages. That's my feeling anyway. You sound like those English actors in films, exactly the same. Like Richard Burton or perhaps Peter O'Toole.'

'Well, Richard Burton was Welsh, and Peter O'Toole is Irish, although he, I believe, was brought up in Yorkshire as a boy. But both of them could put on an English accent when they needed to, as they did when they worked together playing Becket and Henry II. Then again, who knows how people would have spoken in twelfth-century England. And that particular king, who was a Plantagenet, probably spoke more French than English. Anyway, thank you very much for the compliment,' I added. 'I'm glad you like my accent. If only I had Burton's deep voice. You should hear him recite *Under Milk Wood* by Dylan Thomas, I don't know if you know his work, a wonderful poet, and Welsh like Burton . . .'

I thought that I really should stop gabbling, which could be interpreted as nervousness; my answers were getting far too long, positively professorial. María Viana didn't seem to mind, though; indeed, she seemed genuinely interested, rather than annoyed or sardonic, as if she liked me telling her things, anything. Folcuino, I imagined, wouldn't be the most interesting of conversationalists.

'So you know about cinema and literature too. You even know

where Peter O'Toole was brought up. I haven't seen that film where they appear together. I'll see if I can get an original-language version of it on video.'

'It's very old-fashioned and theatrical, and they both ham it up like mad. As I recall, it's pretty tedious. Anyway, if you live in England, you can't help finding out all about their national treasures, the tabloids have a lot of pages to fill. But I don't think either actor ended up as a "Sir", which is odd, since nearly all their distinguished actors get knighted sooner or later. Actresses do too, although they become "Dames".' I was once again beginning to sound pedantic and didactic. I needed to try and restrain myself when I answered her next question.

'What's the film about? It must have been of some interest for two such famous actors to take part.'

'Well, you probably know about St Thomas Becket. In fact, El Cantuariense is dedicated to him.'

'Really? I didn't know that. But why?' I realized then that, for all her cultivated reading, she had no idea who Becket was.

'He was Archbishop of Canterbury, hence El Cantuariense, and the Catholic Church deemed him to be a martyr and quickly canonized him just two or three years after his murder. There are quite a few churches in Spain dedicated to him. In Salamanca for example.'

'What happened to him? Who killed him?'

'Four of the King's knights, and at the King's prompting. He was killed in the Cathedral cloister, I believe. There are lots of frescos, carvings and paintings of his martyrdom. According to legend, he put up no resistance. He's shown kneeling before his killers, who, it seems, sliced into his head with their swords.' I could remember the names of the knights, Morville, Tracy, FitzUrse and Le Breton, in fact, my favourite poet, Eliot – and I've read everything by him – wrote a play called *Murder in the Cathedral*. Naming them now, however, would, for various reasons, have been unforgivable. 'The film shows the youthful friendship between him and the King, when

Becket was a high-spirited courtier and the King's favourite companion on hunting trips and when out carousing, and how the King went on to appoint him Lord Chancellor, and what happened after that.'

'You mean they were friends and yet he ordered him to be killed? Why?' She seemed genuinely interested, she wanted to know the story.

'Well, if you see the film . . . although I don't think it's particularly true to the facts, which would be difficult anyway, given, as I said, that these things happened in the twelfth century. Anyway, to cut a long story short, and if I remember rightly: Henry II appointed Becket archbishop so that he could carry out his plan to curb some of the Church's influence as well as removing certain privileges from the clergy. The Church was eating away at his authority. However, as soon as Becket was made archbishop, he underwent a complete change and became very humble. He gave away his fortune to the poor, washed the feet of beggars and so on. In his case, if you like, the habit really did make the monk, and so the King's infiltrator into the Church proved a great disappointment, turning out, instead, to be a major obstacle to his ambitions. In a fit of rage, Henry ordered him to be killed, and the knights raced off to carry out his order before he could change his mind. Afterwards, he did due penance before Becket's tomb and so on, but the obstacle had been removed and that's what mattered. There's always time for repentance, more than enough usually.'

'Ah, so it was a religious matter,' she murmured quietly, as if the story had given her food for thought.

'Yes, I suppose so, but it was a question of power too. Behind Becket stood the Pope of Rome. Religion has produced an awful lot of criminality,' I added. 'Crimes committed both against it and in its favour. Just look at what's still going on in Ulster,' I ventured, just to see how she reacted. She seemed slightly annoyed, but not at my last remark.

'But it's also a source of holiness and kindness, isn't it?' she said.

It hadn't occurred to me that she might be religious. Neither she nor her husband were regulars at mass. I found her objection or correction strange. Perhaps she was only what people now call 'a spiritual person'. I didn't want to argue with her. I leave religion to those whom it touches or consoles. I leave spirituality to those who want to look deeply into themselves and ponder the universe. Just as long as they keep well away from me. I've never needed either to know what to expect or what to do. Nor even to repent of things of which I should have repented.

'Yes, I'm sure. An awful lot of holiness.'

She said nothing for a moment, perhaps wondering whether my response was ironic or not. Not that she was going to try and convert me. She looked down at her tanned blonde legs, as if to make sure she wasn't showing too much of them, nor anything higher up. She obviously thought not, because she neither changed her posture nor rebuttoned a button. Her gaze was always serene, almost to the point of indifference. She regarded things and people as if they were far away, as if she were contemplating them from a lofty, enclosed balcony, from a watchtower or a turret, as if they belonged to a different sphere from the one she inhabited and could not affect her physically. This is doubtless how she gained people's respect, without seeming haughty or disdainful. She was simply contemplative.

The children were splashing about in the pool and their mother María Viana would glance over at them every thirty seconds, and that fleeting glance had a different quality, a touch of apprehension. A mental tic. She changed the subject:

'And what was that poem you mentioned? *Under* what? Is there a way I could listen to it? I'd love to, if it's as good as you say it is, especially if Richard Burton is reading it. Not that I'll understand much, of course. Perhaps there's a Castilian translation I could read at the same time.' Basques and Catalans always refer to our shared

370

language as *castellano*, refusing to call it *español*. But those of us who come from other parts of Spain alternate between the two words, which, for us, are synonyms. Not that this necessarily meant anything either.

'I don't know. I read it in English, although it is very long. If my memory serves me right, Dylan Thomas wrote it for the radio, and there's a recording of it, on cassette or perhaps CD. If you like, I could ask an English friend to get a copy for you. But you'll find it awfully boring.'

'Or maybe not. If it wouldn't be too much bother, do, please, ask your friend. On condition that I pay you for the CD and the postage.'

'Oh, don't worry, it won't be expensive. The title is *Under Milk Wood*,' I said again, enunciating each word very clearly.

If she really didn't understand English (and that poem has an extremely rich and unusual vocabulary and is full of unpronounceable Welsh names), I couldn't help but find it suspicious that she would be so eager to spend minutes and minutes listening to what, for her, would be a stream of unintelligible verbiage, however rhythmic and sonorous and despite Richard Burton's clipped baritone.

'Tell me something else. Could you do other accents – American, Scottish, Irish – or do people tend to get stuck with the first accent they learn?'

Oh, yes, I could do other accents, that had been one of my specialities and my curse, it was that talent for mimicry that had led me to live one life and not another, that and my facility to learn languages as if I were a Croat or a Serb, or even better. It sometimes made Berta uneasy when I put on funny accents or voices, it made her feel I was no longer me, that I had been possessed by strangers from other countries, strangers who were older or younger than me and had led different lives. She had a good knowledge of English herself, and during my years away this had improved enormously. She understood what I was saying, which is why she found my mimicry so unsettling and threatening, as if I had actually been supplanted, as if someone very strange – benign or malign depending on the occasion – had usurped my personality or as if I had been transmuted into him. She hated me joking around or showing off, even though I'd been doing it since my adolescent years, to which she had been a witness, and I rather enjoyed occasionally alarming her.

She would have been really alarmed if she'd heard me when I was living in other places, on one of my missions or impostures, when I really did change into someone I wasn't and would never be, into the very thing I was fighting, an enemy, a criminal. I wasn't so sure now that I wasn't a criminal: a long time ago, I'd killed two men, although in the way that one does kill in wartime – or that at least was my feeling – that is, usually in self-defence or to prevent other people from being murdered, those on our side, and who would themselves be murdered if we failed to act. That isn't why I considered myself to be a criminal, nor does a soldier who has received orders and fought at the front, but has never resorted to needless brutality (some men are so gripped by fear, so overwhelmed by it, that they become stark raving mad before, during and after the clamour of battle).

Berta would calm down, and even laugh a little, once I returned to my own voice, my own self, or as soon as I was again speaking to her in my Madrid Spanish, my Chamberí Spanish, which was her Spanish and ours.

I certainly wasn't going to tell all this to María Viana, nor inform her of my natural mimetic talents, which I hadn't honed to perfection in the former training centre of Inverailort nor in Arisaig or Moidart, but in a hidden-away place in Inverness-shire (the most discreet part of Scotland, the largest and least populated), and later on in a school in London, where I'd had to do endless exercises to practise diction and pronunciation, intonation and rhythm. That would have put her on her guard, well, it would if she were Maddie O'Dea. I realized that, on the other hand, and contrary to what I had thought, it was actually quite a good idea to come over as didactic and professorial, because it's generally believed that policemen and secret agents are not cultivated people with a love of literature or history. Maddie O'Dea would never suspect that she was being tailed by an educated, pedantic person, even if he was only a schoolteacher, but she would suspect someone who could transform himself into whoever he chose to be, or almost, just by changing his accent and distorting and contorting his voice like an actor.

'No,' I said. 'I'm useless at that. Or only as good or bad as anyone else who has a go at imitating a Galician or Mexican or Andalusian accent. Or as good or bad as you yourself, possibly worse, because however well I speak English, it isn't my mother tongue. I'm not bilingual.' Which is precisely what I have been from the moment I began to babble.

This was shortly before the whole nation exploded in outrage. Those four days of terrible anxiety will never be forgotten by those of us who lived through them, but many grown-ups now were only children then or hadn't even been born, and for them the unfortunate protagonist is just a name and a symbol, that is, merely a distant echo and a fast-fading shadow, which, with the passing of time, is the usual fate of symbols and names, and even actual events: 'That happened in a different age, not now.' The calendar has sped past, twenty or so years have sped past.

On Wednesday 9 July, an ETA commando unit, comprising three terrorists, plotted to kidnap an obscure town councillor from Ermua, a town of some fifteen thousand inhabitants in the Duranguesado region, on the borders of Vizcaya and Guipúzcoa, the same young Miguel Ángel Blanco I mentioned earlier. On that particular day, instead of catching the same train he always caught to go to work in the neighbouring town of Eibar, famous for its arms industry, he borrowed his father's car, and thus lengthened his brief life by a day, or perhaps shortened it (the police would then have had another twenty-four hours to search the houses and fields and perhaps find him, or perhaps not, so it might well have all turned out the same). The unit consisted of Javier García Gaztelu or 'Txapote', José Luis Geresta Mujika, alias 'Oker' or 'Ttotto', and Irantzu Gallastegui Sodupe, alias 'Amaia' or 'Nora' (there's so often a woman involved in this kind of thing). However, on Thursday 10 July, Blanco did not escape: at around half past three, when he stepped off his usual train, 'Amaia' or Irantzu approached him, presumably pretending to hold him up at gunpoint, and made him get into a car. Or perhaps she played a trick on him, charmed him or asked for his help in resolving some difficulty or problem: she was twenty-three or twenty-four at the time, and in the photos now available on the Internet she had a warm, ready smile and a pleasant face, and a certain skinny allure; it's difficult to view her objectively, that is, once you know who she is or was.

Only three hours later, at half past six, the terrorists issued a statement demanding the immediate transfer of all ETA prisoners to prisons in the Basque Country, setting a deadline of only forty-eight hours for the government to agree to their demand: if, at four o'clock on the afternoon of Saturday 12 July, the transfer had not begun, they would execute the councillor they were holding hostage. The whole country knew this deadline was utterly impossible, that no democratic State could yield to such a threat, not because of what we tend to call its 'dignity' (a concept almost no one could define nowadays), but so as not to set a dangerous precedent that would embolden ETA and encourage them to repeat and replicate their methods. Agreeing would be tantamount to inciting more kidnapping, extortion, blackmail and murders either multiple or individual. Everyone knew this, and yet the whole country – beginning with the majority of Basques, who were genuinely angry, perhaps for the first time – clung to the hope that the ultimatum would be extended or would turn out to be pure bluff, and that twenty-nine-year-old Blanco would not die at the hands of his captors. So everyone hoped, despite knowing full well that ETA usually did carry out their threats, especially their most heartless threats. Not to have done so would have brought discredit on them among the Basque nationalists or chauvinists, who, for decades, had so successfully protected them, urged and egged them on, and who have now pretty much made saints of them. They would have been accused of being weak and pusillanimous, because some people wanted to see blood, the more blood the better.

The reaction throughout Spain was unanimous and simultaneous. There were massive demonstrations everywhere calling for the release of the modest young councillor, whose only crime was being a member of the Partido Popular, which ETA loathed as much as, if not more than, the Socialist Party, the PSOE (left and right were all the same to them, they saw both as oppressors of a people who had never had their independence, nor, for centuries, had they wanted it, a prosperous people who had gladly participated in all Spain's most important enterprises). Blanco didn't represent anything, and outside of Ermua almost no one knew of his existence. I don't remember now how many people repeatedly came out onto the streets during the seventy-two hours of waiting, the crowds were huge, people painted their hands white and held them up in a gesture whether of peace, innocence, supplication or surrender, I'm not sure. The placards contained hopeful messages, 'Miguel, we're waiting for you', things like that. I do remember that in Valladolid, a city of some three hundred thousand inhabitants, sixty thousand people took part; in Ruán, with a much smaller population, more than forty thousand came out onto the streets; in Bilbao, the Basque Country's industrial capital and largest city, the demonstrations were as large as in Barcelona and even Madrid.

The country waited expectantly, keeping one eye on the clock as hour upon hour upon hour ticked by, hoping that the various police forces, who were all working together on this occasion, would strike lucky and discover the hiding place of both kidnap victim and kidnappers (they scoured an area of eleven and a half square miles) and that some improbable piece of bad luck would upset the kidnappers' plans and their poor victim would be saved. On Saturday 12 July, the country saw the lunchtime news come and go, then waited until four o'clock that afternoon, which would mark the end of the deadline.

That great clamour of voices proved utterly futile, ignored by ETA and by the commando unit, who were doubtless pleased as punch to have kept the whole nation on tenterhooks for two entire days. At around five o'clock, an hour after the deadline, two locals or hunters from Lasarte-Oria in the province of Guipúzcoa, about five miles from San Sebastián, were walking their dogs along the Oztarán valley. One of the dogs, with a particularly keen sense of smell, wandered off to investigate the stream beneath an old bridge. The hunters followed and found a man; he was barefoot and lying face down, and at first appeared to be asleep. When they went closer, they saw that his hands were tied, and that although he was bleeding from the head, he was still conscious and breathing deeply. They tied up their five dogs and ran to the nearest house to get the telephone number given out by the Ministry of the Interior for any information relating to the councillor's whereabouts. The men either didn't know who he was or were unfamiliar with the face of the wounded or dying young man, but they quite rightly feared the worst.

An ambulance from the Red Cross drove him to a junction less than a mile away, where a medical unit tried unsuccessfully to resuscitate him. A local man who saw him there said he was wearing the same clothes as on the day he was kidnapped, that he still had his hands tied, that his face was yellow and that one eye was puffy and swollen, while the other was open, and he was still breathing. They took him to a hospital in San Sebastián, where it was confirmed that he was in a coma and had received two bullets in the head, both of which were lodged inside, with no exit wound. They could not operate. He died in that hospital in the small hours of Sunday 13 July.

It would seem that the members of the commando unit were in a hurry, which made people think that this was a 'short kidnapping' and that they had intended to kill their hostage regardless of the government's response. At ten minutes past four in the afternoon of Saturday 12 July, the terrorists had bundled him into the boot of a car, a dark-blue Seat Toledo apparently, and driven him to a clearing near Lasarte-Oria. Irantzu Gallastegui or 'Amaia' stayed in the car, while her companions – Gaztelu or 'Txapote' was also her romantic or sexual partner – forced their prisoner to walk a few yards down a path. Then – according to the sentence delivered in 1998 at a trial where the accused were judged *in absentia* because they had not yet been caught – Geresta Mujika or 'Ttotto', who had killed other unarmed people in cold blood, shot Blanco twice with a Beretta 22LR semi-automatic pistol. The first bullet entered his head more or less behind his right ear. The second, the *coup de grâce*, entered the back of his neck and was the one that ultimately killed him.

The country was gripped by rage, fury and frustration at the outcome of that sinister countdown. Every town and city saw more huge demonstrations, as angry as they were impotent, and ETA had never been so hated or so despised, not even after the 1987 bombings in which Magdalena Orúe O'Dea had participated, although I've never found out quite what her role in that had been. In the days prior to the killing, even ETA prisoners had called for the councillor's release. In the Basque Country itself, where ETA had many followers and a few armchair supporters, most people turned on them, boycotting businesses and shops run by ETA sympathizers, who had never concealed their support, but had, on the contrary, boasted about and even benefited from their close relationship with the terrorists; in some places there were attacks on and attempts to burn down the headquarters of Herri Batasuna, ETA's political arm which, while it has since changed its name, has not changed at all (except that now there's no violence and no 'armed struggle'). When the police defended these buildings, demonstrators yelled at them: 'Why protect them? They'll kill you tomorrow!'

The PNV, the Partido Nacionalista Vasco – which, apart from one brief interval, has governed in the Basque Country since the restoration of democracy in Spain – were the first to throw a generous protective cloak about the *batasunos*, as they were and still are known, and rescue them from the general wave of repudiation rapidly engulfing them. They spoke out against intimidation, which they had never done before nor did they do so later, when the people being intimidated were those who had dared to challenge ETA and who were being permanently harassed and threatened by them and their acolytes, who sometimes put up posters in the streets bearing their opponents' faces in the middle of a target. For days, the PNV threw all their energies into calming people down and even managed to rescue the pro-ETA people from the catacombs into which they were about to be hurled during those days of revulsion and revolt at the reign of terror that ETA – and those who favoured them or were favoured by them – imposed on their fellow Basques, with very few exceptions.

In 1999, Geresta Mujika or 'Oker' or 'Ttotto' was found dead on the outskirts of Rentería in Guipúzcoa with a bullet in his right temple and with two of his teeth having been brutally extracted. Police and legal sources spoke confidently of suicide, but not the *batasuna* press, of course. The fact that two of his teeth had been yanked out was very strange, and pointed up the absurdity of the situation, namely, that Geresta Mujika, who was right-handed, was found with a gun lying next to his left hand, the Astra 6.35 pistol with which he would have dispatched himself to the next world. Some time later, in 2001, in a newspaper interview, the ex-General Sáenz de Santamaría, the anti-terrorist adviser to the PSOE government between 1986 and 1996, referred to that death in distinctly unambiguous terms: 'Yes, I suppose there is such a thing as an irregular war.' He preferred the word 'irregular' to 'dirty'. 'Commando units don't just hand themselves in. Some people have even turned up dead with a tooth or two wrenched out. That's not something you do after someone has died.' And he added: 'I'm not saying this as a criticism. We have no option but to wage irregular war on guys who will happily shoot you in the back. Democracy is all well and good, but we can't take it to its logical conclusion, because if we did, we'd be putting ourselves in the hands of the terrorists.' He had said the same thing in an interview in 1995, as Pérez Nuix had pointed out: 'In the fight against terrorism, there are things that should not be done. If you do them, you shouldn't speak about them. If anyone does speak about them, you must deny it.' Six years later, he failed to follow his own advice. He did say 'I suppose', because by then he was no longer a government adviser. In 1996, he had been brought before a judge and charged, but it went no further than that. He gave a statement to a magistrate who granted him release without bail. He died in 2003 aged eighty-four.

In 1999, after the discovery of Geresta Mujika's body in Rentería, I couldn't help thinking of Jorge Machimbarrena, although not of Tupra, because his wars were different and he wouldn't always be doing favours for his friend 'George'. And by then, I was no longer available to help either of them.

Irantzu Gallastegui or 'Nora' or 'Amaia' wasn't arrested until 1999 in France, where she had been in hiding with her companion, and he, if I'm not mistaken, wasn't arrested until 2001. I'm not sure if they're still in the prison in Huelva to which they were sent after they were sentenced. They were allowed to stay together, by which I mean she was in the women's section and he in the men's. I think I read somewhere that they had two children there. The press sometimes talks about their imminent release and how they'll be received as heroes in their fiefdoms; and they may have been granted parole. I don't know and I don't particularly care. It seems, though, that they have never shown the slightest remorse for their respective or sometimes shared crimes, on the contrary. The murder of the young councillor from Ermua was just one among many, just one more.

Some terrorists do show remorse, whether genuine or not, who knows, but in principle, whichever faction they belong to, they can't allow themselves to express remorse without demolishing and destroying the whole of their previous existence, and you can't expect that of anyone, not even of the inhabitant of Berchtesgaden, had he had a few years during which to reflect, either in hiding or in prison. I don't imagine this could be expected of me either, and I'm not and never have been a terrorist. But then I've never been very interested in knowing myself. Too much life has passed, and it was what it was.

Tupra, then, phoned me on the day it was confirmed that Miguel Ángel Blanco had died, that he had, for some reason, been kept alive for a few hours in the hospital in San Sebastián. Perhaps right up until the poor councillor took his last breath, they were hoping against hope that he might pull through, or perhaps they wanted to let one whole night pass so that the country could fully absorb the news it had already assumed to be true when it went to bed. Perhaps they preferred the public response, in the form of more protests and demonstrations, to be not entirely spontaneous – the rage would only have increased since his death and the grotesque manner of his death – but, rather, to begin in an organized fashion on the morning or afternoon of Sunday 13 July.

I therefore had no class with the twins on that day, nor on the previous day. On Friday 11 July, though, I did go to the Gausi house, and it was then, when the air was still full of uncertainty, anxiety and tension as the clock ticked on, that Folcuino irrupted into the garden looking absolutely furious, accompanied by one of his hunting or business buddies (or so I assumed, since he was carrying a rifle hooked over his left forearm), and whom he called alternately 'Marquis' and 'Morbecq', addressing him in both cases as *tú*. I assumed this was how his name was spelled, rather than 'Morbec' or 'Morbeek' or 'Morbecque' (like the French town close to the Belgian border), perhaps by association with the celebrated wine producers Domecq, established in Jerez in the eighteenth century by an Irishman. I also assumed, from the way Folcuino spoke to him, that he was the Marquis of Morbecq or, rather, a relative of his, to whom the title had been extended as a joke, given his youth. Gausi didn't bother to introduce me, well, why would he, it was as if, for him, I were just another tree or shrub, albeit one that was speaking to his children in English.

He was outraged and furious about the ETA kidnapping, and, as if his friend or protégé Morbecq's homicidal rants were not enough, and perhaps also in order to see how María Viana would react to the situation (he and I both shared that interest) or to the insults and abuse he heaped on the terrorists, he began holding forth and venting his rage in the garden. In this he was no different from other irate Spaniards, who monotonously labelled them cowards, bastards, murderers, sons-of-bitches and so on. The fact that his children were there didn't stop him bellowing out the crudest and most bloodthirsty words imaginable. Nor did it stop Morbecq, who perhaps took too many liberties in imitating him.

When I'd first arrived at the house, María Viana had looked terribly sad.

'What a dreadful day,' she murmured, her face drawn and desolate. 'I very nearly rang to tell you not to come, but then I thought the children might be less aware of the tension if they had their lesson as usual.' And she added in a still quieter voice (one doesn't raise one's voice when making a statement of fact), 'What vile people. It's quite unbelievable. Just when you think they can't do anything worse, they do. That poor boy will probably still be hoping he'll be all right, what else can he do? But we know there's no hope, don't we.'

That 'don't we' was purely rhetorical, but just in case, I said:

'I don't know much about these things, but I think you're right, there is no hope.'

Then she took a seat at another table (she must have thought it inappropriate to lie on the recliner on such a dark day) and, as she often did, amused herself a little by listening in to my lesson, but said nothing more until her husband and Morbecq burst into the garden, the latter's rifle making him look more like a guard than a hunter, or perhaps a rural Sicilian with a *lupara*, because of the leather waistcoat he was wearing, with no jacket on top, which was rather odd attire regardless of whether he was paying a social visit or had come on business. He and Gausi had probably been practising their own crude version of fencing, and the Marquis, in a fit of rage at the news, had snatched up that hunting rifle. The expression on María Viana's face was the same as that on everyone else's face: nervous and unsettled, filled with foreboding.

During the brief time that Gausi remained in the garden, he spoke mainly to her, not of course to me or to Nicolás and Alejandra, who were simultaneously frightened and excited by the sight of that weapon, nor even to Higueras, who came and went as usual, in a purely supervisory capacity. And Gausi kept darting her quick, fiery glances, as if expecting her to endorse his words or at least show her approval.

'If it were up to me, I'd fill the Basque Country with tanks and impose a general curfew. You can't talk or reason with scum like that, those fuckers only understand one thing . . . mass arrests, and the interrogation of any suspected collaborators . . . That's what Massu did in Algiers when things got out of hand. He and de Gaulle had fought against the Nazis, and were lifelong democrats, but they changed their minds when they saw which way the wind was blowing. Until, that is, de Gaulle lost his nerve, and then the OAS tried to assassinate him. People called the OAS fascists, but a lot of their members had fought in the Resistance during the Second World War. Massu was far bolder: he used paratroopers, helicopters, whatever was needed.'

I was surprised to learn that Folcuino knew who General Massu was, although, of course, he had read *The Jackal*, where Massu probably got a mention. If he really did know about him, then he was proposing some very brutal ways of dealing with ETA: Massu had used helicopters to drop napalm on the rebels, ahead of the Americans in Vietnam; he had authorized the use of torture during interrogations, which he sometimes carried out himself. I seem to recall that he actually defended those practices in public, and didn't even rule out summary executions or extrajudicial killings. Later, I read that he'd boasted about trying out the electric prod on himself, urging his subordinates to follow his example, so that they could see for themselves that it really wasn't that bad, which would then allow them to use it on others with no pangs of conscience, no doubts.

'We're democrats too, but we're not going to be taken for fools,' the Marquis of Morbecq declared passionately. 'We'll save the helicopters for later, but if the bastards were here right now, why I'd shoot the whole damn lot of them, one after the other.' And he took aim at the top of the tallest tree in the garden.

María Viana leapt to her feet in great alarm:

'Marquis, will you please take that rifle back into the house now. There are children here. How could you even think of bringing it into the garden and waving it around like that. Tell him, Folqui. And anyway, what were the two of you doing with it in the house?'

I could see from the enthusiastic look on the faces of the twins that they really wanted the Marquis to fire that rifle, because they immediately turned to gaze up at the treetop, hoping to see a few leaves blown to pieces or a branch broken off under the impact. The influence of too much television.

'Yes, best put it back in its place, Morbecq, you wouldn't want to get overexcited and fire it by accident. It's loaded, damn it, they all are, just in case.'

'Loaded?' the Marquis repeated incredulously, for as well as young (I don't think he was even thirty), he was, by any reckoning, utterly puerile. His incredulity immediately morphed into excitement, and his desire for revenge saw an opportunity to find satisfaction symbolically or vicariously and, without further ado, ignoring María's and Gausi's warnings, he again took aim and opened fire at the tree, with such brilliant marksmanship and such horrendous luck that he hit a hoopoe that had just alighted on a branch and begun its monotonous song. The bird dropped like a stone onto the lawn, its colourful crest and long beak suddenly drooping, its lovely cinnamon-pink body and its black-and-white wings trembling for a moment on the ground, then lying still.

The children, who had so wanted him to fire the rifle, hadn't expected it would produce a corpse, that it would end the life of a living creature, and they immediately began to scream and cry. Children relate so well to animals, consider them to be their fellows, as if they shared an unwitting bond of irrationality. Nicolás and Alejandra were both over seven, which, until recently, had been the age at which children traditionally reached the age of reason, with surprising precision too. But they were filled with horror to see the poor bird lying there, limp and inert, near the edge of the swimming pool; they covered their eyes, became hysterical. I didn't even want to think how they would have reacted had they seen the way their father had kicked one of their beloved little dogs, as I had on screen.

The highly disciplined Higueras rushed into the house only to return with gloves and a newspaper, ready to pick the bird up and remove it from the scene. Gausi brought him up short:

'Hang on, that's today's paper and I haven't even read it yet. Don't be such a moron and go and fetch another one.'

The man did as he was told and returned at a run. However, when he approached the corpse, he hesitated, covered his nose and recoiled in disgust at the stench. His kiss-curl became displaced and lay horizontally across his forehead, like a sticky spider that had perched there. He may have received many uppercuts in his youth, but he couldn't take a pong like that. It was too soon for decomposition to have started, but hoopoes, though so attractive to look at, do emit a stink as a way of fending off predators. Of course the predatory Marquis hadn't gone anywhere near the bird when he killed it: whether deliberately or not, he had done so without experiencing its natural stinkiness.

I stood up and gestured to Higueras to give me the gloves, as if to say: 'I'll deal with it.' It wasn't my job at all, but I've smelled far worse, whereas Higueras had only had to endure the smell of liniment, blood and a lot of sweat, all of which are more bearable and even stimulating for professionals and fans of gymnasia and the boxing ring. I picked the dead bird up by its battered crest – the way people pick up severed heads by the hair – and held my breath. Slightly embarrassed, Higueras led me round to the rear of the house, where the rubbish bins were.

'You'd better bring me two or three plastic bags, yes, make that three,' I said, still without letting go of the bird. 'I'm afraid the smell will only get stronger.'

'What if we bury it in a corner somewhere out of the way? We wouldn't have to dig very deep.'

'Yes, if you like, but I'll leave the digging to you,' I said, dropping the remains into one bag, then another, then another.

'Hey, what about my gloves,' he cried. 'They're almost new.'

They were gloves intended for manual work or possibly for doing the washing-up.

'You can keep them if you like, but they're pretty stinky. Best throw them out, don't you think?'

I went into the bathroom, washed my hands thoroughly and returned to the garden. Folcuino and the Marquis were still there, I thought they would have taken the opportunity to disappear and thus avoid both María's wrath and the children's screaming. Instead, she and the children had left; she had doubtless taken them inside to console them after the shock, for they were slightly timid, fragile creatures. Rash, obtuse Morbecq hadn't even put away his avicidal weapon. He was frozen to the spot from which he had fired the shot, whether out of pride or shame I'm not sure, but he certainly cut a ridiculous figure, standing there stiffly in his leather waistcoat, his shirtsleeves rolled down and buttoned at the wrists and his rifle on his shoulder as if he were a soldier on guard.

'We've got a lot of work to do, Pretoriano, but I waited here especially to thank you.' Folcuino had forgotten my name, I realized, but I was amused by his very Roman confusion. 'You acted with a decisiveness my employee entirely lacked. He used to be a boxer and thinks he's a hard man, but he did suffer a few injuries in his day, so you'll have to excuse him, he sometimes gets dizzy spells and vertigo, and that smell, well . . . Anyway,' his tone changed, became mournful, 'those bastards still haven't killed José Ángel, although he's as good as dead already,' he had also forgotten Miguel Ángel Blanco's name, a name that had been repeated over and over in the press and on television, 'and they've claimed another victim now, a poor little robin, and in my own garden too.'

He had, needless to say, also got the wrong bird. And he excused his friend for the crime committed, presumably because he could so easily understand that violent impulse or possibly even share it; perhaps he would have done the same as the Marquis had it occurred to him to pick up that rifle as they were about to come out into the garden.

'They're a load of pelota-playing pansies, they are, with their little earrings and their frigging monkish haircuts. Dickheads the lot of them. You can spot them a mile off, but that at least makes them easy to arrest. The police are too soft, that's the problem. Fucking terrorists. But they do a lot of harm. I mean, for fuck's sake, José Ángel will be their seven hundred and seventy-eighth victim.'

'We should shoot the whole lot of them, the arseholes,' said

Morbecq, and he again pointed his rifle at the tree, as if he couldn't wait to join a firing squad.

'Cut the big talk, Marquis,' Gausi said at last. 'You've caused quite enough fucking damage for one day.'

At least the children were spared all those swear words, although they would already have heard their father use quite a few, not that he would have cared anyway, absorbed as he was in his moment of rage, or perhaps he was the same at every moment. ETA's body count would continue to go up; at the time, I think it was nearly nine hundred deaths.

'That's OK, Señor Gausi,' I said. 'It was best to remove the evidence of the crime as quickly as possible; the children were really upset.'

'What do you mean "crime"? What crime?' Morbecq retorted indignantly.

With a calming gesture of his hand, Folcuino told him to be quiet, then he remained thoughtful for an instant before saying sadly:

'True, they are on the sensitive side. Their mother spoils them. It would be quite a different story if I had my way.'

X

I hadn't entirely neglected Inés Marzán or Celia Bayo, or only a little while I devoted more attention to that third person who had been completely inaccessible to me for months, I had to make the most of that opportunity, and without arousing suspicions. The truth is that none of the three women was exactly open to scrutiny, each for her different reasons. As I've explained, Celia Bayo was, at least apparently, the most diaphanous; she seemed such a very simple mechanism. So, yes, I did neglect her the most, in fact, I was ready to dismiss her almost from the start (largely because of her cheery, easy-going nature and her salacious relationship with Liudwino: I continued to be an occasional witness to the couple's outlandish sex sessions, which while they began differently, always ended with the same explosive yelps).

Such scrutiny is always a slow and careful process, especially if you bear in mind the maxim that the best deceiver and dissembler is also the one who has the best chance of getting what she wants and escaping punishment. The problem is that there's no way of knowing for sure if she is dissembling and deceiving. Science, which has made so much progress and so many discoveries, has yet to come up with an infallible method of ascertaining when someone is being honest and when they are lying, something that, to a layman, would seem far simpler than sending a spaceship to Mars or carrying out surgery on a patient remotely, from thousands of miles away; and for all the talk now of extraordinary machines that will soon be able to read our minds, I'm not convinced, because our mind is such an oscillating, contradictory, elusive thing, never stable or still, like the gusts of a hurricane-force wind. I know there are people capable of keeping up a front for many long years, so much so that they end up becoming their mask, and the mask then becomes their real face, and they achieve the fiction of obliterating or abolishing their memory, at least temporarily. Even with all those reservations in mind, though, with each day that passed I was more and more inclined to cross Celia Bayo off the list.

In the days after Blanco's kidnapping, days of anxious collective waiting, and in the days that followed the grim news of his death, I carefully observed the reactions and the behaviour of the three candidates. Tupra gave me a brief extension, once I'd convinced him that it was important to study the women after the killing had taken place.

As I've said, the inhabitants of Ruán and of towns throughout Spain rushed out en masse into the street, and nearly everyone I knew attended the demonstrations pleading with ETA to show clemency, and almost all of them painted their hands white. Among them, of course, there were individuals who would have subscribed to the ideas and the sabre-rattling of Morbecq and Gausi, both men and women (there are fierce women everywhere, whose ferocious self surfaces all too easily, just as there are compassionate and conciliatory women, who, fortunately, are in the majority), or who, had they been in possession of a gun, would have shot down doves, sparrows, thrushes and magpies just to emphasize their rage or make a big deal of it. But in the days before those two shots fired at point-blank range, the second in the back of the neck with the victim kneeling, most people were very quiet and appeared sad and upset rather than belligerent and indignant.

True to her style, during those supplicatory marches, Celia Bayo wept uncontrollably and abundantly (although not in an exhibitionist way: silently). If something saddened her, it always saddened her intensely and what distressed her almost overwhelmed her, and she couldn't stop thinking, not for a second, about the panic the councillor and his family must be feeling, although we hadn't yet seen his family, or not, I think, as much as we did in the ensuing years. She could perfectly well imagine their suffering and their anxiety, she could put herself in their shoes and feel what they must all be feeling, both the hostage and his family, the latter waiting for the much feared phone call, bringing either relief or despair, the call that would tell them he had miraculously been released or that the sentence had been carried out. Every time the phone rang, their hearts must almost stop, she said.

Inés Marzán was there too, despite her reserved and singularly ungregarious nature. She was colder and more sober, but she walked in silence among the throng with her white hands raised and a fatalistic look on her face. She was harder than Celia, or else had more experience of what to expect from situations that are, from the start, warped and distorted, she knew they never straighten out of their own accord, and in this case, no one could do anything – apart from the police in some small measure – except wait and gather together to plead for mercy from people who didn't know the meaning of the word or who despised it or would never even be prepared to allow themselves to feel it. As I said, we all knew this, and Inés Marzán was little given to cherishing vain hopes, she had made that clear when she spoke to me about her daughter.

After the slow cooling of our sexual relationship – or was it a pause? – she had begun discreetly to seek me out, and I had shown myself willing to go back to meeting more often, for our meetings had become less and less frequent, and I had grown quite fond of her. My impression was that she didn't particularly miss the sex – sometimes we had sex and sometimes we didn't, and when we did, it was almost out of habit or politeness or inertia – but that, despite being a very self-sufficient woman who didn't need a man by her side, she had, in a way, become used to my sporadic presence and company, for we never talked very much. During those days of tense waiting, I noticed that she seemed sad and resigned, as if convinced that Miguel Ángel Blanco would not be saved. The most explicit thing she said to me about it was: 'Those people don't step back, not once they've started something. They're like a machine that can't be stopped even if they wanted it to stop. That poor young man is already a ghost. Naturally, he won't want to believe that. None of us would in his place, none of us.' However hard I tried to see some first-hand knowledge in her words, these were words that could have been spoken by any sceptical or realistic person or anyone who preferred not to cherish false hopes.

María Viana and Folcuino also joined those vast demonstrations, and with their hands painted white too, although he would doubtless have thought this a lot of silly nonsense and would hate having to soil his hands unnecessarily. Yet, as leading lights in Ruán, they had to be in the front row, heading the demonstrations along with Mayor Valderas and all his councillors, the always contrary opposition party, the little princes with their gleaming bald pates or their immaculately coiffed hair, and all the other financial and industrial worthies. Liudwino moderated his attire for such a solemn occasion, but not entirely successfully: he replaced his garish greens with a dull, very pale grey, but resisted toning down his accessories: he didn't even tame his quiff or shave off the horrible little tuft of hair growing immediately beneath his lower lip; but his cheeky charm meant that he could get away with anything.

Almost anyone with a reputation to defend, however small, was there, you had to prove that you roundly condemned ETA's actions and that you did so sincerely. I saw Dr Vidal Secanell and Dr Ruibérriz de Torres, and other very eminent people, the notary Gómez-Notario and the barkeeper Berua, the talkative girlfriends that Inés Marzán sometimes spent time with on her free evenings, the head teacher of my school and those of other schools along with their respective staff, the deans of the various university faculties and the Rector of the university, and all the ecclesiastics, slyly elbowing each other aside in their attempts to get to the front of the demonstration and thus be more conspicuous, ordinary priests competing with the bishop. The latter refrained from smearing their hands with white because their purity was taken for granted and there was no need to flaunt it. The reddish stain that was Florentín glowed in the second row, and he walked along taking notes. Even Comendador and other such nocturnal rogues were present, keeping somewhat shyly to the margins so as not to embarrass their respectable clients and oblige them to say hello, even with the lift of an eyebrow.

And there was I with the palms of my hands painted white too, as befitted the teacher Centurión, even though, given my real job, and knowing that these mass expressions of outrage or frustration only indulge and reaffirm those in power, the whole thing seemed to me a lot of well-meaning but sterile nonsense, albeit perfectly forgivable: in situations of absolute impotence, people feel impelled to do 'something', anything, even if it will change nothing. They are like close relatives who cover the coffin with flowers that the dead man can no longer smell or see, or speak to him or write notes or letters, knowing that he can no longer hear or understand. People feel they must accompany someone who no longer needs or wants any company, when really it's the living who are consoling and accompanying the living, and they do find consolation themselves in treating with guilty superiority and relieved condescension the person who has died, murmuring or whispering 'Poor thing, poor thing'. (What everyone deserves is a slow drawing-down of blinds.)

I fear that in my sceptical view, but only in this, I agreed with Folcuino Gausi. He looked thoroughly fed up.

As best I could, I observed María Viana clinging to his arm, as if she needed his support in order to be able to walk in a straight line.

397

She seemed utterly downcast. Unlike Celia Bayo, no tears coursed down her cheeks, nor did she appear grim and disillusioned like Inés Marzán. On her alluring, delicate face, I saw a kind of profound despair that was not confined to that moment, to the kidnapping and foreseeable murder of the young councillor from Ermua, but was more all-embracing, as if to confirm that everything always ends in the worst possible way; that is, as if she knew very well that this happens all too often, as if she were recounting her own experiences and answering old questions, and the answer was always the same, attempt after attempt, time after time, experience after experience, decision after decision, and incident after incident: 'Why so much effort, why so much dodging and diving, why so much running away and so much dread and torment, if everything simply carries on regardless, and we will inevitably be trampled beneath the marching feet of an army. Or beneath the hooves of a single cavalryman – or two or three.'

Tupra would only give me permission to remain for a couple of days longer in Ruán if I abandoned my plan to stay over in Madrid. And so I put off visiting Berta and the kids until my return, besides, I hadn't even had time to warn them, I might do that from London; or not, because I didn't want to risk Berta vacating the apartment just to avoid seeing me, or telling me bluntly that I wouldn't be welcome and not to bother. I had once again failed to keep my word: my time in Ruán was dragging on far longer than was so optimistically predicted by all involved, and I hadn't once escaped to Madrid, even though it was hardly an enormous distance for someone like my old self. Ruán, though, had drugged me and I had grown lazy, or perhaps, who knows, had become fearful of the outside world.

And so when I set off, I went straight from the train station to the airport with my hand luggage, and, during the flight, my mind was still filled with images from the impassioned demonstrations that had taken place before the botched execution in Lasarte-Oria and those held after the killing, which were, at once, more despairing and more enraged, those two states of mind alternating every few minutes or every thousand slow steps, the people taking part so stunned, so lost for words, that they no longer knew what they were feeling or what they wanted to feel. I get the two phases mixed up now, but I know it was during the second phase that people began putting their hands behind their head and shouting the slogan 'Hey, ETA, here's the back of my neck,' as well as other more traditional insults. Miguel Ángel

Blanco hadn't even had the good fortune to have lost his head with one clean, accurate blow, as had Anne Boleyn and Marie Antoinette.

The behaviour of my three women had not changed greatly during the demonstrations that took place before and after. The one whose behaviour had changed most was, without a doubt, Celia Bayo, who as well as continuing to weep copiously, now yelled out slogans with surprising ferocity. It was also true that, when she got angry, she got really angry, especially when faced by injustices, and the perpetration of vile acts of cruelty so enraged her that I did wonder sometimes if she wasn't being suspiciously over the top; although I realized at once that she wasn't, because her reactions were generally very basic and unpremeditated; not that she was the only one to completely lose it after the murder. Folcuino Gausi, for example, who had looked awkward and reluctant when walking along with his hands daubed with paint in order to fit in with his fellow citizens (something he would normally avoid like the plague), was now excited and positively vibrant: and had it not constituted an irresponsible call to arms, he would have turned up with all his rifles and his swords, ready either to riddle with bullets or to skewer any young man sporting an earring or a monk-like haircut, neither of which were exclusive to ETA supporters; 'hipsters' and 'anti-establishment' types from Ruán, Catilina, Puente Levadizo, Mazón, Entrerrieles, Catapultas and other even smaller towns could also be seen sporting earrings or monk-like haircuts and, anyway, fools always rush to imitate whatever appears on TV. Folcuino was in his element calling for war and firing squads, and he strode along at the head of those demonstrations with a livelier, more resolute step, despite his broad hips and effeminately bouncy gait.

As I said, Inés Marzán and María Viana barely changed; at most, their bitterness or fury became more visible on their faces, the one tormented, the other distraught. Neither of them shouted more loudly than was necessary, or only enough not to appear out of place among the crowd. Flying to Heathrow for the first time in ages, I had to admit that, despite my decades-long career and my subsequent scepticism as regards such public displays of emotion, feeling part of a crowd had, in a way, fired me up, had moved me. The same thing had happened a year earlier, when I'd spontaneously taken part, as Tomás Nevinson and no one else, in the vast protest march (they reckon eight hundred and fifty thousand people joined in) that filled the centre of Madrid following the murder of the historian, jurist and ex-President of Spain's Constitutional Court, Francisco Tomás y Valiente. An ETA member (his name was Bienzobas or 'Karaka') had mingled with students and wandered along the corridors on the day before the attack and on the day itself. Having made sure that Tomás y Valiente was alone, he slipped into his office at the Universidad Autónoma de Madrid and shot him three times at point-blank range – at least once in the face – while Tomás y Valiente was talking to a friend on the phone, just minutes before heading off to invigilate an exam. For years, Tomás y Valiente had had a bodyguard, but not at the time, and there he was at the university, utterly defenceless.

Throughout that demonstration, as I had been during the smaller-scale marches in Ruán, I was filled with a feeling – it never really coalesced into an idea – that such a mass expression of revulsion could become something more than just shared grief. Needless to say, this proved false, because for years and years afterwards ETA continued to kill, as stonily unmoved as are all such organizations that never forget anything, still less the lies they themselves have invented or that have been invented for them by their respective priests, older men who encourage malleable young people to risk their necks and commit their crimes convinced that they're right to do so. But the sheer passion of the protesters, the unanimity expressed in the slogans they chanted and in the songs they sang, the sense of one's own individuality being dissolved into something much larger that cancels out consciousness, the coming together in grief and rage and sorrow

with so many thousands of other souls on that slow, sad march . . .
This sometimes made me forget what I knew all too well, perhaps
better than any of my fellow marchers: that the members of those
organizations are mentally armour-plated or mentally void, and that
nothing ever touches them. Nothing that might come from those
whom they can and do destroy: it was typical of ETA supporters to
slip into cemeteries and desecrate the graves of their heroes' victims,
as if they were annoyed that they'd already been killed and thus could
not be killed all over again, two or three or four times.

I had noticed this same mental vacuity in Spain, but far more often
and from closer to in Ulster, on the part of both groups, whereas here
in Spain there was only one group, with the exception, that is, of the
parapolitical GAL in the 1980s and early 1990s, and, of course, the
use of torture by certain policemen on ETA prisoners was not, alas,
that infrequent.

Perhaps it was now my turn to become another of those exceptions, at the service of someone who did not as yet hold an official
position, Machimbarrena, and in my role as a 'foreigner' doing a
favour for my former superiors, who were also foreigners. Mutual
support for secret services worldwide, or for their imitators or usurpers. Tupra was neither of those things, he had always held official
positions. However, he paid little attention to the rules and, with his
variable and various names, was hard to pin down, and always had
been. Our first meeting, all those years ago, had turned out to be a
deception, as I found out far too late. How was it possible that I had
agreed to have dealings with him again and was flying back to see
him and listen to him?

But my thoughts on that British Airways plane kept drifting off to
more recent events. And I thought: 'You should never join in such
mass gatherings, such secular communion services, even if you're
tempted to do so by a sense of civic responsibility that gets you all
excited and fired up. That's why people keep organizing them. It

402

doesn't matter how just the cause, how justified the protest, there's always the danger of throwing reason to the wind and becoming caught up in pure sentiment, which is what all manipulators, religious or otherwise, patriotic or otherwise, from the left or right, try to do in order to gain power over people's minds. It's impossible entirely to resist that pull, and we end up doing what had never been our own solitary intention and that never will be again: people lynch, insult, spit, attack, applaud beheadings, destroy buildings, dismember others and beat them to a pulp, become intoxicated as they plunge into *le frémissement d'un bain de foule*, as the French say, the thrill of the crowd. Being part of a crowd feels good, it's comforting being a rabble with no personal obligations. However cowardly and treacherous the murder of Tomás y Valiente in February 1996, I shouldn't have taken part in the protest, not alongside eight hundred and forty-nine thousand nine hundred and ninety-nine complete strangers all lulling me, soothing me and drawing me in, it didn't matter that among them were those closest to me, Berta and Guillermo and Elisa; nor should I have joined the protests in Ruán at the tragic death of Miguel Ángel Blanco, although in that case I had to go, as the Miguel Centurión I was, or, as Gausi would have it, Miguel Pretoriano: my absence would have been noticed, I would have been spurned or censured. Perhaps Magdalena Orúe O'Dea would have felt the same pressure, as owner of La Demanda restaurant, as a fellow teacher at my school or as the respected wife of a local construction magnate. Any of them could have been pretending just as I was, for I did manage to hold on to a certain sceptical lukewarmness, although not very successfully when passions were running high. The woman who was Maddie O'Dea might not have disapproved of the kidnapping or the blackmail or the grim countdown or the execution of the young man as he knelt with his hands tied. Or perhaps she would, if she had evolved, if she had repented of her past actions and even succeeded in occasionally forgetting what she had once been. In that case, the episode would have acted as a reminder and brought her a double dose of anguish and torment: because of the young man, of course, and because, at another time in her life, she might have been the one to approach and ambush him at the train station in Eibar, or the one to carry out the execution in Lasarte-Oria.'

I sometimes forgot that the woman was more Northern Irish than she was Spanish, just as I doubtless continued to be slightly more English than *madrileño*, given my long trajectory in defence of the Realm. Magdalena Orúe had spent most of her life in Spain, and had been living in that town in the north-west for eight or nine years, but really, or originally, she had been 'on loan' from the IRA to ETA (the Catholic group was much older and more experienced), although I never really knew in what capacity, if she was a great strategist or an explosives expert who would instruct and assess, if she took decisions or merely carried them out and contributed to making any actions taken as damaging and demoralizing as possible.

Tupra kept me in the dark until the last moment, as he always did, that was something that would never change: the less the workers knew about the reason for their task, the stronger the wall, tower, citadel or pyramid they were building would be. Perhaps his and Machimbarrena's motives were different, but with the same objective: the latter's intentions would be more punitive than preventive, no one who had taken part in the 1987 attacks should go unpunished, and all those who had were demonstrably dangerous, although that was a secondary matter; for Reresby or Dundas or Nutcombe the fear would be that, with a solution or a truce in Ulster so very close, there would be reckless elements among the old guard (the old are often as implacable as the young, except that the former are not green and inexperienced but crafty) who could ruin any agreement with untimely attacks. If Maddie O'Dea was a fanatic with deep roots, she would condemn and rebel against any cessation of the armed struggle, having supported it for half her life.

I was going to see Tupra and receive his instructions, but, I told myself during the flight, there was little hope of getting any information out of him. When he wanted he could be hermetic, authoritarian and disdainful, he would never have become upset or excited – not for a second – on some mass protest march, whether supplicatory or funereal; perhaps because he himself came from the 'rabble', and he would find it neither consoling nor novel to join forces with them, he had run away from all that and slowly left it behind doubtless not without a degree of sacrifice and effort and some hardening of the heart. I remembered, though, that he was married now, for love, he had said, so perhaps, with the years, something in him had succumbed to ordinary sentiments. The Tupra I knew took whatever he wanted from other people but gave very little or nothing in return, this was one of his greatest abilities. He would never be able to say: 'Nought's had, all's spent.' At most, he would subscribe to the second part of that quote from Shakespeare, because throughout his life he had spent and spent and spent. And yet his coffers never seemed to empty.

After that period of upheaval, mourning and outrage, during which almost all business and other activities stopped, thus, to all effect, transforming it into a prolonged public holiday, I had phoned Higueras to warn him that I would have to pause my lessons with the tsarish twins for a few days and to check that this would not prove too inconvenient. I didn't mention my trip to London, which was no one's concern but mine. I merely said that certain urgent matters required my presence in Madrid.

'Is there some serious family problem? What family do you have there? Parents, siblings?' This seemed too inquisitive for my taste, as if he were taking the opportunity to pry into my private life. In Ruán, it was assumed that I was single or divorced, and with no conjugal ties. Although, the fact is, no one had inquired about my civil status, a sure sign that Ruán had once been 'a very noble and loyal town', whose people were as discreet as they were reserved.

'No, nothing serious fortunately, but I haven't been back for several months, and there are a few things I need to put in order.'

'I'll ask María. A sudden interruption to the lessons might mean the children will forget what they've learned. I'd better ask her. And you won't, of course, charge us for those days.'

'No, don't worry, I won't charge you.'

'One moment, please.'

He kept me waiting for five long minutes, and when he returned, he sounded surprised and annoyed, as if irritated that he wouldn't be able to place some obstacle in my path.

'Well, María says not to worry, that it might actually be for the best. The children are still badly affected by recent events, and, of course, there's no way of hiding these from them, but they're particularly upset about the incident here on Friday, about that crested bird, and it might do them good to have a few days with no school-work of any kind, until they've got over it. That's what she says anyway. Now, if you care to know my opinion,' this is what a lot of people say when their opinion is entirely unwanted and unnecessary, 'I think that, at this rate, they'll turn out to be a pair of namby-pamby wimps. Don Folcuino is quite right, their mother spoils them and is overprotective. Seeing a bat or something fall from a tree is no big deal. But anyway, it's up to her.'

Higueras clearly worked for Gausi rather than for María Viana. She was just 'María', whereas he was 'Don Folcuino'. 'You won't charge *us*,' he had said, as if he were the guardian of the family fortune. They could do what they liked, I really didn't care.

'I'll take the rest of the week off then, shall I? Well, it's already Tuesday. Please give my thanks to María.'

'It's not up to me. As far as I'm concerned, you can take two weeks off. Just let us know when you'll be back at work.'

Perhaps he saw me as an unexpected competitor, an intruder on his territory. Perhaps he couldn't forgive me for having witnessed his distinctly pathetic response to the stench given off by the hoopoe, and for having, unintentionally, embarrassed him.

In London, I instinctively headed for the same square where I'd sat endlessly waiting some four or was it three years ago (one of the consequences of an itinerant or vagabond life, a life of constantly changing identities, appearances and personalities, is that you lose all track of time, be it urgent or pressing or long gone, or the time that is presumably still to come), during what that pretentious young man, Molyneux, had called 'an interregnum' between my prolonged exile in that medium-sized provincial town and my definitive and disillusioned return to Madrid. Except that then, with Molyneux as intermediary or link, they had given me temporary accommodation in an attic apartment that was perhaps still the property of the secret services, in 1 Dorset Square, where the legendary Special Operations Executive or SOE, charged with organizing intrepid commando units in Europe, North Africa and beyond, had had their headquarters during the Second World War. This time I had, at my own expense, booked myself into the Dorset Square Hotel, very close to Baker Street and its Sherlock Holmes museum and to Madame Tussaud's, the place where I had uncovered the deceit that had been practised on me in my youth by Tupra and his lieutenant Blakeston, who had been such an admirer of Montgomery that, despite being tall and burly and bordering on plump, and having a sometimes irrepressibly hysterical laugh, he went around disguised as Field Marshal or Viscount Montgomery of Alamein.

Yes, in Madame Tussaud's, I had observed, followed and finally spoken to a boy and a girl, Claire and Derek, who turned out to be the children Janet Jefferys could not possibly have conceived or given birth to during a good part of my haphazard existence. How far away Janet seemed now, and to think I hadn't even known her surname until her supposed murder, the woman I came close to being accused of strangling with one of her own stockings, a grotesque imagined death. How far away she seemed, that transient lover from my student days, who worked in Waterfield's antiquarian bookshop in Oxford; there had been no real love between us, and yet she had marked the whole of my subsequent life, and perhaps I had marked hers until she really did die a long time afterwards, in a road accident according to her children.

Despite that bitter memory – that deceit – this had become my favourite part of London, the part where I had felt safest, having grown used to it during that time of patient waiting and a certain degree of freedom, when my name was David Cromer-Fytton and I had nothing to do, and I saw myself merely as a dead man who wouldn't even be remembered by those who had loved me, or indeed by those who had loathed me. I felt only the death of air, as the poet says, nothing more. Or just dead air.

Tupra wanted to see me straight away, the day after my arrival, and unlike on our last London encounter, he urged me to get to his office early, he didn't leave it to me to choose a time. He wasn't in that same building, one I already knew, but in another building with no name in a wealthy area, close to what for two centuries had been Admiralty House, possibly in Cockspur Street, although I'm not sure now, since that was the only time I went there. From what I could see, it was a light and airy place, and at the door I was asked to show proof of identity and explain why I was there, before being invited to empty my pockets and have a metal detector run over me; and this was four and a bit years before the attack on the Twin Towers and the Pentagon and the subsequent disappearance of the way we used to live in the twentieth century.

I wouldn't have been able to smuggle in my little Charter Arms Undercover in my raincoat pocket as I had on that previous encounter in a café in my area, that is, near Dorset Square, an encounter filled with reproaches and disgust and a sense of relief at saying farewell to all that. It seemed so implausible that my disgust could have been so easily appeased, my sense of relief destroyed, and that I had agreed to meet Tupra again in Madrid on that 6th of January; that I had allowed myself to be trapped once more by giving my consent and then moving to Ruán, where I had been living for months, and that I was now again deferring to his orders. My passivity and apathy were to blame, my inability to live any other way, the fact that, having lost everything, or almost everything, during my long years of absence, I didn't have much to lose; that I had realized how unbearable it was to be outside once you had been inside, and that we all, however inexplicably, feel loyalty to somewhere or someone.

The building in Cockspur Street, if it was Cockspur Street – it was a very short street – was another official building, but lacking any name or plaque, as was sometimes the case with the more secret establishments of MI5 and MI6 and the former NID or Naval Intelligence Division and its successors. The fact that Tupra had a light, comfortable, carpeted office on the third floor meant that they were looking after him, that he must have been promoted, that his plans were respected and taken seriously by his remote superiors. I seemed to recall him mentioning (I couldn't remember whether it was in Madrid in January or in London in 1994 – time in Ruán multiplies and expands and embraces more than it should) that he was organizing a special group made up of a few chosen people, all of them extraordinarily gifted. He hadn't told me what the group was for (or only vaguely) and I don't think I asked.

On the one hand, I felt curious about whatever he was up to (being in the know is part of being 'inside'), on the other hand, I didn't give a damn what he did, once he was out of my sight and my life, what machinations were afoot, what new games he was playing, games in which I had no part. As I opened the door to his office, though, I felt inside me a faint whisper of resentment that I was and would be forever excluded.

Tupra was not alone nor was he seated at his desk. He was pacing up and down in his office, holding a cigarette in his left hand and an ashtray in his right, obviously keen to avoid any fallen ash singeing his grass-green carpet. He must have decided to remain standing while he waited for me, for the scrupulous functionaries down below would have warned him of my arrival. The image that leapt out at me, however, was of the woman wearing high heels and sitting on a comfortable sofa with her legs crossed. The office was spacious enough to accommodate two 'environments', if I can call them that. One was reserved for work and the other for visitors, the latter furnished with a sofa, a coffee table and three armchairs. I noticed that in the 'social environment' there was also a fireplace, whether real or fake I don't know. Every inch of Tupra's very large desk was occupied by papers, files, photos and a computer. Apart from his chair – on wheels so that he could easily move about – there were two conventional chairs, one opposite where he would sit, and another to one side, intended perhaps for a secretary, male or female, to whom he would dictate letters and so on.

He didn't shake my hand (people tend not to in England, unless they're being introduced for the first time or are saying goodbye for ever), he merely shifted the ashtray very briefly over to his left hand and patted me on the shoulder, as if he were the grown-up and I the little boy, for he was incorrigibly paternalistic with almost everyone. We had seen each other in January, so there was no reason why he should have changed, but whenever I hadn't seen him for a while, I was always amazed at how little he had altered in the twenty-five years or so since I had that first blind date with him at Blackwell's in Oxford, and the three of us – him, Blakeston and me – walked along Broad Street and St Giles' together. It came to me in a flash, just as it had when we had met after my exile in that provincial English town, that Tupra was one of those rare individuals who somehow freeze or crystallize at a certain age, or at a point when they acquire an almost violent degree of willpower, which they then deploy in order never to grow any older than they deem tolerable. There were his grey or blue eyes, so bright and all-embracing and appreciative, looking straight at me, mockingly, palely, probing the past and rendering it present again so that he could scrutinize and give it due importance, rather than simply dismissing it as old hat or insignificant. Unlike most other people for whom whatever is past no longer counts.

Therein doubtless lay the secret of his persuasive powers and his charm, especially on a first meeting, for in that initial moment undying loyalties were often mysteriously forged: he managed to make the other person feel listened to and important, feel that he found their very ordinary stories fascinating, that their insipid griefs were, for a few minutes, heard and recognized as being, to Tupra's eye and ear, life-changing vicissitudes, which were quite enough to keep anyone awake at night. And he was a great interpreter of women: he could sense who needed to be flattered or made to feel younger, who wanted to be desired and who wanted to be treated rather severely; who was full of complexes and who just wanted company, who wanted to compete and who wanted to be considered his equal, as if relationships between men and women were not inevitably sexual (among heterosexuals that is), as if that factor didn't always lurk beneath the surface as a possibility, even as a horrific, rejected possibility. He adjusted to their needs, and he had an infallible eye, he could see what they needed and give them precisely that. And for some unfathomable reason, unfathomable to me that is, many women found him irresistible. I hoped this would not have been the case with Berta, whom I suddenly missed intensely and remembered vividly with abstract or retroactive jealousy. What would she be up to now, who would she be with?

He had probably proved irresistible to the woman sitting on the sofa in his office. And yet I had the instinctive impression that, with her, he may well have failed; perhaps it's true that falling in love makes us less acute and clouds our faculties. He introduced her to me as 'Beryl', without adding 'My wife' or 'Mrs Tupra' or anything of the sort, and yet I immediately knew who she was, for she was clearly not just a visitor who had arrived before me or a member of his staff. Perhaps it was the way she was sitting there –her extremely long legs crossed, her very tight skirt revealing the beginning of her thighs – serenely smoking, as if she were perfectly at home and didn't have to ask Tupra's permission or fear his reaction or that he might say no. Her name struck me as very slightly plebeian, if you can apply that adjective to names, like Meryl, Myrtle and so on (Folcuino and Liud-wino are quite another matter).

She didn't get up, she merely held out one beringed hand, which I shook briefly, and yet I could nevertheless see that she had a very good figure. She wasn't exactly pretty, her expression was too friv-olous, by which I mean superficial, distracted and vain, although I wouldn't go so far as to say arrogant. Not because she lacked class, which has nothing to do with arrogance, a quality available to anyone with money or ridiculous titles or honours or some important, mid-dling or even minor political post, but because she lacked interest or conviction; her life must have been very dull, I thought completely arbitrarily and doubtless quite unfairly, as if one glance had been enough for me to see her whole character. But that's how it was.

Contradictorily, she both did and didn't seem a suitable match for Tupra. She would certainly be a match for the prehistoric Bertie Tupra of my imaginings, the ambitious, impatient, unscrupulous lowlife he would have been before his degree in Medieval History at Oxford and perhaps occasionally afterwards as well, or when alone at home, or when he returned to his old haunts, if he ever did. I never knew if he had parents or siblings, if he went to see them and took care of them or if he avoided them in order to suppress certain embarrassing memories. Outside of work, he seemed to me a lonely, isolated man, with no roots or ties, almost without a past. The only thing I had sensed or grasped, given his knowledge of the world and the occasional vague or enigmatic remark of the kind he would no longer make, was that he knew all about the mafias with which 1960s London was infested, especially the one run by the famous Kray twins, Ronnie and Reggie, who had moved from the East End to the West End as the owners of nightclubs fashionable in the bustling 1960s, and had become celebrities in what was known as 'Swinging London', rubbing shoulders with actors such as Diana Dors, Barbara Windsor, George Raft and Judy Garland and, so the story goes, with Frank Sinatra, as well as with aristocrats and members of Parliament like the Hugh Saumarez-Hill of my youth. One MP, Lord Boothby, apparently had an affair with Ronnie Kray, the most unbalanced and violent of the homosexual twins, which meant that the Tories had no hesitation in distancing themselves from and taking proceedings against the brothers, fearful lest they, too, became tainted by that connection and that scandal. The same happened with Labour MPs, one of whom had also been linked to the unpredictable Ronnie Kray. They were protected for a long time by their aura as social celebrities, and it was only at the end of the decade, in 1969 I believe, that they were arrested, tried and sentenced, even though they had been involved in many other murders (some in person and before witnesses who, however, kept obediently shtum). If Tupra had served in their ranks, or in those of their rivals at the time, the Richardson Gang from south London, it would have been as an apprentice gangster, intimidating people or beating them up, because he was only a few years older than me, I'm not sure how many, and I was born in 1951.

Beryl, on the other hand, was certainly not a suitable match for Reresby or Ure or Dundas, for the powerful, resolute individual the rest of us saw, a man of wide culture, certain refined tastes, and possessed of a strange charm. His qualities and abilities were so many and various that the staid pinstripe suits and waistcoats he often wore seemed almost incriminating and to strike a discordant note. Nor was she at all a match for the person he was in his profession, ruthless when necessary, often mocking and ironic, always astute and keen-eyed, his sole loyalty being to the Realm. If my intuition was telling me that he had failed with her, it was because I immediately felt that he hadn't finished the job and hadn't won her over unconditionally; that is, he loved her more than she loved him, which is what tends to happen in couples, but if that was obvious to me . . . 'That's bad news for Tupra,' I thought, 'for someone like him who's never caught off guard and never allows for any weaknesses.' I couldn't work out what her secret was, what it was about that Beryl woman that had made him surrender and decide to put an end to the 'temporary additional sadness' involved in loving someone else in vain, which was, more or less, what he had said to me in Plaza de la Paja.

This is always unknowable terrain, including for fellow travellers like me. It occurred to me, immodestly but realistically, that, in my case, it was Berta who had loved me with determination and persistence, even when she thought me dead. Tupra had convinced her of this, because he felt that, for me, it was the most beneficial option and the best safeguard, and he hadn't even given me permission to phone her from the limbo in which I had spent so long dead. 'I am and always will be indebted to her,' I thought, 'it's time now for the tables to be turned and for me to become the unconditional lover, the eternal suitor, the one refusing absolutely to lose her. And yet, despite that, off I go, quite unnecessarily, to live in Ruán, hardly the attentive lover making every effort to win her love, instead, I'm losing her a little more with each day that passes. It's probably too late now and I'll never be able to win her back.'

'Lovely to meet you, Tom,' said Beryl or Mrs Tupra, addressing me confidently as 'Tom', she was probably the kind who would address the Duke of Edinburgh familiarly as *tú* if such a thing existed in English. 'Bertie has told me such wonderful things about you that I feel as if I know you already, and I've long wanted to put a face to the name, a very pleasant face if I may say so.' She gave this compliment with perfect aplomb. She then got to her feet, picked up her handbag and added: 'Right, I'll leave you two alone now. You'll have a lot to talk about. I'll see you at supper, darling.' This last remark was intended for Tupra, of course – at least she didn't address him by some awful twee term of endearment ('sweetie-pie' for example), and then she planted on his soft, pliable lips a loud but perfunctory kiss, the kind of kiss you would plant on a child's cheek, or a child would give to an adult because he has to, even if it's an adult he loathes.

As she left, I saw that she really did have what in English – in less politically correct times – used to be called 'an hourglass figure', and which in Spanish, for we have no word for it, would be indicated by someone drawing the shape of a guitar or a Coca-Cola bottle in the air. In the days, as I say, when such gestures did not receive a stern rebuke and the women who dared blithely and gaily to display such a figure were not lambasted, actresses like Marilyn Monroe, Sophia Loren, Jayne Mansfield or the more moderately curvaceous Rhonda Fleming. This was all well and good, but a mere trifle when it came to embracing an additional sadness and getting married in order to alleviate that sadness. Perhaps what had captivated Tupra in Beryl was her fundamental indifference and her narcissism. At the end of the day, I told myself, it was no concern of mine. I really didn't care who Tupra married or indeed that he had married, or that, in doing so, he had added or subtracted a sadness. Indeed, I didn't care what he did in the present, let alone in the future. From now on, I would keep well out of range.

'You certainly took your time coming, I just hope the delay was worth it, that it proved useful, that you have something worth telling me.'

These were Tupra's first words after inviting me to take a seat in the 'social environment' his wife had just vacated. At least he didn't give me the chair reserved for petitioners and subordinates on the other side of his desk. And he asked not one question about my journey, said not a single friendly word, indeed, he seemed slightly anxious, which was unusual in him, but not unknown, it happened when things were refusing to go to plan.

'Not very useful, no,' I said. 'In any tense, emotional group situation, it's easy enough to know how to behave. You just have to imitate those around you.'

He then rather plonked himself down on the sofa (he had given me an armchair to sit in), a gesture that denoted exasperation or something similar. He was slightly lower than me, and when he took out and lit another cigarette, I did the same and lit mine deliberately slowly, so as to make him wait. However, he didn't wait. He had already waited two or three days for me to arrive, depending how you counted them, and he appeared to be thoroughly fed up with a situation that really wasn't his immediate responsibility and was, besides, of no real interest to him, and which was distracting him from his other English chores and machinations.

'As I said on the phone, Tom, you're making me look bad, very bad. What's going on? What's wrong with you? I was sure you'd have the matter resolved in no time at all, which is why I made that promise to George Machim-whatever.'

He was incapable of saying, or indeed remembering, that long Basque name, a name that, to me, had initially rung false, but was probably authentic, perhaps Machimbarrena was a real Basque from affluent Neguri or from San Sebastián via the private, Jesuit-owned University of Deusto, or something along those lines.

'You've been there, what, five, six months? And not a single result. After what happened with Blanco' – he had no problems with that name – 'people in your country are getting very nervous. Yes, as I understand it, there's a general turning against ETA and their lot, as never before in the Basque Country. Given what's happened in the past, though, this just makes that gang even more dangerous. They're not intimidated by popular outrage and protest, they're like the IRA in that respect too. The more they're booed and whistled at, the more determined they are, like certain footballers who like to provoke the crowd. They might be a little bit frightened now, well, even some ETA prisoners have condemned their actions or are rumoured to have done so. Do people know about that there? They'll soon get over it, though, and then they'll do far worse things: "Oh, so you didn't like that, did you? Well, here's a double ration." The folk in Madrid are afraid the Blanco incident might be only an aperitif, the beginning of an unimaginable escalation of violence. They're in a hurry to neutralize anyone who could cause still more damage either immediately or in the not-too-distant future. The more of them we neutralize the better, it's a question of strengthening our position by any means. Yes, by any means,' he said again. 'There's no time to lose. It's not an easy situation. France is going to do what it can, and Portugal too, they're all horrified at the sheer coldbloodedness of that kidnapping and the countdown, but they're very good at making promises. We'll do what we can here, but there are hardly any known members of ETA on British soil, and you certainly can't expect any help from Ireland, they see the Basques as pupils, or, rather, copycats, but there you are. Those most likely to attack in the next few weeks are the sleepers, the ones who've spent time in the shadows or are burned out or apparently retired; no one's tailing or watching them, there are too many active members for us to waste energy on the inactive ones. The latter include your Mary Magdalen O'Dea, and we — George and his people, Pat, you, and me by delegation or commission — are probably the only ones who remember her. I've told you time and time again: our job consists in never forgetting what the rest of the world forgets. So, please, don't tell me you still don't know who she is, that you don't even have your suspicions. That wouldn't be like you, Nevinson, it really wouldn't, not the Nevinson I plucked from nowhere, whom I moulded and trained. At least tell me you have a candidate. Or that you've got one of them earmarked. Come on, Nevinson, what's happened to you?'

He stood up for a moment, as if accepting that he needed to give me a chance to consider my response and get up steam. He opened a drinks cabinet and poured himself a small glass of port. Before returning the bottle to its shelf, he raised his thick eyebrows interrogatively. I nodded, even though it was only half past nine in the morning (early in England means after nine o'clock, because contrary to what many foreigners believe, it's not a country of early risers). If he was going to drink a glass of port, I wanted to be equally charged up for that conversation, which, while it was beginning with warnings and gentle reproaches, would inevitably change in tone, of that I was sure, and altogether it was not going be a pleasant encounter.

'The one I plucked from nowhere, whom I moulded and trained,' he had said, as if it were a matter of indifference to him where he had snatched me from and what wiles he had used to entrap me. Tupra was very vain. He tended to take all the credit for anything that worked out well (he would just do this once, but once was enough), and I had been a credit to him for some years. He wasn't being entirely untruthful, though; he had taught me a lot (I had no choice), I had learned from him (what alternative was there, if, at first, I was a terrified greenhorn?), although I hadn't absorbed all his lessons. He was too draconian sometimes, and when in doubt, tended to take extreme measures, just to be sure. Better to regret what you *had* done than what you hadn't, missed opportunities. Had he been Walter Pidgeon or Captain Alan Thorndike, he wouldn't have just played at firing his rifle initially nor would he have wasted precious time, he would have realized straight away what lay within his grasp, or within one squeeze of the trigger. He would have realized this from the moment Hitler appeared on the terrace and entered his field of vision. He would immediately have loaded his rifle or had the rifle already loaded. In an instant, he would have adjusted his sight and shot him in the head or the chest. In July 1939, as quick as a flash, Tupra would have thought: 'I might not get another chance. I don't want to spend my life regretting having given in to a scruple,' and he wouldn't have hesitated to pull the trigger. Yes, he was too draconian for my taste and for my character, but what a good outcome in both instances, in both fiction and the anodyne reality of a gloomy, almost deserted Munich restaurant, with a few waiters and a few customers, none of whom would have moved, people are easily frightened and freeze at the sight of a weapon that has already spat out a bullet or two or three.

Just as, for forty years, everyone had frozen when an ETA gunman walked calmly or nervously into a café or a bar or a tavern and blew out the brains of some unarmed, unsuspecting individual sitting having breakfast or enjoying a beer: a businessman who hadn't paid the so-called 'revolutionary tax' they were demanding, a brave, outspoken journalist, a politician who neither accepted nor connived in their terrorist tactics (and there were quite a few, from devout

420

conservatives to a few Basque communists), the owner of a newspaper kiosk whose treacherous customers had accused him of being a drug dealer or a nark (as far as I know, in all those long years, they never attacked a priest). No, no one moved until the murderer had bolted and disappeared. Reck-Malleczewen and his friend Mücke would have left the Osteria Bavaria and no one would have stood in their way or stopped them, the gun still smoking in the writer's hand, once he had given in to the impulse of the moment. He might have felt some remorse later on, but, at the time, he would have done what he wanted to do. And he would have done the world an enormous favour.

If you could know beforehand, if you were sure of what you sensed or suspected or even saw, if you were absolutely clear in your mind that it was right to kill there and then . . . Fortunately or unfortunately for him, Tupra believed he did know things beforehand, or, rather, he not only believed he knew, he did know.

Although he had been receiving periodic reports from Pérez Nuix or Machimbarrena and even possibly from Molyneux (they were, of course, all one and the same and all had me as their sole source), he wanted to hear from my own lips my version of the state of play and in detail. I had the impression that, over the months, he had paid very little attention to the reports he received. He would have been busy with the negotiations in Northern Ireland that would result in the Good Friday or Belfast Agreement of 10 April the following year, 1998, and, above all, with consolidating his personal projects in one of those buildings with no name, which was currently in Cockspur Street, and before that somewhere else and tomorrow who knows where. As I've said, the business in Ruán was not his concern: he'd been asked to do someone a favour, had earmarked the person to carry out the mission, had convinced that person to say Yes, had set things in motion, and then pretty much forgotten about it. Until the events of 10, 11, 12 and 13 July, and the subsequent anxious complaints and grumblings from the man he was doing the favour for.

It was now up to him, briefly, to take charge, at least as far as I was concerned (I was his responsibility and his representative, I really was 'his man', however unpleasant and improbable that seemed to me after my years in retirement), and he wanted to be properly informed about my inquiries and my progress, my conjectures, my doubts, my dealings with the three candidates, my well-founded or purely speculative suspicions and my hypotheses, my advances and retreats, my irritating inhibitions. He had reluctantly decided to devote some time to the bothersome task of being an intermediary agent, well, at least for that one morning, we would see. He picked up the phone to ask for sandwiches, white wine and soft drinks to be brought to us around midday, and then picked it up again to make a few other requests as I proceeded to give him my report. He always made these requests politely but authoritatively, he was, after all, issuing orders.

I set out what I knew and admitted how much I still didn't know. I told him about my friendly-cum-sexual relations with Inés Marzán, my amicable work relationship with Celia Bayo, and my very recent and almost ancillary relations with María Viana. I described the husbands of the second and third of those women. He laughed out loud when he heard about them (we always shared a laugh, even in our lowest moments), and despite his extreme Englishness – it was a shame for him that his surname should be so indecipherable for any pure Englishman – he understood the absurdity of their first names: 'What kind of saints are they, to go ruining some poor wretch's entire life?' he asked in amazement; he had obviously forgotten that these names would have appeared in the reports I had been given at the start.

I told him about Inés Marzán's moderate liking for cocaine, and about her dealer Comendador's home deliveries. I explained that none of the women spoke English as a bilingual person would, or so it appeared: Inés Marzán's English was what one would expect and what would be deemed acceptable in the owner of a restaurant, one that was becoming more and more popular with wealthy foreign tourists; Celia and María seemed not to know any English at all or only what most presumptuous Spaniards, male or female, would claim to know, having made shopping trips to Harrods and Fortnum & Mason, or even, in a sudden fit of cultural enthusiasm, that eighteenth-century bookshop Hatchards. None of them had come out with a single sentence or word in our language (Tupra's and mine) that would have betrayed them as being half Irish, even though

I had very warily tempted them to do so. María Viana, I added, followed my lessons with her children with great curiosity and perhaps understood more than she would admit, that, at least, was my impression. Her twins, though, had no facility for languages at all, and that is something one tends to inherit. I even risked mentioning that the concealed cameras in the houses of Celia and María had proved almost useless, except for some pointless prying: they had been placed in rooms that were rarely used and were thus extremely dull, if I could put it like that, a big mistake (and with this remark I got a dig in at Machimbarrena, simply to share out the blame for what Reresby would see as a failure). I described Inés Marzán's diaries, for I had subsequently borrowed others from different years, all of which contained the same unilluminating notes and abbreviations, and that mania of hers for giving only people's initials. I had, nonetheless, patiently jotted them down in my notebook, and I showed these to him, just in case he could see some meaning in them that eluded me.

He again reached for the phone, and a couple of minutes later a fellow called Mulryan appeared, and Tupra asked him to make photocopies of the relevant pages and to study them.

Tupra may have been draconian, but when it came to applying himself to a task, he was, above all, meticulous, probably far more than I was. That's why, among other reasons, he was the one who conceived and directed operations. The mere fact of giving him an account of my months in that town in the north-west was helping me to see even more clearly how feeble my achievements had been, how meagre my discoveries, how vast my ignorance and how few my non-existent certainties, and how many lacunae remained to be filled. The mere fact of putting them in some order helped me to shake off the mental numbness induced by Ruán's bells and mists, by its sweetly flowing waters and its monotonous, cosy routines, all of which were like a lullaby, a lethargic rocking. It was like living in a hammock on the banks of the Rhine or the Avon, or more like the Avon as it passes through Bath, where Tupra had sent me once to recover from a wound that had affected one lung, two weeks in a now distant summer, and he had kindly paid all my expenses.

He asked me about the different social circles the three women moved in, about their friends and acquaintances. They either had too many (this was the case with Celia Bayo, who, in superficial, frenetic fashion, had dealings with the whole town, although with no visible consequences) or else had almost none worth mentioning (this was the case with the other two, each of whom was, in her own way, reserved and discreet; Inés Marzán had only Comendador, her occasional harmless supper or TV companions, her former lovers or suitors with whom she presumably always made a clean, unrancorous break, and the local powers-that-be whom she knew vaguely because of her position and her profession; María Viana had only her beloved offspring, the staff who worked for her, a few little social princesses and possibly the odd lover or sweetheart of whom there was not the slightest evidence, or just the suspicions of cold, indifferent Folcuino Gausi, whose duel-induced erections I also described to Reresby, and which again made him laugh. Needless to say, I also spoke to him about Inés Marzán's daughter supposedly lost to a prohibitive ex-husband who lived in some unknown place, unknown to her and to me).

'You mean you don't even know that?' he said, tut-tutting. 'Is there no one else? I thought you Spaniards were always madly, unstoppably mingling and mixing.' That morning, I was Spanish, at least to start with.

'Yes, there was someone else, an old friend of Inés Marzán's according to her, who was just passing through and who she'd happened to meet at mass or on the way out of mass, on what was a kind of public holiday. A fat man, much older than her, fifty-something or more. I chatted with him for a while at Inés' place. He had a rather low opinion of democracy, which, according to him, was hedged about with problems, although he didn't go into detail. He was no fool though. His name was González de la Rica. Does that name ring any bells?'

'No, but then why would I know anything about some fat Spaniard? How do you spell his name?' I wrote it down in the notebook he held out to me. He stared at the name blankly, then said: 'Of course you can hate democracy and still not be a fool, if only the people who oppose it *were* all fools, we'd have much less to do. Could you describe him? So that we could have a drawing made and compare it with others in the archive.' Then he added in a bemused tone: 'At mass, you say? Is she a believer, then? Or just a Catholic like the rest of you Spaniards, I suppose.' That day, he definitely considered me to be a true-blue Spaniard.

'Yes, I found that odd too, and so I asked her about it. She said she wasn't so much a believer as "spiritual", whatever that means nowadays. And that she found it comforting to feel part of the community now and again.'

'The community? Being part of the crowd, you mean?'

'More or less, yes. The spiritual crowd.'

'Well, who doesn't enjoy that on big occasions? The rabble wraps around you like a warm blanket.'

Tupra used the word 'rabble' casually and unashamedly. Not in a demeaning or disdainful way, I think, but because deep down he considered that he himself had come from the rabble. He might even consider himself to be 'riff-raff'. In my mouth, let alone in the mouth of that obsessive hunter Morbecq, the word would have a very different effect.

'It was some months ago now, but, yes, I could describe de la Rica to you.'

'Not to me you don't,' he responded, as if he were saying 'Who do you take me for?' and he again took up the phone.

Shortly afterwards, in came another man, who was introduced to me as Rendel or Rendl (Tupra pronounced it with a very strong accent, as if it were an Austrian name, not English), accompanied by a young woman wearing large glasses, Miss Pontipee, who turned out to be the artist and my designated listener. Her very unusual surname sounded to me like a joke, for it was the name of the uncouth brothers in the famous 1950s musical *Seven Brides for Seven Brothers*. Tupra said 'Miss' not 'Ms', for in 1997 few people used that stupid, cacophonous form of address, intended to avoid revealing whether a woman was married or not. It seemed to me that either Tupra's group was not as small and select as he said, or else its members were always dancing attendance on him, always ready to file into his office to fulfil his every need or desire.

Miss Pontipee sat down on the sofa, keeping her (round, compact) knees close together, and on them she rested a large sketchbook on which, as she listened to my description, she began rapidly drawing with a piece of charcoal and various stout coloured pencils, like those people who used to make Identikit pictures. Well, at the time, they still did. Then again, everything to do with Tupra had a slightly antiquated air, as if technological advances weren't his thing, or as if he preferred to carry on working on paper as being more reliable and trustworthy. The computer on his desk did not in any way contradict this, he probably didn't use it at all, he would summon one of his subordinates, male or female, to do that. I was finding it hard to work out what exactly his group did, still less what their shared talent was.

Miss Pontipee would show me each fresh attempt, and I would suggest she correct or adjust certain features, and she would then resume her ever faster drawing, before showing me again. After five or six of those sketches, I couldn't recognize de la Rica at all, and his features were becoming confused and muddled in my head. Either she wasn't particularly skilled or I was very inept in my descriptions, or too detailed and rigorous. Perhaps for reconstructions based on mere words you need to be more succinct. It was very boring, anyway, even though the young woman – her glasses really were huge and made her eyes look bigger, all they needed to be a mere parody of themselves was to be made in the shape of a heart – was like a juggler with her pencils and charcoal, and she finished each portrait, one per page, in a veritable trice.

Tupra wasn't fooled, he could see I was dissatisfied. Rendel, who hadn't moved from the spot since he arrived, was watching Miss Pontipee's work with huge admiration, if not fascination.

'It's just amazing, Morag, the speed at which you draw those portraits. And they're all the work of your imagination,' he blurted out.

Morag is an eminently Scottish name, while Mulryan is Irish, although I've met a few Mulryans in Spain too, the descendants of those who, in another century, had been exiled on account of their religion; Rendel, as I said, sounded like an Austrian Rendl rather than an Anglo-Saxon Rendle or Rendell.

'If you draw slowly, nothing comes out,' she explained, without looking up from her sketchpad.

'What do you think?' Tupra asked me after the seventh attempt, and doubtless feeling as fed up with the whole process as I was.

'I can understand how difficult it must be to be exact, and it's probably entirely my fault, but none of them is quite right, although the penultimate one comes closest.'

'Fine. Rendel, get them to compare this with other portraits and photos in our archives, and if there's no acceptable match, then consult Scotland Yard's archive too. This might take a few days, Tom. If we find anything, I'll let you know. Or Pat will.'

Nothing had changed, it seemed, and why would it? The Secret Service was in charge and prevailed over the police and the military and, with the occasional exception, over almost everything else in the country. Not over the Prime Minister, of course, but they could always conceal things from him and fail to keep him informed.

'Now, please leave Nevinson and me alone. We still have a lot to talk about.'

'*Do* we still have a lot to talk about?' I asked after the docile departure of Rendel and Miss Pontipee, the latter having left behind her
sketches, which had made a slightly unpleasant impression on me, as
if she were a rather mediocre disciple of that sordid artist Lucian
Freud, with the addition of the occasional, equally sordid, Bacon-
esque eccentricity or deformity.

'Yes, we do. You still haven't really told me anything, and so how
much we still have to talk about depends on you. Do you have a solution? Do you have a plan of action? Time is pressing, this can't drag
on for much longer and you can't stay in Ruán *sine die*.'

We had been together for about an hour and a half. I was growing
weary of sitting there before him and having to report to him as if to
a superior. He had reverted to being my superior, and yet he wasn't
any more, I could just abandon the whole project without there
being any very grave consequences now. He could, of course, always
pull a few of his many strings and have my contract at the embassy
in Madrid cancelled, and stop the extra allowances that allowed me
to live very comfortably and to provide for Berta, Guillermo and
Elisa (Berta earned a decent enough salary, but it was hardly a fortune), as well as for the invisible Meg and Val.

'What do you mean I haven't told you anything, Bertie?'

I realized that I tended to call him by that familiar diminutive
'Bertie', as in our better days, whenever he succeeded in irritating
me. An indication of affection, but also of disrespect. In fact, my own

429

thoughts had irritated me more than he had, the confirmation that my main sources of income depended in large measure on his benevolence or appreciation or magnanimity. And you never could tell with Reresby. He was perfectly capable of simply cutting off that income, he had done just that with certain collaborators who had proved disappointing or were no longer useful. Previous services rendered didn't always count, and with him the past didn't count. Neither with him nor with MI5 or MI6. And I assumed it was the same with the CIA, the DGSE, the SISMI and the BND, and even with CESID, and, needless to say, with the FSB or the GRU.

'I've hardly stopped speaking since I arrived. What more do you want to know?'

'Tell me how you're going to resolve this matter, Nevinson. What would resolve it?' He probably went back to calling me by my surname whenever he was getting impatient or cross with me.

'There clearly is no resolution, Bertie. If what you need is enough evidence to justify an arrest, for charges to be brought and a criminal trial, that's just not possible. There simply isn't the evidence. And I don't think there will be any time soon, unless our Maddie O'Dea suddenly opens her heart to me and confesses all or else makes some huge blunder, which, at this stage in the game, seems highly unlikely. And in all the time I've been there, neither Pat nor George's people have been of much help. I've received only very basic information. They could at least have made an effort to find out where Inés Marzán's daughter and ex-husband are living. They sent me there expecting me to join up all the dots myself. If they're now in a hurry because of what happened to Miguel Ángel Blanco and what that might unleash, that's hardly my fault. Maybe I need more time, I don't know. Or perhaps I'm doomed to failure. If that's what you think, then replace me with someone else.'

Tupra took out another cigarette and whistled under his breath, his cold gaze fixed on the floor, like someone considering what to say next. He still smoked, as did his wife, and as did Berta and me.

'No, no, it's my fault,' he said as he lit his cigarette, and I couldn't tell if he was being sarcastic or if he actually meant it; and what he went on to say failed to clarify this: 'I gave them too many guarantees, I had too much confidence in you. When you agreed . . . well, I imagined you'd be the old "you", the "you" you were before. I was wrong. The "you" before you became James Rowland (that was your name, wasn't it?) in that dull-as-ditchwater town, with its river, its mediocre football team and its hotel. Becoming that passive individual, the father of a little girl, ruined you. What other explanation is there? We're running out of time. It's too late to replace you. We're not going to start all over again.'

'You were the one who kept me there all those years. I don't think I had ever been someone else, so unvaryingly someone else, I mean, for such a long time. I probably just got used to it.' And I *was* being sarcastic.

Tupra noticed, but didn't respond.

'Damn it, Nevinson, at least tell me what you think.' He may have come from the rabble, but he was rarely foulmouthed, and hardly ever swore, except when he needed to frighten or terrify someone, and he must have learned that from the Kray twins or the Richardson Gang, probably from the Krays, whom he would have seen in action. 'You must have found out something in the months you've been there, you must have some inkling. Choose one of them, that's the least you can do. I don't know those women, but you do. I mean, for God's sake, Tom, you're having it off with one of them.'

There he opted for a medium term, he didn't say 'you're screwing one of them' or 'you're fucking one of them', nor, of course, 'you're going to bed with one of them', that would have been far too namby-pamby for a conversation whose waters would gradually grow choppier, although, as yet, this was happening only slowly and blandly. Machimbarrena would have launched straight in with: 'Stick it in her up to the hilt'; fortunately, though, he wasn't there, because he would have been a real pest.

'Easy to say,' I thought. 'Choose one of the three and perhaps condemn her to death, because there's no way she'd get sent to prison.' This was precisely what I didn't want, to choose one of them when I still wasn't sure, wasn't certain, to choose one of the three and perhaps simply by pronouncing her name – María, Celia or Inés – deprive her of life's fitful fever, possibly, as Pérez Nuix had hinted in Madrid, with my own hands. Or if not that, then pass her on to someone more skilled, someone with 'their finger at the ready', a Sicilian expression to describe those who are prepared to finish off anyone at a moment's notice and without asking any questions. Yes, there are always people with their finger at the ready, among us as well, and when a war or a revolution or an insurgency breaks out, their numbers gaily, easily multiply.

Gaztelu or 'Txapote' would have his finger at the ready, as he had just shown, as would Gallastegui or 'Amaia' and Geresta or 'Ttotto', who knew precisely how things would end the moment they picked that city councillor up at the station. So would Bienzobas or 'Karaka' in 1996 when he entered the office of the jurist Tomás y Valiente and shot him in the face at point-blank range. So would Caride, Troitiño and Josefa Ernaga, who in 1987 had loosed their ball of flame – the explosive mixture stuck to the victims' skin like napalm – in the Hipercor shopping centre, and so would Santi Potros, who had given the order. As would Magdalena Orúe O'Dea, who would have known precisely what they were making – ammonal, petrol, glue and soap flakes – and helped in its preparation.

That woman was still at liberty and was carrying on with her life – unlike those others, with the exception of the three who had recently kidnapped and killed Blanco – and even though she hadn't taken part in anything since 1987, either in Ulster or in Spain, it was nonetheless possible that she might organize another bloodbath, and I knew her and had dealings with her without having the slightest idea which of the three she was. And perhaps I went to bed with her now and again, and kissed her and let her kiss me, caressed her and let her scratch me, in our mutual search for pleasure. Suddenly that possibility seemed utterly repugnant. According to Tupra and Machimbarrena and Pérez Nuix (according to that parallel Spanish division or whatever it was that George was currently in charge of before he took over at CESID, if Tupra was right in his predictions), there was no doubt that Magdalena was one of the three: Inés, with whom I, and possibly others, did indeed have it off; Celia, with whom Liudwino, with great imagination and theatrical gusto, had it off before my concealed gaze, although in their case there was definitely no one else, given how much they enjoyed each other and given his intense jealousy; or María, with whom, inexplicably, no one had it off, or so it seemed. But who knows.

'Magdalena Orúe O'Dea probably deserves to die far more than Marie Antoinette did and more than Anne Boleyn too,' I thought. 'Ten years is both a long time and no time at all, it's a long time in one individual's life, and nothing in the great tally of times recorded and unrecorded. But we don't know how to judge ourselves by the latter, we can't see ourselves as an infinitesimal part of the world's accumulated time: if we could, no one would ever get out of bed or do anything, because in that dimension, everything is futile, stupid and transitory, and all efforts are vain, even those that seem crucial in our insignificant day-to-day existence: saving someone's life, avoiding misfortunes, preventing mass killings, none of this matters in the onward march of the universe that crushes all before it, crushes and overwhelms. Tupra knows his Shakespeare, or at least his *Macbeth*: "Duncan is in his grave . . . he sleeps well . . . nothing can touch him further." Yes, in the vast land of afterwards, what does anything

433

matter? Best forget about it or we risk becoming paralysed. But even in our meagre, limited space of time, in our crude way of counting how much is a lot and how much a little, everything is diffuse and debatable and uncertain. With very few exceptions, the laws decide when crimes and misdemeanours can be considered to have expired; they set limits on the punishments they hand out, and some murderers patiently count the years, months, weeks and days that remain before justice can no longer touch them and the slate can be wiped clean. After twenty years – I'm guessing – what was done is erased and no longer exists, and you can only settle accounts with the murderer outside of the law. There comes a moment when a single date becomes decisive, and after that, nothing matters. That date signifies impunity, and yet, in fact, it's meaningless, unjustifiable, mere arithmetic and chance, or the hand on an old-fashioned clock. Patricia saw this very clearly when we spoke in Madrid. Why today and not tomorrow? Why this minute and not the next? What kind of reckoning is that? The young are very vengeful, and Patricia, being young, didn't believe in prescriptive periods or statutes of limitations. I tried to make her see that what happened long ago has automatically expired. No one seeks to punish what happened one or two or more centuries ago, however appalling. That very real horror gradually becomes abstract, historical, a fiction. We relive it in fictions, we relive it as if it were happening again, and in real time, before our very eyes. But both the film and the book come to an end, and when we emerge from the dream we're horrified and filled with regret that such a horror could have happened, that all those people no longer in this world should have suffered, just as those who tortured or enslaved or ruthlessly, needlessly, put others to the sword are no longer in this world. All we can do is sigh. On the other hand, as far as justice is concerned what can still be remembered, what has been experienced personally near or far does have an expiry date, but not for those who suffered or witnessed it, which is why vengeance remains a beating pulse in the world, even if the law forbids it. For the parents of the children killed in the barracks in Zaragoza and in the Hipercor shopping centre in Barcelona nothing has expired or lapsed, nor has it for the family of Tomás y Valiente who was murdered a year and a half ago, nor for the family of Miguel Ángel Blanco, whose countdown has only just begun and will continue for as long as each family member remains alive. Justice can obscure, can wrap everything in a mist as time moves on, and when it expires, it can erase and cancel out, can decree that what happened didn't happen or has ceased to happen. We are neither the victims nor the family of the dead, but we are memory, those who never forget. In that sense, and only in that sense, we are like the terrorists and the mafias from whom we differ in one vital detail, as Tupra reminded me on that January day: 'They're also ahead of us when it comes to hatred. But hatred isn't our style, as you know. That's unknown territory for us.' That's true and as it should be, for we must always remain immune to the five contagions as taught to us by our former legendary instructor Redwood. 'Cruelty is contagious. Hatred is contagious. Faith is contagious. Madness is contagious. Stupidity is contagious. We must avoid all five.'

XI

'Sometimes, Tupra, you surprise me with the nonsense you come out with.' It didn't bother me in the least to bat one of his own arguments – or were they attempts at blackmail? – straight back at him. 'Call someone an idiot who isn't and you'll see how they react, how they try to please you and make amends so that your respect and admiration for them is in no way diminished; an intelligent person will immediately feel insecure, whereas a fool or a brute will not.' This, if I remembered rightly, was another of Redwood's teachings. What a pity that Tupra and I had had the same instructor, which meant that he knew exactly what I was talking about. 'Just as having it off with a woman doesn't help us to know more about her or to know her better. It tells us nothing about her past, nor about her capabilities or her character.'

'Really? It tells you whether or not she's the passionate type, hot stuff.'

'That kind of passion doesn't count and reveals nothing. Some people really do change in bed, but only briefly, then they revert to their unpleasant or anodyne or timid self. It has nothing to do with the actual person. Even someone who gets a bit violent in bed isn't necessarily violent in every other aspect of their life. And the same goes for someone who goes all soppy and schmaltzy. They can prove to be surly and abrupt and even tyrannical in their other dealings with people. And having sex with someone never tells us whether that person would be capable of killing. Unless you realize that he or she is a psychopath, but that doesn't often happen.'

I realized that I was lying to him or partly concealing the truth. The chasm between Inés Marzán's wild, over-the-top reactions whenever we had sex and her mechanical coldness immediately afterwards had always given me food for thought, and had subsequently even sent a shiver of fear through me, however vague and imprecise. Not fear for myself, but a more all-embracing fear. At first, I'd put that contrast in behaviour down to a desire on her part to let off steam, to forget, to stop thinking just for one beneficent moment. That it was a precautionary measure, the defensive tactic of someone who knew about life ('*Elle avait eu, comme une autre, son histoire d'amour*') and who says to herself as soon as she relaxes and drops her guard: 'What are you doing, you fool, have you still not learned to believe in no one, to expect nothing from anyone, to take it as read that everything is transient and changeable? What seems certain today will be uncertain tomorrow, smoke that rises up and is lost. What is enthusiasm today will be tepid emotion tomorrow. ("Put out the light, and then put out the light.") What are heartfelt promises today will be melted snow and lamentations tomorrow. What is joy today will, tomorrow, be insalubrious suns and empty apologies for having caused you pain.' Later, though, I wondered if those seamless transitions, from a flattering, over-the-top voracity to a kind of bureaucratic asepticism, as if what had just happened hadn't happened at all, was, rather, an exercise in a deep-rooted detachment, natural in someone who lacks all scruples and sees other people as mere tools or obstacles – tools to be used until they broke and obstacles unceremoniously eliminated – and for whom there was nothing else, only the cause, the cause, whatever that just cause might be.

I preferred not to explore too deeply the idea that Inés, that possible Inés, was very like me. I, too, had used sex in a utilitarian manner, and more than once, in order to obtain something, information or whatever, to win a woman's trust or pity and to undermine her. There had even been a time long ago when my sexual relations with Berta had also been only an egotistical way of shaking off anxiety and tension. However, since I was never that interested in knowing much about myself – since I never really focused on myself or took pleasure in contemplating my navel – there was no point in creating parallels between me and Inés. What did it matter if we were alike? *She* was the object of this study, not me.

I had not, of course, been to bed with either Celia Bayo or María Viana, so I couldn't make any comparisons in that area, and my having seen the former in action with another man really didn't count. But if I told Tupra of my fears regarding Inés Marzán, I would be pointing the finger very slightly at her – and that might be enough for that keen-sighted, draconian individual – which was precisely what I wanted to avoid, to point at someone with no proof or certainty or even any real hunches. Just telling Tupra about my adventures in Ruán had helped me to see things more clearly, which was one of the effects he had: almost without saying anything, he somehow obliged you to see better, to illuminate suspicions hitherto rejected or silenced or hidden, of the kind that would never otherwise emerge however hard you looked or scratched at the surface.

He regarded me with affectionate irony, as if he were waiting in compassionate, albeit bored, silence for me to end my brief disquisition on the opaque nature of sexual relationships. He allowed himself a sigh, a sigh, how can I put it, yes, of affectionate commiseration.

'I clearly can't count on you for the project I've been involved in for years now, for what I've set in train here. I would recruit Pat in an instant, because she has a gift that you lack. Now don't take that as an insult, Tom: you're brilliant at languages and accents and mimicry, I don't think I've known anyone better. And you've been a magnificent agent, disciplined and full of initiative, which is a very valuable combination and quite rare too. But you're not good at people, you don't dare to look at them boldly and, therefore, clearly. Not that you really needed to in the past, you were almost always given very detailed reports and instructions. One can't have everything, anyone who thinks they can is either arrogant or a fool. In the case of Mary Magdalen O'Dea, I thought that your capacity for investigation and improvisation would be more than enough, and that you would pick up in an instant the slightest slip in her pronunciation, in English if she spoke English and even in Spanish. I'm not blaming you: there probably was no such slip, after all, Mary Magdalen O'Dea has spent eight or nine years waiting and on guard. I'm sure, though, that if I'd sent Pat instead of you, she would have identified her by now, perhaps not with any firm proof, but because of that gift of hers. And without having to go to bed with any of them initially. Although ultimately, who knows.'

'And what is that gift, if you don't mind my asking?'

'There's no point in asking. If you don't have it, it's really none of your business.' He paused and made a failed attempt to sound less standoffish. 'Really, Tom, there's no point in asking.'

This response wounded me, more than anything because he was excluding me from his mysterious project. However old a hand you are – even if you left in disgust and have returned only as a remedy against emptiness and as a one-off – unflattering comparisons are always troubling, especially when the person making the comparison is clearly saying that you're just not up to it and don't even deserve to know more. Tupra couldn't possibly have any doubts about my ability to keep a secret: I'd remained silent over and over throughout my life, I'd even remained silent with Berta, before, during and afterwards. Yes, that remark had wounded me. After all, everyone feels loyalty for some thing or place, and once you've been inside, it's unbearable to be outside. I responded with barely concealed irritation:

'To be honest, Bertie, I really don't give a toss about your little games.'

Tupra ignored this comment. He had already moved on, he'd never had any time for people's hurt feelings.

'What I'm asking you is perfectly within your grasp, or, rather, your finger, Tom. All I'm asking is for you to indicate one of those three women, the one who seems the most likely candidate. You must have a favourite after all these months, more months than we assigned to you. You've had your time, and now time has run out. The events of the last few days have put an end to it. You must choose. If you don't, we'll have to cut to the chase, and that, as far as you're concerned, would be the worst possible option.'

I knew Tupra too well to fail to understand his intentions. And yet I found these so disproportionate, and so very grave, that I asked him to clarify or, rather, confirm what he meant.

'Cut to the chase. Coming from you that sounds really ominous. I'm not sure I've quite understood . . .'

'Of course you have, Nevinson, don't act dumb, it doesn't suit you. Cutting to the chase means cutting out the infected part of the wound. Or the uninfected part, yes, even those who aren't guilty, so as not to leave any guilty party on the loose. What is it that you don't understand? Your failure, your timorous response, leaves us no alternative. Or, rather, leaves George no alternative. Here we carry out the orders, that's what the favour consists in, but he's the one giving the orders.'

'Do you owe him that much? Enough to sacrifice all three women, knowing that two of them had nothing whatsoever to do with it?'

'Yes, I owe him something,' he said, clearly piqued. 'But what I want above all is for him to owe me still more, to transfer my debt to him, just in case.'

'Really, Bertie? What, just for some medium-term strategy of yours? Just to get your bishop in a better position on the board? You can't be serious.'

I seem to recall that it was then that Reresby called for more sandwiches, wine and soft drinks to be sent up. He must have been feeling hungry (what he would have given then for some *patatas bravas*), and so he called a halt halfway through our discussion, and that halt lasted until the waiter, or whatever he was (he wasn't wearing a uniform), had left the room. Then, in between taking small bites of sandwich, he resumed our discussion as if there had been no parenthesis.

'Strategy is everything, Tom. In the medium and in the longest of long terms. You either failed to learn this or have forgotten. You always were too well brought up, you always lacked vulgarity, and without vulgarity, you're lost. You've managed to get around that limitation . . . boldly, shall we say, in difficult situations, when you had to save an operation or save yourself, and when you have to save your own skin there's always an element of vulgarity involved. Now, though, you've gone cold, and have grown more delicate, more fragile. A few years ago, you wouldn't have questioned what I was telling you to do or even suggesting. You accepted that you can't leave any loose ends untied or any flanks unprotected. You understood that three individuals are as nothing in our universe. That their disappearance is never a catastrophe, not in the great scheme of things: they're just part of the inventory. In wars, innocent people always die, as they do in battles that don't quite become battles or are only partial wars, hidden away in the basement so that the population won't get too alarmed. It's sad and it's unpleasant, I agree, and it would be preferable if it didn't happen. And yes, these are small personal tragedies, but they're not national disasters. They are individual deaths, of which there are many everywhere; they're not collective deaths like those in 1987.' He stopped talking for a few seconds, took a sip of wine and another bite of his sandwich. 'What do you expect, Tom? If you can't take someone to court, which is what you're telling me . . . then you have to throw a very big ball at them in order to knock that someone down, and it's extremely difficult to knock down

444

just one skittle if there are others standing right next to it. You're bound to knock them down too. At least two of them. What you absolutely can't do is leave all three standing.'

I took a bite of sandwich too. I was feeling hungry despite the grim, sinister turn the conversation had taken.

'You're not expecting me to do that, are you, Bertie? You definitely can't count on me. That isn't what we talked about. That isn't what we agreed.'

Suddenly, unexpectedly, my peaceful sojourn in Ruán, with my view over the River Lesmes and the bridge, had turned into a 'blood mission', another expression used in Sicily and, subsequently, all over the place: criminal and prison jargon is becoming fashionable and is prospering in our incorrigibly vain society, which adopts that language so as to feel more adventurous. I stopped for a moment to think clearly, to assimilate what Tupra had presented to me as a solution: three individual civilian deaths, that of María Viana, that of Celia Bayo and that of Inés Marzán. Far too bloody a mission, whole rivers of blood in a place where blood was rarely shed. I knew that, with Tupra, there would be little point in objecting on moral or compassionate grounds, and so I took a practical approach.

'Just how would you justify three homicides, three violent deaths in a short space of time and in a low-crime town like Ruán? The murders of three women, all well-known figures and all relatively young. That would sing out as loudly as the three tenors all belting out an aria, it would certainly set alarm bells ringing, and people would be sure to make connections between the three deaths.'

Tupra lit a cigarette halfway through his lunch, and I quickly followed suit. His grey eyes were smiling, his thick, effeminate eyelashes closing over them. He seemed to be amused, which made me think that he wasn't being entirely serious. I remembered, though, that he was the sort of man who is being serious precisely when he appears not to be. Sometimes, not always.

'Who said anything about homicides or violent deaths? Well, a violent death can happen anywhere, that's just bad luck. But there are many ways of dying, as you well know, you've studied most of them and seen them from close to. There are sudden, reasonably instantaneous illnesses, there are fatal heart attacks and strokes, road accidents, mishaps at home and at work, someone climbs a ladder, puts a foot wrong, falls and breaks their neck, with no need for anyone else to intervene. There are suicides, far more than are ever made public. There are undetectable poisons that look perfectly harmless, ones you don't even have to swallow, you just apply them to the skin: the FSB and the GRU often use them without the world, that great criminal, turning its back on them or breaking off relations with their country. There are even plenty of violent ways of dying too, so many that there would be no reason to connect them. There are hit-and-run drivers, drunk or high on drugs, who simply drive straight off after running someone over. There are brutal muggings, or some fellow on a motorscooter grabbing some poor woman's handbag and dragging her along with him, splitting her head open in the process. There are settlings of accounts over debts and out of envy or because of some long-held grudge. There are uncontrollable fits of jealousy and thefts of some footling bit of booty, a watch for example. There are sexual assaults, rapes that end with a knife wound and then bye-bye world. And there are, of course, overdoses and fatal combinations of drugs, people can be very careless.' He made a brief pause, as if this long list had tired him out and he wanted to reach the end. 'There are also assassination attempts, ETA shooting one of their deserters, I seem to recall that happening to a woman at some point. There would be a certain poetic justice in that, having an ETA collaborator die at the hands of that same organization. And there are always gratuitous, inexplicable murders committed by complete nutcases and that are never resolved. There are all kinds of deaths, whether violent or not, Nevinson. All kinds.'

I'd heard of 'Yoyes', Dolores González Catarain, who was killed by her former ETA comrades in 1986, when she was just thirty-two, while she was out for a stroll with her three-year-old son in her home town of Ordizia, in Guipúzcoa, having previously left the organization and discreetly, but never publicly, criticized it. The IRA had taken similar measures against a few so-called 'traitors', and Tupra would know about those cases, which would be very useful to him when he managed – albeit rarely – to anticipate those dealing out the punishments.

One can never completely leave behind such places or fraternities, just as we cannot completely leave our place here, which is not a fraternity. I had thought as much in Madrid: 'Once you've started, once you've taken the first twisted step, you have no alternative but to continue along that twisted path and take another twisted turning.'

I was angered by Reresby's combination of frivolity and sadness as he gave that list.

'You mean inexplicable like Janet Jefferys' death, Tupra? Another unsolved murder.'

Tupra wasn't going to go on the attack that day. He wasn't in the mood to be drawn into an argument. Nor to get upset or angry about anything I might say. It was one of those days – I knew them well – when he had no intention of diverging so much as a fraction of an inch from his plans and his instructions, that is, from his own decisive and practical will. Because of me, he was having to neglect his projects with Mulryan and Rendel and Miss Pontipee, in order to douse Machimbarrena's raging fires. He was the one who should be reproaching me, the one taking me to task in his provisional headquarters in Cockspur Street in London, the one whose judgement was being called into question and all because of my diminished powers of perception, my waning abilities and my indecisiveness. He responded to those two angry questions of mine like someone brushing ash off his sleeve:

'Don't worry, don't get irate. There's no way I would expect you to remove all three women from the picture.' This was an expression he quite often used. On another occasion, I'd heard him say: 'Just make sure he's out of the picture,' which was slightly more ambiguous than 'Dispose of him' or 'Get rid of him,' but coming from Tupra it didn't sound so very different. 'Neither violently nor gently nor through natural causes. You're not up to such a whirlwind of activity. Removing one of them from the picture, possibly, but not all three. It's a bit of a nuisance, of course, and will involve some travel, but, if necessary, we'll have to send someone more efficient and with

448

fewer scruples, it's just a shame we can't ask the Spaniards. Then again, it would probably only take a couple of days there and back.'

'Three killings in the space of two days? That's practically an epidemic. You're not serious, are you?'

'Of course I am. People would simply see it as a run of bad luck in Ruán, such things do happen, according to popular wisdom, misfortunes never come singly, but in twos or threes. People will certainly find it odd and will make a huge fuss about it at the time, but eventually everything passes and they'll forget. One erasure would bear no resemblance to the other two, and no one would make the connection.'

He fell silent for a moment, and sat looking at me to observe my reaction; he also took advantage of the pause to nibble at another sandwich; they had been brought to us on a tray, with no wrapping, but I thought they probably came from Marks & Spencer. All this seemed to me pure fantasy. What concerned me was what he had said earlier.

'So you would expect me to remove one of them from the picture?'

'Yes, of course, that's the least you could do,' he replied at once. 'If we were to limit ourselves to removing only the guilty party, that, naturally, would be your job, given that you know the territory and are there *in situ*. Besides, you were warned.'

'Was I?' I childishly pretended not to remember. 'When? Who by?'

'Pat warned you. In Madrid.' And that was the end of the matter. He didn't tell me off for pretending, he left such superfluous nonsense to one side. And I did not insist. 'So you have to choose from among your three girlfriends, between your lover and your two girlfriends. If you want the innocents to be saved, all you have to do is tell me which one is guilty, which one is Molly O'Dea. You say you're incapable of doing that, but I think you're perfectly capable. If you really can't or you refuse, that's bad, very bad: you'll have to bid farewell to Celia, María and . . . who was the other one? Oh yes, Inés. Time's spent, Nevinson.'

He certainly knew his *Macbeth*, he was the one who had reminded or inoculated me with those lines when we met in Madrid, and now one of them reappeared, with a variation. It wasn't 'all's spent', but 'time's spent', which often, but not always, comes to the same thing, one hopes. It's far worse if all your money or your energy is spent, or your ability to keep dragging yourself along, to get up in the morning and have the patience to wait, when the bells have not yet started tolling and there's still a long way to go.

'He's using that rather clumsy threat to force me to act,' I thought. But Tupra wasn't usually clumsy, and so this thought came with some reservations. 'He's threatening to send in a hitman to Ruán, a *matador*, to remove all three women from the picture, just so that I will name one of them and remove her without delay, so that I'll do the job myself without the need for anyone else to cross the Channel. He's coercing me into condemning one of them when I can't and shouldn't, not without any proof or certainty, when I simply don't know. But he's presenting me with an alternative that really is bad, very bad. Sacrifice one and save two, who could refuse such an offer, knowing that two of the women are completely untainted and do not in any way deserve to die, just as the poor victims of the Hipercor bombing did not deserve to die, or the children in the Zaragoza barracks, or the jurist Tomás y Valiente or the young councillor from Ermua or any of the many, many others. I don't know if Magdalena Orúe deserves to die, possibly she does. I know that the other two don't, not the jolly schoolteacher, not the unhappy but wealthy wife of a rich, surly husband and the mother of twins whom she adores, not the independent, hard-working, solitary owner of a restaurant in Ruán. I don't know which of them is Maddie O'Dea, but I know that two of them are not. Tupra isn't joking, but neither is he serious, an old trick, a way of piling on the pressure. But with him, you could never be sure if he was being genuinely serious and actually meant what he said, there had been times when I thought he wasn't being serious and he really wasn't, but there had been others when I thought he wasn't being serious and he was. This is the problem with people who deceive and admit and acknowledge that they deceive, the professional deceivers, who know that their interlocutor knows this too: you can't believe them when they tell the truth or when they lie, nor can you *not* believe them when they lie or when they tell the truth. I, too, have been a professional deceiver, but it wasn't always like that. He has probably been lying since the day he was born in Haggerston, Hoxton or Bethnal Green or some even worse place, and the first time we met, when I went to him in search of help, he pretended to help me and instead deceived me with a major deception that has determined my life and will until the very end, because although my time isn't all spent, too much of it has passed for there to be any going back.'

I didn't know how to resolve this dilemma, how to get out of this bind. The only thing that occurred to me was to shift the responsibility over to him. I took another bite from another sandwich just to look casual and confident (a full mouth provides a good excuse for not speaking), then I said:

'If you think me perfectly capable of identifying her, that must be because you've seen something in what I've told you that I have failed to see. So, Bertie, tell me, go on, tell me which one is Maddie O'Dea. If your people here have the mysterious gift that I lack, a gift that seems to be that of divination or interpretation, please, lend me a hand and advise me. Or open my eyes if, according to you, they are closed.'

Tupra stood up and paced around the room, went over to his desk, circled around it a couple of times, briefly sat in his armchair again, then, returning to the 'social environment', he stood right next to me, as if I were his secretary and he was about to dictate a letter. He was, as usual, wearing one of his many waistcoats.

'No, not closed, Nevinson, rather, half closed, or with your vision slightly blurred, or perhaps it's the mist brought on by being too close to the situation that's preventing you from seeing clearly. Or perhaps it's the mist brought on by unacknowledged affections, the kind you don't even know you feel, and which are always the worst and the most paralysing, and extremely difficult to defend yourself against. But you can see more than you think.'

That shifting of responsibility had had an instant effect, for Tupra always liked to enlighten, to illuminate the path ahead. When he was in expansive, festive mood, he always wanted to have lots of company, to go out partying at night, to clubs and discotheques, perhaps recalling his time with the Kray brothers, a mixture of bestiality and revelry, perhaps recalling his youth. He enjoyed having an audience then. It wasn't night now and we weren't in a club, and I was the only audience. But I was still an audience, because I'd offered him the opportunity to light my way through the dark forest and was prepared to give him all my attention. And I was doing so because it was worth my while, and in my own interests, and might perhaps save Celia and Inés, or María and Celia or María and Inés, by delegating some of the responsibility to him. To save two of the three, assuming removing all three from the picture was not merely an empty threat.

'You may be right,' I said. 'Go on, then, tell me what I'm not seeing that I should see.'

For a while, he remained standing beside me, almost behind me, and even placed one hand on my shoulder, as if to confirm that we were fine like that and not to move. That way, I couldn't see the expression on his face, it was as if he were holding a kind of Oxford tutorial, I remember that kindly Mr Southworth would sometimes remain standing or pacing about when he gave his tutorials, while I sat taking notes, his face invisible to me, but that was a whole eternity ago. Tupra would have had tutorials with Wheeler when he studied at Oxford a few years earlier than me.

'We've been looking at the footage you've been sending, that you sent to Pat.' He was referring to the footage from the cameras hidden in the houses of Celia and María. I'd sent some of it to Pérez Nuix, and assumed she would show it to Machimbarrena, but had no idea she would have sent it on to London. 'True, it's not very revealing, but what speaks volumes is that they were unable to put microphones or cameras in Inés' house. There are no images or recordings of her voice, only photos and your reports and descriptions, and that's not enough. If I remember rightly, there was no guaranteed safe place to hide them, according to George that is, although I find this hard to believe. He said that wherever they put them, they would be easy to find and deactivate. You know her apartment, so what do you think? I'm afraid George is surrounded by incompetents, or are you Spaniards as slapdash as the Italians? More? Or less? Anyway, if what he says is true, there could be a reason: perhaps she's a woman who has had to play it very safe for years now, which isn't the case with the other two, maybe because they have nothing to hide and have never had to live with the fear of being pursued or wanted. I can assure you that Mary Magdalen O'Dea will not have known a single peaceful night in her woeful bed,' and again he was quoting from Shakespeare, from *Richard III* this time – that's an Oxford education for you, 'not since she disappeared in 1987 or '88, since she sought refuge in Ruán and turned herself into Inés Marzán.'

'But we knew about the microphones right from the start. I hardly needed to go there in order to find that out.'

'Don't be impatient, Tom,' he said, and he squeezed my shoulder in a vaguely scolding manner. Seeing the expression on his face could sometimes be disquieting, but not seeing it was even more so. 'Among the many other things we do here is to study people. Directly when we have them here in the flesh or on videos if not. As you rightly guessed, we decipher them, interpret them. We've done that with your three girlfriends, with the two we were able to see.'

He stopped for a moment, and I seized the opportunity to ask:

'By here, do you mean Cockspur Street?'

'The place doesn't matter. We had that other place you were familiar with, and we'll have others too, because we're often obliged to move. We're considered both experimental and old-fashioned, and they always put us in buildings with no name or number. One day, they'll consider us to be essential, as essential as Sefton Delmer was in Churchill's day, two men who were true visionaries. Not that I'm complaining; working in a building with no name suits us well, that way, no one can be sure what we are or what we do. And as you yourself know all too well, not even existing is always the best strategy . . .'

He paused again, as if reflecting on his old aspiration to exist without existing and as if he had lost the thread of the conversation, something he never did. Just in case, I brought him back to the matter in hand.

'And what did you see when you studied that footage?'

'Obviously, we can't simply rule out María and Celia. Some people are very astute, and can dissemble to perfection or even come to believe that they are who they've decided to be and yet are not, you've had experience of that yourself, as have I in my day. Nevertheless, my first instinct is that neither of them is Molly O'Dea.'

'Why do you call her that?' I was curious to know why he used that diminutive, alternating it with her full name, Mary Magdalen. He didn't even bother with Orúe.

He once more became thoughtful, or so I assumed, for I still couldn't see his face, but could feel his hand motionless on my shoulder. Then he made what seemed to me a confidence, or a concession:

'George wants her for the part she played in planning the 1987 attacks. As well as doing him a favour, I'm also looking for her because I know, as I told you before, that her collaboration was a purely temporary loan. If Molly O'Dea returns to active service after all this time, as I fear she will, she won't do so in Spain or with ETA, but in Ulster or in London, and that concerns me far more. In reality, she's more Northern Irish than anything else, just as you are more Spanish than English, or more English than Spanish, well, only you can know which. The loan was from the IRA, her loyalty is to them and not to those Basque idiots. Calling her Molly O'Dea is a reminder of that, and seems more appropriate, don't you think?'

'Operating in Ulster from Ruán? That seems highly unlikely.'

'How did you get here, Tom? People travel, you know, there are planes and trains and hovercraft. And people can disappear from a town overnight, without a word of explanation or a goodbye. That's what your Jim Rowland did, didn't he? Don't underestimate the "sleepers". They wait and wait and wait, their whole life consists of waiting.'

'I thought the Troubles were coming to an end.'

This was how English people referred euphemistically (the word was very similar in Irish too – Na Trioblóidí) to the irregular or intermittent or low-level war that had, at the time, been going on for almost thirty years, mostly in Northern Ireland, but also in England and Ireland and even on the Continent, and during which about three thousand five hundred people had died, at least three times more than the number of ETA victims, among them two hundred children. Of course, as I've mentioned before, there were two gangs doing the killings, with one doing rather more than the other, and that was the side Tupra was concerned with.

'So they say, or so it seems. But you never know. I don't trust any agreement, still less any promise. Besides, even if an end to the violence is near or in sight, there's certain to be a backlash in its dying moments, there always is. No one abandons a long struggle without going out with a final flourish, without a farewell performance that serves as a warning: "We're going, but we might be back." As you know, snakes take a long time to die, and sometimes they recover and revert to their old selves or worse.'

He paused again, he really seemed to have plunged into thoughts from another era, perhaps his youth, or the moment when he had crossed the line, when he'd abandoned his criminal or thuggish activities to devote himself to averting misfortunes and being on the side of the law. A more unstable, more dubious law, it's true, one that could be obeyed and occasionally flouted or indeed both things at once. I said nothing, and it was doubtless my silence that prompted him to go on.

'So we need to find our Molly and remove her from the picture, not just because George is in a hurry, but in defence of the Realm too, our Realm I mean.' He finally removed his hand from my shoulder and sat down on the sofa his wife had previously occupied. On seeing his eyes again, I saw that they were alert and resolute, and not at all digressive, as his voice had been while he stood beside or behind me. He spoke then in a different tone of voice: 'Look, Nevinson or

Centurión, you're resisting making a judgement, choosing one of the women, and that's perfectly understandable, no one wants to be responsible for someone else's fate. But there's no avoiding it, it's up to you. Any avoidance will prove still more painful, more troubling. And I think you do lean towards one of the three. That's clear from what you've told me and from the way you refer to them. You have no proof, but you have a sixth sense. More than that, you do actually know. You can see Molly O'Dea. But you so regret being able to see her, that you prefer not to recognize her.'

Now I was the one to get to my feet. I had grown tired of sitting down, my shoulder ached a little or was that just my imagination? Tupra's slow, gentle siege was making me nervous, and suddenly I found myself encircled. I could refuse to cooperate. No, I couldn't. If Reresby wasn't bluffing . . . Yes, if he wasn't bluffing, he was capable of sending Blakeston or someone younger to kill all three women, he was perfectly capable of that, and I couldn't risk just standing by until he finally showed his cards, because when he did show them, it might be in the form of the first dead woman, María, Celia or Inés, and in the certain knowledge that the other two would follow. He went over to the phone and asked for some coffee to be sent up.

'And who, according to you, should I recognize? Perhaps you should point her out to me.'

'As you wish,' he said from his place on the sofa. 'But all the information comes from you, I'm just helping you to look at it head-on and less fearfully, that's all. Which of the three is the only one who has no family or has a lost daughter who may well be pure fiction? Just to get your sympathy. Which one can close or sell her business most easily, and have ready cash to take with her? Who has failed to make any really strong connections in Ruán? Who would be least missed? Who introduced you to a friend of hers or introduced him to you? Who has least to lose, who would lose nothing of any great importance if she were to leave town? Who could most easily up sticks tomorrow and go and live in Belfast or in Derry, in London or in Armagh or in Dublin?'

'None of that is exactly conclusive, Tupra.'

'No, of course it isn't, that's why I'm going to give you another two weeks, or at most three, *if* you make real progress in the first two weeks. Nor am I going to submit to George's insolent naggings if the job can be saved. I'll humour him, but not submit. And that's it really. See if you can find out more about the other two as well, especially María, now that you have access to her garden. Hers is a very strange marriage and hard to fathom, and it may be, as you said, that Folkwin does know all about her, which is why he can keep her under his thumb: if she made any real attempt to leave him, if there were the slightest sign of disobedience or serious rebellion, he'd call the police and that would be that. And don't cross Celia off the list either, even if she does seem smug and happy in her insubstantial life with the light-fingered Ledwin, both in the videos and in your descriptions.' He had immediately, for his convenience, anglicized those two eccentric Christian names. 'We'll check the initials in Inés' diary too, even though they'll probably lead us nowhere. You get the same initials turning up all over the place. Mine less so, there's Bernie Taupin, Booth Tarkington and that French film director, Bertrand Tavernier. You share yours, though, with Michael Caine, Montgomery Clift, Michael Crichton, Marcus Clarke, Mariah Carey, your very own Miguel Cervantes, and so on and on.'

I had never heard of Taupin or of Clarke, and for some reason I associated Tarkington with Orson Welles. Tupra was a walking biographical dictionary. It was clear, too, that for him I was now definitively, irremissibly Miguel Centurión, my designated role.

'And they might well, of course, refer to people's pseudonyms. We'll also compare Miss Pontipee's drawing with our archive of images, and see if anyone resembles your fat friend, de la Rica, eh? To be honest, I don't hold out much hope: he might have been thinner once, or worn a beard or bought new dentures or had a nose job. Anyway, we'll do what we can.'

Yes, Reresby had set to work from a distance, he had got involved and made the mission his own, and was clearly going to help me, he already was, and this, in him, was a way of urging and egging and driving me on. If a mission failed, he would take it on the chin, accept it with some displeasure, but without making a drama of it, as just another occupational hazard. What he didn't like was leaving a mission unfinished, out of carelessness or cowardice. He may have deemed me guilty of both.

'That will take us a few days. Go back to Ruán and I'll let you know the results, either directly or through Pat. Go back tomorrow, today if possible, Tom. Don't waste any more time, because the deadline is looming. But let's not go overboard: now that they've brought the coffee, why don't you have a cup? It's good stuff, Italian.'

They had, in fact, brought the coffee very promptly. He poured himself a small cup without even waiting for me. He wasn't much good at playing the host. Not on that day anyway, and I was what I had always been, his subordinate. It probably wasn't the wisest thing to do, but I couldn't help commenting:

'As I told you, I was thinking of making a brief stopover in Madrid. In fact, I was thinking I'd do that on the way back, since I couldn't do so on the way here, because in that respect you did submit to George's urgings. It's been far too many months since I saw Berta or my children. And after all, I'm not expected to start lessons with the Gausi twins until next Monday, that's what we agreed.'

He drummed his fingers rapidly on the coffee table, and I realized that he considered our meeting at an end, that he had little else to say to me, having already given me a good few hours of his time. He took a sip of coffee, burned his soft lips, and swore, then, incongruously, drank some wine to soothe the burn.

'Do what you like with the deadline, Nevinson. The time is yours, so do as you wish. You can fly off and spend a whole week in Madagascar for all I care. But whatever you do, you know what will happen when the deadline expires.' He raised his index finger and closed his hand, then raised his little finger, his ring finger and his middle finger, all the while regarding me with an incomprehensible mixture of affection and severity. It was a fleeting gesture, but I understood it perfectly: 'Either one or all three.' 'Just don't come to me with any more tales of woe, all right?'

On the plane back to Madrid, it occurred to me that, as far as he was concerned, all my doubts, reservations and scruples were just that, 'a tale of woes'. I couldn't quite remember which word he had used in English: 'sorrows', 'misgivings', 'woes' or 'grievances', not that it really mattered. That hadn't been the last thing he had said, he had added a few more encouraging words of advice: 'In any case, think of various possible ways, it's always a good idea to have already clear in your mind the best, the least suspicious, the most risky and the most efficient ways to act. When the time comes, don't improvise. Thank you for your visit, and we'll be in touch. Goodbye.' And then he opened the door to his office and ushered me out.

I understood what he meant, I had spent many long years understanding him, had even anticipated what he would say. By 'ways' he meant ways of carrying out my duty, ways of killing a woman. I never dreamed I would be given such an order, having been brought up the old-fashioned way and all that. Still less that I would be given such an order after I had freed myself from taking any further orders from him when I returned for good to Madrid in 1994 or 1995, I wasn't even sure of the year, time is always elusive and diffuse for anyone who has led the kind of life I've led. But whether it was in '94 or '95, I was convinced then that I would be free from all orders. How had I allowed myself to be tempted back in, to become re-entangled, how had I found myself here?

The worst part, during what seemed like a very long flight, was being forced to recognize that Tupra was right. He had put me in a dreadful, impossible situation, and it really would be better if just one of the women died at my hands rather than all three at the hands of the now aged Blakeston or that cruel snoop Molyneux or who knew who else, some brutish Kray twin lookalike, we had such men in our ranks and, if not, you could find them anywhere, they didn't even have to be English. And it was advisable to think of the how, that, too, was true.

I had still not got used to the idea or the idea was still rather abstract, for none of those women had been clearly pinpointed, not María or Celia or Marzán. However well I knew them or however little, while I was on that plane they were all still just 'a woman'. I couldn't really believe it, nor did I feel capable either of doing the deed or of living with the knowledge that I had done it until the end, my end. But the woman still had no fixed name, and so, as I flew over the Channel, I began to think about the 'how'.

Yes, I had killed two men in the past and had lived with that without too much difficulty, or only the inevitable, reasonable degree of difficulty, when I went to bed and when I woke. You can persuade yourself that certain crimes are somehow less criminal, depending on who commits them or who they're committed against, and depending on the why as well. The actual moment of committing them is very hard, because you can't help seeing – as both executioner and witness – how the life of the person dying escapes through the wound you opened and how the blood gushes forth, you see his panic and his ultimate powerlessness, or is it, rather, his collapse or surrender or his will grown weary; or the victim's initial surprise when he realizes that he's mortally wounded and thinks (but he is only thinking this, as if death had not yet arrived and wouldn't arrive) that this is his end. You see in his eyes a glimmer of incredulity or desperate denial, you feel the dying man is thinking something along these lines, not expressed the way a living man would express it, but falteringly and with a childish hesitancy: 'No, this can't be happening, this is pure imagination, it's simply not possible that I will never again see or hear anything or utter another word, that this still-functioning mind will stop or fuse like a lightbulb, this mind that is still so full and unceasing and that continues to torment me . . .'

On that British Airways flight paid for by someone else, I thought that I really couldn't face doing such a thing again, especially not to a woman. Nevertheless, I began to mull over the 'possible ways' like a writer pondering the plot of a novel or a director imagining a film, both of which are territories where everything is feasible, because there is no real risk, where, fortunately, nothing that happens really happens, only in the mind of the viewer or the reader, for whom it really does happen, to the point, in a really successful work, where they're unable to forget it and even incorporate it vividly and clearly into their own experiences. For them it not only happens, it goes on happening and will always happen. In that spirit, I allowed myself to consider the problem, weighing up what would be the least suspicious, the most efficient and the most risky ways, as Frederick Oxenham had put it, for that was another of Tupra's many aliases when he chose to use it, and on that occasion he had seemed to me more Oxenham than Dundas or Ure or Nutcombe: disdainful and with staff at his beck and call.

It still frightens me to recall that among those 'possible ways' I prefigured a real murder that actually took place five years later, in July 2002, in a town rather like Ruán in size and pace and pride, with a murder rate way below average (two or three per year), except that it has the sea but no river. When it happened, and I read about it in the papers, it really shocked me, partly because I'd already imagined it on that flight back to Madrid, and partly because the murdered woman occupied, if I can put it like that, the same world as me, or could have; she was someone I didn't know, but whom I could very easily have known, a teacher of English Language and Literature at a

British school in Madrid, who had, until that 7th of July, been leading an apparently quiet, normal life.

Her name was Natividad Garayo and she had reached the age of forty-four, a few years younger than me or Berta. In the photos published in the press (which, I imagine, can still be found on the Internet), she appeared to be a pleasant, attractive person. Those close to her said she was the very last person anyone would take a dislike to or wish to harm, a gentle, responsible, cheerful woman, devoted to her students. (Of course, the nearest and dearest of most victims would say the same, especially if the latter had met with a violent end; but in this case it appeared to be absolutely true.) She was the mother of three children, and happily married to a public prosecutor.

She was in Santander on that day almost by chance. She had travelled there on a Friday to attend a cousin's wedding on the Saturday, and when it turned out that her husband wouldn't be able to go with her because, on those same dates, their children would be heading off to Ireland, she had even been about to cancel the trip. Finally, she decided to drive (a journey of four or five hours) along with her brother and her niece, and they were almost tempted to give up and turn round when they got stuck in a terrible traffic jam on the motorway out of Madrid, a typical summer weekend. The wedding breakfast took place in Santander's Real Sociedad de Tenis, next to the Palacio de la Magdalena, which is famous as a venue for summer courses. It's an exclusive members-only club with a restaurant, spacious gardens and tennis courts. The party went on until late, although some guests left slightly earlier, among them Natividad Garayo's brother, who gave her twenty euros so that she could take a taxi if she couldn't get a lift, she was staying at the house of an uncle of hers, a magistrate, about a forty-minute walk from the party.

She left alone shortly before three in the morning, and the porter thought it odd that she should set off walking at that time of night and in her party clothes too. But Santander is a quiet, safe place, and perhaps she fancied getting some air and having a walk. The area was neither dark nor dangerous, in fact the street where she was found dead is very upmarket, a well-lit avenue lined with stately mansions owned by the wealthy upper-middle classes, including a few famous bankers, and most of the houses are equipped with various security measures, with guards, cameras and alarms working 24/7.

According to a report by Mónica Ceberio published in 2007, a cutting of which I still have, no one saw or heard anything. No drivers, no neighbours, no guards or partygoers, no waiters in the bars along the nearby beach, which were still open and full of customers on that Saturday in July. One of them, from the restaurant El Balneario de la Magdalena, passed very close to the scene of the crime at the very moment it was being committed, but noticed nothing. A young man on his way to pick up his girlfriend was the first to discover poor Natividad Garayo, when it was too late to do anything. She was kneeling down, almost in a foetal position, with her head resting on the ground and her hair over her face, in the middle of a pool of blood and about three yards from some steps that lead down to the so-called Playa de los Peligros (the Beach of Dangers). He called the police, and just ten minutes after the porter at the tennis club had lost sight of her in her sequinned dress and flat shoes, sirens could be heard. Her little handbag was still there with the twenty euros her brother had lent her. The rather pricey jewellery she was wearing remained untouched. Her dress hadn't been torn and there was no sign of any sexual assault. There was no theft or rape to explain the thirty-five stab wounds she had received. The police found no telltale prints or stains or hairs, not a trace of anyone's DNA on her body, on her clothes, in the street, on the beach. Natividad Garayo had some cuts on her chin, which suggested she had been attacked from behind. The many wounds on her arms, hands and wrists indicated that she had defended or protected herself as best she could, instinctively and futilely.

When Mónica Ceberio wrote that report, five years had passed since the murder, and she described how the policeman who had been in charge of the investigation in Santander was still obsessed with the case, and that he showed the file to all the students attending his courses on homicide in the hope that some bright young police officer might come up with an idea that would allow him to advance the investigation or even solve it.

The last time I read something in the press about that poor English teacher who could so easily have been a friend of mine was a couple of years ago, when nearly twenty years had passed. Exhaustive inquiries were made at the time of the murder. The police questioned her husband and dozens of their acquaintances, people from her private life and from the school where she taught, just in case the killer bore some grudge not against her, but against some member of her family; they traced all the calls and messages received and sent from her mobile during the previous six months, in case she had made arrangements to meet someone in Santander, which might explain why she had decided to walk back from the party so late at night. They considered every possible hypothesis: a contract killing (but it had been a last-minute decision to go to the wedding and it made no sense to bump her off after a party in Santander when she could otherwise be found in Madrid almost every other day of the year), an act of revenge (but they could find nothing strange or unsavoury in her life, nothing that others might find offensive), a spurned lover (but she had no lover, well, they were as sure of this as anyone can be about such secret matters), or that some tramps or winos had picked on her when they saw her walking past in her finery and that things had then got completely out of hand when she turned on them or confronted them (but could things really have got *so* out of hand, besides, tramps and winos tend to be pretty shambolic, and if they do attack, it's entirely unpremeditated, on the spur of the moment, in a fit of rage, and they would have left their DNA everywhere), or that it had been some macabre kind of role-play in which the unfortunate Natividad Garayo was, unbeknown to her, assigned a role by some brainless idiots (something like this had happened three years earlier in Madrid, when two young men had killed an innocent bus driver simply in order to complete their mad fantasy). As for the culprit being a serial killer whose sole motive was to add another victim to his list and satisfy his murderous urges, there were no such killers in Santander at the time nor had there been since.

All these hypotheses had been rejected and, as far as I know, the case has never been solved; it remains veiled in mystery, lost in the void. It isn't even known for certain if it was the work of a single attacker or two: of the thirty-five wounds, thirty-four were inflicted with a small single-bladed knife, but the round lesion on the inside of her thigh must have been caused by a double-edged weapon, like Folcuino Gausi's old Katzbalger sword. An attacker using two weapons only to inflict a single wound with the second one just didn't make sense. Nor did the idea of a second attacker who only stuck his knife in once while his companion engaged in a brutal bloodfest. The likelihood of the police finding DNA traces would have doubled had there been a second attacker. The murderer or murderers had disappeared instantly with inexplicable professional promptness. If they had left on foot, surely someone would have seen them, for they would have been covered in blood. If they had escaped by car, it must have been there waiting, and the sound of screeching tyres or a speedy getaway would have been noticed by the many vehicles still around at that hour, because to travel from the famous Sardinero beach to the city centre, you have to cross and often drive down that brightly lit avenue, named after Queen Victoria.

I have often re-read Mónica Ceberio's very thorough article, almost to the point where I know it off by heart, which is how I have partially reproduced it here. And I've read other articles too that appear now and then evoking that enigmatic murder, such a terrible stroke of bad luck for someone who was simply there on a visit to that safe, tranquil city of fewer than two hundred thousand inhabitants and which, in summer, is abuzz with good cheer and bustle, for someone who could have stayed in Madrid that weekend and continued her apparently discreet, contented, inoffensive life with her husband and her children.

And yet I must confess that during that flight back to Madrid I imagined something similar, with the aggravating factor that I would be the one to commit the crime. The more gratuitous the crime, the harder it is to explain, I thought. The more fortuitous and inexplicable and motiveless, the more we tend to put it down to just that, to pure bad luck on the part of the victim: it was their turn to die just as it could so easily have been ours, just as Miguel Ángel Blanco must have been chosen by those *etarras* in a kind of mini-raffle or by the throw of a dice, because, at the time, there were plenty of Partido Popular councillors in small, obscure towns in the Basque Country. And, in the end, people simply shrug and slowly forget, what else can they do, because they need to forget or, rather, to succumb to lethargy and thus dull the pain; yes, in the end, they give up and say to themselves: there's nothing more to do or to think, that crime drives

468

out and supplants each and every tomorrow, as the young do with the old, 'fragile as the mist that the wind drives away', until they dissolve into exile and become 'dead shadows who wander the night', disoriented and adrift in the dark.

Perhaps that Santander policeman mentioned in the 2007 article is still stubbornly going over and over what happened in his quiet city in the early hours of 7 July 2002, even though with each day that dawns it's moving ever further off; perhaps twenty years on, and for however many more years may remain to him, he's still determinedly seeking clues and facts or fresh ideas, perhaps, if his memory doesn't fall asleep or grow as fragile as the mist that the wind drives away. Perhaps like us, he's condemned never to forget what society forgets, even what the victim's family do manage to forget, somehow shaking off their crushing grief in order to go forward and take a few more steps, it's the first step that's difficult and those that come afterwards, and to give the lie to those lines by Eliot that I read distractedly for the first time in Blackwell's in Oxford: 'We die with the dying: see, they depart, and we go with them.' And leave out the lines that follow: 'We are born with the dead: see, they return, and bring us with them.'

That 'possible way', the one that, five years later, was used on poor Natividad Garayo, the brutal, apparently motiveless murder of an innocent woman walking back from a wedding party – which is, of course, how bad luck and accidents happen, as well as illnesses, catastrophes, good fortune and bad, and trees felled by lightning – no, that wasn't the only 'possible way' I considered while I was flying back to Madrid from London. There were other less messy ways too, like the strangulation with a stocking that never happened to Janet Jefferys and for which, in my youth, I became the main suspect, fool that I was. A hard blow to the back of the chosen victim's head, or two or three just to be sure. An undetectable poison added to a glass or a cup, as they used to do in the Renaissance and in the Agatha Christie novels that Folcuino Gausi read, and in Balzac's novels too, with their dastardly offspring impatient to receive a miserable inheritance from their father. One shot from my old Charter Arms Undercover revolver that had been with me all those years. A nighttime hit-and-run accident. A gentle shove from behind on a balcony, oh dear, she jumped, she fell. A settling of accounts by ETA or by the IRA, both of whom continued their attacks and remained equally unforgiving of any deserters. Morbecq with his rifle mistaking a woman for another hoopoe. An overdose of cocaine that would stop a heart weary of so much running away and being afraid and hiding . . . Yes, the number of possible ways remains infinite.

I realized at once, as I sat in my seat on the plane, that I had said all this to myself ingenuously (ingenuousness never entirely disappears): 'a hard blow to the back of the chosen victim's head'. But nothing was decided, I had two weeks, or three if I made good progress, to investigate and probe better and more deeply and be prepared to run any necessary risks (I had lost my old abilities and grown cautious), in order to try and obtain a recorded confession or some solid proof that would incriminate and bring that person to court, and thus avoid me having to use my own hands or to wait resignedly for the arrival in that town in the north-west of an inoffensive tourist, a traveller invisible to everyone, a businessman or woman who would resort to using his or her hands three times, on Inés, Celia and María, in no particular order. I had, at all costs, to prevent this, I would prefer to choose one of the three myself and then at least there would only be one corpse, hopefully the one who, ten years before, had contributed to leaving twenty-one corpses in Barcelona and eleven in Zaragoza, many of them children and most of them girls, I've never known what happened to the little girl in the famous photo, the one being carried by a young civil guard, bareheaded, his face smeared with blood, his eyes filled with a mixture of determination and profound sorrow, incredulity and deferred rage; the girl with one foot half blown off.

But I was painfully aware of two things, for my ingenuousness was short-lived, it lasted only for as long as we were crossing French skies, but did not survive into Spanish airspace: I knew I would be incapable of achieving anything certain and unappealable in that fifteen- or twenty-day deferment, working against the clock, with an oppressive sense of urgency. If I had failed to identify Magdalena Orúe O'Dea during a period of months – as had everyone else for years, including Machimbarrena the Impatient and Calderón, the then head of CESID who I presumed had been kept informed – she wasn't going to make some blunder now that would give her away in what remained of July, or in August or September.

I also knew that I was, in theory, going to be the one who had to choose, and that while Tupra had urged me not to dismiss María Viana or, for that matter, Celia Bayo, at the same time, at my own cowardly request (I didn't want to be the one to pass sentence, to sign and rubber-stamp it, because one thing inevitably leads to the other), he had clearly pointed the finger at the guilty party and, therefore, the future victim. With reservations, of course: he didn't pronounce sentence on anyone he hadn't seen and heard, either in the flesh or on video. And he had not only used his own finger to point, he had attributed that to me and implicated my finger too: 'You have no proof, but you have a sixth sense. More than that, you do actually know. But all the information comes from you, I'm just helping you to look at it head-on and less fearfully, that's all,' those had been his words, which he followed only with a few eloquent questions that had rung out like statements of fact.

No, he was quite right, as he had been all too often for as long as we had known each other. And so when he was summoning up the 'possible ways' like the novelist he wasn't, in every situation I could already see the look of terror on Inés Marzán's large, broad face as I stabbed her, her huge mouth gasping for air as I strangled her, those enormous greenish eyes (the pupils, whites and irises all enormous) grown even more gigantic as the poison took effect, her endless legs lying bent and broken on the road after being hit by a car in a spot where there was no need for speed or haste. Her super-sized, intimidating body, with all its roundnesses and curves, prostrate on the bed and about to explode with an overdose of cocaine, the briefly passionate, then instantly impassive body that I knew so well, and to which I had enjoyed access easily and indifferently, exploring at leisure her magnificent contours, scrambling up the slope of her enormous knees and thighs, and sometimes in summer, that season of insalubrious suns . . .

No, there had been no summers in the company of my not-so-young thirty-eight-year-old giantess, this was the first and would be the last, and it hadn't yet got beyond its first stage. On the other hand, the suns would definitely be insalubrious because my task had suddenly become a 'death project', to use another Sicilian expression exported worldwide. Pérez Nuix had warned me, it's true, but at the time it had seemed such a remote possibility that I had barely paid it any attention. I should have remembered that sometimes the remotest possibilities do break through and grow and instal themselves without us even noticing they were there. Who would have imagined that an Austrian boy from Braunau, an aspiring painter, a mediocre soldier, the leader of a marginal group of heartless thugs, a grubby soul full of self-loathing, would end up becoming the German Chancellor, to give one of the clearest, most extreme examples of improbable disasters.

Now, inevitably, Inés Marzán appeared in my imaginings as the woman I would have to remove from the picture so as to save the other two, who would never have done anything wrong or provoked mass killings or been the cause of any misfortunes.

I knew a third thing too, the main thing in a sense or perhaps the biggest obstacle: even though I had killed two men in my twenty-or-more-year journey (I told myself that one every ten or eleven years really wasn't that many for such a bumpy ride), my finger was definitely not ready to squeeze the trigger, still less take aim at a woman, it made no difference what she had done in the past. No, it did make a difference, when I remembered Josefa Ernaga, a member of the unit responsible for the Hipercor bombing; or Irantzu Gallastegui who had approached Miguel Ángel Blanco when he got off the train, in the days before we all knew his name; or Dolours Price, who as well as planting a car bomb outside the Old Bailey, which killed one person and injured two hundred, and who, a few years before she died, admitted to having participated in the kidnap and murder of Jean McConville, a widow with ten children, the youngest of whom watched in horror as she was taken from their house never to return.

I tried to regain the desire for punishment and revenge (they're not easy to differentiate) that had flashed across my mind when I eliminated the man whom I killed coldly and without a struggle, and the subsequent thought that I still repeat to myself: 'I removed a foul beast and doubtless liberated my world from further calamities, and, in a way, considering what he had done, I dispensed justice.' On that return flight, though, such thinking was all in vain. I didn't feel like that about Inés Marzán ('not yet, not yet', I said in my more optimistic language). I still wasn't sure, and, besides, she was a woman, that was different: a foolish childhood superstition, an insuperable consequence of my old-fashioned upbringing, although perhaps in 1997 it didn't seem quite so old-fashioned as it does in this idiotic, unscrupulous century that is blithely casting aside our beliefs, one by one, and, even worse, our ability to reason.

XII

I had finally phoned Berta from London to tell her I'd be making a brief stopover in Madrid, and to ask her to let Guillermo and Elisa know in case they could leave a small gap for me in their frenetic, youthful lives. It's only normal for young people to be both busy and egotistical, and I wasn't at all convinced they would interrupt any of their activities to see me. In my case, I totally deserved their egotism, I had, after all, been an absent and dead father, and, on my return, they had received me with curiosity and suspicion, vaguely intrigued and with a degree of sympathy for the adventures which, with only the haziest basis in fact and a few sketchy explanations from me, they imagined I would have experienced during my decease or my exile. I could only satisfy their curiosity (I was still subject to the Official Secrets Act) with a few minor, invented anecdotes, all sordid or violent details removed, and the kind of picturesque lies children like to believe; but they were no longer children, and my invented repertoire soon ran out of steam. They came to realize that at least I wasn't intrusive and didn't aspire to exercising any authority or control over them, not even in the form of some fatherly help or advice, unless, that is, they asked for it. They felt I had no right to any of that, since they had always been, and would continue to be, under Berta's exclusive jurisdiction. Not interfering in their affairs or trying to draw them out made it easier for them to accept me, and so whenever we did coincide, they greeted me with a certain deference and a kind of instinctive superficial affection – Elisa more than Guillermo – but

477

they didn't incorporate me into their lives, I remained a semi-stranger who happened to be their birth father, but nothing more.

Nor, given their age and indifference, did it occur to them that I was the main breadwinner, the one who had allowed and still allowed them to live a comfortable and even reasonably cushioned existence – Berta did also work, of course, and brought in money, but much less than my various emoluments; that I was the one who paid for most of their education, their food, their faddy tastes in clothes and their amusements. No, it didn't occur to them to think that, still less to thank me. This was only natural and right, for if, from the cradle on, children have never known penury or poverty, they take almost everything for granted. Just as I hadn't thanked my parents for sending me to Oxford – something that proved, alas, to be a bad move.

And then, of course, only two or perhaps three years after my return, which I had intended to be definitive, off I went again, this time to Ruán; and despite all my promises, I hadn't been back to Madrid once in six months. I had again been infected by the poison of being active, the illusion of being useful, and had been hijacked by both those things body and soul. As in the many other places I'd been sent in the past, I had felt half dissatisfied and lonely and half perfectly at ease and lonely, troubled or weighed down – and sometimes shaken – by my discoveries, my obligatory betrayals – which were no less bitter for being planned and anticipated – and by the holes I got myself into, but, at the same time, happy to be someone else, with a borrowed or imaginary identity and personality, and for that other me to be the one who experienced all the worst parts and, from the point of view of the enemy, committed extraordinarily vile deeds.

Best to be someone who doesn't exist, at least temporarily, and thus protect oneself a little, sharing the guilt and the burden with your non-existent self. Not being the same person all the time makes the years more bearable – the years that continue to pass and simultaneously linger and leave. I had become accustomed to that: putting

Tomás Nevinson on hold and both blurring his identity and exonerating him, and certainly replacing him, and this can become a habit impossible to break. I had tried to break it on my return to Madrid, and had languished and languished until I almost withered away. Tupra had convinced me that I had not yet exhausted what could and should happen to me. That there was still something more.

The fact is, though, that, since going to Ruán, I hadn't set foot in Madrid or seen Berta or Guillermo or Elisa, my head too full of the bells and mists, the bridge I could see from my window and the river, that ancient tree, the Olmo de las Melodías, the one hundred churches and the Barrio Tinto. Too busy seeing evil everywhere, something that always enlivens and alerts the mind. Now, on the other hand, after all that time, I couldn't see it anywhere, I mean, in any of those three women I had got to know or had spied on in those video recordings, and with whom I'd become familiar in my role as voyeur, companion or somewhat passive lover. I hadn't even managed to see it in Inés Marzán, the candidate favoured by Tupra, and he wasn't often wrong.

It was in that state of fear and trembling about what awaited me in the weeks to come – when the finger hesitates and repents and withdraws and hesitates again – that I landed in Madrid on the evening of 17 July, in the lingering or suspended summer light. I had to catch the train to Ruán on Sunday, which left me that Thursday night, the Friday and the Saturday. Tupra had probably warned Pérez Nuix of my arrival, and even Machimbarrena, and doubtless suggested they meet or make contact with me. If that happened, my plan was to dodge the issue or make myself scarce, for I was in no mood to receive reprimands or admonishments or to take part in any superfluous interrogations, nor to have them repeat what Reresby had already told me, which could not have been clearer. I would do what I had been charged with doing when I had no alternative, and once I had explored a little more the very few possibilities that remained to me of legally incriminating Inés or Celia or María, it didn't matter which. In reality, I saw these possibilities as non-existent and had lost all confidence in myself, in my rusty, if not defunct capabilities (Oxenham clearly had more confidence in me than I did, given that he had extended my deadline).

I wasn't going to submit to a tetchy, impatient weekend siege. I preferred to spend the time reacquainting myself with my apartment or attic in Calle de Lepanto, and, when I was allowed, walking across the square without changing pavements and visiting my old family home in Calle de Pavía, which, for fifteen years, had belonged solely to Berta and her children, they had still been children then, now they were busy young people.

I also felt an instinctive affection for them, although for me this had its basis in distant memories: I had been there at their birth, I had cradled them in my arms and sat them on my knee, I had seen them excitedly rushing to meet me at the end of the day, seen their first tottering steps as they scampered unsteadily down the corridor to embrace me and be picked up; I had seen their eyes fixed on my lips – as if struggling to understand where the melodies were coming from – while I sang 'Auld Lang Syne' or 'Camptown Races' or 'My Darling Clementine', and I had heard their very first hesitant words, when they still didn't even know they were speaking. It had been exactly the same with Val, the child I would never see again, either while she was still a little girl or as a full-grown woman, the child I had left behind, along with her mother, and without a backward glance, in that English town also built by a river, like the Spanish town in the north-west, where I would not be leaving a new young life behind me, but instead removing either three lives or one.

Yes, I had given up many things, initially because I had been deceived, inveigled, and later out of conviction, even enthusiasm. Those memories existed in me or in the me I once was, but not in Guillermo or Elisa, nor would they survive in Val's mind. I didn't think any of the three children would remember me as part of their childhood. Val's childhood was just beginning, while Guillermo's and Elisa's were now long gone, and they would feel no nostalgia for the image of a young man in Calle de Pavía. That same man was not so young now and was only there on sufferance. Without understanding that this is how it would be, without realizing, I had handed in my keys for good on 4 April 1982, in order to fly to the other side of the world and make myself useful in a miniature war between the arrogant Thatcher and the brutal Argentinian military regime, a war that was fast fading from people's memories and that would occupy few pages in future history books: I went first to the Falklands, then to that capital city that so longs to be European and which, whether it likes it or not, is a long long way from us. My enduring death began on that distant date, and when I woke each morning I was still not sure if that death had ended or if I continued to live it, or if I had been dying from start to finish, with the finish added on to each day. It had been far too long anyway.

Berta wasn't free to see me until Saturday, because on Friday, she was teaching a class on Henry James in the morning and had other, long-standing commitments in the afternoon and evening, just as Guillermo and Elisa had too, although theirs were more spur-of-the-moment: they'd been invited to a friend's house in Riaza the day after my arrival, and wouldn't be back until Sunday, and would therefore miss me. Obviously, they weren't going to abandon their plans for the weekend just to spend time with me, whom they hadn't seen in months. I found this perfectly natural, after all, I had made no attempt to visit them, not a single movement or gesture, so why should they alter their more exciting plans now?

Anyway, Berta received me in her apartment at around one o'clock, without having told me beforehand if she was expecting us to have lunch together. That had been the scene of our last encounter, when I was about to leave Madrid, six months or so ago, in the middle of winter, 12 January if I remember rightly. I'd told her I would be going away, had mentioned meeting Tupra, and had said goodbye, while she was doing the ironing, an image that had returned to me now and then during my immersive existence in Ruán: an attractive image, Berta with one hand on her hip, the iron in her other hand, regarding me with clear-eyed disappointment and taking the news very calmly, the kind of look you would give an inveterate gambler who admits he's gone off the rails and doesn't now dare to make any more promises about mending his ways; the look, too, of someone who knows that the gambler in question never does actually lose all his money and somehow always manages to climb out of the hole he's in, even after he's been buried. Perhaps what had annoyed her most was that this latest escapade had been prompted not just by my feelings of restlessness and a sense of loss, but by Tupra's particular interests and manoeuvrings, indeed she had immediately said: 'Ah, that explains everything. He made you feel useful and active.' In my current circumstances, it infuriated me to admit that she had, all unknowing, been absolutely right. And she had added: 'The persuasive Mr Tupra, capable of persuading anyone to do anything, even something that would never even have occurred to them, that they would never so much as dream of doing.' And when I asked her why she said this, as if he had persuaded *her* to do something extraordinary, she had snapped back at me:

'He convinced me you were dead, Tomás. Isn't that extraordinary enough? For years I thought he must be right, for years I believed him and tried to forget you.'

Perhaps that's why, because of that hint of scorn in her voice – or was it pity? – at my spinelessness, I was surprised when she welcomed me with something bordering on joy, her eyes quietly shining, clearly unable to conceal her delight at seeing me again, as usually happens with people we've known all our life, those who know us and who we've known ever since we were very young or as children, and who inevitably grow fewer in number as we age. When we meet such people again, there's always that irrepressible glimmer of joy, that fleeting, involuntary smile, even if we're angry with them or parted on bad terms. It's a treacherous feeling and not to be trusted, but still very pleasant, the feeling of being 'at home' again, the sense that 'home' does still exist; that after all our vicissitudes and mistakes and hardships and unspoken griefs, there is still someone who belongs to that 'before' and who is as instantly recognizable as they were on the very first day.

Soon we would both turn forty-six, but to me, Berta hadn't changed since she was fifteen, twenty or twenty-five. I didn't dare hope that she would feel the same about me, but it was possible, and certainly not *im*possible despite my various scars and my ever-changing face. Besides, in our case, we weren't exactly angry with each other (I certainly wasn't angry with her) nor had we ended up hating each other. We hadn't even really parted, or not with the unmistakable sign that marks definitive endings, namely, a sense of relief. Those at least were my feelings.

I certainly couldn't complain about her treatment of me, but she had plenty of reasons to complain about me and our life spent together-apart. But then she always had been a kind, considerate woman, and her naturally cheerful nature meant that she would never be rude to me or shout at me. What I did notice sometimes was a long look of melancholy reproach, as if she were thinking: 'How unimportant I've been to you during our life together. What a small role I've played in your life, which mostly took place far away.' When I met that thoughtful gaze, I would tell myself that she was quite right and that, outwardly, I did appear to have relegated her very much to the background, like some poor pathetic wretch. What I had never told her out loud, because it would have seemed inappropriate, was that, for me, she was the perfect embodiment of the famous lines written by Yeats in 1893, so famous that they've even been quoted in films, despite which they have remained uncheapened, the poem that begins: 'When you are old and grey and full of sleep, and nodding by the fire, take down this book and slowly read, and dream of the soft look your eyes had once, and of their shadows deep . . .' Whereas I embodied the second stanza of the poem, and doubtless would until the winds finally drove away my mist. While I watched her and pretended to help her prepare some lunch (she hadn't mentioned it because she had taken it for granted that we would have lunch together on that Saturday), I recalled those lines — in English, of course, since that was the language in which they were written – and thought that it would never make any sense to unleash those words on her, words she would doubtless know; to appropriate them as lyrical youths often do with poems they love. However, if I did ever say them, it would have to be in the language in which we usually spoke to each other, in the translation I had made a long time ago and carried around in my head. There would be still less justification or sense in reciting the second stanza: 'How many loved your moments of glad grace . . .'

We each got on with our own lives now, and once in a while those lives coincided or crossed, and our bodies embraced for no very clear reason; perhaps because her life had never followed a different path, by which I mean she had never met another man who would detach her from my ghost; not that Berta needed a man to do that if that was what she wanted, she was very self-sufficient, and my ghost grew ever paler. She never told me about those individuals who, for short periods, had aroused her curiosity and provided some distraction, and for me they were purely imaginary, or, rather, inferred. It seemed unlikely they had never existed, but then again how could I be sure? Anyway, my impression was that any such experiments were short-lived, that luck proved elusive or else she quickly wearied of or grew bored with them, preferring to concentrate on teaching her students to read Dickens, Conrad and Melville, Emily Brontë and Gaskell and Stevenson, Sterne and Fielding and Marlowe and Shakespeare. Or perhaps she was too demanding and had grown accustomed to wait-ing for something that takes a very long time to arrive and never does. And as long as nothing did arrive, I was still around, absent and present, as I had been ever since I went off to study in England, leav-ing her in Madrid as usual.

Over lunch, we inevitably talked about what had happened to Miguel Ángel Blanco (people were still very shaken and spoke of little else), even though I tried, within reason, to avoid the subject;

the last thing I wanted during that brief respite by her side was to be reminded of the task awaiting me. Berta was up in arms, as was the entire country, including some ETA prisoners and Basque football fans, of the kind who before, at demonstrations and in sports stadiums, used to yell out the slogan: 'ETA, kill them!', as if they were addressing the whole world or at least the whole of Spain. She said:

'Those people don't deserve to be treated with a clemency they never give anyone else. As you know, I thought the GAL death squads were an aberration, on a par with Franco's secret police or the people involved in the 1977 Atocha massacre.' On one now distant occasion, she had compared my work with that of the Francoist Brigada Político-Social, for whom she had felt total contempt ever since her student days, and that comment had both offended and enraged me. 'But at times like these, I can understand the temptation. I've lain awake trying to imagine what that young man must have experienced and through no fault of his own either. Well, no, I don't *try* to do that, but I do wake in the middle of the night and find myself thinking about it. Especially when they moved him from the place where they'd been hiding him. It must be just dreadful to be held captive, you must pray that nothing changes, that everything stays exactly the same, immutable. You'd end up feeling almost safe in your cell, and every time a prison guard burst in, you'd think it was a really bad omen, and your heart would be in your mouth. Perhaps when they dragged him out and put him in the car, he thought they were about to release him, he might have gone on thinking that right up until the final moment, even when he was kneeling down on the spot where they shot him in the back of the head. But he would also know precisely what was about to happen, and how on earth does anyone deal with that? Those people are identical to the very worst of the *franquistas*, ruled by the same vicious mindset. They're so repugnant, I don't want to see them arrested or tried or in prison. I just want to see them dead, and I don't care how.'

Berta was a naturally compassionate person, as most people are at a distance, but she was also compassionate from close to. She was normally very calm. In fact, it was some twenty years since I'd seen her so angry, and that had been when she'd told me reproachfully how she had feared for Guillermo when he was so small that he only left his cradle to be held in someone's arms, usually hers, but sometimes mine, for at the time I was still immersed in my training and my complementary studies, in my travels in other countries. Feeling her own home to be under threat and imagining her own child in flames, she had proved as implacable as mothers always are when they feel their child is at risk of dying. It had taken quite a while for her to get over that fright, if she ever had. I had no idea, we didn't talk about it any more, not once I considered the matter resolved, because, since I was the indirect cause, I preferred not to speak of it, and Berta preferred not to recall it. I had to assure her (albeit obliquely and by implication) that the Kindeláns who had deceived her were no longer around, and she had seemed fine with this, as long as I didn't set it out too clearly or in detail, not that she asked for details and not that I knew them, having left the matter in the hands of other members of 'us', as I have described elsewhere.

She had seemed fine with that, I thought at the time, just as the majority of citizens would be fine with fast-tracking the elimination of the perpetrators of such attacks, who are now mostly jihadists. They don't say as much, though, and if it leaks out that this is precisely what has happened, with no arrest, no formal charge being made and no trial, they raise their voices in outrage and accuse the secret services of being a gang of murderers, while, at night, they breathe and sleep more easily knowing that they are less at risk. 'Unless the Lord watches over the city, the watchman stays awake in vain,' say the Psalms. Since there is no such Lord nowadays, we are the Lord, the nasty angels. We're used to such hypocrisy, and even find it understandable: journalists, columnists, people chatting after a lively supper party, they all love to show how ethical and moral they are, and how eager to defend the sacred rights of some rapscallion.

Despite her fundamental decency and her reasonably firm principles, Berta was no different from them. Were someone to attack her children or threaten to do so, she would think the only sure way of preserving and protecting them would be the complete annihilation of the attacker. Seeing how upset and furious she was about the events of that July, it occurred to me that, had she been me then, had she known what I was up to, she would have gladly taken my place and not hesitated for a moment to remove Miguel Ángel Blanco's murderers from the world, along with the perpetrators and collaborators of the 1987 killings, in which so many children had perished. If she had known that I was pursuing one of those women, that the time had come for me to slide a real bullet into the chamber of my rifle, to brush aside the leaf obscuring my rifle sight, or perhaps several leaves that had accumulated over the past six months, in order to take aim with mathematical precision and squeeze the trigger; if she had known that I was within an inch of converting that person into a useless piece of junk, an obstacle staining the ground she lay on, mere detritus, to be removed like a squashed cat from the road, she might perhaps have offered me her finger so that mine did not hesitate.

I was tormented by this prospect and convinced that my finger would be sure to hesitate if my predictions were confirmed, and they could hardly be more pessimistic, indeed, from my point of view, they could not have been worse. Berta may have noticed my sly attempts to divert the subject away from ETA. She could see that I agreed with her as regards her feelings of alarm and fury, which I shared – albeit tempered by my profession and by what I knew – and by the whole country, but she could also see that I was trying to steer the conversation along other paths. After all, we hadn't seen each other for ages, although we had spoken on the phone nearly every week, with me phoning her, never the other way round, to ask about the children more than anything. As regards her, I'd restricted myself to inquiring about her health, her work and if there was anything she needed, but never about how she was feeling or how she was getting on or about her personal life, which is often a euphemism for some-one's sexual or romantic life. That would have been indiscreet on my part, and, besides, I really didn't want to know, not that she would have told me anyway. Now, unexpectedly, I found her in a more sym-pathetic, more cheerful, even affectionate frame of mind, as if after this, my umpteenth unexplained absence – this time, it's true, unfore-seen or 'unplanned' – she had decided to view me once again with kind or pitying eyes. Perhaps during my six-month absence in yet another unknown place, she had come to accept that these disappear-ances were inevitable, that it had always been like that, at least from very early on, prior to our marriage, ever since my enforced enlistment, whose circumstances she still knew nothing about after more than twenty years. And as if, despite that, she had long ago opted to remain by my side, or at least be near me in spirit, and why go back on that decision over a situation that was very far from being new?

Or perhaps, who knows, she could see that I was distressed, and this activated her compassion and her concern for me, which, nourished over far too many years, were sure to reappear one day. She saw that I was depressed and exhausted, perhaps filled with an anticipatory sense of desolation. No, I had never killed a woman, and didn't feel I was capable of doing so, but if I didn't . . .

I had once again been duped, thinking that Tupra needed me and that he really was asking me to do him a favour. Tupra, however, never asked for favours nor, of course, did he say thank you; he always ended up giving orders and making the person doing him the favour feel, instead, like his debtor. And he was very good at urging you on, simultaneously encouraging and offending, dealing out a few low blows if necessary or planting in your mind the one intrusive thought you were constantly trying to banish. I realized that it was not pure chance that, in the Plaza de la Paja, while he was golloping down those *patatas bravas*, he had reminded me of the two occasions in my long career when, to use his words, I had lost my head: the two occasions which, in principle, he alone knew about – apart from the dead, but they no long remember or complain or tell tales – and which I hated being mentioned or alluded to or touched on. Tupra was very far-sighted, and on that day in January he probably already had that possible dodge or trick up his sleeve: placing me, if I failed to take the right path, in a dilemma where the two alternatives were both worst-case scenarios. If I opted for the least worst, I would tarnish myself indelibly; while the other option didn't even bear thinking about.

What had that woman done, the one now disguised as Inés

Marzán, Celia Bayo or María Viana? What was she guilty of, that half-Northern Irish, half-*riojana* Magdalena Orúe O'Dea with such strong ties to the Basque Country? Tupra had never told me, and had even admitted that he himself didn't know: 'I don't know exactly, and it doesn't really matter,' he had said when I asked him, and I hadn't pressed him further. Then he had added: 'George will doubtless know more, but I haven't asked him for details. It would be discourteous, and it's not what we usually do. That's how we work, I scratch his back and he scratches mine. We help them with ETA and they help us with the IRA, just as those two organizations give each other moral and financial support. We can't afford to lag behind them, can we?'

But that 'them' was particularly obscure in my remit, as was that 'we', even if Tupra, as usual, was its embodiment. Machimbarrena didn't belong to CESID at the time: 'For the moment, he's an outsider, doing his own thing.' And then to make matters still more opaque, Tupra had included himself in that: 'And I won't lie to you, as far as this particular matter is concerned, I'm pretty much doing my own thing too.'

David Spedding, the no longer very new head of SIS – no one had even informed me of his appointment (when I left, McColl was still in post) – clearly knew nothing about this operation, or so I understood after Tupra's dissertation on the subject in between *patatas bravas* and before he launched into his unpleasant and ill-intentioned reminder (again in between *patatas bravas* and while being driven up the wall by that garrulous fellow Puddington or Buttcombe, whom he managed to terrify with a thrust of his little plastic fork): 'In our job, Tom, orders are labyrinthine things . . . As for knowing anything, very few high-ups want to know everything, that way they can get angry when things backfire or can justify going too far with whatever measures or actions or, indeed, reprisals they take. But anyone can lose their head. You yourself know how difficult it is to keep your head at all times. Sometimes your head has a will of its own, which is what happened to you a while back, remember.'

The whole story stank. It had right from the start, something that had certainly not escaped my notice. The high-ups of MI5, MI6 and CESID, organisms of the Crown in all cases, would know nothing of my activities in that town in the north-west and would never have authorized them. Or perhaps they did know about them and were pretending not to, those labyrinthine orders do not always begin at the top, but do always end up at the bottom, with the person who has to carry them out, with the 'sword' who crosses the Channel or comes from elsewhere. However, I hadn't been lured in by that unacknowledged, concealed suspicion of legality. It was the longing to be back inside and the pleasure of hearing Tupra asking me for a personal favour – him personally, and not the 'us' that bound me – given that he was definitely not the sort who would ever stoop to depending on his subordinates, still less asking for their help. It was now, beneath the weight of that dilemma and my fear of choosing the worst path (even if it was the least worst path), when the stench hit me. I felt pinned to the wall by it, as I never had before.

In the midst of her indignation and her feelings of powerlessness, Berta, needless to say, could sense my dread and my anxiety, from which there was now no possible escape: I would inevitably inflict harm, yes, I had to inflict the 'further harm' that would no longer touch Duncan once life's fitful fever had been ended by that nocturnal stabbing. Now he was safe, or that, at least, is how the person who had entered his unguarded bedroom and murdered sleep attempts to console himself. But how to convince someone of this when they have not yet died and will not die a peaceful death?

I transferred my problem to Berta, hypothetically that is. She had made it very easy for me.

'Really?' I said. 'But what kind of death? What if you had the chance to kill them yourself. Imagine if Miguel Ángel's murderers were handed over to you and you were given a gun or a knife, and were assured that no one would ever find out what you did to them, and that you would suffer no consequences for having taken justice into your own hands. You said they don't deserve to be treated with a clemency they've never given to anyone else. That's easy enough to say at a distance, in a fit of rage, here in your own home, safe in the assumption that others will execute them. Perhaps those same others of whom you've always had such a low opinion and of whom I am one, not that I've ever had to act with such base cruelty – fortunately. Would you shoot them in the back of the head, would you slit their throats?'

Berta bowed her head, conceding defeat. And then she smiled a knowing smile, as if acknowledging that I was quite right, and that I had placed her in an impossible and, for her, inconceivable position.

'You know I would do neither of those things, that I'd be quite incapable of that. Besides, you shouldn't take my words so literally.'

'I'm not. I know you too well. I've known you all my life. But let's imagine another scenario. *You* wouldn't kill them, but perhaps you wouldn't mind if those who took part in one of the many organized mobs of recent days were to fall on them and tear them to pieces. Would you approve if they lynched them? Up until now, everything has been very public-spirited, hands clasped behind heads, hands painted white, "mob" really isn't the right word, that's unfair. But if that commando unit, those kidnappers and killers busily checking their watches, were there before that crowd, at their mercy, I doubt very much that the multitude would have remained so stoically public-spirited or continued shouting "ETA, here's the back of my neck." You say you'd like to see them, not in prison, but dead some-how or other. What? Strung up from a lamppost or a tree by an anonymous crowd that would go unpunished? Or daubed with tar and set fire to?'

I was deliberately dredging up those barbarous forms of punishment from the past, when mobs really were mobs and there was no one to stop them; those methods could easily make a comeback, as can anything that one assumes to have been eradicated; they were sometimes still deployed in small towns in America, you occasionally read about such incidents in the newspapers. Yes, whatever is buried always rebels and struggles to throw off the earth piled on top of it. You have to keep shovelling on the earth.

Berta shuddered, she found that possibility even more horrifying than the idea of having to kill someone herself, which is probably what most people feel when they're alone and at home and not mingling with those poisonous masses egged on by poisonous leaders or exposing themselves to Redwood's five contagions, which often appear together with no antidote in sight, a solemn, scowling conjunction, which cares only for superficial feelings.

She didn't smile this time, the images I had offered her were too chilling.

'Stop it, stop it,' she said, like someone repeating a magic spell. 'You're quite right. I wouldn't want that either, it wouldn't satisfy me in the least. On the contrary: I would rise up against the lynch mob just as I would against those who led Miguel Ángel into the woods, forced him to kneel down with his hands tied and then shot him, poor boy, such needless suffering, what did they achieve apart from being hated by everyone except their fellow terrorists, who applaud them from the stalls. How many people have they killed so far?'

'I don't know. Over seven hundred, I think.' I did, in fact, know exactly how many with a precision that was possible at the time. More than seven hundred and seventy, including the young man from Ermua.

'That many? How can there have been so many deaths?'

'We tend to forget that there have been far bloodier years than this. In 1978, there were more than sixty murders; in 1979 more than seventy; in 1980, more than ninety. And we endured them all.'

She remained silent for a moment. People banish uncomfortable memories, and numbers both overwhelm and habituate, people don't think about what's happening while it's happening. Tupra had been right in that regard: 'we' are the only ones who don't forget, well, us and organizations bent on revenge. 'Hatred is an emotion unknown to us, and we must not succumb to it. We don't "do" passion, but time doesn't pass. For us, what happened ten years ago is yesterday or even today, and is happening right now.'

'What a waste,' she said at last. 'But you're right: they should catch them and put them in prison, and catch them as soon as possible, so that they don't do the same thing again.'

Yes, that's the most widespread feeling, far more so than the idea proclaimed by virtuous and hypocritical souls who demand that murderers be rehabilitated and reassimilated into society, distorting the words of the great Cesare Beccaria and other just men and women. This was also the idea that had led us to the decision to neutralize Magdalena Orúe by whatever means, her demise precipitated by events, and we were at serious risk of being entirely unjust, even mere murderers, but of the kind who will never undergo rehabilitation and who are already assimilated into society.

'Precisely,' I said. 'So that they don't do the same thing again.'

She again fell silent, a silence that was thoughtful and sad, rather than angry. I had managed to steer her away from the subject filling everyone's mind at the time, mine being filled in turn by the duties that awaited me. I was sure Berta wouldn't insist, that she would let the matter rest. It was now my turn to disperse the mist she had created, to return her to less sombre subjects, to continue our lunch. We had both been sitting there, knives and forks in hand; luckily, it was a cold lunch.

It wasn't that difficult to divert her, thanks to her basically cheerful nature, which quickly grew bored with glum, surly states of mind. And she had not changed, even though she had more than enough reason to. It helped, too, that she was feeling unexpectedly well disposed towards me on that Saturday. Yes, she was kind and affectionate, in a restrained, prudent way, nor did she ask me many questions despite sensing how weighed down I was by my responsibilities. After all those years, she had grown used to not asking questions.

The remaining days and weeks in Ruán – I wasn't even keeping count, it might have been three or only two weeks – sped past, as always happens when you don't want them to, when you want time to stretch out endlessly and for neither night nor the following day to come. I didn't honestly think I would make any progress, light rarely breaks through at the very last moment and solutions tend not to rain down from the heavens. But during the day I laboured away as best I could. I tried to spend a little more time with Celia Bayo, whom I had woefully neglected, but having a couple of drinks with her at a fashionable bar served only to confirm that her very simple soul always won through. She had wept bitter, and apparently genuine, tears over the death of Miguel Ángel Blanco, but she was once again busy with her many projects and social activities, and very proud about something or other that Liudwino was planning, but which, for the moment, she had been forbidden to reveal. There would be local elections in 1999, and it occurred to me that he was perhaps intending to stand for mayor, having set up his own party with the support of his many beneficiaries. If he did stand, he stood a good chance of winning, for, as I said earlier, he had a talent for impressing people, and it would take years for them to be undeceived, such processes are always very slow, or they were before the advent of social media, no, what am I saying, *with* social media the process is even slower. Far stranger things had happened, for example, in the south, in Marbella, a wealthy population had completely fallen under the spell of a coarse, vulgar, grotesque individual with a criminal record. One must never forget that Spaniards from all over Spain – even those who don't consider themselves to be Spanish – have a deep-seated tendency to elect the worst possible leaders on offer and to cheer on whatever tyrants are imposed on them, as long as they make nice promises and seem pleasant enough, even if they have larceny written all over their faces and are clearly very nasty pieces of work.

I didn't try to draw Celia out, so as not to tempt her to say more – it would be easy enough to get her to talk – besides, her husband's plans didn't interest me in the least. I didn't care what happened in 1999, or what would happen to the *ruaneses* and their once noble and loyal city, I had only a few grim weeks ahead of me there and then I would be leaving. I couldn't waste the few hours left to me on Celia Bayo, and so I took a chance and ruled her out completely, I decided that the reason she appeared on that list of three was overzealousness on the part of Pérez Nuix and Machimbarrena, because of when she had arrived in Ruán and because her past was somewhat obscure. However, that's how it is with most human beings, the past is, by definition, obscure, even for those of us who can remember it.

On Monday 21 July, I returned to María Viana's garden, as we had agreed, in order to resume my lessons with the children, which were supposed to last for the rest of the month and for the whole of August. When the moment came to stop them, I would invent some excuse. The moment when I would have to put an end to my sojourn in Ruán and disappear for ever.

No one knew my true identity, and there would be no record of Miguel Centurión Aguilera anywhere, he would not appear in any archive or registry: and if some honest local policeman – like the one years later in Santander investigating the death of Natividad Garayo – did try and track me down and find me, I could always seek temporary refuge in England, and Tupra would use his infinite list of contacts in positions of power to shut him up. And no one would miss me, I hadn't formed any strong bonds there as I had in that English town a long time ago; a time that was gradually fading into nothing. Soon, in that Spanish town in the north-west, I would be just a shadow that passed and left no trace, a mist driven away by the wind and by the bells.

In the final throes of my investigation, María Viana seemed to me potentially more interesting, not that I saw her as the embodiment of Magdalena Orúe either. This feeling doubtless had its basis in the fact that I found her so attractive, but the blame lay more squarely with Tupra, who had so clearly pointed the finger at Inés Marzán – attributing that clarity of vision to me – and fixed that idea in my head. Nevertheless, I felt obliged to try again with María, even though that particular road was closed. There was no way of probing further, the only possibility was to get her to talk and talk until she made some inadvertently revealing comment, but I didn't go to her house in order to chat with her, and once my English lessons ended, I would be surplus to requirements.

We gradually, imperceptibly, lengthened out those fragmentary conversations: the week beginning 21 July, I offered to go there on a daily basis to make up the hours we had lost, and she accepted gladly. It was on Thursday the 24th, when Folcuino, together with that unrepentant hunter Morbecq and some other lout from Cangas de Onís sporting a silly *franquista* moustache, had gone off to Ribadesella or Ribadeo for the weekend festivities of Santiago the Apostle and to sort out some business affair or other, and when she was presumably feeling more communicative or simply bored, that she invited me to join her solitary lunch (the children ate earlier and took a long siesta to protect them from the hot sun).

We chatted about the usual things people talk about when they don't really know each other and don't want to launch into their life story, which no one is interested in anyway, besides, María Viana was always very reserved and I had no choice but to be equally reserved: we talked about novels and films, and agreed that really good authors – who, according to her, were getting fewer in number – managed 'magically' (her rather affected word) to make us believe their stories and passionately engage with them, even when they made it plain that the stories were false, the product of their imagination, pure invention, that they did not exist in the reality that both they and we inhabited.

'It's not really so very odd,' she said after this prologue. 'It's not even that surprising when you consider how ready most of us are to believe what others tell us. I know nothing about you and, besides, you seem very honest, but if you were to start recounting your life à la David Copperfield, I would believe it all however improbable. We are predisposed (well, I am) not to question, not to be suspicious, to assume that no one, fantasists and fabulists apart, would bother lying to us for no reason. We are easily deceived and not only by stories. We can be persuaded by theories, speeches, lies and sermons. There are people determined to explain the world, or a part of the world, and to persuade us that their view is the right one. There are people who promise us happiness or stability or security for our children; or who declare their unconditional, eternal love, swearing that they will always be by our side whatever happens, that they will protect us from persecution and threat. These are convincing promises, but, however well intentioned, impossible to keep, and yet we believe them when we hear them. And when you think about it, the main reason for that is quite absurd: we simply don't see why we shouldn't believe them. We think: no one is obliged to commit themselves, and if they do, then they must mean it. Why would anyone lie to us for no reason; why would anyone give us an adulterated version of history that leads us to believe we have been treated unfairly and are victims? No one wants to feel like a victim, and yet nowadays, it seems as if we're all actively encouraged to feel like victims, cursed since the beginning of time.'

I didn't really know what she was referring to but, just in case, I clung to what interested me most, and which current events were handing me on a plate, without my even trying. That word 'persecution' had aroused my interest, since it didn't fit María Viana's situation at all, but it certainly chimed with that of Magdalena Orúe. But that was all it was, a word. I said:

'To a large extent, something of the sort has just cost that poor young man Miguel Ángel Blanco his life, and many others before him. An adulterated version of history that has triumphed over too many others. It's not like the Irish problem, where there is, after all, a great deal to justify it. Northern Ireland should, I suppose, be part of Ireland, although I don't know a lot about the subject. But the Basque Country, or its territories, voluntarily joined the Crown of Castile in the fourteenth century, I believe, preserving all of its privileges, and the Basques were never oppressed by anyone. One indication is the number of Basque names you find in the Americas, many of them important, powerful people, or among bankers and politicians and industrialists all over Spain. They have never been marginalized, on the contrary. They've been involved in the country's biggest enterprises and projects, and wield a lot of influence. Anyway, that's my impression and what I've been led to believe, not by what I was taught at school, which is obviously not to be trusted, but based on what I've read. Not that I've studied it in depth, because I find all those different nationalisms deeply boring. Maybe it's because I'm from Madrid, but all that stuff about ancestors, fairy-tale histories and comic-book mythologies, about traditions and attachment to the soil, just depresses me, I can't help it; it just grates on me. I find even Ruán's pride in itself rather odd.' And then without a pause, I added: 'Your surname comes from Navarra, doesn't it? Well, Viana is in Navarra, which, of course, the imperialist Basques and ETA aspire to annexing. Isn't Cesare Borgia buried there?'

María wasn't interested in this particular line of conversation, or for some reason she found it awkward. Nor did she seem prepared to talk about her origins. She merely dismissed my modest trap by brushing it aside:

'Oh, there are Vianas everywhere, there are dozens of them even in Madrid, and of course I'm not from Navarra. Do I look as if I was? As for Cesare Borgia, I've no idea. What would he be doing in Viana? I always imagine him in Rome poisoning people, so he's more likely to have died in Italy.'

I didn't want to go off on a tangent and tell her what I knew about the subject, so I let it ride, hoping she might say something about the Basque question, or about Northern Ireland. She was the one who had mentioned the adulteration of history and the need to feel like a victim, although who knows what was in her mind at the time. After a few seconds, when I still said nothing, she returned to what appeared to interest her most, so much so that she spoke meditatively as she stirred her coffee (we had already reached the coffee stage by then) as if she were unmelodramatically condemning herself.

'My big problem has always been that I'm too gullible, so it's hardly surprising that I swallow good novels and films whole, just as I did when I was a child. As you get older, you convince yourself that you've left that gullibility behind you, that you've put an end to it, but it turns out you haven't. It must be a character flaw, a weakness for which there is no cure, not at least in my case. Age doesn't change it, nor do experiences or disappointments or disillusionments. Nor does regret. At the very next opportunity, you're taken in all over again, you trust what anyone says unless they're a flagrant fraudster like our friend Liudwino. It doesn't matter how often you find out someone has lied to you. Each time is like new, each new person is new and you daren't condemn them out of hand. You, I fear, could easily deceive me, after all, you're new. I know, it's the fate of the ingenuous. Or worse, of idiots. Almost no one will admit to being an idiot, just as no one will admit to having bad taste or being a bad person. I accepted that I'm an idiot a long time ago. It's not a nice idea, but there are worse things. I'm not complaining, and I would not, of course, consider myself to be the poor victim of those who have deceived me or encouraged me to make wrong or even disastrous decisions, you don't know they're wrong at the time, you think they're the right decisions. Every deception requires the collaboration of the deceived, who is equally responsible for her actions.' She paused and lit a cigarette. 'The other person is just doing his job, isn't he? He's pursuing his goal or his whim, or looking to profit from it. He would get nowhere if it wasn't for the credulity of the gullible, and I have come to accept that I am very gullible. I'm not perhaps such an imbecile that I can't get through life without falling over again and again, but I've done my fair share of that. At this stage in my life, I'm not going to beat myself up about it, after all, things haven't gone that badly for me.' And she gave an appreciative look at the things around her, the garden, the servants, the house. 'Would you agree that blame has to be shared? Not fifty–fifty of course.' She quickly drank her coffee, and appeared to emerge from her abstracted state, from the serene malediction she had placed upon herself. 'Are you gullible, Miguel? Or are you a natural sceptic? If the latter, I envy you.'

She had never called me by my first name before, or indeed by any name: 'Listen, would you mind . . . ?', 'May I ask you a favour? If it's not too much bother . . .', that is how she usually addressed me, with no name. Her question caught me by surprise, even though the long preamble should have prepared me. I took a little time before replying – the time it took me to light a cigarette and lean one elbow on the table to look as if I were giving the matter deep thought – Centurión should really be the one to answer, not Nevinson, and

Centurión was a grey fellow in principle, whose biography contained few remarkable events. In fact, he lacked any history, few details had been invented, it hadn't seemed necessary. However, she caught me in one of those moments or days when those of us engaged in this profession are suddenly unsure who we are, or find it hard to entirely renounce the person we have been for most of the time, since birth and childhood.

My recent encounter with Berta was probably the reason for this: it had provoked in me a vague desire to go back to being Tomás Nevinson. Not the one who had returned in 1994, disenchanted and exhausted after his long demise, not the reflective, worn-down soul, immersed in all his very worst memories, in a near vegetative state, the one who had half-heartedly resumed his work at the embassy and occasionally sought distraction with the vigorous Pérez Nuix. Not the one who had gradually been fading away since the reappearance of Tupra on 6 January 1997. That one was useless and apathetic. No, the Tomás Nevinson from early on: the Tomás Nevinson of the British Institute and the Colegio Estudio, in the Madrid streets of Martínez Campos and Miguel Ángel, as well as Calle Jenner, where he lived with his parents and his brothers. The one who did not see evil everywhere, who had neither suffered nor inflicted 'further harm' or any harm at all . . . However fanciful, this did not attenuate my desire. A vague desire, but a desire nonetheless.

Yes, I could deceive and, indeed, was deceiving that self-confessed gullible fool, María Viana, just as I was deceiving the simple mechanism that was Celia Bayo, although for her this would have no grave consequences, and of course the independent, sceptical Inés Marzán, for whom there might be one irreversible consequence. I had devoted a large part of my life to the unsuspecting and even to the suspicious and cautious, trying and succeeding in getting the latter to lower their guard and fall asleep while on sentry duty.

Once, years ago, when I had to confess to her, without going into detail, what I did as a profession, Berta had criticized the nature of my activities. She had reminded me of a couple of scenes from *Henry V* and placed them before me like a kind of mirror that both contradicted and cornered me, I could remember it well even though some time had passed. I had fallen into her dialectical trap – she always had been clever, very clever – but I had devised a way of partially refuting her arguments: that this is the nature of wars, and there always are latent or subterranean or hidden wars, all of which have a basis in deceit, besides, someone has to be responsible for the defence of the Realm while you others blithely come and go about your daily business with not a thought for anything else, with no fear of being the victims of explosions or gunshots; we are the ones who allow apparently normal life and peace to exist, for the trains to leave on time and for the metro and buses and bakeries and postmen to exist, all those things that we barely notice and take for granted, when in reality, their existence is a miracle; well, I can't quite remember now what exactly I said in my defence. And yet, and yet . . .

At the time, I had become an enthusiast convinced of the importance of our work, even a patriot of England, the country I was serving. Now, though, as I sat talking with María Viana, I felt weary of deceiving, because, for no reason I could identify, I respected her and also felt secretly, powerfully drawn to her, an attraction that would remain forever unspoken. Perhaps I felt weary because what awaited me was the most unpleasant task of all, the one that ran most counter to my ideals, and I might even have to carry it out on that self-confessed gullible fool who did not deserve to die, certainly not on that afternoon. However, I couldn't shake off a sense of alarm and couldn't help speculating about what wrong, regrettable decisions she was referring to and that even repentance could not cure. She was doubtless thinking about her private life, about her acceptance of conditions that turned out to be an abject disappointment, about the husband who treated her with such scorn and who kicked small dogs and no longer desired her, whereas wielding a sword was enough to give him a hard-on. But it was also possible that she was remembering what she should remember every day: the acts and omissions of Magdalena Orúe O'Dea, which did warrant repentance, for those who do or can repent, something terrorists find an uphill struggle. Who knows.

Her question was still floating in the air. Yes, I, too, was gullible, I had been in my youth and I still was, however unlikely or embarrassing that might seem. I must have been to have ended up where I was now, lost in Ruán and in the unimaginable (I didn't count Pérez Nuix's warning in Madrid, because, at the time, it seemed too remote and unreal; I should have known that she rarely spoke in jest). Finding myself obliged to go against my most deep-rooted beliefs: you don't raise your hand against a woman and you certainly don't kill her. Women are sometimes spared in massacres, even if only so that they can grieve and tell their stories and be the warning voice.

'Yes, I'm afraid I am gullible,' I said. 'As are most people. You have to be pretty cynical to dispense with trust altogether. But I'm not sure what you mean. What disastrous decisions did you take? And why so many regrets? One wouldn't think so to look at you. All in all, things don't seem to have gone that badly for you.' And now it was my turn to take in our surroundings with one eloquent glance.

María gave an embarrassed smile.

'Forgive me, Miguel, for ranting on like that and for no reason. I just let myself be carried along by my absurd thoughts, it must be the hot summer sun. They're the kind of thoughts that keep me awake at night, on some nights anyway, when they catch me off guard. They don't usually bother me during the day. And you're right, I should keep any complaints about my life for when I'm alone, because we all complain about our lot when we're alone, don't we? We all have our discontents, our frustrations and a long list of mistakes we've made. But just as I freely admit to having been foolish, I also agree that I've been very lucky. Who knows what hole I might have ended up in. Forget about it please, and forgive me.'

I could get nothing further from her. I tried to return to the subject a few minutes later, to draw her out in the hope that she would confirm that she was thinking about her marriage and the despotic Gausi, who was perhaps holding her prisoner, and not about something more serious, about crimes committed. But she had abandoned her meditative tone, had turned off that particular tap. She was probably astonished that she had turned it on in the first place, that she had allowed herself to do so in the presence of a new person, a stranger, and a temporary employee. She came close to resuming that tone shortly before we said goodbye, for it was high time I left: she was definitely in need of a siesta and I needed time to mull over what she had said.

'Thank you very much for lunch, María. It's been most enjoyable,' I said.

'We can do it another day, if you like. We still have the whole summer ahead of us.' This sounded like a polite formula, not a real offer or the expression of a sincere or insincere desire on her part.

'I'm not sure your husband would be particularly thrilled to have lunch with me.'

She smiled again, with no embarrassment now, but as if to make light of what she was about to say, for it was not in her nature to speak ill of her family members.

'Well, you never can tell. He only likes what he likes.' This was a complete tautology, an elegant way of saying nothing. 'And he likes to keep very much to himself. Besides, you've only met him a few times.'

I couldn't tell her that, in my videos, I had 'met' him far more often than she imagined. Both him and, of course, her.

'I suppose so. A man in his position can choose to do only what interests and amuses him. If only we all had that privilege.' I held out my hand in a gesture of gratitude, although the Spanish custom between a man and a woman is to kiss each other fleetingly on the cheek. This is precisely what she did, as if to tell me that, in her eyes, I was not a mere employee. 'There's just one thing – if you don't mind.' That gesture had intrigued me. 'You said earlier that you could have ended up in any hole. I don't know how you ended up where you are now, but I find that hard to believe. I mean, I can't imagine you ending up in any kind of hole, given the way you are and the way you look. You know you enjoy the respect of everyone in Ruán, don't you? No one criticizes you or envies you, which is really quite extraordinary in Spain.'

She smiled for the third time, modestly, but without blushing.

'Yes, it would be extraordinary if it were true. That German word to describe feeling pleasure at someone else's misfortune should have been invented in Spain. No region is immune from it, however hard they try to pretend they're completely different from all the others. Yet another reason to feel how very fortunate I am. But anyone can fall down a hole at any moment in their life. Even those who have prospered and appear to be untouchable. Just look how many of them have ended up in prison. There are no guarantees in life, and we should know that.'

Yes, that night, looking out of my window at the river and the bridge, I went over in my mind what María Viana had said. Unlike Celia Bayo, I could not, to my great regret, rule out her completely. Of the three candidates, she was the one I had grown most fond of, the one who inspired in me the most sympathy and the most compassion, however unjustified. When you view someone with compassionate eyes – my gaze was not lascivious, merely thoughtfully sexual – this inevitably clouds your vision, or conditions and skews it, and inclines you to judge or think favourably of that person. If you're a teacher, and I had now pretended to be a teacher twice, in two different towns and in two different countries, you unwittingly fix your gaze on the face you find most pleasing or that inspires most confidence. Nevertheless, her post-prandial, summer ramblings were too ambiguous, too open to interpretation for me to strike her from the short list that was far too long for my taste.

During those highly charged July days, everything seemed too much, I wished there were no list, I wished I could erase from my life that wretched day in January when I had refused to look at the photos of those three women, only to take them home with me. The last thing I wanted was to put a bullet in that body, that face, down some alleyway with my old revolver, or for my hands to close about her slender neck. Perhaps as slender as Anne Boleyn's. But I wasn't going to use a swift, merciful sword, like a whistle once it has left the lips or like a sudden strong gust of wind.

XIII

It was the evening of Monday 28 July when the phone rang, and Tupra's very English voice interrupted my contemplation of the lethargic waters of the Lesmes river as they slipped into the dark with exasperating slowness, exasperating for anyone impatient for night to fall and for the false oblivion of sleep. I made the most of every moment of inactivity or respite, the kind of respite the world provides even in the worst of circumstances or when the mind is at its most agitated. In fact, I sought out such moments, watched for them. Not that I forgot about the task in hand, given how crucial it was for the two innocent women, but I allowed the deadline given me by Reresby in London to slide – he had given me two weeks or, if I was lucky, three – and more than one week had passed already, I preferred not to keep too close an eye on the agonizing passage of time, on the contrary: I tried to make each day resemble that holiday when 'the countryman sallies forth in the morning to view the fields after the hot night of endless, cooling lightning, the thunder still rumbling in the distance . . .'.

In the days before and after that call, I visited places and monuments I had only seen distractedly or in passing, if that. I went on a guided tour of the Cathedral and listened to the guide's explanations like any other tourist. And, naturally, I visited Santa Catalina and El Cantuariense, San Bernabé and San Juan Puerta Latina, as well as Santa Águeda and Santa Decapitación, even though, at the time, those two names seemed like doom-laden reminders, bad omens, the latter for obvious reasons, the former because I knew the legend of that saint born in Catania, Sicily, in the third century no less. She was a beautiful woman from a noble family, who, having made a vow of chastity, rejected the amorous advances of Quintiniano or Quintiano, who was prefect during the brief reign of Emperor Decius, and, in response, she met with a terrible martyrdom, including having her breasts pincered and mutilated. According to Jacobus de Voragine in his *Golden Legend*, St Peter appeared to her in prison and healed her wounds, but Agatha or Gadea, as she is also known in Castile, was so stubborn that she would only allow Jesus Christ in person to heal her, and the apostle had a very hard job persuading her that he really was who he was and that the Lord had sent him. Once her breasts had been fully restored, she was then subjected to further cruel tortures at the hands of that vulgar prefect. Apparently, people invoke her name as protection against fires and lightning strikes, she is the patron saint of her native town of Catania as well as of bell-ringers, which would explain why Ruán has for centuries had a beautiful church dedicated to her. Despite Jacobus de Voragine being a thirteenth-century Dominican friar, and therefore bent on dealing out justice, I do read him now and then to frighten and amuse myself in about equal measure.

During those troubling times, I wasn't keen on the name El Cantuariense either, since I shared a name with Thomas Becket, to whom the church was dedicated. According to Voragine, that shared name means 'abyss' and a couple of other completely different things, but I'm not sure how reliable he was as an etymologist. I hadn't been friends with María Viana or Inés Marzán, unlike the long friendship that existed between the Archbishop of Canterbury and his inadvertent executioner Henry II; given that they had been boon companions in their youthful adventures, who would have thought that the latter would end up calling out loud for someone to rid him of 'this turbulent priest'? (Well, I suppose you might say that I'd had a few adventures of my own with Inés Marzán, what else would you call them?) But what awaited me now was to carry out just such an act of betrayal, or something similar, for it was definitely a death project or a blood mission. Again according to that very righteous Dominican, who usually applauds the excesses both of divine wrath and of his heroines and heroes (such zeal was rewarded, for, in 1292, he was appointed archbishop of Genoa), St Thomas Becket made a mistake after his death or, rather, his remains did: when news spread that they could work miracles (restore sight to the blind, hearing to the deaf, the ability to walk to the lame and even life to the dead), an English lady made a barefoot pilgrimage to his tomb before which she prostrated herself, and her frivolous request was for the saint to change the colour of her eyes so that she could appear more beautiful. As a punishment for her frivolity, she stood up and found that she couldn't see at all, and so she immediately pleaded with the saint to return her eyes to their original colour and condition, which the saint agreed to do with great reluctance and much tut-tutting. As for the impulsive knights who had slain the Archbishop in the Cathedral cloister, they suffered a cruel posthumous revenge, as Voragine recounts with punitive pleasure: one bit off his own fingers; the body of another suddenly began to putrify; the third was paralysed; while the fourth fell victim to several terrible attacks of madness. They were very vengeful things, those restless relics.

Although I was obliged to anticipate what I must do, I didn't foresee myself doing anything very terrible, on the contrary: I was thinking only of the gentlest, least painful methods possible, so that my victim wouldn't even know what was happening or hardly at all, so that I could avoid causing her any great harm, as if there were any greater harm than death itself. My intention was to achieve for her what is promised in those words of John Donne's and which I have never entirely understood: 'One short sleep past, we wake eternally, And Death shall be no more.' With poetry, being bilingual doesn't always help.

This is why I was dreading that phone call from Tupra. I was almost certain that when it came, it would be to tell me, 'Right, time's up,' and that he would add one of his characteristic phrases in the language in which we spoke together: 'Don't linger or delay.' This was usually the unequivocal signal that he had seen the whole panorama and had taken a decision, which must be carried out at once and with no slacking – it was impossible afterwards to go on thinking 'Not yet, not yet'. He had said it to me in the past and I had heard him say it to others too, usually accompanied by some other polite formula ('if you wouldn't mind', 'please, please'), which I knew was a bad sign, an ill omen, the prelude to a telling-off or an argument if you resisted or offered a counter-argument. Those words merely underlined the fact that the order must be carried out urgently.

During those days of waiting and wandering in that town in the north-west, I listened to the news almost obsessively for any further action on the part of ETA. I would breathe more easily each night, relieved that the day had ended with no new attacks or murders. I felt a sense of personal relief: it meant that Magdalena Orúe O'Dea had not been woken up and was still asleep, and that, given the general fear that the terrorist organization would again marshal its resources, her actions had become even more my responsibility. It had been two weeks since Miguel Ángel Blanco's murder, and, for the moment, ETA had not gone on the offensive or responded angrily and arrogantly to the general repudiation they had suffered. Their members and their 'armed wing' had been shaken, perhaps for the first time, when they discovered that many Basques – including those who would normally cheer them on loyally – had condemned them and turned their backs on them. True, the PNV and their leader Arzalluz did what they could to redeem them. However, despite the fears of the upper echelons in government and of Machimbarrena in the shadows, the ETA leaders appeared to have retreated to their lair to lick their wounds, something previously almost unknown.

In fact, they did not kill again until 5 September of that same year, 1997, this time, it was a policeman blown up by a limpet bomb attached to the underside of his car. And in what remained of that year, they only killed another two people. I say 'only' because in the first six months of 1998, when they felt they had regained support and had even been forgiven, six people died, including the wife of that councillor from Seville I mentioned before, shot in the back like him, a doubly 'heroic' deed, with both victims unarmed, as had been the case with so many others. We didn't know then that ETA would wait fifty-five days – which was a long time for them – to spill more blood after the Blanco killing, and so every new dawn was a threat: terrorists, with a few exceptions, tend to kill early in the day, around breakfast time, when sleepy, unsuspecting people are going to work.

I hadn't forgotten the words of warning Tupra had given me in his office in Cockspur Street: 'If Molly O'Dea returns to active service after all this time, she won't do so in Spain or with ETA, but in Ulster or in London. In reality, she's more Northern Irish than anything. She was on loan from the IRA, so her loyalty is to them and not to their idiotic Basque imitators.' He was very dismissive of the latter, as we are of things we don't have to deal with directly. And so, as far as I could in Ruán, I also followed the news from Belfast and London, when there was any news. Things seemed to be on the wane there and had been for some time. After all, in less than nine months' time the Good Friday or Belfast Agreement would be signed (on 10 April 1998, but we didn't know that then), and its preparation, its advances and retreats, were slow and costly, as are all renunciations that suddenly deprive generations of conscientious murderers of a purpose; and in that long intermittent war there were murderers on both sides, as it's always worth repeating and reminding people today, when no one knows anything about anything.

A few months or weeks ago, I read in the newspapers that young Basques under thirty, with very few exceptions (it was not dissimilar in other regions either), had no idea who Miguel Ángel Blanco was nor what ETA had done to him. Quite a number had only very vague memories of the terrorist organization itself, or else believed the airbrushed fallacies passed on by their elders and their slavish followers. It's just over two decades since 1997. It isn't as if they were being asked about historical figures like Daoiz and Velarde or King Joseph I, who, despite all, appears on the list of Spanish monarchs: he reigned for fifteen years and took certain initiatives, not all of them bad. But assassins also have the ability to minimize or erase their crimes (I don't mean justify them, that's part of the job); to blow away their fetid mist with the wind or with an insistent breeze that finally transforms them into an illegible stone or ash on the sleeve of an old man who then brushes it off. Easy enough to do in complicit, shamefaced societies.

Tupra's voice startled me and made the sombre waters of the Lesmes river suddenly flare into life. And before he could even say a word, I was already imagining the worst, assuming that the moment had arrived: one woman must die by my trembling, clumsy hands, or three by other more expert hands, just as, four centuries earlier, other hands had crossed the Channel to carry out their task with delicacy and skill, except that, on this occasion, they would be heading the other way, towards the Continent.

'Hello, Bertie, how are things?' Absurdly I addressed him with that familiar diminutive, as if this might temper whatever he had to tell me.

'Listen, Tom, I've had some interesting news. Nothing definitive, because it can't be, but you can judge whether it's enough to clear up any final doubts.'

Those words pronounced sentence on Inés Marzán, my personal *géante*, whose slopes I had scaled rather more directly than Baudelaire. At any rate, this was an added inconvenience; once you have consensually entered another's flesh, it's almost impossible to inflict violence on it, or so I assumed, although the news is continually proving the opposite to be true. I had never been in such a situation, I had never even slapped a woman.

'What's happened?'

'Well, nothing really. Ruán is the place where things should be happening. Is there anything you should tell me? You haven't phoned since you were here in London, and that was days ago. And according to Pat, you haven't phoned her either. You've made very little use of her in fact. Anyway, George is still getting very uptight and keeps urging me to make haste, people so easily forget that a favour is a favour not a commitment, and suddenly start making demands. And when I say George, that's tantamount to saying his bosses-to-be. It's not enough for them that the terrorists haven't yet killed again, because who knows what they might do tomorrow.'

I hadn't told either Pat or Tupra about my post-prandial chat with María Viana. On the one hand, the things she had said and which I had found so troubling were too inconsistent and could be understood in various ways. On the other hand, I didn't want to make it easy for Tupra to point the finger at her or to think that I was. He saw more and saw more clearly than I did, that much was true, and this meant that he sometimes saw what wasn't there. He could even see without using his eyes, through words and other people's descriptions. As I said earlier: fortunately or unfortunately for him, Tupra believed he did know things beforehand, or, rather, he not only believed he knew, he did know; even more unfortunate were the people upon whom his sharp, suspicious, intuitive eye alighted. There was no point having him fix his sights on María, not for a single moment; I had grown accustomed to the idea that, one unreal night, or on some as yet hypothetical day, I would take Inés Marzán's life. I had found it almost unbearable, the process of accustoming myself to that very real possibility. And Tupra was nothing if not efficient: he was capable of broadening out that death project, just to be sure. 'Take out the two most suspicious ones and, in exchange, we'll let the third one live. Better to go too far than not far enough.' I couldn't rule out that response either, he, too, was prone to forget that a favour is a favour and not a commitment.

'I didn't call you because there was nothing new to report here,' I said. 'But you do have news, you say.'

'There are two elements which are actually one and the same, or at least point in the same direction. We've made an exhaustive comparison of Miss Pontipee's drawing with other images in our archive and other archives too. As you see, it's taken us a while.'

He made a pause, which he perhaps intended to be dramatic. In this he failed. I wasn't going to appear impatient, I wasn't going to give him that pleasure. I said nothing and waited. When he continued his pause, though, I showed the bare minimum of interest:

'And?'

'As I told you, we can't be certain. Miss Pontipee is very good at drawing portraits, but all she had to go on was your description of that man de la Rica.'

'I know. I gave her that description, I was there, remember.'

'That's enough, Tom. Enough.' He was annoyed with me, and I had achieved my tiny goal.

'All right, Tupra.' I went back to addressing him by his surname. It was clear that he was going to give me some bad news and some even worse orders. 'Does he look like someone already known to you, someone on your files? Does he resemble someone from ETA or the IRA?'

'There is quite a likeness, a resemblance. It's just a shame you didn't take a photo, after all, you had the means at your disposal. And don't say "known to you". Say "known to us".'

At first, I took this jibe on the chin – they always hurt more, jibes made by those who are at fault and have no right to come out with them – then I returned it to him with a dig at his friend Machimbarrena, that spoiled Spanish brat whose *franquista* aroma escaped Tupra.

'It's even more of a shame that your dear friend George couldn't instal microphones and cameras in Inés Marzán's apartment. Then you wouldn't just have an image of the fat guy, you'd be able to hear him talking and see him moving. Then again, given how "clever" they proved to be in placing them in the other houses, we would probably just have a video of him having a pee, if, that is, he went to the bathroom, I can't remember now.' Tupra ignored my remark, as if it had nothing to do with him, and so I responded then to his other jibe. 'When you say "known to us", do you mean that I'd seen that fellow de la Rica before?'

'I'm not sure if you met him in person, but you might have seen a photo, I don't remember. Of course, we lost track of him twenty years ago, that's the date of the last image we have. People can change a lot in twenty years. Or not. Anyway, didn't you say that when you met, he stopped to look at you, to observe you? As if he recognized you. That's what you said, isn't it?'

I might have mentioned this, and it was certainly true: for one or two seconds, when he first saw me, I had the feeling that he either knew or recognized me. But since I didn't recognize him, I assumed his look of momentary acknowledgement was merely the kind of spontaneous or automatic sympathy everyone tries to show when a friend, male or female, whom 'we've known for ever, who is almost family', introduces us to a friend of theirs. And who knows, perhaps, as they walked back from the church where they had met as they were leaving, Inés Marzán had explained to him the more intimate nature of our relationship – she would never have said 'promising', that would be too strong a word for a woman like her, a natural sceptic when it came to matters of the heart, or whatever people call them nowadays, when every word is under surveillance.

A faint light dawned, a dull light like that of a lighter flickering out and immediately burning your fingers, because I preferred not to tie up loose ends that were being tied anyway whether I liked it or not: it was equivalent to recognizing that I had made a considerable blunder, or accepting that my memory had definitely got worse. We all think this is something that happens to other people and not to us, and yet it was perfectly normal that it should happen to me, after such an unstable life full of hard knocks, including a period of non-existence. Besides, time passes and fills up with new incidents and episodes that drive out those that have expired or that you had assumed were closed. As far as I was concerned, the episode at which I had not been present, and which I only knew about from Berta's desperate report, was as dead as those who had unleashed it. One should never believe what people tell you, still less their version of events.

'Do you mean that Berta *did* see him in person?' I finally dared to ask, so as to get used to the idea little by little by little.

'If it's him, yes, she did for a time, and she certainly won't have forgotten him, his face will be burned onto her memory,' said Tupra in a matter-of-fact tone, apparently unaware that he really should have followed up this figurative expression with an 'appropriately enough'. 'That's if it is him. Your description was a pretty good fit. He wouldn't even have changed that much, apart from the greying hair. He must look younger than he doubtless is. We don't even know his age. In fact, we haven't actually had news of him since then, some twenty years ago, because he doesn't appear to have done anything. There's something else, though, the second element, although again it doesn't prove anything. Coincidences are natural, as you and I both know, but two coincidences are less natural than one.'

While I was talking to him on the phone, I continued to gaze out at the bridge and the river, for we do tend to fix our gaze on an object when we're listening to bad news, and the scene minimally calmed my growing agitation, which I was trying to conceal in my voice and the way I was speaking, I wanted to face up to that news with as much aplomb as possible and it helped me to see that landscape and those people, all utterly indifferent to my problems, which did not exist for them and, therefore, up to a point, did not exist at all.

It was one evening towards the end of July, with night coming on, in that slow, slow way it has at that time of year in Spain and in England, the sun seemingly reluctant to set. The bridge was very crowded, for as I mentioned before, Ruán did not empty out in the summer, on the contrary: its comparatively cool climate attracted tourists and summer visitors who swarmed to north and south, most of them in search of relaxation or fun or getting sozzled. La Demanda would be packed to the gills, because during the summer season it was open every day and its owner didn't take a single night off, well, she had to make the most of that boom time.

I imagined Inés Marzán gliding busily about between the tables accompanied by the soft tack-tack of her stilettos, moving as if her feet didn't even touch the ground, but hovered above it, as she did her best to keep her composure and her cheerful demeanour despite the clamour of voices and the rudeness of some of her coarser customers. Dressed for summer in lighter, briefer clothes, her curvaceous figure, her firm, almost abundant breasts, her large, strong calves, her pert, prominent buttocks could not fail to attract the attention of her randier, more drunken clients. I thought frivolously: 'She may have a large, strange and distinctly unkissable face, but she'll be quite a loss.' This, to my surprise, was a thought worthy of Tupra, and unforgivable as were so many other things my former boss came out with. But that is what I thought, and hopefully it was only a thought, like the one that crossed the mind of the writer Reck-Malleczewen in the Osteria Bavaria, and which had no consequences. If only it had, but at the time he didn't know the full scale of what would happen, killing is not such an extreme act if you're fully aware of who it is you're killing and how many will be saved as a result, but this is something almost no one knows and so almost everyone recoils from the task. Perhaps you had to adopt Tupra's cool view of facts and events, either past or future, perhaps that was the only way I would be able to confront my future actions. I also considered going to have supper at the restaurant as soon as I hung up, to see her working and alive, she probably wouldn't have many more such nights. But, unless I had booked, there would be no free table.

'And what's the other coincidence?' I asked at last. Much less time had passed than the time it has taken me to describe that pause, the time it took me to accept and take on board that Gonzalo de la Rica probably was who he was, that he was still in the world despite Blakeston's assertions all those years ago, the man who had been introduced to me in Ruán one day of mist and wild bells, without me suspecting a thing. Why would I, given that I'd never met him in person, someone from twenty years ago, and yet he had recognized my face at once. I'd heard Berta's description of him, and it was pos- sible that Blakeston or someone else had shown me a photo later on and another of his supposed wife, Mary Kate O'Riada, I seemed to recall that she had a slight squint, but who can remember a snapshot taken two long decades ago, if, that is, I ever saw one. Perhaps I had met him once and chatted with him for a while in a polite, indifferent manner. With that talkative man who had threatened our son, Guillermo, when we didn't even refer to him as 'Guillermo' but as 'the baby', because he really was tiny then and completely defenceless. I felt a pang of humiliation, not that this mattered, humiliation is soon cured, unless you're one of those people who chooses to wallow in it and feed it throughout their lives as a way of justifying base deeds.

'You would never have missed it before, Tom, not in the old days.' He never let slip an opportunity to point out the diminishment in my mental acuity, my memory, and my faculties in general; this was simply how he was, and I ignored the comment. 'We've made a close study of the notes you made from that woman's diaries, all those cryptic annotations, which were apparently only of use to her. You really weren't thorough enough. Or perhaps you just became bored with all those initials. A bad decision on your part, because, if you really try, you'll always find something useful.'

'Really? And what was it that I missed? Are you going to tell me or simply keep piling on the criticisms?'

'Of course I'm going to tell you, I already am. On 11 December 1987, Inés Marzán was in New York and Boston a few days before the Zaragoza attack, right? Goodness, what a terrible Christmas those poor families must have had. It will soon be ten years since it happened. I don't know if you noticed, but it was the tenth anniversary of the Barcelona attack just a month or so ago. And Magdalena O'Rue O'Dea is still as free as the air.'

This time, he gave her complete name, as if this underlined her impunity; but he pronounced her Basque name just as I have written it, converting it into a doubtless non-existent Irish name. He pronounced the second part as if it were 'O'Day'. 'Rue' means 'regret' or 'repentance', it's not a word much used now by English speakers, although some English versions of *Don Quijote* translate the book's subtitle 'El Caballero de la Triste Figura' as 'The Knight of the

Rueful Countenance'. Tupra may have wanted to evoke those two words – 'rue' and 'rueful' – but it was more likely that he could think of no other way of pronouncing 'Orúe'.

'I've known those dates by heart ever since 6 January when you came to see me and begged me for my help.' I always made a point of reminding him that he had asked me a favour, a big favour, not that it made any difference at this point. 'And what's the significance of that journey?'

'According to your interpretation of the abbreviations, on the 5th of that month, Inés Marzán dined at the Waldorf in New York with seven other people whose initials, I have them here, are BS, BE, RS, RHK, MRK, MW and SM. None of them leapt out at you, I assume, which again isn't like you, or, rather, the person you were.'

I was in no mood to respond to his barbed comments. Suddenly, the penny dropped, because, for some minutes, I had been thinking only about Miguel Ruiz Kindelán or the person who had answered to that name, the man who had approached Berta in my absence and had so wheedled his way into her confidence that he had ended up sitting in our living room, him and his real or fake wife, Mary Kate O'Riada or O'Reidy.

'How can you expect me to connect those initials, that scribbled note, with someone I believed to have been taken out twenty years ago, I left the matter in your hands because, at the time, I was occupied with one of your other pressing emergencies, you know: "don't linger or delay".' I deliberately said 'your' not 'our'. 'Blakeston assured me that neither I nor Berta need worry about that couple again. He said he would take care of them, and I understood what one would usually understand from that expression, that he was going to take them out of the picture. Was that yet another of your deceptions? You have an unfortunate habit of inventing deaths that never happened, starting with Janet Jefferys, then me and finally that fat arsonist, if you're right, of course, and it was him. It all seems purely circumstantial, pure conjecture. Those initials could belong to lots of people.'

'I agree, Tom, I'm not denying that. They could belong to Moorhead Riordan Kennedy, or Marcus Reilly Keefe or Moultrie Rowe Kelsall and many others.'

'I've no idea who those people are.'

'They're not anyone, just possible names. Well, the third one did exist, an actor friend of mine, but he's been dead for years. However, as far as I know, the only MRK in your life is Kindelán, and that is the second coincidence. And don't forget the main piece of evidence, Miss Pontipee's drawing.'

'What happened to him? And to his wife? What did Blakeston actually do?'

'I don't know exactly, Tom. I can't, nor could I at the time, deal with such secondary matters. I asked him yesterday, though, just to see if he could remember, but he's not the man he was either. He's older than us, and he's aged quite a lot, not to the point of being useless, but he's not as sharp as he was. He told me they were rather unimportant, occasional peons. That they passed information on to Sinn Féin and occasionally tipped off the IRA, but that was all. They had no blood on their hands. He thinks he probably just put the fear of God into them, either in person or over the phone, as you know, an anonymous phone call can frighten the cowardly far more than an actual visit. They were a slippery pair, he does remember that. Then he lost track of them, so perhaps they really did take fright. As I said, Kindelán hasn't done anything since, as least as far as we know.'

'Don't you think he'd done enough? In my own apartment and to my son?'

'You really shouldn't let the personal blur the difference between what happened and what didn't happen. Nothing happened to your son, nor to Berta. Yes, it was probably the worst moment of her life, but no one was harmed. Besides, we don't take just anyone out of the picture, that's always an extreme measure. We don't remove peons who haven't committed any serious crimes, you know that as well as I do. We're not ETA or the IRA nor are we Protestant paramilitaries or the mafia. Imagine the endless line of corpses there would be if we didn't distinguish between amateurs and professionals, between sympathizers and murderers. Blakeston concluded that the Kindeláns were just that, sympathizers and amateurs.'

'And yet there he was with Maddie O'Dea, who is neither one thing nor the other, having supper at the Waldorf in New York just six days before the mass killing at the barracks. That's what you're saying, isn't it?'

'No, I'm not, I'm just not ruling it out. If it's true, then we would have made a big mistake twenty years ago. Blakeston will have made a mistake or whoever it was he sent to check them out and track them down. We all make mistakes sometimes. If we didn't, there would be no such attacks, and regrettably there are and will continue to be. If Kindelán was a sleeper, then I have to recognize that he was very good at it. Very patient, very elusive. As patient and elusive as Molly O'Dea, but, as far as we know, much less bloodthirsty.' He paused briefly, and I heard the click of his lighter. 'Or else we're completely wrong, and he's just a snitch, an errand boy, a go-between eager for brownie points, but without running any real risks. It's not worth dirtying your hands with someone like that.'

'Let's assume MRK is Kindelán. Doesn't it seem odd to you that two IRA collaborators or possibly ETA collaborators too (him, I mean) should be having supper at such an expensive hotel? Those organizations aren't exactly swimming in money, or if they are, they use the money for other things . . .'

'I don't know about ETA, but the IRA gets shedloads of cash from the United States. And if the RHK in the diary was Ralph Hynes Killen, for example, he would have paid the bill for all eight guests as easily as someone giving a tip.'

'Who's he?'

'An American industrialist, almost an industrial magnate, who finances various things both openly and in secret. The Republican Party of course; anti-Clinton campaigns; Sinn Féin and presumably the IRA. His father was a big supporter of the John Birch Society in the 1960s, they say he was behind the Kennedy assassination. He's of Irish descent, as his name suggests. Who knows, he could be distantly related to John Killen, a rebel executed in Dublin in 1803. He was accused by two pedlars of having taken part in an insurrection and having murdered a man in cold blood. More respectable witnesses denied this and swore that Killen hadn't moved from his lodgings during the night of the unrest. The judge and jury, however, believed the pedlars, and Killen, despite his desperate protests from the dock to the gallows, was executed on 10 September. Since he really was a rebel, they took advantage of the charges to get rid of him. Such a flagrant act of injustice is remembered in families *per saecula saeculorum*, especially if they're Irish families, who, as you know, have a real vocation for revenge. Especially if they're born in "the new country". They love finding out about their past or inventing one. There are companies devoted to doing just that and to coming up with fantastical genealogies, it's a growth industry.'

Sometimes Tupra revealed a most unlikely knowledge of the most various subjects, especially the subject he had studied, Medieval History. But there was nothing medieval about that man John Killen, still less about his improbable distant descendant, Ralph Hynes Killen.

'How the devil do you know that? Have you been swotting up in some fat legal tome just to fuel your conjectures?'

I wasn't in the best of moods, but I couldn't resist asking that question.

I heard him laugh at the other end of the line, his pleasant, infectious laugh, the same laugh provoked by the story of Enrique the Mourner and his ungainly wife, Catherine of Lancaster. On that occasion, I had been the one to play the erudite scholar, courtesy of Wheeler. What, I wondered, would have become of him and of Mr Southworth? It seemed an eternity since I had heard from either of them. They would probably still be in Oxford, immutable, intact, in that city that preserves in amber those it welcomes and gives shelter to.

Tupra was still laughing. He obviously had nothing else to do on that evening of 28 July. He had brought to a close his day of frenetic activity, and he never had known how to stop. His sun would take longer to set than mine, I was further to the west and he further to the north. Perhaps Beryl was away travelling, or out with her girlfriends.

'You have to do your homework, Tom. In this job, you have to know everything. Well, in any job, although people appear to have forgotten that. RHK is a third coincidence, and three coincidences is most unnatural.'

It seemed that the action, the act, the deed was getting closer. And that I would not escape. One always nurses the vain hope that something will crop up, that the sentence will be commuted (even a prisoner on the scaffold has his hopes), that the orders will be rescinded or cancelled, that someone will back off at the final moment. And if that doesn't happen, you appreciate and treasure each day's delay, each hour's deferral, each minute of procrastination, anything that allows you to keep telling yourself: 'It will be, it will be, but not yet, not yet.'

Tupra was right. He hadn't said anything new or original. He had merely reminded me of something that we all know, even the most stupid of us: nothing has happened until it has happened, nothing is certain until it is irreversible. I was hoping that the action, the act, the deed would not, in the end, take place. But that conversation with Reresby was an exact reflection of what Eliot had written in the poem that had accompanied me ever since the morning when I first met Tupra in the second-hand section of Blackwell's in Oxford. Every word he spoke was 'a step to the block, to the fire, down the sea's throat . . .'. I had known these words since I was a young man and I would sometimes add my own variants so that it wasn't always the same in my head, as it always is in the printed text: always drawing things down, down to the depths.

I wasn't heading towards the illegible stone, I was the person leading someone else there, hand in deceiving hand, a woman; I was going to be the instrument, the guillotine, the executioner. 'I'm doing this in order to save the other two women,' I kept repeating to myself, and yet. 'Quick now, here, now, always . . .' I wasn't in the here or the now, or the 'quick': all that remained to me was a little slowness, a little calm, like the day resisting becoming night and the river's tranquilly flowing waters, in summer the water level gets very low because it hardly rains and it never snows after June. 'Dust in the air suspended marks the place where a story ended.' That dust was not as yet suspended in the air, nor had the story ended, and it would be Inés Marzán's story that would be interrupted, not mine. And, as it turns out, I have lasted quite a lot longer than expected. The proof is that I'm still here and still talking.

'When it suits you, no coincidence is natural,' I said. 'RHK could be any number of people, as could MRK, as you yourself said. It's the same with all those other initials.'

'Yes, it could be Robert Henry Killoran or Rose Heather Kennington or Randolph Hearst Kirby, there are endless possibilities. But the one that tallies best is Ralph Hynes Killen, just as MRK tallies with Berta's visitor. Don't forget the drawing, Tom, the drawing.'

'Would he be likely to use the same name, all those years later?'

'How many years have I spent swapping names? And you too. You've been Ley or Fahey or Breda more than once. Besides, he was in America on that day, not in Spain, so it wouldn't have mattered. We don't know what name he was born with. He hasn't been very important until now, and so no one took any interest. If he was fluent in your language, he's probably half Spanish or half Irish or Northern Irish, like Molly O'Dea. Ruiz Kindelán could well be his real name and he's attached to it and uses it when he's among trusted friends.'

'There's no such thing as trusted friends.' I didn't have any, they were all purely superficial.

'True, but a lot of people don't know that or refuse to know it. We all need to believe in certain loyalties, and to have them as well. The loyalties we cling to tend to be our weakest point.'

'I shouldn't think you have any loyalties, Bertram. Not even to the Crown, I mean, you're acting outside of it right now, just to do a favour to some imbecile.'

'What would you know? Look, don't presume to know me.'

'Oh, don't worry. No one really knows *you*.' It was strange and paradoxical, given all that he had done to me, but Tupra was perhaps the closest thing I had to a friend, even if only because of our shared experiences and because he knew more about me than anyone else, certainly more than Berta. 'And why would Kindelán have come to see me in Ruán, if, that is, he really was de la Rica?'

'Tom Tom Tom, it couldn't be clearer. He went there in order to see your face, even though you've changed, to check you over and report back to Inés Marzán. After all, she was the one who took him to her apartment when you were there. You don't believe you ever met him in the flesh, or don't recall any such meeting, but he knew you. Otherwise, why would he have approached Berta all those years ago? If I remember rightly, he asked her if she was your wife, or took it for granted that she was. He'd met the two of you at diplomatic receptions, that's what he said, isn't it? That's what you or Berta told me. No one really registers anyone at events like that. It all happened ages ago, but it will still be in some file or other.'

Yes, that was possible. That is what would happen, someone would be sent to identify you through photos, to make sure. It's what I had dreaded all those years ago, during my exile in that English town by a river, when a certain Mrs James Rowland – James Rowland was my name during that endless period in hiding – Vera Rowland, had come looking for me at the school where I was teaching. She would have returned day after day if I hadn't finally shown my face, and so, taking every precaution, and with my trusty old revolver in my pocket, I went to the Jarrold Hotel where she was staying, and she immediately sent me packing, disappointed that I was not 'her' James Rowland, the husband who had fled or disappeared, who knows, she was very brusque and to the point: 'I was hoping to find another Jim Rowland, but you're not him. Forgive me. It was a mistake. You have exactly the same name. I'm so sorry to have put you to any trouble.' That had been one of those seemingly unnatural coincidences, but there must be quite a few James Rowlands in England, it's not such an unusual surname.

For weeks, or possibly months, after that strange visit – by a woman whose accent I didn't have time to pinpoint accurately, and who verged on the ugly, but nevertheless managed to be rather attractive, despite her yellowish eyes – I had lived with the anxiety that my next visitors would be some hitmen, to whom she would have confirmed that I was indeed I, thus signing my death warrant: 'Yes, that Jim Rowland is definitely Tom Nevinson, the one who's done so much damage to the organization. People suspect he may have killed one of our members. You can go there right now and take him out.' I had awaited their arrival and remained alert and awake like a watchman, but the Lord had kept the city safe, as the Psalms say, and quite rightly too: once you've been found out, once you've been discovered, the watchman is of little use, and there's not much you can do to defend yourself.

Then time passed and 'the killers' did not appear, and I gradually lowered my guard, which no one can keep up indefinitely; or else the condemned man resigns himself and decides not to keep running away or to put up any resistance when the moment arrives. This has often happened: the man in hiding grows weary and abandons himself to his fate with something approaching resignation or meekness, or with what people used to call fatalism, as if they finally accepted their situation: 'I took a chance, I made my wager, and I lost; now I have to pay.' This had not been my case then, I didn't feel so utterly discouraged or worn down, I still felt I was useful, even though the implication was that I had outlived my usefulness.

Now I was, once again, useful, but I had, alas, been found out. My usefulness was a poisoned one, my first step poisoned, and as that witty woman said to the French cardinal, only the first step is difficult . . . But all steps are difficult, the last as much as or more than the first.

'In that case,' I said to Tupra, 'Inés Marzán will have known who I really am ever since that day. Well, she would have headed off to mass without knowing and, on her return, she would have known. De la Rica would only have to make a particular gesture when he met me or utter a pre-agreed word. She had, after all, spent the night with me.'

'Yes, that probably is what happened, Tom,' said Tupra in the condescending tone that escaped him either unwittingly or not. 'It's likely that she didn't even go to the church, but instead went to meet Kindelán at the train station and brought him back to see you, so that he could take a look at you. The worst thing isn't that Inés Marzán knows who you are, but that Molly O'Dea does. According to our reports, she isn't one for niceties or for weaknesses of the sentimental kind.'

'But perhaps she is now,' I broke in. 'Perhaps she's changed after so many years of inactivity or retirement. Perhaps she's a different woman, the contented owner of a restaurant, and all she wants is to carry on being just that.'

'Don't talk nonsense. People like her never change. Did you ever know one of them to change during your time in Northern Ireland? They never repent or only when they're playing to the gallery, and once they've already been caught. And they all do once they're in prison, just to see if their sentence will be reduced, and that is definitely no coincidence. As you know, the only reason anyone repents, and not just murderers, is failure. When things go wrong. They don't regret the things that went well or that went unpunished.'

'It's not always like that. Even you knew of one such case: an ETA leader who decided to leave, a woman nicknamed "Yoyes"; she got bumped off by her comrades in cold blood, and not after any lengthy deliberations either. That happened in 1986, and there have been a few other such cases. Everyone remembers her because she was a woman and because she was killed in front of her three-year-old son. Besides, you and I have rarely seen things the same way.'

'A couple of exceptions aren't enough to disprove the rule.' That was how he dealt with my objection, almost as if he hadn't heard it. 'The only strange thing about it is that Molly hasn't had you taken out and shot.'

He used that rather military expression, for he did sometimes like to emphasize the military nature of the secret services to which he had devoted half his life – the services that almost everyone forgets – as well, of course, as his high rank: by that time, he would have been commodore or captain (if he belonged to the Royal Navy), something that is usually kept secret even in the James Bond novels and films, although keen fans know that both the spy and his creator, Ian Fleming, held or had held the rank of commander of the Royal Navy. Precisely because of that sense of hidden pride, it infuriated Tupra that all the terrorist groups called themselves 'armies' and their members 'soldiers', an added offence. To him, they were criminal gangs, 'would-be murderers, who just want a reason to kill', a 'motley crew of scoundrels', 'bags of shit'.

'We have no reason to believe that she's ever killed anyone with her own hands, perhaps she hasn't. But if she preferred not to sully her hands or didn't know how, others would rush to her aid – she would just have to say the word – and they would do the job for her and finish you off. There would have been no shortage of volunteers in Belfast or Londonderry, where some would remember your name, or the names you adopted there. But, yes, that is odd. How long is it since she introduced you to Kindelán?'

'I can't recall right now, but I'll have noted down the date somewhere. But it was some time in the winter and pretty cold. I remember thinking that de la Rica wasn't dressed warmly enough.'

'A matter of months then. She's had more than enough time. That doesn't mean she won't be waiting for you tomorrow ready to wield the axe. Or that an Irishman with his hair crushed down by his hat won't turn up in Ruán tomorrow. That, if I remember rightly, is how Rebecca West saw them: "as they went about their performance of menial toil or inglorious assassination".' He laughed softly at what seemed to be a quotation or a paraphrase. 'She was exaggerating, of course, and considered them all to be more or less the same. She could be funny sometimes too, like all brilliant exaggerators.'

'Rebecca West? What's she got to do with it?' I couldn't contain my curiosity. I only knew her as the author of a novel and an extraordinary book describing her travels in the Balkans.

'Haven't you read *The Meaning of Treason*?' He sounded genuinely shocked. 'Everyone should read it, because at one time or another everyone has either committed treason or been the victim of it, however major or minor, and, besides, treason is necessary for the State. She writes about William Joyce, among others. He was Lord Haw-Haw, that American-Irishman who made the war more difficult for us with his Nazi propaganda broadcasts. He'd have to be Irish, wouldn't he?'

Generally speaking, he didn't like the Irish, either the Catholics or the Protestants, he thought they were all hopeless cases. Not that this had stopped him from using collaborators from Ireland or from Ulster; in fact, Mulryan was one of them. He said 'made the war more difficult for us' as if he himself had fought in the Second World War; as I said, he bitterly regretted having missed out on that.

'How odd that you haven't read it. Redwood always recommended it, and it's become a basic text for us, a key text.' He remained silent for a few seconds, then returned to Inés Marzán. 'She could also have left town as soon as she knew who you were, but she hasn't. She's known about you for what, six months? And she hasn't done any-thing. You'd better be careful.'

'That's if Inés is Maddie O'Dea and de la Rica is Kindelán, all of which is pure conjecture . . .'

I was resisting accepting as definitive something that wasn't defini-tive at all, and which, besides, brought with it a death, which had fallen to me like a prize in a raffle. Tupra cut me off:

'No, as far as I'm concerned, those are certainties. As they are for George and Pat, or for . . .' He prudently didn't finish his sentence; he was about to pronounce a name he shouldn't pronounce, perhaps Spedding himself or his Spanish equivalent. 'As far as we're con-cerned that is. As certain as they are for you, given that you were the one who pointed the finger at her without actually pointing a finger,' he said. 'That's more than enough. We've acted on far less evidence in the past. We've condemned someone on the basis of far fewer coincidences, both natural and unnatural. You used to be far readier to condemn someone, basing yourself on gut instinct, intuition. Or have you developed more scruples, is that it?'

I didn't want to recall the past, because I had been exactly as he described, and I had only developed more scruples in my years of remembrance, inactivity and torpor. I had almost never been wrong in my interpretations, and I don't believe I ever condemned anyone unjustly. But this was different. Then I had been caught up in the maelstrom, there had been a sense of urgency, of innocent lives threatened, I'd had to make very quick decisions. Now, as far as I could see, there were neither urgencies nor lives at risk, or only hypothetically, all too hypothetically. I gazed out once again at the river and the bridge, I was growing weary of holding the telephone and wanted to put an end to the conversation.

Everything was finally growing dark, the streetlights were now fully lit with their cheerful yellow light, and I saw a wagon slowly crossing the bridge, drawn by a mule or a donkey, a rare sight in

1997. It was like an image from another age, from my childhood, when, even in Madrid, you would often see carts drawn by mules or donkeys or horses, and, however unlikely it might seem, these coexisted with the many cars that were already filling the streets then as well as thirty years later. Animals had not yet been expelled from cities, they were useful, not mere toys or ornaments or playthings for kids, they quite rightly shared the city because they contributed to its functioning. For a moment, I allowed myself to envy the driver of that wagon, who would be oblivious to the world's problems, and perhaps to its worst meannesses, not beset, like me, by dilemmas. He, like everyone else, would have his dilemmas, doubtless simple ones. My envy was frivolous and short-lived, that of someone who wants to escape and would be prepared to change places with anyone in order to flee and not have to confront what he had to do. The driver would doubtless be poor, would have a thousand and one problems and possibly children to feed, the load on his wagon would also be poor and archaic and absurd (I couldn't make out what he was carrying), and destined soon to disappear, to succumb, just as other such drivers had from nearly all over Europe, even though he believed that his day-to-day existence would last for all eternity, which is what we all believe, more or less.

'Can you believe it? I'm watching a mule-drawn wagon crossing the bridge. In a town of almost two hundred thousand inhabitants or whatever, perhaps less. When it's almost the year 2000 . . .'

'Now what nonsense are you spouting? What are you talking about? What on earth is happening to you? I tell you that you have to take action and there you are going on about a mule on a bridge.' He sounded annoyed, he must be equally weary of holding the phone, although he was probably doing so with his hands free, especially if he was in his office.

'I'm the one who needs to be absolutely sure,' I said, as if that interlude with the wagon had been a mere auditory figment of his imagination. 'Not you or that moron Machimbarrena or that conceited little madam Pérez Nuix or the bigwig you came so close to naming. After all, I'm the one who's going to have to take her out of the picture. It's not going to be you or her or him, and certainly not some carpet-pacing nabob.' Now we were both getting angry, or perhaps not.

'No, Tom, you're wrong. As I've already explained,' he responded, having recovered his usual ironic tone — a matter of about two seconds — 'you're not the one who's going to do the taking out, we are or will be. We're just giving you the opportunity to act in our name and save the other two women. Just think of them, and the enormous favour you're doing them. And think of the misfortunes you'll have averted.'

XIV

Fairly or unfairly, rightly or wrongly, Magdalena Orúe now had a name, and that name was Inés Marzán, or so it had been decided by those authorized to make such decisions. And as on far too many occasions, Tupra was right: I tried to console myself with the thought that not only were Celia Bayo and María Viana safe – now that their names, as if by magic, had been struck from the list of three – their faces, their bodies, their persons would be forever beyond suspicion, always bearing in mind that, in our work, 'forever' almost never exists; someone who appears to be innocent could be found guilty tomorrow or in a year's time or vice versa, in the latter case, rectification often comes late, and then . . . Well, these things happen, it's just bad luck, a brief period of regret and contrition, even Henry II, barefoot and wearing a sackcloth shirt, made a pilgrimage from St Dunstan's Church to Canterbury Cathedral to do public penance before the tomb of Thomas Becket, the friend and companion of his youth, whom he had subsequently called on others to murder. It bears no comparison with what good St Denis did nine centuries earlier: unlike the martyr, who walked five and a half miles, the King only walked about two, and without the bother of carrying his own head under one arm.

The fact is that, if Inés were ever exonerated, too late, I couldn't imagine Tupra or Machimbarrena or Pérez Nuix traipsing from Puerta Latina or Santa Águeda or Santa Decapitación to Ruán's gothic Cathedral, however short a distance. As far as they were concerned, these things happen, it's just bad luck, a bad call, you can't always get it right.

And yes, it also forced me to think hard about the misfortunes or possible massacres that would be averted, which is our main mandate and our principal mission as the rather nasty angels. I found this difficult though: I couldn't see the present-day Inés — and I had known no other – collaborating in some mass killing, still less shooting an unarmed person in the back at point-blank range in a street, in a bar, at a festival or in a restaurant. And yet everything was possible, and it was no longer my job to speculate further, but to carry out orders and complete my mission, to take the first step, and thus conclude my task and immediately leave town. At least she wouldn't die like cattle, part of a herd, not like the victims of the Barcelona and Zaragoza bombings in which she would have played a part ten years earlier, although I never knew how or to what degree she was involved. The passing-bells would ring out in her honour, the bells of Ruán, where, while not exactly loved, she was respected and appreciated as a useful, active member of society. She would be missed, more out of habit than genuine loss, because even her apparent friendliness had always been reserved and opaque. It occurred to me that, ironically, in that proud town, I was perhaps the person who had loved her most, although in a strange, peculiar, lukewarm, unsatisfactory way, and only very recently too (perhaps in the way one might love a giantess during the voluptuous season of insalubrious suns, except that, in my case, this had been during the seasons of snow and mist, and only very briefly in the summer heat).

Given the circumstances, the word 'love' clearly had no place in our relationship, that would be excessive or even a joke. I had, though, seen the charm of that simultaneously winged and clumsy woman, who, at the restaurant, wove nimbly in and out between chairs and tables, seemingly barely touching the ground, and who, at home, was always bumping into the furniture and sending objects flying. Seeing someone's charm is the fundamental, necessary condition for falling in love, for becoming infatuated, fond and unconditionally attached, I had been the victim of neither the first nor the second nor the fourth, but definitely of that third state: I felt for her the usual fondness one feels after repeated skin-on-skin encounters or after having known someone in the flesh, or however the Bible puts it when criticizing or forbidding or advising against such things, it's all the same.

Despite having focused on María Viana during July, the woman for whom I felt a theoretical infatuation, I had not been neglecting Inés, nor had she distanced herself from me. As I said before, she may have been so lonely, so intrinsically lonely, that she had become accustomed to my company, however fleeting and occasional. It's a source of pleasure and contentment to know that someone is waiting for you, that you're important and exist, even if you're only that person's penultimate choice. This had been my interpretation in the days of anxiety and unease prior to the murder of Miguel Ángel Blanco, and in the days of mourning that followed. Now, though, I wondered if Inés' desire to not entirely lose track of me was actually a desire to watch and keep a check on me, or even a way of biding her time so that, when it suited her or when she gave the order, she could have me taken out and shot, to use Commodore Nutcombe's or Dundas' or Ure's half-solemn, half-jocular expression. 'You'd better be careful,' he had warned me, although he had said this only once. He would have thought it paternalistic and superfluous to say any more to a veteran like me.

Even if she was Magdalena Orúe O'Dea, half Northern Irish and half *riojana* of Basque descent, and as ruthless as Josefa Ernaga or Irantzu Gallestegui or Idoia 'The Tigress', I still couldn't feel afraid of Inés Marzán. It's hard to feel afraid of someone you're planning to kill. You inevitably see yourself as so malign and menacing that this, absurdly, eliminates all sense of what danger might be lurking in the other person. When Captain Alan Thorndike had Hitler in his sights, with his rifle loaded and his finger stroking the trigger, he doubtless saw Hitler as a defenceless little lamb and just as easy to eradicate, why, it was almost done already; and the very real Reck-Malleczewen failed to take out his pistol in that restaurant because Hitler seemed to him like a character out of a comic strip and fundamentally stupid, and because he didn't yet know what was to come. Those who manhandled the thirty-year-old Marie Antoinette as if she were a sack of potatoes, manoeuvring her neck into the place where the blade would fall, had probably forgotten all about how dangerous and despotic she had been in the not-so-distant past; just as the merciful 'swordsman of Calais' wouldn't have seen the thirty-year-old Anne Boleyn as the slightest threat to anyone, still less to him. Inés Marzán was also in her thirties, a few years older than those two queens. But given how much longer people live now in comparison with those who lived in the eighteenth and sixteenth centuries, she was quite a lot younger, and there was no reason why she wouldn't live for many more years.

Anyway, I knew that not being conscious of how potentially dangerous Inés could be was an error worthy of a cocksure beginner. It happens to inexperienced hitmen, who think that because they have been commissioned to take someone out and are ready for their baptism of fire, that person couldn't possibly anticipate them and take them out instead. Most finish their careers before they even begin. And besides, Tupra was right: any day, any night, an Irishman with a long memory, summoned by her or by Kindelán, could turn up in Ruán. Or some young kid with no memory, but who had been told certain stories. As the narrator says in an old novel set in County Kerry: 'You'll learn, if you stay in Ireland, that forgiveness by your enemies means nothing. There are always others waiting to take up the quarrel and make it their own.' It's the same in Ireland and in Northern Ireland, as it is in so many other places where to live consists solely of waiting and storing up resentments.

What I've just said is inaccurate and unfair, because not all of Ireland is like that, and, besides, I don't know the country that well; no place is ever wholly like that. Every country has its share of ingenuous, well-intentioned individuals, and delightful places that know nothing of resentment. But there are also places that abound in toxic hubs (whole villages and valleys, and even the occasional town dominated by malice) whose capacity for contamination is so strong that they sometimes impregnate everything else, thus eliminating or corrupting or converting hitherto cheerful, candid souls. As everyone knows, it happened in Hitler's Germany, but not only there and then. It's still happening today, in my two countries, in the unknowable one I served and in the other all too knowable one.

Inés Marzán must have been more than familiar with such places, although in fact you don't need to have set foot in them to notice the stench they give off, the essence of some pestilence or some possible monstrosity. Or rather, what you notice from a distance, the thing that seeps and spreads across borders, is precisely as described by Reck-Malleczewen when, writing not about Hitler and his henchmen, but about himself in relation to them, he writes (in a slightly modified version): 'For as long as I can remember, I have thought hate, have lain down with hate in my heart, have dreamed hate and awakened with hate.' This is precisely the air you breathe in far too many countries, the air they exhale into the world, and then the only solution is decapitation, burning is never enough. In those places they inculcate their children with the five contagions from the cradle up, every single one of them, contagions that grow with age: it's simultaneously terrifying and pathetic to observe how, in their later years, those people positively brim over with them and use their final days to inoculate any new arrivals and thus perpetuate the contagions for all eternity.

Since my visit to London and my last conversation with Reresby, our ears pressed to our respective receivers, what echoed in my mind were the words spoken by Inés Marzán when the whole of Spain was watching and waiting for what might happen after the kidnapping of that town councillor from Ermua (her words had taken on a different, more ominous tone): 'Those people don't step back, not once they've started something,' she had murmured. 'They're like a machine that can't be stopped even if they wanted it to stop. That poor young man is already a ghost.' Suddenly, these did not seem to me merely the embittered thoughts of a pessimist or sceptic, of someone with no illusions or hopes. Now, retrospectively, I could hear something similar to what we tend to call 'the voice of experience'. As if she knew precisely what she was talking about, as if she were speaking from first-hand knowledge. Such is the power of suggestion, from which no one is immune. If, at the beginning of my time in that town in the north-west, I had seen evil everywhere, now, inevitably, it was all concentrated in Inés Marzán.

I suppose that, in my eyes, there was an element of unconscious deliberation, if you'll allow me that complete contradiction in terms; or, rather, sheer necessity. When you find yourself being propelled towards something that appals or repels, your only option is to convince yourself that it really isn't so very bad, so very dreadful, you have to do a kind of mental spring-clean and come up with a justification. I was well aware that this is exactly what the most despicable of murderers do, those who seek kudos by becoming terrorists, who, deaf and blind to all reason, 'obey a cause'. I did not forget either that, after I had been unwillingly plunged into the activities of MI5 and MI6, and as the years passed with no possible escape, I had gradually persuaded myself that my work was beneficial and had a certain nobility about it, even if our methods were often ignoble and involved treachery and deceit.

I ended up embracing what I had once explained to Berta, who condemned the very nature of my profession. I had said many things, that war has always consisted of deception and betrayal, from the Trojan Horse onwards and possibly before. I had gone further: 'Sometimes you simply can't act within the law or go around asking permission for everything you do. If the enemy has no scruples, then the side with scruples is doomed to defeat. That's how it's always been in time of war, for centuries. The modern concept of "war crimes" is ridiculous, stupid, because war consists of crimes being committed on all fronts from the first day to the last. It comes down to this: either you don't embark on wars or, if you do, then you have to be prepared from the outset to commit whatever crimes are necessary, whatever you need to do to achieve victory or simply to survive.' And when I felt cornered (Berta is an excellent debater, it's best not to take her on, and she had laid a trap for me with that scene from *Henry V*), I had defended my work with unexpected grandiloquence, I felt ashamed now to think of it: 'We are the watchtowers, the moats and the firebreaks,' I had said, no less, 'we are the lookouts, the watchmen, the sentinels who are always on guard, whether on duty or not. Someone has to remain alert so that everyone else can rest, someone has to detect those threats, someone has to anticipate them before it's too late. Someone has to defend the Realm so that you can go for a walk with Guillermo.' When you feel forced to do something, the solution is to convince yourself not only that you have to do it, but that it's the best possible option. You can always find a reason for everything, or two or three or more, there's nothing easier than coming up with reasons and thus feeling, quite impartially of course, that you have right on your side.

This was what I had to do in those last days of July, clear away any doubts, banish all excuses and steel myself to act. To forget my strange fondness for Inés Marzán and see that it was vital that she should no longer tread this earth, to make her an objective, a target, an enemy bereft of present and future, someone who must pay for her appalling past, since her past had been judged to be appalling. This was what I had to do, but couldn't. I tried to think back to when I was younger, when I could work like a machine with a purpose and a mission, or like a mere cog in a large, respectable machine. Yes, I was still a cog, a pawn, and I didn't even know the details of that appalling past, of what exactly Magdalena Orúe had done.

Tupra's methods had not changed, although the large machine of which we were a part was neither clearly defined nor respectable. I, however, had changed. I had grown disillusioned, jaded, and had left. I had returned out of a sense of emptiness, which is another form of vanity. I had not been cured of the illness afflicting María Viana and which afflicts us all, gullibility. But time had undermined and diminished that, and this had affected my resolve. All I could do was focus on the decisive point, the diabolical dilemma: if I didn't act, Inés would die, and I would be condemning the other two women to die as well.

Tupra had not set a precise deadline, he hadn't said ominously, 'If the deed isn't done by such and such a date . . .' or anything like that. There was no need, I knew what he meant, and his order or advice over the phone had been 'Get to work,' which didn't mean that I should rush things or risk doing a botched job, but that I should act in such a way that guaranteed success and impunity, and yet implicit in those words was one of his favourite sayings, 'Don't linger or delay,' which was what he always said once he saw that the way ahead was clear. Fortunately, he was intelligent enough to realize that I needed time to assimilate his discoveries – the portrait, the initials and, above all, the inevitability of it all – and that to do so would require a couple of wakeful nights, half sleeping, half waking, full of superficial, troubled dreams, not to mention a sense of incredulity. Had he issued me with an ultimatum, I might have rebelled.

In the last month, Inés and I had seen each other only sporadically. There were the days of waiting for Miguel Ángel Blanco and the days following his murder, then came my departure and my absence with, as my only explanation: 'Family problems. I'll need to be in Madrid for a week or so. I'll let you know when I'm back.' And she, of course, had so little free time in the summer season, La Demanda was chock-a-block for lunch and supper, she was working herself to death. We only met during one of her breaks, when we would go for a short walk in the park and sit down opposite the Olmo de las Melodías, or have a quick drink in one of the bars in the Barrio Tinto before her first shift. We would talk about trivial things, exchange the latest town gossip, and I would tell her about the invented problems my invented siblings were having in Madrid, conversation was never our strong point, we got together for other reasons or she got together with me (I had my own spurious reasons). I assume she found the forty-five-year-old me attractive; I was back to my normal weight and Sigfrido the hairdresser and his Ruán successor had, as far as possible, restored my hair to its youthful self, reminiscent of that famous French actor Gérard Philipe, who drove the women crazy back then and reached godlike status. We, of course, were living in a different age, and Inés would have no idea who Gérard Philipe was. I also shaved off my moustache in an attempt to look younger.

It may not have struck her as so very odd when, one morning, seated opposite the Olmo, I complained about our long period of abstinence, if I can put it like that. Nor was it entirely normal, because we never complained to each other about anything, we hadn't entered the domain of reproaches, explanations, annoying or simply excessive interrogations, we had eschewed the unbearable Spanish habit of asking questions; as I said, she avoided talking about herself with me or with anyone else. This, for obvious reasons, suited me down to the ground, since I didn't want to talk about myself either. I had never gone in for pointless navel-gazing, which didn't interest me in the least.

What *was* strange — a deliberate strangeness, in order to observe her reaction — was that I made my complaint in English, a language which, as I've said, she spoke well enough to deal with any foreign customers at the restaurant, but no more than that. Even stranger was that I, Miguel Centurión, should put on a Belfast accent, Belfast being the Northern Irish city I was most familiar with, for, according to others, I had an exceptional talent for imitating accents, indeed, that was how I came to be recruited as a student, first by Wheeler, then by Tupra. I was hoping that Maddie O'Dea would automatically respond in English, like that British officer in *The Great Escape* to whom a Nazi says 'Good luck' as he's getting on a bus. The officer had passed himself off as Swiss and exchanged a few words with the Nazi in excellent German. Out of habit, and without realizing, he answered 'Thank you', thus signing his own death warrant and that of another escapee travelling with him. It's the same when someone unexpectedly hands us some plates: knowing that they'll fall to the ground and break if we do nothing, we instinctively hold out our hands to take them.

And yet nothing of the sort happened: either she was better pre-pared than Gordon Jackson, the Scottish actor playing the prisoner unmasked by a simple trick about which he himself had warned all his fellow escapees hundreds of times, or she wasn't Magdalena Orúe. I couldn't or shouldn't think the latter. If, during my months in Ruán, I had nurtured the hope that none of my women were Maddie O'Dea and that Machimbarrena had made a mistake, now I fervently wanted Inés to have been responsible for crimes so appalling that they would merit neither pardon nor pity however much time elapsed.

'Why are you talking to me in English?' she said. 'What's that about? Are you going to test me or something?' And she asked me this in Spanish.

I wasn't afraid that I might have blown my cover by imitating that Belfast accent. I had said very little, and, if Inés was O'Dea, she would have known who I was ever since that now distant visit by her friend de la Rica, always assuming he was Kindelán. Why had she done nothing about that, and, even more importantly, why did she continue to meet me and even go to bed with me now and then, with almost as much zeal as on that very first occasion? Tupra found this less of a mystery than I did – he was just surprised that she hadn't had me taken out and shot. We were in one of those situations in which you know that the other person knows that you know, and yet you both behave as if you didn't know. Such situations are tactical, games of watching and waiting, with each of you looking out for your next opportunity, or perhaps that reciprocal knowledge neutralizes you both and you choose to ignore what you know and, to use a chess term, agree to a stalemate. If it had all depended on me, I would have washed my hands of the whole business and gone back to Madrid. Alas, that wasn't the case.

'Oh, nothing, it was just a little joke,' I said. 'But I could help you improve your English if you wanted. After all, I earn my living teaching it to children, and it would be a useful skill for you to have. No, that's a bad idea, forget it. It would all be very artificial.' When she still did not respond, I said: 'But you understood what I said, didn't you?'

'I half understood, I think. You're sorry that now we hardly ever get together in my apartment, is that it? It is, isn't it?'

And when she said this, I realized that she felt flattered, and spoke in an almost timid voice bordering on excitement, or was that pure imagination on my part, for, as I've explained, she was only ever effusive 'during' but never 'after'. Inés Marzán was accustomed to being desired in a primitive, animalesque way, rather than herself offering satisfaction, submitting. That's how it would always have been, with her fellow militants as well, for in that respect they were no different from anyone else or were they perhaps more cynical than anyone else, after all, they were always keen to add another notch on their gun? She was probably less accustomed to being desired more persistently, by someone who had already satisfied his elemental curiosity (what certain fools would now call *morbo*) to hold a very large, tall woman in his arms, to see a vast body taking up the entire bed, naked, dominating, carnal, almost intimidating. Some men would have repeated the experience, but would not have persevered, with the exception of the father of her daughter and who knows who else. And there might well have been a few inconsiderate types who had, accidentally on purpose, covered her face with a sheet or taken her from behind, and not out of pure lust. I myself had thought of doing this just a few days before: her face really was most unkissable, despite the lovely colour of her eyes, everything about it was excessive, lacking all delicacy.

I felt rather sorry for Magdalena Orúe, for Inés Marzán. She was probably disillusioned, resigned, sceptical, but perhaps unable to resist the pleasure of being desired, almost no one can resist that. Far too often, she had been the object of mere prurience, nothing more. She could not help but feel flattered that I, who had so often repeated the experience, should miss it, should yearn for our intimate encounters, should complain and ask for a resumption of activities. That hint of excitement in her question made me feel uncomfortable, which was absurd, since there were far weightier reasons for me to feel truly terrible and this was a trifle in comparison. However, it's very hard to separate out a person's various facets, which mingle and conjoin. It's equally hard to separate out what you know of her in your day-to-day dealings, especially if these are of an affectionate or sexual nature. Until you know that you're about to be betrayed or sacrificed by someone, all that accumulated experience interposes itself and denies what we know to be true: 'No, there's some mistake,' we say dismissively when we're in his company and the other person is his usual self. 'No it's just not possible, I know him, and it's not true.' In the end, though, insidious suspicion prevails, in the end, the facts, what we've been told, prevail.

'Yes, that's it. Well done,' I said. 'Except that I put it rather more explicitly and crudely, which is maybe also why I resorted to English. Lewd words come more easily in another language, don't you think, if you're not actually on the job, that is. But I don't mind saying it in our language, in the middle of the park and with children around: we haven't fucked for ages, and I'm just dying for it. Couldn't we arrange to meet one night after you finish work? Or on Saturday morning, before you go in? I'm not teaching the twins then, nor on Sunday either. But I don't know if you're as hot for it as I am. What do you think? Or maybe you don't fancy it at all.'

I had suggested meeting at night or in the morning, although the former would suit me much better. If she didn't turn up at the restaurant before lunch, her employees would take action, they'd call her and, when she didn't pick up the phone, would go to her apartment to find out what had happened, if perhaps her alarm clock had failed to go off. At night, though, she wouldn't be missed for several hours, twelve or at least ten. I was taking a risk, because if she did choose the worse option, I would have to find a way around it. The fact is that when you do plan some dirty deed, you immediately begin to worry that others will realize, especially the object of the deed, who, in this instance, knew who I was. Yes, I had to take it for granted that she knew, Tupra's view would have to prevail, there was no going back. What Inés would probably not believe is that I was about to do to her what I was being obliged to do. She didn't know there were other suspects, she would be convinced that she was the only one; and even though whole months had passed since de la Rica had revealed or confirmed my identity to her, I had still done nothing, I had continued to treat her kindly and respectfully and with appropriate salaciousness. Nothing had changed between us, although things had cooled off a little, which is normal after the initial urgency and impetus of any new relationship. Nor would she know exactly what my mission was in Ruán, she would assume it had been the same as it had been only weeks or days before: to find her, unmask her, and come up with enough evidence to take her to court, and she must have felt confident that I had failed to achieve the latter; she'd had eight or nine years to eliminate all trace of her past, and since then, she had been Inés Marzán and no one else. Or perhaps she imagined that Tom Nevinson had convinced himself that she no longer represented a danger, that she had retired and repented, and he had decided to leave her alone, to complete his allotted time in Ruán and say nothing. She probably considered me to be a decent person, and saw no signs of fanaticism on my part.

'Of course I do, how could I not? I don't forget past pleasures that quickly, Miguel. The trouble is that after a night at the restaurant I'm absolutely shattered, it's high season now, and I can't afford to take any time off. And on Saturday and Sunday mornings, I'm so exhausted that all I can do is sleep and sleep.' She paused and then added without a hint of flirtatiousness, which wasn't her style, 'Well, I suppose I could get up and open the door to you, but I'd be like a zombie, which is hardly ideal. You'd find yourself lying next to a lifeless body. But if you wouldn't mind that . . .' This did sound almost like a joke, but I couldn't be sure because she didn't usually make jokes. 'I'd love you to come over, but I just don't see how. July and August are completely crazy, although the money we earn certainly makes up for all our hard work. Then, in January and February, it's almost as if there was no one in town at all.'

'You're not expecting me to wait a whole month, are you? Come on, would it be so very grave if you didn't go into work on Friday or Saturday, or if you finished at eleven instead of one o'clock in the morning? I'm sure Transi could cope perfectly well without you.' People had very strange names in that town. Transi was her second in command, short for Transfiguración.

'One o'clock! I wish. It's usually more like two o'clock or later.'

'Even more reason, Inés. You can't spend a whole two months working your socks off. Please, I'm begging you. Sort it out and reserve Saturday night for me, even if it's very late, please, show some mercy. We've had such a hard July, what with the Miguel Ángel Blanco business, which left its mark on all of us. We deserve a little light relief, don't we? If we weren't surrounded by people, why, right now, I'd . . .' I broke off, I didn't want to go too far and overdo the crude language. Most women will take a certain amount, but you should never lay it on too thick. Not at least in a public place.

She smiled with her huge mouth. Her smile was not without charm, but she usually only lavished it on her customers. Whoever she was, whether Magdalena or just Inés, she wasn't immune to flattery. Officially, she was thirty-eight, in 1997 that was young and today would be even younger. She might have been older, but, as I said, she had chosen to be timeless in the way she dressed, which is another way of being ageless. Her very pronounced widow's peak gave her a certain air of severity.

'What? What would you do?' she asked, still smiling. 'Come on, out with it, be bold.'

'I'll tell you on Saturday night, if you agree to see me'

I placed one hand carelessly, distractedly on her thigh, as if I had no intention of advancing further, although the suggestion was there. Her long legs were her best feature, long calves, long thighs, which seemed endless when you ran your hand up to the top – or, to put it more coyly, its culminating point – and which, once she had you in her grasp, would squeeze hard in a simulacrum of strangulation, so hard it almost hurt, until the pressure eased and morphed into pleasure.

She allowed herself to be touched, making sure we weren't seen, for there were passers-by and families everywhere. She put her handbag (which was more like a briefcase) on her lap to cover as much of my hand as possible. I went no further, I mean I didn't advance, this was hardly the place to take risks. However, she then guided my hand upwards, a little more and a little more. Under her slow guidance, my fingertips reached the softer fabric of her knickers, her skirt was pulled down low enough for no one to suspect what we were doing in the middle of the park, opposite the Olmo de las Melodías, where, fortunately, there was no band playing, otherwise the place would have been packed with people. Still urged on by her, I slipped my middle finger under her knickers and immediately felt how wet she was. If Inés wasn't seeing anyone else – she never told me about her life apart from me, and I never asked – it must have been some time since anyone had touched her there.

As for me, despite my sombre mission, I couldn't help having an almost forgotten erection, because I wasn't seeing anyone else either. Nothing had happened with Berta in Madrid – given our situation, that simply wasn't on, although I had been tempted. And I must confess that – to add a further act of villainy, albeit far lower down the scale – when I felt that wetness in Magdalena or Inés and responded with an erection, I automatically thought of Berta. I would have to cover myself now as well, although I wasn't in my pyjamas like Folcuino Gausi when he was playing with his swords. Should anyone look, my erection would be less conspicuous, and he, that poor brutish brute, had assumed he was alone and with no witnesses. Anyway, I had nothing to cover myself with, and so it seemed prudent to remove my hand and abandon the field.

Inés Marzán shot me a glance that was a mixture of disappointment and regret at my sudden retreat. I don't know how far she was intending to go. Whatever the truth of the matter, I had aroused her lust, if it wasn't aroused already. She would be more likely now to give in to my request.

She removed her handbag, put it down on the bench and said:

'I'll think about it and let you know. I'll see what I can do.'

It was Thursday 31 July, and I had suggested, *he* had suggested, Saturday 2 August.

Miguel Centurión preferred that date for two reasons. He had spoken to Tupra on Monday, and didn't want to give him too much time to grow impatient and genuinely angry and decide to act on his own account by sending someone more expert or perhaps even two people. And he was hoping that on that same afternoon or on Friday he would somehow or other receive what he had requested from Pérez Nuix. On that occasion, it would not have been wise to ask Comendador, or anyone else from Catilina or Ruán.

'It's just two days away, Inés. Please decide quickly.'

'Why? Have you got other plans for that night? Can't you keep that Saturday free until I find out if I can make it or not? Or do you want to find a substitute? That's not very flattering, Miguel.'

Centurión immediately corrected himself. Inés Marzán seemed to be speaking seriously, until it became clear that she was joking. He decided to try a different tack, even at the risk of making matters worse.

'For you, I will wait as long as it takes, until Judgement Day itself.'

This sentiment clearly pleased Inés, because she lowered her eyes and smiled.

Centurión did not forget that Magdalena Orúe might have her own death mission in mind and could have decided there and then to have him executed that very Saturday. But he couldn't see her as a danger, not Inés Marzán, besides, she wouldn't have enough time to summon some guys from Belfast or Dublin with their hair crushed down by their hats. On the other hand, there would be time for men in Basque berets and sporting monkish haircuts to arrive from Rentería or Lequeitio or from San Sebastián itself, all of which were within driving distance of that town in the north-west, and they could be there in a matter of hours. It occurred to him that, from then until Saturday, he would greatly regret the absence of microphones or cameras in that apartment he knew so well. Any phone conversation, any phone call during that period could prove vital, which is a word that usually means the exact opposite, namely, mortal. And yet he couldn't believe this, because, in his mind, he was the threat.

That same afternoon, in fact, an informal messenger, not a courier, handed him the small package sent by Pérez Nuix from Madrid. Since he knew what it contained, he didn't open it immediately, nor did he rush to check its contents; he left it unopened on the sill of the window from which he had so often spied on Inés Marzán's movements in her apartment, on her voiceless image, for he never did find out what she talked about on the phone. During all those months, she had continued to receive the same few visitors and no one else: her cleaner, the gunman Comendador with his Stephen Stills-style sideburns, the girlfriends with whom she occasionally watched TV, or, more likely, a film on video. As far as he knew, of course: he wasn't on permanent watch, he didn't keep a check on her every hour still less her every minute, and minutes are all it takes to prepare anything, a murder, a bloodbath. While he was teaching the Gausi children in their garden or getting to know Ruán's churches and monuments, Inés might be receiving a visit from some guy with a monkish haircut or with his hair crushed down by his hat, or, who knows, by Kindelán himself, if he had never actually gone away and often visited the town, and Centurión would never know, would have no idea.

The package could wait, just as he would have to wait, although he was almost certain Inés would fall into the trap, not knowing it was a trap, or half knowing, or possibly not at all. It didn't matter, the date was chosen and fixed and, in his own interests, Centurión could not afford to wait another day. Indeed, his impatience or his unease or indeed his reluctance led him to announce the date and commit himself in advance, without waiting for Inés to confirm. Since he still feared Tupra and feared that he would make his move first, he succumbed to temptation and phoned him that same Thursday at nightfall, using the number Tupra had given him in January; how very far away all that seemed now, that cold January day in the Plaza de la Paja, the woman reading Chateaubriand, the plaque commemorating Clavijo, Henry III's ambassador to the Great Tamorlán, that gabby individual Puddington or Buttcombe whom Ure (doubtless bolder than Reresby or Dundas) had terrorized with a small plastic fork: mentally or psychologically, it didn't feel that almost seven months had passed since then, it felt more like a bubble of eternity.

Centurión was anxious to return to Madrid and yet, at the same time, he was sorry to bring to an end his sojourn in Ruán, for he knew he would miss the town's essentially placid, routine life. But as his itinerant, transitory past existence had taught him, you must never become attached to a place and must always be prepared to leave it.

Following his retirement, though, he had changed, and the best or the worst of that change was that he had become more considerate and had opened the door to the most superficial brand of affection (the kind that attaches you not only to your loved ones, but to mere acquaintances, the pharmacist on the corner and the waiter at the local bar) to a degree he would have found unimaginable two or three years ago. It was possible that now, in 1997, he would not have had the courage to abandon his daughter Valerie, nor perhaps her mother, both of whom adored him. That is why, out of consideration, he preferred the small package to remain intact until he was obliged to make use of it, or at least until Inés had given the go-ahead for what would be her final night. Telling Tupra was a way of making himself do the deed, 'don't linger or delay'. At least in principle. Because until the deed is done, as long as it's in the future tense and not the past, one can always step back.

'Hello, Tupra,' I said as soon as he picked up the phone, and he immediately recognized my voice.

'What's happened? Why are you phoning me on this number? Is the deed done?'

'Stop, don't rush me. When we spoke on Monday, you didn't set a precise deadline.'

'I gave you a deadline a while ago, and you're running late.' He couldn't resist correcting me.

'Actually, you weren't very exact. I can't remember now whether it was in London or here, but I know you said two weeks or, at most, three. And I don't bother counting the days when it's not clear how many I've been given.'

There was a tiny pause. Perhaps even he did not remember that.

'So what do you want then? Look, you've caught me at a bad moment, I'm having supper with Beryl.'

And I did actually hear him swallow something, whether liquid or solid I couldn't tell. From the little I had seen, if anyone was capable of bringing him to heel and demanding his exclusive attention it was that woman who had so unexpectedly prompted him to change his marital status. Tupra was in love, and had married in order, in his words, to spare himself an additional sadness; to enjoy it without regret however long it lasted, he was quite clear about that: 'a few years, and then it will probably end'.

I couldn't resist repeating the little joke I had made in Madrid.

'Give my regards to Mrs Dundas, Mrs Oxenham or Mrs Ure, depending on who she is tonight.'

'Oh, enough of your stupid jokes, I don't have the time and I'm not in the mood.'

'Don't worry, I'll keep it short. I'm phoning to tell you that it will be Saturday night. The day after tomorrow. I thought it best to forewarn you, so that you don't take any hasty or unfortunate initiatives.'

'Me? Hasty? I've never been that. Unlike you and so many others,

I set things in motion only when the moment is right, neither before nor after. Is that all? You really needn't have bothered to call to tell me that.'

I was tempted to remind him of a distant occasion when he had definitely been hasty, and when his haste had brought about the failure of an operation. But I had said nothing at the time, you don't point out your boss's defects and faults, and at the time I was disciplined, and I had to do the same now too, not so much out of discipline and respect – I had lost all respect for him after meeting Janet Jefferys' children – as fear.

'Yes, that's all, there's nothing more.'

'All right, duly noted. Luckily for you. Otherwise, I'd have to set in train what I should have set in train ages ago. Keep me posted. That's a phone call I *will* want to receive.'

I bit my tongue, there was no point in responding, but I did add a further impertinence. That was the least I could do.

'So that you can run and tell Machimbarrena, I suppose, your very pressing friend. I mean, this is all about pleasing him, isn't it?'

As expected, this comment did not sit well with him, because he didn't even bother to answer. He hung up without saying goodbye, although the real reason was probably the disapproving look Mrs Reresby or Mrs Nutcombe was giving him: if there were no other guests, she would be getting bored with hearing half of a conversation that she wouldn't understand at all and about which she wouldn't feel the slightest curiosity. Sitting opposite him, chewing and staring into space.

Inés Marzán didn't get back to me until late on Saturday morning, as she was about to head off to La Demanda to supervise and organize the lunches. Centurión could see her from his window, while she was phoning him. She was already dressed and ready, with her handbag or pseudo-briefcase in one hand, she had waited until the last moment, perhaps in order to make him suffer, if such a verb were not an exaggeration from her point of view, after all, postponing a shag never inflicts real suffering. For him, though, the verb was no exaggeration.

'I finally managed to sort things out for tonight,' she said. 'I've told Transi that I'll be leaving at eleven, once all the tables have been served. We could meet at half past eleven or twenty to twelve, which would give me time to have a shower. I'll have been at work all day.'

Centurión felt a pang of regret, a remnant of frivolity he had so far failed to banish. The dress she was wearing really suited her, and he would have enjoyed taking it off. Or, even more arousing, leaving it on. He had still not fully absorbed what was going to happen.

'Did you tell her why?'

'I don't give unnecessary explanations to my staff. You know I dislike talking about myself.'

'But Transi is a friend, isn't she?'

'That depends. Not to the extent of telling her what I do or with whom. She knows nothing about you, for example, well, I certainly haven't told her. She'll know what the rest of the town knows, that we go out together now and then. And they can put two and two together if they want. So, see you at twenty to twelve?'

'I'll be there on the dot, and I'll wait as long you want me to. Impatiently patient.'

She laughed politely, that is slightly dismissively.

'Oh, come on, it's not that big a deal.'

Centurión did now open the package sent by Pérez Nuix. He had more than enough time, but it was best to be prepared. He was surprised to find that it contained two drugs, the one he had asked for plus another one. The one he'd asked for was Rohypnol (I think that's how it's written, but I'm not sure because I've never seen the packet since and 1997 is a long time ago), which, as its name suggests, has a hypnotic effect, or, rather, it stuns and cancels out the will: there's a total or near total loss of consciousness, time is erased, making it difficult or impossible for the person to remember what happened while they were under its influence, or perhaps there's only a kind of deep-seated confusion, for no one can be sure that what a few flashbacks or retrospective hallucinations are telling you happened really did. It depends on the individual, but sometimes there's a complete blank. It was quite widely used from the late 1980s on to rob the unwary after first seducing them or after sex. It was used by rent boys and prostitutes, who carried out the first part of the job (the seduction and plying the victim with a spiked drink) then alerted their colleagues so that they could skilfully, swiftly burgle the house or apartment. The after-effects were non-existent or minimal: struggling to wake up, feeling as if your mind were wrapped in a dense mist or impenetrable clouds, and, more often than not, there would be a complete void, with the victim never knowing what had happened while he or she was unconscious, or only able to guess from the visible results. Cunning repeat rapists also made use of it, reluctant to use force and fearful of the law. They would send their victim to sleep or wait until he or she was completely out of it, some victims were even unaware they had been raped and so didn't report it; if, afterwards, they noticed stinging, irritation or even pain, they usually came up with some strange, random reason to explain it away; unless they were virgins, they wouldn't even notice they'd been penetrated, especially if their assailant had done so only with his fingers. I'm afraid that the most cowardly rapists and those who act as a gang still use that drug. This wasn't a widespread practice in 1997, however, when even the criminals were less savage and brutish.

Such memory blanks were not that unusual or so hard to achieve. Centurión had never resorted to using such methods himself, but he had, in his time, been with two different women on two separate occasions, both of whom had drunk so heavily one night that, a few days later, they had asked quite genuinely, and without a hint of alarm, purely out of curiosity: 'Listen, did we have sex the other night or not? I have a feeling we did, but I can't be sure. If we did, I can't remember a thing.' In those two cases, they were quite right to remember nothing, because nothing had happened. Their question indicated, though, that they would have been willing, or might even have wanted it. Centurión cleared the matter up for them, much to their relief or perhaps disappointment, but he made a mental note to himself for any future occasions.

The name of the other drug consisted of just a few letters: I have only a vague memory of these, but it was something like GmbH, although I have a feeling that this collection of upper- and lower-case letters is what appears in the addresses of some German companies, and I've no idea what they mean. Whatever they were, in the brief note attached – which Centurión burned after reading and memoriz- ing it – Pérez Nuix told him the correct dosage and explained that this substance – in powder form – had similar properties to Rohyp- nol, but was even more effective and not available commercially. She left it to him to choose one or the other, and Centurión preferred to stick to the one that had already been successfully used by Spanish robbers and rapists. His only concern was that, like the 'swordsman of Calais', he wanted to carry out his task as considerately as possible. (His intention, or his desideratum, was for Inés Marzán to fall so deeply asleep or be rendered so completely unconscious that she wouldn't know what was happening to her, while it was happening.) This was as incongruous as was the trouble people took to avoid Anne Boleyn's backside being displayed to those gathered to watch her execution, if she were obliged to rest her chin or her cheek on the block to facilitate the work of the axeman, which is why the axe was replaced by a nobler instrument. Then again, there are always incongruities in extreme or final situations.

Centurión appeared punctually at Inés' place at twenty to twelve. From his window, he had seen her arrive just five minutes before, so she wouldn't have had time to shower. Nevertheless, he didn't wait, keen not to leave things too late. He made sure that no one saw him standing outside her building, or, rather, that no one noticed him. On Saturday nights, people were too pleased to be out and about, and frequently too drunk, to pay any attention to anyone else. The old street door was opened from above. He went up the stairs, pausing briefly on each landing in case he could hear footsteps or a door opening or closing or the lift, it would be best not to meet anyone, although some of the neighbours would already know him by sight. He rang the bell, and immediately heard the click-clack of the slender but not too high heels on which Inés glided so nimbly about among the tables at La Demanda, which meant that she hadn't even taken off her shoes. After looking through the spyhole, she opened the door. At least she didn't seem too hot and flustered from hurrying or from the heat, it was only the 2nd of August, and the first thing she said with a shy smile was:

'Sorry, there was a bit of a problem at the restaurant, and I got delayed. I haven't even had time to have a shower and change.'

Centurión was determined to be gallant that night, even

passionate, although without overdoing it (anything more would have been suspicious, since passion wasn't their style).

'All the better,' he said. 'I love your dress *and* your natural smell. The stronger and the more unadulterated the more I like it. Plus it's been such a long time . . .'

Cottonwool vanity, as our Spanish philosopher called it, a quality he attributed to poets, is always rather touching and ingenuous, unlike narcissism, pride and a feigned superiority complex. A lot of women back then clung to that vanity or that illusion, and Inés Marzán was one of them. Revealing her almost African teeth, she smiled again, more openly this time, clearly flattered.

'First, let me get myself a drink. I'm dying of thirst.'

'I'll get it for you. You just rest. What would you like?'

'Gin and coke on ice. Three cubes.'

'Heavy on the gin?'

'Fairly heavy. After all, we're not going anywhere, are we?'

Those words troubled Centurión, she didn't know that she wouldn't be going anywhere ever again, but he did. He went into the kitchen, made her a gin and coke, then so as to avoid mixing the drinks up, made himself a whisky and coke on ice (what used to be called the 'whore's drink'). He emptied the powder into her drink and stirred it with a teaspoon to dissolve it. It left not a trace, undetectable to the eyes or the nose and, apparently, to the taste. Then he washed and dried the spoon to get rid of any fingerprints, and put it back in the drawer. 'I've taken the first step, or was it two,' he thought before going back into the living room. 'It's the first step that's difficult, but I'm going to have to take a few more that will be far more difficult. But we, of course, know nothing of hatred and it will be "A murder, nothing more", as Athos said to d'Artagnan, and we still liked Athos.' He forced himself to stop thinking.

Inés had lain down on the sofa, she must be tired after the hustle and bustle of the day. Her skirt had ridden up quite a lot when she lay down. Her long legs, bare as one would expect in summer, smooth and waxed and attractively tanned, the slope of her vast thighs. She wasn't slumped on the sofa, just relaxed, her slightly parted thighs allowed one to imagine what lay beyond, but not enough to ascertain if she was wearing underwear or not. She still hadn't taken off her shoes because she knew he liked her to keep them on, sometimes even right up until the end. Centurión hesitated, and couldn't help but think that if he did start having sex with her, he might not finish. In part, this depended on how quickly the drug took effect; or he could have sex with her once she was completely out for the count.

'That would be an utterly base act worthy of a rapist,' he thought at once, as if what would follow were not far baser. 'But since she's always very hot and eager for it with me, would that be rape?' Scruples come and go and are often contradictory, respectful of some things and not of others; even pity can fluctuate. 'It would still be a base act though, because she wouldn't get any pleasure.'

Best not to get nervous or overthink things. Inés Marzán was no fool, nor, from what he had been told, was Magdalena Orúe. On the contrary, they were both highly intelligent, and Magdalena was very astute. The latter had not put in an appearance, the collaborator or terrorist would not have succumbed to flattery if she had sensed any danger, not at least with such a genuine smile. I felt really sorry for Inés, I couldn't help it, I felt really really sorry. Of course she could be pretending, which was something she would be good at. She would have spent eight or nine years in that town in the north-west pretending impeccably, and without arousing even a hint of suspicion. She had confided in him in a way that, possibly, in all that time, she had not done with anyone else: about her lost daughter, always assuming that story was true. If it was, at least her daughter would not mourn her or miss her, being accustomed to her absence. Just one confidence, made only once.

Inés Marzán drank down her gin and coke with genuine thirst, as if it were water or plain Coca-Cola. She finished it in three gulps, barely pausing in between, and in those brief pauses we immediately began snogging and touching each other up – well, it had been many days and quite a number of weeks – to use the language boys would use in my adolescence, and some expressions never die. Centurión suggested moving into the bedroom and asked if she wanted another drink.

'What would you like? More of the same?'

It would be helpful if she kept drinking alcohol. He didn't offer her any cocaine, though, because that might have livened her up. Nor did she ask for any cocaine or look for her own supply, which Comendador continued to provide. Perhaps she preferred feeling slightly dazed, and lucidity would have been out of place.

'Yes, the same again, please. I don't know if I'm going to be up to much, you know, I'm dead on my feet. As I said, by the end of the week, all I can think about is sleeping.'

'You go into the bedroom and lie down. I'll bring your drink to you.'

The bedroom was next to the bathroom, not too far for him to carry her when it was time, which would be soon.

He returned to the kitchen and made her another drink. He didn't add any more of the drug, one dose was enough according to the instructions. As I made the drink, I kept obsessively or superstitiously repeating to myself: 'A murder. Nothing more. Nothing more.' In that same cold, confident way (what more could there be, what more is there?), Athos the musketeer had played down the fact that, in the distant past, he had hanged a woman from a tree – and he himself was about to kill a woman. Athos had in fact killed his own very young wife, a mere girl, who had, however, miraculously survived and gone on to spread her wickedness everywhere, the wickedness she apparently already harboured within her. When you first read those words in Dumas, you barely notice them, if, that is, they appeared in the children's version, which they probably didn't. Centurión wasn't sure who he was killing, that was his particular curse, and so he also repeated to himself, trying to summon up an anticipatory envy, trying to downplay the action he was about to take: 'Better be with the dead . . .' But no envious feeling came.

Inés was no longer in the living room, she had done as he suggested and lain down on her neatly made bed, for she always made the bed before going off to work. She had left the shutters half open, and he carefully closed them, for, having so often viewed that room from afar through binoculars as if watching a stage, he knew that someone else might also have binoculars. She was still fairly awake, but he could see that she was already reluctantly succumbing to somnolence. She had lain down on her side and slipped her arms under the pillow, almost like someone settling down to sleep. She was still thirsty though, or perhaps her mouth was dry, and she again drank greedily, sitting up to do so. He took advantage of this position to stroke her thighs and undo the top button of her dress, then the bottom one, the third from the top then the fourth and fifth from the bottom, then the sixth from the top, leaving three still buttoned, best not to undo them all. Her dress was navy blue, with buttons from top to bottom and a belt around the waist, the belt having already fallen off; perhaps, dare I say it, more the kind of dress María Viana would wear. Centurión saw now that she was wearing a bra but no knickers.

He was surprised that she had spent a whole long day at the restaurant like that, going back and forth. Her dress was dark enough not to reveal anything, and she did tend to wear close-fitting knickers, which would have stuck to her skin and made her feel still hotter. Or perhaps she had taken them off before he rang the bell. Not her shoes, but her knickers. Even lying there on the bed, she still had her shoes on, doubtless to please him. I was touched by that desire to please as she lay on what would become her 'woeful bed', in that language that was also hers.

She responded to his caresses, his left hand on her breasts, his right on her thighs and further up, although without going all the way. She became instantly aroused, as she always did, her arousal being more physiological than mental, for the body does sometimes respond to stimuli quite independently of the will, or even imposes itself on or contradicts the will. Inés was not putting up the slightest resistance, not that Centurión could ever recall her doing so, out of passivity or indifference; on the contrary, even after the most minimal of preambles, she was gripped by a certain urgency. Until she fell asleep, no, until she lost consciousness, he would continue as usual, and he realized that this would be easy enough, if he didn't focus on that difficult face of hers, and this thought made him feel ashamed, his scruples vacillating and incoherent. He sensed, however, that Inés would not have the energy to show her usual urgency or ardour. He could see that she was exhausted, or perhaps the substance had already started to take effect, it apparently worked very fast.

'I really do feel very tired, and sweaty too,' she said. 'Let me see if a shower would wake me up a bit. It won't take a minute. Do you mind waiting?'

'Of course not, but you seem very weak. You'd better not stand up until you get your strength back, you might fall over. How about me running you a bath, would that be better?'

'Good idea. It won't take long.'

I left her lying on the bed and turned on the taps, warm water, I didn't want her to get too cold nor, of course, to be too hot. I intended, absurdly, to act as delicately as possible, when there was nothing remotely delicate about what I was planning to do.

I ran the water for a while, testing the temperature with my hand, memorizing which surfaces I touched so that I could wipe them down afterwards with a cloth, there are no fingerprints in water, no, not in water. I waited there, smoking, standing by the bath, waiting for the bath to fill, which meant I wouldn't hear any voice or groan coming from the bedroom, and I preferred not to look. I turned off the taps, and waited another minute or two, until I had finished my cigarette, then I threw the end down the toilet and flushed it away, watching it disappear.

'Not yet, not yet', there are times when you can make that 'not yet' last, if it depends solely on you, but that's often not the case. Magdalena would have got up that morning thinking, perhaps as we have all been thinking for decades: 'It didn't happen yesterday, or the day before, or in the last five or ten years, which have passed so slowly night after night and day after day. But who can assure me it won't happen today, when I step nonchalantly out into the street; or that someone won't poison my food; or that a friend won't knock at my door and be the one to put a bullet in me.' No, no one could assure her of that, and now it was today.

When Centurión returned to the bedroom, Inés was fast asleep, out for the count, unconscious. The sound of running water must have helped to relax her, not that she would have needed any help. Centurión touched her, moved her, rocked her from side to side like a puppet, and stroked her skin just to see if he could wake or disturb her. No, she was completely gone, apparently peacefully asleep, her breathing soft and regular, not a glimmer of consciousness, as if she were anaesthetized. He couldn't put it off any longer, it was best to get it over with, then leave and move on to other things, because he had other things to move on to, and she did not. And, yes, it was unfair. But it had been unfair on the victims of the bombings at the shopping mall and the barracks, who would also have had nothing more to do after those two days in 1987 about which no one had forewarned or advised them. Just as it would be unfair were Celia Bayo and María Viana to have their futures cut short at the hands of strangers come from far away, for they were almost certainly not Magdalena Orúe and they had never committed a crime in their lives.

He needed to pluck up his courage, except that's not the right word: he needed to pluck up a sense of righteousness or a desire for revenge that was quite alien to him, as well as feelings of pity for those victims past or future, two contradictory feelings. For a few brief moments that contradiction set him in motion.

It was now very easy to take off her clothes, no one gets into a bath with her brassiere or bra on. He carefully removed her navy-blue dress, finished unbuttoning it and took it off. What came next was more complicated. Inés was large, awkward to get hold of and very ample, but she wasn't that heavy. I would carry her in my arms or, if not, I would drag her to the bathroom, which was only a matter of feet away. The first option was the better one; the edge of the bath wasn't that high, and it would be easier to place her in it from above. I tried to pick her up and succeeded, even though, in the circumstances, she was what we usually call a dead weight. I took the precaution of carrying her through the door in the same position as she would be in the bath, head first, feet last, the plug would then be at her feet, that all-important plug. I paused for a moment, holding her body aloft, as if it were the body of a bride being carried airily over the threshold of her new home or of a hotel room. But I couldn't stand the weight – as on so many occasions, fatigue was the deciding factor – and I lowered her slowly into the water, there was no way I was going to drop her in, let her fall from on high and possibly startle her, and cause splashes or even puddles. I rested her head on the shelf or edge, where she kept sponges and various bottles: soap dispensers, conditioners and shampoos, and who knows what else. Her dark hair immediately became wet, the tips that is, the crown of her head remained dry for the moment, her widow's peak still conspicuous. It looked to him then like the point of an arrow, or silent accusation.

He looked away, the first piece of advice given to hitmen and execu-tioners is to avoid the eyes of the person they are about to kill, not to meet their gaze, because that can cause you to hesitate and falter, and you rarely get a second chance, the exception to this rule being exe-cutioners, who are allowed to make a hash of things and keep on chopping. He was in no danger of meeting Inés' gaze because her eyes were serenely closed. There was danger, though, in her face and its large features, for in sleep they softened and gave an impression of utter helplessness. Centurión paused, knowing full well that he shouldn't, because thinking is the other enemy, you mustn't look and you mustn't think. But he couldn't just push her head under the water, he needed a transition between placing the body in the bath and the end. He remembered that false dead woman Janet Jefferys. This time the dead woman would be real.

'You decided to adopt the appearance of an ageless woman, Mad-die O'Dea, eternally timeless.' Calling her by that name might help, he thought, might drive him on. 'That is your real name, just as mine is Tomás Nevinson not Miguel Centurión or MacGowran or Fahey, Hörbiger or Avellaneda, Rowland or Breda or Ley or any of the other names I have since forgotten. Now we both know who we are, and you have known who I am for far longer. You decided not to confront me nor to pre-empt me in an act of self-defence so as to save yourself. Now you are like the duellist who fires his first shot into the ground or the air and leaves himself entirely at the mercy of his opponent, who might well do the same and go home in peace or else ruthlessly put a bullet between your eyes and not even thank you for showing such restraint. You took a big risk and now you're at *my* mercy, Maddie O'Dea. I have no idea if you knew it or not, if you were too trusting or if you knew it would be today, that's an unknown that will never be resolved.'

Thinking leads not only to doubting, it can also prove unstoppable once set in motion, it was the same with 'those people' of whom Inés Marzán had spoken before the poor local councillor from Ermua was murdered, for the 'commando' had clearly avoided looking him in the eye before killing him, choosing, as usual, a bullet in the back of the head. She knew them: 'They're like a machine that can't be stopped even if they wanted it to stop,' and that is what he, Centurión, must be like now. But he had stopped, he hadn't acted promptly and was delaying the end. Idiotically (as he would have said in English, his other language), he again tested the temperature of the water, worried that she might be feeling cold. It had definitely grown cooler, and so he turned on the hot tap to warm it up a little, taking care to move her feet out of the way so that they didn't get scalded by the boiling water, which, he feared, might also wake her up a little, and that was the last thing he wanted, because he would be forced then to resort to violence or, rather, to a more explicit violence that might involve a slight tussle, and he really didn't feel capable of that. Doing so while she was completely unconscious was very different from doing so while she had a tiny scrap of understanding or consciousness, struggling to shake off her torpor, fighting to achieve at least some form of wakefulness.

Why had Inés Marzán not taken precautions to save herself, why had Magdalena Orúe not done so, she who didn't bother with niceties? Why had she not warned her colleagues in Bergara in the Basque Country or in Magherafelt in Northern Ireland to help her out immediately? Why had Ruiz Kindelán not told them? The only explanation for this was that she, being a higher rank than him, had expressly forbidden it, but why would she do that? Centurión didn't think Inés had grown so fond of him that she would save his life at the possible cost of her own later on. But he might be wrong, it's very hard to gauge the feelings we inspire in others, because we are the object not the subject. And for the same reason we're also a bad judge of what we imagine others are feeling, perhaps Inés thought he was half in love with or even devoted to her, and therefore 'neutralized' and almost harmless. Some people are secretly vain and conceited and proud, but never show it.

Or perhaps it was simpler than that, a mere question of weariness. Yes, weariness dictates all kinds of attitudes and inhibitions and actions, who knows how many give up everything out of sheer weariness. Perhaps for some time now she had been thinking the same as Ole Andresen in Hemingway's famous story and as the racing driver disguised as a teacher played by John Cassavetes in the film *The Killers*, which is partly based on that story: 'At last they've found me. I shouldn't complain. I was given a little extra time. Useless, meaningless time, but nevertheless a little extra time to spend in the universe. And since all such respites must have an end, so be it. I won't defend myself and I'm not running away either.' Imagining Inés being so resigned to her fate further undermined me. As did the idea that she might feel unreasonably fond of me. Centurión could not allow himself such a feeling, he must put an end to it.

He still did not look at her face. 'It's safer to be that which we destroy than dwell in doubtful joy after its destruction,' well, that's a rather inaccurate version of the quote, no matter, it was a question of envying the victim in order to have the courage to be her executioner. He looked at Inés Marzán's feet, her neatly trimmed, pedicured, varnished nails. All he had to do was tug on her feet with his two hands, since she, being in a state of limbo, would know nothing about it, and she would leave the world unwillingly but also without rebelling. She couldn't have been so innocent as to think that our day-to-day existence will last until eternity. She wasn't the driver of a cart drawn by a mule who had been crossing the bridge over the River Lesmes for centuries. She would have known a lot of fear in her life, and when you're afraid you reflect and prophesy and predict, you foresee all that has been and will be, he had experienced this himself and he knew exactly how it was. She wouldn't be so very different from how he had been.

He tugged at her feet, her ankles, and immediately her head began to go under the water until it was completely submerged. All he needed was to hold steady and allow a little time to pass, counting the seconds, one, two, three, four, five, six, seven, eight, nine; and ten. He had made a start and so allowed himself a pause, knowing that this could well prove to be a fatal error, but he needed to make sure that she wasn't reacting to her incipient drowning, that she wasn't aware of how imminent it was, that she wasn't regaining so much as a tiny flicker of vague consciousness, which is what he most feared and felt least capable of dealing with. He couldn't tell if she had already swallowed water, he imagined she had, but she was asleep and completely out of the waking world, and she didn't even cough or choke or take a desperate inbreath. She was breathing though. He gave himself and Inés a respite, although perhaps that was cruel on his part; nearly five centuries ago, when there was little compassion, they had sent for the skilled 'swordsman of Calais' to avoid pointlessly prolonging the victim's agony. No, he wasn't being cruel – he was simply allowing time, and time is always civilized – because Centurión could not allow her ever to be able to say anything along the lines of 'No, this can't be happening, it's just not possible that I will no longer see or hear anything or utter another word, that this still-functioning mind will stop and be snuffed out, this mind still so full of tormenting thoughts; that I will never again stand up or move so much as a finger and will be thrown in a ditch or be burned like a lump of firewood albeit without giving off the same pleasant woody smell, that my body will become a cloud of smoke if, at that point, I am still me. I will be me in the eyes of the person who killed me and those who see me and pick me up and manhandle me away from the scene of the crime, who will continue to recognize my features as if I were alive, but I won't be me in my eyes or in my consciousness, because, it seems, I will have no consciousness . . . Later, some of Ruán's bells will toll for me, but I won't hear them.'

No, Centurión would not allow that tiny glimmer of thought. And so, after that brief pause, he again tugged at her feet and fully submerged her in the innocuous bathtub that she would have entered every day. He didn't count this time, no, he didn't count, that would compromise his objective, his obligation, besides, he had no alternative; and so he didn't count. He didn't know how many seconds passed while Inés began to drown, perhaps a minute or slightly more. And then the same thing happened as happened with one of the two men I had killed in self-defence or in order to avert terrible misfortunes, in a life that I could recall but no longer recognize. When he realized he was dying, that man looked at me entirely without rancour, at most with a slight hint of reproach directed not so much at me as at the order of the universe, which had brought him to that place without his consent, had enwrapped and entangled him for as long as it chose to keep him there, and was now suddenly, without a word, carrying him off again, was expelling and expunging him. Then, at the very last moment, Inés kicked furiously with her feet, very fast it seemed to him in his imagination, as if she could still run and flee. She was lying down and her feet weren't touching the bottom, they were running in the empty air in a vain, final, posthumous attempt to escape, when, in reality, those same steps, at once so light and so very weary, were leading her into non-existence.

I couldn't see the look in Inés Marzán's enormous eyes, she wouldn't be able to raise her eyelids however hard she tried, but it didn't matter, I could feel that look: I felt that slight hint of reproach directed at the order of the universe, which is what leads us all to gamble and to lose. What I did feel in my hands, though, and this was not my imagination, was her feet struggling to free themselves. I was so frightened that I let go, and then I saw them kicking, very fast it seemed to Centurión in his imagination, as if she could still run and flee. Only water around her now, no air.

And then I couldn't, I just couldn't go on. Those feet were the leaf that happened to fall from a tree and cover my rifle sight. For a moment, I lost my line of sight, but that moment was decisive and I did not recover my position. Those vainly kicking feet were the bare, defenceless, pedicured feet of a woman. ('Perhaps,' I thought, 'what we cannot tolerate is that we should be killed by someone else, that others should decide the time and manner of our death, and faced by that, we rebel like savages, sometimes not even knowing what we are doing.') Because a falling leaf is enough for time to end, inconsistent, indeterminate time.

As I grabbed her under the armpits and pulled hard to get her head above the water – she lacked the will or the strength to sit up, and even the survival instinct isn't strong enough if you're drowsy and absent – I realized the consequences of my action or omission: 'I'm condemning Celia Bayo and María Viana, and I'm not saving Inés Marzán either. A murder, nothing more, and now all three will fall, sooner or later.' However, another egotistical thought occurred to me, or, rather, a conviction: 'It won't be today, and what hasn't yet happened might never happen. At any rate, it will not be me, I will not be the one to do it.'

XV

Nothing had happened, I could stop trying to memorize everything I had touched, there was no need to erase every fingerprint, every trace. I immediately removed the plug and the water gradually drained away. I waited until she had dried off a little once the bath had emptied, for the night was still hot. I took the biggest towel I could find, almost the size of a sheet and spread it out on the bed. It would be more of an effort getting her out of the bath than lowering her in. I managed to lift her up though – she seemed heavier – and carry her over to the bed. I patted her dry, including her feet, then briefly wrapped the towel around her, taking care to place her face down so that any water she might have swallowed would dribble out. She was breathing quietly, having suffered no apparent harm, she didn't seem distressed or agitated, she can't have been dreaming, certainly not about what had happened to her; perhaps I had kept her under for less time than I thought, thirty seconds at most, it was impossible to know now.

I remained sitting beside her, on the edge of her woeful or not quite so woeful bed, observing her, guarding her, watching over the city without the sleepy or attentive eye of the Lord. Some areas of her skin were slightly crinkled, but she hadn't been in the water that long, then again perhaps my pauses or respites had lasted longer than I imagined. She didn't seem to feel either cold or hot, although I felt quite feverish, my pulse faster than normal. I steadied myself, reached for an ashtray, lit a cigarette, and blew out a cloud of smoke, smoking calmed me. Otherwise, I didn't take my eyes off her, alert to any change. There probably wouldn't be any change or no significant change, but I felt uneasy at the thought of setting about tidying up, restoring order and covering her with the sheet before leaving her there alone. I shouldn't have been afraid, but I was. Nothing had happened.

After a few minutes, I began to grow bored and was filled by inopportune thoughts, the thoughts that are always lying in wait for us. I looked at my watch, which I had taken off earlier, I hadn't looked at it for a while. It was a quarter past one, I had been in her apartment for an hour and a half, I wasn't sure if I should stay any longer, if I should spend the night there like a sentinel, which wouldn't, after all, seem so very odd. What would she remember the next day and in the days to come? Perhaps absolutely nothing, perhaps more than was desirable. There would be no trace of what had happened, but I would find it embarrassing to see her again and talk to her, because I would certainly remember, I knew everything and wouldn't forget, how could I?

It would be an hour earlier in England, a quarter past midnight, still too late for Tupra, I thought, although this was a call he would be interested to receive, indeed, he might have postponed going to bed in order to wait up for it, eager to know and tell Machimbarrena. Or instead of phoning him, I could phone Pérez Nuix, who certainly wouldn't have gone to bed yet, not on a Saturday night in Madrid, but nor would she be at home – she was a night owl – and she didn't have one of those prehistoric mobile phones Tupra had in 1997, one of the privileged few. The truth is that I didn't want to phone either of them. In their eyes, I would be giving them some very bad news that would anger them both, and no one wants that. I was under no obligation to phone them immediately, they knew my date with Inés would be late at night, that something unforeseen could happen and that things take time. Not so much the murder, but the preparations.

I could simply not phone, there was no reason why I should. They could seek me out in vain, feeling justifiably suspicious. I could always refuse to answer . . . 'Although, one day,' I thought, 'I'll have to answer, because every day comes around, however remote and unlikely that seems.'

I opened the shutters, there was no need to keep them closed now, and looked across at my apartment opposite; as usual, I had left a couple of lights on, to give the impression that someone was in. I looked at the bridge, which, as on any summer Saturday, was heaving with people. I looked at the waters, which were, by contrast, very still and peaceful. It didn't make much sense now to stay on in Ruán, nor to return to Madrid where it would be swelteringly hot and when Berta and the kids would be in San Sebastián, that holiday town, for it was the time of the summer exodus, and these were still the boom years. I would fulfil my commitment to teach the twins for the rest of the month, which would mean I could keep an eye on what happened to those three women who were now in grave danger. Not that I could do much if one or two guys turned up when least expected. Nor could I be in more than one place at a time, or be more than one person; but at least I would know, I would find out *in situ* and not from somewhere far away. Any death in Ruán would be an event and cause a real upheaval if it were a violent death, as happened years later in Santander to that poor visitor from Madrid, Natividad Garayo; Florentín would devote pages and pages to it in *El Esperado* and whole hours on the local television channel. In Madrid, on the other hand, the press would give it a miserable half-column or not even that if it was disguised as an accident or a sudden heart attack.

It was two o'clock by then or slightly later. Inés Marzán or Magdalena Orúe was still asleep or unconscious, probably more the former the latter. Anyway, she was in a deep sleep that looked likely to last, if such things can be predicted. She was alive, she was still alive. I was intensely relieved, I even felt a kind of inner euphoria. And yet I was also beginning to feel worried. What if Tupra was right, as he usually was? What if I had reprieved the Berchtesgaden cat, always bearing in mind the insurmountable differences and taking such a comparison with a large pinch of salt? What if, in the short or medium term, E T A made another attack, or the I R A did so in Ulster, which was on its way to a peace accord, an attack in which she was involved?

I cursed my luck, my endless quandaries: I had taken on a very different responsibility, with many lives at stake and not just one. I would have to be alert to what happened not only in that town in the north-west, but in the rest of Spain and in Northern Ireland too, dreading each day, combing the newspapers, feeling alarmed and always fearing the worst. I suddenly eyed Inés with suspicious, anticipatory reproach. But what could I do? Refill the bath and put her back in? No, it was too late for that. No one could guarantee that the same thing wouldn't happen again, and I would spend the night changing my mind, doing and undoing, contradicting myself; at some point, I might go a step too far, and then there would be no going back. No, the moment had passed and I would have to face the subsequent risks.

She was now completely dry. I carefully rolled her over to remove the towel without waking her; I hung it on the rail where I had found it, it might drip a little, but that didn't matter. I returned to the bedroom, drew back the sheet and covered Inés' naked body, and once again I saw her as she was, long legs, long arms, ample curves, no longer shrunken or diminished. I emptied the ashtrays into the bin. I removed the bottles and carefully washed both glasses, as thoroughly as if somehow I were tainted too. I had come so close that perhaps I was, that's how it would be viewed today, in an age that judges and condemns thoughts, intentions and temptations, people in the last century were less hysterical and authoritarian. That night still belonged to the twentieth century, although only just, and with each day that passes, we look back on that century with a certain nostalgia.

Before turning off the lights, I went over to the front door and looked around. Once I had left and closed the door behind me, there would be no going back; if something unexpected happened to Inés after that, she would have to fend for herself. As she would have done on any other night. I had neither the desire nor the courage to stay and sleep by her side, with one eye open. I needed to get out of there.

And yet I again retraced my steps as far as the bedroom door and went in. She was still there and alive, I drew back the sheet for a few seconds to check that her body was intact, with no worrying marks of any kind: a superstitious gesture, just as before you set off on a journey, you check five times that you've turned off the gas. I would find out how she was the next day, if she contacted me; as for me, it would be best just to let time pass, although that was most unlikely. I walked back to the front door, but still did not open it. Order was restored, and the world would carry on as if that night had never happened. I mean the night that I alone had lived through. It hadn't existed for anyone else, or so I hoped and would prefer. No one had dared disturb the universe, or at least I had not.

Tupra contained his probable impatience – or perhaps he sensed that I had failed – and left me in peace on the Sunday, the eve of the Queen Mother's birthday – she had been born in 1900 and would live for a few more years yet. I said nothing to him, neither to him nor to Pat Pérez Nuix. Unlikely though it might seem, they were both apparently observing the local days of obligation. In 1997, when the phone rang, you couldn't tell who was calling, and so my only options were either to pick it up or not. If I heard the voice of one of my 'guards', I had decided to say nothing and put the phone down, at least on that day, I didn't need any shocks or scoldings or arguments, I needed slowly to calm my nerves. The person who did phone was Inés Marzán before she left for the lunchtime shift at La Demanda, and I was definitely prepared to speak to her. I was still concerned about her recovery and was dying to know.

'Hi, Miguel. Just a quick question, I haven't got much time,' she said quite casually. 'I wanted to ask you what happened last night. I woke up with such a heavy head and a monumental hangover, and I can't remember a thing. I was lying in bed naked, so I presume we went ahead with our plan, but I'm not sure, my mind is a complete blank, can you believe it, as if someone had wiped it clean with a sponge. Forgive my frankness, but I can't remember a thing about what we did or didn't do. What happened? What happened to me?'

She didn't appear to be pretending, but you can never tell. And if she was Magdalena Orúe O'Dea – and now that I had left her alive and free, I was inclined to believe she was – she could easily be lying, having spent years lying every day and to everyone. To lie would be her first instinct.

'Yes, poor thing,' and I resorted here to the most colloquial expressions of pity, 'you were so exhausted, practically ready to drop, just as you had warned me. It really wasn't a good idea for us to meet. Forgive me, I was the one who came on all heavy and insistent.'

'No, I wanted it too, but what happened? It really distresses me not to be able to recall a thing about last night, not so much as a single moment. The last thing I remember is waiting for you to arrive. I've never experienced such a complete and utter blank before.'

'We had a couple of drinks and fooled around a bit. Well, I managed to get you half undressed, but then you said you felt all sweaty and still smelled of food from the restaurant and that you wanted to take a shower or a bath. You had a funny turn in the bath, a combination of exhaustion and the booze, I suppose. It was just as well I was there, you could easily have drowned. You were so far gone I had to lift you out of the water and dry you before putting you to bed. I stayed for a while to keep an eye on you, then left. I'm really sorry, it's all my fault for insisting.'

I tried to keep as close as possible to the facts, just in case she had noticed some sign of what had happened in the bath or the wet towel, in case she felt as if she had swallowed water and had a slight cough, details that could be explained by my version of events.

'So we didn't make love, then?'

'No, we didn't get around to fucking.' I couldn't bring myself to use euphemisms, I didn't have the right. 'You were in no fit state for that. What you needed was to sleep. I think you must have drunk some wine at the restaurant too . . .'

'Well, I reckon I slept for ten hours straight, possibly more. What time was it when I had that funny turn, more or less I mean? Any idea? Getting myself to wake up properly and get going this morning was unbelievably difficult, but that's sometimes what happens when you oversleep: instead of feeling rested, you feel shattered.'

'I don't know, about half past twelve or perhaps a little later, maybe a quarter to one. You didn't manage to stay awake for long actually. The alcohol and the bath finished you off.'

'Anyway, I've got a really thick head and I'm running late. I'm glad to know, though, that we didn't fuck after all, because it's just not like me to forget something so completely. We'll have to try another day when I'm not so tired, and next time, no alcohol. Why didn't you offer me a line of coke to spark me up?'

'That would have been pure selfishness on my part. It really didn't seem a good idea to mix drink and drugs.'

'OK. I must run now. Shall I give you a ring in the week, just to check in?'

'Of course. Call me whenever you like. I'll leave it to you to decide, when you're feeling more rested. I'll be here. And again I'm really sorry, it was wrong of me to put pressure on you like that.'

I breathed a sigh of relief. It had all turned out as I'd hoped. She didn't remember a thing, and had no idea how close I had come to killing her. Just as well. I would still feel embarrassed to see her again though, let alone have sex with her, because I did remember and I did know what had happened. It would be best to leave it to her to phone me, to take the initiative. I could always play the unavailable card with her as well, or just hang up without answering. Besides, it was impossible to believe she was being totally genuine. Perhaps it had all been a pantomime, that ingenuous conversation. She hadn't even asked me how it was that, according to me, she'd been in danger of drowning, given that it's not that easy to drown in a bath. If she *was* being genuine, she must simply have thought I was exaggerating. If she wasn't, it would be because she preferred not to delve too deeply or to admit that she did know what had happened, and then, when we next met, she'd be waiting for me with a vengeance. I was clearly still very upset because I was getting my languages mixed up: 'with a vengeance' doesn't mean what it seems to mean in English, and has nothing to do with revenge. She had a very cool head, Magdalena Orúe, and I couldn't discount the possibility that she would repay me in kind on another night of love. She was now the duellist whose turn it was to shoot.

The truce ended on Monday the 4th. I set off early, and by late morning, on my return from teaching María Viana's twins, I found four messages on the answer machine, three from Tupra and one from Pérez Nuix (Machimbarrena didn't deign to contact me directly). Tupra was brief and to the point: 'I've been waiting to hear from you since Saturday and have still heard nothing. Ring me as soon as you get this message. There are a few people anxious to hear from you,' was the first one. The second was even more pointed: 'I'm still waiting, Tom. Don't make me waste any more time.' The third was irritated and urgent: 'Call me back.' Pérez Nuix's message was longer: 'Why haven't you been in touch? What happened? Did it turn out badly or did you back off at the last moment?' – and so on. And by way of farewell, she added: 'Bertie's absolutely fuming. We don't want him to catch fire. That would be bad news for all of us.'

Never a truer word said. Tupra on fire was indeed bad news, all it would take was for him to lose his rag for one second – just one – and make some rash decision that would then be difficult to rectify once reason was restored. And so I picked up the phone, dialled the number of his pre-mobile phone and said as confidently as I could (an entirely bogus confidence, as he sensed instantly):

'What's up, Bertie? Why so urgent and persistent? I assumed that, by now, you would have guessed what had happened, with no need for any explanation.'

'Are you a moron or what? You've turned into a complete twat, Tom, and you never used to be.' He really was fuming. 'If you say you're going to call me, you call me, right? Yes, I did guess, but I wanted to hear it from you. Did things go wrong or did you?'

I wasn't going to invent some twattish excuse, to lie, to hide, to give him the chance to set me another deadline and provide me with another opportunity. Whatever for?

'*I* did. I couldn't go through with it, what can I say, I just couldn't. I came very close, and it was all going well, but, at the last moment, it just didn't feel right. I didn't see things as clearly as you. That's all I can say.'

'Oh, so it didn't feel right.' However coolly he said this, he found my choice of words scandalous, infuriating.

'Instead of sending her to peace to gain our peace, I sought my own. If I sent her into war against us, I'll be very sorry, of course, but that remains to be seen.'

I was sure that, however angry he might be, he would recognize that paraphrase of those lines from *Macbeth*. He knew the play by heart, like any truly cultivated murderer. He had caused more murders than I had, but they didn't weigh on him: they were just part of the job, that's all. He had been brought up among the savage Kray brothers, whereas I had grown up in Madrid, in the peaceful, civilized Chamberí district of my adolescence and childhood.

'The war isn't being waged against us, Nevinson. They're waging war on anyone and everyone, on a mother playing with her children in the park, on an old man with a stick walking down the street. *That* is the war you have failed to avert. As for the war being waged against us . . . well, we can defend ourselves, but they can't, Nevinson, they can't.'

I found it odd that he should resort to pathos, or was it demagogy? But he knew what he was doing. For a moment it worked. I said again:

'That remains to be seen.'

'Of that you can be sure. If we don't sort things out quickly, we'll certainly "see" sooner or later, in a month or six months, in a year or two. And all because you were too much of a wimp to go through with it.'

He wasn't pulling his punches, and he was right. I had no answer.

'Look, one thing is clear: you were wrong to come to Madrid. And I was wrong to take on the mission. But the initial mistake was yours.'

'Well, we can take that as a given,' he said somewhat peevishly. 'But you know what's coming next, don't you? I warned you.'

'I know, I know, but that's your business, not mine. I'm finished – again.'

'Oh, you're definitely finished, Tom.'

He hung up. So did I, and that was that.

Afterwards, before the days of desolation began, I called the head teacher at the school to tell her that I wouldn't be able to continue teaching in September. Unforeseen family problems, my indispensable presence in Madrid. 'Oh, please don't leave me in the lurch like that, Miguel,' she said.

According to Tupra, Miguel had left far too many people in the lurch, and with far graver consequences. Inopportunely, into my head came those lines from *Diary of a Man in Despair* – that never-ending doubt: 'If I had had an inkling of the role this piece of filth was to play, and of the years of suffering he was to make us endure I would have shot him without a second thought.' I had had an inkling, but only by inference, and that hadn't proved to be enough. I consoled myself superstitiously and in anticipation, much as Reck-Malleczewen had: 'It would have done no good in any case: in the councils of the Highest, our martyrdom had already been decided.' This wasn't actually true, but it helped.

Then began the long period of waiting, like so many other long periods of waiting in my life, and in Berta's life too, I never forgot that, I never forgot her. No, 'never' is an exaggeration, a lie. I had sometimes been too absorbed in my deceptions and my activities, but not when I was in that town in the north-west, in Ruán. Our last meeting in Madrid had left me feeling hopeful, and I thought about her more with each day that passed. I wasn't deceiving myself: I took refuge in her image, in the idea of her, because that was all that was left to me of affection and importance and value, and in such cases one tends not to distinguish between longing and lack, between desire and need. Something to hold on to, a lifeline.

That time of waiting would be either long or not depending on what steps the IRA and ETA took, depending on Tupra and his envoys, probably not the ailing Blakeston or the idiot Molyneux, but brutes like Patmore and Hurd, both of whom I knew by sight and, above all, by reputation, the first was an obedient mass of muscle, the second a weakling who wore round-rimmed spectacles and was a nasty, cold-blooded piece of work, and both were perfectly capable of removing anyone from the picture.

I stayed in Ruán for all of August, spending the mornings fulfilling my commitment to María Viana and her children, and spending the afternoons and evenings half as a hermit and half as a libertine, as I said, in the summer there was always plenty going on. On some evenings, I would find an excuse to phone Berta in San Sebastián, and we would chat for a while in a superficial, friendly manner, I had told her that I should be back in Madrid at the end of the month, to which she had responded: 'Good.'

I charged Comendador with keeping me informed of any 'strange new arrivals', for he was constantly going back and forth between Catilina and Ruán and frequented all their various social circles. 'What do you mean by "strange"?' he asked quite rightly. 'You know, foreigners who don't look like tourists, especially if they arrive as a twosome. They could also be Spanish. People who look as if they had a particular reason for being here, other than to see the sights and get drunk in the bars. It's hard to explain.' 'What's up, is someone after you, on your tail?' 'No, I don't think so, but, yes, it's as if someone was.'

I woke each morning feeling anxious. Now I waited eagerly to read *El Esperado*, flicking through its absurd pages as I sat on the terrace of the Hotel Childe, a hotel that was first opened in the nineteenth century, and had since been tastefully refurbished and modernized – perhaps its original owner had been a fan of Byron. Even though anything that happened to María, Celia or Inés would have made the front page, I even read the news in brief, in search of clues, quite what I didn't know. Buying English newspapers in Ruán was difficult, plus they often arrived late, and the Irish press was impossible to find, as it probably was in Madrid too. I bought all the Spanish newspapers and studied them closely. The IRA had gone very quiet, so presumably the secret negotiations were continuing to progress, and they would indeed conclude eight months later with the Good Friday Agreement of 10 April. Although more agitated, the Protestant paramilitaries were still not actively torpedoing the project. As for ETA, ever since Miguel Ángel Blanco's murder and the repudiation they had suffered even in their own fiefdoms, they were lying low, inactive. I was convinced they would kill again, but they were clearly in no hurry, which ran counter to the fears of

Machimbarrena and his unofficial superiors – who weren't unofficial, but anyway – in CESID or the Ministry of the Interior.

By the time I was due to return to Madrid on 28 August (Berta, Guillermo and Elisa had done so two days before), nothing bad had happened in Ruán. María, Celia and Inés were still alive and unharmed. Not that this meant a great deal, but each day that passed with no shocks or deaths felt like a reprieve to me. During the week, I saw María in her garden, which was still occasionally infested by Morbecq and that tacky guy from Cangas, who was now sporting a bizarre pair of tennis shoes, so, in that respect, it was business as usual; I sometimes coincided with Celia in the street and we would chat, such chance encounters were always very easy in Ruán. Inés, though, didn't get in touch, not once. I wondered if she had remembered more of what had happened on that night or had her suspicions. One day, I phoned her and said:

'I'm not going to be in Ruán much longer. Some family problems have cropped up, and next term I need to be in Madrid. I thought we'd see each other soon, and I left that up to you, not wanting to put pressure on you again, because I know how busy you are. If we met now, it would only be to say goodbye, although I'll probably come back for the odd weekend. I've got used to life here. And to you.'

She sounded as reassuring and genuine as she had the day after my failed murder attempt:

'Oh, I'm so sorry, really I am, but there was no way we could have got together, I haven't stopped for a moment all month. I haven't had a night off since we last saw each other. I was sort of assuming we could leave getting together until September, which isn't far off now, and by then things will have calmed down. But what a shame, what a shame. When are you leaving?'

'On the 28th, barring any new problems.'

'So soon? Why didn't you tell me before?'

'These problems have really only just arisen. I didn't even know

I'd have to leave until this Saturday just gone. Nor that I'd need to stay in Madrid.' I didn't think Inés was in touch with María Viana or the head teacher, who had known of my plans for a few weeks.

'So it's something pretty serious, then?'

'I hope not, but my parents are getting older now and I need to look after them and be there on the spot.' So Miguel Centurión still had parents, I discovered or invented.

'That's really disappointing, Miguel, because I'd got used to you too.' This sounded to me like someone merely returning a compliment, but who knows. 'We'll have to find a moment before you leave, Miguel. We must. Let me see what I can do, and then I'll call you. The 28th you say.'

A reassuring, perfectly natural conversation. Perhaps too natural, especially given that the days prior to my departure passed and she still didn't phone, not even to say whether we could or couldn't meet. I didn't insist, because I still really didn't want to see her, I would feel more comfortable not seeing her and not confronting that difficult face which I had been on the point of turning into a rigid mask for all eternity. She didn't know that, but it's horrible to come face to face with someone you had tried to kill. If you succeed, you'll never see that face again, but I had failed, I had stepped back. Not having done the deed was hardly of secondary importance, and yet somehow it was: in my mind, I *had* done the deed, as had Macbeth. Like him, I had taken advantage of my victim's sleep, and worse, I had brought about that sleep. 'The sleeping and the dead are but as pictures,' which makes it easier to erase them. I didn't use to be like that, but now Lady Macbeth would have scolded me as she did her husband: 'You do unbend your noble strength, to think so brain-sickly of things.' Doubtless one of the consequences of being outside after having been inside is that it does make us brain-sickly. And that's unbearable too.

I went back to my apartment or attic in Calle de Lepanto, just a hop and a skip from Calle de Pavía and from Berta Isla, my youthful love who had never faded. The first day of September fell on a Monday, and that day, as agreed, I returned to my post at the embassy in Madrid, which, since time immemorial, had become accustomed to treating me with every possible consideration. That's one of the advantages of being inside for decades, and in an official capacity, not extra-official as I had been during my stay in Ruán.

Even though I had commanded Comendador to inform me immediately of any change or event in that town in the north-west, especially anything that affected my three women (I gave him a very large sum as an advance on a whole year's worth of information), I couldn't resist walking to Puerta del Sol every morning before work to buy *El Esperado* in one of the well-stocked newspaper kiosks there and – when they had it – Ruán's other less significant paper. The English, Scottish and Irish press were all waiting for me in my office, and I would spend my first hour at work leafing through them quickly but attentively.

ETA did not wait long before taking up arms again. Not even two months had passed following the murder of the councillor from Ermua. On 5 September, they attached a limpet bomb to the underside of a policeman's car in Basauri, and the man died. A month later, on 13 October, two terrorists gunned down a Basque police officer when he tried to stop them placing explosives outside the

Guggenheim Museum in Bilbao. After twenty-six hours in Basurto hospital, he died. Two scares followed by two egotistical sighs of relative relief, because I thought, albeit not as cynically as it might sound: 'At least that killing doesn't bear the stamp of Magdalena Orúe, assuming, of course, that her stamp *was* on the 1987 attacks in Barcelona and Zaragoza. Tupra always avoided telling me precisely how she had collaborated in them, and now I can't ask him.' I found the abortive bombing of the museum very worrying though, because, depending on how powerful the explosives were and when they would have been detonated, the ensuing massacre would have resembled those of ten years before.

No, I couldn't ask Reresby. After our final strained and disappointing phone conversation (disappointing for him, that is), he didn't deign to show any sign of life, not even in order to worry, shame or mortify me, or to amuse himself by winding me up; and I didn't dare pester him with questions he would never answer. I assumed that he felt only infinite scorn for me and wanted nothing more to do with me. At least all of August and September had passed and half of October without any of his threats materializing: the three women were still alive and leading their normal Ruán lives. I wondered what he was waiting for, because he didn't usually make empty threats. I was also thankful and suspected that perhaps he was playing a very old game, a subtle game, one that wears the opponent down and undermines him: torture by hope. The only antidote for this slow poison consisted in refusing to hope and accepting that there was nothing to be done; alas, I didn't have that antidote to hand, by which I mean that I was incapable of doing either of those things, and I lived in daily fear of *El Esperado*'s front page or of receiving a sudden call from Comendador. In November, Patricia Pérez Nuix left. We had hardly seen each other while we were both in Madrid. She avoided me and treated me coolly and even contemptuously, I suddenly found it hard to believe that we had occasionally been to bed together. She was young, passionate, impetuous and totally disciplined when it came to following orders. I think she couldn't stand seeing my image as a much admired veteran crumble into dust, or else Tupra had infected her with his scorn for my extraordinary show of weakness. I assumed she was moving to London to work with him on that new project begun years before and for which someone like me was quite unsuited, and had been even before Ruán. A few days before her departure, I passed her in the corridor and asked her straight out:

'Are they sending you to London? To the building with no name?' She knew what I meant.

'For some months now, Tom, that has been none of your business,' was her curt reply, and she continued on down the corridor with barely a glance in my direction.

I realized that this was Tupra's mantra, and that I was now outside for good. For the moment, of course.

There was the occasional skirmish in Ulster, but any more serious hostilities appeared to have been suspended or postponed. In Spain, they would continue for many more years, although two months passed before ETA's next murder: on 11 December another Partido Popular councillor was shot in the head while in a bar in Irún, and on 9 January 1998 another councillor from the same party died in Zarauz after a limpet bomb attached to his car exploded. Again neither of those attacks seemed to bear Maddie O'Dea's stamp, or what I had decided, with no foundation in fact, was her stamp.

I didn't see that stamp in the attacks of 30 January either, and they were especially cruel. Their target was another councillor, this time a local councillor in Seville, Alberto Jiménez Becerril, I do remember his name. They shot him in the back, at night, when he was walking home from a restaurant with his wife Ascensión. The additional cruelty or sadness was that they killed her as well, shooting her in the back too, and neither of them had the remotest chance of defending themselves. Because of that additional sadness I also remember their names (and have mentioned this murder more than once here).

ETA didn't stop, they just didn't stop. They were not in the least influenced – and why should they be, people rarely imitate positive models – by the Belfast Agreement of 10 April, which put an apparent end to the more than three thousand violent deaths caused by both sides there. On 6 May 1998, in Pamplona, they shot and killed a councillor from the Unión del Pueblo Navarro while he was sitting in his car, and only two days later, in Vitoria (as if to make up for their temporary cessation of activities), a retired lieutenant in the Civil Guard was shot in the head not far from where he lived. On 25 June, someone else was killed in Rentería, there were so many, so many, that it's impossible to remember them all or the circumstances. And yet there were fewer killings in those years compared with the 1980s, when, as I mentioned, in one year alone there were ninety murders.

As with all the ETA attacks since the restoration of democracy and since its members were granted an amnesty (even some attacks that occurred under Franco, if they were particularly vicious and the victim particularly innocent), I felt a mixture of rage and regret, and, like other Spaniards, I thought they would never stop. But one's own feelings always intervene, and can attenuate or exacerbate things depending on the situation. I couldn't see Inés Marzán being involved in the murders that took place in 1997 and 1998 after I had left Ruán, and I would console myself thinking – 'console' isn't the right word, but you know what I mean – that none of them would have been avoided if I had held her head under the water for two or three or four minutes; or five to be absolutely sure. The murderers would have murdered their victims anyway, in Basauri, in Bilbao, in Irún, in Zarauz, in Seville, in Pamplona, in Vitoria and in Rentería. The bloodshed wasn't going to stop regardless of what I did. Regardless, too, of what the heartlessly frivolous Machimbarrena did.

The gang killed three hundred and forty-three civilians, *civilians*. And in Madrid alone – after the Basque Country, Madrid was the region that suffered most attacks – they murdered one hundred and one people during the democracy. We have grown used to counting the murders that took place under the dictatorship separately. Perhaps that's unfair, perhaps not, I don't know.

Absurdly – because orders can always be issued at a distance – I was also reassured to know that Inés was still running La Demanda in Ruán. At least I was until 30 May, because the following day, a Sunday, I received an unexpected call from Comendador. And a few hours later an even more unexpected one from Tupra, Reresby, Dundas, Nutcombe, Oxenham or Ure, one never knew which he was going to be when he woke each morning. Perhaps even he didn't know.

'Hi, look, I know it's a Sunday,' said that phoney Wild West gunman. The last time I'd seen him he was still wearing his leather trousers and his curly Stephen Stills-style sideburns, and he had a tattoo on his forearm, an idiotic thing for an outlaw to do. 'But there's been a big change you should know about.'

'What's happened?' I asked, instantly gripped by anxiety, afraid that the corpse of the first of the three women, or even two, had just been found.

'Yesterday was La Demanda's last day,' he said. 'There was a notice on the door saying "Closed due to change of ownership". Inés has either leased it or sold it without saying a word to anyone and has literally vanished overnight. She didn't turn up for the evening shift, but she had been there at lunchtime and behaved perfectly normally. There's sure to be an article about it in *El Esperado* tomorrow. It's caught us all by surprise, including her employees. And once they'd all gone home, someone or other must have dropped by to put up that notice.'

'So it caught you by surprise as well? Didn't she mention her plans, didn't you have your suspicions? Was there no indication? And you mean no one so much as dropped a hint to you who know everything?'

'Well, not everything, but quite a lot,' he said. 'But no, I knew nothing about it. She didn't even say goodbye, the rotten cow, and after all these years too. It's as if the ground had opened up and swallowed her, and no one knew a thing. She did it all in secret, no, it was more than secrecy, it was stealth.'

'Does anyone know who she sold it to? The buyer must have known about it.'

'Not for the moment, no. Rumours are rife, as you can imagine. But since it's Sunday, there aren't many reliable sources to go to, no one's answering the phone at the town hall, for example. People are saying it was all done through intermediaries, through a company. Florentín will find out more later on, he won't let anything get in his way. Meanwhile, he's absolutely seething, because the news really caught him on the hop, with his trousers down if you like. For the moment, no one has a clue, there are only rumours. People are saying she's also sold her apartment, which she owned apparently.' I had forgotten that, but it was true, it was in the preliminary report I was given. 'If that's true,' added Comendador with a touch of frustration, 'then she's left us for good.' Perhaps he felt frustrated because he had lost a regular, loyal customer, or perhaps because he felt his affections had been spurned. 'Anyway, you asked me to let you know of any changes, and this is a big one. La Demanda was a real institution here. Who knows what will become of it now.'

'Thank you, you were quite right to phone. Update me when you know more. So no one has any idea where she's gone, where she might be?'

'How could they, Centurión?'

To the people of Ruán I would continue to be Centurión. And Centurión didn't like that change of ownership at all. More than that, it alarmed and upset him. I made myself think up some stupid possible reason. She might have received a call from the father of her daughter, telling her the girl was dying, and she had shot off to wherever they happened to be living. What nonsense, I told myself. It isn't even certain that the daughter exists, and no one carries out complicated negotiations in the middle of an emergency. It didn't look good, and my Sunday had suddenly turned sour. I tried to read a novel, an essay, but couldn't take anything in. I tried watching television, and it was the same. The day turned sourer still when, in the late afternoon, the phone rang again (I'd spoken to Comendador at around midday, or one o'clock more like) and I heard Tupra's unmistakable English voice saying in a wounding, sarcastic tone:

'Well done, Nevinson, you deserve a round of applause. I assume you know what's happened.'

He spoke to me as if we had only spoken the day before yesterday, when in fact it had been ten months. There was no preamble, he didn't even say 'Hello', but then someone who's about to stick a knife in you doesn't usually say 'Hello'.

'Good evening, Bertie. How did you find out, if you don't mind my asking?'

'How do you think? George is beside himself, and I don't blame him. We had Maddie O'Dea in our grasp, and off she's flown to some unknown destination. It took years to track her down, to locate her, identify her, and it's all come to nothing. I really must congratulate you, Tom.'

I couldn't resist throwing this back at him.

'You should congratulate yourself and George too. What happened to your "drastic plans"? I left Ruán more than eight months ago, and as far as I know, all three women are still alive, and you had sentenced them all to death. Did you lose your nerve or something?'

'Look, I can't spend my life worrying about what's going on in that backwater, I have more important things to deal with here. Besides, knowing as we did that the other two didn't represent any danger, there was no sense in executing them. We're not thugs. Nor are we the mafia or terrorists who don't care if they kill one person or a hundred. You know that as well as I do.'

My counterattack had hit home, and he had gone on the defensive.

I took advantage of this to go a step further. That phone call, after so many months, had, to put it concisely and crudely, really pissed me off.

'And what about Inés? If you were so convinced . . . If she *is* her, which is still not clear, then several of us have failed.'

He didn't like being included among the failures.

'I was asked for help and I gave it. I sent you, but you turned out to be a total waste of space. Then I washed my hands of the whole business and left it up to George. Everything takes time, and you squandered all the time we'd invested in it, which meant we had to start all over again. Or do you still believe that she was totally unaware of your little attempt at drowning her? That would have left her even more on the alert. I think George was waiting for her to make a move.'

'Well, it seems she has. He obviously waited too long.' It was no easy matter to leave Tupra speechless, but for a few seconds he said nothing. I changed my tone and added: 'The fact that she's sold the restaurant doesn't prove anything anyway. It's not a crime as far as I know. People often do things in secret and for any number of reasons. It does look bad, I realize that, but George is such a hothead, and there's really no rush to find her. Can't she be tracked down again? Using passenger lists and so on?'

He too changed his tone and became more collaborative.

'They're looking into that, but it won't help. She'll have changed her name, and it's anyone's guess what her new name will be.'

'I didn't find any passports in her apartment.'

'She wouldn't keep them there. They'd be in a safe deposit box in a bank to which there'll be only one key, hers; they'll investigate further tomorrow. If she caught an early flight from Madrid, by now she could be in Boston, in Philadelphia or in New York, or on her way to San Francisco, with an impeccable American passport. They treat European terrorists very well in America, where there's a kind of latent hatred of Europe, with you and us at the top of their list.

They can't forgive us for making them what they are, the good and the not so good. They understand terrorists there, justify and support them, especially if they're Irish. Haven't you ever noticed that the *New York Times*, the *Washington Post* and other prestigious media outlets almost never refer to ETA members as "terrorists"? They're "separatists" or "Basque nationalists" and so on. There's even more sympathy for the IRA. Maddie O'Dea will have lots of wealthy friends over there, and some poor ones too.'

'So you don't think she's moved to Ulster?'

'Look, in the absence of a final, official count, it seems that in a referendum on the Agreement, 71 per cent of the population of Northern Ireland have just voted in favour, Protestants and Catholics alike, because after thirty years people just can't take any more bloodshed. And next month there'll be elections. I don't think she would have much to do there at the moment, but who knows. Anything could happen now, thanks to you.'

We had been speaking for a while quite normally (we had done this for years, analysing situations together and collaborating), but suddenly he returned angrily to the charge. This time, I took it as a joke and did not hit back:

'If she allowed herself to be drowned in the bath while she was still conscious or half-conscious, then she's certainly not lacking in sangfroid, she must have the supernatural blood of a vampire.'

Tupra had recovered his incisiveness, his truces tended to be short-lived, even when he allowed himself to see the funny side.

'Or she simply knew you better than you know yourself. Some women have that ability. They know at once what a man is and isn't capable of doing. Physically, I mean. Especially if they've been to bed with him. Pat has that ability and she warned me about you. She said that, when it came to it, you would chicken out and step back.'

I preferred to ignore that remark. Pat was a blabbermouth and, as yet, a nobody.

'The kind of women who notice everything, Tom Nevinson, are the ones who pretend to be distracted, to be not paying attention, when in fact they're making a note of every detail and every symptom in their keen, brain-sickly brains.'

'You do still owe me one thing, Bertie. In what way did Maddie O'Dea collaborate in the attacks on the shopping mall and the barracks? I've never known, and you've never told me.'

'Why should you care about that at this stage in the game? If you must know, she was one of the organizers in charge of logistics, especially raising funds and financial support. She's brilliant at fund-raising, and terrorists have to live, they need money to buy their weapons and explosives. Bank robberies, extortion and kidnappings don't bring in much dosh. Their days drag as much as they do for anyone.'

This was on Sunday 31 May 1998, Whit Sunday or Pentecost, which I've always considered to be my personal holiday, because of the gift of tongues that has determined my life and led me, night after night, day after day, to today.

Now all I could do was wait and hope, as usual. Hope that nothing would happen in the world – in my worlds – nothing that bore the stamp of Magdalena Orúe. Yes, torture by hope. Who can ever refrain from hoping?

XVI

And so I had no alternative but to settle into the state of mind described by the poet as waiting without hope, and I had entirely run out of that. However many doubts I'd been assailed and paralysed by on 2 August 1997; however hard I'd resisted believing that Inés Marzán was the evil I saw everywhere, I was now almost certain that Tupra had been right from the start or, as he pointed out, that I had been right without realizing it. I stopped worrying about Ruán, nothing more would happen there. Tupra had acknowledged that he wasn't going to sacrifice two innocent women. I reached the conclusion that he had threatened me with that, first, in order to put pressure on me, then to punish and torment me, to keep me dangling. This was very characteristic of him, especially if anyone ruined his plans or disobeyed his orders. I knew of former agents whom he had kept on tenterhooks for years, afraid their money would be cut off or that they would be accused of violating the Official Secrets Act, something we've all done, if we live long enough; we all end up telling someone something, or one night, out of pride, drunkenness, anxiety or a very bad conscience, accidentally let something slip.

Now I was worried about the whole of Spain, the French Basque Country and all of Northern Ireland. Each day that passed without a single massacre felt like a small victory. The trouble was that one day is always followed by another, and so the countdown begins again. I've already recorded the murders committed by ETA between me leaving Ruán and 25 June, all of whose victims were individuals. In Ulster there had been minor or abortive attacks in Moira, Portadown, Belleek, Newtownhamilton, Newry, Lisburn and Banbridge, the latter on 1 August, a bombing by a new organization called the RIRA, the Real Irish Republican Army, whose leaders intended to replace the IRA, whom they considered to be cowardly traitors for signing the Belfast Agreement. There are always people who are opposed to everything (the turbulent Dolours Price spoke out publicly against it, and claimed that the IRA had threatened her because of that), there are always people eager to carry on fighting and killing. Fortunately, there were not, I believe, any fatalities in those attacks, but many were wounded, thirty-five in Banbridge. These attacks seemed to be the familiar death throes of the unrepentant few, I just hoped that the referendum and time would finally bring about their dissolution. And so it seemed until 15 August 1998, when Ulster saw the worst atrocity of all thirty years of the Troubles – it's strange that such a gentle euphemism should have become the accepted term for more than three thousand violent deaths over a whole eternity.

It happened in Omagh, County Tyrone, a town of some forty-five thousand inhabitants. It was a busy Saturday in the streets, and although it sent shockwaves around the world, few outside Ulster will remember it now. But then history barely teaches us anything, or only in a simplistic or distorted form, and recent history is often hidden away, so that it doesn't besmirch the living who were the main protagonists; so it's very easy to forget, and even easier to know nothing. I do remember because I was still combing the English and Irish press every day, which is why I can recall those names: Moira, Belleek, Newry and so on, and not only Omagh, no, not only Omagh.

The bomb, 500 pounds of fertilizer-based explosives, was placed in a red Vauxhall Cavalier that had been stolen in Ireland a few days before. Some Spanish tourists took a photograph of two of their companions standing next to it, when it was still just a rather smart car parked in Lower Market Street. The man and the child perched on his shoulders who appear in the photo both survived; the person who took the photo did not.

As is always the case in these mass killings, there were warnings which were, perhaps deliberately, confusing, and afterwards there was the usual exchange of accusations. The first warning, preceded by the codeword that the Real IRA had used two weeks before in Banbridge ('Martha Pope') was sent to Ulster Television: 'There's a bomb, courthouse, Omagh, main street, 500lb, explosion thirty minutes'. Only a minute later, the second warning arrived: 'Bomb, Omagh town, fifteen minutes'. And the next minute, the third one was received in the Coleraine office of the Samaritans: 'Bomb, Omagh main street, about 200 yards from the courthouse'. This information was passed on to the Royal Ulster Constabulary. Slightly more than half an hour after the warnings, the police were evacuating the area near the courthouse when the bomb went off, at around ten past three in the afternoon.

There is no street in Omagh called Main Street, Market Street is the town's principal shopping street. The evacuation began in the buildings and the areas closest to the target, the courthouse, but the red Vauxhall Cavalier was parked about 365 yards from there. Many people were caught directly in the blast, and the images taken immediately after are very similar to those from Barcelona and Zaragoza in 1987, and from Vic in 1991, and similar to those of any brutal destruction of buildings and bodies anywhere in the world. The area was packed. Twenty-nine people died like cattle, not all at the moment of the explosion, and there were about two hundred and twenty wounded, some of whom lost limbs. For a time, I could recite the names of all twenty-nine victims, now I can only remember the names of the youngest ones: Oran Doherty, eight, James Barker, Séan McLaughlin and the Spaniard Fernando Blasco, twelve, the latter's compatriot Rocío Abad, twenty-three; Gareth Conway, eighteen, Aidan Gallagher and Julia Hughes, twenty-one, Deborah-Ann Cartwright, twenty, Brenda Logue, Jolene Marlow and Samantha McFarland, seventeen; Alan Radford, sixteen, and Lorraine Wilson, fifteen; Breda Devine and Maura Monaghan, both only one; Avril Monaghan, thirty, was pregnant with twins, swallowed by the sea's throat or dwelling now in the dark back of time, perhaps the most densely populated area of all, the resting place of what existed and what did not exist. Protestants, Catholics and even a Mormon died, the bombers didn't discriminate between religions.

The police accused the RIRA of deliberately directing people towards the bomb; the RIRA accused the British, Irish and American intelligence services of possessing prior information about the attack, which they did not pass on to the local constabulary. They said they had not intended to attack civilians and apologized. This exchange of accusations went on for years, and more or less everyone ended up either avoiding responsibility or begging forgiveness for their negligence, ineptitude, slowness or lack of coordination, including the chief of the Royal Ulster Constabulary and a few double agents from MI5 who apparently failed to pass on vital information to the right people. None of this interested me, neither then nor in 2008, when a monument to the fallen of Market Street was finally unveiled.

I know that nothing would have happened if that ephemeral dissident organization had not packed that car with explosives. I say 'ephemeral' because it broke up shortly afterwards, following the outrage expressed across all of Ireland, north and south, at such carnage. Too late for the twenty-nine dead and the hundreds of wounded, burned and mutilated of Omagh. The repercussions were far-reaching, and that action, which sought to torpedo the difficult, fragile, precarious peace agreement reached on 10 April, was condemned by the Queen, by Prime Minister Blair, Pope John Paul II and President Clinton, and even by the Sinn Féin bigwigs McGuinness and Adams, who had not been exactly critical in the past. The

Prince of Wales visited the town. And ultimately this only helped to strengthen the Belfast Agreement.

It's not that long since 1998, and yet few people in the world now know what happened. After all, it was just an ordinary Northern Irish town almost no one had heard of. It's the same in Spain, even though two Spaniards, a young woman and a boy, died in the attack. The speed with which we forget grows faster with each year that passes, and what happened two years ago or even the day before yesterday is already prehistory.

The reason why I remember it so vividly is because, as soon as I heard the news (that summer, Berta and I were holidaying in Cantabria; the kids were already off leading their own lives), as soon as I found out . . . Ah yes, then I did see Magdalena Orúe O'Dea's stamp, the one I had attributed to her. She had been at my mercy twelve months earlier, that season of insalubrious suns; twelve months and a few days, lying defenceless in the water with the child-like face of a sleeping giantess, the face of my occasional lover Inés Marzán, there in the town of Ruán.

I held back on that Saturday and on Sunday too, but on Monday the 17th I could stand it no longer, and this time I was the one who phoned Tupra, hoping that he hadn't changed that private number and that it remained live. Not much time had passed since his last impertinent call at the end of May, after La Demanda was unexpectedly put up for sale or else changed hands.

'Tupra, it's Nevinson,' I reverted to surnames again so as to sound more professional. I was opening myself up to more woundingly sarcastic comments, but I was prepared to take them on the chin if I deserved them.

'Ah, Tom, how can I help? I thought you didn't want to have anything more to do with me. But you've said that on other occasions too, and it's always turned out not to be true.'

He knew why I was phoning, but he wanted to make me say it. This was also a price I was prepared to pay.

'Please tell me that Maddie O'Dea had nothing to do with the killings in Omagh the day before yesterday. I know she wasn't actually there, that a few blokes stole the car and parked it in the wrong place. But then she wasn't in Barcelona or Zaragoza either was she, and yet you've always considered her to be responsible.'

I heard Tupra sigh.

'She's obviously terribly refined and dainty, and hates the sight of blood. From close to, I mean. From a distance, though, you can neither see nor smell it, nor smell the burned flesh either. It becomes mere information.'

He wasn't going to answer me straight away, he would doubtless keep me waiting. If, that is, he answered at all, for he could easily refuse.

'Was she involved or not?' I said, knowing that to insist was always a mistake, counterproductive.

'What makes you think that? Omagh's a very long way from Ruán and from the Basque Country too. And what makes you think I would know? Keeping track of that woman is no longer my business. It was, but not any more, not since you let her escape. That's when I departed the scene, because when one of my agents fails it always reflects badly on me. It's just as well it was all extra-official.'

This remark left me unmoved. He was perfectly within his rights to taunt me and 'with a vengeance, to boot'.

'You once predicted that, if Maddie O'Dea ceased to be a sleeper, it was far more likely that she would be involved in actions in Ulster than in Spain. That's what you said, do you remember? And I know, too, that any loose ends will always be your business, even if it's not your fault. Keeping track of her may well be someone else's affair, but I'm sure that, until she's finally neutralized, you'll still be keeping a close eye on her. That's why I think you'll know. What happened on Saturday will have set alarm bells ringing for you, just as it did for me.'

Tupra gave a short, possibly irritated laugh. He still intended to humiliate me.

'Look, Tom, even if I did know something, I wouldn't be authorized to tell you. I'm not part of the Omagh investigation, and you're not part of anything any more. You're outside, outside of everything – your choice. You might as well be the postman or the baker asking me. You're just another curious onlooker now.'

'But *they* didn't have her life in their hands, Bertie. Tell me what you know, please. You owe me.'

His laugh now was openly sarcastic with a touch of indignation.
'*I* owe *you*? You're the one who owes me.'

'Our story didn't begin in Ruán or in Madrid. You owe me Janet Jefferys, Bertie, and that's a debt you can never pay off.'

He remained silent for a few seconds. He was very adroit at side-stepping awkward questions. When he spoke again, he did so as if we were just beginning the conversation. He was equally brilliant at erasing at a stroke all trace of anything that disarmed or displeased him:

'There's still no conclusive evidence, Tom. It's very early days, and there could be a lot of people behind the RIRA, here, as well as in Ireland and in America. All I can say is that it does look like Maddie O'Dea's work. You never really believed me, but she's a real fanatic, of the kind that won't allow thirty years of struggle to be tossed in the bin by an agreement between despicable politicians and despicable repentant terrorists. If you want my opinion, then you can take it as read that she definitely took part.'

'But how? Do you know where she is?'

'She could be anywhere,' he said, and I caught a note of despair in his voice. 'How? Well, the usual way, raising funds and finances, proselytizing from a safe distance. Nowadays, you can do that kind of thing from the farthest-flung corner of the globe.'

Despite everything, I respected Tupra's opinions, he was right far too often. Fortunately or unfortunately for him, Tupra believed he did know things beforehand, or, rather, he not only believed he knew, he did know. His 'you can take it as read' was enough for me. I tried to press him a little more, taking advantage of the fact that the conversation was suddenly flowing quite normally. I wouldn't have many more opportunities, certainly not in the short term.

'Do we know who she sold the restaurant to? As far as I can make out, the folk in Ruán are still in the dark about that. All they tell me is that the place is still closed.'

'No, she was very clever about it. The intermediary company have been forbidden to reveal the buyer's name. She could even have sold it to herself. It's one of those opaque companies, whose real ownership is hidden, perhaps registered overseas.' He suddenly stopped, as if remembering his rank. 'Anyway, I don't want to waste any more time on you, Tom.'

And he hung up.

Yes, his words were enough to enrol me in the same club as the untroubled Alan Thorndike in Berchtesgaden and the very troubled Reck-Malleczewen in the Osteria Bavaria in Munich, the same club as the idle and the inert, as all those who believe ingenuously that they will get another chance. Thorndike took a while to realize who he had within his sights, Reck-Malleczewen still didn't know the magnitude of what was about to happen. Inés Marzán wasn't the Führer, no one could be, or perhaps they could, I can see a few candidates shaping up for the role right now. But this did nothing to quell my unease. 'Unease' is a very weak and self-indulgent word, I know, but it also pretty much covers everything.

After putting the phone down, I felt that I could have avoided those twenty-plus deaths in Omagh if I had just tugged a little harder on that woman's bare, helpless, pedicured feet. Killing is not so extreme or difficult or unjust if you know who you're killing, what crimes she's committed or is prepared to commit, how many evils people will be spared, how many innocent lives will be saved in exchange for a single bullet, a few knife thrusts or a drowning, it lasts only a few seconds and then it's done, it's over, it's finished, and life can carry on, it almost always does, lives can sometimes be very long and nothing ever stops completely. Dumas said as much, or put those tranquil words into his hero's mouth. That story, of course, took place in the seventeenth century, when murder was a less serious offence or at least more common.

And yet, and yet, I did ask myself what it would have cost me to keep her head under the water for a couple more minutes. I had taken the first step, which is always the most difficult. My problem hadn't been delay or ignorance exactly, although you can never truly foresee anything. Tupra had been convinced, and deep inside I was convinced too. But those depths proved unfathomable to me and I wasn't sure who I was killing and I didn't want to be the one who did it. It seemed too extreme, too difficult, too unjust, perhaps as a result of my upbringing. So much so that I couldn't do it.

I felt terribly gloomy for the whole of the rest of that day and the subsequent sleepless night. I remained so during our last week in Cantabria, before our return to Madrid. I tried to hide it as best I could, i.e. not very well. I went to the beach every morning, made trivial comments about our fellow bathers, we had lunch in nice restaurants and Berta slept during the siesta, while I did not, although I pretended to. We went for walks in the evening, heard the vespers bell being rung at a convent and dined at the hotel, where I preferred them to bring something up to our room, serrano ham, some cheese, smoked salmon, I could only eat light things or apparently light things.

But Berta was very perceptive and had spent her whole life observing me, albeit intermittently and with vast gaps. She immediately noticed my tormented state, and quite rightly too, because I was more or less thinking what was said to that Shakespearean character in his troubled dreams: 'Let me sit heavy on thy soul tomorrow, let me be lead within thy bosom, and may you end thy days in a bloody battle.' Twenty-plus dead people would be saying that to me every day, including two one-year-old girls who, in their briefest of brief lives, wouldn't even have learned to speak, still less tell their story.

During the twelve months since my return from that town in the north-west, which I have been calling Ruán, Berta and I had grown much closer. I don't know what her reason was, but I know my own a little better. What she did, who she went out with, who she saw and who she went to bed with, if she went to bed with anyone – and I assumed she did – none of that had been any of my business for a long time and I had never dared ask her about it. She also knew, and had done for an even longer time, that I couldn't tell her about the part of my life that took place behind her back and at a distance, not even if I wanted to. I preferred not to calculate just how large a part of my life that had been. I imagined that anything she had experienced of an emotional or personal nature had been only so-so or bad. Perhaps such experiences had worked for her occasionally, I'm sure they had, but not in the long term, nothing had persisted or endured.

We were both forty-six when I returned to Madrid and forty-seven after our trip to Cantabria, me in August and her in September. When she was young, she had loved me in the primitive, obsessive way young people often do, purposefully and determinedly, with love as her justification. At that childish age, she had childishly decided that I would be the person with whom she would share her life, and those early decisions, long pondered and precious, prove very hard to revoke, because an element of childishness remains in all of us into our old age, more so in some of course than in others. I had even seen certain childish traits in Tupra, it's something as tenacious as the lingering gullibility of which María Viana had complained.

Perhaps Berta found that I was what remained for her. If so, this was, in my view, a rather hasty decision, because she could still have started a new chapter, at the end of the twentieth century she was still young and, in my eyes, very attractive, and presumably in the eyes of other men too, since I'm no different from them. Her growing closer to me didn't mean that she wouldn't start any new chapters, I didn't deceive myself in that respect: I considered myself to be purely temporary.

As for me . . . after my earlier return in 1994, I had spent far too long in a state of hibernation, immersed in bad memories, feeling displaced and outside of everything, yearning to be active again, despairing because I had been written off as burned out and useless. Despite my qualms, Tupra's visit in January had brought me back to life, and, after initially playing hard to get, I had embraced the mission fully. It had been a complete and utter failure; this, however, did not take away from that initial impulse, but changed it, rather, into a feeling of resignation.

Since September 1997, I had – at last – become fully integrated into the life of the embassy and began to take an interest in my work and found it easy to cultivate friendships that, up until then, I had rather scorned, after all, my life had consisted of making friends with the most unlikely and inimical people, with the enemies I was setting out to destroy. And I found that Berta Isla, my classmate of thirty years before, who, more than anyone else, had been my personal fitful fever, had neither upped sticks nor gone away; she was still there, just a few steps from my apartment, in the same apartment that had belonged to us both. She was intelligent, desirable and very funny, above all, she was still full of good cheer, which was what I lacked. What more could I want, given that she had left the balcony door open for me?

During our last week in Cantabria, she refrained from asking me any questions, although I was walking around with an almost visible cloud hanging over me, as if I were a character in a comic strip or a cartoon. In Madrid, though, the gloom persisted, and one night when she stayed over in my apartment in Calle de Lepanto (she never let me stay in her apartment in Pavía) she noticed that something was weighing on my dreams like lead within my bosom. These were the voices of Séan McLaughlin and Oran Doherty and James Barker, of Fernando Blasco and Lorraine Wilson, of the little girls Maura Monaghan and Breda Devine, and all the others. I tried to console myself each day with the thought that perhaps the phrase Tupra had used and that I had presumed to be true, 'take it as read', could have been a lie intended to punish me and make me suffer; that Magdalena Orúe or Inés Marzán had played no part in Omagh, and that, even had I shown greater presence of mind or greater resolve, I would not have succeeded in averting those deaths. It was no use though. And I often thought about Inés Marzán. If Gonzalo de la Rica had told her who I was, why then had she continued meeting me and going to bed with me, why had she allowed herself to be led to the scaffold like that? No one could possibly have that degree of sangfroid and no one could possibly know a merely temporary lover that well. Or perhaps they could, perhaps.

The day after that night of fog and filthy air to which she was a witness, Berta invited me over to supper in Calle de Pavía and during the meal said:

'I suppose I still can't ask you anything. For example, what you were doing last year during all those months away, and where you were. Tupra came to Madrid and you left, and for almost eight months you came back only once – was it once? – even though you said you wouldn't be away for long and wouldn't be far from Madrid, which meant that you could easily pop back.'

Yes, we all end up telling more than we should, although probably to only one person and only once. I don't know what it was that made me answer her question that time:

'No, I wasn't very far away, and I could have come back here more often. But things always become more complicated, or more than that, they become all-consuming. You focus entirely on your mission, and it's as if everything else almost ceases to exist, or becomes a memory, a figment of your imagination. I don't like that, I never have, but it always happens. It's a state incompatible with memories, it drives them out. And until you've completed the mission, there's no future either, or you don't think about it.'

'And how did the mission go? Not very well, I'd guess. I've never known whether you were good at your job or not. I've taken it for granted that you were very good given how often you've been called away. Only someone who gets results is going to be in such demand, right?'

Now I was the one who had left the balcony door open, simply by answering her question. It was only normal that Berta should, very cautiously, take advantage of that opening.

I put my knife and fork down on the plate without finishing my food. I lit a cigarette and said:

'It went badly. And although I used to be good, I'm not any more.'

'So badly that you're still having those horrible nightmares a whole year later? Last night, I thought you were going to die.'

'Yes, and there'll be more nightmares to come.' I could have stopped there, but instead I continued. I felt very close to Berta, I felt she was my companion. Not the one I had at school, but my future companion. I feared, too, that I might regret telling her, but I went on: 'I had to find and identify a particular person in order to bring them to justice. And I failed. Tupra identified the person for me, with information that I had given him. It was decided then that they must be killed, and I was the one chosen for the job. To avoid more crimes, more horrendous crimes. As horrendous as if that man Kindelán really had set fire to Guillermo.'

Berta wasn't expecting to be given so much information, such a frank confession. She was disturbed and frightened.

'You? And what happened? Did you kill that person?'

'No, I couldn't. She was a woman.'

I sensed her relief, her enormous relief. She was essentially a very kind person, but she was also discreet and said only:

'Good.'

'No, Berta, not good. Had I been capable of killing her, many people might still be alive now, and it's made no less terrible by the fact that they died far from here.'

'You mean Omagh?' It was only natural that she would make the connection. I had grown still gloomier since the day of the bombing.

'Yes, Omagh.'

She had the delicacy not to question me further. She showed still greater delicacy in resisting asking me if, on another occasion, I had killed anyone else. Given that they had ordered me to kill now, this was highly likely. Perhaps it wasn't so much delicacy as respect for certain secret bitternesses, and she preferred not to risk my confessions going too far, much too far. Once you begin to talk, you might not know when to stop, and some knowledge is so ineradicable that it destroys trust and crushes hope, and, at the time, she must have needed both. As did I, however I had exhausted both trust and hope. No, her need would be greater than mine.

Yes, it's true that we almost always do carry on, regardless of what we have or haven't done, regardless of what happened or didn't happen without our intervention. Nothing ever stops completely if we live long enough, and out of sheer inertia each new day stretches out before us, until it feels like an eternity. We're often tempted to say: 'All's spent, nought's had. I should have known that before I began squandering everything.' And no, nothing is ever all spent.

I focused all my efforts on making sure that Berta's bed would never be a woeful bed, never again, even though I never slept in her bed and she only slept in mine occasionally, sometimes. There was no hope for my bed, it was condemned to be 'woeful' and, yes, 'rueful' too, because of Magdalena O'Rue, as Tupra pronounced her first surname, lending her a suitable semblance of Irishness. Berta's bed would have been restless or sad for many years, and I would do my best to ensure that it would not be so in future years. That's not very much to ask, to be able to go to bed more or less serenely after the troubles, frustrations, upsets and shocks of the day, and yet there are many women and quite a few men who draw back the sheets with a feeling of infinite dread, as if they feared suffering further harm in their sleep. No, for those who do not live a life of endless grief, incessant remorse or desperation, it's not that much to ask.

She spent New Year's Eve in 1998 in my bed, which she kindly graced with a little of her perennial good cheer, and she suddenly asked me:

Will you go away again?'

'No, not like that, I don't think so. I will have to travel sometimes, but not disappear. Not to the point where you won't know if I'm alive or dead, no, not like that.'

She looked at me slightly sceptically, and her response was sceptical too. She was wearing a dark-blue silk nightdress.

'You told me that four years ago. Or you implied it anyway.'

We Spaniards are always saying and writing twee things, almost all of which ring false and are not even remotely sincere, their sole purpose being to allow us to swagger and strut and make a good impression. My English half, or perhaps my character, won't let me do that. However, it was my turn to come out with one of those schmaltzy sayings, my feelings and the occasion demanded it, and it's easier to do that in a language not your own, as if another you were speaking. Or to use someone else's words, as adolescents do. The problem was that English and Spanish were both equally my languages. This time, I didn't just recall those famous lines written in 1893, more than a century ago, I recited them, the part I liked best. And I did so in her language, because that is the one in which we spoke to each other.

'I know I haven't exactly played a major role in your life, and mine has largely been lived elsewhere, but I can say this to you now: "When you are old and grey and full of sleep, and nodding by the fire, take down this book and slowly read, and dream of the soft look your eyes had once, and of their shadows deep." '

She still had time to interrupt me and comment ironically:

'Assuming we both make it that far.'

She probably knew the poem – possibly by heart – but seemed to like hearing me recite it, because her irony was accompanied by a smile that was half amused and half fond. And so I plucked up my courage and recited the next verse too: 'How many loved your moments of glad grace, and loved your beauty with love false or true, but one man loved the pilgrim soul in you, and loved the sorrows of your changing face.' Yes, I said those words, even though I had been the one who had inflicted most of her sorrows and turned her shadows still darker, and had done most to change her face.

For some seconds, she said nothing, then she asked:

'Is that what you're saying to me?'

I don't know if I blushed or not, I'll never know.

'Yes, unless you're the one who goes away.'

She stroked my cheek at the spot where there had once been a scar I had lied to her about. She smiled again and said:

'Possibly. You never know.'

October 2020

Acknowledgements

Given that the world is now so full of pernickety, uncultivated detectives – thanks to the Internet, anyone can track down quotations or 'appropriations' with no need to have ever read anything – it's probably wise if, as far as I can, I record those that appear in this book.

The authors of some of the quotations are clearly stated (although certain quotations have been deliberately altered or paraphrased): William Shakespeare, Friedrich Reck-Malleczewen, Thomas Stearns Eliot, John Milton, Fernán Pérez de Guzmán, Charles Baudelaire, William Butler Yeats, Alexandre Dumas, the Psalms, Rebecca West and John Donne.

Others that appear in quotation marks but without any mention of the author (I didn't want the narrator to come over as too pedantic) are Wilfred Owen, Friedrich Hölderlin, Gustave Flaubert, Dante Alighieri, Michael Powell, Heinrich Heine and William Blake, again sometimes slightly altered.

Of those that appear with no quotation marks, there is the occasional brief quote from Russell Lewis, Joseph Weisberg and Louise de Vilmorin, although in her case those words may come via Max Ophuls, I'm not sure. There is also a sliver of an idea which comes, I believe, from John le Carré. Finally, one substantial paragraph that appears on a couple of occasions is an adaptation or reworking of a far better one by Giuseppe Tomasi di Lampedusa. And needless to say, there are numerous references to, even quotes from, my previous novel, *Berta Isla*, of which *Tomás Nevinson* is not so much a continuation as a 'companion piece', shall we say. And those are all I can remember.

Lastly, I would like to thank Mercedes López-Ballesteros and Carme López Mercader for their help in researching certain topics, tracking down documents, and in many other intangible ways. I hope I haven't left anything or anyone out. If I have, so be it.

Javier Marías

Translator's afterword

When you translate a particular author's work for thirty years, their departure from this world feels very much like a bereavement, because the relationship is rather like a marriage, except that you are married not to the person but to their voice, their way of using language and, indeed, to their fictional world. Now that Javier has gone, it's strange to think that no more 600-page novels, written in that familiar voice, will arrive at my door and plunge me once more into that world and that way of writing.

As with so many things in life, I became Javier's translator purely by chance. Guido Waldman of Harvill wrote to me in 1991 to ask if I would be interested in translating a novel by a Spanish author. The novel was *Todas las almas* (*All Souls*), and the author was Javier. This was his sixth novel and my sixth novel translation. I had already translated some fairly difficult texts, but this was the first time I was translating an author who had impeccable English – a prospect that was both reassuring and daunting. Javier asked me to send him my final draft and went through it line by line. He did pick me up on various things where I had either misunderstood (I *was* something of a novice) or had perhaps, in his view, chosen not quite the right word; however, he always made it clear that I, as the native speaker and the translator, had final say – and this was typical of his combination of meticulousness and generosity. He never again asked to read through the whole translation, hopefully because he trusted me, but possibly because he didn't have time (by then, he was becoming a big name with many translators), but he did always have time to answer my queries and would share his other translators' queries with me too.

I had no idea at the time, of course, that I would still be translating his wonderful prose thirty years later.

All Souls was my first encounter as a translator with such long sentences (which did, I think, become longer over the years), but I plunged gaily in, translating a sentence at a time and polishing each one before moving on to the next. People often comment on Javier's long sentences, as if these were somehow unusual or an obstacle to be clambered over or tampered with or, heaven forbid, cut up into shorter ones. English doesn't like long sentences, they say, but this simply isn't true. Modern writers may not like them, but English is such a wonderfully flexible language that it can easily accommodate long sentences, with the help of commas, semi-colons and dashes. A long sentence can take an idea or a feeling and investigate its many crannies and contradictions, and Javier's books are very much about ideas and feelings, about holding them up to the light and testing them out. Listen to this extract from *Tomás Nevinson*:

> But that thought cannot erase the memory of seeing a person's life escaping through the wound you caused, the blood pouring forth, of having been a witness to his panic and his final impotence, or to his initial surprise at finding he was wounded, and imagining (because one only ever imagines it, as if it had not yet arrived) that this was the day he would die. You catch in his gaze a glimmer of incredulity or desperate denial, you believe you can see in the dying man's mind something along these lines: 'No, this can't be happening, it's just not possible that I will no longer see or hear anything or utter another word, that this still-functioning mind will stop and be snuffed out, this mind still so full of tormenting thoughts; that I will never again stand up or move so much as a finger and will be thrown in a ditch or a river or a ravine or a lake, or be burned like a lump

of firewood albeit without giving off the same pleasant woody smell, that my body will send up a pestilential cloud of smoke, and I will stink of scorched flesh if, at that point, I am still me.

That one sentence takes you on a brief journey through the minds of both killer and victim, as well as through the concept of what it is to be alive, to be an individual. And the length of the sentence, and the rhythm (that's why I say 'Listen'), is all part of that exploration. It simply wouldn't be the same in a more staccato prose.

Javier delighted in language, be it poetic or prosaic or positively plebeian. He runs the whole gamut of Spanish, which is what makes translating him into English such a joy, precisely because you are required to use every ounce and iota of your own language.

Here, for example, is the gloriously grotesque Folcuino on one of his scabrous riffs:

'Today, I finally got Gausi to kiss arse,' he said (Gausi was a very well-known property developer with operations in Castilla y León, Asturias and Cantabria), 'and as for Valderas, I've got him on such a tight lead, I can take him anywhere I want, it's amazing how quickly I broke him in.' Valderas was his boss, the mayor: 'Pee here, Mr Mayor, now stop here, and here is where I relax the lead for a second so that you can imagine you're free, but now we've got to get a move on, Mr Mayor, and if you need a shit, tough titty. The only one I'm kind of worried about at the moment is Peporro, I haven't yet got him eating out of my hand, and he's still up to his old tricks, but I keep passing him expensive little presents and when he does finally pocket them, he'll be sure to drop his trousers and offer me his cock to tickle with a feather or beat with a whip as the mood takes me. That's what I tell myself anyway . . .'

Humour and a sense of the absurdity of life are another constant thread. In every novel, there are comic characters or episodes, and, like one of his great literary heroes, Shakespeare, Javier could move seamlessly between comedy and tragedy.

As you can see from his acknowledgements at the end of this book (the first time he included such a list), his work is also full of literary references, notably Shakespeare (especially *Richard III* and *Macbeth*, both of which are rife with deceit and deceivers and murderers and their guilt), as well as T. S. Eliot, Balzac, Conrad, Dumas and so on. There are also many references to his other novels, to certain turns of phrase and even to characters who reappear from earlier novels or even emerge from a short story to take centre stage. In this novel and in *Berta Isla*, though, he often deliberately misquotes himself or gives a not-quite-exact version of a quotation used earlier in the text, perhaps taking the unreliable narrator a step too far for the poor translator always wanting to get things 'right'!

His themes remained the same throughout his career – lies, deceit, betrayal, guilt – and also, as he says in this novel, the past as 'an intruder impossible to keep at bay'. In the later books, this past inevitably involves the Spanish Civil War and the Second World War, the wars that left the deepest mark on his two 'countries', for while Javier was profoundly Spanish, he was also so immersed in British and American literature (he did, after all, translate Sterne's *Tristram Shandy*, as well as Thomas Browne's *Religio medici*, and stories by Conrad, Stevenson and Hardy) that, rather like Tom Nevinson, he was bicultural. And then there is Oxford, which left a deep impression on Javier during the two years he spent teaching at the university, and the city and the university are a constant presence in his novels from *All Souls* on.

Above all, though, Javier was fascinated by people in all their complexities and contradictions. Not for nothing does his writing abound in perhapses and maybes and possiblys, as well as synonyms and near-synonyms and antonyms, all of which underline the unpin-downable nature of the human psyche. As he says in this novel:

> Literature allows us to see people as they truly are, even though those people do not exist, but will, with luck, always exist, which is why literature will never entirely lose its prestige.

And Javier's work will certainly never lose its prestige.

Margaret Jull Costa

October 2022

Translator's acknowledgements

I would like to thank Javier Marías, Mercedes López-Ballesteros and my friend and colleague Alexis Grohmann of Edinburgh University for all their help and advice in translating this book.

A NOTE ABOUT THE AUTHOR

JAVIER MARÍAS was born in Madrid in 1951. He was the author of the novels *The Man of Feeling,* which received Italy's Premio Internazionale Ennio Flaiano; *All Souls,* which received the Premio Ciudad de Barcelona; *A Heart So White,* which received the International IMPAC Dublin Literary Award, Spain's Premio de la Crítica, and the Prix l'Oeil et la Lettre; *Tomorrow in the Battle Think on Me,* which received the Prix Femina Étranger, Venezuela's Premio Internacional de Novela Rómulo Gallegos, the Premio Fastenrath (awarded by the Real Academia Española), the Premio Arzobispo Juan de San Clemente, and the Premio Letterario Internazionale Mondello-Città di Palermo; *Dark Back of Time;* the *Your Face Tomorrow* trilogy, comprised of *Fever and Spear,* which won Barcelona's Premio Salambó, *Dance and Dream,* and *Poison, Shadow and Farewell; The Infatuations; Thus Bad Begins, Berta Isla,* which received the Premio de la Crítica; and *Tomás Nevinson,* which received the Premio Gregor von Rezzori. His early novels are *Voyage Along the Horizon, Los dominios del lobo, El monarca del tiempo,* and *El siglo.* He was also the author of the story collections *While the Women Are Sleeping* and *When I Was Mortal;* the stand-alone story *Bad Nature;* a collection of short literary biographies, *Written Lives;* a collection of critical and personal writing, *Between Eternities;* and a selection of articles on soccer, *Salvajes y sentimentales.*

He received the Nelly Sachs Preis (Dortmund, Germany), the Premio Grinzane Cavour and the Premio Alessio (both of Turin, Italy), the Premio Moravia (Rome), the Premio Iberoamericano de Letras José Donoso (Universidad de Talca, Chile), the Premio Nonino (Italy), and the Austrian State Prize for European Literature. He was a member of the Real Academia Española. He was also a highly practiced translator into Spanish of English and American authors, including Joseph Conrad, Robert Louis Stevenson, Sir Thomas Browne, Laurence Sterne, John Ashbery, Wallace Stevens, J. D. Salinger, William Faulkner, and Vladimir Nabokov. He held academic posts in Spain and the United States, and was Lecturer in Spanish Literature at Oxford University.

His books have been translated into forty-six languages in fifty-nine countries, and have sold more than nine million copies throughout the world. He died in 2022.

A NOTE ABOUT THE TRANSLATOR

MARGARET JULL COSTA has been a literary translator for nearly forty years, and has translated the works of many Spanish and Portuguese writers, among them novelists: Javier Marías, José Saramago, Bernardo Atxaga, and Eça de Queiroz; and poets: Sophia de Mello Breyner Andresen, Mário de Sá-Carneiro, Fernando Pessoa, and Ana Luísa Amaral. Her work has brought her numerous prizes. With Javier Marías, she won the 1997 International IMPAC Dublin Literary Award for *A Heart So White*, and, in 2006 and 2010, her translations of volumes I and III of *Your Face Tomorrow* were awarded the Premio Valle-Inclán. In 2000 and 2011, she won the Oxford Weidenfeld Translation Prize for, respectively, *All the Names* and *The Elephant's Journey*, both by José Saramago. In 2008, she won the PEN/Book-of-the Month-Club Translation Prize and the Oxford Weidenfeld Translation Prize for *The Maias* by Eça de Queiroz. In 2015, she won the Marsh Children's Fiction in Translation Award for *The Adventures of Shola* by Bernardo Atxaga, and in 2017, with her cotranslator Robin Patterson, she won the Best Translated Book Award for *Chronicle of the Murdered House* by Lúcio Cardoso. She won the 2018 Premio Valle-Inclán for *On the Edge* by Rafael Chirbes. In 2013, she was appointed a Fellow of the Royal Society of Literature; in 2014, she was awarded an OBE for services to literature; and in 2015, she was given an honorary doctorate by the University of Leeds. In 2018, she was awarded the Ordem Infante D. Henrique by the Portuguese government and a Lifetime Award for Excellence in Translation by the Queen Sofia Spanish Institute, New York.